Praise for the
Daughter...

"Karen Chance... an action-packed adventure with a strong female character that, while tough as nails and a dhampir, is also very human." —SFRevu

"Intensely hilarious dialogue, intriguing and endearing characters, and pulse-pounding action!" —Fresh Fiction

"In dhampir Dorina Basarab, Chance has created a sassy, tough heroine who never says die. Following these first-person adventures is going to be an adrenaline high." —RT Book Reviews

"Karen Chance has done it again . . . a brilliant start to a new series." —Vampire Romance Books

"Karen Chance knows how to write. Not just the action scenes, or having the butt-kicking heroine throw out pithy one-liners, but the setup is clever [and] the involvement of the various factions in the simmering war is well thought-out, as are the repercussions to various actions characters take in the book." —Monsters and Critics

"Glorious fight scenes, eerily still moments of fractured memories, steamy romps that set the heart pounding; it is little wonder that Chance has caught the attention of so many fans. . . . She delivers in every way—utterly staggering." —The Truth About Books

BOOKS BY KAREN CHANCE

THE CASSIE PALMER SERIES

Touch the Dark
Claimed by Shadow
Embrace the Night
Curse the Dawn
Hunt the Moon
Tempt the Stars
Reap the Wind
Ride the Storm

THE MIDNIGHT'S DAUGHTER SERIES

Midnight's Daughter
Death's Mistress
Fury's Kiss
Shadow's Bane

THE MIRCEA BASARAB SERIES

Masks

KAREN CHANCE

Shadow's Bane

A MIDNIGHT'S DAUGHTER NOVEL

BERKLEY
New York

BERKLEY
An imprint of Penguin Random House LLC
375 Hudson Street, New York, New York 10014

Copyright © 2018 by Karen Chance
Penguin Random House supports copyright. Copyright fuels creativity, encourages
diverse voices, promotes free speech, and creates a vibrant culture. Thank you for buying
an authorized edition of this book and for complying with copyright laws by not
reproducing, scanning, or distributing any part of it in any form without permission.
You are supporting writers and allowing Penguin Random House to continue to
publish books for every reader.

BERKLEY is a registered trademark and the B colophon
is a trademark of Penguin Random House LLC.

ISBN: 9780451419064

First Edition: August 2018

Printed in the United States of America
1   3   5   7   9   10   8   6   4   2

Cover art by Larry Rostant
Book design by Tiffany Estreicher

This is a work of fiction. Names, characters, places, and incidents either are the product
of the author's imagination or are used fictitiously, and any resemblance to actual persons,
living or dead, business establishments, events, or locales is entirely coincidental.

If you purchased this book without a cover, you should be aware that this book is stolen
property. It was reported as "unsold and destroyed" to the publisher, and neither the author
nor the publisher has received any payment for this "stripped book."

ACKNOWLEDGMENTS

I'd like to thank all the hardworking people at Penguin who helped to make this book a reality:

Miranda Hill—Editorial Assistant

Jessica Mangicaro—Marketing Coordinator

Andrea Hovland—Production Manager

Tiffany Estreicher—Interior Designer

Alexis Nixon—Assistant Director of Publicity

And, of course, Anne Sowards, a great editor!

Thanks for helping me see it through to the end.

Prologue

Mircea, Venice, 1458

It was freezing. He knew that because he could see other peoples' breath frost the air as they passed, a crowd of shapes that should have been nothing more than dark blurs, but instead were full of light and sound and . . . life. He could close his eyes and still see them, streaks of color against the night, with bright streamers flowing out behind them like the pennants that used to fly from the ramparts at home.

One approached the shadow where he stood; she was so vivid that she almost seemed unreal. Her eyes were blue, shimmering deep and dark, but not cold. Not the color of the ocean, but of the skies, limitless and clear, even shadowed with the knowledge that something wasn't right. That somewhere nearby, a hunter waited.

A strand of red hair slipped out of the hood of her cloak, curling against a cheek that others might have called pale, but which to him glowed peach and pink and warm, like a lantern against the blacks and grays of the narrow street, and the silvered thread of a canal behind her. The colors dimmed and bloomed with every heartbeat, with every sigh of breath that issued from between cold-reddened lips. The life pulsing in her veins called to him like a siren's song, urging him to loosen the night he'd wrapped around himself and take one step into the street.

That was all it would take. One step, one lifted hand to call her to his side, one vague brush against her mind to overcome the fear that hastened her feet and sent those beautiful eyes darting into shadows. Just one.

He didn't take it.

But someone else did.

Mircea saw him even before he moved, not a man but a boy, barely a year out of the grave and without the hard-won restraint Mircea had learned. He must have been local; no one so far gone in bloodlust could have made it this far otherwise. Venice was an open port, where vampire territories were forbidden and everyone was permitted, but this child would have gotten himself killed long before he reached it.

She came closer, the boy trailing her in shadow. Mircea could smell her now, a scent as bright as the daylight she seemed to carry within her, a strange, exotic perfume: bitter orange, honey musk, ambergris, and vanilla, set against the sweet smell of female sweat. His gut twisted, yet he gave no sign.

Because she wasn't alone.

He couldn't see the one who trailed her, like the fisherman following the bobbing of his lure. The light he gave off was dim, almost indistinguishable from the glimmer of moonlight on the water below. So dark, in fact, that even with vision many times sharper than a human's, Mircea could barely discern him, and only because he had known he would be there.

The boy didn't see him. The boy couldn't see anything but her. Mircea remembered those days, not so far in his own past. When the bloodlust took you, it was a terrible thing, like being possessed, to the point that he understood why humans called them demons and thrust crosses in their faces.

Crosses didn't help. Or holy water, or garlic, or wedging bricks into the mouths of the dead, as the locals had taken to doing in a vain attempt to keep them from feeding if they rose. When the demon rode you, only blood would satisfy him and return you to something like sanity.

It was a state the boy had not seen in some time.

The young one slipped closer, in and out of shadow now, visible in glimpses even to human eyes. And audible, too: a strange, low keening issued from between his lips.

This was not the savage predator of legend, capable and cruel, but a half-starved child with no master to tend him, no family to help him, no one to lean on for information or even succor.

Stumbling through the night, all alone.

Mircea knew that feeling.

He'd entered this strange life through an old woman's curse, and hadn't understood what was happening when his skin started to burn in sunlight, when his food became oddly flavorless, when his eyes seemed to acquire a cat's vision, suddenly able to see clearly even in the dead of night. Not until his enemies caught up with him, tortured and buried him, leaving him to gasp his last breath in that tiny coffin underground, had he understood. And clawed his way back to the surface in a rebirth of sorts, as terrified and disoriented as a babe, and as ignorant of the new world he found himself in.

Yes, he understood.

He didn't know this one's story, only that he wouldn't be on his own, crying in need, if he had a family to look after him. So he was one of the thousands who washed up on these shores every year, unwanted, abandoned, lost. Made by mistake, on a whim or as punishment for an infraction, and then cast aside to die alone.

Because vampire death was something of a Venice specialty.

But before they died, they hunted. And ones like these hunted wildly, so driven by hunger that they no longer cared for their own safety, much less that of their prey. And while the Vampire Senate allowed them the right to feed here, on the massive festival crowds too drunk to know the difference, mangled corpses were treated seriously.

Members of the city watch, the special ones with the Medusa-head armor and the Senate's backing, had a hunt of their own, rounding up those who killed when they fed and carrying them away to tiny prison cells. Where they could scream themselves hoarse, or shred their hands battering warded walls that would never yield, and slowly starve surrounded by silence. As if they, too, had been buried alive.

But that wouldn't happen here.

Because something else hunted tonight.

When the trap sprang, it took place in an instant, almost too fast even for Mircea's eyes to follow. The boy leapt, with a strangled cry of defeat and desperation, as if he'd been holding himself back but could bear it no longer; the girl turned with a cry of her own, lips parted, eyes wide and frightened; the darkness surged around them.

And the next thing Mircea knew, the girl was alone once more, her breathing rapid, her lips trembling slightly, one pale hand gripping her throat.

Until the darkness whispered something that even Mircea couldn't hear, and she turned and stumbled away. Walking hurriedly, almost drunkenly, down the street, not a woman but a trap. One that had been sprung and was now being deployed once more.

Mircea waited, unmoving, unbreathing, as the girl and the strange, dark shadow that followed her passed him by.

And then he slipped out into the street, quiet as a breath of wind, and cloaked in a shadow of his own.

And followed.

Chapter One

The truck was old army issue, built back when even regular cars resembled tanks, and it could easily eat a Hummer for lunch and spit out the bolts. At least, it could have in its prime. But the years had not been kind, resulting in it landing at Stan's Auto Emporium, a junkyard/car dealership in which it was often hard to tell the difference between the two types of merchandise.

"It's as dependable as they come, Dory," Stan said, patting its rusty hood. He was a tiny man, four foot something, with the something being mostly chutzpah. "This truck is rugged."

I crossed my arms. "This truck passed 'rugged' a long time ago. This truck couldn't find 'rugged' with a map. This truck is—what's the phrase I'm looking for? A hunk of junk."

"A hunk of junk you can afford, sweetheart."

He had a point.

"How much?"

"Two hundred."

"*Two hundred?* I could practically get a limo for that!"

"But you don't need a limo."

"I don't need a hole in my wallet, either."

Stan crossed his arms and silently chewed tobacco at me.

"I just need it for the night," I told him. "I can have it back in the morning."

"Fine. That'll be two hundred bucks." Something hit the concrete below the cab with an ominous rattle. Stan didn't bat an eye. "Okay, return her in good condition and I'll take ten off the price."

"Good condition? You mean something other than the way it is now?" But I forked over the cash. Normally, I'd have driven a harder bargain, but I'd promised to help a friend and I was running late. And nowhere else was going to have the kind of steel-gauge construction I needed. This thing might be a hunk of junk, but it was solid.

Yet, fifteen minutes later, as my team filed in, it was also sagging and groaning, to the point that I feared for the tires—all six of them. It wasn't hard to figure out why. I peered into the cavernous interior, and found it alarmingly full of troll.

"Here's the thing," I told the nearest four-hundred-pound slab of muscle. "We're going to need room to transport the illegals, assuming we find any, not to mention the slavers. And I don't think they're gonna fit."

Nothing. I might as well have been talking to the brick wall the guy closely resembled.

"I'm not saying that everybody needs to stay behind," I offered, trying again. "Just, you know, two or three of you."

Nada.

I waited another moment, because troll reasoning faculties can be a little slower than some and I thought maybe he was thinking it over. But no. The small, pebble-like eyes just looked at me, flat and uninterested in the yammering of the tiny human. I sighed and went to find Olga.

The leader of the posse currently straining the hell out of my truck was in her headquarters, which consisted of a combo beauty salon and what looked like the back room at *Soldier of Fortune*. It would have been an odd marriage in the human world, even in Brooklyn, but there weren't many humans shopping at Olga's. And the local community of Dark Fey seemed to like buying their ammo and getting their nails done all in one place.

I found the lady herself pawing through a cardboard box of suspicious items in the storeroom. Like her squad of volunteers, she was of the troll persuasion, weighing in at something less than a quarter ton—but not a lot less.

Not that she was fat; like most trolls, she was built of muscle and sinew and was hard as a rock, all eight-plus feet of her. I don't know how she found clothes, but she usually managed to be more stylish than me.

That had never been truer than tonight.

For the evening's sortie into New York's magical underbelly, I had selected jeans, a black T-shirt, a black leather jacket, and a pair of ass-kicking boots. It didn't make me look tough—when you're five foot two, dimpled and female, not a lot does—but it hid a lot of weaponry and didn't attract attention.

Olga did not appear to be worried about attention.

Instead of well-worn denim, she was strutting her considerable stuff in pink satin clamdiggers, a matching sequined butterfly top—cut low to show an impressive amount of cleavage—and glossy four-inch heels. The heels were nude patent leather, possibly so they didn't clash with the toenails poking out the end, which were the same fire-engine red as her hair.

I regarded it enviously for a moment. It made the paltry blue streaks in my own short brown locks seem dull and lifeless by comparison. I needed a new color. Of course, for that, I also needed to get paid, which meant getting a move on.

"You're coming, right?" I asked, as she flipped over the OPEN sign.

"Moment," she said placidly.

"I just wondered because, you know." I gestured at the acre of sequins.

Olga continued sorting through the box.

"Not that you don't look good."

Zilch. I was starting to get a complex.

"So, listen. We've got a problem with the truck."

She finally looked up. "It no go?"

"No, it's fine. It's just, uh, sort of packed."

"Everyone not fit?"

"No, they're in there. But I don't think we're going to be squeezing in any more."

"Slaves make their own way home, once we free them." She held up a fistful of the type of charms her kind used to pass as more or less human.

"Okay, but that still leaves the slavers."

That got me a long stare.

"Olga," I said, getting a sinking feeling. "I have to bring them back for questioning. We'll never stop the selling of your people if we don't know who's behind it."

"That vampire behind it," she said, stuffing the charms into a sleek pink clutch.

She was talking about a rat fink named Geminus. Until his recent, unlamented demise, he'd been a member of the Vampire Senate, the governing body for all North American vampires. But power, fame, and the idolization of millions hadn't been good enough. He'd wanted to be rich as Croesus, too, and found that running the slave trade from Faerie fit the bill nicely.

"He's dead," I pointed out. "And yet business goes on as usual."

"Not for long."

I sighed but didn't bother pointing out that a handful of trolls and a lone dhampir were not likely to bring down a network Geminus had spent years building. Because that wasn't our job. All we were after was a new arrival who had failed to arrive.

That sort of thing had always been a hazard for the Dark Fey who paid to be smuggled out of the almost-constant warfare in Faerie. Sometimes the smugglers took the money and then failed to show up, or left would-be immigrants stranded far from home and on the wrong side of the portal. Others did make it through, only to end up in the usual mess faced by any illegals—lousy jobs, worse pay, and no one to complain to. Although that still beat what was behind door number three.

There are tons of old legends about the fey kidnapping humans. What nobody bothered to record is that we do it right back. A lot of the slavers are dark mages who promptly drain the magic—and therefore the life—out of anybody unlucky enough to fall into their hands. Others are more like subcontractors, finding specimens for sale into nefarious "professions" that usually end the same way.

But lately, thanks to Geminus' death and a simultaneous Senate crackdown on smuggling, the number of active portals was dwindling. That would have been good news, except for the law of supply and demand, which ensured that the price for slaves was going nowhere but up. That had left the smugglers with the ironic problem of having to watch out for other crooks who were trying to steal their illegal cargo. Like the group that attacked a band of would-be immigrants last night.

They'd been lucky enough to make off with an even dozen new slaves.

They'd been unlucky enough to have one of them be Olga's nephew.

If she caught up with them, I strongly suspected there'd be a few less slavers to worry about. Which wouldn't have concerned me except that my job these days—on the Senate's anti-smuggling squad—was to make sure that that didn't happen. Well, not before I had a chance to question them first.

"You know," I said idly, as Olga locked up, "a few deaths, even of scumbag slavers, won't do much to stop the trade. But the info they might provide . . ."

Olga threw me a look, which was hard to see behind her flashy new Dolce & Gabbana shades. They would have seemed odd, because the sun was close to setting, but these shades weren't for keeping light out so much as letting it in. They'd been modified to enhance all light in an area, because troll eyesight sucks even at the best of times.

And I guess Olga wanted to see the leader's face before she bit it off.

"You stubborn little woman," she told me.

"It has been remarked."

She tilted her head. "You take him away, how I know he dead?"

"Because the Senate isn't known for compassion?" She just looked at me. Olga didn't have a lot of faith in the Vampire Senate. Olga knew that they only cared about the smugglers because of the weapons they also brought in, most of which went to the Senate's enemies. Olga knew nobody gave a shit about the Dark Fey, which was why they had to look out for themselves.

"And because I'll take care of it," I added.

"You kill?"

"It's what I do."

She thought this over while I sorted through the pastry box she'd brought for the boys. Tonight was muffins, although I couldn't tell what kind. "What are these?"

"Lemon."

I sniffed one. Human food was still a new experience for the fey, who tended to combine things in odd ways. I took a bite.

"And these green things?"

"Asparagus."

That's what I'd thought.

We reached the truck and Olga climbed in, making the struts groan and drop another inch. I donated the muffins to the boys in back and turned to follow suit. And found a chest in the way.

It was a nice chest, wearing a blue knit pullover in some kind of thin material that outlined hard pecs and a washboard stomach. It was attached to an even nicer pair of denim-covered thighs and a butt that ought to be hanging in a museum somewhere. It even smelled good—a rich, sweet, decadent scent that always reminded me of butterscotch.

The face topping the whole mountain of awesome was pretty nice, too. Even crowned by a mass of auburn, Breck-girl hair pulled back from a manly jaw by an understated tortoiseshell clip. And even if it was currently regarding me sardonically.

"What are you doing here?" I asked.

That got me a raised eyebrow. "Aren't you glad to see me?"

I guess so, since my nipples just got hard, I didn't say, because his ego was big enough as it was.

"It's just a little unexpected."

"I gathered that." Narrowed blue eyes took in the straining truck. "Am I interrupting something?"

"Just . . . going out with some friends."

"Indeed. That is reassuring. For a moment, I thought you might be planning to contravene doctor's orders."

Yeah, I was busted.

"We're going to see the fights," I said, hoping he somehow hadn't noticed the army-issue truck, the armed-to-the-teeth posse, and the half ton of illegal weaponry I had hidden around my outfit.

An eyebrow raised.

Well, shit.

"I enjoy a good fight," Louis-Cesare said, in what had to be the understatement of the century. "I'll come along. Consider it a date."

"A date, huh?" I looked him over. "If I buy you a popcorn, do I get to have my way with you later?"

He took a step, and I suddenly found myself trapped between hard steel and harder vampire. "How big of a popcorn?"

"I don't know. What am I getting in return?"

He bent over and whispered something in my ear.

I swallowed. "We'll see if they have a bucket."

———

They didn't have a bucket.

They did have beer, overpriced and in tiny paper cups, sold by enterprising types out of a repurposed ice cream van that prowled up and down the ridiculously long line to get in. I wouldn't have plunked down the cash for what was essentially highway robbery, but I had my evening ahead to think about. And I wanted to see what the so-cultured Louis-Cesare would do with a half-frozen beer. Because the truck's freezers had not been repurposed along with the rest of it, leaving us with what amounted to beer Popsicles.

Not that I was complaining.

Until I ran into something.

I'd been distracted wondering how the gargoyle-like things driving the truck were managing to reach the pedals, since they were maybe toddler height, when I suddenly stopped moving. The obstacle in my way was skin warm, although it felt more like stone. And looked like it, too, when I turned my head to see so many muscles that some had given up trying to find an appropriate spot and were just bulging out haphazardly, wherever they could find room.

The living boulder regarded me for a second, and the squinty little eyes got squintier. "No," he rumbled.

"No what?"

The rocklike dome, which lacked any sort of hair except for a couple robust tufts coming out of the ears, nodded at a nearby sign.

NO WEPINS, it informed me, in dripping acid green spray paint.

Okay, no.

"They have lockers," Louis-Cesare murmured.

This was true. A stoner with a bad case of Muppet hair was sitting cross-legged on the dirt beside the sign, in front of a row of lockers. They looked like they'd been ripped wholesale off an elementary school wall, complete with bits of happy ducky wallpaper still clinging to the edges. And then piled haphazardly against a sagging chain-link fence, without any effort to secure them to anything. Meanwhile, their only guardian's eyes were starting to cross from a joint the size of a cigar that he was munching on, Churchill-style.

"You have got to be kidding me," I said.

"Move," the boulder rumbled, when I just stood there.

"Then let me in."

"Then lose the hardware."

"You just let her in." I nodded at a tall, model-pretty chick in a leather catsuit, with bright purple hair, carmine lipstick, and a half ton of lethal accessories. She disappeared through a gate in the chain-link and immediately flickered out of view, masked by whatever glamourie was being used to hide the night's festivities.

The spell wasn't perfect; every so often it let out a split second of raucous music, or a glimpse of smoky darkness lit by odd smears of light. But mostly it held. Meaning that the only thing I could see past the sagging fence was an overgrown lot strewn with grimy police tape, some pools of water from this afternoon's downpour, and the fire-gutted building that had brought us all here.

Fly-by-night pop-up events like this preferred disaster areas, because any damage could be written off as part of the previous catastrophe. But this one was a little more catastrophic looking than usual. The sun was setting, making the old brick building appear to still be on fire, with the last rays boiling in broken, smoke-clouded glass.

Glass that looked a lot like jagged teeth, framing the solid black maws of burnt-out windows, which could be hiding anything, anything at all.

Yeah.

"Imma need my weapons," I told Boulder Boy.

"Know her. Don't know you," he said slowly, answering my previous comment. Because lightning fast was not the processing speed we were dealing with here. But then, most people didn't want to pay for a bouncer who could think. Most people wanted a bouncer who could follow orders, and I was getting the definite impression that once an idea got lodged in that rocklike cranium, it didn't get out again.

Well, not without some help.

"Hold my beer," I told Louis-Cesare.

But then backup arrived. At least, I guess that's what it was, because an arm the size of a small bus reached out of the glamourie and grabbed, not me—because I know how to move when I have to—but a guy standing behind me. Who had also come armed for bear, but not armed for whatever the hell had just grabbed him. And had now turned him upside down and was shaking him like a maraca.

For a moment, all conversation stopped as the line watched the shakedown. A couple knives, five guns, a set of brass knuckles, and half a dozen extra clips fell out of the guy's coat and jeans and various useless holsters. Because they weren't meant to stand up to that kind of abuse.

Of course, neither was human anatomy, and he'd looked pretty human to me. But I guess not. Because he was still breathing when the arm dropped him a moment later.

On his head.

"No weapons," the bouncer told me.

"Gotcha."

It was finally decided that one of the trolls, a small mountain named Sten who was nonetheless looking at the arm with respect, would take my stuff back to the truck and babysit it. That left us a man down, but I was somehow less concerned about security, all of a sudden.

The stoner cranked off a bunch of tickets from a roll that looked like the kind you got after stuffing quarters in a Skee-Ball machine, and Olga accepted them with a regal inclination of her head. She swept through the gate, with Louis-Cesare and me on her heels. And I guess the rest of the trolls brought up the rear, but I wasn't sure because—

"Holy shit!"

Chapter Two

I don't know what I'd expected. I knew we were going to an illicit, no-holds-barred fight of the kind that would leave the UFC writhing in envy. I knew that said fights were not supposed to be known to the authorities, human or otherwise, and were therefore an open invitation to all kinds of rabble. I knew that we were walking into danger, serious danger, which was why I'd been so loaded down with weapons that I basically clinked when I walked.

Even though I knew all this, I still wasn't prepared for what I saw once we stepped through the glamourie.

I still wasn't prepared for troll carnival.

And I wasn't prepared for it to hit all at once, to the point that my brain could take it in only by breaking it down into different senses.

Sound: hitting like a tsunami that drags you under before spitting you out the other side on a wave studded with audible debris. Which beats and bangs you up, leaving you breathless and disoriented, because it's coming at you from all sides: wonky loudspeakers giving updates nobody could hear; old-fashioned boom boxes blaring every kind of music simultaneously; hordes of gamblers screaming bets around bookmakers standing on piles of smoke-damaged furniture to get above the crowd; and people, all kinds of people, threading through the crowd of vendors' tents and lean-tos surrounding the burnt-out hulk like a swirl of colorful skirts. And fighting and laughing and singing and shouting in a couple dozen languages, including some that scratched the brain because they weren't in human decibels.

Smell: a five-foot toddler lurching by on unsteady legs, waving an odorous treat that left scent trails so thick they were almost visible; hawkers in the form of ieles—large bipedal cats—pushing their version of suspiciously mouse-like shish kebab; families tailgating over open fires, with pots so bright with unknown spices that they twitched the nose and fooled the mind, turning the flames multicolored as several senses tangled up and tripped over one another.

Sight: a towering giant, leaning against a tree and scratching his nuts, waiting for the next partygoer with an attitude; a cascade of tiny ashrays floating by in bubbles of water, because they couldn't touch land; humpbacked ogres peering suspiciously at the world from under thatches of unkempt hair; a beautiful blond selkie in human form, leaving watery footprints wherever she walked; · a raucous tent filled with satyrs and mazikeen, flightless fey with iridescent wings often mistaken for angels except for their tendency to really get the party started; and a dozen others I couldn't even put names to.

I'd started to think, after this summer, that I was something of an authority on the fey. My landlord was a Dark Fey princess; I had a basement full of troll in the form of several of Olga's relatives; my adopted son was a half Duergar/half Brownie who'd helped me battle a Light Fey princeling with skills I'd never even heard of until I was almost gutted by them, and yet I'd somehow come out intact on the other side. And, I was quickly realizing, still didn't know shit.

I was realizing something else, too.

"Wait a minute!" I screamed at Olga, who somehow heard me over the din. She turned politely. "What are all the fey doing here?"

That got me a forehead wrinkle. "For the fights."

"Yes, but . . . you told me it was fey being kidnapped and forced to battle to the death! Not that they'd be part of the crowd!"

Large shoulders shrugged. "Fey fight at home. Fey fight here. Fight not problem. Kidnapping problem."

"Okay, but you appreciate it's going to be a little hard to find your nephew in all this!" I waved at the crowd, maybe a couple thousand strong, already packed into the lot. And we hadn't even gotten to the main event yet.

"We not need find him," Olga explained patiently. "Find slaver. Then—" She made a fist.

And, okay, I was pretty sure he'd talk, too. But still.

"But still," I yelled, because the noise level was astonishing. "That doesn't look like it's going to be any easier!"

It really didn't. Especially since the place wasn't packed just with fey. There were also droves of magical humans, who seemed a lot more in the loop than I was, since they were buying booze or haggling a buck off the price of a T-shirt instead of staring around in slack-jawed astonishment. And here and there were dark puddles of stillness that screamed vampires, who I guess had come for the fun, since fey blood didn't nourish them. There were even a few weres, looking like humans but itchy, like a feather tickling up my spine.

Normally, finding the perp in my line of work is easy, since I'm mostly chasing things that go bump in the night amid crowds of humans. Find the supe and you usually find the bad guy, the needle in the proverbial haystack who shows up on my mental radar, all nice and shiny. Only here, half the haystack was made out of needles. And even that didn't help me much, since, this time, they might be the good guys.

"Don't worry," Olga said, clapping a ham-sized hand on my shoulder and almost buckling my knees. "He albino."

That seemed to settle things as far as she was concerned, because she took off, plowing through a gleaming stream of will-o'-the-wisps with a *tchaa* and some flapping of massive hands. They went swirling off in annoyed clouds, and I and my date went stumbling after her.

I didn't point out that this albino, if he was behind the theft, wasn't likely to be hanging around in full view. Or hanging around at all if he realized he'd grabbed the nephew of the widow of one of Faerie's most notorious weapons runners. A widow who still had a lot of connections and a serious hate-on for losing more family members. Hell, he might not even be on the *planet*.

But I didn't tell her that, and not just because of the

noise. I didn't think we were going to find Olga's nephew, not in one piece, anyway. A scared slaver was a dangerous slaver; why risk keeping a witness to your stupidity when a knife through the eye would take care of the problem?

But Olga didn't need to hear that right now. I didn't know what troll life was like back in the old country, but here the community was tight-knit, leaning on one another for support in a world they found as frightening and strange as we did theirs. Every new arrival was valued as a reminder of home and a hedge against adversity, and every death was mourned as a tragedy that affected them all.

So, no, I wasn't going to tell her that we weren't likely to find him. Because maybe we could find the son of a bitch who'd killed him. He should be far, far away by now, if he had any sense, but people often didn't.

Especially arrogant slavers used to calling the shots.

The thought made me smile. And then a glance at Louis-Cesare made me smile bigger, because the French aristocrat with the flashing eyes and dangerous temper and heart affixed quite firmly to his sleeve still liked to believe that he was Mr. Cool Under Pressure. Nothing rattled him, no sirree, not a chance. Except for this, apparently, because he was staring around, as discombobulated as me.

I needed to keep up with Olga's bright red head, bouncing just ahead, so I had to content myself with catching glimpses here and there. Like of his wider-than-normal eyes, reflecting the firelight as he watched ponderous troll jugglers deftly spin torches into the air in amazing parabolas. Or his openmouthed astonishment at a group of Thussers—Norwegian fjord fey—going to town on some fiddles, wildly enough that the closest vendors had shut down their music in deference to the awesomeness. Or his brief smile at a massive troll serving as a "ride" for some diminutive troll children, who were being flung three stories into the air and then caught expertly while they screamed and giggled and demanded something I didn't understand, but which was obviously "Do it again!"

Or the flush on his cheeks when a half-naked nymph

tried to pull him into a dark tent, where sketchy things were happening in corners.

"Not a chance," I told her, and draped an arm around his waist.

She pouted prettily. And while she didn't appear to know English, or any other spoken language, the body was . . . expressive. It somehow conveyed the impression that a threesome was not out of the question if I'd stop being so selfish and learn to share.

"Maybe later," I said, watching Louis-Cesare, who was manfully biting the inside of a cheek to keep from breaking the macho sangfroid he didn't have anyway.

I pulled him off.

"For a moment there, you looked interested," he murmured into my ear.

Olga had paused to round up a couple of the boys, who had been enticed away by some wasps' nests on a stick—three for a dollar!—so we had a moment.

"Intrigued, maybe."

Strong arms wrapped around my midsection. "Are you trying to tell me you're kinky, Dorina?"

I shot him a look over my shoulder. "You're a vampire dating one of the few things on earth capable of killing you, and I'm kinky?"

"Good point." Warm lips found my neck.

They were nice lips. And the body pressed against mine was even nicer. Especially when a cloud of smoke from a nearby vendor's grill billowed past, and the damned vamp took the opportunity to slide his hands under my jacket.

That was better than nice, because Louis-Cesare could have taught the nymph a thing or two. Or, at least, it should have been. Except for the fact that we were already a threesome, and that was without the girl.

Cut it out, I told myself, as those warm hands went roving in all the right places. *Can't you just enjoy something for once? Don't think about her.*

But it was kind of hard not to when the third in our little ménage wasn't someone I could just walk away from. Because she was me—the other me, the monster to my Frankenstein, the Hyde to my Jekyll. The alter ego that, despite the fact that we shared cranium space, I didn't feel like I knew at all.

It was a long story, but essentially boiled down to a stark truth about dhampirs: we're all certifiably nuts. That's why, despite having technically immortal creatures for sperm donors, we rarely end up with even normal human life spans. I suppose it's nature's way of compensating for the fact that we're not supposed to exist in the first place, since dead sperm don't swim.

But half-dead ones do, and rare vampires like my Sire, who was cursed rather than bitten, have a couple days' leeway while the spell takes effect. A couple days in which they aren't one thing or the other. And neither are any children they make in the meantime. Children who end up with greater strength, heightened senses, Olympic-athlete speed—and two natures that try their best to kill each other.

In my case, my vampire half had made a good start on that, growing faster and maturing quicker than my mostly human side, and threatening to tear me apart in the process. So Mircea, the sperm donor in question, who was talented at manipulating the mind even for a bloodsucker, put a wall between us—a mental wall. One that had allowed my two natures to develop separately, never occupying consciousness at the same time. It had saved our lives, and given us a chance to do what most dhampirs rarely manage and actually grow up. But it had also created some problems.

Big ones.

Like the fact that Dorina was pretty damned savage, as far as I could tell, adhering much more to the vampire nature than I ever had. Like the fact that Mircea's wall had eventually crumbled, cracking recently thanks to my ingesting a fey substance that had been labeled a beverage, but acted more like a mind-altering drug. And like the fact that now, for the first time in five hundred years, Dorina and I were leaking through the wall, her into me or me into her—the jury was still out but the point was, there was *contact*. Small, intermittent stuff so far, dreams or maybe memories of places I'd never been and people I'd never known.

But how long would that last?

It was unsettling enough, the idea that all those times I'd passed out in my life, I'd just been living someone else's. Someone who had done things I couldn't remember, to people I didn't know, who may or may not have deserved them, because how the hell would I know? But what was really causing me nightmares was worry about what was to come. Mircea had separated us because Dorina was stronger—was she still? And if she was, and if our brains were now blurring back together, what did that mean for me?

What did it mean if she decided that maybe I'd been in charge long enough, and it was her time in the driver's seat?

"Dory?" I suddenly noticed that Louis-Cesare's hands had stopped. Going vampire-still like the rest of him as he scanned the crowd for dangers he wouldn't find, because they were all locked up in my crazy head. "Is something wrong?"

Nothing I want to try and explain, I thought. *Especially not tonight.* If I didn't have much time left, I was going to enjoy the hell out of what I did.

I grabbed his hand. "No. Come on."

"To where? Olga has stopped."

"Yeah, to round up the boys, so there's time."

"For what?" His eyes flickered to the tent again, as if he was calculating exactly how long we had.

I smacked his arm. "To win a prize," I said, and dragged him off toward a snarl of booths ahead.

This wasn't the most organized place I'd ever seen, maybe because of the limited space the vendors had to work with. Or maybe because troll eyesight preferred the pretty lights all mushed up together. But we managed to forge a path through the tangle nonetheless, to a small booth almost buried in teddy bears.

Huge eye-searingly pink ones.

Now, I hate pink and could give a crap about stuffed animals, but I had a half-breed at home that loved them. Specifically, he loved to chew the shit out of them because he was teething. And, with the number of teeth in that mouth and all of them coming in at once, it was a problem.

I'd tried those amber necklace things, but the razor-sharp canines he was developing kept slicing through the string, and then he'd eat the beads. Which wouldn't have been so bad except he crunched them up like candy, *crunch*, *crunch*, *crunch*, all day long, and the sound had been driving everybody crazy.

So we'd switched to softer stuff, but we were fast running out of pillows, and most of the stuffed animals I'd bought as a substitute hadn't lasted ten minutes. Of course, they'd been normal sized and pretty flimsy, while these . . . I gazed up at them in satisfaction. That's what I'd thought. These had been made for *trolls*.

They looked vaguely like Lots-o'-Huggin' Bear if he'd been made by somebody worried more about sturdiness than hugability. The main material seemed to be some sort of rawhide, with black embroidered eyes that couldn't be crunched off and seams that appeared to have been quadruple stitched. Because troll babies were hard-core.

And there were tons of them, the lack of space having forced the vendor to pile them everywhere, including on top of his stall, where they remained, a trembling mountain of pink sturdiness just waiting to be savaged by my little heathen baby.

"What . . ." Louis-Cesare stood there, staring upward, seemingly at a loss for words. Perhaps at the fact that I'd dragged him away from the nymphs for this. Or perhaps because the bears looked like they might collapse on us at any minute.

"I want one of those." I pointed.

Louis-Cesare blinked a few times, but took out his wallet.

"No, you can't buy it," I said. "You have to win it."

"Win it?" He looked slightly confused.

The carny decided to help me out. "That's right, good sir, step right up, we have a winner here, I can tell, we have a big winner!"

An aristocratic eyebrow went up at the man's cant, and I swear it looked like Louis-Cesare had never been to a carnival before. Which was weird, because I knew France had them, although maybe not this kind. Definitely not this kind, I thought, as the man's assistants popped up from beneath the counter.

And, okay, this was new.

Peering at us over the countertop were a line of wizened little . . . somethings. Grayish green and brown and vaguely hoary, had they been in a glade somewhere, I might have walked right past them and thought they were moss-covered stones. But here, under the bright lights of the carny's booth, they were obviously . . . somethings.

"Spriggans, ride with trolls," the carny said, seeing my surprise. He leaned in. "Don't give them any money."

"What?"

"They'll go off and bury it somewhere, and then we won't have a game, will we?"

"*Do* we have a game?" Louis-Cesare said, because he did not appear to be interested in things that ride with trolls. He appeared to be interested in the bears, eyeing them as if reevaluating his whole impression of me. "You truly wish one of these?" he asked, his eyes sliding to mine.

"Or two. Two is good."

"Two."

"And easy it is, sir, easy it is. Just take these," the carny slid three spiky balls across the counter. "Fix 'em to the back wall there, just anywhere you please. Black circles get you a fine key chain, hand carved by some of the locals—truly stunning work. The purple areas get you a premium box of candy for the lady here," he smirked at me. "And the green circles, well, those'll get you one of these fine, handcrafted—"

"And the pink. Those are for the bears, yes?" Louis-Cesare asked.

"Uh, yes. Yes, indeed." The carny broke off his spiel to nod at three tiny, bright pink circles amid the busy backdrop, which won the top prize. Still, the game didn't look too hard to me. Both the balls and the backdrop were covered in a bunch of Velcro-looking stuff, and ought to stick together nicely—if you weren't a troll with lousy eyesight. I glanced at Olga, who had started ambling this way, and wondered how many we could win before—

Pop!

Something went off like a gunshot, loud enough to make me jump. And then blink and do a double take, because the nearest little whatever was little no longer. In a split second, the spriggan had blown up to the circumference of an oversized beach ball. And in the middle of the stretched, mottled, knobby-looking hide resided a single off-white ball.

Okay, maybe this wasn't going to be as easy as I'd thought.

"Olga's coming," I told Louis-Cesare, who had acquired a small frown in between his eyebrows.

"This will not take a moment," he told me, and threw the remaining balls.

Pop! Pop!

More frowning.

"We can come back later," I offered, as Olga came up behind.

"What you do?"

"Winning a bear."

"Not here," she said, chewing on something with tiny trailing feet and a tail. "He cheats."

"I do no such thing!" The carny looked offended. "This is a game of skill, plain and simple."

"Not with them," Olga said placidly, as the little things watched her with shiny black eyes.

"He's a vampire," the carny said, passing over more balls. "With reflexes far faster than they're used to. It's more than fair—"

Pop! Pop! Pop!

"—why, it's the easiest game anywhere!"

"You know, honestly," I said, starting to wish I hadn't brought it up. Because I'd been watching those little beggars, and they moved like lightning. And whenever they weren't sure they'd be fast enough, they blew up like balloons, instantly covering so much space that there was literally no way to win. "It's fine. Really."

But Louis-Cesare was looking at me again, and he had that expression in his eyes. The one that said we weren't going anywhere. "Three more," he told the man.

"We could be here all night, and we have a match to—"

And then a bunch of things happened at once. The man handed over three more fool's bets; a bunch of coins suddenly flashed in the air, a glittering wave not of silver but of gold, pure and shiny and gleaming under the lights; and a bunch of crusty beach balls deflated and scrambled like mad for the surprise treasure.

And three little Velcro balls landed in three little circles, each one smack-dab in the middle.

I stared at them.

And then at the ground, where the crazed somethings were scrapping and clawing and scuffling in the dirt.

And back up at Louis-Cesare, who was looking smug. "You just spent like . . ." I didn't even know. "A couple *thousand* dollars on a *bear*."

"Three bears," he said complaisantly, and pulled them down from the row above our heads.

"That's—you—wait—" the carny said. And then he said something else, but I couldn't hear him. Because an eardrum-rupturing horn had just gone off, and I thought it possible I'd never hear again.

It time, Olga mouthed, as the whole field suddenly jumped up and started for the house.

Chapter Three

"You're upset," Louis-Cesare said, from amid a forest of bear.

He was carrying all three, one affixed to his belt where his sword usually went when he was somewhere he could wear a sword. The other two were under his arms, with the huge violently pink bodies lolling like drunken children. I frowned at them.

"I'm not upset."

"We won," he pointed out. "Most people enjoy winning."

"We didn't win. You basically bought them."

"That is what is troubling you?" He looked surprised. "We can go back after—"

"No. The man was a shyster. I don't—Why were you carrying *gold*?"

"Gold?" He blinked at me.

"The coins? The ones you threw?" I stopped, hands on hips, to stare at him, because if I'd just thrown a handful of gold at somebody, I'd damned well remember it. And then I almost got run over. Because the whole staircase leading up to the building was moving. Seriously, it was like an avalanche in reverse.

Louis-Cesare pulled me against his chest, inside the blindingly pink buffer zone. "For tips."

"What?"

I thought I'd misheard, because my ears felt like they were under siege. The loudspeakers were screaming instructions, people were jostling and fighting, and a group of inebriated dwarves behind us were belting out what I guess was a fight song. They were not among the more musically gifted of fey, something they were making up for with enthusiasm.

"Tips!" Louis-Cesare shouted, and just made things worse. But then he rubbed his fingers together in the universal sign for stubborn wheel grease and light dawned.

And still made no damned sense.

"For who?" I shouted back.

"The court."

"What?"

He bent his head down to mine. "The servants at court. Whenever they do anything for you, it's considered customary to tip them."

"With *gold*?"

"It's better than favors," he replied, with more cynicism than I'd have expected from him.

Louis-Cesare wasn't just a vampire; he was a senator, and therefore one of the ruling elite of the vampire world. But while most of the people who reached those lofty heights were manipulative, sneaky, and deviously clever, Louis-Cesare had reached them because somebody *else* fit that description. Namely, Anthony, the charming rogue in charge of the European Senate. Who'd realized that having a champion with Louis-Cesare's fighting ability meant that no one in their right mind was likely to challenge him—ever again. Giving Anthony all but absolute power.

Until recently, that is, when Louis-Cesare had gotten tired of playing bodyguard for an amiable tyrant and defected to the Senate's North American counterpart, where his new role had yet to be determined.

But it wasn't likely to be in central intelligence.

Not that he was a dumb jock, or dumb at all. But he was honorable—to a fault. And honest and decent and straightforward, none of which were traits that adapted well to the world of court intrigue. Not in Europe, where scheming Anthony ruled with an iron fist, and not at the court of courts that our own consul was putting together. Which, as luck would have it, had just become the focus of the entire vampire world.

The usually somewhat-turgid and uber-traditional

vamp society had gotten a shake-up recently, when the long-running war in Faerie spilled over into Earth. And quickly became enough of a threat to cause the unthinkable: an alliance of the world's six vampire senates for the first time ever, since for the first time ever they had a common enemy. Other than themselves, of course.

Nobody knew how this was going to work, or if it was, since the senates mostly hated one another. So, normally, I'd have been worried about Louis-Cesare in that unholy snake pit, which was now more like an unholy canyon filling up with opportunists from all over the world, eager to make whatever they could out of the war and the chaos it provided. Because they wouldn't get another chance like this.

Opportunities for advancement were pretty damned rare in vamp society, since immortal butts don't often vacate seats. That was especially true for the highest positions, which had waiting lists that could span centuries. But the war had changed all that, causing previously despised outcasts with useful skills to suddenly be looked at with new eyes.

Outcasts like me.

It was why I wasn't as worried for Louis-Cesare as I might have been, since I was right down there in the snake pit with him. Because, believe it or not—and I still mostly didn't—the newest member of the illustrious North American Vampire Senate, the ruling body of millions of vampires at home and the leading force of the coalition abroad, was . . .

Me.

No, seriously.

No, *seriously*.

Okay, it was actually Dorina, who Mircea had somehow managed to convince people was a first-level master vamp wearing a human suit.

And, yeah, under normal circumstances, that sort of carefree manipulation of the facts would have gotten him a padded cell—or a stake, since vamps don't bother warehousing their problems. But these circumstances weren't normal. The war had taken the lives of half of the old

Senate members and new ones had been needed stat, preferably ones who might be useful in the upcoming fight.

Of course, there were plenty of people who fit that description and would seem a more logical choice than me. Hell, the *garbage boy* would have seemed a more logical choice than me. Dhampirs and vampires are natural enemies, and while I'd recently come to have a slightly more . . . progressive . . . view on the matter, most of them still hissed at the sight of me. Yet the consul had given me the nod anyway, for the same reason that she'd snapped up Louis-Cesare: daddy dearest had promised her that I'd vote the way she wanted.

And with a bunch of new senators on board and not all of her choosing, and with rival consuls and their entourages flooding in to discuss the war, and with everybody watching her every move, just waiting for a chance to replace her as the newly appointed leader of the vampire world . . .

Well, even a dhampir's support had started to look pretty good.

Of course, I could have declined the honor and the Mack truck of excrement probably headed toward the fan of my life as a result. But the family had needed help, Louis-Cesare had needed an ally, and I had kind of wanted to go on living. Something that wasn't likely if the fey flooded through a bunch of illegal portals and murdered us all.

So I'd said okay.

I just hadn't stopped to wonder how a chick who'd spent most of her life as a pariah, scrounging up a living on the fringes of vamp society, was supposed to fit in at the court of courts.

Where people were tipped in *gold*.

"You're going to need some friends, too," Louis-Cesare told me, as if he'd been following my thoughts. And the next thing I knew, my hands were full of coins, old ones with a smirking guy on the front with a big nose and a wig. And before I could respond to *that*, a roar went up, one that made the former bedlam sound like a day at the park and seemed to be coming from directly overhead. I looked up—

And promptly forgot everything else.

Holy shit, I thought, caught flat-footed for the second time in one night.

We'd reached the ruined lobby, which was a working sea of people below, and above . . . was crazy town. It was also mostly missing. The fire damage hadn't looked that bad from outside, where the sturdy exterior walls had masked the carnage within, but now I could see that the entire center was gutted. As if it had acted like a chimney, pulling the fire up and out, and leaving us staring at fifteen floors of mostly open space, bisected by half-fallen girders and ropes of electrical lines, forming a giant echo chamber.

And it had plenty to echo. Hordes of spectators were clustered in working knots on the floors that could still support their weight, jostling for space on the cracked and burnt remains of people's apartments. Thousands had already beaten us to the punch, staking out prime spots while we were goofing off outside, and now they were shouting and stomping their feet and banging on things, which I didn't think was too smart considering the state of this place. And which was sending siftings of black ash down like evil snow, covering everything in drifts of soot nobody cared about, because the fight was about to begin.

Although where it was I had no idea. I didn't see anything that even vaguely resembled a ring, or so much as a cordoned-off section of floor. Of course, it was possible that it was buried somewhere under the massive crowd, which covered every square inch of the lobby, and seemed to want ours, too, judging by the amount of abuse we were taking.

"Dory!" I somehow heard the shout, which seemed to be coming from a towering pile of ruined furniture by a wall.

There were some more stalls over there—the usual T-shirts, hats, and water bottles. And one selling nothing but flashlights in all shapes and sizes, along with ropes of batteries in garlic-string-like bunches festooned everywhere. I almost bought one; it was gloomy as shit in here.

Which was why I couldn't tell who was calling me.

"Dory!"

I finally noticed that the spray-painter had been at work here, too, with neon green arrows flickering in the scattered torchlight, high on smoky black walls. They pointed the way to everything from booze to food to areas designated as toilets that I didn't want to know any more about. To a dripping line that said merely *FIN*.

There was no further explanation offered, but then, one wasn't needed. The hoi polloi of bookmakers might have set up outside, in the mud and muck, and managed to nab some business. But those in the know had bypassed them, because they knew better odds were to be found within.

They knew to look for Fin.

And, sure enough, the face peering at me over the side of the furniture pile was familiar. It was also full of nose, because Fin was of the troll persuasion. But unlike the mountain variety, who sort of resembled their namesake, he was an itty-bitty forest troll. One with a serious admiration for Olga, and no, I didn't know how that worked, but I assumed it was the reason he was beckoning us over.

Fin usually operated his business out of his bar, where you could get a bet down on anything from human and nonhuman sports to how fast a spider could traverse a girder. Fin covered it all, and had a rep for paying up promptly when he lost, which was probably why his makeshift perch looked like it was being besieged. We fought our way through to him anyway, using the bears as battering ram and buffer in one, which allowed us to reach the bottom of the pile more or less intact.

"Been trying to reach you all day!" Fin yelled, while continuing to accept money and write slips. "You kill another phone or what?"

I held it up. "Got it on me!"

"Well, turn it on once in a while! I got news!"

"A job?" I yelled, because Fin had been known to shoot work my way. And while I didn't think moonlighting was normal for a senator, neither was starvation. And nobody had bothered to mention before I took my shiny new Senate job that it didn't come with a salary.

A girl needed to get paid.

"No! A warning!"

He made a disgruntled sound and handed the book-making off to his senior associate. And clambered down the mountain, although not all the way. He found a perch that left him approximately chest high on Olga, which seemed to be a view he liked. Because he simpered at her while she gazed around the lofty space above us, probably searching for the albino.

I poked him. "What warning?"

"There's a rumor going around—some of my competition are already giving odds."

"On what?"

"On how long you'll last!"

"What?" It felt like I was saying that a lot tonight.

Fin nodded. "I'm not taking them, of course, us being friends and all, but others—" He broke off, eyeing the gleaming stash I was still clutching. "Of course, if you want to get a bet down on something else, I can—"

"Fin!" I pushed the gold at Louis-Cesare, who indicated with a grin that his hands were full of bear. Bastard. So I shoved it in my pocket for the moment. "What are you talking about?"

"Just that you're a senator now, and nobody saw that coming!"

"So they think I'm going to get fired?"

"No. They think you're gonna get dead!" he yelled, because some enthusiastic drumming had started from somewhere behind us, loud enough to tear through the din and my head.

I glanced around to see a bunch of trolls emerging from a room across the lobby. They were threading their way ponderously through the crowd, not that they had to work too hard. Everyone was practically trampling one another to get out of the way.

I didn't blame them.

They were the biggest damned trolls I'd ever seen.

The nearest was what I called shadow-on-a-rock, a mostly gray skin tone with purplish highlights in the crevasses, and had to be at least twelve feet tall. He had a torso like the Hulk's and arms thicker around than Olga's entire body. I'd never thought of her as a dainty, sylphlike creature before, but if these were what full-grown male trolls looked like, I was revising my opinion. And he was one of the *smaller* ones.

The biggest was fortunate that the ceiling was mostly missing, because the bits that remained were well below chin height, and that was despite the lobby having had a vaulted ceiling. He was a colossus with sun-kissed-mountain-range skin, mostly indigo with a scattering of orange-copper highlights. They gleamed in the torch-light, along with a map of scars, some new and vivid, some old and stretched, scrawling across the massive chest and back and arms. Advertising just how many of these contests he'd already survived.

I licked my lips uneasily. I'd thought the duo living in my basement were big, but I now recognized them for what they were: scrawny adolescents. And understood a little better why Olga had wanted an entire truckload of backup.

Not that we were looking so formidable, all of a sudden.

There seemed to be two groups, distinguished by the red or blue bandannas they wore on bulging biceps. Or, more likely, repurposed tablecloths, because just *look* at them. Most of the crowd didn't even come up to their *waists*, including some of our garden-variety green-brown boys, while some of the smaller beings scuttling around were in danger of being turned into a greasy spot with one misplaced step.

I didn't see anybody get crushed, but one obviously drunken ogre a few stories above us threw a bottle, and had the good aim or bad luck to have it bounce off the biggest guy's head. I doubt it hurt—the rock-hard cranium was encased in a helmet it didn't need—but I guess it made him mad. Because a split second later, maybe fifteen hundred pounds of muscle had jumped up, grabbed the offender, and landed back on the tile, with enough force to shudder it under our feet and to crack it around his giant ones.

And then he casually flicked the guy *through a wall*.

It looked like that was what the crowd had been waiting for, because they started roaring and stomping even harder than before, giving every impression of enjoying the pregame show.

I barely noticed. I was too busy wondering if maybe I couldn't see a ring because we were standing in it, and how it might be a good plan to, you know, get out, which was what everybody else appeared to be doing. The groaning stairways were suddenly flooded with people trying to get to higher levels, and crushing us against the wall in the process.

"Are you listening to me?" Fin demanded, as even Olga ended up hugging brick.

"No," I breathed, and doubted he heard it. But he must have seen it, because the wrinkled forehead acquired another one.

"Dory! I'm trying to tell you that you're in danger!"

"No shit," I said, as the trolls started scaling the burnt brick, pulling themselves up ruined floor after ruined floor, until the blue and red teams were facing each other, not on the ground, but on the *walls*.

And, finally, I understood. The fight—a free-for-all between a dozen massive guys on each side—was to take place in the demolished open space in the center of the building, up and down fifteen stories as combatants leapt and dove and swung through open air, getting assists from a few dangling ropes the showrunners had provided while dodging the pots and pans, broken bottles, and burnt, ragged-edged table legs many of the fans were wielding. Which they clearly planned to use to help their favorite team by clobbering the hell out of the other guys.

"Interesting," Louis-Cesare said, his eyes shining.

Because he was *insane*.

Like Fin, apparently, who had leaned over to grab me and yell something in my ear.

"What?"

"... warn you ... word on the streets ... seat."

"I can't hear you!"

"Heard ... want ... seat!"

"What seat? It's standing-room only!"

Fin was starting to look frustrated, but not nearly as much as I was, because how were we supposed to find anybody in this? We'd be lucky to avoid getting pancaked by a falling troll. Like, really lucky, I thought, staring upward at thousands of pounds of muscle hanging off barely-holding-together walls as a sound like a thousand trumpets pealed through the air, loud enough to make me actually nauseous. And to drown out whatever the hell Fin was yelling.

"I don't want a damned chair!" I told him, ears ringing, as I tried to pry him off. Which should have been easy, because forest trolls are a lot less butch than their mountain counterparts, only this one was *determined*.

And now he was shaking me. And screaming in my already-wounded ear. "Not a *chair*! A *seat*! They want your *Senate seat*!"

I frowned at him. "What? Who does?"

"Hello." It was the girl with the purple hair and the catsuit, appearing out of nowhere and giving me a little wave.

And the next thing I knew, I was flying.

Chapter Four

For a moment, everything was darkness and disorientation and the disturbing feeling of no longer being properly attached to earth. And thunderous noise, because the crowd was on all sides now, since I'd just been thrown something like three stories straight up. And flipped head over heels in the process, to the point that I only knew where I was by the torches burning in the lobby below, a ring of fire slinging around me as I tumbled through space, getting farther away by the second.

Gravity being a thing, I fully expected to be reacquainted with them shortly, when I hit the floor in a puddle of used-to-be-dhampir. And maybe I would have—except that I hit the side of a moving mountain first. To whom I clung like a limpet, because literally all I could see were thrashing bodies and flailing fists, all of which were bigger than my head.

Way bigger.

And aimed at us, I realized. Team Immovable Object and Team Irresistible Force were meeting with a crash like two freight trains coming together, with me in the middle. Because I'd happened to catch hold of the big boy, whom everybody seemed to agree had an unfair advantage.

So they were trying to take him out first.

Half of the opposing team jumped him, most of them having already found weapons consisting of whatever the fire had spared. Kitchen knives, heavy pieces of furniture, and what appeared to be part of a solid steel girder all came at us at the same time. Causing my ride to do a 360 flip in midair, coming off the wall and going straight up, amazingly fast and balletic for someone his size.

Leaving the would-be attackers to crash into the wall below.

"All right," I breathed, grinning in shock and relief as we righted again, on a broken ledge another story up. "All right! Yeah!"

Which, in retrospect, wasn't the best idea. Because troll hearing works a lot better than troll eyesight, and Big Blue realized he had a hitchhiker. And flicked me off his shoulder like an annoying insect, one headed straight at the opposite wall, which was about to serve as a fly-swatter.

But I wasn't a fly, and I grabbed one of the hanging ropes in passing, somehow getting my knees up and my feet out. And managed to push off from the wall instead of splatting onto it. And ended up—

Right back in the thick of things.

The next few seconds were a kaleidoscope of impressions more than thoughts, because I didn't have time for thoughts. Bodies were tumbling, bricks were flying, blood was spurting—green, oh good. And I was getting smacked around by both sides, because I couldn't see well enough to find a way out.

But not because of a lack of light. The battleground had started off gloomy, with a little moonlight above and some scattered torches below, but it hadn't stayed that way. As soon as the fun began, the flashlights turned on— masses of them. And started waving around everywhere like a thousand tiny spotlights, because everyone seemed to have one. It reminded me of people holding up lighters at a concert, only these lighters were extra powerful and were glinting off everything: ruined metal and broken glass and tiny, angry troll eyes, whose owners were prob-ably pissed that they had to fight half-blind.

Which was why they were going on *movement*, Dory!

I finally realized why I was drawing so much attention swinging around on my little rope, probably looking like a flying fist even as I tried to avoid them—and the bottles and bricks and unidentifiable junk the crowd was pelting us with.

Until I got smart and jumped for a piece of somebody's living room, draped with fallen shag carpeting that gave me a decent handhold. At least, it did until I pulled an ancient TV off the edge. It was built in a cabinet like a piece of furniture and would have taken me out or at least down, only a nearby troll grabbed it first. And flung it at an opponent's head, catching my rope in the process, and sending me hurtling across the gap—

Straight at a bunch of humans crowding somebody's bathtub.

Oh, thank God, I thought, reaching for them gratefully.

Only to have them shove me right back out again, waving beer bottles and cheering.

"Assholes!" I yelled, but nobody heard.

On the bright side, the shove sent me spinning across the void toward another possible perch: a broken piece of hallway that nobody had claimed, maybe because it was no longer connected to anything on either side. But I wasn't coming from the side; I was coming head-on, and I managed to catch it.

With my stomach.

It hurt like a bitch, but so am I, and I snarled and clambered on top. And then just lay there, breathing hard, because it felt like I'd broken a rib. It still did when I rolled over a moment later and peered past the edge, trying to take stock.

It wasn't easy.

The fight had already spread out, with two fallen colossi in the now-mostly-vacated lobby, and two more battling it out on the floor around them, throwing up huge drifts of soot in the process. Everybody else was tearing through the various stories, raining down bricks and dust and debris, which, with the strobe lighting from the damned flashlights, made it hard to see anything. But I nonetheless managed to glimpse a smear of pink, far below.

And then Louis-Cesare, on one side of the lobby. He had a torch in one hand and a piece of rebar in the other, and was holding off an even dozen vamps while still draped in three grinning sidekicks. Because it looked like Bitch Girl hadn't come alone.

It also looked like her backup was a little worried

about the bears. Like why Louis-Cesare hadn't felt it necessary to set them down. Or maybe they'd heard rumors of the crazy swordsman with the old-world manners who would apologize if he stepped on your foot in a fight right before he gutted you. But it was more likely going to be the other way around this time, because he was distracted, his eyes flickering constantly upward.

Looking for me, I realized.

"I'm okay!" I yelled, waving both arms, and saw a brief flash of teeth.

Right before he was swamped by the whole crew at once, who weren't politely waiting to duel him one at a time, like in the movies.

They never do.

Crap.

I started looking for a landing spot that my rope might reach, only to realize that it wasn't a rope. I'd grabbed for one, but in the darkness I'd found something else. Something that spit and sizzled, like a downed electric cable.

Maybe because it was a downed electric cable.

"Shit!"

And then Purple Hair popped up over the side of my impossible-to-reach perch, like freaking Spider-Man.

I blinked at her.

"How the hell did you get up here?" I demanded.

"Miss me?" She flashed some fang.

"No," I said, and stuck the cable to her chest.

Okay, that worked better than expected, I thought, watching her slam back into the void, like she'd been hit by a giant fist.

And then get smashed between two of them, when she sailed straight into the middle of a troll fight.

I winced.

That had to hurt.

And then the cable suddenly coiled around and hissed at me, like some huge black snake. An image that was only reinforced when it started striking down, sparking off brick and plaster and part of a twisted girder, as I ducked and dodged and cursed vampire master powers, the fun stuff they get with advanced age but which I'd managed to miss out on.

At least I know how she managed that throw, I thought, wrestling with the damned thing. And finally managing to loop it around a girder. And tie it off in half a dozen knots until it just stayed there, flailing helplessly.

Like me, when a roundhouse kick came out of nowhere and sent me sailing.

Son of a bitch!

I landed in a rug-burn-inducing slide in a soot-covered apartment somewhere below. One stuffed to the gills with ogres who didn't appreciate the intrusion. Between the pots and pans and somebody's floor lamp they started pelting me with, it took me a second to notice that my assailant's hair was now blond and short, and that she seemed to have changed sexes.

"Who the hell are you?" I asked, staring up at the new guy.

"A dead man," he told me, which was accurate considering the fangs, but weird.

Or maybe not, I thought, as he suddenly staggered backward into the abyss, and I realized that he hadn't been the one speaking.

"Competition?" I guessed, as Purple Hair grinned at me some more.

"Competition," she agreed.

And then she lunged.

But I'd expected it, and got a frying pan up in time, slamming it into her pretty face. It didn't cave it in, exactly, but I had the impression that her features might be a lot flatter once it came off. I decided not to find out and kicked her over the edge.

For anyone else, that would have been it, but anyone else would have already been dead from electrocution. So it wasn't entirely a surprise to see some purple-tipped talons grasp the edge of the floor a couple seconds later, although how their owner managed that I didn't know unless she jackknifed in space. But at least she was looking a little worse for the wear, with her hair a crackling nimbus around her perfectly made-up and now-blood-smeared face.

Not that it seemed to be slowing her down.

I'd gotten back to my feet, but before I could blink, my

ankle was caught, my butt hit the floor, and the only reason I didn't go over the edge was the couple of large ogres I'd managed to grab on the way down.

And the fact that I was slamming my boot into her head as hard as I could.

"Out of curiosity," I panted, while one of the ogres' friends started wailing on me with a toaster, "is there a reason you and Blondie both showed up tonight?"

She spat blood. "You're a hard person to find. You get appointed to the Senate, then immediately get sent out of the country."

And, yeah, the Senate had had a couple errands for me, one of which had resulted in my current, less-than-optimal state. But I didn't see what that had to do with her. "So?"

"So we didn't know where you went, and had to wait for you to get back, and now there's only a week left."

"Until what?"

"Until the swearing in," she said, getting smacked by a determined little guy with a broom handle. "Once you're confirmed . . . no one can touch you . . . until after the war. And by then . . . you'll have made alliances."

I vaguely remembered somebody telling me that duels between senators had been outlawed until after the war, to cut down on the chaos. And because I guess the consul felt like she'd lost enough Senate members already. But we newbies weren't technically senators yet, were we?

"So this is gonna be an all-week thing?" I guessed.

"Oh, trust me." The annoying smirk was back. "It won't take nearly that long."

I was beginning to think she might be right. Because she was somehow managing to drag me, the two ogres I'd latched onto, and what appeared to be their whole clan—all of whom were now holding on to them, with some even bracing in the doorway—toward the precipice. And that was while I did my utmost to punch a hole through that stupid grin.

And I wasn't the only one.

"Die, bitch," Blondie said, coming to the rescue despite having her stake still sticking out of his chest.

"How are you guys getting *up* here?" I asked, but

didn't get an answer. Because a passing troll fight swept them and a third of the room away, and would have dragged me off, too, if the ogres hadn't jerked their relatives back just in time. And taken me with them.

"Hey, thanks," I said sincerely, staggering back to my feet.

And had the whole room charge at me at once.

I had a split second to spot a rope, or end up plunging through space without one. But between the fighting and the dust and the disco-ball-on-acid effect of the flashlights, that wasn't easy. But I thought I glimpsed something off to the left and leapt for it, hoping it wasn't another live wire.

I never found out.

However, I did find out how the vamps were all but levitating around, when I went rocketing toward the roof. It took me a second to realize that I'd landed on the broad back of a troll, who was too busy chasing a blue team member up the wall to notice. And judging by the level of enthusiasm, I really didn't want to be there when he caught him.

Not that that was likely to be a problem, I realized, when somebody jumped off another passing titan and grabbed me.

"Would you get a *life*?" I gritted, watching Purple Hair wrestle with my boot.

"Trying to," she told me indistinctly, while I slammed my heel into her face some more.

I am not a weakling, and I was motivated. But it didn't seem to be making much of an impression. *Of course I could be wrong,* I thought, as a side table, a keyboard, and a La-Z-Boy came flying out of the apartments we were passing, as if pulled by a string.

Or by a determined master vampire who wanted to give me something else to think about.

And she wasn't short on ammo. A bunch of tumbled bricks came streaming at me a second later, like a machine gun spewing huge, rough-edged bullets—half of which were hitting my freaking ribs. Even worse, the barrage seemed to have given my ride's opponent an idea, because we were suddenly being pelted by a ton of stuff from above, as he tried to slow us down. Including the burnt-out remains of a fridge he'd grabbed out of somebody's kitchen and was about to—

Okay, yeah.

I stopped pummeling and twisted, hanging off Troll Boy's bandanna by one arm, getting ready. And, to her credit, Purple Hair wasn't stupid. I saw her eyes widen and her hands fumble for weapons she'd so far ignored, right before my leg muscles bunched and my knee snapped and she was thrown into the path of the fridge, still flailing.

People can say all they want about Babe Ruth, but that troll was the real MVP, wielding that thing like a bat and sending her up, up, and all the way out, through the nonexistent roof and into the moonlit sky beyond.

Hitting a home run if ever I saw one.

"Heh," I said, because it was funny.

And because I never learn.

Suddenly, I had a very unhappy troll's face in mine, a chair-sized hand snatching me off his back, and a wall coming at me too fast to do anything about. This time, the flyswatter connected. A moment later, I was bleary-eyed and barely conscious, scrambling to find a handhold on the rough old bricks.

And I did. I found plenty. Because the wall had been seriously charred here, which left it jagged and broken, with any number of potential grips. Unfortunately, it also left it soft and brittle, and pieces of it kept breaking off under my hands.

My head jerked about, looking for alternatives. But all I saw were ominous cracks racing off for yards in every direction. And the concrete slab of the lobby floor, way too far away to be survivable. And Louis-Cesare looking up, surrounded by a circle of bodies, fear and horror dawning on his face.

And a lump in my pocket that one of my flailing hands brushed against, and that I vaguely realized was the gold he'd given me.

Gold.

A moment later, the whole section of wall crumbled to pieces. And I fell into wind and light and noise, with no ropes, no jutting bits of hallway, and no passing giants to

the rescue. Just a glittering line of coins racing ahead of
me, pattering down on the floor below like golden rain.
And a flood of small somethings surging out of the dark,
scrabbling for them greedily before looking up—

And seeing me speeding at them like a dhampir-shaped
bullet.

Suddenly, the whole, echoing tower of crazy sounded
like the world's biggest popcorn popper going off.

Which is why I hit down, not on a hard concrete subfloor, but on a sea of rubbery, bouncy, inflatable somethings, most of which were still trying to spot the coins in
the soot. And battering me this way and that, sending me
bouncing around like a drunk chick in a ball pit. One
whose boyfriend came to grab her out of the air a second
later, and drag her against his chest, yelling something
inaudible because the room had suddenly gone crazy.

But not because of us.

"Well, shit," I said distinctly, staring upward.

Right before we were buried under a couple thousand
pounds of falling muscle.

Damn, I knew *that was going to happen,* I thought.

And passed out.

Chapter Five

Not surprisingly, I dreamed of trolls.

Not big ones, but normal sized, even a little puny, watching me with tiny eyes blown wide with fear as I tore past, raking backhoe amounts of bricks out of walls and carving the old building into my personal ladder. I couldn't see well, just smears of light that sometimes dazzled, sometimes blinded, when they shone directly into my eyes. And I could barely hear, the surrounding walls reflecting back every sound, from my hoarse breathing to the deafening cheers of the crowd.

Didn't matter.

I could sense my prey ahead, could smell him—an oil slick of a scent, partly the result of whatever he used on his hair, partly him. A little man. A frightened man. A bully, as slavers always were.

This would be easy.

I smelled the others, as well, the ones I'd come with, racing up what remained of the stairs nearby. Because they'd spotted him, too. They were faster than I'd expected, these ponderous-looking creatures, but they had to throw the people blocking the stairs out of the way, and deal with the man's servants, whom he'd left behind to slow their pursuit.

I didn't. And while he might be fast enough to avoid them, he was no match for me. A fact he seemed to realize when we reached the roof, him bursting out of a stairwell and me vaulting through the tattered opening the fire had provided, at almost the same time.

He was panicked; I could smell it in his sweat, hear it in the labored breaths he was taking, glimpse it in those

pale eyes. But not enough. Not like one who has seen his
death and has no way to avoid it.

That look I was intimately familiar with, the pallor of
the skin, the slump of shoulders, the resignation that sets
in, seconds before any damage is done, because they
know it's coming.

It was absent this time.

There was something wrong.

I glanced around, but with the limitations of this borrowed body, it was difficult to tell if he had reinforcements. It was dark, with most of the light below us now, a
moving lattice etching the night that did little to dispel the
gloom this far up. And there was nothing in the air that I
could scent, except soot and smog and exhaust, the acrid
burn of asphalt still warm from the day, and a soothing
gleam of rain behind.

And his weapons, a metallic taste on my tongue that
shouted a warning, not that it mattered.

His toys couldn't hurt me.

But something else might.

I threw myself to the side, hitting concrete a second
before a wall of energy spiraled out of nowhere, tearing
across the roofline right where I'd been standing.

It would have been exhilarating in my old body, a roaring finger of power spearing the night, right overhead. But
in this one . . . it was a problem. The electric flood from
the portal had frightened my avatar as the battle had not,
the strange light searing his small eyes, the strange smell
filling his nostrils. It wasn't fey, it wasn't human, it wasn't
anything he knew, and it was everywhere, leaving him
scent- as well as sight-blind, with no senses he could trust.

It made the huge body huddle and cringe, and swamped
the mind with panic, always the hardest emotion to see
through. He began fighting me, desperate to get away, to
get anywhere that felt familiar. And in the few seconds it
took for me to reassure him, the slaver—

Was gone.

The portal winked out of existence as quickly as it had
come, allowing the blue-black darkness of the city to close
over our head again. I pulled us back to our feet, reeling
from the troll's surging emotions, and the fury of my own.

Because the slaver could be anywhere now. From another point on Earth, perhaps thousands of miles away, to another realm altogether, if this portal connected to Faerie. I had failed.

So why could I still smell him?

I growled, a low thread of anger that matched the troll's changing feelings. His fear was receding as rage took its place, that the creature he so hated had made him cower and cringe once again—and gotten away. To a place where he'd do it to others, the way he always did, the way he always had.

I had a sudden flood of memories, not mine, but vivid just the same: the hulk I was inhabiting once small and frightened, his young wrists scarred from shackles he couldn't break, his child ribs showing through the scraps of clothing he wore, yet being forced to fight nonetheless. Because if he did not, the rod came, the tip of which felt like fire. It hurt; it burned. And, eventually, if used enough, it killed.

So he fought, even though he knew his role wasn't that of victor. He was to be loaned out to battles as one of the bodies carried away at the end of the night, to give the crowd the blood it craved, yet spare the better combatants. The ones who chose to be there, as he did not.

Yet, again and again, they were the ones carried away, and he remained, battle-scarred and seething, growing larger than them all, and waiting . . . for his chance. Not to live; he had nothing left to go back to. He didn't know where they'd found him, who his people were, didn't even know his true name. Only the one they'd given him: Magdar. It meant "cudgel" in some Earth tongue, and that was all he'd ever been.

What did he know of life?

No, his plan wasn't escape, but to do what he'd been trained to do: to kill. This slaver, the one who owned him now; the others, who had had him before—until he became too much to handle; THE slavers, the two who had taken him from his home, who had ripped him from his mother's arms, who had dragged him screaming through a portal.

Into this never-ending nightmare.

Killers. Abusers. Desecrators.

He would have them; he would have them all.

And I will help you, *I promised, while scenting the air, drawing in great bushelfuls at a time, filling the great chest. And no, I hadn't been wrong. I could still smell him, and not just the residue his presence had left behind. But him, although distant now, indistinct.*

And getting more so by the second.

We let out a roar and leapt across the roof, to the side facing the parking lot. With the distance and these eyes, I couldn't make out much, even with the lot lights spearing the darkness. But I could see movement, and a slim, pale shape weaving among the cars, because that portal hadn't gone to Faerie, had it? It had let out somewhere near the bottom of this building, like an emergency slide without the slide, and now our prey was getting away.

And I couldn't catch him like this.

Your shackles are gone, *I reminded the other.* Come find me when this is over. And we will hunt again.

I felt the nod, the way I had when I'd made my initial offer. And then the disorientation of a mental flight hit me, a thousand minds crowding in from all sides, all at once. Overwhelming, exhausting, thrilling . . .

Until I burst free of the building and soared into the night.

I didn't have much time, and not only because of the slaver. I couldn't hold free flight for long; I had to have an avatar, and soon. But there were far fewer options out here.

There were some vendors cleaning up and getting ready for another onslaught after the fight. There were a few drunks under tables and slumped in tents, too far gone to care about the night's revelries. There was a bag lady with her little cart, who had wandered in through the unwatched gate, because its keepers had snuck away to the fights. And who was now staring around, her mouth hanging open.

None of which could help me.

But he could.

The troll my twin had sent to watch her weapons was sitting in the cab of our truck. The door was open, because there wasn't enough room for him to be comfortable inside even with the seat all the way back. He was therefore sitting sideways, one huge leg bent over the other, to bring his foot up to his face.

So he could pick at his toes.

These creatures would have fascinated me another time, how clear, how clean their minds were. With none of the anxiety, the constant worry, the thousand pesky thoughts even a dull-witted human had running in the background all the time. This one was simply thinking about his toe, and the splinter that had somehow wedged itself into the tender flesh around his cuticle.

He was perfect.

And a moment later, he was straightening up, was twisting around in the driver's seat, was grasping the wheel—

And was then just sitting there.

Because neither of us knew how to drive.

I cursed, and felt his apology; he wanted to help. Not your fault, *I told him, and then cursed again, the deep sound echoing around the cab as the albino sped past us in a red sports car. One that screamed its way out of the lot a moment later, but we had no way to follow. The troll didn't know what to do, and my twin's mind was still unconscious, buried under a couple of fallen combatants. Even had I been willing to risk direct contact, she couldn't help me.*

Damn it!

Someone knocked on the door of the cab. I looked out and saw the bag lady from before, hanging off the side of the truck, gripping the mirror. And looking more than a little disturbed. She was babbling and pointing back the way we'd come, as if trying to tell somebody about the madness she'd just witnessed.

Until her bleary eyes caught mine, and she registered who it was, exactly, she was talking to.

She jumped down, surprisingly spry for her age, and took off, her shopping cart speeding in front of her. But I caught her mind—interesting—and made an offer. Not a demand; such things were difficult, and dangerous if the unwilling one was about to be piloting a few tons of racing metal.

But no such pressure was needed.

I saw her slow, saw her shoulders twitch. Saw the question in her mind, and knew the answer. She looked back, the fear in her eyes suddenly replaced by something else.

And then I was sliding over to the passenger side, and she was scrambling into the cab.

She was a strange-looking creature, with half-smoked cigarettes sticking out of her frowzled gray afro in a dozen places, patched skirts bunched up around her wrinkled knees, and the smell of alcohol on her breath.

"I really shouldn't be driving," she told me conversationally, as the engine turned over. "I drink, you know."

"Hit the gas," I growled, and we took off, the truck lurching ahead from a dead stop, and then screeching around a corner.

It had taken us only a moment to get going, but our vehicle was slow, and with the slaver's head start, I was afraid we would be too late. But then I saw him up ahead, stopped at a red light. Because humans are creatures of habit even when running for their lives.

Until he saw us, coming up fast behind him, and shot ahead, barreling through the intersection and getting clipped by a truck in the process.

It spun him around, but didn't do much to slow him down.

But the few seconds it took for him to get oriented bought us some useful time. The trolls we had come with had seen his flight as well, and had rushed down the length of the building, emerging on the sidewalk at a lumbering run as we shot past. And then stopped on a dime, my huge, borrowed arm sticking out of the window to beckon them forward.

They got in.

The truck sagged with their weight, making it even slower than before, but I wanted backup in case he was leading us to some of his own. And then the light changed and we went charging forward, the gas pedal all the way down because our driver had a crazy gleam in her eyes. Maybe she really shouldn't be driving, *I thought—too late.*

But it seemed to be working. And the added weight

ensured that we did not, in fact, end up on three wheels when she took a corner at a somewhat startling speed. "Ha, ha!" she said, cackling and rocking back and forth, the crazy eyes full-blown now.

"Watch the road," I grumbled, and she nodded vigorously.

And, to be fair, while we plowed through a mailbox, a light pole, and part of a florist shop, we did not lose the red car. I couldn't see the slaver too well in this guise, but when I slipped briefly into the old woman's mind, I saw him glance at us over his shoulder, his eyes huge and one of his long, white hands gripping the steering wheel. While the other—

"Gun!" the woman and I said together, as the first bullet tore through the windshield, cracking it all at once.

"Gun, gun, gun, gun, gun, gun, gun!" she informed me, as we started slinging around the road, as if she were trying to dodge the bullets.

"Stay on target," I growled, slipping back into the one called Sten. And starting to climb out of the door when someone tapped us on the shoulder.

I looked back, and the red-haired troll woman draped something over my head. When I looked down again, my borrowed body had transformed into that of a bulky human male with hairy arms. As had those of the trolls in the back of the truck, who could have been my brothers by appearance, yet were staring at me oddly.

"Thank you," I rumbled.

"We talk later," she said, and gave me a push.

Sten and I finished our transition to the hood of our vehicle and paused, to judge the distance.

He seemed to think we could make it, and he was proved right when we leapt from the front of our vehicle and smashed down onto the roof of the small red car. It had already been low to the ground and was now sending up sparks as we slung around another corner. Because the glamourie the woman had provided did nothing to change bulk, and Sten was well-fed.

But not well enough.

Slow him more, Sten told me, and sent a visual of us hanging off the back of the car, digging in our heels.

Better way, *I told him back, and plunged our hand through the flimsy car top, ripping it open like a can and leaving the albino exposed.*

He didn't seem to like that, judging by the amount of bullets suddenly hitting us. Which didn't penetrate even at this distance, but which hurt Sten the way bee stings would hurt a human. And caused him to put one of his huge hands in front of our eyes to protect them.

And before I could explain to him that I couldn't kill something I couldn't see, the car had raced around a curve and plunged down a hill, jittering and juddering as if we were no longer on a road.

Because we weren't, I realized, as Sten parted two huge fingers enough to show us a construction site, which the albino had turned the car into. One crowded with equipment and silvered with moonlight, which was why I could see anything at all. But not in time.

A large girder dangling from a crane came out of nowhere and hit us in the head, sweeping us off the back of the car as the albino tore underneath. And almost causing us to be run over by our own support team, who were right behind. But the bag lady saw us and swerved, sending the truck flying up a dirt ramp and sailing over our heads—

And over the albino's.

He had taken another ramp, this one going down into the ditch that was going to be the foundation of the new building someday. And abruptly realized that he had no way out except back the way he'd come, which was why he'd just spun around. In time to see the huge truck— heavy in its own right, and now also loaded down with troll—come hurtling at him off the edge.

I assume he did not see it hit down, since it landed directly on top of him and the little red car.

The crunch was . . . satisfying.

After a moment, Sten got back to his feet and lumbered to the edge of the ditch.

"Olga all right," *he observed, watching her and the rest of the trolls climb out of the ruined truck and get some distance.*

"Yes," *I agreed.*

"Slaver . . . could be," *he added, sounding less sure.*

And then abruptly stepped back when the car went up, the explosion big enough to engulf both vehicles in a ball of fire and a column of billowing black smoke.

"Maybe not," he conceded.

I sent the image to Magdar, along with the sounds and smells and memories of the chase.

One, he sent back.

I smiled.

Chapter Six

I woke up in a bed that smelled of butterscotch.

My favorite flavor, I thought, stretching. And rolled onto something muscle hard and skin soft that was taking up most of my bed. *Like warm candy,* I thought, my lips finding a nipple.

Strong hands gripped my waist.

"You aren't up to this," Louis-Cesare's voice informed me.

"Neither are you, but give me a minute."

I went back to the candy.

Until I was rolled over, which should have been pleasurable but which surprisingly . . . was not.

"Ow," I said, my ribs protesting vocally.

"I told you."

I opened my eyes to find a curtain of auburn hair falling on either side of my face, my favorite blue eyes looking down at me in concern, and my hands caught above my head to keep them out of trouble.

Damn, he knew I liked that.

It made for a challenge.

The blue eyes took on a rueful gleam, and the delicious chest moved back, just out of reach.

"I'm serious," he informed me. "Doctor's orders."

"Dhampir," I reminded him. "Don't need a doctor. Unless he's doctor *luuuv*."

That got me a burst of laughter and an eye roll. Because Louis-Cesare seemed to like it when I was silly. Especially when I was naked and silly.

I slid along underneath him, and watched those gorgeous eyes catch fire. I'd never known blue could burn before I met him, I thought, right before warm lips caught mine. And, yes, they were very nice lips. And a very nice tongue. And very nice teeth, nipping at me gently.

I wrapped my legs around him, because that was more like it.

And suddenly found myself vertical, with hard hands under my butt and strong legs carting me off somewhere, which turned out to be the bathroom.

I can work with this, I decided, as my backside came to rest on the countertop.

He leaned over to start the shower, and I enjoyed a view of the world's greatest ass for a moment. And then the world's greatest chest, when he stood back up. Which was nice to look at but even nicer to rest my head against, the skin-to-skin contact just so . . . damned . . . good. Warm like the bed had been, and the shower would be— in half an age, because the ancient water heater took its time. Not that I minded, I thought drowsily, my hands sliding over intriguing dips and valleys . . .

And then spazzing out, when I was suddenly drenched by a warm waterfall.

"W-what?" I choked, staring around wildly—

At the inside of my bath.

It looked the way it always did: cracked blue and white tile on the walls, fat old porcelain fixtures on the claw-foot tub, eyelet shower curtain billowing out because my roommate had decorated the place and she's a girlie girl.

And because of the steam.

The shower was *hot.*

"How . . . how did you do that?" I asked Louis-Cesare, who had turned me around to soap up my back.

"Do what?" he murmured, as I braced my hands on the tile and wondered, *What the hell?*

"The water." I struggled to think past the rhythmic soothing of those callused hands. "It's hot."

"Isn't it supposed to be?"

"Yes, but not now. It takes forever—"

"Almost fifteen minutes," he agreed. "You need a new—what do they call it? The device that heats the water."

"A water heater, and no, I don't. I need to know what's going on." I twisted around, because all the stroking was making my brain fuzzy, and I needed to be sharp right now.

Louis-Cesare's forehead wrinkled slightly. "I am helping you to bathe. The doctor said it would relieve some of your stiffness—"

"Not about that! About the *time*."

"What time?" The wrinkle was starting to deepen.

"You just said we've been in here fifteen minutes—"

He nodded. "About that, why?"

"Because I don't remember them. I don't remember any of them!"

I stared around, suddenly feeling trapped. It felt like the curtains were closing in. Only it wasn't the curtains, it was me, and how do you feel claustrophobic in your own skin?

I was finding out.

"Dorina—"

"Don't call me that!"

"Dory, then," Louis-Cesare said, his voice deliberately soothing. Like I didn't know what that was. Like I wouldn't pick up on a vampire suggestion after half a lifetime of them!

Exactly half a life, I thought, my skin going cold despite the hot water pattering down.

I had to get out of here!

"Dory!"

The sharpness of the tone suddenly snapped me back, and I looked dizzily up at a wet master vampire, water dripping off his now dark brown hair, and more drops trembling on his brows and lashes. Louis-Cesare clothed and dry was stunning. Louis-Cesare naked and wet could have stopped traffic for a forty-mile stretch. But my panic didn't seem to care.

"What is wrong?" he demanded, somehow holding on to me, despite my current, soapy state.

"I told you! I don't remember, and Dorina—" I stopped to stare around some more, like I expected to find her hanging off the ceiling or something. Like a bat.

I was losing it.

"She isn't here," Louis-Cesare told me, the wrinkle a full-on frown now.

"Well, she was a minute ago!"

"She wasn't—"

"And how would you know?" I snarled, because he didn't get it. I'd been told I was mad my whole life, but most of the time, it hadn't felt like it. Most of the time, I'd moved through society—a lot of them—perfectly fine. I talked to people, I contracted work, I handled my shit.

Except when she showed up.

But even that hadn't been so bad—okay, that was a lie; it had been fucking terrifying—but at least there were *rules*. Ones I'd learned to understand, to respect, to keep the scary thing inside me pacified and absent. It hadn't been a perfect system, but it had worked.

Until now.

Because this wasn't the rule, this wasn't even close to the rule. I didn't go around just losing fifteen minutes! Not with no threat in sight and when I wasn't stressed, when I was the opposite of stressed—happy and warm and *clueless*, because of course the rules had changed.

Ever since that barrier in my brain went down, everything had.

I didn't know how to control her anymore.

I don't know what my face looked like, but Louis-Cesare's suddenly altered. And then he was hugging me, carefully because of the damned ribs, which shouldn't have helped. Which should have made the whole claustrophobic-in-my-own-skin thing even worse, but somehow didn't. And I was holding on to him when I should have been getting out of here, but I somehow wasn't.

"She was not here," he murmured, after a moment.

"You can't know that—"

"I *can*." He pulled back, so that I could see his face. "I can feel when she's here, instead of you. I don't know how to explain it," he added, when I started to say something. "But it's unmistakable, the difference between a sunny day and a dark night. If she'd been here, I would *know*."

"Then how do you explain those fifteen minutes? I don't remember—" Anything, I realized. And not just from today. "What happened last night?" I asked, my voice suddenly soft and frightened. But I couldn't help it. I was getting flashes, strange and skewed, that didn't make sense. That wasn't how it went!

Was it?

"You fell," Louis-Cesare said, his mouth tightening like he wanted to say more, but was holding back.

I nodded. That much had been memorable. The dizzying fall into nothing, from a height that could turn even a dhampir into hamburger, but hadn't because—

"Those things caught me."

"The spriggans, yes. But not out of altruism. If you hadn't had that gold, and been clever enough to use it—" He cut off, and then his arms tightened again, as memories whirled about my screwed-up brain. Memories of bouncing around on a sea of fey, like bodysurfing at a concert, only bodysurfers don't usually get thrown about that much.

"And then a troll fell on us."

"Two trolls," he said, scowling. "They were fighting and fell together. I managed to brace somewhat, but I didn't reach you in time to do a proper job. Your head still hit the floor. It's likely why you're having trouble remembering things."

I shook the area in question.

That wasn't why.

And I hadn't forgotten everything, after all, because suddenly there were pieces, like of cut-up photographs, crowding my mind. Not of the crazy landing, but of other things: a huge troll, the biggest of them all, racing up a wall; an albino with long, white hair stepping through a brilliant portal, searing my eyes; a feeling of flying, soaring into the sky and then turning to look down at the temporary fairgrounds, trash strewn and windswept, with a few bonfires still burning—

I winced, and shut down the flow, because my head *hurt*.

And because I hadn't done those things. I'd been passed out on a cracked subfloor under a couple thousand pounds of troll, with a ton of bouncy toys and a freaked-out boyfriend. I remembered Louis-Cesare yelling my name; hands lifting me, gentle as a baby; some confused shouting . . .

And rocketing through an intersection in a troll-laden truck, while a witch with cigarettes in her hair laughed and laughed.

Louis-Cesare's fingers gently combed over my abused scalp. "The doctor said there should be no lasting damage, that dhampirs have the hardest heads she's ever seen."

"I'm fine," I told him.

Physically, anyway.

"You won't be if you don't rest," Louis-Cesare said. "You all but passed out on me a moment ago—"

"What?"

He nodded. "That's why you don't remember the last few minutes. You're so tired you drifted off."

"I did not!"

His lips twitched, the worry suddenly eclipsed by what looked like genuine humor. "You look so indignant."

"I'm not," I told him, and then thought about it. "Okay, maybe I am, but I don't *nap*."

Louis-Cesare's lips twitched some more.

"Stop doing that!"

"Then explain to me what is so wrong with a nap? I recall quite liking them once."

"They're"—stupid, ridiculous, weak—"dangerous. To zone out in a fight—"

"But you weren't in a fight. You were home, behind excellent wards, and I was here. It is hard to be safer than that."

I ignored the smug comment, because he wasn't wrong. About that, anyway. "I don't nap," I repeated.

"Not normally, perhaps. But it is as the doctor said: you need time to heal. Time you haven't been taking."

He turned me around again, and started lathering up my hair.

"I'm not hurt," I said—and tried to put some heat behind it, because the magic fingers were doing a good job of making me forget how serious this was. "And that wasn't a nap. Don't you get it?"

"No," he said simply. "Tell me."

Yeah, like it was that easy. To compress a lifetime of fear and struggle and pain into a few sentences when I never talked about it, not with anyone. Because who would care? And because I didn't know how.

Only I guess I did, because it came out in a rush. "I used to try all kinds of things to keep Dorina under control. They didn't always work, but I got pretty good at it. Enough that I could tell when things were about to go bad and smoke some weed, or walk away from a conflict, or punch a tree until I calmed down. But now . . ."

"Now?"

Those damned fingers should be registered somewhere, I thought, unconsciously leaning back into the feel of them. "Now everything's changed. Dorina couldn't come out when I was conscious; the barrier prevented her. That was the whole point of it."

I felt him nod.

"But now it's gone, and without it . . . there's nothing to keep her from showing up anytime she feels like it. And what if she feels like it all the time? What if—"

I stopped for a moment, because I didn't do this shit. This touchy-feely, let's all share our deepest fears shit. It made me feel uncomfortable and vulnerable and a bunch of other things I hated, made me want to run away or lash out at something, which usually worked pretty well to change the subject. But I couldn't do that this time.

Louis-Cesare deserved the truth.

"What's stopping her from just taking over my life," I rasped. "All of it, all the time, and shutting me out? For good this time?"

Like I'd tried to do to her.

I'd always treated this as my life—all mine. Because of course I had; I hadn't even known she existed until very recently. I'd spent years thinking that I just had fits sometimes, that it was the dhampir crazy coming out, and concentrated on finding ways to tamp it down, while hoping that someday, someone would find a "cure" for my "disease."

Only to find out that I didn't have a disease, I had a— *Twin.*

The word floated through my mind suddenly, frighteningly, because I hadn't put it there. Wouldn't have, since I'd never thought of us that way. We weren't twins, we weren't *sisters*, I didn't have a sister! I had a fucked-up mind thanks to Mircea and, yes, maybe it had been necessary to save my life, but I didn't know that, did I? I'd been there, but I couldn't remember any of it.

Like I couldn't remember the last fifteen minutes.

Had I been asleep? Just nodding off in the warmth and security of my boyfriend's arms, because I was that beat? Maybe. It had been a hell of a month, with things coming hard and fast, one after another, before I had time to blink sometimes, much less to heal. And although the family had some gifts in that area, with the war raging, most of them had been in need of help themselves. And, anyway, they could only do so much.

Sometimes, nature just had to take its course.

So, yeah, maybe I'd drifted off when I never did. But I didn't know for sure. And neither did Louis-Cesare, no matter what he thought. He'd only met Dorina a couple of times, and both had been under duress. Would he feel that difference he talked about if she was just . . . there? If she was just . . . watching?

I shuddered, and didn't manage to stop before he noticed.

Louis-Cesare's hands stilled. "You truly think that is possible?"

"I don't know. I don't know anything anymore! I just—" I twisted around, and my damned ribs rewarded me by shooting savage pain up my newly loosened spine. "God-damn it!"

Louis-Cesare's hands dropped unerringly to the source, sending warmth and relief coursing through me, despite the fact that I didn't want it. I didn't want to feel better. I wanted—

I didn't even know.

Like I didn't even know what he was still doing here.

"Why are you here?" I asked wearily, looking up at him.

"Why wouldn't I be?"

"Because, when you hooked your wagon to the crazy, it wasn't this crazy?"

He just looked at me.

"I'm a disaster," I told him plainly. "I always have been, and things aren't getting better. You ought to bail while you can."

It hurt, even more than the ribs, but it was the truth. I'd always known it, but I'd hoped to hold on a little longer, to hold *him*. But things were starting to fall apart—I could feel it—and Dorina—

Isn't here, he told me mentally, because he could do that sometimes.

All vampires could. Even babies could talk to family, and masters could communicate silently with almost anyone they chose. Except for me, who wasn't a vampire and who'd had exactly zero mental gifts for five centuries, until that wall started to fall.

And all of a sudden, I was hearing voices.

But not hers.

She had the mental gifts, not me. I had no idea how to contact her, but she could talk to me any time she wanted. But she hadn't.

Why talk to someone who won't even be around much longer?

Why get to know someone you plan to kill?

"Listen to me." Louis-Cesare's hands came up to frame my face, his eyes fiercer than I'd ever seen them. "I am here. I'm not going anywhere. And no matter what happens, we will find a way to deal with this!"

Looking into his eyes, I almost believed it. But I'd learned the hard way not to want what I couldn't have, not to reach for things out of my grasp, not to hope . . . for anything. Or anyone.

Because who the hell would want to waste their lives on a crazy dhampir?

And for years, I'd been happy that way. Okay, maybe "happy" wasn't the word, but content, at least. Once I'd thought that things were going pretty well if I had a full stomach, a place to sleep in safety, a job to do, and no frightening episodes for a while. That had been the good life; that had been all right.

So when had "all right" stopped being enough?

I had a feeling it coincided with meeting a certain blue-eyed vamp who had somehow retained a measure of innocence that was ridiculous, just ridiculous, in our world. He'd come out of nowhere with all these *ideas*, stupid, antiquated things like chivalry and nobility and decency, the stuff *humans* usually scoffed at, and that vampires . . .

Well, I doubted some of them even knew the words anymore.

I didn't think some of them ever had.

And yet here was Louis-Cesare, a ridiculous contradiction of a creature, determined to ride or die when the latter was a lot more likely, not caring that his girlfriend had a split personality that could kill him, and just might for shits and giggles someday!

He was a naive fool, and I should have kicked him to the curb as soon as I met him.

But, instead, here I was hoping again.

So, who's the fool now? I wondered, and pulled him down.

Chapter Seven

And, God, he was good, because Louis-Cesare was always good. Even in a tub partially filled with soapy water, because the drain mostly didn't. But you couldn't beat the size of the thing, which was six feet long and comfortably roomy, because the Victorians knew how to make 'em, yes they did.

Made you wonder what they got up to, all those upstanding citizens, when the curtains closed.

That, I thought, arching up.

If they were really lucky.

Oh, yes, just like that.

But good as it was, it wasn't what I wanted tonight. Only I didn't know what that was. I just knew there was something—

Something he seemed to understand, because he started kissing his way up my body a lot sooner than normal. Stopping at all his favorite spots until he paused at my neck, right over the pulse point. I swallowed, my heartbeat speeding up, but he didn't bite. Just rested his lips against the hot, soapy skin under my hair, his own falling over my shoulder, his breath tickling my ear.

"What is it?" he murmured, because I'd tensed up, going rigid in his arms.

I didn't answer because I didn't know. Just gripped his shoulders, feeling the hard muscle underneath as he slid against me—and, God, yes, that's what I needed like the air I wasn't getting in panted breaths. My ribs protested, but I didn't care. My ribs could go to hell.

And then he pulled away again.

I stifled a scream—just. "What?" I breathed.

"We shouldn't be doing this," he said, frowning. "Not now."

"Oh, yes, we should."

But he was getting that look again, that stubborn "I know best" look that drove me half-mad even when I wasn't already there. He was hard against my thigh, hot and huge and insistent. And so ready he was shaking with it. Typical of the man to be noble, even when need had turned to agony, too gentle or polite to take what he wanted.

So I did it for him.

With a cry of pure frustration, I flipped us, throwing him onto his back again and straddling him with efficient grace. Wrapping one hand around the base of him and curling the other around the back of his neck, I sat down smoothly. And simultaneously pulled his mouth close enough to kiss, swallowing his protest.

Mine, I thought deliriously, and with a growl, I ground my hips down, setting a ruthless pace, latching on to his neck with my teeth and—

Louis-Cesare froze.

Suddenly, everything slowed down, from the wave of soapy water splashing over the side of the tub, to the shower curtains billowing out to show the bathroom in flashes, to the heart beating hard under my lips.

I told myself to let him go, to pull away, but I didn't appear to be listening. I managed to get my fangs out of his skin before they had done more than dent it. But then I stopped, like I'd hit a wall.

I stared at that expanse of pale flesh and a tingling spread over my skin, like a fever had gripped me. I could feel how it would taste as I bit down. It would be firm and slightly resistant, warm, with faint traces of soap and Louis-Cesare. My fangs would slide in, slick as glass, pushing past his body's defenses until the blood welled up, hot and thick and alive in my mouth.

It was an insane thought to have. I didn't have the bloodlust of a vampire; I never had. Blood did nothing for me: I couldn't use it, didn't need it. But suddenly I could taste it, wanted to, with a craving beyond any I'd ever had—for anything.

I wanted to bite deep into that vulnerable spot where shoulder met neck, not to harm but to mark. To leave an unmistakable brand to everyone who saw him that this one was taken. This one was *mine*.

I heard him swallow, felt the chest beneath me rise and fall faster, as if some of my intent had leaked over. But he didn't draw back, even when my lips ghosted over that exact spot again, when the faintest edge of my teeth grazed him. A shudder rippled through him and into me, and his hands clenched on my body, but to draw me closer, not to shove me away.

His hand moved to my nape, sliding under the hot, wet strands of my hair, pulling me close. My tongue flicked out, laving the warm surface, his pulse beating hot and fast under my lips. His neck was smooth, free of any marks, an unbroken pale expanse that no one had ever dared to claim, because that wasn't how this worked.

The more powerful vamp made the mark, and I didn't know too many more powerful than Louis-Cesare. The damned vamp had held another first-level master, the highest rank of all, in thrall for a century, so I was thinking power wasn't really a problem for him. So, technically, it should have been him marking me, only he wasn't moving.

But he wasn't moving away, either, and I didn't know what that meant.

I also didn't know that I could even do it. I wasn't a vampire; I'd never marked anyone in my life, not like that. But somehow I knew it would work, knew I could leave an indelible trace of our connection on his body, something no amount of time would erase. The urge was so overwhelming that, for a moment, I just clung to him, vibrating, my nails digging into his hip, his shoulder, deep enough that they threatened to leave marks of their own.

"Dory—"

"Don't." I growled, my voice low. "Don't talk."

I turned my head to the side, and gulped in a breath, almost dizzy with the desire to finish this. And knowing I couldn't. Vampires bit often, but they marked oh so rarely. To do so was to make a final claim, an eternal commitment. A formal declaration of alliance that joined houses, bloodlines, and fortunes in a way that made a mockery of human marriage.

And once done, it could never be undone.

Not to have one at your side whom you had marked was one of the biggest signs of weakness possible. It could open him up to attack, to challenge, by those who didn't understand that the one who had marked him wasn't a vampire, wasn't someone who had the right. Wasn't someone who had anything to offer.

Not even herself, since half of me was owned by someone else.

This was another one of those things I couldn't have; I *knew* that. But it's hard to think when your body is full and tingling, your nipple still throbs from his lips, and the rush of lust has made you light-headed. Yet I was trying. Trying to push back against the tide of instinct or desire or whatever the hell was wrong with me and remember all the reasons this would be a Very Bad Idea.

It wasn't working.

I growled again, and felt him shift inside me; clamped down, and heard him cry out. Felt him begin to thrust in thick, stuttering strokes, so unlike his usual easy dominance, as my fangs started to dent that perfect skin again. And it was sweet, sweet, oh God, it was so fucking—

Someone started pounding on the door.

It was loud enough to cause my head to shoot up, my heart hammering, but it wasn't the bathroom door. That was just as Louis-Cesare had left it, still partly open to the next room. It was the one to the hall, where the rapping was loud and insistent enough to count as banging. One of the troll twins, I thought, because Sven and Ymsi had a different definition of a soft knock than everybody else.

Only I guess I was wrong, because a second later I heard a female voice. "Dory?"

My roommate, Claire, with her famously bad timing.

"I made some soup," she called. "If you feel up to it?"

I didn't answer. I'd never been so happy, and so furious, to hear her in my life. But, apparently, Louis-Cesare did not have the same conflict of emotions.

"I think," he told me, breathing hard, "there is a chance . . . that I hate your roommate."

"It's okay," I told him, grabbing a towel. "I kind of think she hates you, too."

"So it would appear."

He lay back against the tub, looking martyred, with a forearm thrown across his eyes while I disentangled us.

"She's just trying to be protective."

"I keep telling myself that," he said grimly, as I started to get out of the tub.

And tripped. Which was not a good sign, since I'm supposed to have better reflexes than that, even on soggy rug- and suds-strewn floors. But today, it seemed like I was off-balance in every way.

Not that it mattered, since I was caught before I hit down, and spun against the wall.

"You're going back to bed," Louis-Cesare informed me flatly, somehow on his feet and in front of me, having moved with that liquid speed all vamps have, but which was somehow so much sexier with him.

"Okay." I perked up.

"Alone," he said severely.

I sighed.

"So you can heal." It was savage. I blinked. "Properly, *finally*. So that I may take you away, somewhere very far from this place, and make love to you until neither of us can see straight!"

Sounded like a plan.

So, instead of getting vamp married, I got a trip back to la-la land. Which sucked as a runner-up prize, but my body didn't seem to agree. Louis-Cesare went to piss off Claire, and my stiff and sore muscles relaxed back into the familiar softness of my bed: old, well-laundered sheets; a soft, threadbare duvet; and a comforter that I'd finally managed to bunch up in exactly the way I liked. It was heaven.

I was out before my head hit the pillow.

————

Mircea, Venice, 1458

Mircea knew before he reached home, before he even reached his street, that something was wrong. He broke into a run, one too fast for wet cobblestones, or for the human his neighbors believed him to be, but they'd gone to bed by now. And he wouldn't have cared if they hadn't.

He could feel her agony in his mind.

He burst through the front door, tripping a little on the warped boards, into the tiny main room of their house. And immediately saw her. She wasn't in her room, in her bed, as she should have been. She was writhing on the floor, screaming loudly enough to wake the whole street, if the rain hadn't been bucketing down tonight.

It was what had made him leave off his pursuit, for not even hunters could hunt in this, and when the storm clouds broke, the strange duo he'd been following had disappeared, along with their prey. He'd turned for home, cursing the November weather, when it felt like it rained all the time. But now he was glad for it, because his old servant clearly didn't know what to do.

Of course, neither did Mircea.

"It started a few moments ago. She was fine at dinner," Horatiu told him, fluttering about.

The kindly old face was splashed on one side with light from the adjacent kitchen. It wasn't much; the coals had been banked for the night, with just a few glimmers of red peeking through the ash. But, for a vampire's eyes, it was enough.

To see the fear in Horatiu's clouded gaze, to see the blood staining his worn nightshirt, to see it ringing Dorina's mouth and glinting redly on her teeth. The ones she shouldn't have had, because she wasn't a vampire. But which protruded past her lips anyway when she had her fits.

Because she wasn't human, either.

"You're hurt," Mircea said, focusing on the old man's shoulder, where the stain was darkest.

"She wanted to leave; I tried to stop her. She didn't like that."

"Here." Mircea reached for him, but Horatiu shook his head. "Her first. After our tussle, she collapsed. I was afraid she'd choke."

Mircea noticed a small piece of leather, from an old belt he'd broken and hadn't yet had repaired, on the floor.

Bitten clean through.

"Go wash yourself," he told Horatiu. "It's easier to heal if I can see the wound."

Horatiu made a disgusted sound. "It's a little thing. She didn't mean it—"

"I know that."

"She was in pain, still is—"

"I know that, too."

"Then help her! Or are you afraid, boy?"

No one else ever spoke to Mircea like that. But Horatiu wasn't just a servant. The old man had been his tutor once, and more, since Mircea had rarely seen his parents while growing up. They were always busy with their own affairs, their own ambitions. Ambitions that had eventually gotten them killed. But Horatiu had made a fine enough substitute, and that was before the curse, and the butchering of Mircea's family that followed it. When everyone else had attacked or deserted him; when his own nobles had tried to kill him and mobs of his people had chased him through the woods; when he was at his lowest, half-mad and starving, unsure who or even what he was anymore, only one person had been at his side.

The one glaring at him now.

For, as much as the old man loved him—although he'd never admit it—he loved Dorina more. Had done, ever since he first set eyes on her. He didn't make a splash of it, but Mircea saw: the extra meat he pulled from his plate to give to the child, who always ate like she was starving; the vociferous haggling he did in the marketplace, shaving a few coins off the price of staples, here and there, to buy Dorina the sweets she loved; the way he painstakingly taught her to read, determined that the scion of the Basarabs would be no ignorant street child, no matter how much she seemed to prefer it.

The way he was looking at her now, the rheumy old eyes shifting from her tortured face to Mircea's and back again, clearly saying: fix this.

Mircea knelt on the boards and gathered his daughter into his arms. It was easy for him to contain the thrashings that had almost overwhelmed his servant. And to cradle her head without danger, even as she gnashed her teeth and fought him. But while that might keep her from injuring her body, it wouldn't help her mind.

Only one thing would do that.

The next moment, he was sinking inside the tortured brain, into darkness and odd flashes of light, and the vastness of her mental landscape—

And almost getting blown away.

Because he'd broken through into what felt like a hurricane. Exactly like, Mircea thought, as the winds picked him up and flung him what felt like a mile before he hit down, rolling. While overhead, a tempest raged, one as strong as the one he'd encountered on the voyage home—

No, Mircea thought, shoving the memory away. *No!*

But he wasn't quick enough.

She ripped the images from his mind, as easily as he could call them up himself. And the next moment, Mircea found himself slammed onto the deck of a ship lost in mountain-sized waves. They loomed on all sides, massive things that dwarfed the vessel that had once seemed so large, and now looked like a child's toy.

One about to sink.

A wave slammed into him from over the side of the ship, washing him into the mainmast and threatening to crack his skull. He hung on nonetheless, trying to think, to concentrate, with waves lashing and winds tearing at him, trying to pull him away from his only support. And almost succeeding, but not because of the environment.

But because Horatiu had been right: Mircea *was* afraid.

Not for himself; he could leave whenever he chose. But for his daughter, who couldn't. She was trapped here, in this hellish place, until the fit passed, assuming that it did this time.

But what if it didn't? The fits were coming closer together now, and were lasting longer. Yet six months after they'd first started, he still didn't know what they were, or why they were happening. Or how to stop them.

Other than the obvious, of course.

Mircea slid down the mast, while the winds howled

and the storm clouds flashed, unleashing lightning bolts that illuminated the rain-washed boards beneath his hands. The storm was worse now, like it knew what he was going to do, and maybe it did. Because the storm was her, the other part of her, who didn't like being caged in this little body.

The one who wanted out.

But out of where?

It's your body, he wanted to yell, to scream at the skies. *There is nothing to escape from. What are you trying to do?*

He'd never received an answer. He wasn't sure that she had one, this other side of his daughter, the one he barely knew. She raged like a trapped god, like a force of nature entombed in flesh, who wanted nothing more than to rip her prison to shreds and break free.

He was terribly afraid that, one day, she would manage it.

But not this day.

Mircea gripped the boards, hard enough to feel splinters biting into his hands. He ignored them. They weren't real, any more than the wind or the waves or the salt that burned his eyes was real. Just manifestations of her power, power that was overflowing her human body, but had nowhere else to go.

Until he gave it one.

The boards under his touch began to glow, first a faint luminescence barely limning his fingers in light. And then spreading outward, brighter and farther, lighting up the bones in his hands and the frayed edges of his sleeves, while he fought to stay in place. Because, yes, she knew what he was doing.

But she couldn't stop him—not yet. They had a connection, the two of them, because of his mental gifts, or because he was both father and Sire in one, or for some other reason he didn't know because he didn't know anything. No one did, not about dhampirs. He'd learned that the hard way, these last months.

The same way he'd learned everything, he thought, as the ship suddenly turned almost perpendicular.

It threw him against the side, where the sea tried its best to drown him and debris to impale him, and a lightning burst almost succeeded in incinerating him but hit a flying barrel instead.

Shards of burning wood fell all around him as the ship slammed back down and rocked to the other side, and half the items on deck went airborne. But not Mircea. Because he'd wrapped his leg in a rope and braced, one arm on a railing and one on the deck. And, once more, the light under his hand began to spread.

He watched it creep outward, illuminating the stains and nails in the boards and the banding on casks and barrels, while the winds shrieked and the waves pounded the little craft, as if in anger. But the light flickered on, across the deck and up webs of rigging above tightly furled sails, turning them white-hot and gleaming. Until the vessel was covered in light, until it looked like he was kneeling on a ghost ship. And the farther the light reached, the more the waves lessened, the quieter the winds blew, and the more Mircea's hand felt like it was about to combust.

And then did so along with the rest of his body when a lightning strike took him, the bolt coming out of nowhere and landing with a ferocity that tore him off the boards and sent him hurtling backward over the side, screaming—

And hitting something with his whole body, hard enough to bruise.

It took him a moment to realize that the hard object was his own front door, and that the soggy boards he'd landed on were his floor, where the wet had blown in. And that Dorina was quiet, lying exhausted in his arms as he fought for breath he didn't need, and stared at Horatiu, still standing nearby. Who looked back at him with pride in the old eyes.

"It worked."

"This time," Mircea rasped, the power he'd drawn off his daughter thickening his voice and spilling through his skin, lighting the dim room as if someone had decided to burn a hundred candles.

She was getting stronger.

But he was not, at least not fast enough. There was going to come a time when he couldn't drain her sufficiently, and he was desperately afraid that that day would be soon. He had to have help.

And there was only one way to get it.

Chapter Eight

I awoke for the second time with shards of memory poking the soft tissue of my brain. For a moment, weird images overwrote my sunny bedroom: rain laced with wind, huge waves, an old man with blood on his face . . . Shit!

I grabbed my head as a spike of agony lanced through it, courtesy of Dorina's latest blast from the past. Or maybe my headache was food related, because I was also absolutely ravenous. I just lay there, fairly stunned, as the pains in my head and gut fought it out for dominance. Then I shoved them both aside with a snarl, threw back the covers, and headed out the door in search of breakfast.

And only succeeded in scandalizing Ymsi, who was sitting in the hall, just outside my room. The blond head with the incongruously baby-fine hair brushed the ceiling, and the massive hands were busy with something I couldn't see over the broad expanse of back. Not even when he turned to glance at me over his shoulder, and let out a bleat of alarm.

I looked down and sighed, because of course. Louis-Cesare liked to dress me in frilly nightwear, but only when he was going to have the pleasure of removing it again. But since that hadn't been likely this time, he'd left me as I was.

Buck naked.

Not that it should have mattered, I thought, heading back inside. The fey didn't care much about bodily modesty. They felt that clothes were more for showing off than for covering up, and were therefore optional around the house. At least, that had been the attitude of the troll twins, who had been yelled at repeatedly by Claire when they first arrived for letting it all hang out, when the "all" in question was eye-poppingly huge and hard to miss.

In desperation, she'd bought out a fabric store of sturdy canvas cloth and sewn them cargo shorts, and they'd apparently decided that wearing them was better than dealing with my redheaded roommate's famous temper. Although it was still a good idea to yell out a warning before entering their private sanctum in the basement, and the butt crack of doom was often to be seen looming o'er the yard when Ymsi was in the garden, kneeling over a tiny plant that he was encouraging to grow.

However, the same laissez-faire attitude did not apply to me. Not for Ymsi, not since he'd poked his head in my bathroom one day when I was bathing, and I'd been a little . . . stern with him. I'd apologized later, but it hadn't helped. Once trolls get an idea in their heads, you may as well stop talking.

The result was a massive, lumbering teen with the scruples of a Victorian auntie. Who I could hear making weird crunching noises outside the door while I struggled to find a tee that didn't make my eyes water. Damn, I needed to do laundry, I thought, crawling out from under the bed.

Only to see a basket of clean, perfectly folded clothes sitting in front of my closet door.

Uh-oh.

I sat there for a moment, biting my lip and wondering what Louis-Cesare had said to Claire. I shouldn't have left the two of them alone together; I *knew* I shouldn't. But I'd been exhausted and freaked out, and I'd assumed he was just going to decline the soup, since I wasn't awake to eat it. But the question was, how had he declined it? Because Claire had afterward felt the need to do my laundry, and that was never a good sign.

Claire had a problem with vampires, a relic of a time when she was the unwilling guest of my mad, bad, and very dangerous-to-know late uncle Vlad. Which wasn't surprising: most mages felt the same, even if it wasn't PC to say so, and with far less reason than Claire had. But it was a bitch when you happened to be dating one of the aforementioned bloodsuckers, who wasn't anything like

Vlad—seriously, we're talking practically a different species here—but try telling Claire that.

I knew because I had. Which had prompted a begrudging invitation so that two of the most important people in my life could get to know each other. Only that . . . hadn't gone so well.

Guess Who's Coming to Dinner had nothing on her and Louis-Cesare, politely savaging each other over homemade potpie.

Pie.

My stomach grumbled angrily as I remembered flaky crust and Guinness-marinated beefy filling and tender carrots and plump potatoes swimming in the gravy of the gods, studded with onions and little green peas . . .

I quickly pulled on a freshly washed tee and jeans and headed out.

Of course, that required edging around Ymsi, who was still blocking the door, and didn't seem to understand that I wanted him to move. And the serious shoving I was doing probably felt like the wafting of a feather to someone with hide like a stegosaurus. A heavy stegosaurus, I added mentally, grunting and groaning and finally managing to push my way past.

And then stopped and stared, but not at Ymsi. At the hall beyond him. Which was . . . different.

"Did somebody die?" I asked, but only got those weird crunching noises back.

I stared some more, my eyes trying to figure out what, exactly, they were seeing.

At first, it just looked like every flower in the garden had been squashed into my hall for some reason. Which wasn't *that* odd, since trolls have a sincere appreciation for beauty and a love of growing things. Sven, the strawberry blond twin, was currently consumed by the warrior arts, practicing regularly with the Light Fey contingent in the backyard, who Claire's relatives had sent to guard her. But Ymsi didn't seem interested in learning how to kill things; he had all but taken over Claire's already-sizeable garden, adding a whole section just for flowers.

He often brought me the fruit of his labors stuffed into mason jars or old coffee tins, to brighten up my bedside table. But that's not what he'd done here. Or, no, I thought, my concern level ramping up a few dozen notches. Not him. Because Ymsi might be talented, but he hadn't managed *this*.

"Pretty," Ymsi said, stealing a glance at me.

I nodded. That was one word for it. Of course, I could think of a few others.

Because these flowers weren't in jars or vases or cans. They weren't even piled in heaps on the floor. They were growing *out of* the floor—and the walls, and the ceiling.

Especially the ceiling, I thought, staring upward, where great swags of cherry blossoms festooned the old hardwood planks, dipping low enough to brush my head. Some were on new-growth branches that crisscrossed over the plaster; some came straight out of the old, dusty, been-dead-for-a-century-or-so-now boards. And they were thick, like spring on the National Mall, all squeezed into the area by the stairs, just garlands of them, massing overhead and drooping down the walls—where they could find room. Because the walls were already laden with some kind of growth of their own, and what the hell was that?

I looked closer, because it looked like someone had installed moving wallpaper. Bright green moving wallpaper. Which was busy thrusting out little pods that burst open to spew something at us every few—

Oh. I figured it out when I noticed what Ymsi was up to. Because he had a basket in his lap, and some papery brown things cracking in his fist, and was busily doing what trolls did best. Only, this time, the fat green clusters of pecan pods were raining down nutty goodness faster than he could eat it.

Which was pretty damned fast.

Although, in fairness to Ymsi, he was also being besieged by other crops growing up from the floor. The parquet floor, I realized, blinking. Because the ceiling was century-old cherrywood, the house having been built back before such things were scarce, and the walls were—of course—pecan. But the floor was a scuffed old parquet that I'd never paid much attention to, like to wonder what woods, exactly, had made it up.

Magnolia, oak, and apple, I thought, taking in the huge,

white, waxy blooms, the tiny brown acorns, and the rampant pink blossoms that made it look like the floor near the stairs was growing a crazy carpet. One that still followed the zigzag pattern faithfully. Well, except for where Ymsi had harvested parts of it, with the half of his basket that wasn't stuffed with pecans overflowing with the apples that kept bubbling up from the chaos, because the whole growth thing appeared to be set on fast-forward.

"Well, shit," I said.

Ymsi gave me a commiserating look, and proffered an apple.

"Thanks."

I took a bite.

It was good.

Of course it was.

I started wondering if I could fit through the tiny round window at the end of the hall, when Ymsi thwarted my escape plans by picking me up and depositing me in front of the stairs. Where a cascade of apples he couldn't reach had overflowed the floor design and were bump, bump, bumping down the steps alongside my feet. And where the pecan pods hung from actual branches, brushing my head as their produce erupted at me, like brown rain, and then rolled everywhere.

I somehow got downstairs without breaking my neck, and peered inside the kitchen door.

Yep.

That's what I'd thought.

"Dory! You're up!"

I was also halfway turned around and headed for the front door, but the desperation in Claire's voice stopped me. Because her housekeeping frenzy wasn't, as I'd supposed, due to irritation at Louis-Cesare, but to something else entirely. Something worse.

Something sitting at the kitchen table, perched on a stool with a cutting board in front of him, holding out a finger. "Dorina!" The lilting voice made my name sound like a cascade of bells. "Come and see. I am *wounded*."

It was said with all the panache of a dying hero announcing a mortal blow.

I sighed and turned back around. "Hello, Caedmon."

"Come," he demanded. "Kiss it better." He waggled the supposedly injured digit at me.

I sighed again and walked into the kitchen.

Most women would have been happy to kiss it, or anything else Caedmon chose to name. He was Claire's soon-to-be father-in-law, but he didn't look it. I don't know how to adequately describe how he did look, because there's simply no practical equivalent. We're talking seven feet of finely muscled leanness; hair like actual sunlight, as in it glowed from within; eyes like genuine emeralds, deep green and glinting with an odd mix of wit and wisdom; and a face that would have been literally stunning if it wasn't currently pouting like a child.

Or maybe not a child, I thought, as one side of those sculpted lips edged upward, barely a fraction of an inch. And yet miraculously changed the expression from sass to seduction. He waggled the finger at me again.

"Healing's not really my specialty," I told him, leaning against the table. "I'd only hurt it more."

The not-smile edged up another tenth of an inch. "How much more?"

He sounded intrigued.

"Let me see your knife."

"Dory!" Claire sounded a little shrill, like she was afraid we were going to duel it out right there in her kitchen. Which wasn't likely, even if I'd been in any shape to take on a king of the Light Fey. Because where was the room?

The kitchen wasn't as bad as my hallway, but there had been some . . . additions. Caedmon was king of what was known on Earth as the Blarestri, one of the three great houses of the Light Fey. It wasn't their real name, of course—which we mere mortals weren't good enough to have—just a placeholder meaning "the Blue Fey." But it was descriptive of their realm, high in the mountain fastnesses of Faerie, with blue skies all around and lush greenery everywhere. Because nature loved Caedmon.

Literally, I thought, as a little vine tried to twine itself in his long, flowing hair.

"There, there," he said absently, and pulled it out, to wind it around the back of a chair instead.

It had a lot of company.

Claire's window-box garden, where she grew the herbs she used for cooking, had exploded, for lack of a better term. It was now a window jungle, one leaning not outward, toward what looked like late-afternoon sun, but inward, scrawling across sink and countertops and floor like a toddler's drawing. And then climbing here, there, and everywhere, just to get a little closer to the glowing fey sitting at the table.

It wasn't the only one. The bedraggled pot of begonias that Claire had brought inside and placed on top of the fridge had draped the appliance in dark green leaves. They were huge and healthy now, and framing clusters of crimson flowers that brushed the floor on either side. They made the old, dented fridge look like it was wearing a long red wig, one more luxurious than Claire's currently frazzled locks.

"Stop it," she muttered, as another mass suddenly plopped over the fridge front, like bangs, making the resemblance that much more startling.

"What's for dinner?" I asked, because priorities are priorities. And if I had to deal with Caedmon, I was going to need energy.

"Soup," she said curtly, and then jumped when a spider plant, including pot, suddenly slammed in the screen door from the outside, pulling itself along on its weird little handlike protrusions, earthworming toward its god. "Oh, for—Dory!"

"Got it," I told her, scooping the crazed thing up. And presenting it to Caedmon, who sighed as it wound its creepy little vine-hands about him, in a fervent embrace.

"At least something loves me," he said soulfully.

"What are you doing here?" I asked, taking the— thankfully glass—cutting board and wailing on some carrots before they sprouted. Because he was clearly too injured with his paper-cut-like wound to manage it himself, and I wanted to eat already.

"Helping with dinner."

Claire, looking tired and sweaty, shot him a glance over her shoulder.

He failed to notice, being too busy petting his new admirer. "I always like to be a thoughtful guest."

"Uh-huh. And why are you guesting, exactly?"

The beautiful green eyes widened. "Why, to see my grandson."

"And?"

"Oh, how remiss of me." Caedmon took my hand and kissed it playfully. "And your lovely self, of course."

I sighed and looked skyward—

And got clobbered by a bushel of apples. Because a tree branch had inched its way in from the hall, pushing aside the old boards of the ceiling until it found a more formidable foe in the brass ship's lantern in the center. And then dropping half a bushel of fruit during the epic battle between them.

Onto my head.

"Caedmon!" Claire whirled on him, hearing my surprised yelp. And then hurried over, wiping her hands on her apron and reaching for me, because her old profession— before she traded it in for fey princess—was nurse.

"I'm okay," I told her. I'd managed to dodge most of them.

"By luck! She's supposed to be recuperating," she told Caedmon furiously.

"Really?" He looked me over. "Ill?"

"Injured."

"Ah, I can relate."

"You are not injured!" Claire snapped, grabbing a box of Band-Aids from a cabinet and slamming them down in front of his paper cut.

Caedmon looked at them sadly. They were Sponge-Bob, which I suppose he felt was lèse-majesté. He opened the box anyway.

"And can you please stop this?" She gestured around at the leafy carnage.

"It will stop on its own in a bit," he assured her.

"I'd prefer it to stop *now*," she said, as several apples plopped into the soup.

Claire went to scoop them out, while I watched a little tendril on Caedmon's shoulder wind around the point of his ear. "Why can't you stop it now?" I asked.

"The same reason I don't simply heal my wound. Too much power buzzing about."

"What?"

He grinned, and flexed SpongeBob at me. "I might grow an extra finger."

I decided to quit while I was ahead, but Claire was braver than me. "And why do you have so much power 'buzzing about'?"

The perfect lips made a slight moue. "There was a bit of a dustup getting through the portal. Oh, nothing serious," he assured us. "Although it's sweet of you to be concerned for me."

Claire didn't look concerned; she looked pissed. And sounded it, too. "Dustup? I thought you said everything was fine at home, and that's why you could afford to leave?"

"Well, yes, it is," he agreed. "At home. But we weren't at home—"

"We?"

"Heidar and I."

And now Claire did look concerned, and with reason. Heidar, her fiancé and Caedmon's son, had recently gone on a scouting trip into territory controlled by another great fey house, and not one of the nice ones. The Svarestri—aka the Black Fey, due to the color of their armor—were heavily involved with the group currently trying to go Chuck Norris on our asses.

"You were with Heidar?" Claire said sharply.

"Yes—"

"Where is he? Is he all right? You said there was an attack—"

"It was nothing," Caedmon said, soothingly. "I sent him through one portal, and took another myself, although it was a bit of a ride to get there—"

"Why did you take another?"

Caedmon looked like he was debating something, possibly lying.

"Caedmon!"

"The first disappeared . . . somewhat abruptly. The Svarestri caused a landslide—"

"Landslide?" Claire suddenly sat down.

"Heidar made it through well before," Caedmon assured her. "I sent him back to one of our staging areas and fought my way clear—"

"And came here. And not to see Aiden, as you said!" Claire accused, talking about her and Heidar's child, and Caedmon's current heir.

"I do want to see him," Caedmon protested.

"That would be a first!"

Caedmon looked put-upon. A little cactus in the middle of the table bristled, as if about to come to his defense. Claire threw a dishrag over it.

"You know we've been through this," Caedmon said. "Our women raise the male children until they are old enough to handle a sword, after which the men in the family take over. To do otherwise would break tradition, and also make him appear—"

"Caedmon!" Claire's complexion was getting dangerously close to her hair color. "Why. Are. You. Here?"

He sighed prettily. "Oh, very well. And while I was visiting my charming grandson, I was wondering if I might borrow a little something."

"Borrow?" Claire looked confused, probably wondering what we had that would interest a fey king. "Borrow what?"

"Nothing much, just—ah, there he is!" Caedmon smiled and held out his arms. "My boy!"

I looked up to see a towheaded Aiden, still in his jammies, because when you're a year old, any time is jammie time. He was looking angelic, all big blue eyes and blond hair like his daddy, and standing in the kitchen doorway next to my own little bundle of terror. Who was Porky-Pigging it in a ratty T-shirt and dragging a battered pink bear, which had already lost most of an ear. I sighed.

"Gran'pa!" Aiden raced across the kitchen floor, which had mercifully not yet sprouted anything, and jumped. And was plucked up and spun around by an obviously delighted fey king, who, okay, maybe *had* wanted to see his grandson a little bit. Because he was grinning hugely.

"How you've grown!" he told Aiden, lifting him overhead, where the apples politely drew back out of the way. "Such a fine, handsome boy."

I picked up Stinky, who was not a fine, handsome boy, but deserved some love, too. "Do you like your bear?" I asked him, which had traces of soot on it in addition to the badly mangled left ear, but was otherwise holding up pretty well.

He nodded, but I clearly didn't have his full attention. The wizened, fuzzy face, which sort of looked like a monkey, a Muppet, and a snaggletoothed cat had met up in a blender, was focused on the sword at Caedmon's side instead. It was a beautiful thing I hadn't noticed because he'd been sitting down. And because I'd never seen him feel the need to go about armed while inside before.

"Not yet, dear boy," he told Stinky, smiling down at the face of his grandson's staunch friend. "That day will come soon enough. Enjoy the time you have now."

"Caedmon!" Claire was nothing if not persistent. "Borrow *what*?"

He looked back at her, blinking, while holding Aiden up again so that he could pick a fruit. "Oh, nothing much, my dear. Just a few dozen dragons."

Chapter Nine

I was saved by the bell—the one on the front door, to be exact, which took that moment to start clamoring for attention. I gladly gave it some, because the decibel level in the kitchen was mounting. And because I was hoping it was the Girl Scouts, since it didn't look like I was going to be getting dinner anytime soon.

It wasn't the Girl Scouts.

It took me a second, because it looked like I had a bunch of clean-cut Mormons on the stoop, who'd decided that they needed extra support for the crazy house, so had brought the whole congregation. But then I noticed that the smiling faces were a little too fixed, the eyes were a little too blank, and the air above their heads was shimmering a little too much. And, suddenly, it was like those dot paintings when you finally see the real picture hidden by the pattern.

Or when you see the large creatures hidden by glamouries that didn't fit, because Mormons are not twelve feet tall.

I'd have been worried, despite still being inside the house's formidable wards, because we'd gotten some less-than-friendly visitors in the past and some of them had been tricky. But I had Stinky on my hip, who had a sixth sense for trouble yet was just calmly gnawing on his bear. And then I noticed a familiar pink satin clutch tucked under one burly guy's arm.

And felt my spine relax.

"You wouldn't happen to have any muffins?" I asked hopefully.

"Not today."

"Worth a shot."

I got out of the way.

The missionaries shoved their way in, and despite the fact that the front door was a double one, it was a tight fit for a few. At least, that was judging by the scraping sounds and the paint flaking off on either side. And by the heaviness of the feet causing the glass in the transom to chime as they passed underneath it.

And, okay, that was weird. Because I knew Olga's boys, and they weren't *that* big. Most of them were family, various relations she and her late husband had helped come over and who she was sponsoring until they started to figure things out.

These didn't strike me that way, and not just because of the size. The adolescent trolls I'd met had a cheerful innocence about them, like Ymsi with his flowers or Sven with his sword practice, which had caused even the jaded royal guards to crack a few grins, although they usually stifled them when they saw anybody watching. But the point was, the twins were endearing.

These guys . . . I wasn't sure what vibe I was getting, but I didn't think "endearing" fit.

I led them to the dining room, because it had the only furniture likely to support them, a sturdy old hardwood dining set built back when craftsmen took their jobs seriously. And because I wanted to check them out before I let them loose on the rest of the house. Not that I didn't trust Olga, but she didn't usually have an entourage.

I was glad I'd made that call when I suddenly found myself confronted with a strange group of large, scary-looking fey.

And one small one.

"What's with him?" I asked Olga, as the little guy was deposited in a chair by the troll who'd been carrying him.

I guessed he was a troll, too, although it was hard to tell. He was smaller than me and scrawny, like a deflated balloon. Where there should have been bulging muscles, there was just loose skin. Where there should have been bright, round eyes, there was only a pair of slits, cloudy and vague looking. And where there should have been a nice greeny brown skin tone, there was a dull ashen color, with patches that looked almost black.

Bruises, I realized.

I hadn't known trolls could get those.

"Escaped from slavers," Olga said, taking Stinky from me. She used to babysit him, and had a soft spot for the little guy. But today she looked like she just needed someone to hug.

"Be back in a sec," I told her, and ran off to find Claire.

She was where I'd left her, yelling something at Caedmon that I didn't bother to listen to, because I was afraid we were about to have a corpse on our hands. "Got your kit?"

She stopped, mouth still open, and blinked at me. "What?"

"Troll, half-dead. Or maybe more than half. Olga just brought him in."

Claire blinked again, and I could almost see the transformation. From harassed mom with in-law problems to competent nurse on a mission. "Where?"

"Down the hall."

She grabbed a bag from a cabinet, and was on my heels in a second flat.

We entered the dining room to find the trolls seated on groaning chairs; Stinky with his chin propped on his bear's head, watching everything with inquisitive eyes; and the little troll out cold, facedown on the table.

"Help me get him up," Claire muttered, and I hurried to comply, a little worried about just how easy it was to lift this particular troll. He felt like a bag of bones, and looked it, too, after we laid him on the table and Claire ripped open his shirt to reveal little more than a lattice of ribs. And—

"Fuck me."

That was me, of course. Claire is usually able to convey emotion without profanity. But she wasn't saying anything at the moment. Just looking down with the kind of expression you hope to never see from your doc.

"You help?" Olga asked, looking from me to Claire.

Neither of us answered. Claire was busy examining the little one, her mouth pinched almost to nonexistence, while I was realizing why my hands were wet. The dark patches I'd noticed on his arms were a black lake on his chest, one composed of old, caked blood and some fresh. I wiped my hands on my jeans and left greenish black smears behind. And looked up to see Claire's face mirroring what was probably on mine.

"There's no open wound," I said, looking for some kind of hope.

"It's internal. Trolls bleed through their skin if it's bad enough," Claire said shortly.

"And it's bad." It wasn't a question.

She looked up at me, answering with her eyes the question I hadn't asked. She couldn't help him. And if Claire couldn't, nobody could. Her last name was Lachesis, and she belonged to one of the oldest and most respected families of healers anywhere.

They'd once been known for something else, back when poisoning had been the nobility's favorite pastime. But over the centuries they'd grown out of their dodgy rep, into a respected family of potion sellers. Not that their concoctions would help the fey, who did not respond well to human medicine, if at all. But Claire hadn't specialized in human illnesses.

Even before she'd found out about her own . . . unusual . . . genetics, she'd been drawn to the fey. She'd worked in R & D, looking into the potential healing properties of fey flora, which was one reason we'd ended up as friends. She was the only person I'd ever met compassionate enough to want to help a half-mad dhampir.

Which was probably why she was tearing up now—and rooting around in her bag, I guess for something to ease the little one's pain, at least.

Until she suddenly stopped, and just stared at the wall for a second. Before dropping everything—literally, the bag scattered its contents of precious bottles and handmade plasters all over the floor—and running out the door. And before I had a chance to go after her, to ask what the hell, she was back.

And hell had come with her.

Or so you'd have thought, when a tableful of massive trolls suddenly surged to their feet, and a dozen weapons flashed under the dining room's dim lighting. One of them was close enough to have given me a shave had I been the type to need one. That was happenstance, though, because the weapons weren't aimed at me.

They were aimed at Caedmon.

He stood in the doorway, shimmering softly, because he'd drawn down the glow that the Light Fey tended to have in our world. Not that it helped. I'd always heard the expression "You could have cut the tension with a knife," but in this case it would have taken the sword gleaming by my eye socket, because it was so thick I could barely breathe.

"Stop," Olga said suddenly, because nothing intimidated Olga.

Something that sounded like a cross between a word and a growl came from a huge specimen on the far end of the table. He could only stand while bent over, despite the high ceilings of the room, which flattened the top of an impressive mane of white hair and allowed braids the size of my arms to brush the tabletop. And he was so heavy with muscle that he was the only one at that end of the table, because no one else would fit. He wasn't speaking English, and nobody felt like translating, but I didn't need it.

His expression was . . . eloquent.

"Caedmon can help," Claire said, which didn't.

"Claire." I licked my lips, having seen what a bunch of pissed-off trolls could do and not wanting to see it again. "Why don't you take Aiden and—"

But Claire wasn't budging.

"Gessa!" she yelled unnecessarily, because the little au pair was never too far away. In this case, she was already peering in the door worriedly.

She was another relative of Olga's, on her late husband's side, who had been a forest troll like Fin. Also like Fin, she was tiny, only a little over three feet tall, and cute, with big brown eyes—for a troll—and a mop of brown curls that always seemed to go everywhere. She'd been brought on board after Olga got her business up and running again, and hadn't had time for babysitting. Then Aiden came along, and now she cared for them both, with a gentleness that belied her ability with a double-headed ax, if anyone threatened her charges.

She was looking around now, like she was thinking of getting the ax, until Claire took her son from Caedmon and handed him over. "Take the boys outside," Claire told her. *To where my guards are* remained unsaid.

Gessa nodded.

Stinky didn't want to leave, but a firm pat on the backside from Olga and a stern look from me, and he loped off with Gessa, one small hand in hers and the other dragging the huge bear.

Leaving just us grown-ups.

Except for the small troll, who didn't look that old to me.

Or to Claire, I guess, because she moved *toward* the forest of blades before I could stop her. "He's a child, and he's dying!" She stared around the table, green eyes flashing. "What is *wrong* with you?"

"You help," Olga told her again, subtly getting between Claire and the male trolls.

"I can't help!" Claire said, shoving frazzled red hair out of her eyes. "You should have come to me sooner—"

"Just found."

"He's your nephew?" I asked, because I really hoped not.

"No. Slave. Ran away last night, after fight."

"What happened?"

"Slaver's men found. Tried to kill."

"So he couldn't rat them out," I guessed.

She nodded. "We find, but they find first. Killed them." It was nonchalant.

Good, I thought.

I'd find some more to question.

Ones who hadn't tried to kill a child.

"Listen to me," Claire said, looking around the table. "I don't have the skill for this. Do you understand? I need *help*."

Nothing.

Nobody moved; nobody breathed. A bunch of humans would have had tired arms by now, holding weapons that heavy that still for so long, but the trolls hadn't so much as blinked. They looked like some kind of Renaissance tableau—a deadly one, with small, dark eyes reflecting the overhead lighting, which also glimmered on the swords and axes and knives. And on the scattered pieces of armor that some of them wore, despite the fact that I'd rarely seen trolls think they needed it.

"Listen!" Claire said again, because it didn't look like anyone was. "I can't help your friend. But *he* can."

She pointed wildly at her father-in-law, who also hadn't moved, not so much as a finger. He was still in the doorway, hands loose, weapon still in its sheath. Not that it mattered. Every damned person in the room knew how quickly that could change, which probably explained the standoff.

Well, partly explained it.

"I thought you guys were okay?" I asked Olga, looking from her to Caedmon. They'd seemed to get along at a dinner party they'd attended at my crazy uncle Radu's recently. Who was absolutely the kind of guy to put Dark and Light Fey at the same table and think nothing of it. Yet, somehow, everything had worked out.

More or less.

But the less hadn't been because Olga and Caedmon were at each other's throat. They might not be friends, because fey didn't really understand that term the way humans did, but they also weren't enemies. At least, I hadn't thought so.

"We okay," Olga agreed, and several of the nearest trolls growled.

This did not appear to faze her.

"He not hurt us," she pointed out, with a little more liveliness than I was used to from Olga.

And got an almost shockingly long comment in return from White Hair. I couldn't understand it; I don't speak troll. But compared to the one-, two-, and three-word answers I was used to, it was positively loquacious.

It also wasn't appreciated.

"She can't help," Olga said, using the language everyone understood, because she had manners. "He can!"

"No!" This was another troll, shorter but even more well muscled than the last, with a shock of gray hair and a face that looked like it had been dragged behind a truck at some point. Some point a long time ago, because it had healed and scarred over, yet still had little bits of gravel embedded in it, all along one side. They glittered in the low light, reminding me of the big guy from the fight, the one with all the scars, except this one lacked the exotic coloring. He was the same greeny brown as the rest, but looked like he'd lived a harder life.

Much harder.

And he wasn't having it.

Which sucked for him, because Olga was.

The next thing I knew, she was up on the table, crossing the expanse of shining mahogany faster than I could blink. And, okay, that did not help the tension any, I thought, as the other trolls stiffened. But she didn't pull a knife, didn't have any weapons that I could see at all. He did—a short sword, which in this case meant slightly less than the six-foot length of some of the others', and it was out. But he didn't turn it on her.

I waited, but nothing was said for a long moment, as they faced off. Literally: there wasn't so much as a millimeter between the two of them. It was nose to nose, eye to eye, and while it might not sound like much, just two people looking at each other, it was somehow more intimidating than any of the chest-beating and wall-thumping I'd seen last night.

Suddenly, I could barely breathe, my arms broke out in goose bumps, and my hands flexed, wishing for a weapon, any weapon. I glanced at Claire, and she didn't look any better. Her face was flushed, her eyes so green they almost looked electric, and her hands were gripping the back of the nearest chair, like she was thinking of throwing it at somebody. But then the bigger troll looked away, even turned his head slightly. And while nothing was said, the tension snapped like a rubber band, hard enough to stagger me.

I had no freaking clue what had just happened, but I didn't have time to worry about it.

Because Caedmon was doing something.

He didn't touch the little troll, or even move out of the doorway. But a light suddenly shone through the cracked and darkened skin of the small one, as if he'd been lit from within. It was soft at first, gentle, visible only because the room was dim.

And then it flashed outward, shining up through pores and mouth and eyes, turning the skin translucent and highlighting the too-fragile bones and organs beneath.

It was almost as good as an X-ray, a truly impressive display that danced on the ceiling and everyone's faces. It was also useless, because there was nothing left to save. The internal organs were all but pulverized, from a beating so savage that even a couple of the trolls made noises. The slavers who had done this hadn't just intended to kill; they'd intended to write a message in his pain: come after us again and this could happen to you.

But Caedmon must have helped a little, because the small eyes opened after a moment, and a hand raised, trying to grab Olga's.

She'd shuffled back down the table, to squat by the little troll's head. She took the hand. His jaw was fractured, off-center and sagging, but he managed to whisper something anyway. I didn't catch it, and wouldn't have understood if I had, but Olga did better.

"Yes." Her fist hit the middle of her chest. "Swear."

He nodded slightly and said something else, and her expression grew confused.

Then the light died, and the small face went slack, and I thought that was it.

But I'd reckoned without fey stubbornness, and I don't just mean the trolls'. Because a second later, I was knocked aside by someone glowing like a small sun. The sudden radiance eclipsed the electric lighting, caused the trolls to throw arms over their eyes, and prompted Claire to make a sound of distress, probably worrying that somebody was about to attack her father-in-law.

But no one did. Even when he got his hands on the child, pressing them into the little chest, almost hard enough to crack it. And then all that light, all that power that had allowed a fey king to fight his way to a portal in enemy territory, that had practically seared our shadows onto the walls, that had caused havoc all over the house because it needed a place to go—

Found one.

It poured into the little body, a flood of power that looked like it would rip him apart, but instead did the opposite. I stood there with my mouth hanging open, because it was like watching a film move backward: rebuilding tissue, plumping muscle, brightening eyes. Which opened in pain and panic and confusion halfway through, with only Olga's hand on the boy's shoulder stopping him from getting up and trying to flee.

But he didn't.

He just lay there.

And I continued to stare, as healthy color flooded over gray, as the cap of scaly skin on his head sprouted with hair, as blood dried up and flaked off, and ribs, cracked and scattered and broken, began working their way back into some semblance of order under his skin.

Then the light cut out, not fading away, but all at once, like a switch was flipped off. Caedmon staggered and almost fell, but Claire and I caught him. And Olga stepped protectively in front of him, palms out and arms extended, because showing weakness is never a good thing among the fey.

But nobody tried to take advantage of it.

Nobody, in fact, was looking at him at all. The other fey were gathering around the child, who was still sprawled on the table and looking far from well. He had some very unnatural dents and bumps in his chest, some mottled skin on his hands and arms, and a jaw that still didn't fit quite right on his face. But he was alive.

And, like me, nobody seemed to quite know what to do with that. Until Olga threw her head back, and spoke for us all. And *roared*.

Chapter Ten

"Well, that was intense."

I'd given up on dinner, and was hanging off the back of the porch, a longneck in one hand and an ice pack in the other, because my head hurt.

Olga nodded. She was in the porch swing with her own beer, which looked entirely inadequate in those huge hands, but it didn't matter since I'd brought a bucket full. It was sitting on the weathered boards between us, along with a pillow, some blankets, and half a dozen apples, because there was every chance I might not get up again today.

I hated convalescing, but if you had to do it, this was the place.

The late-afternoon sun slanted across the backyard, glinting off the ice in my bucket and striping the blanket where the boys were supposed to be playing, only they were running after fireflies instead. Or, rather, Stinky was, his long arms making the chase at least somewhat competitive, while Aiden was mostly falling on his ass. But he looked like he was having fun.

So did a horse over by the fence—Caedmon's, presumably—which was poking fleshy lips between the slats, trying to reach Mrs. Luca's roses. And Claire's guards, who were roasting something they weren't supposed to have over a fire pit and laughing with the boss. He'd recovered about as fast as you'd expect for a guy who kept a bunch of crazy fey wrangled most of the time. But he also looked like he'd be happy sitting around for the rest of the day, shooting bull and drinking beer, instead of performing any more heroics.

The king of the fey looked pooped.

"Fish, tracks, door," Olga said suddenly.

I looked up at her. "What?"

"Fish, tracks, door. You understand?"

"No."

I lay back against the boards. They were sun warmed and velvety smooth, the way wood gets after being worn down by weather and feet through the years. They went nicely with the buzz of bees raiding the garden, the creak of chains holding up the old swing, and the tinkling sound of an ice cream truck in the distance. It didn't come down this street anymore for reasons, but still gave a melodic accompaniment to the scene.

Nice, I thought sleepily, and seriously considered taking a nap. Which I absolutely was not going to do, because dinner was almost ready. Assuming we had enough to accommodate all our extra guests, that is.

Because the trolls hadn't left.

From what I understood, they were some big shots in the local troll community who had been at the fights last night and offered Olga their help. She had been glad to accept, since apparently all hell had broken loose shortly after I passed out. The slaver had ended up dead somehow, and as soon as they heard, the slaves had started to flee.

That wouldn't have been so bad, even if most of them were new arrivals who had no idea how to navigate the human world. Worst-case scenario, they'd be picked up by the Corps, a bunch of nosy mages who think they're the supernatural police, and sent back to Faerie. Best-case scenario, somebody like Olga would find them, and they'd get adopted into the local Dark Fey community. Or, at least, they would have, except the slaver's assistants had preferred to kill them rather than let them escape and give evidence.

Hence the hell.

The fight had quickly devolved into two camps, although not exactly the way you'd think. Some of the slaves had sold themselves to the slavers in order to escape the wars in Faerie, which were even more likely to get them killed. They'd been promised money and a new start if they survived so many fights, and those nearing the end of their contract had been persuaded to help the slavers in return for an early payoff.

Others had sided with the slaves, like the big scarred guy, who had torn a swath through the slavers' initial advance. Larger trolls like him had given the smaller ones—mostly water boys and cut men there to help with the fights—a chance to flee. But the slavers had called in reinforcements from their compound in Queens, and somebody else had called in the Corps, which caused a panic, since a good percentage of the spectators were just as illegal as the fighters.

The lot had quickly turned into a knock-down-drag-out—literally, the Corps had been dragging people out—which explained why Olga was still in her sparkly pink outfit. She hadn't gotten a wink of sleep. She and her guys had been on a mad scramble to find the slaves before the slavers did, while somehow avoiding arrest, since not all of Olga's people were exactly legal, either.

Fortunately, she'd had the charms to help with the latter and the former had been simpler than one might expect, because we're talking trolls here. Young, hungry trolls—because the bastard slaver had only fed the guys who were going to fight and needed to bulk up. So, of course, every escapee had made a beeline for the nearest source of food.

Olga's group had fished one guy out of a mom-and-pop grocery, where he'd been going to town on the produce. And a couple more who'd popped open a semitruck and were helping themselves to a bounty of Tastykakes, wrappers and all. Olga said their digestion would take care of it. I had decided not to ask what that meant. And a third group who had broken into a local brewery, and been found with bellies so distended by all the beer that they'd had to be carried out because they could no longer walk.

So, yeah, she'd welcomed help from the Elders, which was the best translation of the big guys' titles. Together they had managed to recover a number of slaves, including the tiny one currently asleep in the trundle bed in the boys' room. However, relations appeared to have soured all of a sudden. I wasn't sure why.

I just knew that the boy had been carried upstairs by Olga herself. And that, when the other trolls tried to follow, they'd had their faces smashed into a ward that she'd flicked on as she went past. That had not been appreciated, especially by Gravel Face, and a somewhat . . . lively . . . conversation had thereafter taken place in the middle of the hall. It was still going on, only without Olga, who had left halfway through.

I didn't blame her.

Those guys were dicks. . . .

"It what child say," she told me, suddenly.

I jerked back awake, which was a surprise, since I hadn't recalled drifting off. "What?" I stared around. "What is?"

"Fish, tracks, door."

I frowned, trying to get the brain to work when it didn't want to. "What child? The troll child?"

She nodded.

"Just now? When he was about to—" I blinked. "What did he say, again?"

She repeated it. I sat up. The motion made me dizzy, which pissed me off. I drank some beer and told my body to deal with it already.

"What does that mean?" I asked.

Olga shrugged.

"Well, it must have been important."

"What's important?" Claire asked, coming out of the back door.

I looked up. The sun was setting in her hair, making it almost look like it was on fire. "Fish, tracks, door."

She frowned at me, like maybe I'd hit my head harder than she'd been told. "Are you all right?"

"More or less."

She frowned some more, put down the crate of dishes she was carrying, and started pawing through my hair. "You have quite a bump."

"It'll go down by tomorrow." If she'd stop poking at it, I didn't add, because she was trying to help.

"I can get you an ice pack," she began, before I held up my dripping one.

"Got it covered."

She seemed to accept this, because she let me go. "They want to see you," she told Olga, who sighed, but got up and lumbered inside.

That left the swing free, but Claire sat down beside me instead.

"Are we eating soon?" I asked hopefully, eyeing the dishes. They were for the picnic tables that we used far more often than the dining room, since it was nicer out here in the garden, and we couldn't fit everybody inside anymore, anyway.

"As soon as the pizzas arrive." She shot me a chagrined look. "No way to stretch soup that far."

I nodded. I'd seen trolls eat. And those were what I was coming to view as normal trolls, instead of the hulks I'd been encountering lately.

"How many pizzas?" I asked, feeling like I could eat a whole one all by myself.

Claire didn't answer.

She had one of those faces that was in turns perfectly plain and completely beautiful, all depending on her mood. When she was in a temper, the emerald eyes flashed, the ivory skin flushed, and the bright red hair, only a shade or two off from Olga's fiery locks, seemed to have a life of its own. She was almost half human, but I swear, when she was really, truly angry, she didn't look it.

She wasn't angry now. Now, the eyes were a dull olive, the cheeks were pale and pinched, and the freckles on the long, thin nose stood out clearly. The hair reflected her overall mood, sagging dispiritedly around her face.

"Want a beer?" I asked, and passed one over when she nodded.

She looked like she could use a bit more than that, like maybe a shoulder to cry on for some reason. Only I didn't know how to offer one without making things worse, because Claire could be touchy. Comes with the territory when her recent history involved almost being killed by her slimy cousin, who'd wanted to inherit the family business; being spirited away to Faerie by a handsome prince; getting pregnant; having a kid; having said kid almost killed by a murderous fey court who didn't like the idea of a part-human heir; and escaping back to earth, where she was now living in a crazy house with a dhampir, some adolescent trolls, and a bunch of royal guards camped out in her backyard, stepping on all the vegetables.

It was enough to make anyone cranky.

But she didn't say anything, just drank half the beer, like she could use it, then narrowed her eyes at the fey across the yard. "What are they cooking?"

I tried on an innocent look. "Couldn't tell you."

"Don't lie." She leaned forward a little, and the sharp eyes narrowed on a pile of something that I don't think she got a good look at, because a fey flicked a cape over it a second later. She started to get up, then sighed and sat back down again. And drank the rest of the beer.

"Are *you* all right?" I asked, because Claire always took care of everybody else, while often forgetting to do the same for herself. And it was hard to remind her, because sensible people backed off when she said "I'm fine" in that certain tone, and her eyes flashed.

Of course, I've never had much sense.

"You don't look fine," I said idly, and passed over another beer.

She looked at it. "I'll get drunk."

"Off two beers?"

"Off an empty stomach and two beers." She took it anyway. "And a truckload of stress!"

"Why are you stressed?" I asked, and immediately regretted it. If storm clouds could grow a face, that would be it. And, okay, stupid question.

"Oh, I don't know, Dory!" she said, throwing out an arm. But she didn't say anything else. Just chugged the beer in a way that would have won her another round in any campus bar, then set the bottle neatly by the porch post, where I'd been piling mine.

And lay back against the sun-warmed boards, her hair going everywhere, like she enjoyed the feel, too.

I decided to join her. For a while, we both just stayed there, watching a spider build a web across a Victorian curlicue in the top of the railing. Gessa could be heard telling Stinky to let go of something, and then wrestling him for it when he predictably declined. Aiden laughed. A horse we shouldn't have had whinnied. I sighed.

The portal had a setting that let out into the garden, but for security reasons, it didn't work the other way. The only entrance was in the basement. So, to get the illegal animal out of here, we faced the prospect of leading it through the house and down a narrow flight of stairs. And then across a crowded basement where the portal light would probably cause it to freak the hell out.

At least, that's what had happened last time, and no one had thought it fun.

And since the troll twins didn't trust the Light Fey in their sanctum, and the Light Fey didn't trust the trolls with their precious horses, it was probably gonna be left to me again, and frankly—

"It's getting worse," Claire told me abruptly.

I rolled my neck over to look at her. "What is?"

"You know what. I think—" She swallowed but didn't turn her head to look at me. "I think it's getting stronger."

I didn't say anything for a minute, because yeah. I did know. Because Claire and I had a similar problem, if for totally different reasons.

I was stuck with a crazy other half because of a weird mental operation Mircea had done, once upon a time, without really understanding what he was doing. I didn't blame him; nobody else had known what to do, either. Dhampirs were so rare that there was no money in figuring out how to help us. My condition, or whatever you wanted to call it, might have been around forever, but it hadn't preoccupied the attention of anyone in the healing profession.

Until Claire. I hadn't understood why she, who was mainly interested in the fey, would want to help a human/vampire hybrid. Especially a crazy one. But she had, cultivating some extra-powerful fey weed for me that calmed the beast when nothing else could. But, lately, I'd come to believe that maybe I did know why she'd given a damn. Even if she hadn't known it then, we weren't that different.

Because Claire was a hybrid, too.

Her mother had been human, with a tiny bit of Brownie in the mix somewhere. That wasn't particularly odd for the magical community and hadn't seemed to affect her. But her father . . . well, her father was something else altogether.

It was why Caedmon was here, trying to bum assistance for whatever he was up to in Faerie. It seemed that the fey had their own version of shape-shifters, just like our weres. Or, no, not just like. Because while weres could be terrifying, especially in large numbers, none of them held a candle to their fey cousins.

None of them morphed into a two-thousand-pound dragon.

Claire hadn't realized that her mother's lover—who had been in human form when they met, obviously—was anybody special. Nobody in the family had ever said anything, and she'd never shown any signs of peculiar abilities. Until she took a trip into Faerie with Heidar, and discovered the hard way that she was something known as two-natured among the fey.

The revelation had been a little traumatic, from what I'd heard. And apparently, things hadn't improved since. Her other half was still an adolescent, because living on Earth had stunted its development, but lately, it had been making its presence known.

"Still craving rare steak?" I asked. Because Claire— the old Claire—was a strict vegan, something her other half was not on board with.

She waved the question away, with a flutter of long, white fingers.

"Yes, but I can handle that. I can't—" She stopped, her throat working. And then she blurted it out. "How do you do it?"

"How do I do what?"

"Not explode!" She sat up, her face white, but her eyes bright. "I felt it, what you carry inside you—all that anger, all that rage—every time I pulled it off you. The first time, it was such a shock. That you could even *function*. And in the garden that night—it was amazing. Just amazing." She shook her head.

Yeah. That was one word for it, I thought uncomfortably. She was talking about an incident a couple weeks ago, when Louis-Cesare said something that offended Dorina, and she'd almost gone ballistic, threatening not only him but everybody else we'd had over that night. Including the commune that lived across the street, and as far as I knew, were one-hundred-percent human. It had been terrifying, because I'd been fighting with everything I had, but I still couldn't control her, and I didn't know what she'd do if I let go.

Thankfully, Claire had been there, and even more thankfully, her human half is what is known as a null witch, someone capable of pulling magical energy off other creatures. That was how we'd met. She'd been working at an auction house after fleeing her homicidal excuse for a cousin, calming down the odd little items they had up for sale, some of which could be dangerous if a null wasn't around to drink all that excess energy. I'd been shopping to bulk up the arsenal, and we'd started talking. And had ended up as roommates because our abilities complemented each other. I'd kept her safe from her weird-ass family, and she'd kept me . . . well, more or less sane.

Except for that night, when even she hadn't been able to drink it all, because Dorina was *pissed*.

Luckily, Louis-Cesare had old-fashioned manners, and had apologized the way that one master did to another, by kneeling and offering his neck to her sword if she'd had one. It was archaic, but then, so was Dorina. And it had done what nothing else could, and sent her back to sleep.

Leaving the rest of us seriously weirded out, especially me, because I wasn't used to being awake when she emerged. Not that she had entirely, but it had been close enough to shake me. And, apparently, it hadn't been any better for Claire, and now I was kicking myself for not even thinking about that.

"I'm sorry—" I began.

But she was already shaking her head. "It's okay. I just meant—you fought it, somehow. If you hadn't, I wouldn't have had time to do anything, and who knows what would have happened? I need to know how to do that. I thought I understood, that I could handle my . . . problem . . . like I did yours. But that was something from outside of me, someone else's emotion. It was distant, you know?"

Not really, but she was looking at me hopefully, so I nodded anyway.

"But now . . ." She bit her lip. "Dory, I almost lost it in there. When they wouldn't let Caedmon help, when they were just going to watch that child die, I almost—" Her eyes met mine, and there was genuine fear in them. "It wasn't distant then. I wanted to kill them, to rend them, to hurt—" She put her face in her hands.

I sat there, feeling awkward. Because I wasn't used to having friends—the fits had always made it too dangerous—much less to comforting them. I sometimes looked around at all the people in my life now with sheer amazement, and no little fear. That I wouldn't know what to do in any of the roles I suddenly found myself in: parent, lover, best friend. Because I'd never played them before.

But Claire had been there for me when I really needed her, and she clearly needed something from me now. But I didn't know what. So I just hugged her, remembering how much it had helped when Louis-Cesare had done the same for me. And after a startled second, she hugged me back.

"I wanted to *eat* them, Dory," she whispered, her voice cracking. "I wanted it so . . . damned . . . much. And I just . . ." She hugged me harder, and it hurt, because my ribs were apparently never going to freaking heal, but I didn't say anything.

She was hurting more.

"How do you do it?" she asked again, sounding fairly desperate. "I can't turn into this thing. I won't!"

I didn't know what to say, because the truth wasn't something she wanted to hear. The fact was, anger management had never been my specialty. I'd learned a few tricks, but it was always a crapshoot whether any would work. Mostly, I'd learned to live with it by letting my emotions out on a regular basis when I hunted, which helped to calm them the rest of the time.

And calm emotions kept the door locked on Dorina.

But Claire was a vegan nurse; she didn't hunt.

I didn't know what that meant for her.

But I didn't say that, or anything else. Because the back door suddenly slammed open and a bunch of trolls spilled out. And they weren't looking happy.

Chapter Eleven

"What *now*?" I said, as Claire scrambled to her feet.

"Is the little one okay?" she asked, looking worried.

But the trolls weren't stopping to chat. They were already off the porch and halfway across the garden, leaving me and Claire looking at each other, because they were obviously heading for Caedmon. And I don't think either of us knew what to do about that.

But the royal guards didn't seem to have that problem. They went from relaxed and mostly supine, lounging around the fire in that boneless, catlike way the fey have, to on their feet in a row in front of Caedmon, swords out and game faces on, in about the time it took for me to blink. I sometimes wondered why the hell I spent so much time worrying about hurting people, when I was probably the weakest one around here anymore.

That didn't change when Olga came out of the door a moment later, and then just stood there, hands on hips, looking pissed. Because she'd clearly had enough of the macho brigade for one day. She started down the steps, but Claire grabbed her arm.

"What's going on?"

"They being stupid," Olga said.

"Is the boy all right?"

She nodded. "He asleep."

"Then what—"

"They want to know why he help," Olga said, gesturing at Caedmon. Who was on his feet now, too.

"Why wouldn't he? He had the power to spare—"

Olga started to say something, and then just gestured

at them. Because yeah. Inside voice was apparently not a thing in trolldom.

We took off for the latest crisis, despite the fact that we could hear them from the porch. And so could half the neighborhood, not that they'd probably understand what they were saying. I sure didn't.

But not because of the language barrier.

"Boy has no clan. No one pay for him. You get *nothing*!" That was the big troll with the scraped face, and yes, I'd been right. Now that we were in better lighting, I could see that it was definitely some kind of black, sparkly gravel embedded in his skin, from temple to neck, and glinting redly in the setting sun. The skin had grown back around it, in scarification-like swirls, as if it had been in there for decades. Because sure. Why pull it out, right?

I didn't understand trolls at all.

And it looked like Caedmon didn't, either.

"I don't recall asking for anything."

It was said mildly enough, but for some reason, it seemed to enrage the trolls, several of whom took a step forward. To the point that they were almost touching the shiny tips of the royal guards' swords, which no one had lowered. And which a couple of the boys looked like they'd enjoy having an excuse to use.

Claire must have thought so, too, because she started forward, only to have Olga hold her back. It would have been funny under other circumstances, because Olga's gesture was that of a mother reaching an arm across a child during a sudden stop in a car. But Claire wasn't a child, and she didn't look like she appreciated it.

Like, really didn't.

And, suddenly, the hairs on the back of my neck were standing up.

"I have a grandson," Caedmon was saying, apparently oblivious. "The boy is scarcely older. I wanted to help—"

"No Light Fey help Dark! Not for no reason!" Gravel Face looked pissed.

"*He* did. Boy fine. Go home," Olga told them, but nobody was listening.

Possibly because a lot of them wanted a fight. The royal guards were bored out of their minds, with nothing to do all day but hang around Claire's garden. And the trolls—well, I frankly didn't know what their problem was, but they definitely had one. Making me wonder what the hell they had expected to happen.

"Did you want us to just let the kid die?" I demanded.

I didn't really expect an answer, but for some reason, I got one.

"He too sick, can't get to healer in time," Gravel Face said, still staring down Caedmon. "Olga say she know another, so we come. But not to *him*!"

"But . . . he saved him—"

"And now we owe debt! He want us fight for him, die. We not die for Light Fey king! No more!"

The garden exploded with the chant, and with chest-beating and growling and half lunges toward the guards, who planted their feet and stood their ground. Even though the only thing keeping Dark Fey blood from smearing the tips of those swords was the thickness of the hide battering into them. Great.

"He doesn't want you to fight for him!" I yelled, to be heard over the racket. I looked at Caedmon. "Tell them!"

"I'm always happy to recruit new auxiliaries—"

"Caedmon!"

"—but that wasn't what I was doing today. You owe me nothing."

"See?" I asked, and Olga nodded. And then threw up her hands, because they clearly didn't see.

"You say that now," White Hair said, in perfect English. So I guess he'd just been being a dick inside. "But when the time comes, you'll call in the debt, and throw us in front of your own troops to spare their blood. We know how you see us, fey king. We know how all of you see us, as nothing but animals—"

"My daughter-in-law is not an animal," Caedmon said, his eyes on her.

Like mine should have been, I realized, because Claire was looking a little . . . odd.

It wasn't physical. She was the same slender girl in an old-fashioned floral print dress, which should have made her look dowdy but somehow never did. All she needed was a big, floppy-brimmed straw hat, her hair in messy braids, and a wheat field to model for one of *Vogue*'s "Girls of Summer" covers.

And a different expression.

A really different expression.

"Claire?" I said, and got a low, rolling growl in return. Uh.

"Maybe we should go inside? Check on that soup?" I began, only to be cut off by raised voices from the crowd.

This time, they weren't in English, so I don't know what they said. But whatever it was prompted a quick interjection from Olga, who wasn't looking so concerned with etiquette anymore. There was some yelling and gesturing and then—

"You *lie!*"

It was Hothead again, and I was beginning to understand how his face got like that. I was hankering to chain him to the back of my car and drag him for a few miles, and I'd just met him. But if pain hadn't taught him something before, it probably wouldn't this time, either.

Not that I got a chance to find out.

Not before he jumped for Claire.

Annnnnd that probably wasn't his best move, I thought, stepping abruptly back. Or what he'd expected, judging by his expression when his back slammed into the ground, hard enough to tremble it. And to add some rocks to other parts of his anatomy as he thrashed around, in full-on panic.

And went nowhere.

Because the taloned claw suddenly pinning him to the earth didn't belong to the girl I knew, or even to the cute baby dragon I remembered. But to something else entirely. For a long moment, I just stared.

The first time I'd seen Claire in her alternate form she'd been . . . well, frankly, adorable. I'd still been weirded the hell out, because dragon, but even then, I couldn't help noticing the absurd tuft of purple hair between the two little glasslike horns on top of her head. And the tiny black wings squashed against the ceiling in the hall, because she'd transformed in a too-small space. Or the, um, healthy thighs and butt, neither of which those wings were gonna be lifting anytime soon.

Of course, I could have been wrong about that.

Because it looked like baby was all grown up.

The fat little haunches were currently sleek and gleaming with a river of pewter scales. The wings were huge and thick and heavily veined, blocking out much of the sky. And bisected by a ridge of amethyst that had been just a smear of color up the spine last time, but was now a line of crystalline structures, like they were literally carved out of semiprecious stones. And the ridiculous tuft of hair was now a full-on mane, falling between two massive, translucent, curled horns.

She was beautiful, if a twenty-foot embodiment of death can be described that way. Or, rather, twenty feet if you didn't count the tail, which was long and spiked and thrashing around, digging out great swaths of grass and telegraphing her mood all at the same time. A mood that could obviously be summed up as face-eating furious.

I didn't want to see her eat the troll's face, despite not caring for it much.

Because I did care for Claire, and I didn't know how she would take that once this was over.

Scratch that. I knew exactly how she'd take it, considering that she planted freaking marigolds around her garden to ward off pests, so she didn't have to kill them. So, yeah. Time to save the asshole troll.

Only problem was, how?

I glanced at Olga, but she wasn't much help. She was just standing there, blinking slowly. Because yeah. She hadn't been there before, had she? And while she'd known what Claire was, knowing and seeing are two different things.

Very different.

So it was up to me.

Only I was unarmed—seemed to be a theme, lately—and even if I hadn't been, I didn't want to hurt Claire. Not that that was likely. Because the talons at the ends of those huge, scale-covered paws—the ones that had previously been the size of my handy penknife—were now somewhere between butcher and machete range, and razor-sharp. The one pinning the troll down had a slight *scritch-scritch* motion going on, hardly anything really, barely enough to notice.

Except for the line of green-black blood dripping down his rock-hard chest and side, the ones that the fey swords hadn't even managed to dent.

I swallowed, and licked my lips.

"Uh, Claire?" It was soft, tentative, almost a whisper. Yet a split second later, the huge, finely tapered snout was in my face, and I was staring into a pair of eyes that had once been pansy colored and kind of silly, but weren't so much right now.

Now the nictitating membrane that had freaked me out last time slid across irises of fiery orange, burning yellow, and, at the very edge, a ring of pale purple. That would have been intimidating enough all on its own, but for today's serving of extra crazy, the striations . . . weren't static. The little lines that radiate out from the pupil in a human's eye just sort of stay there. I'd thought the same had been true of Claire's, even in her transformed state, although I admit to being slightly freaked out and not nearly this close last time, so maybe I just hadn't noticed. But I was noticing now, and these . . . were not.

These spread outward in an ever-moving kaleidoscope of light and color. Orange lines pierced the yellow; yellow radiated back into the orange; the purple flared and blurred with barely contained elemental fire; the whole a hypnotic dance of color and movement and . . . and . . .

And *shit*, I thought, shaking my head, feeling dizzy. And warm and happy and kind of sleepy, because she'd almost had me. Without even trying, she'd almost had *me*, a gal who had thrown off vampire suggestions all her life, like water off a duck's back. But I had almost been hypnotized just standing there, swaying lightly on my feet until I *made* myself stop, and shook my head again before looking back up at her defiantly.

Because not today, Claire.

Not fucking today.

"You need to stop this and go back inside," I told her, my voice a lot stronger this time. "Right now."

Only that swishy tail didn't think so. It casually destroyed a stone garden bench, reducing it to rubble without apparently noticing, and scattered the pieces far and wide. Meanwhile, the talon continued to press into the troll, a little harder now, judging by the size of that trickle. And the vertical pupils, like the fucking eyes of Sauron, met mine with what I swear was a challenge in them.

I got a sudden flash on Mrs. Nedermeyer's cats, and the snake that one of them had found in her yard one day. Just a little thing, a bright green grass snake, harmless and kind of cute. But that hadn't mattered to the cat. Who had stayed on its haunches, its tail swaying side to side, right in front of the little creature. And every time it had raised up its snaky head, thinking maybe it would make a slither for it, the cat would put out a paw.

And bop it back down.

Because cats like to play with their dinner, don't they?

Just like dragons.

"Stop it, and go in the house!" I said, more forcefully.

The sunburst eyes narrowed. She didn't like that. Like I didn't like the snout suddenly thrust the rest of the way into my face, to the point of literally touching my nose. It was a dominance move, and a pretty damned good one, with the great chest heaving, and the huge jaw cracking, and the tornado of breath billowing through a really impressive collection of teeth and feeling like it was about to set my hair on fire.

For the record, staring a dragon in the face is . . . intimidating. It makes you feel small and vulnerable in ways that short-circuit the brain, and send your mind on odd flights of fancy, like wondering if you taste good. It also makes you forget what, exactly, you had to say that was so damned important, but that your brain can't seem to remember right now because it's kind of busy gibbering in a corner.

"Uh," I said, trying to look intimidating and having a really good idea how badly I was failing at it.

But I still didn't move.

Not even when the great snout started sniffing around me, with huge wheezing breaths that ruffled my hair and felt like they might be giving me a sunburn. Or a dragon burn, I thought, my brain snapping out of it for a sec to decide that our final thought would be flippant, because sometimes my brain is an ass. But I didn't lose it and run screaming across the yard, although I don't get any points for that considering that my knees had just locked and I couldn't seem to move.

I don't know what would have happened next, whether Claire would have remembered me or whether I'd have ended up as an appetizer. Because the main course took that moment to show up. I heard the old fence gate squeak its way open; saw someone in a bright red ball cap come in carrying a tower of pizza boxes; smelled meaty, cheesy goodness spreading across the lawn.

And screamed: "Claire, *no!*"

But it was too late. I hadn't even gotten the words out when the huge body turned in a flowing motion, elegant yet quick as lightning, like a striking snake. Only she didn't need the advantage. Because the poor delivery boy didn't even see her, thanks to the huge pile of boxes.

Not that it would have helped if he had, because a second from now he was going to be a memory, and there wasn't a single thing I could do —

About it, I thought, my brain not keeping up with the action, but fortunately, someone else's was.

Namely, Olga's was, because she'd moved — I didn't know when, since I'd been kind of busy. But she'd used the distraction I'd unwittingly provided to do something, since the rest of us were just standing about, hoping not to get eaten. Only what she could do, I wasn't sure.

Until I saw Aiden.

She was standing between Claire and the house, looking impossibly tiny despite being eight feet tall, because of the contrast. Yet, there she was, not too far from the clueless delivery guy, holding Aiden up in the air like Rafiki holding Simba. She didn't say anything, and neither did Aiden, but then, they didn't need to. Because, if there's one thing every mother knows immediately, instinctively, it's her own child.

A second later, the delivery guy was forgotten, the big neck was curving, and the huge creature was delicately snuffling her only son. Who did what you'd expect a one-year-old to do in that situation, and started wailing. I knew the feeling, I thought dizzily.

But Claire obviously didn't. The huge head reared back, the very nonhuman face somehow managing to convey a very identifiable progression of emotions: horror, chagrin, dismay. And then pain, the depth of it searing my retinas before a flash of golden light made us all cover our eyes.

When I looked again, a hysterical, naked woman was running for the house, sobbing; Olga was cuddling a very confused Aiden; and the pizza guy was just standing there, the boxes scattered around him and trodden in the mud, his face slack with disbelief.

Before he suddenly shuddered, a deep, all-over motion, and leapt for the fence, fumbling with the gate for a moment before deciding, "Fuck it," and jumping across, and then ignoring his car in favor of running down the road, screaming.

On the plus side, the trolls didn't give us any more trouble after that.

Chapter Twelve

Several exhausting hours later, I was huddled on the porch under a makeshift tent eating a popular type of toaster pastry. And wondering why it was popular. It was chalky and overly sweet, and had too little filling. And most of that had never seen a piece of actual fruit in its life.

The turnovers Claire made were a thousand times better, buttery and flaky and stuffed to overflowing with her own vine-ripened crops. Only I didn't have any of those. Of course, I didn't have anything else, either.

That was the problem with boarding two adolescent trolls: food disappeared as fast as it was brought in. They were like teenage boys, aka bottomless pits, only with stomachs many times as large. Even with a sizeable backyard garden to draw from, the cupboards were always empty.

That was true even today, when we'd had a second harvest inside. I'd been too preoccupied to wonder where the troll twins had been during all the excitement, but I guess that term is relative, isn't it? So while we were yelling and fighting and facing a sudden dragon problem in the backyard, the twins had been busy gathering up all the apples and carting them off to the basement. Where there was some grand project going on to turn them into cider, or possibly brandy if they could figure out how to work Claire's uncle's old still.

I just hoped they didn't blow up the house.

Anyway, as a result, there wasn't a single whole piece of fruit left in the place. Or any pizza, most of which had gotten crushed under a giant-sized heel. There *was* soup, but by the time I'd tried to talk to Claire, who was sobbing in her room and wouldn't open the door; and called up the pizza place, to make sure they had been paid and we wouldn't get blackballed from yet another delivery service; and got hung up on because too late; and rescued Stinky from the trolls, because he was trying to fight them; and watched them leave in a huff before they were thrown out bodily; and made up the spare room for Olga, who'd decided to stay the night; and checked on Claire again, who still wasn't talking; and took a phone call from Louis-Cesare, reassuring him that, yep, I'd just been hanging around the house all day, no problems here, I discovered that it was all gone. And my cooking skills mostly involve making grilled cheese, only I didn't have any cheese.

That was okay; I didn't have any bread, either.

But then I found out that somebody, probably the damned guards, had drunk all the beer, and that was the last straw. So I was hermiting inside my tent with an attitude and the last piece of food in the place. Because there are certain things even a troll won't eat.

I saw a shadow approach from outside, and then pause, before a familiar blond head stuck through the flap where the blankets overlapped. And eyed my dinner. I snatched it away quickly, the little cellophane wrapper reflecting the light from the lantern Caedmon was holding. There may have also been some growling involved.

This did not appear to deter him. "May I come in?"

"No." I shoved the last of the so-called pastry in my mouth, because I wasn't taking chances.

He came in anyway.

I'd have had something to say about that, once the chalky mess cleared my throat. Only a scent hit my nostrils before then, a rich, decadent, meaty aroma emanating from something in the hand that wasn't holding the lantern. Something that wasn't terrible pastry with inadequate filling. Something that looked a lot like—

"Izzatme'?" I asked, hopefully.

"I beg your pardon?"

I swallowed, and it was tough, because some asshole had drunk all my beer.

"Is that meat?" I repeated, and snatched the plate he was holding out.

Caedmon said some word I didn't know, and then smiled at my expression. "Yes," he said simply. "It's something of a specialty of mine. I think you'll like it."

I liked it.

It tasted like duck: dark, sweet, and tender, with an acid undertone that probably came from the wine. The same kind he handed me a skin of while he tried to find a comfortable position. He ended up cross-legged, hunched over, and fidgety. Then said to hell with it and reclined, golden head propped up on one fine-fingered hand, silken hair cascading onto my last blanket, long legs protruding out onto the damp boards.

It was raining, hence the tent. Of course, we were under shelter, but the sky kept throwing handfuls of water at me through the sides of the porch, because it was that kind of day. But Caedmon didn't look like he minded. In fact, he looked entirely too happy altogether, which probably boded badly for me. But right then, I didn't care.

"Good?" he asked unnecessarily, considering that I was all but inhaling it.

"Never had swan," I said. The park down the road boasted eight or nine of the ill-tempered things—or it had. The old people were going to get a surprise when they showed up to feed their pets tomorrow.

"These were fine, fat cygnets," Caedmon agreed, looking pleased.

I didn't say anything.

I was kind of complicit at this point.

"I'm not talking to Claire for you," I told him, in between bites.

"I thought you'd already talked to her. Else why were you banished?" He gestured around the little tent.

"I'm not banished."

A golden eyebrow went up.

"I'm out here to get some sleep."

"And you cannot do that inside?"

I rolled my eyes and ate swan. "Listen."

He cocked his head to the side, and the fine lips pursed. "Is that—what is that?"

"Olga. She's sleeping over."

"It's . . . astonishing." He listened some more, to what

sounded like a cross between a wounded buffalo and a dying rhino, with a little elephant trumpet there at the end sometimes. "Can you imagine," he asked, after a moment, "an entire cave or village, hundreds of them, all sleeping at once? It must be deafening."

I thought one was pretty deafening.

Dhampir hearing is a bitch.

"And yet, they can be so silent when they want," he continued, "so stealthy, that even my men have missed them at times."

"The slavers didn't seem to have any trouble," I pointed out, thinking of the little one.

The smile on Caedmon's face faded. "He was likely never trained. Even my people do not move as they do without practice."

"Maybe he'll get some now."

Caedmon shook his head. "I did what I could, but the damage was too severe. He'll limp for the rest of his life, if he walks at all. It will make him of little use to his people, who rank someone's value by their fighting prowess. If he goes home, he will always be considered *mótgørð.*"

I looked a question.

"A nuisance."

I scowled, but didn't say anything. I hadn't lived in unceasing warfare for centuries. I had no room to talk. "You understand their language?"

"Well enough."

"What did he say in there, right before you helped him?" Olga was usually pretty good at getting her point across, but her English was a little . . . rudimentary. And "fish, tracks, door" didn't make a lot of sense.

"He asked her to rescue his bones."

I frowned. "What?"

Caedmon switched to his back, looking up at the lamplight playing on the roof of the tent. I didn't know why he'd brought it. He gave off enough light of his own, and for a darker night than this, if he wasn't drawing it down like he was at the moment. I wondered why he bothered. To seem more normal, more relatable? To make it easier to talk me into something?

Maybe. Or maybe he just didn't want the neighbors to

ask any questions. Of course, other than the commune across the road, who were high half the time and didn't trust their eyes anyway, most of our neighbors were about a hundred and wouldn't have noticed anything unusual if he'd been standing in front of them. Except to remark on how tall he was.

At least, that had been old Mrs. Epstein's comment when she accidentally came through our gate instead of her own one day, and had a group of "such nice young men" take her back to her front door. She'd never know that she'd had an escort of royal fey guards, and they'd never know that I'd seen them, several times since, hopping the fence to help her take in her weekly groceries.

It was strange how . . . human . . . people could be, given a chance.

"It is my people's belief that Faerie is a living thing," Caedmon said, "an organism with a soul of its own. And that each of its children are parts of that soul, experiencing life in different ways: as a tree, a breath of wind, a person. When one of us dies, our soul rejoins the soul of Faerie, and will one day live again."

"So reincarnation, then."

"In a way. Although, from what I understand of your Earth religions, they view the cycle of rebirth negatively, as something to be escaped. They long for the peace of nonexistence, or at least for an end to the cycle, something that would make very little sense to my people. We look forward to experiencing everything life has to offer, in all its many . . . permutations."

He smiled suggestively at me.

I shot him a look. "Then why do your people hate the Dark Fey, and vice versa? If you're all part of one soul—"

"I, for one, do not hate them," Caedmon demurred. "And I did not say that everyone believes so; indeed, many do not. But the little troll does, which is why he asked to have his bones returned to our soil."

I waved a swan leg at him. "How would a bunch of bones help with that?"

"The fey view the soul and body as inseparable. The idea that our bodies could be one place and our souls another, separated after death as some of your people believe, is quite . . . disturbing." He actually did look disturbed for a moment, before his good humor returned. "It is thought that the soul bonds particularly well with the bones, which are so much sturdier than the fleshy bits—"

I removed his hand from one of my fleshy bits.

"—and thus the *íviðja* swore to help him live again, by returning his bones to Faerie, to be reabsorbed. The fist to the chest gesture you saw is a solemn vow among her people. She would have to do as she swore, or die trying."

"But she didn't know him," I pointed out. "She'd risk her life going back there for someone she doesn't even know?"

"She is probably one of those who believe that if Faerie's children do not return, they cannot be reborn. That their souls will remain trapped here, where their bodies lie, and be forever lost. Both to their people and to Faerie."

"So the fey who die here . . . they're all sent back?"

"That has always been the practice among my people, certainly." He thought about it. "Well, most of the time."

"Most of the time?"

"There is the story of the dastardly Princess Alfhild Ambhọfði—a cautionary tale of greed and pride still told to children."

I put on my interested face, and Caedmon laughed. "Do you know, I haven't told a bedtime story in some years?"

"Then you can use the practice. For Aiden."

He sighed. "I need to spend more time with the boy. Claire is right about that."

"But you don't."

"Things have been . . . tense lately."

"Want to tell me why?"

"Yes, in fact," Caedmon said, surprising me. "But I don't know that I should."

"Why not?"

He picked up my greasy hand and kissed it. And then mouthed away a little swan grease that had fallen into the well between my thumb and forefinger. It was . . . surprisingly erotic. I pulled my hand back, and he looked pleased.

"Because, my dear Dory, I do not know if I am talking to you or your father."

"My father isn't here."

"Isn't he?" He scanned my eyes for a long moment, and then he sighed. "Perhaps not. I should certainly like to think so."

I decided not to ask why.

"Still, I think I would do better telling you about Alfhild," he continued. "She lived what you would call once upon a time, in a kingdom at the foot of a great mountain. There were hundreds of petty kingdoms then, some barely larger than the castle walls of the main keep, others with vast lands under their control. Alfhild's was neither particularly small nor overly large, but she—did I mention that women could rule then?"

"Must have forgotten it."

"Well, they could. Until Alfhild. She serves as a cautionary tale for that, too."

I considered smacking him, but I was feeling mellow and was busy gnawing some bones. I settled for a look. "I take it she was a bad ruler?"

"Oh, no, quite the contrary. One had to be skilled to survive then. The petty kingdoms were always squabbling among themselves, making treaties and breaking them, and going to war every spring as soon as the new buds flowered on the trees."

"Did you ever fight her?"

Caedmon feigned shock. "Just how old do you think me, Dorina?"

"Pretty damned old."

He grinned. "What is it they say? Age is but a number? But my number does not go that high."

I frowned. "How old is this story?"

"It goes back a bit, even for us. For you . . . let's just say, when the need arose, there were no scribes yet among you to write it down."

I frowned some more. "'When the need arose'?"

He patted my leg. "Alfhild was ambitious and, despite having a prosperous land, was dissatisfied with her lot. She therefore used her beauty to seduce her neighboring kingdoms into a coalition. One she planned to use to attack the large, peaceful, and prosperous land belonging to one of my ancestors. It was in the mountains then, too, but had several verdant valleys under its control that Alf-hild coveted."

"I assume she lost the war?" Otherwise, I guessed, Caedmon wouldn't be here.

"There was no war. Her coalition members realized that, instead of attacking a well-equipped and, of course, very valorous kingdom—"

"Of course."

"—they could attack her instead. Thus taking a smaller but more certain reward, instead of risking a war they weren't sure they would win. And that, even if they did, might see the spoils end up more under Alfhild's control than theirs, allowing her to pick them off, one by one."

"So they picked her off first."

"No, but they should have," Caedmon said, suddenly grim. "Instead, they exiled her to an island in the middle of a large lake, and ringed the small fortress there with spells. They thought it would hold her, at least long enough for them to have the victory feast!"

"It didn't." It wasn't a question. His expression was eloquent.

"No, it didn't. The legend says that she somehow escaped, gathered her most loyal supporters, and while the five dastardly kings who had betrayed her feasted well into the night, she struck—"

"And killed them all!" That was a story I could get behind.

Caedmon nodded gravely. "Yes, she killed them all. And then she killed their families, down to the last child, still in the cradle. And then she killed their generals and their families, their nobles and their families, the leading townsmen who had supported their war efforts by taxation, the merchants who had sold them arms, and even the cooks who had fed them. A bloody great slaughter of virtually everyone who had had anything to do with their treachery."

I blinked at him. "Damn."

"Oh no." Caedmon looked at me, his eyes gleaming. "We're not to 'damn' yet."

Chapter Thirteen

"Do I want to hear this?" I asked him.

He cocked a head. "I don't know. Do you?"

I debated it. But I'd polished off the bird, and I'd come this far. "Yes. Finish it."

Caedmon obliged. "After the slaughter, it is said that Alfhild had a great caldron made, out of the basin of the large fountain in front of her castle. In it, she cooked up the flesh of the perfidious, boiling them whole, and then served them to those she'd seen fit to spare. They were forced to continue the feast well into the next day, until every scrap was consumed, and they had utterly devoured the bodies of their relatives and friends."

Okay, I thought sickly. *Really glad I'd already finished that bird.*

I drank wine.

"I'm guessing there was some payback?" I said.

"Not at first. Having thoroughly cowed what was left of her old 'allies,' she absorbed their lands into her own, and turned the entire production capacity of her new realm to war. She had one enemy left, you see."

"Your ancestor."

He nodded. "My great-uncle, in fact. Who she believed had bribed her supporters to turn on her, in order to prevent the cost and loss of a war."

"Had he?"

Caedmon shrugged. "Probably. War is expensive and he had a great reputation for parsimony, and such things are commonly done. But Alfhild was apparently not one to understand subtlety, or perhaps she simply wanted to continue her expansion, now that she had the means. In any case, it was her undoing."

"Because your uncle was so clever," I guessed, only half joking.

Caedmon was no slouch.

"Well, of course." He smiled. "But it was also a factor that Alfhild didn't stop to consider that she had just killed most of the coalition's experienced generals, and that many of the ones remaining secretly despised her. Their troops surrounded her as she took her place on the battlefield, and when my uncle gave the signal, everyone turned on her at once. His troops watched her own people take her down."

"And Alfhild?" I leaned forward. "What on earth did they devise for her?"

"What on earth indeed." Caedmon's voice had taken on a slightly vicious edge. "For her crimes, it was determined that killing her would be poor justice. She would simply reincarnate, and where would we be then?"

I frowned. "Nowhere. I mean, assuming all that . . . stuff . . . is even true, she wouldn't remember anything, right?"

A blond eyebrow lifted. "Ah, but there's the rub, as your Shakespeare would say. For some of our people claim to experience flashes of past lives. I myself once had an incredibly vivid dream of what it feels like to be a tree, shivering in the wind. It was quite . . . sublime."

The conversation was making me vaguely uncomfortable all of a sudden; I wasn't sure why. "People dream all the time," I pointed out. "And some feel incredibly real, when you're in them."

"And when you come out?"

I didn't answer, thinking of a few I'd had lately.

"Ah, well, you're probably right," Caedmon said, toying with the knife I'd been using to eat apples, when I'd had any apples. "But I have heard a young child give a battle cry from a long-dead language while playing with his friends. And seen a girl weaving a pattern she thought she'd invented, but which was once the standard of an ancient king. And watched a bard sing a song that hadn't been heard in ten thousand years, and quiet an entire hall."

And, for a moment, so did I. A huge hall of gray stone

rose up around me, with tables running along three sides, and an old man—or a fey, I guessed—sitting on a stool at the center, and slowly rising to his feet along with his song. It echoed off the walls and out the windows like a blaze of trumpets, startling several birds from the rafters. While among the fey, food trembled on spoons untasted, wine went undrunk, and the whole chamber stayed utterly silent, mesmerized by the long-lost ballad come to life once more.

Then the image winked out, as abruptly as it had come, leaving me blinking and swallowing and shaking my head.

Damn, I wished he'd stop doing that!

I drank wine, and wished for something stronger. This sort of thing happened around Caedmon occasionally, and it was . . . unsettling. At least with Dorina, I'd actually seen the stuff; I just didn't remember it. But with Caedmon . . .

Sometimes Caedmon freaked me out.

I caught him watching me, and I shook my head to clear it. I wanted to ask if he'd done that on purpose, but if he hadn't . . . I didn't want him knowing that Dorina could pick up his thoughts, even stray ones. Caedmon was as secretive in his own way as a master vamp, and I didn't think he'd care for that.

"So you're telling me you're a believer?" I said, a little hoarsely.

"I'm . . . open-minded. I know you humans think us so old, me especially"—he flashed a grin—"but it doesn't seem that way to us. Quite the contrary; there never seems to be enough time to experience all of life's wonders. I take some comfort in the idea that, perhaps, we will have a second chance."

"And Alfhild? Did she get a second chance?"

He gave a quick bark of laughter, but there was no mirth in it this time. "No. The view was that she'd already had one, and no one wanted to see what she would do with a third! And not just in this life; they were also worried about the next. What if she came back? What if she *remembered*? Would they ever be safe? Would their families?"

I narrowed my eyes. "So they did . . . what? Take her back to the tower to molder some more?"

"No. They took her to Earth. And killed her here, it

was said, in front of a great throng of those she had wronged. My great-uncle swung the blade himself, lest any of his people be targets for her partisans' revenge. And afterward, her bones were burned, releasing her spirit into a cold, alien world, ever to walk unfamiliar pathways, moaning and crying and dreaming of revenge she'll never have. For she can never now go home."

I shivered; I admit it. The story was bad enough, but Caedmon's delivery was worthy of an Oscar if they have one for "seriously creepy." And then he suddenly stopped, dead still, and turned to stare at something outside the tent.

"What is that?"

I dropped the wineskin and grabbed the knife. "What is what?"

"Not sure, but I feel a sudden chill . . . something ominous . . . something cold . . ."

I started to head out, but he grabbed my arm.

"No, wait. I think . . . I think . . . oh. Oh no!"

"What is it?"

"Dory—"

"What?"

"I think it's Alfhild!" And then he lunged at me, from zero to a hundred in about a nanosecond, and I jumped and yelped and smacked him, over and over, and he laughed and laughed and laughed.

"You bastard!"

"I assure you," he gasped, "my parents were married with great ceremony!"

I smacked him some more. It did not appear to help. "Some bedtime story! Do *not* tell Aiden that one!"

Caedmon grinned at me from the floor, where he'd ended up. "Well, not until he's older."

"Not at all! Or God help you if Claire finds out!"

He watched me from under spilled golden hair. "Claire must stop smothering the boy. I understand her concern; we all do. And it is not without merit. But keeping him here, on Earth, tied to her apron strings—"

"He's a year old!"

"Yes, but he won't stay that way. Sooner or later, he must come back to court."

"Maybe when you've figured out who tried to kill him!"

Caedmon frowned. He didn't like to be reminded that his grandson was here because he'd been in danger in Faerie. But it was nonetheless true. If Claire hadn't been unable to face one more dinner among a court whose lips smiled and smiled, and whose eyes shot daggers, Aiden wouldn't be here now.

She'd decided to take her baby for a walk, because he was fussy and teething and it seemed to soothe him, rather than hang out at the high table. And when she went back to the nursery, it was to find the maid on the floor, in a puddle of blood, and an unknown assassin probably lurking nearby. So she turned around and ran, and didn't stop until she reached New York, and who could blame her?

Caedmon, apparently.

"You don't approve," he said, watching me.

"Of Aiden going back to Faerie? Hell no. But it's not my call. It's Claire's."

"My son did have a small role to play in the boy's conception."

"Uh-huh. And if you want him to be able to conceive anymore, you'd better not drag him into this." I looked pointedly downward. "Or get involved yourself."

Caedmon looked pained and crossed his legs. I knew he was joking with me, but I didn't think he realized that I wasn't. If he got Aiden hurt, Claire would freaking geld him.

I decided to get back to the point. "So, the Light Fey, barring batshit-crazy fey queens—"

"Princess. I think she was going for queen."

"Whatever. But barring people like Alfhild, all dead fey go back to Faerie?"

He nodded. "Of course, I cannot speak for the Dark Fey, as I do not know their habits here. But I would suspect that, at the very least, their bones are sent through a portal."

I thought about that. It was interesting—I hadn't known much about fey beliefs before—but it didn't help with my original question. "So, Olga promised to send the boy back if he died, and then he said something else. Just a few words. Do you remember?"

"Vaguely." Caedmon's head tilted. "It seemed mere nonsense. Was it important?"

"I don't know." It was probably nothing, just confusion from the pain and shock. But I decided I'd have Olga ask him when he woke up.

I don't like mysteries.

"Are you done?" Caedmon asked, watching me wrap up the remains of my feast, not that there was much left. I hated to admit it, but swan made for a damned fine meal. Especially fat young swan raised on popcorn and peanuts by the locals.

"Yeah." I agreed. "All ready for bed."

"Excellent idea."

I put a hand to his chest, which was infringing on my space suddenly. "Alone, your majesty."

"Why so formal? Call me Caedmon."

"Okay, then. *Alone*, Caedmon."

"You know, I always find that I sleep better after exercise." I suddenly found myself on my back, with a randy fey king on top. "Wanna wrestle?"

"Get off me!"

"Don't tell me you're still toying with that annoying vampire."

"Louis-Cesare. And yes."

"And here I thought you'd be bored with him by now."

"Not bored."

"Give it time."

"Caedmon—"

"I'll tie one hand behind my back," he offered.

"Tie both, and your legs while you're at it!"

"Ah." Green eyes glimmered down at me, so dark they were almost black. "But that would leave me at your mercy, and I suspect that could be . . . dangerous."

I flipped him, and a second later the knife he'd been playing with was at his throat. "You have no idea."

His eyes flashed, but his lips slid into a purely evil smile. "But then, danger has always been something of a hobby of mine. I'll spot you both arms—"

"You'll behave or I'll kick you out!" I said, and climbed off. He sighed, but didn't look too displeased. Probably because toying with me was just the overture, wasn't it?

The main event hadn't even started.

I grabbed the wineskin and leaned back against the side of the house. I didn't offer him any. Consider it a beer tax. "What are you really doing here?" I asked. "And don't lie."

"I never lie."

"My father says the same thing. It's even true, most of the time. Yet somehow . . ."

"Your father is an excellent diplomat. Prevarication is part of the skill set."

"And you're a king. What's the skill set for that?"

He ran a finger up the side of my bare foot. "Everything. And just when you think you know it all, you discover that you require something else. It's why I learned long ago to arrange help where I need it."

"Like you need it from Claire?"

Dark eyes met mine, shining in the lamplight. "She likes you. Trusts you. After that little display today, I can see why. You could do her a service—"

"Her or you?"

"Does it have to be exclusive?"

"And what service would that be?"

"Persuade her to contact her father. He has the resources I need, but reaching him has been . . . challenging. But she could arrange a meeting—"

"Caedmon—"

"—here, on neutral ground—"

"Caedmon."

"—we're in-laws, after all, or will be soon. We should have met already—"

"Caedmon! Did you not see what happened today?" I gestured at the garden. "Did you somehow miss the massive freaking dragon tearing up the place?"

"No, she was magnificent."

"Or the horrified woman running off in tears after she changed back?"

"She lost control, and was embarrassed. It happens—"

"That's not what happened!"

I drank wine, and debated whether I should even be talking about this, because it was Claire's business, not mine. But I knew Caedmon, and I didn't see him going away without some kind of explanation as to why his plan, whatever it was, wasn't going to work. And I thought Claire had enough to deal with without taking on her father-in-law.

"It's getting stronger," I told him, after a moment.

"What is?"

"Her dragon half."

"Of course. She's growing up—"

"Maybe she doesn't want it getting stronger, Caedmon! Maybe she doesn't want to think about it at all!"

"And why not?" He sounded puzzled. "Power is safety, in your world as well as ours—"

I laughed, and drank more wine. "It's not always safety."

"Yes, it is." He still sounded puzzled, but also vaguely wary, like I'd just suggested that the sun comes up in the west or something. I wondered again what Faerie was like, that Caedmon, a being so old and—presumably— wise, couldn't conceive of a single question to which more power might not be the answer.

"It's not safe if it takes over," I told him shortly.

"Takes over . . . what?"

I waved the wineskin around. "Her. Her life, her family, her garden, her kid. Everything. Everything that matters, anyway."

"Dory. What are you talking about?"

"I'm talking about getting your life stolen, right out from under you. About thinking you're finally someplace that almost makes sense. You have people around that you care about, and who seem to care about you. You're in a good place, or as good as you're ever likely to be, and then—*bam!* It's all gone. Not because you made a mistake, not because you got something wrong, but because life just decided that today, you lose."

No matter what you do.

Caedmon took the wineskin away. Just as well. It was mostly empty now anyway.

"Are you drunk?" he asked me. He looked concerned.

I lay on my side, pillowing my head on my arm, and sighed at him. "I wish."

"Then make some sense—please. I am starting to worry about myself."

"So is Claire."

"Claire is worried about me?"

"No. She's worried about her other half. The one that's getting stronger every day, to the point that stuff is starting to happen. It was hard enough to manage when it was younger, and smaller. But now . . ."

"Power isn't an asset," Caedmon said, like he finally got it.

"Not when you can't control it."

He didn't say anything for a moment, just looked at me. And then reached over to brush a bit of hair out of my eyes. I was sleepy, so I didn't object, and his expression softened.

"Maybe it isn't about control."

"What else is there?"

"Letting go."

I just lay there, silently, because that didn't even compute. Or maybe I was just too sleepy to figure it out. I yawned, and he smiled again, a little ruefully this time.

"You're never what I expect."

"What do you expect?"

"Tonight?" He leaned over to kiss my cheek. "Nothing. Go to sleep, Dory."

It was the last thing I remembered.

Chapter Fourteen

Mircea, Venice, 1458

The rain hadn't stopped; if anything, it was heavier now, splashing down on the canal and the top of Mircea's gondola. It should have blotted out the lights on the palazzo ahead, just as it had smothered the moon and gutted the torches outside the other great houses they'd passed. But the palazzo defied the weather, burning so brightly that it almost appeared to be on fire, with every window flooded with light and flickering with the moving shadows of guests.

The gondola hit the dock, a gentle bump, and Mircea leapt out. To no reception, because the guards who should have been there were huddled under the loggia, trying to stay out of the rain. And mostly failing; the wind kept blowing it in the sides.

One of them glanced at him uninterestedly as he approached, hurrying through the wet with his cape clutched around him. He should have been known to them, after the numerous times he'd visited during the past two months, but there was no recognition in those eyes. A vampire not even twelve years out of the grave wasn't worth remembering.

He did not ask how old they were. He didn't have to. The bright silver breastplates with the Medusa-head design, the rich green silks, and the short-bladed falchions they wore were all impressive, but less so than the power they were radiating. Which threatened to burn him even yards away.

The city watch was supposedly there to keep order in the vampire population, but in Mircea's experience they were the guardians of the elite. And as these were guarding the most elite of all, he supposed it made sense that they were so bright with power that his inner eye could barely look at them. They could have reined that in while he fumbled around under his cloak for the letter granting him admission, but they didn't. Watching him squirm was probably the most entertainment they'd had all night.

Until he couldn't find it.

Damn! He'd been in such a hurry that he must have left it at home. And there was no possibility of getting in without it. He knew that even before one of them gave him a friendly shove that almost resulted in his taking a bath in the canal.

"Run back to your master, dog. Tell him you broke your leash!"

Mircea's hand reached unbidden for his boot, and the knife therein. And then froze, stock-still, like the rest of him, when two swords suddenly flashed in his face. He hadn't even seen them move.

"Or maybe we'll tell him ourselves, when we deliver your gutted carcass."

Mircea backed slowly away, hands where they could see them, and they let him go. The impression conveyed was that it was more from a desire not to get wet than any concern over him, or the feelings of his nonexistent master. A vampire forced to use one such as him as an errand runner wasn't worth fearing.

But that was the thing about power, Mircea thought, as he nipped down an alley and started scaling the side of the palazzo: it made a person complacent. The guards out front were impressive in size and outfitted luxuriously, right down to the stone in the pinkie ring one had sported on a meaty finger, which exactly matched his emerald silks. But they were there more for show than anything else.

After all, who would be crazy enough to burgle the praetor?

The term was an old-fashioned way to designate the leading magistrate in a territory. And since Venice was one of the wealthiest and most influential vampire territories in all Europe, its praetor was rivaled only by the awe-inspiring consul herself. Mircea had a healthy respect for that kind of power.

But he was also running out of time to help his daughter, and he wasn't going home empty-handed. Not when he knew that the praetor's pinch-nosed bastard of a secretary always kept his window open, to air out his fetid work space. Fortunately, that was true even in a rainstorm, which was why all the papers near the window were already soggy even before Mircea slid neatly over them.

And then almost broke his neck anyway, because the place was a wreck.

The pompous creature insisted on calling it a *studiolo*, as if he were Petrarch, hard at work on his latest scholarly achievement, surrounded by art and antiquities. In reality, it was a cramped cubbyhole off the vamp's bedroom, filled with dirty wineglasses and smelly plates of anchovies he kept forgetting about, which slowly moldered under tall piles of books, clothes, and household accounts. Which was why Mircea had to crawl under a table to get out of the mess.

But he managed it. And once he shed his soaked cloak in the quiet corridor beyond, he looked almost respectable. He ran a hand through his hair, stashed the cloak behind a vase, and joined the party.

And quite a party it was.

Mircea made his way through a chain of rooms, some devoted to dancing, some to gambling, and others to lounging and deal making, and all of them awash in people. For this wasn't merely a party, just as it wasn't merely a house. It was the vampire counterpart to the Doge's Palace and every bit as splendid, with the same type of inlaid floors, mural-covered walls, and fine paintings and statuary.

Normally, he had to force himself not to dawdle in front of the latest piece of art, because there was always something new. But tonight, he felt his steps quicken, not slowing even at the sight of a faun caught in perfect, fluid marble. Or at the fascinating snippets of mental conversation that he wasn't supposed to hear, but that floated his way anyway, thanks to his growing abilities.

"—merely pointing out that age isn't the question; it's all about power—"

"And you think the praetor is more powerful than the Lady?"

"Not now perhaps, but in time—"

"How much time? The consul is two thousand years old! If you really think—"

"I don't think anything. Except that power ebbs and flows, like the tide. Best watch the current, see which way it goes."

Mircea normally would have paused at that, because he had reason to have some loyalty to the consul in question. But there were always schemes and power plays, and he had more immediate concerns. And the consul was perfectly able to take care of herself.

Of course, the same could be said for the object of his search, whom he finally spied in an open courtyard at the end of the hall. And who spied him at almost the same time, lifting a glass and laughing. "Mircea! Come join us!"

The husky, somewhat masculine voice belied an elegant appearance, which could have stepped right off an ancient plinth. It helped that the elaborate hairstyles preferred by Venetian ladies, full of swags and braids and buns, mimicked closely those of old Rome. And that the current favorite style of evening gown, with its low-cut top and flowing draperies, could, if one squinted, be mistaken for ancient attire. Her coloring was perfect for the part, too: burnished olive complexion, huge brown eyes, and high, arched brows as dark as his own.

She drew the eye, but that wasn't why he was here. It also wasn't why she was surrounded by sycophants, flatterers, and hangers-on, who coveted the vast patronage she controlled. For the praetor, the most powerful person in Venice and one of the leading lights of the vampire world, was a woman.

It was one of the many things that Mircea was still adjusting to in his new reality, where either sex could make Children, where power trumped everything else, and where none of the old rules applied.

But he was getting used to it. Like he was getting used to the perpetual parties, because Lucilla seemingly did business nowhere else. Which probably explained why there was such a throng in the garden.

Although there might be another reason, Mircea realized, finally breaking through the crowd to see what all the excitement was about.

The little party within a party was situated in the open courtyard at the heart of the house, although it was half covered tonight by a series of awnings to keep out the wet. They seemed to be working, at least enough to protect the lamps burning here and there along the walls. But in the center—

Mircea jumped back, along with the crowd around him, as something huge came sailing at them out of the firelit darkness. It hit down on the wet flagstones where he had just been standing, then snarled and righted itself, ignoring the blood turning the puddles beneath it a darker color. It took Mircea a moment, despite the fact that he was almost on top of the thing, to realize what he was seeing.

He pulled away as it resumed its feet, a huge brown bear shaking wet fur onto the squealing partygoers, and taking off—

For the house.

"No, no, my cowardly creature. Not that way."

The booming voice was coming from someone standing in the center of the garden, where the awnings didn't reach. A man was laughing in the deluge, a bloody sword dripping onto the stones around him, a hand raised. Or no, Mircea thought, as a series of doors slammed shut behind him without human aid, not a man.

A mage.

As if to underscore Mircea's thought, a whip spiraled out of the mage's hand, formed from some kind of blue-white light. It snapped through the air as the injured animal reared back, its one avenue of escape cut off, and a cascade of sparks rained down on the pavement. They hissed in the water, and the vampires around Mircea pulled back, their instinctive fear of fire overcoming their enjoyment of the entertainment.

The animal, on the other hand, had nowhere to go.

It turned, fur wet with both blood and rain, dragging

a back foot that leaked a crimson line across the wet stones. It was injured and vulnerable, surrounded by fire and gleeful faces laughing at its distress, and cheering for the death that was inevitable now. It roared in pain and confusion, and scuttled away from the strange light it didn't understand.

"No," someone said, a soft cry of distress.

Mircea glanced around, because that had sounded like a child's voice, and he couldn't imagine what one would be doing here. But he saw nothing. Except for the faces of the crowd, splashed with fire and now with spell light, enjoying the mage's version of a bear baiting. Which was even less fair than the ones in the Campo Sant'Angelo, where the bears were chained to a stake before the dogs were turned loose on them.

"He *cheats*?"

The same childish voice came again, sounding outraged. Mircea looked around once more, and once more saw nothing. But that was less surprising this time, with the people around him crowding closer, their momentary fear forgotten, as animal and man circled each other, looking for an advantage.

The bear wouldn't find one, because the mage wasn't using magic just to fight it. He was also using it to slow the creature down. Mircea didn't know how, but he had seen enough bear baitings to know that an injured animal becomes more enraged, more deadly, as it feels the end approaching.

It doesn't look around vaguely, as if half-asleep, and stumble drunkenly even on the legs that hadn't yet been injured.

The mage was taking no chances, it seemed. Which put this out of the range of sport, if such it had ever been, and into that of slaughter. And lost whatever mild interest Mircea might have had.

But that wasn't true of someone else.

"He can't do that! He'll kill it!"

Mircea's head whipped around, his heart suddenly pounding. Because this time, he had recognized the voice. And yes, it had been a child's—his child's.

"Dorina!" he whispered, staring about, and wondering

if he was going mad. There was no possible way she could have followed him here. Not when she was well, and certainly not when he had left her in such a state!

"It's only bad when we're both awake at the same time," she told him, matter-of-factly. And then the crowd roared again, as that strange lash connected, sending the animal limping back in pain and the mage bowing and twirling and showing off. "Daddy, make it stop!"

"Make what stop? Dorina! Where are you?"

"That man hurting the bear. Make him stop!"

Mircea was turning around in circles now, scanning faces, tubs of ornamental bushes, awnings sagging low under the weight of water, putti on plinths. And not seeing his daughter anywhere. He probably looked mad, and would have been receiving more attention, except that the fight had just escalated.

"Make it stop! Make it stop!" Dorina sounded frantic, as the bear acquired another jagged wound.

"I can't make it stop," Mircea said, feeling more than a little frantic himself. "The creature doesn't belong to me."

"Then I'll do it." And the next second, Mircea had the very disturbing feeling of something peeling off his skin, almost like he was shedding it.

But instead he was shedding something else. Something that flitted across the open space like a ripple of air, and sank into the wounded body of the bear. Which shuddered all over, as if in the throes of its final moments, causing a roar to go around the garden and the mage to bow some more, encouraging the applause.

Which is why his back was turned when the bear suddenly leapt up from the ground and struck.

The mage must have been shielded, drawing the barrier down enough that it was indistinguishable from his skin, to make it seem that he was risking more than he was. Because the blow would have dropped him otherwise. As it was, it knocked the sword from his hand, and sent him staggering.

And by the time he regained his footing and turned, it was to the sight of a large brown bear, wet and bloodied and furious—

And holding the sword.

Mircea did a double take, and then just stared. Because he'd seen dancing bears and fighting bears and even a little bear cub on a leash that went around with a bag tied to its neck, like the trained monkeys some of the panhandlers used, collecting donations from the festival crowds. But he'd never seen this.

He didn't understand how he was seeing it now, because how the hell—

Oh. That was how. Because the sword that the grandstanding mage had been using wasn't the usual, lightweight sort carried for personal safety. Perhaps he hadn't thought that one of those would work against such an opponent, or perhaps he had simply wished to show off.

Instead, he'd brought one of the new type being developed at the Venetian armories for the export trade, and designed to be used in battle. One with a thick, two-edged blade and an unusual pommel, where the old handguards had been woven together to form a sort of basket to protect the user's hand. And which the long, curved claws of a bear could snag quite effectively, it seemed, even without human dexterity.

Not that dexterity appeared to be a problem, because the bear was wielding the weapon like a trained swordsman. Or a trained swordswoman, Mircea thought grimly, recalling Horatiu's frequent complaints that Dorina was running around with the local children again. And fighting up and down their narrow street using the wooden swords someone's grandfather had made, playing knights and pirates and whatever else their imaginations could devise.

And, apparently, someone had given them some instruction, because the bear's stance wasn't half-bad, Mircea thought, and then shook his head, because he was clearly losing his mind.

Only, if he was, so was the rest of the garden. Everyone was in flux, yelling, laughing, squealing, and pointing. Or pulling back out of the way of the chase, which was quickly moving around the confined space. Or jostling for position with all the newcomers flooding in to see what the fuss was about.

Everyone, that is, except for Mircea.

Who knew he should do something, but had no idea what.

For a moment, he just stood there, hugging the wall and staring like everyone else. Both because the spectacle deserved it and because, while he wasn't sure what to do, he knew instinctively what not to do: he must not give any indication that he had any special knowledge of what was happening. The farce of a man being chased about by his own pet, which was now spanking him with the flat of the sword every few steps or so, might look amusing, but that could quickly change.

Very quickly.

Mircea had recently brokered an agreement with the Vampire Senate for his dhampir daughter, whom they would normally have killed on sight, to remain unharmed— as long as she stayed under his care and in Venice. Even then, the agreement was good only until she grew up, but at least it gave her a modicum of safety. A modicum that would last exactly as long as her mental abilities remained unknown.

For his kind respected power above all things—as long as it was theirs. But power they didn't have and couldn't counter, in the hands of a despised dhampir? Dorina would be dead the moment they knew.

Dorina, Mircea thought softly, careful not to raise even his mental voice. Because many of the vampires here tonight were senior enough that they might pick up on a stray thought, as he had done. *That is sufficient. Go home now.*

He'll hurt the bear some more if I do!

I don't think he's going to be hurting anything tonight, darling, Mircea thought, which was an understatement. The mage was hysterical, staring around between blows, yelling the names of other mages whom he seemed to believe were pranking him. And then tripping over something, Mircea didn't see what. And huddling in a little ball, arms over his head, whimpering every time a sword smack landed.

Can you get home alone? Mircea asked. Surreally, the bear looked his way, and nodded.

He swallowed. *Go then.*

And she did. Because Dorina was always obedient, although one had to remember to state exactly what was required. Otherwise, she had an impressive ability to find ways around even some of his most carefully worded instructions.

Like that one, he thought, as the sword was discarded, flung away into some bushes.

In favor of the whip.

No, no! Mircea thought, but it was too late. Because the whip, which had been sizzling against the ground like a snake made out of lightning, was even easier to use than the sword. The bear scooped the nonburning handle into its mouth, and turned toward the doors to the main part of the house, which were open again thanks to everyone coming this way.

Everyone who suddenly found themselves facing a huge, angry, fire-wielding bear.

Things went about the way one would expect after that, with Mircea being all but trampled as a houseful of finely dressed people screamed and fought and stepped on one another in their panic to get away.

By the time he made it back to his feet and into the house, it was to see overturned tables, shattered vases, burning draperies, and a long, blackened, still-smoking line on walls and floors and furniture, showing where the bear had been. He ran to the front door, just in time to see a fiery whip flaring in the distance, appearing to levitate down the bank of a canal. Because the dark hulk that carried it, and that his softhearted daughter was not about to leave behind, was no longer visible against the night.

Mircea sagged back against the wet bricks of the palazzo, feeling dizzy. And watching two finely dressed guards crawl out of the canal, cursing. And wondered, not for the first time, if he was up to this.

Parenting, he had discovered, was harder than he'd thought.

Chapter Fifteen

I awoke to rain seeping in the side of my tent and a crick in my neck. I poked my head out of a flap to see deep blue darkness spread over the lawn like a blanket, fey tents glowing faintly in the gloom, and somebody moving around in the kitchen. Well, okay, I technically heard the latter, not being able to see them from here, and because they were cursing softly.

My stomach growled. It seemed that half of a large swan hadn't been enough to satisfy it. And I knew the drill: it was either stay here and stare at the top of my tent, because I wasn't going back to sleep, or get up and do something about it.

I unfolded myself, cracked my neck, and padded into the kitchen. And found one of the royal guards staring at the coffeepot in annoyance. I grinned, and not just because the fey loved coffee, although they refused to admit it, since that would also require admitting that something about the human world was superior to their own. But because they refused to understand how electricity worked.

I plugged in the pot, and it started gurgling and burping its way toward heating some water. "Thank you," the fey told me, looking slightly abashed. "I always forget to do that."

"No problem." Coffee sounded pretty good. My body was all wonky from sleeping much of the day; I could use a pick-me-up. Of course, I could use some food, too.

I mentally started running down the list of takeaway places open at one a.m. that might still be willing to deliver to us, when a package of something appeared under my nose.

"I don't know that humans will like them," the fey said, a little awkwardly. "But they go well with coffee."

"They" turned out to be hard little wafer things, which could have passed for biscotti if I hadn't been given them by a glowing blond god with a basketball star's height.

I tried one.

They did, as it turned out, go well with coffee.

The fey and I sat at the kitchen table, chowing down. He wasn't one I'd had any contact with, and he looked young. Not that they all didn't. I'd yet to see a wrinkle or an age spot, even on Caedmon, who looked maybe thirty on a rough day.

This one didn't look much younger, maybe twenty or so, but he *felt* younger. The easy assurance with which Caedmon did everything, as if he were an actor on the final take after days of rehearsal, was totally missing here. This one had not only forgotten to plug in the coffeepot; he'd also been standing in the dark until I'd switched on the light, which had made him jump. And seemed fascinated by the self-sealing coffee bag, with its little zipper closure. And was now examining the condiments in the center of the table, delicately sniffing the Tabasco sauce before rearing back in alarm.

And blinking at it worriedly.

"We don't usually put that in coffee," I told him, and he nodded, setting it back in place.

I got up and rummaged through the cabinets, which were pretty much back to normal. There were a few oak sprigs poking out here and there, but nothing that interfered with functionality. And the apple tree was completely gone—a pale scar cut across the ceiling boards, some of which were still out of alignment, but other than that, you'd think it had never existed. Even the old ship's lantern was back in place and shining smugly, because I guess it had won.

Okay, it had definitely won, I thought, noticing a discreet pile of apple logs stacked by the stove. That was a little disturbing, but not surprising. This house had had issues long before the fey showed up.

The big old Victorian had been built a century ago, right smack on top of a vortex. Yes, one of *those* vortexes, the wells of power created when two or more ley lines cross. And, yes, *those* ley lines, the rivers of magical energy that flow across our world and then beyond, serving some purpose in the grand scheme of things that nobody has quite figured out yet.

Some people think that they're the result of two universes rubbing together, ours and the one Faerie resides in, like great tectonic plates, with energy bubbling up like lava along the fault lines. Others believe that the planets act as giant talismans, collecting the magical energy of creation and distilling it into rivers of current, which they then send rocketing across metaphysical space. Still others believe that the earth itself generates them as a kind of by-product, like gravity or lightning, just one that's not detectable to nonmagical humans.

There were a thousand theories, and no one knew which, if any, were right. But that didn't stop people from sussing out vortexes, and building structures on top of them to benefit from all that free energy. Of course, the main whirlpools of power, those that weren't too strong to use, had been claimed centuries ago, but not all were so obvious.

Some vortexes had formed on cadet branches of the lines, little ones that didn't go anywhere interesting, and thus didn't get much traffic. Or that weren't well explored, because the ley line system hadn't been known about for all that long, magically speaking. And then there were those that formed in a field of vortexes, such as the one that lay all over New York City, allowing them to hide in the glow and remain undetected.

At least, long enough for someone to plop a house down on one.

That someone, a retired ship's captain, hadn't known what he'd had, but Claire's uncle Pip did, and snapped it up as soon as the old boy died. And started layering his treasure with protection spells, which in themselves hadn't been a problem. The trouble came when he decided to link said spells, not to his own power or to a talisman, the magical equivalent of a battery, but *directly into the vortex itself.*

And then to just leave them there, to do their own thing, for decades.

That *had* caused some problems, because spells aren't meant to last forever. They peter out if not renewed, or expire with the death of the caster—which is actually a good thing. Because it prevents them from becoming weird.

Unattended magic can become problematic over time, as the rules of the original spell become confused, or get overwritten by pieces they borrow from other spells around them, or link up with the wild magic of the earth. The upshot was that the house had become a little ... eccentric ... over the years, almost like it had a mind of its own. Or a personality, anyway.

Specifically, that of a crotchety old woman who didn't like people messing with her stuff.

Really didn't, I thought, glancing at the hall. Where a bunch of small things were writhing helplessly under sheets of faded floral wallpaper, which had previously been shredded by burgeoning pecan pods. And which were now whole again and set on revenge.

Watching them caused the same kind of creeping horror as watching a sweet old lady in a lilac-covered housecoat slowly strangling a small animal to death. Until I quickly looked away, and continued to rummage. Hey, I had to sleep upstairs, okay? If the house wanted to murder some pecans, that was its business.

A moment later, I'd gathered everything up and set a line of creamers in front of the fey. There was everything from peppermint mocha to caramel macchiato, because Claire is a flavored-coffee nut. He just stared at them, apparently overwhelmed by the choice.

I pointed at the coconut crème. "That one's good, and the amaretto. I'd stay away from the butter pecan." I glanced at the hall. "At least right now."

The fey eyed the little bottle warily, as if I'd told him it was poisoned. And opted for the coconut. "That's nice," he said, looking up at me in surprise.

I nodded. "Claire really likes that one. I use her for my barometer on all things fey."

"Your . . ."

"Gauge? Measure? Test?" I guess they didn't have barometers in Faerie.

He nodded. "Thank you. I'm supposed to be improving my English, but there are many words I don't know."

"That's why you're here? Other than to guard her, I mean."

"I don't think she needs much guarding!" he blurted out, and then looked mortified when he realized what he'd said. "I—I mean—"

"I know what you mean."

"No! No, you—" He stopped, realizing that he was halfway off his stool. And with a hand reached out as if to touch me reassuringly, which he quickly drew back. Because the fey are famously lacking in the whole touchy-feely department.

Well, except for Caedmon.

But he was a rule unto himself on a lot of things.

"I'm sorry." The young fey sat back down. "I'm also supposed to be working on my . . . my ability to speak as though I had thought about it beforehand."

He sounded like he was quoting. "Caedmon told you that?"

He shook his head. "My father. He is one of the king's chief counselors, but I . . . just say things. I don't mean offense, but—"

"But people take it that way."

A miserable nod. He had a longer-than-usual neck, even for a fey, and was drinking coffee while we spoke. He was starting to remind me of those mechanical drinking birds. Nod . . . sip . . . nod . . . sip. It was kind of hypnotizing.

"Don't worry. I do the same thing," I said. "Only I usually intend to piss people off."

The kid just sat there, clutching the coffee cup in his hands, and looking unsure of himself. As if he was trying to parse both the language and the humor, and was having a problem with it. He didn't seem to multitask well.

Or maybe it's your "humor," Dory, I thought wryly. *Stop teasing the infant.*

But he recovered pretty fast. "I . . . just meant that she's so powerful. And she has you. And the *jötnar*. She is well guarded."

"Then why are you here?"

Again a pause. "Me or . . . everyone?"

"Both. Either." I didn't really care that much, but I was enjoying the cookies.

"Well, we're here—the group of us, I mean—as . . . I suppose you would call it . . . an honor guard?"

I nodded, since he seemed to like that gesture.

"And because, well, you're not powerful just by having power; you must know how to wield it. And the king says—"

"Claire doesn't know how yet." He nodded, looking relieved. Maybe because I'd said it, so he didn't have to. "And you?"

The fey didn't answer. His eyes were on Gessa, who had just come in, her curly brown hair even messier than usual, a yawn threatening to split her face. She dragged a stool over to the counter, climbed up on top to pour herself some coffee, then plopped her butt down on the all-purpose piece of furniture to drink it.

"Gessa, do you know—" I looked at the fey.

Who was looking at the little nursemaid with an expression somewhere between curious and concerned. Like a sleepy, three-foot-tall au pair was a potential threat. Gessa yawned again.

"You have a name?" I asked the fey, more pointedly.

"What?" He blinked at me. And then blushed when he realized he'd been staring, not that Gessa seemed to care. She was staring now, too.

At his cookies.

"I . . . yes. Hemming," he said, watching her scoot her stool over the floor and brazenly take half his stash. "But, uh, they don't call me that."

"What do they call you?" I was familiar by now with the fact that the fey had about fifty names each. But for some reason, this request only made him blush harder.

"Soini," he finally said, like he was admitting something.

Gessa snorted into her coffee.

"What's funny?" I asked her, but she just shook her head.

"It means 'boy,'" the fey blurted out. "I'm . . . not as old as the others."

No shit, I didn't say. Because, despite what certain people believe, I do have manners. Sometimes.

"So, what are you doing here?" I asked instead. "Or do they regularly take boys on trips like this?"

"I'm not actually a boy," the boy hastened to assure me. "I just haven't really gone anywhere before, and my father thought—"

"Earth would be a good starter trip?"

He nodded some more, but this time, he was more animated. "I'm glad he did. It's so *interesting* here. Home is beautiful, but nothing ever happens. I've only been here a short time, yet there's been so much, well, happening."

"We like to stay busy."

Gessa rolled her eyes. I kicked her under the table. She stole my last cookie in retaliation, and I still had coffee left. I sipped it resentfully, and Soini looked back and forth between the two of us, apparently confused.

"So, you're doing the tourist thing?" I asked. And got more confusion in return. "You're here to explore, maybe take some pictures," I rephrased.

"I—well, my father does want me to get more experience, but so far, the others haven't let me out of the yard—"

Gessa opened her mouth. I kicked her again. She grinned unrepentantly and chewed at me.

"—but it's mostly that I have a . . . sort of talent."

"A talent?"

"Yes, a rare gift among my people," he said, looking confident for the first time. "At least, it is these days. They say there used to be more of us, but some skills have diminished. But it's thought to be really useful—"

"Useful how? What do you do?"

"It's difficult to explain. It's usually described as a kind of far-seeing, but that's not really very accurate. I mean, we do see far, but—"

"So you're a clairvoyant?"

"What? Oh, no, no—"

"Because Gessa here reads runes. Don't you, Gessa?"

She shook her head at me, her mouth full of stolen cookie.

"What do you mean, no? You read mine a week ago—"

She swallowed. "Stinky take."

"Take what? The stones?"

She nodded.

"He didn't eat them, did he?"

"No, not eat." She thought about it for a moment. "Probably."

I sighed. With Stinky, that was the best assurance anyone could give. "Then what did he do with them?"

Gessa ate the last bite and hopped off her stool. "Come."

I'd finished my coffee, and all the cookies were gone, so I followed her out of the kitchen. And across the hall, into the living room we rarely used, because the garden was roomier. And less full of dusty old furniture that never got any less dusty, because of one of those spells Claire's uncle had put in place.

It was supposed to be a housekeeping spell, which would have been great, except that it didn't exactly clean things. It just kept them the way they'd been when it was first laid, and Claire's uncle had apparently had an inability to see dirt—or dust, at least. So the spell would clean up a dropped soda, for instance, if you left it there long enough, but afterward, the old boards would still have as much dust on them as before.

It infuriated Claire, who was a bit of a neatnik, but the house didn't care. The spell had taught it to see the vaguely tidy but sort of old and dusty interior as the perfect version of the world, and by God, it was going to stay that way. Forever.

Gessa, however, didn't seem to mind the dust, or the ugly furniture, or the fussy drapes, and of course the boys only cared that the TV worked. As a result, the living room had become a playroom that was more toy strewn by the day, including the large cardboard box in the corner that Gessa was now peering inside of. And swearing loudly.

"What is it?" I asked, hurrying over.

The sides of the box had been decorated with taped-on pieces of paper with bright blue skies, fluffy white clouds, and rich green hills scribbled on them. And at the bottom was a chessboard that had been a gift from Olga, and had become the boys' favorite toy, although not because either of them was interested in strategy. They just liked to watch the fights.

And, since this was a troll board, that's exactly what they got. One side was made up of angry little ogres and the other of tiny pissed-off trolls, which had been enchanted to be pretty darn lifelike. The board was enchanted, too, to ensure that the two groups didn't see a cardboard cell, but rather a large, rolling world in miniature, full of open fields, shaded grottos, and velvety forests. A world they would battle to the death to defend.

Or, at least, to the end of the game.

Only, lately, that time never came, because the boys never put their toys away. So instead of chess we'd ended up with a social experiment, in which both sides spent less time battling and more time building villages, hunting for food in the tall grass, and fishing in the little streams. The last time I'd looked in, they'd managed to construct some rudimentary huts out of the grass, only I guess that hadn't been good enough for Stinky, who had donated Gessa's runes for building materials.

The trolls had piled them up into what looked like a cave formation, while the ogres were constructing actual tiny houses. Or they had been. But I didn't see anybody moving around right now.

That was strange; there was usually somebody carrying in game, punching up one of the tiny fires, or scratching his miniature ass.

And then, belatedly, I saw what Gessa had, which probably explained why she was crawling around on the floor, still cussing. A bunch of fern on a table above the box had all but exploded out of its pot, thanks to Caedmon's overflowing magic. Which would have been fine, except that a single frond had dipped into the box, like a piece of Yggdrasil, the mythological world tree, fallen to Earth. And had changed everything.

Because while we'd been dealing with the drama of our day, the little chess pieces had been having some of their own. To us it was just a piece of fern, but to them . . .

it was a ladder. A stairway to heaven, because it gave them a way out of the game.

And into a house that didn't like competing magic and already had a serious snit on.

"Is something wrong?" Soini asked, looking from me to Gessa.

"Uh, probably not," I said, trying not to think about the two cats lounging on the sofa, watching us uninterestedly, which weren't really cats. They were yet more wards, created by Claire's uncle because he'd been running an illegal still in the basement that he hadn't wanted anybody to find. And nobody had, partially because the cats could suddenly expand to the size of prehistoric sabertoothed fluffiness and freaking end you.

"Shit," I told Gessa, who nodded.

"Must find."

Yeah, before the house enacted who knew what kind of revenge.

"Spread out," I told the troops. They quickly did so, Gessa taking one side of the room and throwing pillows off couches, and Soini lighting up the other, and gingerly swishing aside drapes. I took the hall with the murderous wallpaper, in case any of the little pieces had made it this far.

And, sure enough, I spied a tiny guy all the way at the end of the hall, near the front door.

Making a run for it.

Only, weirdly enough, he appeared to be running this way. "Gessa, do we have a box or something?" I asked, wondering if the little thing had gotten into some paint somewhere, because he looked kind of red.

And then the whole room did, when a giant fist came out of nowhere and sent me flying.

Chapter Sixteen

The blow felt like a sledgehammer backed by a semi. I hit the stairs hard enough to stun me; hard enough that my nerves started blaring all kinds of warnings from virtually everywhere; hard enough that I looked up and found myself already in ultra slo-mo, the way movies are filmed when the shit has most definitely hit the fan.

It works the same way for vampires, when their brains realize they're in over their heads. Time, of course, doesn't actually slow down, but their perception of it does, giving them what feels like a few added seconds to evaluate a situation. It's one reason they're so deadly, and why they move like quicksilver in battle, their every move looking precise, calculated, and well thought out—because it usually is.

That state had always been a rarity for me, and only in extremis. Probably wasn't a good thing that my brain already thought I needed it, huh? Or the fact that it didn't seem to be working right.

The hallway was fine, having taken on the familiar underwater feel of slo-mo: I saw Gessa through the door to the living room, looking up in concern, her brown curls bouncing slowly around her head; I saw a piece of the railing I'd hit on my way to destroy my rib cage flipping leisurely through the air; I saw little siftings of dust raining gently down from where the force of my impact had shaken them loose from the ceiling. Everything was exactly as I'd have expected.

Except for the fist slamming into the stairs, right by my head, still fast, still deadly, and still looking like it was in real time, to the point that I barely managed to dodge it.

Which meant that whatever was assaulting me was fast—very fast. Faster than me, I thought dizzily, trying to assess the situation while scrambling backward up the stairs. And attempting to avoid a second blow while still reeling from the first.

That wasn't working so great, and wouldn't have worked at all, except for the house. Because the latest massive hole that the Hulk-like fist had left in the stairs had just closed up around it, like a wooden maw clamping down—and clamping hard. That left me half a second to focus my bleary eyes on my attacker, only that didn't help much.

Because I'd never seen anything like it.

It was roughly the size and shape of a large troll, only it wasn't one. Not unless there was some kind I didn't know about, made out of lava right before it hardens, with a cracked, reddish crust on top and fiery-looking stuff inside. Which would have been worth a double take or maybe two, but I didn't have time.

Because the damned thing had two fists, didn't it?

The second crashed into the wall beside me, because I'd dodged at the last second, sending shards of hardwood into the skin of my cheek and neck. I stumbled backward, half-way up the stairs now and still dizzy—because it had been all of a couple seconds since this whole thing started. And because we had wards, damn it! About a thousand of the things, many of which weren't legal anymore, if they'd ever been, and all of them on steroids from sucking on an energy teat for much of the last century.

So how did the damned thing get in?

Make that damned *things*, I thought, looking past the huge, thrashing, rocklike beast, which now had both fists trapped by a pissed-off house.

And saw its backup—like it needed any—spiraling up from the floor.

That's the best way I can describe it, although it doesn't do it justice. More of the small things I'd mistaken for toys were running at me, a whole line of them from the direction of the door, and getting bigger and meaner with every step. And more like Pig-Pen, because it looked like all the dust in the house, even that sifting down from the ceiling, was curving, was flowing out, was joining up with the rock-hard bodies they were forming like little stairsteps— and forming them fast.

They were cleaning the house for maybe the first time ever, which unfortunately I wasn't going to live to see because I couldn't take this many.

But something else could.

Suddenly, out of every room along the hallway—the kitchen, the dining room, the guest bath, even the living room, prompting a startled "*Eep!*" from Gessa—came the cavalry. I was busy trying to get back to my feet while a roaring rock monster thrashed in my face, and my ankle, which had gotten injured along with everything else, kept trying to give way on me. So for a second, I didn't understand what I was seeing.

And then I did, and I still didn't believe it.

Because the huge bodies suddenly flinging themselves at our attackers looked a lot like—

The missing chess pieces.

They had the same mottled brown or dirty green skin tones. They had the same patched leather armor and dull iron and steel weapons. They had the same little tusks on the ogres and the same beady little eyes on the trolls, although "little" really didn't work as a descriptor anymore.

Because they were huge.

For a moment, I thought I must have hit my head too hard, but then I saw it.

Or, rather, I saw *him*, a troll different from all the rest, darker of color and wilder of eye, because he'd seen some shit in his short life. And I'm afraid I mean that literally. Because Stinky, who eats everything that doesn't try to eat him first, had accidentally swallowed him along with some animated circus cookies that Olga had brought over from a troll bakery. They'd been galloping and neighing and generally stampeding around the kitchen table, and Stinky, never one to miss an opportunity, had opened his mouth and let them just fall in.

Only something else had fallen in as well, and gone for the ride of its life.

We'd managed to retrieve the little troll after his journey, but he'd never been quite the same again. Including his hardened leather battle gear, which was sadly acid eaten and useless by the time he, uh, popped up. So Stinky, who had been made to understand that you don't eat little sort-of-sentient creatures even if they only got that way because of a spell, had made him a new set.

Which was why one of the suddenly massive former chess pieces was wearing soda can armor.

Only the house, which I guessed was what was doing this, had fiddled with that, too. The familiar red background and white curly letters of one can were now a thick, molded breastplate that Batman would have been proud of; the formerly flimsy red, white, and blue logo of another was a shield Captain America might have envied; and the bright blue and green pauldrons and orange and white shin guards could have been borrowed directly from Iron Man.

Who I really wished would show up right about now, because we were still getting hammered.

Maybe because our attackers didn't feel anything. Or if they did, they gave no sign. Even when I got my shit together, grabbed a jagged piece of wood that the trapped monster was shredding as fast as the house could regrow it, and started trying my best to shove it through its eye.

Only it didn't have eyes, although it could obviously see. But there was nothing inside the vague indentations in the skull but darkness and more rock. And when I did finally manage to break off a chunk, it didn't seem to care. Just kept coming at me, only now with the added horror of doing it sans a third of its face.

I turned around and ran.

"What is it?"

That was Claire, pulling on a dressing gown and coming out of her room as I half ran, half limped into mine.

"You know that learning curve you've been on?" I said, throwing open my closet door. "It's been accelerated."

"What?" She'd come in behind me. "Dory—"

I grabbed a duffle bag in one hand and her arm in the

other. "Get to the kids. You're the last line of defense. Anything gets past me, burn it to the ground."

I didn't wait to see if she got it or not. Because, in the short time I'd been away—and it had been fucking short— the lead creature had broken loose from the house and leapt up the stairs—

Only to be blown all the way back down, into the line of backup headed this way. And with a new, basketball-sized burning hole in its torso, the blackened edges still on fire when it landed. And sent the others falling into what had become a battle of epic proportions and was about to get more so, because the duffle I'd grabbed wasn't black.

There was nothing in my usual stash that would work on these things; I wasn't even going to try. So I'd gone straight for the red sack of special-occasion toys I rarely use since none of them are legal and all of them would normally be massive overkill. But it always helps to be prepared, I thought, ratcheting the special shotgun again.

And cutting loose.

The nice thing about buying magic from dark mages, I thought, is that they just don't give a damn. There's none of the hand-wringing, permit needing, or side-eye giving that you get from the legit places, not to mention that the selection is, oh, rather better. Because this little baby was the definition of one shot and done.

Except when used on these guys, apparently. Because while this thing would put down a charging bull elephant— or a freakishly huge rock monster—in a single shot, the latter didn't stay down. Like the first creature I'd hit, who had ended up sprawled on a pile of his buddies, but who was already getting up, was closing the wound, was coming for me—

And was getting his head blown off for a chaser.

But even that didn't seem to matter, to him or to the others I was busy turning into Swiss cheese. Because they healed the same way they'd formed: by pulling dust and dirt through the air, or through cracks in the floorboards, or from under the front door. And there was no way to stop it, because the wards, good as they were, had been designed to keep out normal threats—spells and hexes and more mundane stuff like bullets.

They weren't designed for this.

That thought connected to something in my brain that had been nagging at me, like maybe it was important. Only I didn't have time to worry about it right now. Because I was going to run out of rounds before they ran out of dirt, which meant, okay.

No more Ms. Nice Guy.

Which is why the next minute or so saw thirty grand's worth of next-level, badass, lethal-as-we-wanna-be magical weapons go up in smoke. And fire. And a hail of flying steel shavings that buzzed through the rock like a drill bit through wood, leaving only dust clouds behind.

Which immediately coalesced into more rock monsters!

It quickly became apparent that, while my toys worked a wonder on flesh, nothing works on *dirt*. And that includes the ever-nasty, always-favorite, terribly expensive dislocator, the kind of pretty bauble that, once it explodes in your face, you no longer have a face. You have ears growing out of your knee and a smile on your ass and brains where your kidneys ought to be, because your entire upper body has just been dislocated—to somewhere not conducive to life, hopefully.

Because the damage is not reversible.

Unless you happen to be a freaking rock monster. In which case, you just turn dusty for a second, and do a little twist-and-writhe that hurts the brain of the person watching you, because torsos aren't designed to turn into Escher-like knots. And then hey, presto!

Good as new.

Okay, that was . . . fairly impressive, I decided, digging furiously around my pack for something, anything, that might work on these things. But while a bunch of auto garrotes disrupted the next charge up the stairs, popping off heads that I thereafter kicked back into the fray, it was a momentary victory. Like the potion bombs that ate huge craters into the next assault. Or the cloud of fighting stars that a war mage had enchanted for me, which zipped about, glittering impressively in the gloom, since most of the lights had been shattered by now. But didn't do much else but ricochet harmlessly off rock and I was running out of options!

And yet another charge was forming, or trying to, because they really wanted up these stairs, didn't they?

But they were being opposed by our no-longer-little chess pieces, who were splitting heads and cleaving limbs much more effectively than before.

They'd been having trouble at first due to their blade weapons shattering on the stonelike surface of the enemy. But they'd figured out that massive fists and iron maces and huge, heavy wooden shields were more effective. As a result, the hall and rooms branching off it had turned into a sea of churning rubble, spotted with flotsam in the form of lamps and pieces of furniture and Gessa, passing by like Rose after the *Titanic* sank, riding a piece of door while jabbing at re-forming rock monsters with a pike.

And then yelling at me, I didn't know why.

Until I realized: a new monster had formed out of the pieces of his fallen brothers on the stairs. And had stayed low, until he was whole enough to make a surge upward. And grab me by the throat.

There was no way I was breaking that hold. Not in time, and probably not at all. But there was time to make a gesture.

And small though it was, it worked. Because, sure, you can save a few bucks here and there, on sales of ammo or two-for-one grenades at that one guy's stand at the local gun show. But there are things you simply pay the asking price for and don't argue.

Because, one day, they're going to save your life.

Like my little stars did for me. Because all of them suddenly paused, midair, and zoomed back this way. And kamikazied the massive stone arm, like a magical jackhammer. And, while most of them got stuck in the rocky hide, or went ricocheting off, bent out of all usefulness, their combined force was enough to crack the forearm, allowing me to finish the job with a savage upward blow.

The arm cleaved and shattered, I fell back, gasping and choking—and had the other fist come at me, almost before I could blink.

But this time, I'd expected it, and managed to get my legs up, including the one with the possibly broken ankle, because there was no other choice. Leaving me with the giant fist in both hands, keeping it back from my face, my legs on its chest, pushing it away with everything I had, and my body shuddering in pain, because any second now—yeah, there it was. *Make that a definitely broken ankle,* I thought, screaming in the beast's face, because why the hell not?

My duffle was just a few steps away, half-buried under rubble, but I couldn't reach it. It was taking everything I could to hold the creature back, who was freakishly strong, like a couple of vamps' worth, only he weighed a hell of a lot more. And that was before my ankle bent in ways a bone isn't supposed to, and gave way entirely.

I would have screamed again, the force of the break echoing through me. But all the air had just been forced out of my lungs. The creature slammed me back against the stairs, my one good leg shoved against my chest, my body bent almost in two, while a red, amorphous face thrust into mine.

Staring into those dark pits of eyes, I suddenly remembered what had been nagging at me earlier. Because, no, I'd never seen these things before. But I had seen something like them, only that time they'd been strangely beautiful and made out of water. A *manlikan* was a fey construct formed from the elements. It wasn't human; it wasn't fey; it wasn't really anything except transport for the mind behind it. Because the creature didn't pilot itself; there was no consciousness there.

Except for the maker's looking out through its eyes.

And enjoying watching me die.

"You first," I mouthed, and spat in the thing's face.

And, oh yeah, there was a personality in there, wasn't there?

Because the ugly thing reared back in fury, to get the leverage to crush me against the stairs. But that also left me a second and a tiny bit of wiggle room. I used it to shove the great fist to the side, to twist, and to lunge for my bag. And to miss, because my head was suddenly gripped from behind and slammed against the railing.

Repeatedly.

I screamed, in pain and fury that this was the way I was going to go out—to the fey version of a fucking drone.

Until I noticed that, while I hadn't gotten a hand on the duffle, I had gotten a foot. And yes, it was *that* foot, but right then I didn't care. Because in agony or not, the leg still worked. And so did my reaching arms, grabbing the bag that it sent flying through the air and slamming it against the massive chest, as I screamed the word I'd paid a dark mage five thousand dollars for.

It was worth every penny.

I watched the space above me wrinkle, and flatten, and bend. And then turn strangely triangular, like I was suddenly looking at everything through a piece of abstract stained glass. And then the body, so large that, towering over me like this, it was literally all I could see, folded up like a deck of cards.

And disappeared.

Chapter Seventeen

There was something wrong with my head.

No, no, it was my ankle that was hurt, a bright, stabbing ache. I liked some pain in battle—gave me an edge. But this was off-putting. Nauseating. It *hurt*.

But I couldn't concentrate on it.

There was something wrong with my head.

It had been hit, a few times, against a very unforgiving railing, and you had to give it to those old shipbuilders who had put this place together. The captain had some of the guys from the docks work on the house, and damn, if they didn't know how to build a railing! Nobody was falling off this ship, nope, nope.

There might be something wrong with my head.

I blinked and there was a tree limb in front of me, as big around as my body and covered in hoary old bark, like it had been there forever, only I didn't think so. Because a blast of dirt and rock came with it, like somebody had just unloaded a dump truck on me. It made me cough and gag, because I'd had my mouth open, and now on top of everything else, I could barely breathe.

And then some apples fell on my head.

Probably not a good thing.

There was already something wrong with it.

But at least the limb seemed to have taken out a couple more rock creatures, like a bark-covered fist shooting out of the kitchen. Where I guess the apple logs had sprouted again, and slammed into two assailants I hadn't noticed until what was basically a sideways tree smashed through the middle of them. And sent a crap ton of fruit bouncing down the stairs.

I just lay there, watching it go, because I couldn't do anything else. The limb was lying across me like it meant business, and anyway, my brain didn't seem to be taking orders right now. But I wasn't too concerned, and not just because of the comfortable darkness that kept trying to eat at my vision. But because of the crashes and yells and renewed *clang, clang, clang* of metal on stone.

The fey had arrived, lighting up the hallway as if dawn had come in a moment. I flashed on that scene with Gandalf showing up with the Rohirrim at Helm's Deep. Because even half-dead, I am a huge fucking nerd.

"To the king," I whispered, laughing, and then couldn't remember why.

There was something wrong with my head.

And this time, I could name it, because it was weirdly like static, only no.

Static didn't hurt this much.

I think I screamed. I'm not sure, since all I could hear was that awful white noise, but I felt like screaming—and rending and tearing and stabbing whoever was repeatedly sticking an ice pick in my fucking *ear*. But there was no one there.

Except for Caedmon, who was looking slightly weirded out.

"What?" I said, as the static retreated, and watched him blink at me. It seemed to take a long time. But maybe not, because then he was gone again.

I heard the front doors slam open, and peered over the tree limb to see everything start to get sucked out. Or blown out, because it seemed like the wind was coming from in here. I didn't know. I just knew that pieces of wood and other debris, even some of the smaller rocks, went flying. And disintegrating, in the case of the latter, as they sailed through the air outside. I could see them through the transom, puffing away into nothingness above the streetlights, like dirty fireworks.

Big dirty fireworks, because a few of the creatures were getting blown out, too.

It looked like some of the fey had tiny whirlwinds in their hands that they were throwing at the rock monsters, but obviously not.

There was something wrong with my head.

"They can't hold their form too far off the ground," Caedmon yelled, because he was back again, his long blond hair whipping around his face.

I nodded.

That explained why they hadn't just formed upstairs to begin with.

Good to know, I thought, dizzily.

And then I blacked out, because there was something wrong with my head.

———

I woke up on the kitchen table, screaming in pain. "Be still!" Caedmon said, holding my ankle and looking harassed.

Normally, it would have been funny to see him with his shining fall of hair a frazzled mess, his shirt sleeves rolled up, and his face red.

But not when his hands were red, too. Because it looked like I hadn't been the first one on the table tonight, and wouldn't be the last. There were several battered and bloody fey sitting on stools, their heads resting against walls or cabinets, as if they were too tired to hold them up. It looked like the *manlikans* hadn't gone down without a fight.

And then somebody else started screaming, and he sounded worse off than me.

"I said, be still!" Caedmon snapped, but I barely heard him because it was back again, that terrible static that sounded like a swarm of bees.

Angry bees.

Angry stinging bees, *inside my skull.*

Caedmon appeared in my vision, grabbing the sides of my head, saying something. It looked like it might be important, and felt like he was pouring power into me, but I couldn't concentrate on anything but the bees. They were making my body jerk and strain from their constant stinging, dozens and then hundreds of them, all at once. I tried to read his lips, until my field of vision was overlaid with static, too, like an old-fashioned TV on the fritz, where sometimes you got a clear picture, and other times it was just snow.

Stop it! I told myself. I'd had enough shocks for one day. I didn't need my brain deciding to break a little more for no apparent reason.

Only there was a reason; I could *feel* it.

I just didn't know what it was.

And then I was screaming some more, because it hurt that bad.

––––––––––

I awoke to light and pain and noise, which wasn't unusual. And to a glowing being bending over me, holding my head between his hands, which was. I realized I was screaming and stopped, caught his shoulder and swung my legs off the side of a table before pushing him against some counters.

He looked surprised, but not as much as I was.

What . . . was he?

It was hard to tell. He glowed so brightly that he was difficult to see. Liquid light, white-hot and yellow, outlined his body, and boiled through the middle in a shimmering dance of—

Gah! I didn't know. I couldn't look directly at him, not for long, and even when I did it was useless. I'd never seen anything like him.

I glanced to the side, quick flicks of the eyes, trying to see where I was, and so that he had no opportunity to break away. Not that he was trying. He was simply standing there, permitting the scrutiny, because he knew it didn't matter.

I couldn't take him.

The realization struck deep in my stomach, like a thudding blow. It had been a long time, a very long time, since I had felt outmatched. I could be bested by numbers or taken down by trickery. But sheer power, in one being?

That . . . was rare. And even when I'd felt it, I'd never been sure of the outcome. Battle is fickle; the strongest doesn't always win. A thousand things go into it: strategy,

*patience, experience, determination. The outcome was
always in question—*

Until now.

I couldn't *take him. I felt it resonate in my bones, with
an assurance it had never had before, felt my lips pull back
from my teeth, in anger and denial. What* was *he?*

Not alone, *I thought, because there were others in the
room. Scattered about, all of them tense, unhappy, wary.
And glowing softly in my mental landscape.*

Fey.

*They were wounded but on their feet, with weapons out,
despite the fact that one could barely hold a knife. He was
shaking, imperceptible to a human, but I saw. Ready to fall
with barely a strike. But the others were combat ready, despite their wounds, and still more ran through the door.*

*These were almost untouched, with only a few cuts and
bruises that showed up as dark patches in my mind, not
even enough to slow them down. But it didn't matter. They
weren't attacking. They were looking to the one I held for
guidance, as if they weren't sure what to do.*

And for the first time in a long time, neither was I.

*"One of my people is injured," the creature told me.
"Will you let us help him?"*

*The request was quiet, measured, calm. The blinding
energy of a moment ago was gone, drawing back inside
him. He looked like a fey, I realized.*

He wasn't one.

*But he wasn't attacking, either, and he'd drawn his
power down. I hesitated, feeling strangely off-balance. He
wasn't even looking at me now, but at something behind
me, near the door to the outside.*

*Where a fey lay on the floor, I realized, arching up in
pain and screaming.*

*I didn't know why. There were no wounds of conse-
quence on this one. He seemed to be—*

*And then I understood, when something hit me, too,
like a wave of acid.*

It hurt—God, it *hurt*—like nothing I'd ever felt before. And
that was saying something, I thought, staggering against

the counter. Caedmon was there, grabbing me before I hit the floor, holding on while I writhed and screamed. I wasn't usually the screaming type; I'd trained myself out of it years ago, because it doesn't up your chances of survival if you broadcast to the enemy both the fact that you're wounded and exactly where you are.

But this time, I couldn't seem to stop.

And then it cut out, as abruptly as it had come, leaving me panting and bent over. And then straightening up and staring wildly about, knife in hand. But all I saw were confused-looking fey.

"Dory?" Caedmon said carefully, concern in his voice, because yeah. I was acting crazy.

With good reason, I thought, still trying to spot the attacker.

Because there was one. Something the fey had missed. Something *I* had missed.

"Someone's here," I heard myself say, and it was my voice, but lower, deadlier, almost unrecognizable. I saw a nearby guard's eye twitch, 'cause yeah. *Not bored anymore, huh?*

Neither was I.

"Dory." That was Claire, getting up from where she'd been kneeling by a fey. Soini, I thought, recognizing the baby fey, who didn't look like he was enjoying his vacation, all of a sudden. He was white-faced and panting, and looking like I felt. For a moment, we just stared at each other.

And then Claire was touching my arm, and the cool feel of her power was swamping me, trying to soothe, to help—

"No!" I jerked back. That wasn't the kind of help I needed.

———

I flinched, suddenly back in control, but I hadn't been for a moment. I knew that, even though it felt like no time had passed, because there was a knife in my hand, and I was suddenly in a different position. It was disconcerting, confusing. I took control and kept it until the job was done. I didn't slip like that; I never slipped!

My back hit the counter and I snarled, my eyes flicking around the room, trying to assess the threat. But for the first time in memory, I couldn't do it. Not for all of the ones right in front of me, the ones I could see.

Much less the one I couldn't.

The one that was sending waves of excruciating pain that were causing my brain to malfunction. Or to switch consciousnesses in a desperate attempt to ward it off, I realized. Flipping between me and my twin whenever one of us became overwhelmed.

Which was happening every few minutes now, and I didn't even know what I was fighting!

"Dory—"

That was the woman called Claire, my twin's friend. She was standing nearby, beside the fallen fey. There were several more fey behind her, well armed and outside her field of vision, but she didn't seem to care. Perhaps she didn't have to be careful; she was powerful, too. I could see them, the eyes behind the eyes, staring out at me, curious, wary, strange.

But not afraid.

Like I was, I suddenly realized.

And blinked at the shock of it.

I was afraid, and with cause. I could take the fey; I could possibly even take the dangerous creature staring at me from behind Claire's eyes, should it choose to attack. I could not take the glowing one. And I could not even see the other to assess its power.

But I could feel it building. A pervasive heaviness in the air, an electric frisson up my spine, a metallic taste in my mouth—not like blood, but like I was biting onto a sheet of metal, chewing on foil. It made my teeth hurt and my brain ache and it seemed to be coming from everywhere, all directions at once.

I'd never felt anything like it.

I realized that there was a sound issuing from my lips, and it was unfamiliar, too. Pained, fearful, dangerous. Like an animal that knows it is beaten, but will fight to the death anyway. We might die, but it would be with our teeth buried in someone's throat!

And then the attack increased, and I screamed, screamed as I never had, my brain feeling like it would explode in my head.

———

"What is *happening*?" Claire screamed, although I could barely hear her. Because other people were screaming, too: Soini, on the floor, convulsing like his spine would break, and someone else—

I abruptly realized it was me.

I cut it off, breathing heavily, and mentally slapped myself.

Get a grip*!*

"Dory?" That was Caedmon, while Claire stared at me, her eyes wide. And then she snapped orders at the fey, who rushed to help hold Soini while she forced some black, horrible-smelling draught down his throat.

It must have tasted as bad as it smelled, because he fought it, but she won. And it seemed to do him good. It knocked him out, almost instantly, and I watched the long body relax into sleep.

"I have more," she told me, looking up, but I shook my head.

"Dory. Who is here?" Caedmon asked, his hand on his sword hilt.

"I don't know." I sounded hoarse, probably from all the screaming. I shook myself and started moving around the room, searching for some hint, some glimpse. Which would have been easier if I knew what I was looking for.

And if the static would stop and let me think!

The static.

"This way." I still didn't know what was going on, but I knew that every time I got closer to the door to the hall, even by a single step, the static grew worse. Whatever this was, it didn't want me out there. And that meant—

And then I was running, slamming through the door, my newly healed ankle throbbing, my heart pounding. Because I'd held the stairs, somehow, against every advance, but there was no one on them now. Just pockmarked holes trying to heal, all other signs of the battle scoured clean, even the usual layer of dust still gone. Leaving an open path, straight up to—

I hit the stairs, practically flying, and was knocked back by a wave of pain so breathtaking it was like a physical blow. And the annoying static in front of my eyes was suddenly a blizzard. It would have stopped me, all on its own, except that I knew this place so well I could have navigated it blind.

Which I almost was by the time we reached the second floor, where Olga's snores—and how the hell had she slept through all that?—echoed strangely in my distorted senses. They were as loud as a freight train one second, and almost silent the next. Like the corridor flickering in and out of view.

"It's here," I said, and it was a growl that time, full-on and feral.

"Check them!" Caedmon snapped, and I felt rather than saw guards stream by me. I heard Olga's snores pause, and then continue, and a fey call out that they couldn't wake her. Heard people tearing through my and Claire's rooms, careless in their hurry. Something shattered against the floor, knocked off by an untucked elbow, but there were no warning cries.

They hadn't found it yet.

And then someone yelled, and I sprang forward, only to be hit by an avalanche of agony, all at once. It was staggering—literally, I would have fallen if someone hadn't grabbed me. And excruciating, leaving me writhing in that someone's arms for a second. But only a second, because the shouts were coming from the boys' room.

"Let me go!" I snarled, and tore away, into a blizzard of static and pain and noise.

That suddenly cut out, all at once, as soon as I crossed the threshold. It left me gasping and staring around: at Aiden, huddled against a wall, blue eyes wide and terrified; at Stinky, standing protectively in front of him, a toy sword clutched in his fist; at Gessa, slumped on the floor, unmoving.

And at Ymsi, blood smeared and dazed looking, standing over the small troll.

Who was still in the trundle, his eyes closed, his face almost peaceful.

Except for the dagger sticking out of his heart.

Chapter Eighteen

The assassin was quick, but I was quicker. Tearing loose from my twin and soaring into the air, right on its tail. And then following as it fled the house and headed for its avatar, the one who couldn't pass through the wards like it could, a dark figure I spied waiting beside a car down the street for its master to return.

But its master couldn't risk that, not when we were still too close to the house, and to the dangerous creatures inside. Like the fey king, who had just caught my twin before she hit the floor. Or the two-natured one, who had run into the room to kneel by the troll girl, and start snapping orders. Or the sobbing man-child, currently weighed down under a mass of Light Fey, debilitated more by what had just happened than by anything they were doing.

Because the force required to commandeer a mind against its own wishes was damaging, both to the host and to the attacker, leaving them weakened and vulnerable.

Like the murderer was now.

So, no, it couldn't go back.

It also couldn't communicate with its avatar, not in free flight, which is limiting in almost every way. I could return and warn those in the house, could send someone after him. But that would take time, and I would lose the more dangerous enemy in the process.

The one that flitted ahead of me, just out of reach, not faster than me but more experienced, and far more panicked.

It knew it was weakened, knew a hunter like itself was on its trail, knew it had to get away—

But it hadn't expected this. No, no, it had not. It had known about the boy, the one they called Soini, and had sent the terrible static to hurt and sideline him. But it had not known there was another of us.

It had not known about me.

It did now.

And it had made no preparations for this. Without its avatar, it had only free flight, and that would not spare it long. Will you risk it? I wondered. Risk the great void, the nothingness of a scattered consciousness, the death that is more than death? *Because the body could come back, in so many ways, but the mind . . .*

Once lost it was lost forever, and no, it wasn't willing to risk that. Was terrified of it. So terrified that it wasn't waiting for the designated avatar to realize that something had gone wrong and catch up to it.

Instead, it was taking another.

A bird suddenly burst out of a tree, startled out of its nightly rest by the demands of a strange mind. Wild of eye and swift of wing, it almost flew through me. And then darted off, eating up the sky and rapidly increasing the distance between us.

So, it was a race. And one I wouldn't win, because I didn't have the enemy's experience on my side. I could take avatars by force as well, but it was exhausting, a constant battle. My strength would fail, and fail quickly, and I would lose my prey.

I needed a willing host.

So I woke Dory as I never had, as I never could, before now. And sent images, feelings, the uncertainty that gripped me. Allowing her to make the choice.

A split second later, she was sitting up, staring about. And then bolting out of the king's arms and down the stairs, grabbing something from a pegboard before bursting through the kitchen door. The king was on her heels, asking questions she ignored. She ran instead for a vehicle parked alongside the house and jumped in, the king beside her. And then the car was roaring down the road, barely missing the shadowy avatar that she didn't care about any more than I did.

We were after bigger prey.

So, it was a race, then.

I found a bird of my own, a falcon, and with its help soared up into the crisp cool air of a rain-strewn evening, the moon bright overhead, even in the midst of boiling clouds.

And tore after the enemy.

It wasn't easy. The creature might have been weakened, but it was experienced, breathtakingly so. It led me through a bewildering succession of avatars, grabbing a new one whenever the old tired and slowed, as easily as a human would change clothes. First several birds, then a deer, then a woman in a car who veered and swerved all over the road for a moment before the murderer released her. Because, when you take complete control, the avatar's mind can't help you.

And my prey did not know how to drive.

But there were things I didn't know, too. Like how to make the four legs of a deer work together, instead of landing in a tangle on the ground. Flying had been easier, not because I knew how to do that, but because I'd instinctively fallen back on old patterns. Instead of trying to take full control, I had suggested to the bird mind that easy prey lay ahead.

I tried that again, but deer are not predators, and their food is everywhere. And planting the suggestion that a hunter was coming only panicked the poor thing. Which untangled its limbs and scampered away in the wrong direction. But I couldn't yet join my twin in the car, not while keeping track of an enemy that was ignoring roads, eschewing bridges, and traveling overland. We were out of the city and moving quickly, as my twin was not, being caught in traffic behind me.

Until she suddenly wrenched the car off the road, traversed a shallow ditch, bumped across a patch of open ground behind a gas station, and tore through a fence. And somehow skirted the traffic snarl, slinging out onto the bigger road below us. And then did something that caused the car to shoot ahead.

* * *

"—say something!" Caedmon said, grabbing for the wheel, why I didn't know. Like a fey could drive better than me.

"Cut it out!" I told him. "You're going to make us crash!"

"You appear to be doing that well enough on your own! Have you gone mad?"

"Years ago! And the wheel only steers. It doesn't make it go!"

"Then what does?"

"This," I said, and floored it.

I was really wishing I'd grabbed my car, but it had been parked in front of the one Claire had recently bought. Because, while she might be a princess in Faerie, she didn't rate that level of scratch here on Earth, where her bank account had only ponied up enough for a beater convertible. One with a top that was a pain in the ass even when you weren't flying down the road at something like a hundred miles an hour!

I struggled with the thing, which was flapping around like it was trying to take off, while Caedmon peppered me with questions despite having his long legs braced and one hand gripping the side of the car like it might just fuse there. Whatever dealings he'd had on Earth, it didn't look like they'd involved high-speed car chases.

Ones made even more fun when the damned top decided to detach altogether.

Damn it!

"Was it supposed to do that?" Caedmon asked, looking worried.

And that was before maybe a hundred deer decided to jump out in front of us.

"*Shiiiiit!*" I yelled, the wind in my face, and white tails flashing on all sides. I just knew we were about to crash and flip end over end. And without a top on the car, that was—

Not going to happen, because Caedmon, looking a little pale, had done something that caused the deer to jump clean across us. We plowed through the middle of a herd of what appeared to be every deer in New York

State—a tunnel of brown and white bodies and leaping legs—without hitting one, and burst out the other side. Only to have another car peel off the side of the road after us, red lights flashing and siren blaring.

And wasn't that just all I needed?

"I believe he wants us to stop," Caedmon said, turning around.

"I know he wants us to stop!"

"And yet you are not," he pointed out.

"If I do, I'll lose them!"

"Lose *who*?"

I didn't answer, being busy trying to figure out how to shake a tail on an open road while not also shaking that tentative link to my crazy other half, who was somehow flying overhead, although I couldn't see her.

And then it started to rain again, and I couldn't see anything.

Because it wasn't a gentle pitter-patter on the windshield and my head. We drove into a torrent that had been left over from Noah's day, thick and white and pounding down, like a million tiny strokes of a lash. Which hurt like hell and appeared to be trying to drown us. And was doing a pretty good job, because I didn't have a top on the damned car!

What I did have was the cop car, whose red flashing lights suddenly went from annoyance to godsend, giving me a beacon in my rearview mirror, allowing me to stay centered in the road. It wasn't easy, because it felt like we were hydroplaning about half the time, but it was all I had. And it was working!

Until he ran into a ditch.

Son of a—

I swerved to avoid doing the same, and a second later, broke through the deluge onto an open stretch of road, spluttering and blinking and very surprised.

And grateful as hell.

Until I looked to my right, and came face-to-face with a furious king of the fey.

I thought it might be because he was a soggy mess: the glorious hair was straggling around his face, the casual shirt and leggings were drenched and dripping, and the

inch or so of water that the car had managed to acquire
was sloshing around his feet. But all that was true of me,
too, and you didn't hear me complaining. I was just glad
to be alive.

Although how much longer that would last was debatable, because a heavy hand had just descended onto my
neck.

"We need to talk."

*I watched from the air as a large herd of deer simultane-
ously pricked up their ears and turned their heads. And
then charged the long ribbon of road below, converging on
the one spot of color fleeing through the night, the small
white car my twin and the king of the fey were using. As fast
as they were going, even a single impact might well prove
disastrous. But the king must have done something, for
they sailed over the car like a brown river, never touching it.*

The creature's trick hadn't worked.

*But it wasn't the only one it knew. For I'd barely had
the thought when a rain squall blew up, looking oddly like
the herd, with every cloud in the surrounding area suddenly focused on one target. It utterly blocked my view,
and I couldn't imagine that my twin was having better
luck.*

She was going to crash.

*So I sent my latest avatar diving through rain-battered
skies, straight at the small eagle my prey had recently acquired. It was quick, just a dark smudge on the sky. But I
was currently riding a peregrine falcon, favored hunter of
the kings of old, which nested in abundance in this new
city of glass and steel.*

And was faster than anything in the skies.

*I felt our talons sink deep, felt our prey struggle and
fight and cry out, felt it start to fall—*

*And felt the rain cut out, abruptly, as the murderer's
concentration broke.*

*It was impressive, nonetheless. Just as whatever spell
had been used on the herd had been. I could not throw
spells; none of my kind could. But even had that been a
possibility, I did not think I would have been able to manage it and hold an unwilling host at the same time.*

But this one could, and could do it weakened.

I did not know what to think about that, like so many things today. It felt strange, to have a rush of new experiences after so long, to feel curious and off-balance. I spread my wings, feeling strangely exultant, free, reborn—

Until a shadow circled overhead.

And hunter became prey.

"What do you mean, your other half?" Caedmon demanded.

"Can we do this another time?" I yelled, because we were getting hit with scattered showers, as the big one broke apart, making me have to concentrate on the road. And because I didn't know the answer to most of his questions myself.

"No! Explain yourself!"

It was like night and day: the amused would-be lover, toying with me because he was bored or because he wanted something, which had been most of my experience with Caedmon until now; and the sharp-eyed, serious, powerful king of the fey I was getting acquainted with tonight. And wasn't it fun? I thought grimly, switching gears.

"I'm dhampir," I said shortly. "You know that. It means you get a two-for-one deal, with one being batshit insane."

I glanced upward, at the boiling gray skies, and wondered which of us that was. Because, seriously, either some next-level shit was going on tonight or I really did have something wrong with my head. More than usual, that is.

"And your other half is . . . up there?" Caedmon said, gesturing at the sky. Although that weird, intense, slightly creepy look he was giving me never wavered.

It was starting to freak me out.

"Look, I don't know anything more than you do, okay? We're not supposed to be awake at the same time! But the barrier my father put in place fell recently, or got a big hole blown in it, thanks to your fey wine—"

"Fey wine?" It was sharp.

"Yeah. Not actual wine, but that weird stuff you guys export for the druggies. The kind with the herbs—"

"I know what it is!"

"Well, I didn't! I thought it was just helping to control my fits—that's when Dorina used to come out, you know?"

He nodded grimly.

"Because it worked even better than Claire's weed. But it also weakened the mental barrier Mircea had put in my head, something I didn't know until—*bam!* No more barrier. Or not much of one. Parts of it are still there, but it's pretty damned ragged and not really preventing contact anymore."

"And now you are finding out about . . . hidden talents . . . on the other side of your brain."

"That's one possibility!" I yelled, because the rain had picked up again.

"And what would be another?"

"That I've finally gone crazy and think I'm a bird!"

And then I did go flying, all right, but not because of wings. But because the car hit something and skidded wildly, careening us off the road and up a grassy rise of ground. And then flipping us over, and damn it!

Fortunately, I was tossed into a soft hillside, and didn't break anything else. I did go rolling and cursing down said hill afterward, however, since much of the rain-soaked ground gave way with me, in a miniature mudslide. One that left me filthy and banged up and seriously pissed off.

And sliding to a halt at the feet of a couple of grinning vampires, one of whom was holding the end of what looked like a grappling hook on a cable.

The other end of which was attached to the back seat of my ride.

"You wrecked my roommate's car!" I said, putting it together.

"Don't worry," the blond from the troll fight told me. "You won't live long enough to have to explain it."

And then he gave the cable a gentle tug, sending the convertible flying through the air like a giant mace.

One aimed directly at me.

I rolled frantically to the side, only to find myself facing off with Purple Hair.

"I thought . . . you two . . . were competitors," I said,

trying to get my breath back, while dodging kicks, blows, and stabs, because Bitch Girl had gotten herself a spear.

She was pretty good with it, too.

"We are," she informed me, doing the rapid-stab thing all around my contorting body. "But you're kind of annoying. So we're teaming up till you're dead, then going to fight it out between us."

"You teamed up with *that*?"

'Cause Blondie had just tugged on his cable, trying to reposition the car, instead of helping her.

Only to reposition it onto his head.

She scowled. "You gotta do what you gotta do."

"Couldn't agree more," I said, got a leg over her spear, and snapped the heavy shaft in two.

She looked from it to me, and the scowl grew more pronounced. "Bitch, that was my favorite spear."

"Not anymore," I said, and went for her with the jagged end, which made a quite serviceable stake.

Because vamps and wooden weapons don't mix, no matter how good they think they are, but I didn't have a chance to demonstrate the point.

But not because of her.

Because I was suddenly hit with a jumble of *slurring, cloud-filled skies, clawing talons and sharp, tearing beaks.*

Pain ripped through me, and I looked down at my side, expecting to see a jagged wound, but there was nothing there. Just like there was no sky full of feathers, and strong flapping wings, and blood spurting as two predators fought it out, somewhere above me. Which was going to get me killed down here, because my brain wasn't used to doing a freaking split screen!

And because my opponent didn't have that problem.

Fortunately, she did have another.

One that reached down with a huge, hoary hand and grabbed her, right before she could shove the shiny end of the spear through my eyeball. And snatched her off the ground and into the air, maybe thirty feet, maybe more. Whatever the height of the copse of tall trees just behind us.

Of course, her buddy was no help. He crawled out from under the car he'd just jerked on top of himself, in time to see another tree branch curving like a giant's hand and reaching down for him. Then the two vamps were getting introduced to the ground by the treetops swaying violently this way and that, as if in hurricane-force winds, grabbing them up and smacking them back down, over and over and over and over.

I could watch this all day, I thought dizzily.

And then a couple of birds splatted onto Claire's windshield, and the split screen became one seriously messed-up brain again.

One that was no longer even trying to keep up.

Well, shit, I thought.

And passed out.

Chapter Nineteen

Mircea, Venice, 1458

"Damn it, Mircea!" The praetor's color was high, but not from embarrassment. She stepped out of her lovely gown, giving Mircea a glimpse of a beautiful bronzed figure, lean of thigh and high of breast, the opposite of the Venetian preference for rounder, paler forms.

The Venetians were idiots, Mircea thought, as the praetor's ladies hurried to help her into her bath.

It was unusual, too. The Venetian norm was the same as everywhere else: a high, wooden tub lined with cloths to reduce splinters, and, for the wealthy, soft, scented soaps and thick towels. He hadn't had a bath like that in a while, being relegated to the local public bathhouse when he had the fee, and to an overlarge bucket Horatiu had found that left his knees up around his ears whenever he didn't.

This was like an indoor fountain, a depression in the floor decorated with mosaic tiles and featuring streams of fresh water coming from decorative fittings in the walls. It was ridiculously pretentious in a town that received its water exclusively from rainfall caught in sand-filtered wells. Behind the luxurious facade, some poor servants were laboring to carry buckets up four stories so they could fill some reservoir that allowed her to pretend she was still in Rome.

Mircea remained stoic, but the sheer waste colored his appreciation for her beauty.

That, and her cruelty.

"I had one in sight tonight," he told her. "I saw one boy taken and the trap set again. If the skies had stayed clear—"

"But they didn't, and you lost him. Leaving me precisely where I was before."

She paused to summon a maid mentally. *Goat cheese, and pears stewed in red wine.* The girl hurried to bring her mistress a late-night snack that Mircea couldn't taste, thanks to his age, not that he was likely to be offered any. He hadn't even been offered a chair.

This was not going to be a long audience.

"I know where they hunt now," he said urgently. "I *will* find them—"

"Not soon enough. Jacomelo is kicking up a fuss, and the Lady wants answers."

"I understand—"

"Do you?" The other maid began washing her mistress' arm with soap smelling of musk and cloves. It was a heady, rich scent, and wreathed Mircea's head in fragrance. It did not seem to improve his patron's temper, however. "She's at war," she said flatly. "She needs her allies kept happy, and losing his son has not made Jacomelo happy. It didn't help that the damned boy was the only one in his family who could count!"

No, Mircea supposed not. Jacomelo was the head of a powerful vampire family with extensive business interests in Venice and abroad. He was also a longtime, vocal supporter of the consul. Had she failed in her attempt to overthrow her Sire and take control of the Senate, his blood would have run in the streets alongside hers. As it was, he was a senior member of her government, with a great deal of power.

Power he was using to find out who had kidnapped, and presumably killed, his son.

There had been rumors about vampires disappearing for a while, but the usual targets were the masterless hordes that no one cared about. Whoever had taken Jacomelo's son had probably assumed he was one of them. When he wasn't running his father's vast empire, the boy had been fond of slumming in Venice's stews, dressed as a commoner.

Until one morning, when he didn't come home.

"I will solve this," Mircea promised again. "Soon."

"And when you do, you will have your reward."

"But I need—" Mircea stopped the blurted words, because she didn't care. It was one thing the nobles of his new world had in common with those of his old. Telling them what you needed—even desperately—was beside the point. They saw only their own, selfish points of view.

"My daughter's illness takes up a good deal of my time," he said, more diffidently. "I fear her condition grows worse. I spend as many hours as I can on the streets, on this project of yours, but—"

"Project of mine?" the praetor interrupted. "Say, rather, the consul's; she's the one who ordered it, but gave me no men to aid with it. They're needed for her war, it seems."

"I understand—"

"You keep saying that." She crossed her arms on the edge of the pool, laying her cheek on them as the maid moved on to her back. "Of course, you've met her, so perhaps you do. Others see her beauty, her charm, her power—so much power! It blinds us poor mortals."

"But . . . you're not mortal," Mircea said, confused. The praetor was said to be almost as old as the consul herself. Old enough to remember when Venice was founded, not that she was here then.

Like so many of her kind, when old Rome fell to the barbarians, she merely moved to one of her estates—in Spain, Mircea had heard, somewhere near the sea—drank her wine, watched generations of her servants cultivate her olive trees and . . . waited. Vampires as old as she had watched empires come and go more than once. They had time to wait for the next one.

"Yes, that's the story they tell the young, to sway them into the fold," she agreed. "For what does youth fear but age? Yet, how many do you see, from all those centuries past, who still remain? One day, death finds us all."

"Then she is mortal, too." He dared to sit on the edge of the bath, although he had not been asked, but she only looked at him in mild amusement.

"Says a boy, barely grown. She's managed to avoid death for a millennium and a half. And her Sire was said to be ancient, perhaps five thousand years old. They are difficult to kill, that family."

"Yet he died, too," Mircea pointed out.

She laughed, and it sounded genuine. "You always know the right thing to say," she told him cryptically, and waved the girl away. *Go find out what's taking Colleta so long.*

The praetor rinsed herself under the streams of water, taking her time, while Mircea fought not to vibrate with impatience. But he said nothing, and kept his expression blank and dutiful. His old habits did him little good in this new society, where bluster and bravado were the habits of children, and where time, always the bane of mortal existence, stretched long.

Like the silences.

He watched the candlelight flicker in the dark water. The rain had stopped and someone had opened a window, letting in the scent of clean air, roses, and wine, because several servants were indulging themselves after a hard night's work, somewhere below. Mircea wanted to elaborate on his previous theme, of how his daughter's illness was keeping him from giving his full attention to the praetor's matter, and how helping him to cure her would therefore benefit them both. But there was an odd stillness in the air. Something weighty that made him pause, and wait for her to resume the conversation.

And she knew he would wait, as long as required. She was the only one who could give him what he sought. Where else was he to go?

"Hand me my robe," she finally said, and Mircea made himself move slowly and deliberately to retrieve it, as if it were a matter of complete indifference to him how long it took.

He turned to find her drying off—alone, because her servants weren't back yet. And smiling at him, a brief twist of her lips, amused and a bit wistful, all at once. "I remember when things were so important," she told him. "When I, too, vibrated with need."

"Praetor—"

She held up a hand. "I know what you want. You know you haven't earned it. But unlike our dear consul, I understand . . . exigencies. You may have until dawn. Do not waste it."

"No, praetor. Thank you, praetor."

She nodded and waved him off, her mind already on other things. Mircea bowed several times until he reached the door, trying to contain himself. And then he ran.

―――――――

From rain-drenched Venice, Mircea tumbled into a world of dust so fine that it moved like water, sloughing off under his frantic feet and down a hill, before cascading into the valley below. The sky, which had cracked open with all the power of a lightning storm to release him, now snapped shut again, leaving only dancing red images in front of his eyes, like laughing demons. Which was fitting, Mircea thought, rolling over and trying to get to his knees.

After all, he'd just been in hell.

People called the rivers of lightning he'd traversed "ley lines," a term that made no sense and was pathetically inadequate in any case. They weren't *lines*. They were terrible, raging torrents that battered his flimsy shield as if desperate to consume him. As desperate as he was to get away from them.

But they allowed him to do what nothing else could, and travel hundreds of miles in a few moments, to visit the greatest healers of the age and search for a cure for Dorina. Not that that had been going so well, but then, he'd been able to see but a fraction of his list. Because, while the ley lines were owned by no man, and were therefore free, the shields required to traverse them safely definitely were not.

He wasn't a mage; he couldn't make his own. And he damned well couldn't afford to buy one! Which is why he'd made his deal with the devil, or at least, with the praetor.

Who was going to kill him—quite, quite literally—if he lost her damned orb!

He scuffled about in what felt like an ocean of sand, for a round object the size of his palm. It looked like nothing more than a ball of glass, something the artisans of

Murano might make as a toy, yet it was worth the price of a palazzo—a large one. He finally found it, and lay back against the sand, half-dizzy from relief. And noticed that the moon was up. Unencumbered by the clouds that draped it in Venetian skies, it was another pure, clear orb, lying low on the horizon.

He didn't have much time.

Mircea got to his feet, dusted himself off, and looked around.

One of the praetor's mages, who had been here once when he was younger, had spelled the little device to take Mircea to his destination. He'd also described the place, and it looked like it hadn't changed in all the years since. It was nothing like Mircea had expected.

The great magical families of Venice lived in mansions every bit as fine as those owned by the wealthiest of merchants. This . . . was not one of them. In fact, Mircea hesitated even to call it a house, considering that it was half buried in sand, and what was still visible had a tree growing out of it.

Or sort of a tree. It was old, withered, and bleached a silvery gray by the harsh sun that was shortly to revisit this landscape. It had no leaves. It was a ridiculous excuse for a dead tree, and yet, there it was, poking out of the roof like a misshapen chimney.

Mages, Mircea thought in disgust, and slogged up the hill.

The little house sat at the very top of the rise, overlooking the small village that Mircea could see in the distance. It was dark and quiet, and Mircea hesitated before knocking. Humans rarely liked being awakened at this time of night, and human mages even less so. There was every chance the man would curse him.

But he'd curse himself far worse if he lost this chance, so he knocked.

Nothing happened.

Mircea swore under his breath, and tried again, louder this time.

Still nothing.

He could break down the flimsy excuse for a door, but there were undoubtedly wards here. Mircea couldn't perceive them, even at the lowest range of his hearing, but that didn't mean they weren't there. He hesitated, biting his lip.

Then sent a mental feeler inside, sliding past the worn wood, and into the small space within.

And was promptly slapped by something that felt like a lightning bolt, one that sent him flying backward through the air and tumbling down the hill, trying to curse but finding that his mouth suddenly didn't work right.

Neither did anything else.

The hand clutching the orb was locked tight around it, unable to move, while the other was flapping about randomly. He rolled to a stop and just lay there for a moment, watching it flutter here and there on its own, while the shock of the curse or whatever it was still echoed through him. He finally decided to attempt to get up, and found that his legs were just as useless, absolutely refusing to bear his weight, or even to let him crawl.

Not that he needed to. Because, a moment later, he was picked up from the sand by an unseen hand, and jerked back up the hill again. Where the strangest-looking creature he'd ever seen was waiting for him.

One would think that the great Abramalin could afford a better class of servant, Mircea thought, staring at a knee-length grizzled beard; a dirty loincloth over a scrawny, nut-brown body; and a pair of eyebrows so bushy that they were like little beards all on their own hanging down in front of the man's eyes.

Mircea couldn't tell if the creature was staring back because of the eyebeards, but he supposed so. Because a harrumph issued from between unseen lips after a moment, forcefully enough to blow out the regular beard a little. And then the creature turned and went back inside, prompting Mircea to call after him, and try to explain.

And to sound like one of the goats on the way to the abattoir back home, bleating its last, because his lips still didn't work!

But a moment later, he found himself floating feetfirst through the doorway, into the small room with the tree. Which had all sorts of shelves nailed to its dead trunk, strewn with strange-looking devices and potion bottles and some things that might be shriveled body parts. Mircea felt himself swallow, and wished he'd had the forethought to have the praetor's servant write him a letter of introduction, not that the creature looked like he could read. . . .

The man lit a little clay lamp, illuminating the rest of the room. And explaining why the shelves were on the tree. Because virtually every other surface—walls, floor, even part of the ceiling—was stacked with books and scrolls and collections of parchment.

The man toddled over with the lamp, and thrust it in Mircea's face. And said something in a language Mircea didn't know, and couldn't even identify. And coming from a busy port like Venice, he found that disturbing, all on its own. Like everything so far!

"Do . . . do you speak Italian?" he asked, very carefully, so that his still-numb tongue wouldn't trip over the words.

"Do I speak Italian?" the man mimicked, and flapped his arms around, like a bird. It caused the lamp to flap, too, and spread dancing shadows everywhere. Mircea stared.

And not just because of the strange mockery or whatever it was. But because the house had only one room, and there was no one else in it. Just a pallet on the floor, a small bench by a wall, where food was obviously prepared, and a wild-eyed hermit.

Who, Mircea was coming to suspect, might not be a servant after all, because the place didn't look like it had one.

Mircea had been warned that all mages were at least a little mad. He should have thought to wonder where on the spectrum someone who chose to live out in the Egyptian desert, in a tree house, might fall. But he hadn't, and now he was in the man's power and the sun was soon to rise, and he didn't know what to do.

But he knew that he couldn't go home to Dorina empty-handed.

"I have a little girl," he blurted, and the man—the mage?—who had been fussing about, fixing breakfast, looked up.

"Liar."

"What?" Mircea blinked at him.

"You're a vampire."

"Yes. But . . . but I wasn't eleven years ago! Almost twelve now, back when I lived in—but that doesn't matter; you don't care where I lived—" *Get control of yourself, man!* He was babbling, but the creature was listening, or he seemed to be, and Mircea didn't know how long that would be the case. "I'm sorry to wake you," he said, trying again. "But she's dying. My daughter. And I don't know how to stop it, and neither does anyone I've tried—"

"And who have ye tried?" The man took a swig of something from a bottle.

"I live in Venice, so I went to the great healing houses there first—Piloti, Lachesis, and Jalena—"

"Ha! Filthy poisoners. They deal in death, not life, boy!" The shaggy head shook.

Mircea swallowed. "And then to Zoan of Napoli—he didn't have another name—but I was told—"

"Oh, he had one. His family stripped it from him after the last scam." The man took another swig. "Toad doctor."

"What?"

"Picked it up on his travels. Britain, I believe. Hang a bag containing a live toad around an afflicted person's neck."

"And . . . and what does that do?"

An eyebeard went up. "Absolutely nothing. Hence the scam."

"I—"

"And before that, he was selling wool soaked in olive oil, supposedly from the Mount of Olives. Said to cure all sorts of ailments, when coupled with a long-winded story about a soldier named Longinus—"

"—healed of his blindness by the blood of Christ," Mircea finished, feeling sick.

The old man cackled. "Got you, did he? Ah well. The old tricks are the best tricks."

"Do you know anything that aren't tricks?" Mircea said, more sharply than was wise, given that he still couldn't control his movements. But he'd spent a small fortune on that damned bit of wool, and that was after

searching through half the bars of Naples for the bastard.
And all for nothing!

"Oh, perhaps a few things," the mage said, pausing to
sniff something in a pot. Mircea watched him hopefully,
until the man shrugged. And spread whatever it was on
some bread.

Mircea swallowed his anger, and tried again. "I've been
to healers in Paris and Rome, Tripoli and Antioch. All for
nothing! Nobody knows anything about dhampirs—"

"Dhampirs?" The old man turned around, holding his
breakfast. "Ye didn't say anything about dhampirs!"

"I'm sorry!" Mircea said quickly, because the man was
already shaking his head. "Please! I'll pay anything
you say!"

The bread went in the beard, and crunching sounds
were heard. "Don't look like ye have anything to pay. No
gold or jewels, clothes're nothing special, cloak's been
mended—"

"I can get you whatever you want. I *will* get it—if you
help her."

Some more crunching ensued. It was all he'd done all
night, Mircea thought. Sit by—or levitate by, in this case—
and watch people eat. People who weren't in a hurry at all,
despite knowing what was at stake!

The man walked over to the tree, and stood musing
awhile, before picking out a small bottle. He came over to
Mircea. "You're from Venice, y'say?"

Mircea nodded.

"Good, good. Give this to the little one, three drops at
a time, in water. No more, no less. It will calm her fits—for
a while." He tucked it into Mircea's sleeve, because flappy
hand was still flappy.

"Thank you. I—"

The man tutted. "Don't thank me yet. 'Tis not a cure.
For that, I'll need a little something."

"What? Anything—"

Black eyes glittered at him through veils of hair. "Some
associates of mine have been having trouble getting a certain ingredient. We use it in many of our potions, but it's
scarce as a virgin in a brothel these days—"

"I can get it for you. Just name it—"

"It's not about a one-time shipment. We can arrange that for ourselves. It's the trade we want resumed, and right quick. Problem is, this particular ingredient only comes in quantity from one place: Venice. But somebody's been fiddling with the flow, likely trying to up the price. You get it moving again, and I'll take care of your girlie— and not by hanging a frog round her neck! How's that, vampire?"

"I—yes." Mircea didn't know much about trade, despite living in a city based on it, but he could find out. He would find out. "Yes, I can do that. What ingredient are you interested in?"

The old mage grinned, showing a mouthful of blackened and half-missing teeth.

And then he told him.

Chapter Twenty

For the second time in less than a day, I woke up to a man in my bed. Only this one was little and uncomfortably hot, and was wearing a pair of *Star Wars* Underoos, because putting him in something he liked was the only way to keep any clothes on him. And more than SpongeBob, more than Transformers, more than Lucille Ball—don't ask—Stinky loved *Star Wars*.

Of course, he'd wanted to be Boba Fett, which had worried me, but lately he'd been leaning more toward Rey. Which opened up a whole different set of questions, but I decided I could figure them out later and started to get up. Only to find myself pinned to the mattress.

"C'mon," I said sleepily. "Move."

Nothing. I knew he'd heard me, because those long fingers and toes had just gripped the mattress even tighter, which wasn't going to work. Because Stinky and I had wrestled before, and I always won. Except for today, apparently, when my best efforts left me right where I'd started.

Of course, I couldn't do my best work, because something else was snuggled into my right armpit. Or make that *someone* else, I thought, recognizing Aiden's silky head. And chubby little baby hand, which had just batted at me to stop moving around, because he'd had a hard night.

You and me both, kid, I thought, wondering what had happened after I zonked out. But all I got was a rush of memories, some crazy, some confusing, all overwhelming. So I shut that shit down, and waited for somebody to come and tell me.

Only no one did.

I glanced at the bedside table. Somebody had gifted me a small violet in a pot—one guess who—about a week ago, which had been a charming thing with three shy little blooms. But Caedmon must have had some more excess energy, because the table was no longer visible, being draped in a mass of purple flowers that spilled down from the surface and were spreading across the floor.

There was nothing else to do, so I watched them for a little while. Fortunately, they seemed to be slowing down, so maybe we wouldn't be smothered in violet exuberance in our sleep. That was good, I decided.

Then I was out again.

The next time I woke up, it was because of food. A wonderful, earthy smell turned out to be coming from a bowl of soup somebody had shoved under my nose. Thankfully, that somebody was Olga, who had a proper notion of what a portion size is.

I sat up, my bed warmers having gone off somewhere, probably to get their own soup. And, in the case of Stinky, had left a couple handfuls of coarse gray hair behind. "I think he's shedding," I told Olga blearily, which of course got no response. Trolls don't care about such things.

Fortunately, they do care—passionately—about food. Which was why the tray she was setting over me contained not only what looked like a whole tureen of homemade vegetable soup, but also half a loaf of fresh-baked bread, about a stick of butter crammed into a little pot, a couple of longnecks—hallelujah, somebody had bought beer—and some soft cheese that went great on the bread I'd already slathered with butter. There was no meat, but I didn't mind.

I dug in.

Olga sat on the end of the bed, causing me to go almost perpendicular due to mattress sag. I managed to rescue the tray, while she scowled at the flimsy human furniture, then went out again. A few moments later she was back, carrying a sturdy wooden chair from the dining room. She put it down by the bed, and took a moment getting comfortable.

I watched her over my bread-and-butter-and-cheese feast, which was seriously good. The bread wasn't long out of the oven, the butter was melting into all the little cracks, and the cheese sat on top, being silky smooth and warm and—God. I was starting to sound like a troll. I certainly had the appetite of one, and Olga didn't interrupt.

Food time is sacred time to her people.

I don't know how long it took me to clear the tray— maybe twenty minutes, despite the fact that I had my head down, shoveling it in the whole time. I finally fell back against the pillows, utterly replete, and noticed that Claire had come in while I was busy. "My compliments to the chef," I told her, and got a small smile.

I started to set the tray on the bedside table before remembering the floral profusion. Which was gone now, I realized, with just a few well-shorn lilacs peering at me over the top of the pot, looking properly chastened. I completed the movement, wincing when pain shot through my shoulder.

But it was a little pain, and didn't seem to be echoed in too many more places. For once, I felt pretty good. "Hey," I said. "I feel pretty good!"

I started to throw back the covers, and, once again, was stopped.

This time, by two fierce looks from two fierce women, which had me sliding back onto the pillows meekly.

I didn't feel *that* good.

"So," I said, looking between the two of them, "is there a reason I can't get up?"

"You can get up whenever you want," Claire said, frowning.

"Of course," Olga agreed.

I reached a hand toward the covers, and I swear somebody growled at me.

The fact that I wasn't sure which of them had done it was kind of concerning.

"We just want to talk, and downstairs is still"—Claire looked like she was reaching for the right word—"messy."

"It a pit," Olga agreed, which made Claire tear up, because it was her house. And because she usually ran a tight ship. And because she looked like just about anything could set her off right now.

But she didn't argue the word choice, so it was probably bad.

"Maybe I could help," I offered, but didn't try getting up again.

I'm reckless, not stupid.

"Oh, it's fine, Dory!" Claire said. "The guards are helping—"

"The guards? What guards?"

She blinked at me. "The royal guards. Who else?"

I grinned. "You have the royal guards cleaning up? Since when?"

The fey had this whole hierarchy I didn't understand, because I didn't care, about who could do what and when. It was familiar to me since it was the sort of thing vamps did, making up a hugely complex system of rules because, when you live hundreds or even thousands of years, what else are you going to do to pass the time? But I did understand enough to know that royal fey guards didn't do the mopping up.

Or anything else, as far as I could tell. Except hunt and laze about, polishing their weapons and waiting to accomplish deeds of derring-do. Of course, last night they'd pretty much managed that, so I guessed I should cut them some slack.

"They do when Caedmon tells them to!" Claire said, and got up, but not to leave. Just to pace around, because she looked like she was about to come out of her skin. And considering what that looked like, I was all for the pacing. "I had my hands full with our patients—and the boys, who were scared out of their minds!"

"They seemed okay earlier," I said, "unless I was dreaming them being in here."

"No." She turned around, looking apologetic. "I hope they didn't keep you up, but there was nowhere else. My room was taken up with injured fey, and Gessa and the little troll were in the boys' beds, and I was constantly back and forth and would have woken them anyway—"

No wonder she looked tired, I thought.

And then what she'd said registered.

"The little troll? You mean he's not dead?"

"Not yet," Olga said darkly.

"I was up with him all night," Claire told me. "And with Gessa, who had a slight concussion after Ymsi—"

She broke off, biting her lip.

"Wait." I sat up and shoved another pillow behind me. My thoughts were still a jumble, but there was some stuff that I remembered clearly. Like a knife sticking out of a kid's chest.

"Caedmon was with me," I said. "And that knife was through the heart. So how is he alive again?"

"Troll heart on other side," Olga told me simply.

I blinked, and filed it away for future reference. "I didn't know that."

"Someone else not know, either."

"Or maybe they weren't aiming for him!" Claire said heatedly.

"Aiden not stab," Olga pointed out, with the tone of someone who had said it before.

"Aiden?" I looked at Claire. "You think this is about your son?"

"Who else?" She shoved extra-frizzy hair out of her face, because I guess she hadn't had time to do anything with it today. "Gessa said those things went straight for the stairs, not once but numerous times. If you hadn't been there—"

"They'd have met an angry mother dragon a floor up. They were better off with me."

"Stone doesn't burn, Dory," Claire said, her arms tight around her, her face white. "It's how the goddamned Svarestri win against the Dark Fey—how they've always won! Our element is fire; theirs is earth. And earth smothers fire. . . ."

Leaving you armed only with a maw of daggerlike teeth, ten-inch claws, and a tail that can crush a man in one sweep, I thought, but kept my mouth shut because this wasn't the time.

"Aiden is probably the best-protected little boy on the planet," I said instead. "Plus, he's wearing that thing, isn't he? That rune we spent so much time tracking down?"

It had been an ugly, discolored item, old and cracked and strangely heavy. Not something you'd expect the heir to one of the major thrones of Faerie to have in his possession. Or on his person, because it melted into the skin once on the body, becoming invisible—and making the wearer virtually invulnerable.

That didn't mean he couldn't be hurt; if Aiden had been stabbed, he'd have definitely felt the pain, and borne the wound until it healed. But it would have healed. Because wearing one of the last remaining Runes of Langgarn granted certain privileges.

So whatever had happened to the rest of us last night, Aiden had not been in danger.

But that raised the question: who had? Because they'd sure wanted somebody. Gessa had been right—they'd made a beeline for the stairs and never so much as looked at anything else.

"Why do the Svarestri want a troll kid dead?" I asked.

"They *don't!*" Claire said, whirling around.

Olga didn't say anything, but the look she gave me was eloquent. She didn't agree with Claire, but she wasn't going to argue with a frantic mother who was low on sleep. That never got anybody anywhere.

"It's that bitch Efridis," Claire told me. "She'll do anything to see her son inherit!"

And, okay, Claire was the type who ran on nerves, even on a good day, and she hadn't seen many good days lately. So she was a little distraught. But she nonetheless had a point.

Efridis was a bitch.

The beautiful blond fey queen was Caedmon's sister, but other than for looks, I didn't see a lot of resemblance. For example, she'd used her position to steal the rune now guarding baby Aiden for her son, a piece of work named Æsubrand, who was the Svarestri heir apparent. Yeah, I know. The names kind of get to me, too.

But, basically, Caedmon's sister, who had married the Svarestri king, had stolen baby Aiden's protection to help her own son, who dreamed of a Faerie united under his rule.

And one land means one throne, doesn't it?

Æsubrand had planned to inherit Caedmon's kingdom, merge it with his own, and then go conquer everything else. And the fact that Caedmon had a son hadn't really thrown a spanner into the works, because said son—Claire's fiancé, Heidar—was half-human. And Blarestri law required their king to have more than half fey blood.

Which was good for Heidar, since it kept him out of the hot seat.

And was bad for Aiden, because it put him right in.

Because the law had neglected to say *what kind* of fey blood was required. So Claire's, although Dark Fey, still counted. And she was slightly over fifty percent, thanks to that Brownie great-something grandma. Meaning that, while Heidar couldn't inherit, his son could.

Thus making Aiden the target. His birth had knocked out Æsubrand's chances of succeeding to his uncle's throne, something the Ice Prince had been kind of hot about. So much so that he'd tried to kill Claire while she was pregnant to prevent Aiden from ever being born. Yet, afterward, he'd also said that he wouldn't hurt a child, but would wait for Aiden to grow up to duel him for the throne.

I would have laughed at that, but I'd asked around, and it seemed that, yes, the fey had the view that a baby wasn't a baby until it was born. So, while Æsubrand could retain his honor and kill it in the womb (killing an innocent human mother apparently didn't count as an honor ding), his rep would take a hit if he murdered a child. And we'd eventually gotten the rune back, making future assassination attempts on Aiden much less likely to succeed anyway.

So, end of story, right?

Only no. Because Æsubrand had done us a favor recently, and pimped on his batshit-crazy dad's plan to bring back the gods. One that had almost worked.

Aeslinn had attacked the consul's home, where all six vampire senates were meeting, to try and knock the vamps out of the war by destroying their leadership. That would have given a huge black eye to the war effort, since vamps are almost the only creatures who can fight effectively in Faerie, where human magic doesn't work. If they dropped out, there would be no one to take the war to Aeslinn, allowing him all the time he needed to find a way to bring the old gods he worshipped back into this world.

And, presumably, to kill us all.

His plan had been a good one, but Æsubrand and his mother had come to warn us first, so we'd had a slight heads-up. Yeah, you read that right. After trying to assassinate Claire, almost killing all of us over the rune, and generally being a massive douche nozzle, the prodigal son had returned to the fold and dragged momma along with him. It seemed that, while his father was happy at the idea of being a godly flunky, Æsubrand actually wanted to rule his own kingdom.

And that did not include being a puppet to anyone.

Of course, warning people who have every reason to view you as an enemy is not easy. They tend to be too busy trying to kill you to listen. But that wasn't a problem for Efridis, who had conjured up a glamourie, disguised herself as a cook, and snuck into the house along with a bunch of servants Louis-Cesare had loaned us.

And drugged the whole lot.

I'd arrived to find everyone out cold, including Claire, who had been slumped over a table in the backyard, while Efridis and her spawn held on to the two kids. It's the closest I've ever come to a heart attack. But they hadn't hurt the boys, just used them as hostages to get me to listen.

Yet now they were suddenly trying to kill Aiden again? When they, of all people, knew that he had the rune? It didn't make sense.

"You don't believe me, do you?" Claire demanded, watching me.

"It's not that. I wouldn't put anything past those two. It's just . . ."

"Just what?"

"What Olga said. They didn't stab him, Claire," I said gently.

And immediately flashed on that old saying about not poking a bear, especially when the bear is a dragon.

"No, *Ymsi* stabbed him," she told me, her voice low and furious. "With that bitch riding him! And troll eyes are notoriously bad, especially in the dark—"

"Wait. What?"

"—and the boy only arrived today, and unexpectedly,

so Aiden and Stinky were the only two people supposed to be in that room—"

"Claire, hold up."

"—and Stinky snores to high heaven! There's *every* reason to believe that anybody walking in there would assume—"

"Claire!"

She looked at me, eyes wide and startled, because that had practically been a shout. But she'd just said something important, and I needed to grab it before my wonky brain let it slip away again. "Riding?" I asked.

"What?"

"You said 'that bitch' was riding Ymsi. What—"

She threw out a hand, in a gesture that somehow managed to be elegant and exasperated at the same time. "Caedmon told me what happened with you and Efridis. I know—"

"Me and Efridis?"

"Well, who else are we talking about, Dory?" Claire stared at me. "Who else do we know who desperately wants Aiden dead, who probably knows how to remove the rune, *since it's her family heirloom*, and who also happens to be a *vargr*?"

"A what?" I said, because I was trying to keep up and not doing so great.

And, suddenly, everything stopped.

It was almost funny. Claire had been gesturing again, with her arm up and her mouth open, about to say something that never made it past her vocal chords. The only thing that did was a small "Oh."

And then she abruptly sat down again.

"What I say?" Olga asked her mildly.

Claire was still looking at me, her face almost tragic. "Caedmon didn't tell you," she said softly, a hand on my leg.

And, okay, getting freaked out here.

"Tell me what?"

The two exchanged a look. Claire shook her head, and bit her lip, obviously passing the buck. Olga sighed.

"You remember spriggans?" she asked me.

I had to think for a moment.

"Those little round things at the fair?"

She nodded. "Old days, spriggans used as spies. Look like rocks. Blend in. Troll *vargar* ride them far away, all directions."

I blinked a little, because my brain was suddenly sending me the disturbing and quite hilarious image of a thousand-pound troll riding around on top of a crowd of those little things. Just this mass stampede of tiny, straining creatures, each with a bit in its mouth, the reins held by the troll. And dust flying everywhere as they thundered o'er the—

I cut it off.

I was losing it.

"*Vargar* rare now," Olga said sternly, as if she knew I wasn't taking this seriously. "Used to be many. Spriggans put on all borders, even into enemy lands. We see far—"

And, suddenly, something connected. "That young guard," I thought for a second, and then snapped my fingers. "Soini. He said that's why he's here, something about far-seeing—"

Olga nodded. "Light Fey also have, but not so many. Boy is young, but he will learn. Be important one day." She looked at me shrewdly. "Like you."

I laughed. "Oh, so I'm a spriggan, Olga?"

She shook her head. "Spriggan *eyes*. Send where you want to see, nobody notice. Like bird or animal."

And then it hit me, a memory of cloudy night skies, beaks and feathers and blood, and a breathtaking fall, dizzyingly far, and ending in—

I jerked up, blinking, and swallowed. Because being in an animal when it dies is not fun. What the *hell*?

"Not spriggan," Olga said gently, catching my attention again, and gently touching my forehead. "*Vargr.*"

I decided I needed to lie down again.

Chapter Twenty-one

An hour later, I stepped into the shower, which was much less fun without Louis-Cesare. And stayed there for a while, and not just because the hot water felt so damned good. But because I was trying to straighten out my head.

Part of that was easier than I'd thought. Memories of the attack last night were coming back, and were easier to parse than whatever had happened at the fights, I suppose because I'd been conscious this time. Or half-conscious, or superconscious, or whatever it was called when two minds are awake and acting at the same time.

I called it freaky.

Olga had another word.

The best I could figure out, *vargar* were some kind of fey shamans or mystics who could throw their consciousness into other creatures. They'd gotten the name from wolves, because their favorite ride had once been fast-moving wolf packs. Which was why they were shown on Viking monuments riding around on wolves like horses, and why some of the sagas had fey witches and trolls doing the same thing.

But, eventually, they'd noticed that mentally tagging along with wolves had its downsides. Like the fact that people tended to notice a pack of dangerous predators, which made spying difficult. And that wolves were easily distracted by game or threats, making them harder to control than other creatures. Like birds, for instance.

Which Claire had been quick to point out were Efridis' favorite avatar.

She wasn't alone. Like Odin, who had seen through

the eyes of his pet ravens, plenty of *vargar* had moved on to birds or boars or other creatures for their rides. A guy named Bothvarr, an early Beowulf type, had liked mentally hitching a ride on a huge bear, especially in battle. It was said that he was never defeated until somebody interrupted his concentration one day, and he lost control of his avatar.

Because *vargar* weren't weres; they didn't become their creatures. They just . . . went along for the ride. Or mentally hopped from one to another, checking out the borders better than any spy cam, because spriggans could move wherever you wanted them.

Giving the fey literal eyes everywhere.

Or they used to. *Vargar* were few and far between these days, although nobody knew why. Just that fewer were being born. Which was why Olga had been so surprised to find one here on Earth.

Only she hadn't.

That's why we'd lost last night. I wasn't fey, so I couldn't be a real *vargr*, and neither could Dorina. We had—or, to be more precise, *she* had—Mircea's mental skills, and from what I could remember she'd been getting inventive with them.

Unfortunately, our attacker had been better at it. And that was a problem, because we were obviously up against the real deal, a powerful *vargr* with a lot more experience than Dorina. Which raised the question, how were we supposed to catch it?

So, okay, maybe even the easy stuff wasn't so easy. As for the rest . . . I soaped up my hair, which cracked with grit from the dust storm last night, and tried not to think about it. But my brain wasn't having it. My brain was worrying the other GREAT BIG THING I'd remembered, like a starving dog with a bone, and wherever I turned, there it was again.

Looking at me.

Okay, I'd think about it. Once. And then that was *it*. Because there was nothing I could do about it anyway.

Dorina's thoughts were still a jumbled mess with big blank spots, probably where I'd had to concentrate on something else. But one thing stood out crystal clear: the idea of a scattered consciousness. She'd said that was what happened if you were in free flight for too long, that you might just drift away and never come back. That you might cease to exist—mentally, at least—if you couldn't find an avatar fast enough.

Leaving, I assumed, a brain-dead corpse behind.

Unless, of course, you were a freak with two consciousnesses. Because that would leave . . . what, exactly? A brain-dead corpse that wasn't brain-dead? But that was normal, with one consciousness, just like everybody else, for the first time ever?

It was that thought that wouldn't leave me alone, that had me using up all the hot water and getting prune-y, instead of getting on with my day. It was what had me pressing my forehead against the tile, and thinking about what that could mean. For both of us.

For Dorina, the benefits were obvious: no more deadweight. I wouldn't be a remora on her side anymore, an anvil around her neck, a useless thing that no one respected, and who she'd been carrying for five centuries now and was probably sick of it. Especially with the gleaming jewel of a Senate seat currently dangling in front of her. And with it, everything her abilities should have gotten her all along: wealth, respect, family, position. She could instantly be all caught up, at the pinnacle of the vampire world, and all she needed for that to happen was for me to just . . . disappear.

And as for me . . .

I swallowed, feeling ill. But the truth was, it wouldn't be the first time I'd wished a part of me dead. I'd spent centuries looking for a way to do exactly that—to kill off the terrifying thing inside me that had made anything like a normal life impossible.

Memories crowded in, not hers this time, but mine. Of running through a briar patch, shredding my feet and legs, too desperate to get away to bother finding an easier path. She'd almost erupted in the middle of an inn that time, where I'd been dumb enough to get talked into a game of cards by the fire. It had been cozy: rain beating down on the roof from a storm outside, a bowl of stew by my side, a tankard of ale in the hand that wasn't holding the cards. A perfect, relaxing night . . .

Until one of the men accused me of cheating, and pulled a knife.

It was a stupid thing; he was drunk. And the brawny innkeeper was already heading our way to settle it. And even if he hadn't been, was a red-faced idiot barely able to hold a knife someone I couldn't handle?

Dorina had apparently thought so, forcing me to run off into the cold, desperate to get far enough away that she couldn't wreck the place. Because she'd wanted to. I'd felt it like I'd felt her, rising like a gorge in my throat, blood filling my senses, threatening to choke me.

And everyone else.

So I ran, like I did a hundred other times. And ended up spending the night in some farmer's barn, curled up among the cattle and hoping I woke before anyone found me in the morning. And was gutted for their trouble.

But running didn't always work. She could take me in an instant sometimes, like the night a group of guys decided to jump me in an alley, just some young thugs, barely armed, who I could have knocked out with their own cudgels. Except the next thing I knew, I was waking up covered in blood and they were all dead.

The same thing happened with some highwaymen, who would have probably settled for the little bit of money I had on me. And with a group of randy soldiers, who were too drunk to outrun me, not that they'd had the chance. And with the personal guards of a stupid lord who thought he'd have a little fun with a peasant girl.

I'd come around inside his coach that time, lying on his lordship's bloated carcass, his men arrayed almost artistically on the dirt outside. I'd stared at them, dizzy and sick, their blood a cloying stench in my nostrils, and recalled the stories about my uncle Vlad. Who, it was said, had liked to arrange his victims in pretty geometric shapes so he could admire their corpses from the towers of his castle.

Guess it ran in the family, huh?

I'd started trying harder to avoid conflict, after that.

Like giving up sea travel, because my other half in an

enclosed space for too long was not a good idea. Like avoiding gambling, because a game gone wrong might end with the accuser strung up by his entrails. And like shunning close friendships, much less romances, because people near me had the life expectancy of a mouse hanging around a cat.

In other words, just as long as the cat didn't get hungry.

I'd never known when my personal monster was going to get hungry, or been certain that I could stop her if she did. And every time it happened, I'd felt more like a failure, more like a bloodthirsty thing that enjoyed killing, more like the monster people thought me to be. So isolating myself had become the norm, not for my sake, but for everyone else's. And that was still true, wasn't it?

It was still true yesterday, when I'd been too afraid to mark Louis-Cesare. I didn't want him tied to me when I didn't know who I was anymore, or who I might become. I didn't want him getting hurt when the crazy came out, possibly for good this time. I didn't want him to wake up and realize that he didn't know the woman lying beside him.

But he wouldn't accept that, wouldn't listen if I tried to tell him, just like he hadn't listened in the shower. He thought he could handle it, that he could handle anything, but he couldn't handle *her*, and neither could I. She was going to do what she always had—any damned thing she wanted, to anyone she wanted, and that included him.

And that couldn't include him.

Whatever it cost me, it *wouldn't*.

———

I finally ran out of hot water, threw on some old gray sweats, and ran a comb through my wet hair. And made my way down to the kitchen, where activity was going on, although not of the cleaning variety. Instead, a couple of mighty fey warriors were peeling apples, another was coring and cutting them up, and a third was standing by the kitchen table with a rolling pin in hand.

Despite everything, I felt a smile twitch at my lips. And not just at seeing the fey put to work for a change. But at the table.

It had been cleared off except for a piece of fabric that

had once been a tablecloth, before it had become too stained for regular use. It had now become a kitchen aide, one that had been liberally sprinkled with flour and was supporting a large sheet of rolled dough. And there was only one thing Claire used that setup for.

Ah yiss, I thought gleefully. *Motherf'king strudel!*

Maybe.

"It keeps tearing!" a fey warrior said shrilly.

The fey was the one by the table, with sweat on his forehead and fury in his eyes. And flour in his hair, which someone, probably the determined-looking redhead standing beside him, had made him put up into a sloppy ponytail. More of it was smeared on his cheeks, where he'd wiped his face with a flour-dusted sleeve, leaving him looking like a toddler at play in Mom's kitchen.

A profane toddler.

He cursed some more in some fey language—I didn't know it, but that was definitely a curse—and glared at the dough. "This is impossible!"

"It won't tear if you roll it evenly," Claire said, which only appeared to madden him more.

"I did roll it evenly!"

Claire gave a disdainful glance at the dough, which even I could see was lumpy and thick in places, and almost see-through in others. Like he'd been pummeling it instead of rolling it with the wooden pin he was brandishing, which still had pieces of dough stuck to it here and there. Ironically, it was almost the only thing in the kitchen not covered in flour.

"You never told me it was this hard!" he accused.

Claire crossed her arms. "You said, and I quote: 'It's women's work. How hard can it be?'"

A fey at the sink choked back a laugh.

The flour-covered one snarled something at him.

"Sorry." Dish Fey didn't look sorry. He looked wet. Like, all down his front and dripping into a puddle on the floorboards, where the soapy mixture was turning the flour into something approaching paste.

Housekeeping did not appear to be a fey specialty.

"Raisins or nuts?" Claire asked me, as the chef went back to aggressively beating up his dough.

"Why not both?"

"Need a better dough for both," she said dryly.

Damn, Claire, I thought, looking at the poor, suffering fey.

That was cold.

A car horn went off in the front yard. I looked out the window, and felt my smile fade. "Be right back."

I slipped through the side door and moseyed out front, where a shiny black Lamborghini was parked catty-corner on the lawn. I'd have had something to say about that, but Caedmon must have done it, since I'd been too out of it last night to drive. I vaguely remembered us starting and stopping and starting and stopping as he slowly figured out this strange Earth conveyance, because the fey don't carry cell phones to call a cab. And flagging someone down when seven feet tall and dressed like Robin Hood can be a problem.

So he'd decided to just drive us home instead—in our attackers' car. And for a first-timer, he hadn't done too badly. He'd even managed to miss the stone frog near the mailbox when he parked it, which I appreciated.

A couple of chop-shop boys I knew would appreciate it, too.

But somebody else didn't.

"What did you do to my car?" Blondie demanded, from the driver's seat.

"Is there a problem?"

"You know damned well there's a problem! It won't go!"

Purple Hair didn't say anything, just stood there, all daytime dominatrix in black leather jeans and jacket, and a low-cut silk shirt the same shade as her hair. She checked me out, in my ratty sweats, and her eyes narrowed in judgment.

Or, you know, because I hadn't bothered to arm myself, and she was wondering why.

"That's a shame," I said, glancing at Claire, who had come out of the kitchen, wiping her hands on a flour-dusted apron. "I wonder what's wrong with it."

Claire just smiled. It wasn't a particularly nice expression. But Blondie didn't seem to notice.

"Damn it! This is brand-new," he told us furiously. "If you've fucked it up—"

A scaly arm reached through the window and jerked him out, because Claire was suddenly beside the car. I blinked. I hadn't even seen her move.

I guess the vamps hadn't, either. Because Purple Hair's hand twitched, in the general direction of her jacket. I tensed, prepared to jump her, but she paused the action, probably realizing that she was about to make things worse.

She had no idea.

So both of us just stood there, watching Blondie kick his heels several inches off the ground, because Claire is a tall drink of water. One who suddenly had a wealth of iridescent purple scales covering one arm. And three-inch talons, shading from black to maroon to milky white, on the newly armored hand.

Guess I knew why she favored sleeveless dresses, I thought, seeing how the finely made scales transitioned seamlessly into the freckled skin of her shoulder.

It was an impressive display, but I wasn't as worried as I might have been. I'd seen this particular trick before, and she'd remained in full control. As far as I could tell, a partial transformation simply gave her more strength without compromising her grip on her other half.

Of course, I could be wrong, I thought, tensing again as something that wasn't a voice slithered out of Claire's mouth. It was low and haunting, with a slight echo, despite not currently having anything to echo from. It was something like the sounds the demon made in *The Exorcist*, only worse, because it vibrated right through skin and flesh both. You didn't hear it so much as *feel* it, like someone scratching the insides of your bones.

So, uh, yeah.

And then the sound turned into guttural words. "My car now."

Blondie swallowed, and looked like he might pass out.

For her part, Purple Hair had gone very, very still. She didn't move; she didn't blink. Neither did I, because I didn't want a repeat of the backyard incident, and I didn't know what small gesture might set Claire off.

And then a small cadre of fey banged the front door open and came out. They were armed, because they were always armed, but they didn't look particularly bothered. Maybe because they were skiving off work. A couple leaned against the house, another propped up the door-frame, and one sat on the stairs, working something loose from a molar with a toothpick. But their arrival broke the tension—slightly.

"What is this?" Blondie demanded, suddenly reani-mating. "What the hell is—"

"Shut up," Purple Hair told him harshly.

"But she can't—she isn't—and my *car*—"

He broke off with a gurgle, probably because the mailed fist had just tightened. Purple Hair closed her eyes briefly, the universal sign for "Why me, God?" For my part, I was listening, but didn't hear any crunching noises. And he didn't actually have to breathe, so . . .

I just stood there some more.

After a moment, Purple Hair looked at me. "The car we wrecked. It was hers?"

I nodded.

"Ah." She looked at Claire. "Your car now."

Claire released Blondie, then turned and went back into the house without another word. He fell to the ground like a sack of potatoes, and stayed there, gasping. Not because he needed the air, but because that's what you do when someone almost decapitates you one-handed.

I walked over, reached in, and took his spare set of keys out of the ignition.

"Fair's fair," I told them. "I knew what I was taking on when I agreed to this job, so you have your week. But that's out there." I nodded at the city. "My home is off-limits, understand?"

"Beginning to." Purple Hair kicked her companion, who was still sprawled theatrically in the grass. "Get up."

"But my car!"

"You wanna take it from her? Be my guest." She looked at me. "Just don't try hiding out here until Satur-day. Fair's fair."

She dragged Blondie off and threw him in the back of a red convertible. They left, and I turned back to see that the fey had come over and were checking out the car. "Does it go very fast?" one of them asked me.

"Yeah."

"As fast as a running horse?"

"Faster."

He frowned, and stuck his head in the window, checking it out.

"Do you think you could teach me how to drive one of these?" Soini asked, looking excited.

I looked back at the house. "Ask Claire. It's her car now."

I went back inside.

Chapter Twenty-two

I went looking for my roommate, to make sure she was okay, but she wasn't in the kitchen. Or the laundry room or the pantry or her bedroom. I'd come back downstairs, intending to try the backyard next, when a fey tapped me on the shoulder. "You have a guest."

I frowned. I wasn't expecting anybody, and despite the myths, Louis-Cesare didn't need an invitation to come in. He had a master power, called the Veil, that allowed him to phase out of this plane of existence for a moment, and bypass whatever pesky ward was in his way. Of course, maybe he was trying to be polite.

"Who is it?"

The fey shrugged. "Says he's your son."

I raised an eyebrow. Then I walked over and raised the door latch and stuck my head out. And found a lump on the steps.

It was an odd-looking thing, wrapped in enough layers to leave it a generic mountain of clothes. In addition to what had to be six or more coats, there were scarves, a hat, dark glasses, what looked like several pairs of gloves, and an umbrella. All this despite the fact that it had to be in the mid-eighties and there wasn't a cloud in the sky.

I leaned against the doorframe. "My darling boy."

"Shut up and let me in."

Apparently, it was an angry lump. "You know, I don't recall having a son."

"I didn't say 'son'; I said 'child'—"

"Which I also don't have, unless you count Stinky."

"—I can't help it if those weirdos you live with don't lis—what? The fuck you don't!"

I clicked my tongue. "Now I know I didn't raise you. Such a potty mouth."

"Yeah. 'Cause if I'd been brought up in your crazy-ass family, I'd be so refined. Now let me in!"

"And them?"

I nodded behind him, to where a crew of assorted additional lumps were huddled together under some umbrellas, similarly attired.

And looking miserable, what I could see of them.

"I hadda bring 'em. It's a long story, and thanks to the damned sun, I can't even think straight. Now get out of the way!"

I considered it. He was talking through a scarf, which muffled his voice enough that I'd have had no idea who was speaking if the fey hadn't said something. And even still, I wasn't taking chances.

"Ahhh! The fuck?" the lump screamed, when I tried to pull down the scarves to take a look. Gloved hands batted at me, and angry eyes glared, barely visible behind black shades. "Are you crazy?"

"I need to verify. So you're going to have to come up with something—"

A string of profanity, impressive in its scope and extent, greeted that comment. "How you expect me to verify when I'm *on fire*?"

"I don't see any smoke."

"Well, you're gonna in half a minute, so I hope you got more of that salve. You can rub it on my whole body this time, 'stead of just my ass—"

I sighed and swung open the door. "Come in, Ray."

Ray came in.

And was followed by a stampede of lumps—and their umbrellas—following him to the dining room and all but knocking me down. I was starting to get déjà vu. They slammed the door in my face, and then screamed at me when I opened it to slip inside.

"All right, anybody on fire?" Ray's voice rose above the din, while I fumbled around for the light switch. Because the dining room had been built before people worried about things like natural light.

The overhead fixture flickered on to show me a bunch of guys huddled in a corner, one sprawled under the table, sobbing pitifully, and a couple more on their knees, trying to stuff some sweaters under the door. I guess to cut off the weak haze of light filtering through the cracks. And then collapsing back a second later, panting for breath they didn't need, while Ray divested himself of several tons of outerwear.

"How's the neighborhood?" a pissy voice demanded, from inside the cloth mountain. "I got a bunch of stuff in the car—"

"Ray—"

"—I think I locked it, but I was in a hurry, and you know this city; can't trust nobody no more—"

"Ray!"

"—and if somebody rips me off, I swear to God—"

"*Ray!*"

He peered at me out of the neckhole of a sweater. "What?"

"What are you doing here?"

Pale blue eyes narrowed. "Well, you'd know if you kept your damned phone on. I only left, like, a hundred messages. I been trying to reach you all day! But you never take a call, and Claire's weird about me, you know?"

"She's weird about all vamps."

"Don't lie. It's the head, isn't it?"

"It's not the head."

"Don't give me that. She keeps doing that thing—"

"What thing?"

"That tilt-to-the-side thing, like she's trying to see where they sewed it back on."

"You're imagining things."

"Check it out sometime. I ain't imagining shit. She's giving me cancer."

"Do you have a point?"

"Just that you oughta keep your phone turned on, 'cause trying to get any info out of your roommate is a pain in my ass. And could be one in yours if you miss out on a great deal 'cause I can't find you."

I felt my eyes narrow. Raymond's idea of a great deal and mine differed slightly. "What kind of deal?"

"The best kind. The we're-rolling-in-dough kind."

"Uh-huh. Which would be why you're here with a carful of your stuff, along with . . . your family?" That last was a guess, but the lumps were vamps under the camouflage, and pretty low-level, or they wouldn't be snoring. Most of them were already out like a light.

And smoking slightly despite the cover-up.

"Shit," Ray said, also smelling barbecue. "Help me out. Gotta figure out which one's burning before he sets the whole group on fire."

I sighed but went to help sort through the pile of what, yes, turned out to be Ray's family. Like their master, they were not particularly prepossessing. Also like their master, they were wearing a lot of clothes, even things like eight or nine pairs of underwear and triple pairs of socks, although that wouldn't help much with the sun.

"The damned hotel," Ray said, when I commented. "They see you take out your luggage, and they wanna get paid—"

"So why didn't you just pay them?"

"Why didn't I just pay them?" It was a falsetto, which would normally have been annoying, but he looked seriously pissed. The small ferret face was pinched and scowling. And the shock of dark hair was quivering with indignation. "Same reason we were living in a damned fleabag. Cheung, that son of a bitch!"

"Cheung?"

"Senator Cheung? My old master Cheung? Bastard ex-pirate who's still a goddamned pirate Cheung?"

"Okay."

"He wiped me out!"

"And by 'wiped out,' you mean . . ."

"Every damned cent! Every bank account I had was also in his name, so he could check up on me, you know?"

I nodded. Until recently, Ray had been a seedy nightclub owner under Cheung's manicured thumb. But a series of unfortunate events had resulted in Ray losing first his head and then his master, when Cheung gifted him to me as a bad joke. Because Ray was obviously about to die and, as a dhampir, I couldn't have vampire children anyway.

But Ray had the survival skills of a cockroach in nuclear winter, having had plenty of practice. The bastard son of a Dutch sailor from the bad old days when raping the locals was considered a friendly greeting, and an Indonesian woman who died young, Ray had considered it a good day if he managed to find something to eat—and he often didn't. And then he became a vampire and stayed short and scrawny forever.

But also plucky, scrappy, and luckier than he thought he was, which was how he'd ended up in possession of Aiden's magic rune for a short time. It had given him some protection; plus, while beheading is no joke even for a vamp, it isn't usually enough to seal the deal. So, long story short, Ray got his noggin sewn back on, Aiden got his rune, and I ended up with a "child" I didn't want and had no way of holding on to without a blood bond I couldn't do.

Not that holding on to him was really the problem. Getting rid of him was more like it, because Ray didn't seem to want to go. And now he was moving in?

"You're not moving in," I told him, while he slapped at one of his children's smoking backsides.

The door opened and Olga looked in.

Ray gave a little shriek, but her bulk blocked out most of the light. And, anyway, he was a master, if a very weak one. He could handle a small exposure to daylight, especially indoors.

Unlike his boys.

"You okay?" she asked, as I threw a coat over a guy's badly blistered thigh.

"Yeah. Could you bring the little pot of green salve from the kitchen?" I asked. "It's in Claire's medicine cabinet."

Olga nodded, and started to leave. "And the vodka," Ray called after her.

She stopped and looked at me.

"No vodka."

"I need a drink! You don't know what kind of day—"

"We don't have vodka."

"Whiskey?"

Olga inclined her head graciously and left. Damned troll hospitality. "You're not drinking all the whiskey, and you're not moving in," I told him, grabbing another limp body.

"Why you gotta be like that?" Ray said. "I never even asked."

"You just showed up with all your stuff!"

"Maybe I'm visiting."

I sent him a look. "For how long?"

"You know. A couple weeks—"

"Ray!"

"Like I got a choice? You think I'd be moving in with Ms. Vamps-Are-Icky if I had a choice?"

"You're *not* moving in."

"Then where am I supposed to go? My club burnt down, and we were living on the top floor—"

"So tell Cheung to give you your money back. He can't just take it for no reason—"

"Like hell he can't. He says it was my fault anyways, 'cause the club wasn't insured—"

"It wasn't insured?"

"It was sorta insured—"

"Ray!"

"And now he wants my head and I can't afford to lose it again! And you can't navigate being a newly appointed senator without someone to show you the ropes."

I rolled my eyes.

"What?" he demanded.

"You're as much a train wreck as I am. And as soon as the war's over, somebody else will have my seat anyway. You think they're going to keep a dhampir on the Senate one second longer than they have to?"

"Well, not with that attitude."

Olga knocked, then came back in with the salve. There were three in the in-need pile so far, and she and Ray started on them, while I determinedly stripped the rest. By the time we were done gooping up the sickly, wrapping them in blankets, and piling them along the walls, *I* needed a drink.

Thankfully, Olga had brought three glasses. Hospitality says you don't let your guests drink alone. It also says you get water glasses full of booze, because troll ideas of a shot are a little different.

I eyed Ray. I supposed I should be worried that he'd belted his back in one go. And then slammed the glass down, wiped his lips, and looked at me. "Okay, about that deal."

———

A couple hours later, Olga and I rolled to a stop by a sidewalk, where a seriously impressed-looking valet ran over to take our ride. He didn't so much as glance at me, despite the nifty silver jumpsuit I was wearing, a recent gift from my fashion-conscious uncle Radu. It was one shouldered and figure hugging, with the material stretchy enough not to be binding. It also had a faint snakeskin pattern in the weave that I secretly thought was badass. And slightly flared trouser legs, although not enough to hide my usual butt-kicking boots, so I'd opted for silver sandals instead.

He also wasn't looking at Olga, who was a vision in gold lamé, along with some troll bling in the form of a necklace that looked like it might leap off her neck and go for your jugular at any second. But it didn't rate so much as a glance. The guy only had eyes for the car.

I couldn't blame him. The sun was setting as we pulled up, and the shiny black surface reflected the colors in bright streamers. I was still gonna have to see my buddies— Claire wanted something less likely to get hijacked—but for the moment, Olga and I were stylin'.

Well, if you didn't count what was following us.

We got out, I handed over the keys, and Claire's new ride purred off around the corner. And was immediately replaced by an ominous rattle, a screech of brakes, and the scent of burning oil. And more acrid black smoke than an old-fashioned steam train.

The battered contraption that rattled to a stop by the curb was part yellow school bus, part ancient semi, and part *Mad Max* movie prop. And all hard-core. Like its occupants, who required a rugged ride, but had been damned cagey about what had happened to the last one.

I watched Olga's posse pile out and frowned. Misplacing Stan's property was no joke. He was connected, specifically to a fat-ass were named Roberto who owned half of Brooklyn and had zero chill. I mentally upped finding Stan's truck a few notches on the priority list, and turned my attention to tonight's errand.

The theatre we'd parked in front of had seen better days. A third of the lights were out on the old-fashioned marquee, there was peeling paint everywhere that wasn't dirty brick, and the COMING ATTRACTIONS posters were so faded behind their yellowed plastic covers that they could have been anything. It wasn't the sort of place you'd expect to have valet parking.

Yet, while I stood there, a Mercedes, a BMW, and a Jaguar hummed up to the curb behind Frankentruck, disgorging a stream of beautiful people headed for the theatre's front doors. Where two neon mermaids were flicking their tails above the name *Delmare*. I'd never heard of the place, but apparently it was owned by an old acquaintance of Ray's from his smuggling days.

Ray's guy had flourished under Geminus, who'd liked the rare and exotic slaves he specialized in. Geminus had had his pick of them for the illegal arena games he was running, and in return, he'd provided the kind of ironclad protection that allowed the smuggler to stay ahead of the law. But Geminus' death had left the guy up a creek, and he was currently looking for a new paddle.

Me.

He'd lost one senatorial protector, and now he wanted another, and Ray had been shopping me around like a side of beef.

I'd have had something to say about that, but Olga's ears had perked up at the first mention of smugglers, and she'd started looking the place up on her phone. I hadn't gotten interested until she pulled up a photo of the flirty twosome up there, in all their neon glory. Who, to a dazed, frightened, and confused little kid, might have looked like a couple of—

"Fish," Olga said, staring at them.

"Yeah."

At least, that was her theory. One she'd acquired after spending all day on the phone with everyone on her late

husband's contact list, in the not-entirely-legal underworld where he'd once worked, and coming up with
zilch. Nobody knew what "fish, tracks, door" meant, and
nobody cared.

Except for Olga, who'd decided that, on what he believed to be his deathbed, the troll kid had wanted to tell
someone what he'd seen. Like maybe where he'd been
brought in from Faerie? Or where his fellow slaves were
being bought and sold?

Of course, he could have just been raving, and we were
wasting our time. But waiting for him to wake up and
confirm the theory was not going to work for Olga. I'd
come out of my room after changing clothes to see her
through the open door to the boys' room, staring down at
the little troll, flanked by the fey Caedmon had left there
to guard him.

She hadn't said anything, but she hadn't had to. Her
lips had been tight, and her eyes wet. She was wondering
if her nephew had ended up the same way.

And one way or another, she was determined to find out.

So here we were. Being given a wide berth by the beautiful people, I noticed. Which was strange because Olga
and the boys were under glamouries.

Sort of.

I turned to see a knot of tough-looking dudes standing
on the sidewalk, wearing white shirts, dark trousers, and
bandoliers of Bibles, because they were having a hard
time figuring out how to conceal all the extra weapons.

It looked like the boys had learned a thing or two from
last time, and stocked up. I eyed a straining backpack
with grenade-shaped bulges, a couple guitars—one with
a scope on it—and a bike that one of the guys had tucked
under his arm and which could be anything, anything at
all. Except a bicycle, presumably.

"Okay. We're absolutely, positively clear on the
no-snacking-on-the-witnesses thing, right?" I said.

Olga looked offended.

"Okay. No snacking until after I've questioned them."

She nodded. Apparently, this was an acceptable compromise. I waited while she explained things to the posse
so they'd actually listen. As a member of the Senate's task

force on smuggling, I was technically in charge of this little squad, but I was pretty sure I was the only one who thought so.

Except for the second valet, who was standing off to the side, and did not appear enraptured with our remaining ride.

"You, uh, you're gonna have to move that," he told me, staring at the deep ridges in the road that had been left by the truck, part of which appeared to have been dragging the ground. Probably the part that was now on fire. Or maybe that was just the oil leaking out of the smoking engine and filling the ridges.

"Seriously," he said, getting in front of the group as they started to move away from the curb. "I'm gonna need you to—"

He cut off when a dozen "Bibles" were suddenly thrust in his face.

He blinked. "What are you guys? Gideons?"

And then a third valet came running over, dressed like the other two except for a maroon sports coat that he was stuffing full of crisp new hundred-dollar bills. "Get in the truck," he told the other guy.

"*That* truck?" Valet Number Two looked at him like he might be crazy. "Are you high?"

"No, but you're going to be off the schedule for a week if you don't get your ass in gear."

"I'm not getting in there! It's a fire hazard!"

"That was not a request."

"Look at it! It's not even a real thing. It's like . . . it's like . . ."

"Frankentruck?" I offered.

"Yeah! Like that! Where the hell am I supposed to—"

He broke off for the second time, when a fan of fat bills appeared in front of his face, like magic. His eyes crossed; my own narrowed. Not at the bills, but at who was holding them. And then smirking slightly when they disappeared, into the pocket of the khakis now clambering into the truck's wonky cab.

A moment later, Frankentruck went belching and burning around a corner and I was left staring down with Louis-Cesare.

"We could have handled that," I pointed out.

"But why waste time?" Tonight he was in a green pullover that looked knitted, but shone like silk. It changed his hair almost to red and his eyes to aquamarine, the same startling hue as his father's, which wasn't fair. Like the jeans, which fit him like a glove but didn't fit the old-world bow he managed to execute flawlessly.

I scowled at him.

"I went to the house," Louis-Cesare said. "I was informed you were here."

"So you decided to stalk me?"

An eyebrow raised.

"I decided to see the show. I hear it is quite something."

The words were mild, but there was a definite challenge in those blue eyes. He knew we weren't here to see the damned show. Any more than he was.

To be here already, he'd have had to be awake well before sunset. And while a master at Louis-Cesare's level was perfectly capable of daywalking, it was still unpleasant. Not to mention burning through power like nobody's business. There was absolutely no reason for him to have been up and about that early.

Except the obvious.

"And it had to be tonight."

"Is there a reason it shouldn't be?"

Yeah. A whole list of them. Which I might have enumerated, except Olga took that moment to step heavily on my foot. And heavily for a troll is no joke. I gasped; she simpered.

"Good show. You come."

Louis-Cesare smiled at her, and kissed the hand she regally extended. "What an excellent idea. I'd be delighted."

And so the whole sorry lot of us went to see the show.

Chapter Twenty-three

Ray went to see his buddy, and the rest of us went to get tickets. Olga splashed out on box seats, probably because the Mormons wouldn't fit in the regular ones. And I guess she wanted to keep an eye on the boys so they didn't get too trigger-happy too soon, so she squashed them all into the same box.

I watched it worriedly.

I hoped it had good struts.

Louis-Cesare and I had the box next door to ourselves. It should have been fairly romantic, with a cute baby chandelier overhead, sparkling like diamonds against rich brocaded wallpaper, the kind of moldings they don't make anymore, gilded and two feet high and carved to within an inch of their lives, and enough red velvet to outfit Olga's entire family. But not under the circumstances.

I shifted a little in my seat, so I could get a better view of the curtain over the stage, which had yet to be pulled back. People were still finding their seats, so I guessed we had a while. Great.

Louis-Cesare came over and sat beside me, so I got up and sat on the front of the box. He's six foot four in his socks, so I didn't get opportunities for a height advantage very often. When I did, I took them.

He didn't say anything, just watched me with curious eyes.

Curious, beautiful eyes, and damn it! I needed to pick a fight, prick that famous pride, get him to go away and stop dogging my footsteps until I could figure out the latest curveball life had chucked at me. Which should have been easy, because fighting with people was what I did best. Except where he was concerned, because he didn't fight fair.

My family got cold and cutting when we fought, like normal, dysfunctional people. We sulked, we avoided one another, and when confronted we lashed out with stuff that had been over for centuries in some cases, because if you're not hitting below the belt, are you really trying?

Louis-Cesare did not.

I wasn't sure if it was the old-fashioned manners, or the fact that he knew it threw me, but he did weirdly unexpected things.

Like reaching over and pulling me into his lap without saying a word.

"Are you planning to give them a show?" I asked, straddling him. A curious troll was peering at us around the wall separating our box from Olga's, his glamourie sliding slightly off center in the process, because it was too small. Leaving him looking like he'd ripped the face off some earnest young man and was wearing it like a mask.

It was kind of horrifying.

"No." The box had plush hangings, which Louis-Cesare reached over and untied one side of, swishing it closed in the troll's face.

It was suddenly darker in here, and cozier, with only half the box still open toward the stage. I didn't know if you were actually supposed to do that, to move the curtains around from their nicely arranged shapes. I'd always assumed that they were just there for show, because it never would have occurred to a peasant like me to try and find out.

Like it wouldn't have occurred to me to bribe the valet instead of just arguing with him for half an hour. Or that golden baksheesh was expected at the consul's court. Or probably a thousand other things, because we didn't live in the same world—we didn't even live in the same *universe*—so what the hell was I doing?

"Are you upset with me?" Louis-Cesare asked, steadying me so that the slippery jumpsuit didn't dump me on the floor.

"No." It came out flat, because it was the truth. I was trying, really hard, to work up a good head of indignation, to call on some of that anger that was probably my foremost character trait, to help me through this. But tonight, when I could have really used it, it wasn't working.

Maybe because I knew him too well.

Despite the bank balance, Louis-Cesare wasn't an overprivileged douchebag, a loser parking his Ferrari in a handicapped zone, because fuck you, that's why. He was an old-fashioned aristocrat who could have coined the term "noblesse oblige," the outdated concept that with wealth and power came a responsibility to help those without, and to fight for something besides just enriching yourself some more. In short, he was a goddamned Disney hero, including the hair, while I . . .

Was not.

And, frankly, his attitude didn't even make sense. Because he *hadn't* been born into privilege. In fact, his background weirdly paralleled Ray's, with a randy father who cut out quick and a mother who didn't die young, but who did abandon him at an early age.

Of course, in his case, the father was a duke and the mother a queen with a reputation to protect, and as far as I knew, he'd always gotten enough to eat. But his meals had been taken in a variety of prisons, where his half brother had locked him away so nobody would find out that their mother got around, and maybe start questioning his own royal parentage. And once Louis-Cesare had finally gotten out, it hadn't been followed by a trip back to the palace where he'd never lived anyway.

Yet you couldn't tell it. He acted like the prince he'd never been, with a casual arrogance that frequently made me want to strangle him, and an overconfidence that made me afraid for him, and an innate goodness that made me want to sit down and have a serious talk with him, because life wasn't a Disney flick. In real life, Prince Charming took a knife in the eye, because he fought fair when nobody else did, and the bad guys won.

That was my reality. Hell, that was everyone's reality, because that was *actual fucking reality*, and yet here he was, acting like none of that was true, none of that could touch him. But it was, and it could; *I* could. Not only wasn't I a Disney hero, part of me wouldn't even have been cast as the villain because she'd scare the crap out of the kiddies.

"You *are* upset," said Mr. Insightful.

"Getting there." And—finally—I was. And it felt good.

Anger was comfortable, familiar, unlike everything else these days. My life had started to feel like a fight against an outsized opponent, where every time you got back to your feet, he hit you again. And back down you went, onto your ass, with the little birdies flapping around your head while you wondered where you were.

And how you got into this.

I sure as hell didn't know how I'd gotten into this. It was like I'd stumbled into some kind of crazy dream, one where I had all these people around me, and a respected job, and a gorgeous boyfriend, and . . . and that wasn't real, that *didn't happen*. Which is why it felt less like a dream, and more like the setup for a nightmare, because I didn't know how this all ended yet, did I?

I felt my hands clench on the thick muscles of Louis-Cesare's shoulders, and wanted . . . what exactly? Reassurance? Life didn't give reassurance. You paid your money and you took your chances, and most of the time, you lost. Like I was going to do, because I didn't deserve—

"I'm frightened, too," Louis-Cesare said suddenly.

I blinked, torn out of my mental battle by whatever the hell that was. "What?"

"I, too, am afraid," he repeated.

I just stared at him. His eyes met mine, hedged by lashes that couldn't decide what color they wanted to be, like his hair. At the moment, both were reddish gold, gilded by a stray beam from outside making it into our little cave. And the eyes themselves were open and honest and vividly blue, because the damned man didn't know you weren't supposed to say things like that.

And then I realized the implication. "I'm not afraid!"

"I think you are."

"Of what?"

"Of this."

The hands on my thighs clenched, and I scowled at him. "I've fooled around before!"

"I'm not talking about that." The disturbing gaze didn't waver. "I feel it, too. I've never been in love—"

"Stop it."

"Why? It's true. I'm in love, and it terrifies me."

"Then why are you here?" It came out harsher than I'd intended, but he didn't flinch.

"Because you're here."

I just stared at him some more; what the hell do you say to that?

"I don't know how to do this," he told me. "I never had the chance to find out. I spent my youth trying to survive. When I finally managed to work my way into a better situation, a stable one, for the first time . . . Christine."

Yeah, irony of ironies, the best catch on the planet had ended up tied to a crazy bitch named Christine, who was even a worse romantic prospect than me. But she'd gotten her claws into him deep, not because he loved her, but because he'd hurt her. To be more exact, she'd been injured, he'd tried to change her into a vampire to save her life, and it hadn't worked. She'd ended up as something called a revenant, a masterless monster that resulted sometimes when a change went wrong, and was supposed to be put down immediately.

But, of course, he hadn't put her down. Instead, he'd kept her around, like a living penance. And, I strongly suspected, because he'd been abandoned by his own Sire, the vampire father who'd left him just as his human parents had done, and he couldn't bring himself to do the same to anyone else. But Christine wasn't a vampire, and she was crazy, and it had all ended about as you'd expect.

"I made many mistakes," he told me quietly. "For a long time, I thought I would end up paying for them forever. Maybe that is why, lately, everything seems so unreal. She is gone and you are here, and I never thought—" He stopped, and his hands clenched again. "I never thought I would have *this*, so I am afraid."

That threw me some more, because it had never occurred to me that Louis-Cesare, of all people, felt anything but confident. He sure as hell never acted anything but confident. Or looked it—

Until now, when there was something in his face I didn't want to acknowledge, especially not with the sword of Damocles hanging over my head.

"You should be," I told him harshly. "I could hurt you. *She* could hurt you. Or worse!"

"And what if she does?"

"What?"

"Or what if I die in the war? Or what if you do? Will being deprived of love for whatever time *le bon Dieu* gives us help in some way?"

I scowled at him, because he still wasn't getting this. "If you're not around Dorina, maybe you won't die at all!"

"And if I am not with you, I will not live at all, not as I have these past months."

I stared at him.

"There are a thousand ways to die," he told me quietly. "There are so few to really live. I would gladly risk the former for the latter, and it is my choice, is it not? To risk whatever I must, my heart, my body, my soul, in order to be with you. Is that not what love is?"

I stared at him some more. And not just because he was doing it again, saying outrageous things that you weren't even supposed to let yourself *think*. But because—

"I don't know. I don't know what it is."

I was never supposed to be asked that question.

Dhampirs were nature's loners, the perfect killing machines, with no friends, no lovers, and no family. And for a long time, that's all I'd been. My own father had rarely talked to me, and my mother had died before I was old enough to remember, so what did I know about family?

But I'd wanted one anyway. Desperately, terribly, no matter how many times I told myself that I couldn't have it. To stop whining and get on with things, and so I had. For a very long time, I had. And just when I got used to that, when I finally started to accept it, when I was actually kind of okay with it—

Fate, or fortune, or the game master up there with the whacked-out sense of humor decided to send me a blue-eyed Disney prince with his heart on his sleeve and words on his lips that I'd never, ever expected to have said to me, and—

And I had no idea what to do with him.

None at all.

"Then let me tell you," he said, pulling me closer so he could murmur in my ear. "Love is sending someone away, because you would rather hurt than hurt them, Love is fighting beside them, bleeding along with them, and putting their well-being above your own. Love is trembling at their touch so much that you do not notice that they are trembling at yours."

"I'm not trembling."

"I am," he whispered, and kissed me.

I kissed him back, because I didn't know what else to do. I never had. From the first time I met him, the only way I'd ever found to deal with him was, well, this.

And it worked pretty well, because he immediately deepened the kiss, one hand sliding under my hair, one remaining on my thigh, gliding up and down the silky fabric. Okay, make that really, really well, and God, this wasn't helping, I thought, biting his lower lip. I was supposed to be pushing him away, not trying to climb down his throat!

Then he groaned and did that thing, that slide-his-hands-down-my-back-to-grip-my-ass thing, and—

What the hell; this fight wasn't going anywhere anyway.

"I never felt fear like when I saw you fall," he murmured, when I paused for breath. "And didn't know if I would be fast enough to reach you—"

"It doesn't matter now."

"It does." He caught my hand, which had gone exploring under that sweater. "I know you don't want me here tonight—I knew before I came."

"Okay." I started working on the jeans, which wasn't as easy as you'd think left-handed.

"You've been independent for so long, it's all you know. I was like that, too. I understand."

"Great. Good to know." The jeans were too tight, especially with him sitting down, and then there was the problem of the damned jumpsuit.

"Can you understand why I couldn't *not* come?"

"Can you just shut up and fuck me?" I gritted out, wishing Radu had sent a dress. Some short little thing that would be easier to—

Screw it.

The jumpsuit ended up on the floor, and I ended up back on his lap, and, oh yeah, that was better, that was perfect.

Damn, I loved the theatre!

Hard hands gripped me, moving over me while also trying to get him out of his own clothes. Which wasn't easy in a chair that wasn't built for two and also had a squeaky spring somewhere inside that was advertising the preshow, not that anybody could see. We were in the top row of boxes, so pretty high up, and the front of the box was fairly tall, and there were no seats on the left of us, where the curtain remained open. Just the stage where some musicians were warming up, but they were in the pit far below.

Squeak, squeak, squeak. Louis-Cesare growled something profane, I laughed, and he rolled us onto the floor.

And, okay, yeah. Better, especially since I'd ended up on top. There was plenty of room in front of the first row of chairs, the plush carpet looked clean, and the dim light filtering in from the theatre was just enough to see by. *Ten/ten, would fuck again,* I thought, and pulled his sweater off.

And stopped halfway, because he'd just caught something in his mouth.

In fairness, it had been swinging in his face, so.

Callused hands slid up my back, pulling me down as he started to suck, sending shivers throughout my body. I didn't have his sweater all the way off. It still trapped his arms, which was nice, which was perfect, I decided.

"You can't get away now," I told him.

I don't recall trying.

"Don't talk with your mouth full."

Mental communication was new to me, mental laughter even more so. And strangely intimate, because I couldn't usually do it with anyone but him. And because it was still echoing in my head when he slid into me.

He was hot and hard and long and thick and *gah*! I

came almost instantly, vibrating before he even started thrusting, with little explosions going off behind my eyes. Like my body had been waiting for this forever; like our whole relationship had been foreplay.

Which was how it felt every time, but something about the trapped vamp and the cozy darkness and the need to be silent and the perfect rhythm that we fell into despite the fact that he couldn't use his hands . . .

Yeah. Oh yeah. Oh God—

His patience broke barely a minute later, and he rolled me over, cursing and fighting with the damned sweater while I laughed and laughed, and while the chair we'd banged into again squeaked and squeaked, and while the musicians below, who had started playing for real now, probably started wondering which of them was making that weird noise—

I bit his shoulder, because it was that or give them a screaming demonstration.

And then Louis-Cesare stopped, and stared around.

"What?" I asked breathlessly. "What is it?"

He swallowed. "We usually get to this point, and your roommate shows up. I believe I've developed a complex."

"Well, Claire's not here." I moved sinuously underneath him, and felt him shudder. "We should come to the theatre more often."

"Or you could move in with me, and we could do this in a bed," he pointed out. "Just for a change."

His eyes were serious, but his head came down, catching my lips again, before I had to answer that, and the mounting rhythm resumed, and damn, it was even better this time. Slow and sweet and hot and—yeah. Might have been wrong about that whole climax thing. Because the shuddering was getting harder, and the fireworks were getting brighter, and I was biting my lip to keep from crying out at every . . . passionate . . . thrust . . . and yeah, oh yeah, right there, *right there*—

The door banged open and someone came in, carrying a tray of something I couldn't see, because I was looking at it from below.

And because the fireworks were in the way.

"Hey, sorry it took so long. The meeting went okay, but

I hadda go down the street for snacks. You wouldn't believe the crap they have at the—oh." Ray peered over the tray, blinking. "Are you guys busy?"

"Out!" Louis-Cesare roared, loud enough to cause the musicians to miss a beat, and flung his nice pullover at Ray. Who didn't have the greatest reflexes, and who promptly spilled a tray of convenience store treats everywhere, including onto us.

Louis-Cesare looked furious and tragic and crushed and half a dozen other things, all in quick succession. I don't know what I looked like, and didn't care. I kicked the door closed, rolled on top of him, and finished what we'd started, complete with cola in my cleavage and Twizzlers in my hair.

'Cause that's what love is.

Chapter Twenty-four

"Well, how was I supposed to know?" Ray said, settling into one of the seats behind us, and handing me some more napkins. "You oughta put a sign on the door. If the balcony's rockin', don't come a knockin'—"

"This isn't a hotel," Louis-Cesare grated out. The mess was cleaned up, and the pullover was back in place, but the hair was still a tousled mess. I grinned at it. And then reached over and tousled it some more. He caught my sticky-with-cola wrist and placed a kiss on it. Ray snorted.

"That's my point. There's hotels all over the city. You two need to get a room—after the show, all right?"

"When's the meeting?" I asked, deciding that I was as clean as I was going to get, despite the fact that the cola had made the jumpsuit cling in all the wrong places. I gave up dabbing at myself with dry napkins and stole some of his Bugles.

"Intermission. Curly said he's got some stuff to do, but'll meet us for drinks."

"Curly?"

"The theatre owner. His real name's Meredith, 'cause I guess his parents hated him. But he goes by Curly, even though he don't have too many anymore." He sat forward. "This oughta be good."

"What ought to be good?" I asked, because they still hadn't raised the curtain.

And then, almost as if they'd heard me, they did, pulling it not up but across, in one huge swish of red velvet.

And I just sat there, a Bugle about to fall out of my suddenly slack mouth. Because that . . . wasn't a stage.

"Okay, oh boy, okay," Ray said, as I took in the sight of a wall of water. It spread over the entire area where the stage should have been, with the bottom disappearing behind the orchestra pit, and giving the impression that it went down a lot farther. With the top and sides hidden by the framework of curtains, it looked like a whole reef had somehow been transported into the theatre. It must have contained millions of gallons. It was *huge*.

Yet that wasn't the weirdest thing about it.

I stared at the setup, which looked like nothing so much as a kid's first aquarium, complete with a bunch of fake-looking plants, some colorful coral, a turreted, backless castle perched on a rocky outcropping, and some bubbles.

But that wasn't the weirdest thing, either.

"Are those . . . What are those?" Louis-Cesare whispered, sitting forward in his seat.

I didn't answer.

I thought it was kind of obvious.

"Huh, huh?" Ray elbowed me as something swirled up out of the darkness. "We're gonna be freaking *rich*."

Yeah, I thought blankly.

Yeah.

The music reached a crescendo, although it was almost drowned out by the audience. Which was on its feet, giving a standing ovation as the cast members arrived, despite the fact that nothing had happened yet. *Sit down,* I thought, annoyed that they were holding up the show.

Until I realized: I was hanging over the side of the box, trying to get a better view, even though I already had what was probably the best in the house.

And was suddenly even better, when one of the "showgirls" paused in the water not twelve feet away from my reaching hand.

For a moment, we just stared at each other.

There was no doubt what she was. But she didn't look anything like the flirty neon cuties on the sign outside. She didn't look like anything I'd ever seen.

"Hey. Hey, get back in here. You're gonna fall," Ray said.

I barely heard him.

The water was dark, or maybe it was just that the lights were pointed at the castle, where something I didn't care about was going on. But it didn't matter. I didn't need it.

She made her own light.

Not like other fey I'd seen, who cast light shadows in our world, how thick and how bright depending on how powerful they were. But like she captured any light that came her way and sent it back in a scintillation of colors. They sparkled off the antenna-like filaments above her eyes, the delicate gills at her neck, and above all, the long, sinuous sweep of iridescent scales beginning just below her waist.

They were completely unlike Claire's. Hers had been lustrous, but thick and hard, like battle armor carved out of semiprecious stones. These were soft and supple, a glide of colors rather than a single hue, the way water takes on the shade of the world around it. I honestly couldn't have said what color she was.

The tail ended in a spreading, translucent, filmy fin, gossamer fine, like the bluish gray hair that ghosted out in the water around her. It was long, maybe two-thirds the length of her body, making her look like she was drifting in a cloud. It was beautiful. She was *beautiful*. . . .

"Dory?" That was Louis-Cesare, because I was up on the side of the box now. It was thick old wood, perfectly capable of supporting my weight. But he had a hand on my leg anyway, probably because of the thirty-foot drop.

Or maybe because I was acting crazy again.

Get down, I told myself, but I didn't get down. I wanted to touch her. I *needed* to—

"Dory!"

His hand tightened on my calf because I'd reached the end of the box and was trying to go farther. But there was no way unless I learned to walk on thin air. I let out a cry of mixed frustration and longing, heard Ray asking Louis-Cesare what the hell was wrong with me, didn't have an answer.

And then I didn't need one, because part of me was able to close that gap, after all.

It was the weirdest sensation, like a film was being pulled off me. I could almost see it, extending out beyond my hand, a ripple in my vision, distorting the darkness. And reaching, reaching, reaching—

The creature beyond the glass or whatever it was seemed to see it, too, or to see something. Because she was pressed against the surface now, her very human hands spread wide across it, allowing me to see the faint weave of skin in between the fingers. Her eyes, likewise, were so human but so strange, larger, slanted, crystalline, with that same noncolor of the scattering of diamond-hued scales that edged them. She looked almost like a statue carved out of crystal, except that she lived and breathed, the gills on the sides of her neck fluttering excitedly because almost, *almost—*

"Dory!"

Louis-Cesare pulled me back, right before I would have taken a headfirst plunge into darkness, but he didn't get all of me. Something went careening out into the theatre, flowing over the heads of an audience who never noticed, if they even could have, being too intent on the assault on the castle that some of the creatures were pantomiming. And then came curving back, through air and glass both, into dark water and luminous, crystal eyes.

Tell me.

And she did.

————

Darting out into the lobby, pushing through a ward over the stairs that crackled and hissed, going down, down, down, two stories, three, five. Out into a hallway with three doors, two normal ones on either side, and a metal submarine-type straight ahead. Some security guards in an office, through the door to the left, watching a row of TV monitors.

"What the hell is she doing?" one demanded.

Another man, leaning over his shoulder: "Dunno. Fucking vampires."

"I think she's a dhampir—"

"Same thing. They're all crazy." He made an annoyed sound. *"Better call the boss."*

Getting tired; couldn't hold free flight much longer. Luckily, two guards were leaving the office. I grabbed one lightly, just enough contact to steady me. Then we were through the metal door, and into a corridor that looked like it was literally on a submarine. There was a narrow strip down the middle of rubberized flooring, and large portholes on either side, looking out onto a huge holding tank.

"I don't like it in here. It's creepy," my guard said. He was younger than the other, tall and thin with an obvious Adam's apple that kept bobbing up and down.

And then stopped, arrested like his breath, at a flash of iridescent green outside one of the portholes.

It was gone in an instant, before I had time to more than glimpse it. Then it reappeared on the other side, hesitating long enough for the young guard to notice. Along with a glimpse of yellow, alien eyes.

He stumbled back, swallowing a cry, and the other guard grinned.

"Aw, it looks like Fairfax likes you."

"F-fairfax?"

"One of the girls in the office named him. Means 'beautiful hair,' or some shit." He shook his head. *"Women."*

"Women," the younger guard agreed, and laughed nervously.

And then screamed and jumped back when something slammed into the metal wall, right beside him.

"Relax, kid. He does that all the time. It's why they don't let him upstairs no more; wouldn't keep on script. Just kept ramming the ward, like he was tryin' to take it down." The older guard grinned evilly. *"Or maybe eat the audience."*

The younger man didn't look like he thought that was funny.

"Could he do that?" he asked, staring around.

"Naw. Redundant system. Got a control upstairs as well as down. You're safe enough."

The older guard started working to get the door at the end of the hallway open, while the younger continued to *stare around. But Fairfax was nowhere to be seen. After a moment, my guard visibly relaxed—*

Until strange sounds started emanating from portholes up and down the corridor, making him jump. They were impossible to describe in any human tongue, because they weren't made by a human tongue. Just strange, underwater sounds, loud and disorienting, causing the young guard to reach for weapons he couldn't use.

"Would you calm the hell down?" the other guard demanded.

"Would you hurry up? I didn't sign on for this!"

"You signed on for exactly this, and stop letting him get to you. It'll only encourage him, and he's bad enough as it is. Be on the pile already, if he wasn't such a good breed—ah. Here we go."

The door gave way, and we were through, into a medium-sized, dimly lit room with curved sides, one of which was made almost entirely out of glass. Or perhaps a transparent ward, considering what the pressure had to be down here. The other walls were piled high with wooden crates, to the ceiling in some cases, along with something on a table, desiccated and dry. A few brown, curled-up bits, like withered leaves, floated to the floor from the disturbance of our entry.

And then Fairfax reappeared out of the murky depths, to throw himself at the ward, battering it with his body so furiously that even the older guard flinched.

"See? I told you so!" That was a short, overweight man with shirtsleeves rolled up and sweat on his brow. I thought he might be the "Curly" my twin's friend had mentioned. He was bald, but had a rim of little blond curls around his head that flipped up instead of down, making him look like he was wearing a hat without the hat.

There was another person with him, a man, judging by the height, but I couldn't see him well. They were standing directly under a recessed light, which gilded Curly's brim of golden curls and danced in his blue eyes, yet the shadows gathered around the other man so thickly that the light couldn't penetrate. A mage, then, cloaking himself for some reason I didn't understand. Surely everyone knew him here?

Curly, if that was who the other man was, certainly seemed to, and was vibrating with irritation. "You can't just come in here and do things like this!" he snapped. "I know how they are, and how to handle them; you don't!"

"It's working so far." The other man's voice matched his appearance: low, with a deliberate rasp that hid its true inflection.

"Does that look like it's working?" Curly demanded, pointing at Fairfax. The powerful tail was churning up the water, the humanoid torso was beating at the barrier with both hands, and the strange, alien eyes were staring, staring, staring—but not at any of us. But at . . .

The girl.

Because that was what was on the table, I realized: not a clump of browned, shriveled-up seaweed, as I'd first thought, but a child. A tiny thing, shorter than the table she lay on. And almost completely unlike the beautiful creature upstairs, who was suddenly animated, too.

I could see her dimly, through my twin's eyes. As well as the scenes she was feeding us through the link. It was her child, and she was deathly afraid, her child, and they planned to—

I flinched, and almost lost my hold on the guard, pain searing through me as it did the female and Fairfax, the child's father. They were punishing him for leading a revolt. For encouraging the others to refuse to play out the pantomimes set for them until their children were freed.

Instead, he was watching his own child wither in air breathable for his people, but in dryness that was toxic over time. The delicate membranes that made up their bodies could not afford to dry out. It would kill her; it was killing her.

"You're too soft with them," the other man said, and looked at the older guard. "Show him what defiance costs."

The man hurried to the wall and slammed his fist down on a button. A high-pitched sound resonated through the room, barely audible to the guard I was riding, but Fairfax screamed, an almost human sound. And writhed in apparent agony on the other side of the ward.

"I said cut it out!" Curly snapped, and knocked the guard's hand away. "You don't take orders from him!"

The guard just stood there, looking nonplussed.

"What are you two doing in here, anyway?" Curly demanded.

"Uh, there's a problem with the show."

The older guard clicked his fingers at the younger one, who walked over and handed a tablet to Curly. It showed the security feed of my twin, along with the entire cast. Every one of whom was now clustered on her side of the stage, the murmuring audience forgotten. I watched the scene through the guard's eyes, and then through my twin's, who was staring into the desperate, pleading face of the mother.

She couldn't understand her, I realized. There was a connection, but she didn't know what to do with it. She knew the creatures wanted something, could feel it like a palpable thing, but she didn't speak their language.

She didn't realize; she didn't need to.

I sent the mother images: the room with the watery window, Fairfax thrashing frantically against the glass, the girl on the table, shrunken and brown. And then emotions, which are the same in any language: despair, need, hope, question?

The mother didn't nod; that gesture didn't exist in her culture. But her hands were suddenly scrambling against the barrier, clawing at it as if she were trying to break through.

Images flashed across my mind. Girl, she showed me. Water, she showed me. Swim.

I tamped down my frustration. Yes, we needed to get her to water, but how?

"What the hell? What's she doing?" Curly asked, staring at the tablet.

The older guard shrugged. "You know vampires. They're all crazy—"

"Give it to me," the taller man said, coming closer. I still couldn't see him well, but there was something familiar about the voice. Something not from my mind, but from my twin's. Something I couldn't place, because he was yelling. "The Basarab girl! You fool!"

I quickly sent the creature an image of the ward over

the tank, strong and thick. It hadn't so much as wavered under Fairfax's relentless attack, and the avatar I was riding was human. Even assuming he was a mage, and that I could force an assault, he didn't have the power to break through. Wards like that were made to withstand a prolonged siege by numerous mages, and I could ride but one at a time.

How? *I showed her an image of the wall breaking, over and over.* How, how, how?

I felt the question fly through the link, saw the female's excitement when she finally understood, heard the answer forming in her mind—

The tablet hit Curly on his bald head, sending him staggering back. The older guard just stood there, looking back and forth between the two men, obviously not sure what to do. And then not having to worry about it when the taller man grabbed him. "Kill her!"

"What?" *Curly grabbed the guard, too, before the man could move, and whirled on his partner.* "Are you crazy?"

"She's a danger—"

"So is killing a senator under my roof! You have any idea how much hell that would rain down on me? And I need her—"

"She's on the task force designed to shut you down!"

"So was Geminus! And she's willing to deal. I have it on good authority—"

"She lied! I've dealt with this bitch before." *He turned to the guard.* "Kill her! Take everyone you have—"

"Remember who pays your salary," *Curly snapped.*

"If you need protection, you come to me," *the taller man said, bending over Curly menacingly.* "We have a deal—"

"No!" *The little fat man had clearly had enough.* "I had a deal with Geminus. One I stupidly agreed to continue with that albino bastard, because he said he was in charge after the big guy's death. But he kept screwing with the deal, and now you—who the hell are you?"

"The one in charge."

"Not here! This is *my* place, and I don't need you anymore. I made a deal for a new protector, and one better connected than you! I don't need any—"

The tall man's arm moved, as quick as a vampire's, and the next second Curly was hitting the wall on the other side of the room, unconscious or worse.

The guards just stood there, their eyes huge.

"I said kill her!" the man hissed. "Or you're next!"

They ran.

Chapter Twenty-five

I woke up to find myself in Olga's box, wrestling a Mormon for his bicycle.

I wrenched the thing away from a pleasant-looking older man with a kindly, concerned face and angry little troll eyes that glittered at me from behind the mask. Then swung it toward the stage like a puppet on a string, with no intention of doing any such thing. But I couldn't seem to control my actions, like I couldn't seem to see properly. The theatre slurred along with me, a wash of brilliant reds, gleaming golds, and glittering jewel tones from the women's clothes, interspersed with more somber smears of the men's.

Somber smears that were suddenly running for the exits, climbing over people, and elbowing others out of the way, chivalry be damned, because spell fire and gunfire had just erupted from below.

People started screaming, which didn't help my head, and neither did the bullets strafing the box. Everyone ducked, including me, although I hadn't told myself to do so. But I hit the floor anyway, cursing silently because I also couldn't seem to speak!

Dorina, I thought furiously. *What are you doing?*

No response.

Give me my body back!

The lack-of-response thing continued, and I remained flopped on the ground, unable to move. But I could hear: people screaming, glass shattering, bullets firing in the distance, or striking like hammer blows against the wooden front of the box. And I could smell: spilled alcohol from someone's glass, acrid gunpowder as the trolls began firing back, and buttery popcorn that had been trampled underfoot.

I could even see a little better, down in the gloom, and realized that my eyesight problems were from double vision: I was seeing both here in the box and wherever Dorina was, some dim room with strange, underwater light crawling up the walls. That other room kept throwing shadows over this one, distorting it, but it couldn't cast shadows on the dark. And then somebody shot out a sconce by the door, which made things even better.

Enough that I could see Olga's jewelry jump off her neck and onto a guard's face, like something out of *Alien*, sending him staggering back—

Into a dozen more, headed through the door.

Curly's boys were mages, and a few even seemed to be pretty good ones. But the fey have a partial resistance to human magic, and the guards didn't look like their hearts were in the fight. Especially after a few Hulk smashes around the box by some of the larger trolls. Had it been just them, they'd have run in seconds.

But it wasn't just them.

"The *fuck*?" Ray yelled, as a vampire leapt over the front of his box and tried to wrench his head off.

He and his attacker disappeared from view, hidden by the wall that separated the two boxes, but only for a moment. A mage was getting choked out on this side and started wildly throwing spells. One set the curtains on fire, another hit a couple vampires that had been leaping for us from the theatre floor, sending them flipping backward into darkness, and a third slammed through the partition, obliterating most of it.

That left Louis-Cesare staring at me through the burning wreckage, a vampire under each arm and his hair alight.

"You're on *fire*!" I yelled, because vamps had the flammability of kerosene-soaked rags.

And then I realized that I'd just said that aloud.

I jumped back to my feet, staring around in confusion, because I was suddenly back in charge of my body and I didn't know why.

Then I noticed: those few vamps had been merely the vanguard—of a legion. They were leaping up from the floor of the theatre, despite the fact that we were two stories high, and crawling over the fronts of the boxes like humanoid spiders. Dozens of them.

The first group had mostly avoided our box because of the crazed mage. But he'd gotten thrown over the side, and now they had a clear field. And even trolls couldn't fight with no blood in their bodies.

As several demonstrated almost before I'd finished the thought, huge living boulders suddenly falling to their knees. And to drain a fey that fast, we weren't talking rank and file here. We were talking—

"Masters!" Ray screamed.

Shit.

The only good thing was that the destroyed wall had left a mass of flaming bits lying around. Shards and splinters of old hardwood, still burning merrily, including on a sheet of paneling directly in front of me. And then in the air after I picked it up and flung it with everything I had at the approaching lineup.

The weight of the slab knocked several of them off the box, the burning shrapnel set more alight and one piece caught a guy straight through the heart. He wouldn't die—his head was intact—but he was out for the count. Unlike several others, including one blond-haired master who I danced with all across the box, weaving in and out of the battle going on inside, and stabbing him three different times while he tried to drain me.

But you need line of sight for that, and I kept dodging behind trolls. I finally saw an opening, slashed hard across his throat then stabbed directly downward. I was using a wooden shard, not a knife, so that should have been it. But he dodged at the last second, so the blow missed the heart. And then, with an elegant somersault backward into the darkness, he was gone.

I leaned over the edge of the box, panting and lightheaded, with a snarl on my lips, because I don't let prey walk away! But he was nowhere to be seen. But something else was. I realized I was wreathed in a faint yellowish green glow, spreading out from where the master had just been.

Geminus' family aura, Louis-Cesare confirmed, before I could ask. I was still getting used to seeing auras, the power signatures all vamps gave off that told their family histories at a glance. They'd been invisible before the wall fell in my head, because the skill for seeing them was on Dorina's side of the brain. But now I could—

And this one made no sense at all.

Why? Louis-Cesare asked. *Geminus' family was huge. The Senate thought they killed all of his masters who were involved with the smuggling trade, but it's reasonable that they missed a few.*

This isn't a few! And Curly just said—

But I didn't have time to go into what Curly had said. Because the next wave was about to hit, with mages as well as vamps. And these didn't look like the pansy-ass guards.

The mages couldn't jump two stories like the vamps, but that didn't seem to be slowing them down any. They threw glimmering strands of magic at the top of Louis-Cesare's box, where they clung like Spidey's web—and acted like it, too. A ripple of white light tore through them, they abruptly tightened, and the mages went flying through the air like they were riding huge rubber bands.

Allowing them to hit Louis-Cesare with half a dozen spells, all at once.

I felt my heart stop, because even a master could go down under something like that. But the spells didn't seem to work. They hit, but he didn't so much as flinch, and nothing happened.

Except that the wounds he'd been healing suddenly started seeping again.

That included a large gash across his stomach that he'd closed so fast it hadn't even had time to stain his shirt. It was staining it now, in a bright red flood that made my heart clench, even before I started to run. And found that my legs had other ideas.

No! Damn it, let me go! But Dorina didn't listen. Instead, she threw me back at the wall, where the bicycle was propped up on its little kickstand, the shiny blue and silver paint job reflecting the fighting and the fire and my desperate face.

Because antihealing spells were a bitch. They'd make a human bleed like a hemophiliac until he bled out, and even for a vamp, they could be deadly. They wouldn't kill you themselves, but they'd slow your healing down enough that an obliging enemy could do it for them. I didn't know how badly they'd affect a first-level master, but it was safe to say that the field had just gotten a lot more level.

But I couldn't do anything about it, because I was busy playing with the damned bike!

My hands moved expertly over it, without any input from me, while Louis-Cesare began ripping chairs from the floor and throwing them and everything else he could find at the mages. It seemed to be working. Half of them were knocked over the side, with several getting tangled in their own safety nets, like butterflies trapped in cocoons. And the rest couldn't seem to dodge and also concentrate well enough to throw a spell. But it left him unable to help Ray.

Who looked like he needed it.

A high-level master was holding Ray's hands immobilized over his head with one of his own. He'd forced the smaller vamp to his knees with a little smirk, but hadn't thought to turn him around. Probably assuming that Ray was too weak to bother with such precautions, because most guys at his level would have been.

Ray wasn't most guys.

He didn't bother trying to break the hold, which probably wouldn't have worked anyway. He just popped some fang and went straight for something below the guy's belt. And a vamp's bite is kind of like a crocodile's; getting one to release when he doesn't want to is no freaking joke.

Which probably explains why the guy turned purple and threw up. And why Ray was able to break his hold, rip his throat open, and then flip him over the balcony. He saw me looking and spread his hands.

"Huh? Huh?"

I didn't say anything, because I couldn't, and because somebody on this side was trying to stab me in the eye. Only to find something suddenly sticking out of his own. The mage fell over, a shocked look on what was left of his face, and I stared upward—at Olga, wrenching a long, skinny blade out of his head, in order to whirl around and slash it through the belly of someone else.

Red splattered and she roared, standing over me with a bloodied sword like a modern-day Boudicca. The sound was echoed by the trolls still in the box and the ones in the corridor outside, where a major battle had broken out. And then everybody went running for the door, because our box was temporarily clear.

Everybody except me.

I looked down to see that the bike's wheels and handlebars had been taken off, along with various other bits. But the strangely thick center piece was still there, now a fat tube bigger than any bike could possibly need for support. And with a little scope that popped up from the base.

Shit. I tried to cry out, to tell someone that something very bad was about to happen, but my tongue refused to form the words. And even if it hadn't, I doubted I'd have been heard over the screaming, which had reached highest-hill-on-the-roller-coaster levels, and the continued gunfire, and the *bam, bam, crunch* of a troll smacking somebody against the floor and walls and possibly ceiling outside.

Meanwhile, I was getting back to my feet and moving to a central position in the box. And resting the no-longer-bicycle on my shoulder, aiming for the bright gold crest over top of the stage. And screaming in my head, because I still didn't know why.

Redundant system. Got a control upstairs as well as down, echoed in my thoughts.

Shit, shit, shit!

The only good thing was that the former bicycle was damned hard to steady, with the whole theatre now in mass-exodus mode, with enough pounding feet below to shake the box up above.

Or maybe that was the shaft of orange light that suddenly speared upward, shattering the boards in front of me and throwing me back against the wall. Along with the remaining chairs, the mountain of debris, and the cute baby chandelier that had been glittering overhead. And was now in pieces raining down everywhere.

I wasn't in pieces, but I hit hard. Hard enough to force

all the breath out of my lungs, and to leave me gasping like a beached fish. Hard enough to ruin Radu's couture with wooden splinters, some as big as knitting needles, suddenly sticking out of it. Almost hard enough to knock the bazooka from my suddenly numb hands.

Almost.

I snarled and lurched back to my feet, and swung the RPG launcher up at the same time. Louis-Cesare was throwing three more vamps off the balcony and elbowing a mage in the face without even turning around. Because he was looking at me.

He opened his mouth to say something, probably to ask, *What the hell?*—which yeah. *Let me know when you find out,* I thought. But then he caught something out of the corner of his eye, and his expression changed.

"Get down!" he yelled. "Get—"

What looked like a bunch of fifty-caliber rounds cut him off, strafing us from a box on the other side of the theatre. They ripped through the old hardwood like it was nothing, tore through the shoulder of a troll in the doorway, sending him staggering back into the hall. And would have torn through me—

Except that Louis-Cesare had just leapt from the neighboring box, taking a whole line of tank-killing rounds while knocking me out of the way.

I hit the floor with him on top, the once-perfect body a mangled piece of red flesh and white bone and—

I tried to scream, horror washing over me along with his blood. But my voice wasn't under my control any more than my body. My head was already turning back toward the stage, my hands were pulling the bloody weapon out from under him, and my eyes were fixing back on target.

What are you doing? I yelled at Dorina. *What the* fuck—

"That."

I felt my lips form the word, but nobody heard. Including me, because I'd just fired a rocket launcher, and didn't have hearing protection. The resulting sound was so loud that, for a second, everything went absolutely quiet and almost still.

I could see blood droplets, flaming splinters, and a lone

crystal from the chandelier, thrown back into space by the impact of the bullets, lazily turning. I could feel the sparks that edged the shell as it blasted out of the end of the weapon, glittering brightly in the gloom. I could trace the thin trail of smoke as it tore across the room—

Just as a magical grenade was palmed and primed and thrown downstairs, all in one swift gesture by another pair of hands.

Two explosions ripped across my vision; two redundant systems failed simultaneously. And the beautiful crystalline creatures dove as one, so fast that I barely saw them move before they were gone. Down, down, down to a flooding room lit by a spiral of light, where a portal's maw had opened, spearing bright yellow beams through the floating debris.

I watched them through Dorina's eyes as they poured through the portal, moving like quicksilver, visible only because of the silhouettes they cast against the light. And they weren't the only things. The huge tank was emptying after them, its contents falling down the portal's maw like water down a drain. Along with the body of the older guard, the floating crates, and the now-empty table, just a square of darkness against the portal's light before it was swept away on a rushing tide of water.

But not enough of it.

Because it wasn't just the wards below that had been taken out. I stared through drifting smoke at the great energy field over the stage, which a second ago had been hard as a rock and slick as glass. And which was now bucking and bowing and shimmering and—

"Get *back*!" I yelled—uselessly.

Because the next second, the ward shuddered and shook and broke, loosing the entire wall of water to come crashing down, all at once. And it looked like it had gone up higher than the curtains as well as deeper, because the heavy red velvet pieces went shooting off into the flood, ripped away by the force of the tsunami that had just been unleashed, right on top of us.

The wave slammed over the balcony, but I couldn't hear it. Couldn't hear anything but the echo of the gun blending with the roar of the water until everything was sound. Like everything was suddenly cold and dark and liquid.

Well, almost everything.

Because Dorina's hold over me had shattered along with the explosions. And as soon as it did I dove for the floor and Louis-Cesare, grabbing him right before the water hit, and clinging as we were swept over the balcony. And out into the room, falling half in water and half in air, before hitting the floor the same way.

Then the rest of the wave came down and tried to drown us.

I grabbed the only thing I could reach—a flat piece of wood that might have been flooring, because it wasn't three inches thick—and held on. The great wave sloshed forward and then back, preparing for another surge this way, and I shoved Louis-Cesare onto the slab and braced over top of him. It was almost the same position I'd occupied earlier, under very different circumstances.

And then we were thrown forward again, the current propelling us and a dozen other stragglers up the incline, through the theatre doors, and across the ruined lobby. Where some ended up slammed into the wall, but not us. Louis-Cesare and I went shooting forward, straight out the front doors and into the street, on a swell big enough to surf on, which was practically what we were doing.

Until I looked up and saw a big white delivery truck and—

Chapter Twenty-six

"Augghhh!"

I screamed and sat up, staring around wildly.

At a darkened room.

My room, I realized, recognizing the mural on the far wall, splashed with moonlight.

And my bed, where I was lying next to—

There were running feet, a door crashing open, and a light flicking on, but I barely noticed. Because Louis-Cesare was beside me, and he was all right. He was all right!

Only, he wasn't. He was out cold, in a healing trance, the kind vamps fall into when they need all their strength focused on repairing catastrophic damage. Damage I could still see in ridges and ripples of flesh, healed over but not yet smoothed out, what seemed like everywhere.

There was a huge indentation over his heart, with new, pink skin puckered and drawn around it. Another where his belly button should have been, except that it had been carved anew by hot metal, embedded pieces of which still ringed the crater the bullet had left. I pushed back the duvet and found a third wound in his thigh, angry and red and seeping into the bandage I pulled away.

It looked like a shark had taken a bite out of him.

There were other wounds, too, smaller but still visible, because a vampire's body isn't like a human's. It prioritizes healing, putting the most dangerous wounds first. So the little lesions, which should have been closed in an instant, hadn't been, because he'd needed, because he'd almost, because—

"Dory?"

There were other people here now, and he was naked. I should have been covering him back up, but I wasn't. I was pulling him into my arms, crying and making sounds that weren't screams, but weren't not screams, either. And staring at the wall, my wall, which should have been comforting but wasn't, because one of those shots had taken his heart. It had taken his *heart*, and if another had torn through his neck, or if a piece of shrapnel had—

"Dory. Dory, take this," someone was saying, and trying to give me a cup of some hideous-smelling concoction.

I didn't take it. I held on instead, rocking him slightly, I didn't know why. Maybe to comfort him, although he didn't know it. Maybe to comfort me. While a litany of *no, no, no* rang in my head, and may have come out of my mouth, but I couldn't tell, didn't care. Because he wouldn't have suffered all that except for me, because he could have dodged any of those things but for me, because he deliberately—and I couldn't—I *wouldn't*—

"Dory!"

Someone snapped their fingers in front of my face, loud enough to make me blink.

It was Olga. I looked up to see her bending over the two of us, her hair in a mess. She had on a baby blue robe over a floral nightgown; I don't know why I noticed that. She took my head between her hands—giant, strong, strangely comforting hands—and looked into my eyes.

"He survive. You survive. It *over*."

But she was wrong. It wasn't over. I'd almost gotten him killed, and it wasn't over at all.

"Olga, can you?"

That was Claire, passing her the horrible brew. Which Olga fed me like I was a baby. It tasted as awful as it smelled, and was a complete waste of time because it didn't do a damned—

The next time I woke up, the sun was shining through the curtains and Louis-Cesare was gone. For a moment, I just stared at the indentation in the mattress, at sheets that still held the scent of his body, at faint traces of blood on the duvet. And then I was up and running for the door, and bursting out into the hall—

Where Gessa was playing with the boys on the sunny boards of the landing.

I stared at them. There were blankets and toys and a large, pinkish bear that had now lost both ears but otherwise seemed to be holding up. It was regarding me quizzically, like everyone else.

I swallowed, and just stood there, swaying for a moment. "Where—"

"He fine," Gessa told me. "He go talk to Senate. He said tell you."

I swallowed again. "Okay."

Stinky came over and offered me a cookie. It was half-eaten and the rest was seriously slobbered on. He was badly in need of braces—if his adult teeth ever finished coming in—and he drooled a lot.

"Thanks. I'm okay," I told him, and went back into the bedroom.

I was not okay. I looked down to see that my hands were shaking, which was absurd. I sat down on the bed, but all I could see were bloodstained sheets. All I could hear was the sound of those bullets hitting flesh. And tearing and rending and—

My breath started coming faster, and I wondered if this was what a panic attack felt like. I didn't know because I'd never had one. Dhampirs didn't. Of course, dhampirs didn't have friends or families or children or—

I got up and went to the bathroom.

My face in the mirror looked like a stranger's: gaunt and dead white except for the burning, half-golden tint of my eyes. They looked like my father's, when he was calling up power. They looked alien.

They looked like *hers.*

I cut that thought off hard. I didn't want to think about her right now. How she'd taken over my body, and forced me to follow her commands, instead of helping him. Together, Louis-Cesare and I could have laid waste; together we could have cleared the fucking *room.* Instead—

I saw my lip curl, showing fang. I wanted to put a fist through the mirror. I wanted—

To look at something else, I told myself harshly. *Before you give her even more control! Calm down!*

I didn't calm down, but I did look away. And let my eyes roam over the bathroom, but that didn't seem to help. Couldn't think; didn't know why I'd come in here.

Until I bent over the sink, to splash some water on my face, and my ribs screamed at me.

Oh.

That was why.

I peeled off the baggy sweatpants and T-shirt someone had put on me, and checked out the damage.

The slinky jumpsuit had provided zero protection, but Louis-Cesare had drawn most of the fire and I'd been surrounded by troll. The worst I'd suffered was a bunch of weird, round bruises, peppering my stomach and thighs, from the porcupine-quill-like shrapnel thrown up by the destroyed floor. They were puffy and sore, with an angry red eye in the middle of each one. My ribs were also pissed off again, I was stiff as hell, and I felt uncharacteristically weak from the blood loss. But it could have been worse.

It could have been a lot worse.

I sat on the side of the tub and put my head in my hands.

I felt like shit, but it wasn't physical. I'd fought in worse shape than this—way worse. But I'd never *hurt* like this.

He's okay, I told myself. *What is wrong with you? Get up, get dressed, get busy! You only have about a thousand things to do!*

I didn't get up. And I already felt busy, like my head was sucking up all my strength, trying to sort out a mess that couldn't be sorted. I didn't have the skill set for this. I didn't even know where to start. My thoughts just went round and round, until they made me dizzy, until they made me want to throw up.

If we hadn't been attacked so ferociously, and thereby held up, would Dorina have drowned a theatre full of people? Would she have pressed that trigger if they'd still been inside? I didn't know.

Like I didn't know how well she'd been following the fight. With her mind literally elsewhere, had she realized how much danger she'd put us in? Did she care?

Or was she confident that she could get me—and therefore herself—out of there, and fuck everyone else? She'd saved the fey, people she didn't even know, but what about the people *I* knew? What about Olga and Ray and—

If Louis-Cesare was anyone else, he'd be dead right now.

The thought intruded on my mental battle, loud and clanging, like a cymbal dropped on concrete. It made logical thought impossible, because every time I tried, there it was again, resonating. Over and over, louder and louder, that moment when he'd pushed me out of the way stuck on repeat in perfect clarity.

I could see the brilliant crimson of his blood, brighter than the acres of curtains; could feel the warm stickiness hitting me in great bursts; could smell it in the air, partially vaporized by the force of the bullets, and rich with power he could no longer use. Shook again as I hit the floor of the box, sliding painfully into the hard wood of the side, unable to stop with his weight on top of me. Felt her throw him off and jerk the weapon out from under him, like it was nothing, like he didn't matter.

Because, to her, he didn't.

I finally got up and took a shower. The water hurt the bruises, but it was a familiar, burning ache, almost comforting. I knew how to bleed; I knew how to heal. But this . . . I didn't know how to do this.

The hot water ran out before I was finished, because we only had about a thousand people taking showers these days. I rinsed in cold, got out, dried off, and put on some clean sweats. I thought about combing out my hair, but it didn't seem important. Neither did the hunger clawing in my belly, the ever-present cost of a dhampir's metabolism. I felt it; I just didn't care.

I wanted to call somebody, to report what I'd seen, but Louis-Cesare was already doing that. The only thing he didn't know was what Dorina had overheard in that underwater room, but that seemed . . . really unlikely. The mage had told Curly that he was in charge, and it had sounded like he was talking about Geminus' family. Only vampire families didn't work like that.

Like really didn't.

Vampires thought of themselves as a breed apart, better, smarter, longer-lived—basically an evolved sort of human. *Homo superior*, I'd heard one say once, and he hadn't been joking. To take orders from a regular old garden-variety human, even a magical one, would be like . . .

Well, like your dog walking you.

It just didn't happen.

And then there was the fact that what I'd heard, or thought I'd heard, had come from Dorina. She'd been riding that guard; she'd heard what was said, not me. So this was secondhand information, filtered through a wobbly link, and from a source I didn't entirely—

Goddamn it!

I'd twisted wrong, picking up a dropped towel, and pain ripped through me. I stood there, panting by the sink for a moment, tamping down a desire to rip it out of the wall. *Screw it.* I couldn't do this right now. Like I couldn't heal if I didn't eat.

I threw the damned towel in the bathtub and headed out the door.

And almost tripped over some fey drinking coffee.

I must have been in the bath longer than I'd thought, because Gessa and the boys had moved on. The fey were in their place, looking like they were taking a break from whatever fresh hell Claire had been putting them through. And eating their version of biscotti, with big mugs of steaming-hot brew.

Or, at least, they were until I showed up, when they abruptly scrambled to their feet.

Okay, that was . . . different.

Because another thing the fey didn't do was to give a shit about their dhampir housemate. They'd always treated me as something between a high-ranking servant—because I traded protection for rent—and a friend of Claire's. Which meant that I was well below them in the household hierarchy, but also not theirs to order around. That had worked out, leaving us on a casual, vaguely friendly footing, with no obligations either way.

Including whatever the heck this was.

"Good coffee?" I finally asked, when the silence stretched a little long.

"You need more," one of them said, holding up his mug, which was the size of a soup bowl. And had another elbow him in the ribs.

"I thought you guys didn't like it."

"We're trying to acclimatize ourselves to your strange Earth foodstuffs," a second one said, but he wasn't looking at me. He was looking at another tall, well-built blond, a carbon copy of all the rest except for his expression.

His expression was . . . well, shit.

"Is there a problem?" I asked, because clearly.

There was no answer. But the stare-down continued—why, I didn't know. I'd spent the day *sleeping*. Pissing off somebody while unconscious was a new one, even for me.

"Reiðarr," a taller fey said, and put a hand on the angry one's arm.

And had it immediately shrugged off.

I looked between the two of them. "Okay, what?"

"It's nothing," Coffee Lover said.

"Seems kind of tense for nothing."

"He's being ridiculous—"

"Watch yourself!" Reiðarr flushed, and his hand flexed. The one on the same side as his sword. "It's my right—"

"It's your neck!" Coffee Lover snapped. "The king likes this one—"

"Then he should have put her under his protection!"

The tall fey, who was also a little bulkier, and who hadn't liked having his hand shrugged off, smiled at him. It wasn't a particularly nice expression. "Maybe he doesn't think she needs it."

Angry Ass didn't like that, turning flashing eyes on his supposed ally.

"You're only doing this because the king's away," Coffee Lover accused.

"He's still away?" I asked.

"He remains at your Senate. He should be back soon." He shifted his gaze to his buddy. "Which is why you should wait until he returns."

"He's afraid he won't allow it," one of the others said. "I told you—"

"Won't allow *what*?" I asked. Because I hadn't had *my* coffee yet—or eggs or toast or anything else—and was getting annoyed.

"Tell her," the tall one said.

"It's my right," Reiðarr repeated, ignoring him. Because I guess I didn't merit an explanation.

His fellow fey just looked at him, with expressions ranging from embarrassed to pissed off. Like when the angry drunk guy who wants to fight everyone is your cousin. Only I didn't think this guy was drunk.

I didn't know what he was, and wondered if I cared.

"It is!" he insisted.

Annnnd the verdict was in.

"Fuck this," I said, and headed for the stairs.

And had a heavy hand grab my shoulder and spin me around, which was not the problem.

The problem was that I was unarmed and it was from behind, and that sort of thing—

Wakes the beast.

It happened in an instant, as it always did. Rage spiraling up out of nowhere, red haze descending, my heart threatening to beat out of my chest. But this time, it didn't come from her.

This time, it came from me.

I felt her start to rise—the familiar, hateful rush—and something in me snapped. I'd spent most of my life containing my anger, trying to tamp it down, to beat it back. I'd spent years learning techniques to quiet the beast.

But not this time.

This time, for the first time, my rage matched her own.

I saw again the puckered skin, the bloody wounds, the glittering pieces of shrapnel Louis-Cesare was going to have to dig out of his healed flesh at some point, yet more pain. Like all the rest he'd suffered for me, but because of her! She'd hamstrung me in battle, almost gotten him killed, like she'd taken over time and time again, blacking me out and using my body to do unspeakable things.

Not this time!

I threw everything I had at her: five hundred years of

pain and fear and hate, a storm of fury with all the raging wildness of a hurricane. And it felt good—God it did! To let go for once, and let her know how it felt for a change!

And it *was* a change.

Because, instead of everything going black, the sunlit room merely darkened. Instead of gutting the fey with the knife that my hand had decided—on its own—to pluck from his boot, I drove it into the floor. And instead of passing out, and leaving my body in Dorina's hands, it felt like there were suddenly two captains on this ship, each fighting for control.

And I wasn't *finished yet*!

But the fey almost was. He was trying to scramble away, after my leg swept his out from under him and we followed him to the floor. But Dorina was faster, grabbing the still-quivering knife out of the floorboards and—*shit*.

The knife was a blur even to my eyes, hitting down a dozen more times in a staccato beat, as she ripped it out of the floor and I drove it back in, over and over, trying to bury it. That didn't work, and it was everything I could do to keep it out of the fey's flesh. Which wasn't helped by his twisting and turning—and squealing, when the latest strike sliced through his trousers in a particularly vulnerable area.

It didn't slice through anything else, but it was close. I needed to get rid of the damned thing—now—and started struggling to throw it out the window. But all that did was screw up my vision, making it look like someone was flipping a switch on and off, on and off, while the damned fey yelled and rolled around some more instead of taking the chance to—

Finally! He'd made it to his feet, but he didn't run. And then things got interesting.

Darkness: She tripped him, grabbed his hair, used it like a handle to bare his throat—

Light: I twisted the knife at the last second, slammed the hilt into his temple, tried to knock him out, hoping that would end this.

Darkness: But he stayed conscious and she latched

onto the idea, jackhammering the thick wooden handle repeatedly into his face.

Light: I shoved him away, toward the wall, and ran for the stairs—

Darkness: She spun us around and lunged for him, catching him before the paneling did, and then crashing his head through it—

Light: So I threw *him* at the stairs, hoping he'd take the hint and *run*, goddamn it!

Instead, he snarled and whirled, face a bloody mess, but eyes flashing, and unsheathed a sword. Immediately, a wave of heightened rage flooded my body, tingled my fingertips, sapped my control. And sucked all the light out of the room in a split second, leaving me fumbling in the dark.

But not unconscious; not yet.

But I was left trying to stop a fight by hearing alone, because she had my eyes now and she wasn't giving them back. And the idiot had a weapon, and if the fey's reputation was anything to go by, he knew how to use it. And his buddies weren't interfering, despite their earlier attitude. I didn't know why; I just knew—

Fuck.

I heard the fey curse, my own voice snarl, and a sword go clattering. Felt my hand closing on a long, pale throat, a pulse beating rapidly in my palm as I *squeezed*. Felt it start to slow, weakening his attempts to free himself, which weren't working anyway, because Dorina had a hand free.

I could track his movements by her responses: blow blocked, foot sweep denied and turned against him, his own momentum sending him to the floor again, half the job done right there. Gut punch arrested before it could land simply by grabbing his hand and pressing the bones until they crunched and he cried out, a barely there gasp for mercy he wouldn't get, and I couldn't help. Suddenly, I couldn't do anything.

And that made it worse than all those other times. She was using my body to murder someone, and I was going to feel every second of it, a captive audience to savagery

I couldn't control any more than I'd ever managed to control her. A useless appendage that couldn't do anything but rage, so I did.

"I hate you!" I yelled, even knowing she didn't care. "I've always hated you! You take every good and decent thing and you *destroy* it! You're the monster they always called us, not me, not *me*, and I *hate*—"

And just like that, the world fell away.

Chapter Twenty-seven

Mircea, Venice, 1458

Mircea was racing the sun, and losing. He'd gotten back late from his visit to Abramalin, but there had been no offer for him to stay at the praetor's. He'd pointed out that he didn't need a safe room, one of the special retreats his kind used to ensure that stray sunbeams didn't set them alight while they slept. Anything would do, he'd assured her servants, even a closet. But the lady was abed by the time he returned, and none of her people gave a damn.

Leaving him fleeing into darkness as death flirted with the horizon. And while his own body betrayed him, because this close to dawn, nothing worked right. Or at all, Mircea thought, clipping a wall at a dead run, and taking half of the damned thing along with him.

Dizzy and confused, he stumbled out of the cloud of dust and debris, only to stare around at a world gone mad.

Buildings loomed inward, as if bending from their foundations to see this most curious of curious things: a vampire about to face the day. Shadows reached for him, cool islands of relief that beckoned him away from the streets, where the thinning night was starting to eat at his skin like acid. But they lied. The sun was coming, and the shadows would dissipate, leaving him to die screaming in their absence. He couldn't stop. . . .

But it was becoming harder and harder to find his footing, as his depth perception fled along with his power. Even worse, his mind was starting to suffer, leaving him looking at a city that no longer made sense. Bricks appeared to float up from under his feet, tripping him, and then sailed overhead, as the street dissolved around him. The shutters of a nearby house detached from the wall and flew into space, like a giant moth. Strange noises called out to him from passing houses, a sibilant whisper one moment, a deafening warning the next, making him jump and stagger and fall. And then lie there, gripping the bricks in confusion, not even sure which way was up anymore.

All he knew was that he wasn't home, and he was out of time.

The first notes of the Marangona rang out over the city. The hauntingly beautiful bell was named after the carpenters who started work at first light. It heralded the beginning of the workday, so dawn couldn't be that—

It exploded behind him, all at once, releasing its terrible fire. The first beams began spreading across the city, brightening old bricks, picking out gilt decorations on palazzos, eating across pathways between buildings. Including the one behind him.

Mircea screamed, and clawed at the street, stumbling back to his feet and into the shadow of a building, away from the terrible light. But it wouldn't help for long, and he didn't know what to do. The bells were deafening, the shadows were fleeing in front of him, the city was falling into fire, and there was nothing, nothing to save him—

Until someone took his hand.

"This way."

The voice was a dark whisper in his mind. Mircea didn't know anything, barely even knew his name at that point, but he recognized that voice. Soft yet strong, and calm, so calm. As if there was nothing to fear and the world wasn't falling apart.

"Come." A tug on his hand, and it was constant, too, even though it felt like his skin was sloughing off. He followed along behind, blind now, as the approaching day stole his sight along with everything else. "No, this way. Hurry."

He changed his course, following the voice. His feet stumbled, and he almost went down again, because how could you walk on a street that was dissipating like smoke?

But the voice beckoned him on, and the hand steadied him, and he staggered onward into nothingness. Until—

"You found him!" A new voice.

"Yes, but he's hurt."

"Of course he's hurt! It's almost day!" Someone grabbed his shoulders and shook him. "What the hell were you thinking?"

Mircea didn't answer. He wasn't sure that the new voice was talking to him. He wasn't sure of anything.

And then the pain became agony, as if he'd been dunked in a vat of acid.

"Run," the first voice told him urgently. "We have to run!"

He ran. The city raged around him, crashes and lightning bolts and thunder like the feet of a thousand horses, like a battle, one he was losing because his skin was fire, his eyes were flame, the moisture in his mouth dried up and flew away, so that his next scream was silent, the desiccated remains of his throat unable to form words or even sounds anymore, just endless, silent screams—

"Shut it! Shut it!" Someone else was screaming now. Something slammed behind him, and something was thrown over him, a heavy, enveloping weight.

"Up to his room. It's still too light in here," the first voice said.

"D'ye mind if I put out the flames first?" The second, irascible voice asked, and Mircea suddenly felt himself being pummeled. Something was burning; he vaguely realized that it was him. And then he was being shoved at what felt like a set of stairs when he fell into them. And pushed and heaved and dragged upward, because his limbs didn't seem to be taking his commands anymore.

But, somehow, he reached the top, and was pushed forward again, and then—

God! Blessed, soft darkness; cool, cool air; pain, so much, so hot, but lessening, drifting away. Like his consciousness. He tried to hold on to what was left of it, tried to get his eyes to work, so that he could see that he was safe. But the darkness had him, and closed relentlessly over his head.

And he was gone.

"Daft!" Horatiu's hand slapped the back of his head again, hard.

"Are you trying to beat my brains out?" Mircea huddled over the little table in what passed for a kitchen. It was a small room on the ground floor of their house, one that stuck out over the sea that raged against the rocks below like a demon. Or maybe that was just his mood.

"Someone ought to, as they're clearly defective!" the old man snapped, and ripped off another piece of Mircea's hide.

Mircea bit back a scream, because it wasn't manly. And because his throat felt as raw as his back, which Horatiu was relieving of a wealth of ruined skin. The stuff had to come off; the charred reminder of yesterday's activities was clinging in places to the new growth trying to come in, and keeping Mircea from healing. But the old man didn't have to be quite so enthusiastic about it.

"Like a damned snake," Horatiu muttered, throwing the latest piece into a bucket.

Mircea tried not to look at it, or at the clothing that had literally melted to said flesh, and was being removed along with it. He stared at his arm instead, the one cradling his throbbing head. It was pale and whole and perfect, having already been dealt with. Only a few reddened patches, where the outer flesh had been stubborn and ripped some of the new away with it, gave witness to how close he'd come. So very close. If Horatiu hadn't—

"Augghhh!"

"That's the last of them," Horatiu said, having just stripped the ruined flesh off the rest of Mircea's back. He slapped the newly revealed skin. "Get up and drop your breeches."

"I can't drop them; they're melted to my legs!"

"Don't take that tone with me," Horatiu said, and pushed him up against the wall.

Mircea had a response on his lips, but it died at the sight of the knife the old man was wielding, like a butcher coming after a fat young calf. A half-blind butcher, because

Horatiu's eyes were getting worse every year. "I'll do it myself," he said, alarmed, and Horatiu thrust it into his hands.

"See that ye do," he sniped, and took the flesh bucket out the back, and tossed it into the sea.

"You didn't have to throw in the bucket, too," Mircea said, watching him.

"As if I could ever use it for anything else!" the old man said, and slammed back inside.

No. Mircea supposed not. But they weren't finished, and now they had no bucket.

He decided not to mention that. Horatiu was more incensed than Mircea had ever seen him, and not without cause. He and Dorina had spent the hour before dawn scouring the streets for him, and only found him at the last possible moment. If they'd been even a little later . . .

Mircea cut off that train of thought, and swallowed, tasting ash. He felt nauseous and really unwell, but thought it unwise to mention it. Horatiu stomped into the main part of the house, on some errand Mircea didn't question, perhaps to give him some privacy. Which was appreciated, since the burnt flesh on the lower part of his body came off like a pair of hosen, in one, excruciating piece.

Mircea lay on the floor afterward, naked and uncaring, panting at the ceiling. He was bleeding from a few dozen new wounds, and probably looked like a plague victim. He felt like one, too, although he would live. By late tonight or tomorrow, the reddened flesh would be pale and perfect again; the broken rasp, which was all the fire had left of his voice, a mellow tenor; and his stiff and reluctant muscles smooth and strong.

It was the one thing you could be sure of as a vampire: what didn't kill you would leave you exactly as you were, with no scars or other reminders of how close you'd come. Not that Mircea needed them. That experience had been seared into his memory, possibly literally.

"Are ye done yet?" Horatiu's voice demanded, from outside.

Mircea sat up, feeling dizzy. "Yes, I—"

A pair of hosen hit him in the face, cutting off the comment. They were followed by a shirt, a belt, and a hat.

"What is this?" Mircea asked, looking at the latter.

"A hat," Horatiu told him sweetly. "Ye wear it on yer head."

"I know what it is! Why do I need it?"

Horatiu didn't answer. He just left again, while Mircea struggled into the huge old camisa his servant had provided, which was threadbare and patched, and so voluminous that he'd taken to wearing it as a nightshirt, since it drooped well past his knees. Even the soft, weathered weave stung his skin in places, but nowhere near what tight hosen or a fitted doublet would have done.

"Here." Something was shoved under his nose, while Mircea was still trying to figure out if he dared to put on anything else. He was leaning toward no, and that was before he realized that the thing Horatiu was holding wasn't the drink he could have really used right now. Instead, it looked like one of the allegorical warnings against sin that pious pilgrims to the city were always snatching up after visiting the brothels, and before stopping by the taverns to drink themselves insensate.

Only hellish painted monsters didn't blink.

Mircea took the little mirror and examined his face. Half of it was more or less normal, the side turned away from the sun, he assumed. But the rest . . . Mircea swallowed again, taking in the naked skull bubbling with blisters, the reddened, peeling skin of his jaw, and the liquid pus oozing out of a corner of one eye, which was so swollen and puffy that he was surprised he could see at all.

And, frankly, wished he couldn't.

"It'll heal," he croaked, and ignored the expletive that sentiment won him.

He turned back to the table, his eye over a bowl, trying to force out as much pus as possible. Horatiu muttered something just outside Mircea's damaged hearing as he cleaned up the latest mess. When he was finished, he pulled out a chair and sat down, with an audible sigh.

"All right," he said, after a moment. "All right."

"All right what?" Mircea asked, feeling pained and put-upon and grateful and irritated, all at the same time.

He appreciated all his servant did for him—he truly did—and he didn't blame the man for looking disgusted. Mircea had felt his own lip curl at that brief glimpse of the creature in the mirror, so how could he blame Horatiu for a similar expression? But in that case, why didn't the man leave him alone? Go look at something more attractive, and leave Mircea to what passed for his ablutions?

"We have to talk," Horatiu said ominously, and Mircea sighed.

Oh, that was why.

"About?"

"About?" Horatiu looked like he was about to smack him again. "What d'ye think? Ye almost killed y'damned self. I hope it was worth it!"

"It was."

Mircea gave up on the eye and sat back against the wall, feeling about as good as he looked. Horatiu got up again, fetching them both flagons of ale and tossing out the little bowl. Guess that was another thing that couldn't be saved. Fortunately, that wasn't the case with other things.

"I have it," Mircea said, as a tankard was put in front of him.

"Have what?"

"What have I been looking for? The solution."

"That's what ye said about the blessed kerchief of the many gold pieces," Horatiu muttered, and drank ale.

"That was from a shyster—"

"And this isn't?"

"No." Mircea drank, to wash the feel of burnt flesh out of his mouth. "No."

"And how do ye know that?"

Mircea told him.

It took a while, and at the end, Horatiu was staring at him in consternation. Or maybe that was the wonky eye. He couldn't see out of it worth a damn.

"Are ye mad, boy?"

Or maybe not.

Mircea frowned. "I thought you'd be pleased."

"Pleased? Ye're talking about killing her!"

"Killing—" Mircea paused, because he obviously

hadn't explained well enough. "No. Just the *disease*. Vampirism is—"

"What you are!"

"What I *have*," Mircea corrected sharply. "A magical disease that I passed on to Dorina, and which is killing her. You know this."

"What I know is that ye're not taking her to some lunatic in the damned desert—"

"I will do what I must!"

"—and letting him carve her up—"

"He isn't—will you *listen*?" Mircea grabbed the old man's wrist, because he'd jumped to his feet, as if he planned to spirit Dorina away while Mircea was too weak to stop him. "He isn't going to carve up anything. He's going to cast a spell that divides her mind, walling off the vampire-based insanity and allowing her to live a normal life. Isn't that what we've wanted?"

"No! That's what ye've wanted! Ye hate what ye are, even now, after all this time. Ye can't accept it, blame it for costing you—"

"Careful." They didn't talk about his deceased wife. They just didn't.

Except for tonight, apparently.

"Why careful?" Horatiu demanded harshly. "Elena's dead because of that damned murderous bastard of a brother of yours, not for anything ye could have—"

"She's dead because I left her! Alone and unprotected! Just like I left Dorina—"

"Ye didn't even know she existed!"

"And that makes it better?" Mircea got up, despite the fact that there was no room to pace in their closet of a kitchen. Or in the rest of the shack he called home these days. A dainty old lady dipping her toes in the surf, the man who sold it to him had said. When the reality was that it was a roof and little else, one that looked like it could collapse into the sea at any moment. He should be glad to have it nonetheless; plenty had less. But he resented it, like he resented having to fawn and crawl to the praetor, to the wealthy so-called healers who had yet to heal a damned thing, to the whole world!

When he was alive, he'd led armies in suits of armor

that cost more than this house, possibly more than the whole street. He'd returned to palatial dwellings, servants, the finest of food. And gold, so much that he'd become careless with it, and had to be chastised by his father, because too much liberality could be viewed as a sign of weakness.

He didn't miss the money—most of the time—or the trappings and finery. He didn't mind living in poverty, in mended clothes and patched shoes, in a city where ostentatious wealth was the only birthright anyone cared about. He didn't even mind the contemptuous glances—

All right, that was a lie. They burned almost as hot as the sun, but he could deal with them. He couldn't deal with this. Watching his daughter die, eaten alive by the curse that had already stolen his life, his wife, everything he cared about. And was now determined to deprive him of the last thing of value he had left.

It wouldn't succeed.

Not this time.

"I can't kill it," he told Horatiu. "It's part of her now. But I can trap it, imprison it, wall it away. This mage said he's done it before, but it takes a fantastic amount of power, more than he possesses or I can afford—"

"Then this is over."

"Like hell it's over!" Mircea rounded on the old man. "He doesn't have the power now, but I'm going to get it for him. And when I do, the vampire part of Dorina will never be a problem again."

"The vampire part." Horatiu's rheumy eyes met his, and there was fire in them. "D'ye hear yourself? Has this latest charlatan rattled your brain, or did the sun cook it?"

"Have a care—"

"I am! I do! And the sense that has somehow left you." The old man gripped his arms, and Mircea allowed it, despite the pain. Because Horatiu looked pained, too. And worried, more than Mircea thought he'd ever seen before. "She's your daughter—all of her—aye, the vampire part, too. How d'ye think we found you tonight? Do ye think a human could have tracked you in time, through the maze of streets around here?"

"She is human." Mircea pulled away, furious that

Horatiu couldn't understand. "She has abilities, yes, because of the disease, just as I do. But it's killing her—"

"And this mage won't? Men like him prey on the desperate, telling ye what ye want to hear, to gain what they want in return. He's fed you a story!"

"He's also the first decent chance we've had! The first to hold out any real hope—"

"Aye, that's how they get you. They're purveyors of hope, of dreams—and nothing else!"

"And how would you know?"

"How would you? Because he told you?"

"No. Because she did." Mircea looked up, in the direction of the room where his daughter slept. "Dorina followed me tonight, to the praetor's. Not in body," he added, because Horatiu was looking alarmed. "Mentally. You were right about her gifts."

"Mentally?" The old man's eyes narrowed. "What does that mean?"

"I'm not sure. But she was there. And when I asked her how she managed it, how she could do anything after what she went through last night, do you know what she said?"

"I'm going to find out," Horatiu muttered, also looking at the ceiling.

This time, it was Mircea who took him by the arms. "She said, 'It's only bad when we're both awake at the same time.' She knows, Horatiu. She knows there's two of her, a light and a dark. The girl she should have been, and the monster I made of her.

"A monster I'm going to shut away—forever."

Chapter Twenty-eight

The vision, or whatever it was, snapped, leaving me staring at Claire's hallway. And visibly shaking and feeling like screaming; I wasn't sure why. I suddenly had so many reasons to choose from.

The fey weren't looking much better. Two of them had naked swords in their hands, but were being held back by Tall Guy. Coffee Lover was plastered to the wall, one hand on his sword hilt and the other clutching his mug, most of the contents of which were sloshed down his front. The final fey was on the ground underneath me, his face red with gore and broken blood vessels, his expression as shell-shocked as I felt.

Because that . . . What the hell was *that*?

Nobody spoke. Sunlight was streaming through the octagonal window, the beams lighting up the dust in the air and putting an ironic halo around the head of Angry Ass. The fey weapons were sliding back into their sheaths, courtesy of a terse gesture from Tall Guy, who must have noticed the change in my expression. Because Dorina's rage—or mine, or a combination of both—was simply gone.

It looked like time had rewound and I'd just come out of my room, except that I was sitting on a fey.

I sat there some more.

Dorina, I thought blankly, but didn't get anything back.

One of the fey cleared his throat. It wasn't the guy on the floor, whose eyes were starting to pop, I realized. I slowly pulled my fingers out of his flesh and a sigh rippled around the hall, along with a fervent sentence from Coffee Lover in a language I didn't know.

I also didn't care.

"Dorina?" I said again, my eyes flicking around, as if I was waiting for her to materialize out of thin air.

Nothing.

"Dorina!" I waited, my heart about to beat out of my chest, my breath coming heavily as it hadn't during the fight.

More nothing. She wasn't going to talk to me. And there was a reason for that, wasn't there?

"I didn't tell Mircea to do that!" I yelled. "It wasn't my fault!"

The silence was deafening. And accusing. But I couldn't defend myself if she wouldn't—

"Damn it, talk to me!" A sudden surge of emotion tore through me: anger, fear, longing, sadness. I didn't know what it was, or why it was there; I just knew I was tearing up. Which made me even more frantic, because there was nowhere for the emotion to go.

She wasn't here.

But she *had* been here, just a minute ago. And now she was gone, because, what? There was nothing left to talk about?

"Dorina . . ." I said, and even to me, it sounded sad and broken and weak.

No wonder she didn't want to talk to me.

Someone cleared his throat. "It is Dory, yes?"

I looked up at Tall Guy, half-blind with tears I didn't understand. He was staring at me along with everyone else, but instead of looking angry or shocked like the rest, his face was almost . . . gentle. It confused me.

"Are you unwell?" he asked, after a moment.

"I . . . don't know."

He crouched down beside me, and I realized that I was still straddling his guy. Should probably do something about that, as soon as I made sure that he wasn't going to attack me again. And figured out why he had in the first place.

I poked him in the chest. "What's your deal, again?"

He didn't say anything.

His face was still too red, his eyes too prominent, and his stare too distant. He looked like he was reevaluating his life choices. Tall Guy didn't have that problem, and after a moment, he answered.

"There is a series of heroic deeds among our people," he told me. "Or 'challenges' might be a better word. Nine in all that, if performed before witnesses, grant . . ." He frowned. "There is no equivalent in English. One is remembered in song and legend thereafter, counted among the bravest of the brave, and greatly admired by one's fellow warriors."

"And that has what to do with me?"

"One of the nine is to defeat a *vargr* in battle," he admitted.

Great.

"Well, I'm not one, so jumping me before I have breakfast won't bring you any renown," I told Angry Ass, and climbed off him.

He flushed some more, I guess at the implication that he'd tried to take me down when I was at less than my best. But he didn't say anything. Maybe because I still had his knife.

Dorina had shoved it in my—our—pocket, why I had no idea. To make the point that she didn't need it to kill him? To keep as a souvenir? To leave me a message?

A spot of blood had run off the blade and stained my sweats. It wasn't much, and it wasn't mine, but it showed that, despite my best efforts, she'd gotten a blade in him. I swallowed, feeling sick.

"What do you mean, you're not *vargr*?" Coffee Lover asked. "The king said—"

"The king doesn't know everything," I rasped.

There was a stunned silence, like I'd blasphemed in church.

"The king doesn't know everything about me," I rephrased, shaking my head to clear it.

Tall Guy looked confused. He had a long, somewhat homely face for a fey, with a slightly bulbous tip to the nose, and eyes that were too small and too close together. It made him look like a puzzled greyhound.

I decided I needed a name for him. I didn't usually

bother, since I couldn't tell them apart anyway, but he seemed to be in charge. Or maybe just older. He had that seen-it-all-didn't-think-much-of-it world-weariness of an old soldier. He was also something approaching eight feet tall, putting him almost a foot above the rest of the fey, including Caedmon. So I thought I'd remember.

"You have a name?" I asked, expecting the usual speech I got from the fey before I'd learned not to ask that question. They tended to rattle off all the nicknames they'd won over the years, I suppose as a way of telling you something about themselves. But it was annoying.

Except for this time, when I got exactly two syllables.

"Olfun."

"Okay, Olfun. I'm having kind of a . . . problem . . . lately. Call it a split personality; call it whatever you want. Just don't fuck with it, okay? 'Cause I'm not always the one in charge."

The confusion didn't go away, but he didn't ask any stupid questions. "All right."

I handed him back his guy's knife, because the fey are weird about their weapons, and I didn't need any more trouble.

"See what I can do about the coffee," I said, and went downstairs.

Mircea wasn't answering his phone. He was probably at the consul's, where the wards played hell with modern tech. I knew that. It didn't keep me from wanting to punch through the wall, however.

I was on the front porch, because I needed some air and it was getting harder to find any place to be alone around here. I'd called Mircea because I didn't know who else to call, but I didn't need him. I needed his daughter, and she wasn't reachable by phone.

Or any other way I knew.

And, honestly, I couldn't blame her.

I didn't even know why I wanted her to talk to me so badly, because what was I going to say? Yell again that it wasn't my fault? I didn't see that helping.

Especially since it kind of was.

I flashed back to a half-remembered dream, one of the ones she'd shown me because I didn't recall the years we'd spent in Venice at all. Mircea hadn't been sure that this barrier of his would hold; Dorina's mental gifts threatened it, and he'd been afraid that if I started to get curious, too, it might undermine the whole thing. So he'd made sure I never would by erasing my memories of the place—all of them.

For centuries, I'd had gaping holes in my past filled with absolutely nothing, which I'd put down to the crazy, but which were actually things Mircea had thought might trigger my curiosity. I hadn't remembered Horatiu, the kindly old man who had apparently been important to me, other than as a servant of Mircea's. I hadn't recalled the quirky house on the ocean, where I'd spent much of my childhood. And I definitely hadn't remembered my child body twisting in agony as Dorina raged inside her little human cage.

Because how was she supposed to develop properly like that?

I didn't know how she'd developed at all. Vampires didn't. Not even those taken as children, which was why it was forbidden to change one so young. But it had happened in the past, when the rules weren't as well enforced, and what had been the result?

Nothing. A child vamp was a child vamp. He got stronger with age and feeding, but never matured, because his growth had been arrested at the moment he was changed. Leaving him as limited in understanding as he'd ever been, no matter how many years of experience he gained, because his brain just . . . stayed the same.

Which had caused some seriously messed-up masters, on occasion, with all the petulance, two-dimensional thinking and tantrums of a child, in a body capable of leveling a small city.

I didn't think that was true of Dorina—the bits I remembered from her memories had seemed adult enough—but I didn't know. Like I didn't know what happened to a vampire's brain when it *did* evolve, when it was forced to change and grow, because the eternally static body it was in wasn't so static. When something meant to be forever the same was ripped apart, over and over again, as the human child it had been welded to in the womb decided to have another growth spurt.

No wonder most dhampirs died in childhood, and the rest went mad!

Or were walled away in a tiny section of my mind, only able to emerge when I was asleep or when my mental grip was compromised through shock, anger, or fear. God! No wonder she hated me!

And once done, the separation had been permanent. Her mental powers had been growing right alongside Mircea's, because a few decades' difference in age is no time at all in vampire terms. He'd told me once that he'd been afraid of lowering the barrier, because once it was down, he might never be able to raise it again. At the time, it had sounded like the truth. Maybe it even was.

Or maybe it was a convenient excuse, a small voice said.

I shifted uneasily.

So, instead of a life with occasional wild episodes, Dorina had had only a fraction of one, and had lived it with the knowledge that Mircea, the father she'd loved, the father she'd *rescued,* didn't feel the same way. Because Horatiu had been right; it hadn't been me that night, scouring the streets for him. Mircea had been saved by someone who spoke to him mentally, something I still had trouble with.

So it had been Dorina.

And since she'd also been the one to send me memories of that talk in the kitchen, she must have been listening. Or maybe riding along again, which made it worse. If someone said something hurtful, you could try to pass it off as their having a bad day, and lashing out. Could convince yourself that they didn't really mean it. But if you were in their head at the time?

She'd known he was serious, that he thought of her as a monster. Or, worse than that, he thought of her as a *disease.* The same one that had stolen everything from him, from his life to his position to his wife. And was now killing the only thing he had left.

Like he'd wanted to kill her.

I swallowed, and put my arms around myself, because what the fuck did that do to you? Growing up knowing your only parent didn't just hate you, but wanted you dead? And that, since he couldn't kill you without killing the daughter he did want, he was determined to lock you away.

Forever.

I felt the old ball of anger and distrust for him well up, the one I'd carried for so long that it felt normal, natural. Mircea had separated from me after I reached adulthood, and the memory wipe that followed had made certain that I thought of him as a cold, distant master vamp, ashamed of the nasty dhampir he'd sired. And who seemed to show up only when he wanted something.

He'd told me recently that he'd been concerned that his growing status would put a spotlight on me, a dangerous prospect, since the deal he'd made with the Senate to overlook my existence was nullified once I grew up. And because he himself might serve as a trigger to all those repressed memories. Maybe it was even true.

But it had left us most definitely at odds, to the point that this recent spate of familial closeness felt strange. Nice in some ways, but strange nonetheless. My default was hating him, or at least seriously suspecting him. I hadn't known what to do with the other feelings that had been bubbling up lately.

Like I didn't know what to do with this.

I sat there on the steps, the sun on my face, but my thoughts dark. He'd condemned Dorina and me to a half-life, but what else was he supposed to do? What would I have done, in his place? Kept looking for another solution while the fits tore my kid apart, fits I could stop with knowledge I already had?

It reminded me of those parents with a troubled pregnancy, the ones forced to select one child to die so that the other might live. Lose one, or lose them both; a horrible choice.

But how much worse was it when the one selected out knew it? When she was aware that she'd been made into a sacrifice? That her life had been deemed less important; her wishes discounted; her hopes, dreams, and ambitions stifled, so that her far less talented sister might thrive? What the hell happened *then*?

The phone rang. I put it to my ear automatically, not even checking first. And, of course, it was Mircea.

"Dorina?"

Wrong number, I thought, half hysterically, and didn't say anything.

"Dorina?"

His voice was as mellifluous as always. He could do wonders with that voice. Could charm emperors and kings with that voice. Could persuade master vampires into agreements they didn't want at all, which was a lot harder than talking to kings.

"Dorina?" It was becoming more insistent.

"Sorry. Butt dial," I whispered, and hung up.

I sat there some more. I felt dizzy, in limbo, uncharacteristically numb. I didn't know what to do.

Not that it was up to me, or to Mircea, either. For the first time, the ball was in Dorina's court. She could do what she wanted, and I couldn't blame her for whatever she chose. Like I couldn't blame her anymore for the life we'd lived. Or for the life *I'd* lived, I corrected, which suddenly seemed like paradise in comparison.

So now what? The thought left me feeling sick and worried, and seriously off-balance. She hadn't banished me, but I wasn't sure whether that was a good sign or not. She might be testing these new waters, making sure that the mental tie we had wouldn't drag her off along with me.

Or maybe she didn't intend to do anything at all. It wasn't like she needed to risk it. As she'd demonstrated twice now, she could emerge whenever she chose, and wrestle control away from me, because she'd always been stronger. And that was with the wall still partially up. What would happen when the last pieces fell?

What would happen when she could trap me in the same hell that she'd been forced to endure, or banish me entirely?

I turned the phone back on and punched in a different number. Because if I couldn't talk to Dorina, I needed to talk to someone who knew her. And better than Mircea seemed to.

"Hello?"

"Uh, hello. I'd like to speak to Horatiu, please."

"And who may I say is calling?"

I sighed, because this never went well. Mircea's masters were better than most, better than the ones at the Senate, who usually hissed at me unless Daddy was around, but it was a matter of degree. Mircea's masters looked like they wanted to hiss, but were manfully holding back because they had better breeding than that.

Unlike me.

"Dory," I snapped, because didn't he have caller ID? "And I don't want a problem, okay? I just want to talk—"

"Lady Dorina, is that you?"

I paused, and looked at the phone. Not because of the words, which could have been sarcasm, but because of the tone. The guy, whoever it was, had sounded . . . delighted.

"Uh. Yeah."

"How wonderful to hear from you!"

I stared at the phone some more. I resisted an impulse to shake it. And then I did it anyway, because happy little burbling noises were coming out of it and freaking me out.

"Can I speak to Horatiu?" I finally cut in.

The burbling stopped. And was replaced by a gushing, apologetic vamp explaining to me what I should have already known, because Horatiu wasn't a master. He was barely even a vampire, since Mircea hadn't gotten around to changing the old man until he was on his deathbed, and those sorts often don't take properly. Leaving the family with a doddering, mostly deaf, and almost completely blind vampire, who because of Mircea's huge fondness for him could do whatever the hell he wanted.

Including sleep in.

"What time does he usually get up?" I almost yelled, to be heard over the effusions of joy that speaking to me had apparently brought to this vamp's life.

There were a lot of them.

"Thank you!" I finally yelled. "Tell him I'll be by later."

And then I hung up, and just sat there, staring at the phone some more.

What the *hell*?

Chapter Twenty-nine

I was sucking on a splinter—my only relic from the fight—
when I entered the kitchen. And found it deserted except
for a harassed-looking fey at the sink, and Gessa sitting
on a stool alongside. She looked the same as always, in a
cute blue sack dress, because nothing rattled her. Including, apparently, teaching a fey how to do the dishes.

He looked up when I came in, relief flooding his face.
Either he was out of the loop or he didn't care about my
supposed shaman status. All he knew was that a woman
had finally showed up to do the chores, and the world had
righted itself.

He started to take off his apron, and I held up my hand.
"Sorry. Splinter."

The weight of the universe came crashing back onto
his shoulders, and Gessa had to turn away to hide a smile.

"You okay?" I asked her.

She nodded.

"And Ymsi?"

She sighed. "In his room. He sad."

Yeah, I'd been afraid of that.

I added coffee to the perpetual grocery list on the
fridge, and wolfed down a giant container of soup, a salad,
three boiled eggs, most of a jar of pickles, and some soft
cheese spread on half a loaf of fresh-baked bread. Then I
headed for the basement.

Or I tried to. But young trolls make human teens look
like neat freaks, and there was so much stuff piled against
the basement door that I could barely . . . get the old
thing . . . *there*! It finally allowed me a couple inches to

squeeze through, so I did. And abruptly stopped, because I couldn't see a damned thing.

That would have been bad enough on its own, without the minefield of items between me and the bottom of the stairs. But Claire's uncle Pip had never bothered to run lights down here, and I didn't feel like taking time to hunt for a flashlight. I slowly started to pick my way down.

Trolls are nocturnal, more often than not, back in Faerie. Not out of choice, but because their eyes don't help them much even in daylight, leaving them at a serious disadvantage among better-sighted creatures. But at night, their superior hearing and smell put the shoe on the other foot, allowing them to hunt in pure darkness.

It was why a lot of them lived in caves. Even a well-equipped contingent of Light Fey hesitated at the idea of descending into a dark-as-pitch subterranean maze filled with creatures that didn't need to see you in order to kill you. And over time, it had just become a thing. Caves might be cold and hard and generally unappealing—until you factored in the advantage of sleeping in safety. And suddenly, they didn't seem so bad.

Which I guess was why the twins had chosen to live in the basement, despite being offered the guest room upstairs.

And why only one of them had adjusted to living in sunlight.

That, of course, was Ymsi, because gardening was easier during the day. But Sven was still mostly a night owl, and had taken to prowling around the neighborhood after dark, dragging back any rubbish that caught his eye. He just couldn't get over all the stuff that people threw away here: cracked birdbaths and old furniture and random two-by-fours and a twisted bike with no back wheel and a painting of triangles and a rusted fridge and a whole box of CDs.

Trolls are not fond of hip-hop, as it turns out, but still—so shiny!

Claire had drawn the line at bags of actual trash, like she'd had to break Gessa from washing used paper towels and setting them all over the counters to dry. The Dark Fey lived on lousy land in Faerie, since most of the better stuff had been taken from them in the wars. I'd kind of gotten the impression that everything was hard to come by, from food to possessions, so nothing was wasted.

"Trash" just wasn't a thing among the Dark Fey.

So garbage day was an endless bazaar of wonders to Sven, because many of the old people put their cans out the night before. Leaving him on an all-night shopping trip where everything was free. And leaving our garbage guys an easier job the next day, because a lot of the discarded junk of the neighborhood ended up back here.

That was especially true of anything metal and shiny that whirred softly when poked. Because, unlike his brother, Sven preferred all things mechanical, and had "rescued" a profusion of broken electronics to tinker with. He'd managed to get an old blender working again, which had delighted him to no end, and had thereafter started a side business with other Dark Fey, trading things he'd found or repaired for things he wanted.

The problem was that Sven had a problem telling trash from treasure, and had begun to demonstrate some serious pack rat tendencies. They hadn't progressed all the way to hoarding, but they were heading that way fast. And Claire didn't play that. If he didn't do something soon, she was going to make good on her threat to open up the portal, and just blow everything to kingdom come.

Which might be the only option at this point, I thought, jumping over the railing for the last five feet, because it was easier.

My eyes had had time to adjust, allowing me to see a dim lantern glowing in the gloom and Sven over by the far wall, holding something. It turned out to be a troll favorite, consisting of potatoes sliced up in a bowl, covered with milk and a cloth, and set in a corner of the basement until it turned into something horrid. It was the Earth version of a traditional troll delicacy and the boys loved it, but it took a long time to make—because apparently it wasn't good until it was *really* rancid—and they guarded their portions jealously.

Which was why it was weird that he wasn't eating it.

He was just holding it, sitting on the floor beside a blanket-covered lump that I assumed was his brother. He looked at me. And then he held out the bowl, in both hands because it wasn't actually a bowl. It was a kitchen sink one of the neighbors had thrown out, and that he'd found and bunged up and used for things like eating three boxes of cereal for breakfast.

Or a whole lotta rancid potatoes.

"He don't eat," Sven said, looking worried. Because that was not a normal thing among trolls.

"Just leave it there," I told him, and he nodded and put the sink down.

Sven levered himself up and, despite his size, managed to negotiate the minefield on the stairs better than me. It reminded me of the big guy at the fights; so graceful despite his size. I stared after him for a moment, with something rattling around my brain, something that felt important. . . .

But then it went away, and I sat down by the lump.

It was a little ripe in here, smelling like a combo of swamp gas and troll ass, and making me curse dhampir noses. But there was no point trying to hurry this. Trolls did not hurry. They considered it undignified, unless it was children gamboling around or in battle. Otherwise, they had an odd sort of gravitas about them, a natural poise you wouldn't expect—or at least I hadn't, until Olga taught me that grace transcended species.

I waited.

It was peaceful down here if you ignored the smell, and dim even with a lantern. There were some narrow windows up near the ceiling, but they'd recently been covered with black paint. I dragged the lantern closer, and Ymsi turned over, the light glimmering in his tiny eyes.

"Did I disturb you?" I asked, wondering if I should put it back.

He shook his head.

We sat there some more.

Despite appearances, trolls could be very restful people to be around. Unlike the Light Fey, who reminded me of jagged bolts of lightning, or hyped-up teenagers, always ready for a fight or an adventure, trolls had a natural peacefulness about them. Like the mountains and trees and deep, quiet fjords they were named after, they didn't seem to need to prove something to the world to justify their existence. They could just be.

I leaned back against the basement wall, and slowly felt the anger, confusion, and worry still knotting my gut start to ease away. Cool darkness wrapped around me, a gentle sort of fuzziness pervaded my body, and my feverish thoughts slowed down, down, down. I took a deep breath, and let it out, suddenly feeling calmer.

It was nice.

A large finger emerged from the blankets, and pushed the heavy vat of potatoes and slime my way.

"Thanks, but I just ate," I said.

Ymsi frowned, probably not seeing what that had to do with anything.

"We humans have tiny little stomachs." I pulled up my sweatshirt and showed him. He regarded it sadly. "And mine's full. Otherwise, I'd be all over that," I said, which seemed to mollify him somewhat.

"You should eat, though," I told him.

He shook his head. I noticed that his eyes glimmered a little more than usual, although maybe that was a trick of the light. *Sure, Dory, and the light is dribbling down his face, too.*

Goddamn, I wished we'd caught whatever attacked him! I wanted to do evil things. But that required finding it first.

"I know this is a bad time," I said. "But I have some questions. Can you answer some questions?"

Ymsi blinked at me, looking surprised. Like he'd expected the usual "it's not your fault, you shouldn't blame yourself" stuff he'd probably heard a dozen times by now. Which was true, but not helpful, because of course he blamed himself. He'd stabbed a kid. And the fact that he hadn't wanted to, and that the kid might pull through anyway, wasn't really the point, was it?

"I'm going to find whatever was here last night, and I'm going to kill it," I told him. "But it would be easier if I had some more info to go on. If you remember anything?"

Ymsi regarded me silently for a moment. I looked placidly back. Troll brains took their time, but that didn't mean they were stupid. Ymsi, for example, could tell you everything about every flower in the garden: which needed sun and which did better in shade, which made the prettiest flower and which smelled the best, which responded to what kind of fertilizer, or needed what kind of soil, acidic or sweet. The guy was a walking compendium of knowledge about his favorite subject, like a human kid knowing all the stats on his favorite sports team, even though he'd just failed algebra.

People are smart when they want to be, and I thought maybe Ymsi wanted to be right now.

"Woman," he finally said, in a low rumble.

"It was a woman who attacked you?"

Again, I got a surprised look, although this time, I wasn't sure why.

Until he told me. "Not attack. *I* attack. I *kill*—"

He broke off.

I blinked. Maybe no one had talked to him about this, after all. "You didn't kill anyone," I said. "He's upstairs resting. Didn't they tell you?"

He nodded, and then shook his head violently. "I try kill. Same thing."

"I don't think the kid would think it's the same thing."

"She say stab. I stab. I can't stop—" He broke off again and, for a moment, sat very still. "I try," he finally said. "I run into things. I break. But no one hear."

Probably due to all the screaming.

"That's why you were covered in blood," I said. Because the stab wound in the kid wouldn't have caused that. The blade might have gotten a little messy, but Ymsi should have been fine. Except that he'd made himself deliberately bloody, not an easy thing for trolls, so that someone would notice.

And if everybody in the house hadn't been in basically the same shape, maybe they would have.

"That was brave," I told him, and got another look, almost angry this time.

"Not brave! I *kill*!"

He threw off the blanket, looking like he wanted to get up and punch something.

I knew the feeling.

"Well, I think you're brave," I said. "You tried to fight

off an attack, all by yourself, with no one to help you. And when you couldn't, you did the next best thing. You stabbed the wrong side of the chest, because you knew what this woman didn't. That troll hearts are on the other side."

Ymsi made a sound, and not a nice one.

It didn't seem like he agreed with me.

I sighed and looked up at the ceiling, which had some old explosion patterns on it, from Pip's still. The boys had apparently halted production of their brew for the moment, because the hulking thing in the corner was silent, just gleaming a little in reflected light. And showing me a dark glimpse of the tortured face that Ymsi was hiding from me.

There was another long pause.

"Light Fey," he finally said, his voice harsh. "Heart same side as human."

"So if it was a Light Fey woman, one who didn't know much about trolls, she might think you'd done the job?"

He nodded.

Sounded like Efridis to me. But that made even less sense now than yesterday, and it hadn't made much then. Efridis of all people knew that Aiden was protected— she'd been the one to steal the rune in the first place. She had to know he was wearing it, so stabbing him would do exactly fuck all.

But if the troll kid had been the target, then it *really* didn't seem like her.

Based on what Dorina had heard in that underwater room, it sounded like Geminus' family were back in the smuggling business, assuming that they'd ever stopped. Geminus had been running weapons, and very dangerous ones. There was serious money in that, particularly in the middle of a war; it would make sense for some of his guys to risk continuing it.

And to kill a troll kid who knew too much.

What didn't make sense was for Efridis to be involved. Claire might hate her, and with cause, but the fact remained that she'd come to warn us when she didn't have to. She'd helped save our asses just a couple weeks ago. Why would she be helping the other side now?

And it wasn't like there weren't other suspects. Aeslinn, for instance, Efridis' estranged husband. He was a leader on the other side of the war who had worked with Geminus in the past. He had every reason to put arms in the hands of his partisans here, and to sow as much discord as possible.

Plus, earth was his element; he could easily raise a *manlikan* force out of it. And he controlled a whole fey kingdom. He could probably also scrape up a *vargr*, if he thought he needed one. Like to frame his faithless wife for a crime he'd committed?

And, finally, there was the fact that Olga had slept a little too soundly the night that the troll boy was attacked. She'd put it down to being up for something like a day and a half, but I wasn't sure. Food and drink are always offered to visitors by trolls; it's seen as a major insult not to. So despite arguing with Geirröd, aka White Hair, and Trym, better known as Gravel Face, she had followed precedent.

After they left, she'd been so sleepy that she could barely keep her eyes open, so she went to bed. And slept like the dead. Which she might well have been, except that Stinky had stolen her half-finished beer.

Fortunately, Duergars are immune to drugs and poisons, which was a good thing. Otherwise, he'd have been dead years ago from all the crap he eats. Seriously, Stinky will never starve.

So, somebody might have tried to knock out or poison Olga, who had brought in the troll kid, and then an attack came that very night that ended with that same kid getting stabbed. Seemed like they might be connected. Especially since she'd said that the two leaders hadn't been keen on coming here. They'd wanted to take the boy to a troll healer, halfway across town, and Olga had made them divert. Because she hadn't thought the boy would survive the trip.

Maybe they hadn't, either.

Ymsi was looking at me over his shoulder, like he was wondering what I was thinking. *Or maybe he wanted some comfort, Dory!* I was bad at that, but Ymsi was a good kid; one of the most genuinely sweet people I knew. He hadn't deserved any of this.

"You couldn't have done any better," I told him. "Caedmon and I tried together, and we couldn't stop her."

And, okay, that finally got a reaction.

Ymsi blinked. "You fight?"

"Yes, we both did. But it—she—got away. She was powerful, Ymsi, but you tricked her. You tricked her and you won." I got up. "You ought to remember that."

Ymsi just looked at me, blinking slowly, like he was trying to process that.

But when I looked down from the stairs, on my way out, the sink was in his lap and he was eating.

Chapter Thirty

My thoughts were still on the puzzle from last night when I reached the hall, and found it full of vampires. That would have been bad, but not surprising, since Ray had come with accessories. Only these accessories were naked.

They were standing in a line from the dining room to the downstairs bathroom, leaving the what the hell stretching almost the entire length of the house. Some had towels wrapped around their waists or draped around their necks; others sported embellishments in the form of flip-flops, shower caps, or bath brushes; and a few even carried baskets of toiletries. But there were also plenty of different-colored buns in view, along with sunken chests, man boobs, and hairy shanks.

And then it got worse.

"Dory?" Claire's voice came from somewhere upstairs. "Is that you?"

I looked up, and I swear my heart stopped.

Holy shit.

I grabbed Ray, who for some reason was completely filthy, and shook him. "What?" he asked.

"Dory?"

I swallowed. "Uh, yeah? Hi, Claire."

"Hi, yourself." The voice floated down from the direction of my room. "I'm just going to change your sheets, okay?"

"Sure," I squeaked. "Thanks!"

"Do you need any towels?"

"Yeah, we could use—" Ray began, before I clapped a hand over his mouth.

"What was that?"

"I said, sure, if it's no trouble," I called up.

"No trouble. I have some fresh ones in the laundry room—"

"No!" The laundry room was downstairs. "I mean, no, I just remembered—I'm fine. Tons of towels!"

"You're sure?"

"Absolutely!" I shoved Ray at the dining room door, but he didn't want to go.

"Mmhfmf!"

"What?"

He pulled my hand away. "What the hell are you doing?"

"What are *you* doing?" I hissed. "Get them back in the dining room!"

"Why? They gotta get baths—"

"Not now!"

"Then when?"

"After I have time to talk to Claire!"

"You haven't talked to Claire?"

"When have I had time to talk to Claire?"

He put dirty hands on terry-cloth-covered hips. "You had time to talk to her last night. You telling me she don't know we're here?"

"That's what I'm telling you!" I whispered, while shoving Ray into the dining room and pushing his guys in after him.

"And I'm telling you this is bullshit!" Ray ducked under my arm. "I'm gonna go—"

"Back inside," I said, and whirled him through the door again.

"Cut that out!"

"Then stop being a dick!"

"I'm being a dick? You—"

I slammed the door on him, and casually leaned against it as Claire came down the stairs. And then noticed, about the same time she did, the small yellow object at the bottom of the steps. She bent down and picked it up.

"I don't remember us having a rubber ducky."

"It's mine." I smiled brightly.

Her eyebrows raised.

She came the rest of the way down the stairs. "Are you . . . waiting for something?"

"Dinner. Starving. You know how it is."

"I saved you some soup—"

"Someone ate it." I smiled winningly. "So hungry."

Claire blinked at me. "I'll, uh, go make you something."

"That would be great!"

I smiled some more.

And then stopped, because it appeared to be freaking her out.

She disappeared into the kitchen, after looking back at me once over her shoulder, and I opened the dining room door and slipped inside.

I tossed Ray the damned duck. "You've got to get out of here!"

"That's what we're trying to do! My boys need to feed—"

"So *go!*"

"Like that?" He gestured at the oily-haired, scruffy-jawed, smelly bunch who were currently congregated in the far corner of the room, staring at me. Because dhampir.

I sighed.

"They didn't eat all day yesterday," Ray told me. "And they're not strong like me. They can't go for days with no food, okay?"

And, sure enough, they had the twitchy, pasty-faced look of vamps in need of a meal.

Shit. Claire was going to love the idea of a bunch of hungry vampires around her kid. Not that they were anywhere close to losing control; they weren't babies. But try telling her that.

Only I didn't intend to tell her that.

I hadn't talked to Claire yesterday because I'd planned to have them gone by now. They'd been out of it last night, trying to heal, and might as well have been the logs they'd resembled, all rolled up in their blankets, safe from the sun. Today, I'd planned to smuggle them out at first dark, only today had mostly been spent recovering.

And it wasn't like I could just rent them a cheap hotel room. A random maid opening the drapes at the wrong time could cook them to a crisp. The only hotel safe enough was the Club, a super-expensive vamp-owned chain for traveling masters, which I couldn't have afforded even if the local one hadn't recently burned down.

"Look," Ray began.

"Shhh!"

I poked my head out the door and then hopped into the hall to take a quick look upstairs. The coast was clear. But knowing this place, it wouldn't stay that way.

I waved at Ray and mouthed, *Come on!*

They came on. Up the stairs on silent vamp feet and across to my room. Olga came out of hers in time to get flashed by the lineup, who reared back against the wall, clutching their towels and looking spooked. Guess they'd been too out of it yesterday to remember her.

She looked at them; they looked at her; she looked at me.

And then slowly took a step back inside her room and shut the door.

The vamps sprinted past, towels flying, and disappeared into mine.

I stayed behind with Ray to gather up armloads of their crap and run after them. It took three trips, but we got it all. Even the goddamned duck.

I closed my door and stayed pressed against it, looking at them. There were a lot. More than I recalled. Ten, twelve, fifteen.

What the hell?

"You can use my bathroom," I said. "To get cleaned up. Then go out the window."

I nodded at the big windows framing the bed, and when they turned to look at them, I pulled Ray back out the door.

"Fifteen?"

"I know, okay?"

"You're too weak to support fifteen!"

"Not when I was with Cheung. I got a boost from him, remember? But I lost that along with my head, so—"

"So now you're trying to support fifteen vamps on your own?" No wonder they needed to feed. Ray likely couldn't give them any help at all.

"What else am I gonna do?" he demanded. "I'm responsible for them, like you're responsible for me—"

"I am *not* your master!"

"See, this is why we have problems. You've never fully committed to this relationship."

"Ray! I'm a *dhampir*."

"You're a senator. The boys are thrilled to be part of your family. Thrilled!"

I opened the door again.

They did not look thrilled.

"Bathe!" I told them, and they jumped, and then stampeded for the bathroom.

I closed the door again.

"They can't stay here," I said. "We're going to have to work something out."

"I *had* something worked out. Then somebody just hadda be a hero. Well, I hope you're happy. Curly's in the wind, his theatre's trashed and, even if he does show up again—"

"Wait. What?"

"—he won't want anything to do with the two of us—"

"Curly isn't dead?"

"—*Nobody* is gonna want anything to do with the two of us if what happened to Curly gets around. We're gonna be known as the people you need protecting *from*."

"*What* happened to Curly?"

"You were there!"

I clapped a hand over his mouth and towed him to the stairs, and then up to my office. It was in what had been the attic, and was pretty well insulated, especially when I closed the trapdoor. And then turned around to see Ray peeling something nasty off his shoulder.

"What is going on? Why do you look like that?"

"Oh, Ray. I'm so glad you're all right." It was a falsetto and nothing like my voice. "I was so *concerned*—"

"I was concerned!"

He looked at me.

"I would have been concerned—"

"Sure, when you remembered I *existed*."

"I remembered! It's been a hard few days, all right?"

"Tell me about it. My old master rips me off, my new

master denies me, and that's after I almost end up buried alive!"

"What?"

He nodded vigorously. "The damned portal sucked in half the street."

"Half the *street*?"

"Okay, maybe not half. But three other buildings collapsed when it pulled the ground out from under 'em. There's supposed to be controls on a portal, you know? So it don't go crazy? Only something must have happened, because Curly's was set on full-bore 'let's swallow the world' mode and almost did!"

I thought of the grenade Dorina had thrown at whatever control they'd had down there.

Yeah, that would do it.

Although where she'd even gotten the thing I couldn't imagine. What kind of security guard carries grenades? Even for dark mage smugglers, that seemed a little extreme.

"—looking like a sinkhole had opened up underneath it," Ray was saying. "With the damned roof sitting curbside! It probably woulda been gone altogether, but the Circle showed up and shut it down. They're still pawing through the wreckage—"

He paused to look around for somewhere to stash the nasty thing from his shoulder, but didn't find anything. "You got a trash can?"

I shoved an ashtray at him, and he coiled whatever it was into it. "The audience got out okay," he added. "Being smart enough to run like hell. But those of us still inside when that wave hit—"

He shuddered.

And, suddenly, I did feel bad, because I *had* barely thought of him. Not that I didn't have about a thousand other things to think about, but still. Ray could have died.

"I could have died!" he told me, flopping down into my desk chair. "I was trying to swim out when that portal sucked the floor out from under me. I got pulled two, maybe three stories down, and couldn't see shit, 'cause there was water and mud and furniture and who knows what else being dragged down on top of me!"

I reached over and touched his arm. "That must have been terrifying."

"Yeah, well." He looked slightly mollified. "You know. Anyway, I finally found a staircase—completely full of mud—and just burrowed my way up. And stepped into freaking air again, and man, you shoulda seen it."

"Seen what?" I sat down on the visitor's chair I kept for clients, back when I had clients, and scooted it around the desk.

Ray looked pleased to have an audience.

"The main auditorium held together pretty well, I guess 'cause the floors underneath were getting chomped on, while it was just kinda sinking. Anyway, it looked like some big, dark underground cave, full of broken shit and puddles and waterfalls pouring down everywhere. It was crazy!"

"So, that's when you saw Curly?"

"No, that's when I almost got scared to death. The Circle broke a hole in the roof and sent some of their boys down on ropes, only I didn't know that, right? So there I am, freaked out, mud everywhere, including in my eyes, and there's this mist of water in the air, making everything sort of foggy. And then one of those assholes starts running at me, and he hadda helmet with a searchlight on it, and looked like some kind of one-eyed monster—" He paused. "You know, a real one-eyed monster, not—"

"I get it."

"Anyway, that's when I saw Curly."

"What?"

"Yeah. He was with one of his boys, some young, skinny guy, and they were booking it across the other side of the theatre. I called out, and I know that bastard saw me, but he just kept going. The guard shot one of those Spidey webs at the hole in the roof and they bounced."

I thought of the young guard who had been Dorina's ride. Maybe she'd managed to get him out, and Curly, too? But if so, where were they now?

"Beats me," Ray said, when I asked. "We used to call him Squirrelly Curly, 'cause he runs at the first sign of trouble. He had bolt-holes everywhere, back in the day. That's why he wanted out of the business. He don't have the nerves for smuggling."

"It looked like he was still in the game to me."

"Where his precious theatre was concerned, sure. Nothing was too good for that thing. Damn, if he's alive, I bet he's *pissed*—"

"Enough to rat out the people he was working with?" Ray stopped. "Why?"

"Something Dorina overheard."

He scowled. "You know it's weird when you talk about yourself in the third person, right? It creeps me out."

"It doesn't do a lot for me, either."

"Then why not stop it?"

"I can't stop it."

"Why not?"

"Because she isn't me!"

"Creep factor intensifying."

"Would you listen? She was roaming around the theatre's guts while we were upstairs, and she overheard—"

"Roaming around? She can roam around now? Like what? A ghost?"

"Not exactly—"

"When did this start?"

"Just recently—"

"I know it's just recently, or I'd know about it!" He glanced around the room, and he was looking genuinely spooked. "Is she here now?"

"I don't know. I don't think so."

"You don't *know*?" He got up.

I pushed him back down.

"Just listen."

"You can't spring something like that on a guy and then say, 'Just listen.' Like it's nothing. Is she gonna keep doing this?"

"Doing what?"

"Just . . . adding more powers?"

"I don't know—"

"Well, what *do* you know?"

"That you're getting on my last nerve!"

We sat there, glaring at each other for a moment, before Ray let out a breath he didn't need. "All right. I'm listening. What?"

I told him.

"Okay, no." He got up and headed for the door.

I caught him halfway.

"Look, Ray—"

"No, you look! Geminus' group was straight-up savage, okay? Everybody knew it; nobody messed with 'em. Until he died. And the damned Senate got involved and cleaned house! They killed every one of his boys who were even suspected of smuggling—"

"I know that."

"—so if anyone decided to go right back to what just got half their family butchered? They are *not* the kind of guys you wanna mess with!"

"I don't want to mess with them. I just want to know who they're working for. If they're in it for themselves, smuggling some refugees or fey wine or whatever, then fine—"

"That's not what they're smuggling. That response last night? You don't get that over wine!"

"That's my point, Ray. If they're working with Aeslinn, they could be bringing in some very bad stuff for the war."

"Then why not just tell the Senate? Have them deal with this?"

"Ray, I'm *on* the Senate. But if I'm going to talk them into diverting resources in the middle of a war, I need to have some evidence to offer. All I have right now is something Dorina overheard, which made it sound like first the albino and then a mage had taken over control of Geminus' family. And you know that's impossible."

Ray shook his head. "It's not impossible. In the trenches, you make alliances where you have to."

"Yeah, only I don't think it works like that for senators. But we know Geminus was working with Aeslinn before he died, and a bunch of dark mages. So, if the mage is Aeslinn's contact—"

"Then the vamps wouldn't be working for a human, but for a king of the fey."

I nodded. "And their ally in the war."

Ray frowned. "So you need Curly to find out if you're right."

"He was working with them. He has to know something."

Ray sighed. "Maybe. Or maybe he just grabbed the first offer he got after Geminus bit the big one. People like Curly and me, we team up with mages or weres or whoever the hell is gonna help us survive."

"Even a dhampir?"

"That's different. You and me, we got a bond."

I started to dispute him, but there was suddenly something in his face, something I'd probably worn on my own, more than once. Ray looked like a guy who was bracing to get hit, with words if not with fists, because he'd just risked something. And every time he did that, every time he trusted anybody, he paid for it.

I'd spent a lifetime like that, and yet, like Ray, I always seemed to come back for more. Always seemed to hold out hope for something . . . I wasn't even sure what. Acceptance? A place I belonged? Some kind of certainty in an uncertain world, that somebody had my back, and would always have it?

So I didn't say anything.

Except to ask if something was wrong, because I'm nosy like that.

Ray sat on the edge of the desk. His dark hair flopped in his face, and his blue eyes were serious. More so than I could remember seeing them.

"My boys . . . they're not doing so good," he told me. "When Cheung cut me loose, he didn't bother to think, or didn't care, that he was doing it to them, too. And then the club burnt down, and most of our stuff went with it. I keep telling them that we got a new place, that you're our master now, but they don't believe it. They tell me, 'What's a senator want with us?' They think you're gonna kick us out, and then they don't know . . ."

He didn't finish the thought, but he didn't have to. Somebody like Ray needed a protector. He was going to have to cut a deal with someone, and soon, and he would not be negotiating from a position of strength. He and his boys were likely in for a very tough time, if they found any place at all. And if they didn't—

Well, in some ways, the vamp world was like the human. It wasn't kind to those of us on our own.

I didn't know how this thing between Dorina and me

was going to play out, and it seemed insane to take on any more responsibilities until I did. But if the worst happened, and if Ray and company had been acknowledged by me, then somebody in the family would take care of them. They'd have to.

We Basarabs stick together.

"Yeah," I told him, after a moment.

Ray looked up. He'd been contemplating his naval, with a crease in his forehead, and his eyes shadowed with worry. He looked like he'd forgotten what we'd been talking about.

"Yeah, what?"

"Yeah. I guess we have a bond."

Chapter Thirty-one

There was a ceremony. There's always a ceremony with vamps. Although, I don't think it normally involves a bunch of guys in towels and dripping hair, some half-shaved, going down on one knee to kiss my nonexistent ring.

They seemed a lot happier, though, by the time I finally pushed the last squashy ass out of my bedroom window to go look for Curly. And then headed downstairs, wearing Ray's worried frown, because I now had to find lodging for fifteen—sixteen, counting him—kind of pathetic vampires, and had to do it soon. Which was why I was halfway to the porch before I looked up.

And saw Louis-Cesare standing just outside the door.

I stopped dead.

Last night, there had been powder burns on one of his temples, a cut across his lower jaw, and a bruise, livid red and purple, distorting his left cheek. Tonight, there was nothing. It was as if the whole thing at the theatre had just been a bad dream.

It shouldn't have surprised me.

As soon as the curses wore off, healing would have been almost instantaneous. That's why most people never saw a first-level master like that; they healed too fast. You were never supposed to be able to trace the indentation left by a bullet, or see the scattered pieces of it shining in the moonlight through half-healed skin. You were never supposed to smell his blood, or feel terror grip your heart at the extent of the damage, because it was gone in an instant, as if it had never been there at all.

But it had been there, and I had seen it.

And, suddenly, I couldn't see anything else.

"Dory!" a lilting voice called. "We were just talking about you."

Shit. I'd been so busy staring at Louis-Cesare, I'd failed to notice that someone else was back, too. And lounging on the swing, his long legs splayed out in casual elegance, his green eyes amused.

I didn't know why Caedmon looked so pleased with himself until I noticed: Louis-Cesare was holding a single rose, a beautiful thing, elegant and bright red and tied with a little white bow. Which would have been more impressive if the porch hadn't been draped with them. Like, to the point that I wasn't sure it wasn't about to collapse.

I didn't know where the others had come from, because they weren't the hothouse variety. But rather big, old-fashioned, pale pink things with fat ruffled heads that shed a subtle perfume. Or they would have, if there hadn't been a million of them.

Then I noticed the bloom-filled creeper coming from next door, where it had crawled out of the neighbor's rose patch and inched along the ground the way this variety didn't, because it wasn't a climbing rose. Or, at least, it hadn't been. Until it scaled a tall wooden fence, dropped over the other side, scrawled across the yard, and set about making our sagging back porch sag some more with a crap ton of heavy pink blooms.

Just to be nearer to the blond in the swing.

And to piss off Louis-Cesare, judging by his expression.

Things were a little tense on the porch, because he and Caedmon had a history, and it wasn't good. And I really didn't want a repeat, considering how much repair work the house still had to do. And then I noticed that Louis-Cesare was in a suit.

It was a nice one, a dark blue that deepened his eyes to sapphire and brought out the red in his hair. He'd matched it with a pristine white shirt and a dark-colored tie, usually a boring combination unless it's draped across broad shoulders and a sculpted chest. I blinked at him, because he looked . . . well, like you'd expect.

Edible.

"Going somewhere?" I asked, and he awkwardly handed me his lone flower.

"I was hoping to take you to dinner."

I didn't say anything. Not because Olga's errand waited, or because I'd already eaten. But because I hadn't expected him tonight and I wasn't ready.

I knew what had to be done, had known ever since I realized that my days were likely numbered. Hell, I'd known it long before that, practically since I set eyes on Mr. Too-Good-for-the-Likes-of-You. But I still wasn't.

"Dory?"

"Uh—"

"We're already planning a feast here. My men are cooking it now," Caedmon said, coming to the rescue with a strange little smile. And with a wave of a languid hand toward the garden, which I hadn't noticed because the roses were blocking half of it. But now . . .

"Did you ask Claire about this?" I breathed, my eyes widening.

"Ask me about what?" Claire said, backing out of the house. She had a tray in her hands, piled with sandwiches, napkins, and a pitcher of homemade lemonade. Which she almost dropped, along with her jaw, when she turned around. "Caedmon!"

She was staring at the fragrant smoke starting to waft this way from numerous campfires. Campfires that had been dug willy-nilly, all over her formerly nice lawn. Including a huge fire pit over which a spit had been erected to hold an entire . . .

Smallish cow? Overlarge sheep? Massive pig? The jury was still out, because I couldn't see it properly through a bunch of guards, who were crowding around to rub the meat with some kind of spice paste.

Others were putting pots on fires, decorating weathered old picnic tables with what looked suspiciously like Claire's best bedsheets, carting in armloads of firewood they'd gotten who knew where, and chasing off a couple of little dogs, which had been drawn by the aroma. Large lanterns were being lit in the trees and smaller ones were being strung on ropes crisscrossing the garden; wooden kegs were being brought out of tents, including one that

splashed Soini in the face when he opened it wrong; and
groups of fey were gathered around large pans, loudly debating sauce ingredients.

Somebody brushed past Claire with a question in a
language I didn't know, but which caused her to spin and
yell after him: "No! And stay out of my pantry!"

Having scared off the fey, she turned her ire on Caedmon, who was still lounging in the swing, still smiling that
little smile and still holding Louis-Cesare's eyes.

"Do stay for dinner," he offered, which for some reason made Louis-Cesare flush almost as dark as his rose.

"Caedmon!" Claire's voice snapped. "What *is* this?"

"A celebration. It's not often we have the chance to
welcome a new cousin, especially one so skilled."

"Cousin?" Claire looked confused.

I glanced around. That was all we needed. Another fey.

"My apologies about your treatment earlier," Caedmon said, looking past her—at nothing, because there was
nobody behind me. "Reiðarr has been informed of his
error. He and the others have been instructed to treat you
with the respect due your new station."

"Station? What station?" Claire asked, looking confused as I met Caedmon's eyes.

And realized that he was talking to me.

A weird sort of chill crept up my spine.

"I told you before I left," Caedmon said, glancing at
Claire. "She is *vargr*. We all saw it—"

"What?" Louis-Cesare said, looking back and forth
between me and Caedmon.

"—and as part fey—"

"*What?*"

"—she is to be welcomed by her family, as is tradition.
One codified by treaty." That last bit had a bite to it, probably because Louis-Cesare's eyes had settled on Caedmon with an expression I really didn't like.

"What? Wait." That was me.

But Caedmon didn't wait, although his smile acquired
an edge. "And as there seems to be no way to tell which
clan she belongs to, after so long, I have decided to adopt
her into our little family. To the newest Blarestri warrior!" he said, hoisting a mug of something.

Suddenly, I was surrounded by fey, dozens of them, laughing and talking and slapping me on the back. And shoving a beer stein into my hands, while Louis-Cesare stared at Caedmon. And if looks could kill . . .

"Dory, what the hell?" Claire and I had ducked back into the hall, while the festivities exploded outside. And while Louis-Cesare and Caedmon faced off, because it had just dawned on my boyfriend that the king of the fey was trying to poach me.

"You tell me. Did you know about this?"

She looked shocked. "No! Or, rather, after last night I knew what you were—are—I mean, what you have to be—"

"Claire! I'm not fey!"

"But . . . you're *vargr*. That's a fey talent. It doesn't exist anywhere else—"

"No, it doesn't. But vampire mental powers do!"

"You think that's what this is?"

"I know that's what it is! My mother was a Romanian peasant girl, and my father—" I stopped, because holy *shit*. Mircea was going to be . . . well, 'pissed' didn't really cover it. Not only did he have a family obsession that this was going to fly straight in the face of, but he also needed me on the Senate right now. And needed badly, or he'd have never persuaded the consul to look at a damned dhampir every meeting.

"Vampires can do that?" Claire said, her forehead wrinkling. "Just mentally ride along with someone? Because I've never heard—"

"Neither have I."

Caedmon had slipped through the door while we weren't looking, a massive pink bouquet in his hands. He laid it in my arms like I was some beauty pageant contestant about to be crowned, which would have been funny except that Louis-Cesare was on his heels. At least, he was until he grabbed the king of the fey and slammed him against the wall.

"You're not taking her!"

I dropped everything—literally: the full stein splattered its contents everywhere and went rolling across the boards, and the flowers littered the hall. But I got in between the guys before a blow landed. "Not here!"

"Damned right!" That was Claire. "What are you playing at, Caedmon?"

"Playing?" A blond eyebrow ascended. "I assure you, I am perfectly serious. The law clearly states that we are allowed to claim anyone with fey blood—"

"I don't have fey blood," I said.

"I can assure you that you do."

"And I can assure you, I don't! I'll take a test, if you like—"

"You already did."

"Funny, I don't recall it."

"Really? I thought it was memorable."

"Start making sense!" Louis-Cesare snarled, and Claire nodded. I blinked. Because seeing the two of them agree on something was . . . kind of creepy.

"It's quite simple," Caedmon said, taking his time, and adjusting his wrinkled tunic. "We have a treaty with your Senate—with all of them, for that matter. As you know, our birthrate is very low. We cannot afford to lose anyone of our blood, particularly one with such a rare gift—"

"We know all that!" Claire broke in. "But Dory just told you—she isn't fey!"

"And she would know?" Caedmon looked at me. "You know who your mother was, but what about your grandmother? Your great-grandmother? Your great-grandfather? How well do you know your bloodline?"

"My mother was a peasant girl," I reminded him. "They didn't keep records back then. Most of them couldn't even read."

"Exactly so." He sounded like he'd just proved something.

It pissed me off. "It doesn't matter! I've told you, it's a vampire skill. I get it from my father—"

"What is?" Louis-Cesare asked.

"I doubt that," Caedmon murmured.

"Dory?"

"Something happened the other night," I told Louis-Cesare. "It's . . . complicated."

"Complicated? How complicated?"

"Merely a *manlikan* army attacking the house, and then an assault by an especially strong *vargr*," Caedmon said, before I could stop him. "Don't worry; we don't expect you to know what that means," he added.

Because I guess Louis-Cesare's face wasn't red enough already.

"Give me a damned blood test, and end this!" I said, because I needed to talk to my boyfriend. Like, now.

"You are dhampir," Caedmon said. "Irrevocably changed in the womb by your father's . . . condition . . . from what you would have been. There are no blood tests that can see through that."

"So much for talk of treaties!" Louis-Cesare snapped.

Claire nodded vigorously.

"—fortunately, we don't need one," Caedmon continued smoothly. "Such tests can be inconclusive for a variety of reasons, which is why the treaty clearly states that there are other acceptable proofs. Such as demonstrating clear evidence of fey magic." His eyes caught mine, and there was steel in them. "Which you most definitely did."

Okay, shit.

"She belongs here!" Louis-Cesare said, pushing against the hand I had on his chest, in an attempt to get in the king's face.

"She belongs with her people," Caedmon said serenely.

"She belongs wherever the hell she wants to be!" Claire said. "And if you two start a fight in my hall, I swear—"

"She's right. The kids are here," I reminded them. Because I'd just caught sight of Aiden, wobbling about on unsteady baby legs, among the tall creatures on the porch. Until one of them picked him up and gave him a sip of beer, which made his face wrinkle and his small fists flail around, and the fey burst into laughter. And miss his companion, who was still on the ground with his nonexistent nose pressed against the screen door.

Until he was suddenly inside, and launching himself at Caedmon.

I grabbed Stinky before actual blood was spilled, not that it helped. Because Louis-Cesare's hand was on his sword, Caedmon's was on his, and both men looked like a battle was brewing just below the surface. And not far below, because I could feel Louis-Cesare's arm flex when I grabbed it.

He wanted a fight, and the king seemed more than willing to oblige—why, I didn't know. He had to realize how this was going to play with Mircea and the rest of the Senate. It was seriously ironic that they were being put in a position to defend a dirty dhampir, but they had done worse in their long lives. And when the choice was between distasteful and dangerous, they'd go for the former every time. And right now, an unbalanced Senate was way more of a danger than a pissed-off fey king.

Caedmon had a fight on his hands.

Yet, despite that, and despite the fact that he had Soini and probably other *vargrs*—since I couldn't see him risking his only one in the wilds of Earth otherwise—he was still pushing this. And still looking at Louis-Cesare like he was one of the main obstacles to his carting me off to Faerie. Which might have been reasonable in the mind of someone as old and traditional as Caedmon, but which made my blood boil.

Time for him to enter the twenty-first century.

"He isn't my guardian," I told Caedmon flatly. "I came of age a long time ago. You have anything to say, you say it to me."

"I just did," the king pointed out, but he was still looking at Louis-Cesare. Until I twisted a hand in his shirt, almost tight enough to strangle him. The stunning green eyes shifted to me, and a beautiful smile broke over the face, almost luminous in its intensity. "And would have when I first returned, but didn't wish to interrupt your talk with young Ymsi. How is he?"

"Fine," I said shortly. "He thinks it was a woman—a Light Fey woman—who attacked him."

"I knew it!" Claire looked daggers at her father-in-law. "I *told* you—"

"Yes, yes." Caedmon frowned slightly. Because while enraged master vampires didn't seem to faze him, his red-haired daughter-in-law was another matter. And if Claire had been pissed before, it was nothing compared to this. Suspicion was one thing; confirmation was quite another. And while this wasn't actual proof of Efridis' involvement, I didn't expect Claire to understand that.

Apparently, Caedmon didn't, either, at least not without some work. "We need to discuss it, at a later time—"

"We'll discuss it now!" Claire snapped, as I released him. Because the man had bigger problems. "I want—"

"I know what you want. But as I've told you repeatedly, it's not that simple—"

"Did you even see her?"

"Yes, I—"

"See her?" I asked.

Caedmon glanced at me. "My sister is currently a guest of your consul—"

Great.

"—and she denies any involvement—"

"Of course she denies it!" Claire said. "Did you expect her to just admit it?"

"Possibly, yes." Caedmon began to look impatient as Claire glared at him. "You lived at court long enough to know better than this. My sister is not only Blarestri royalty; she is the queen of another powerful court—"

"Who she betrayed!"

"But that does not mean her husband would not come to her aid if she were imperiled. Her honor reflects on him. He might arrange an accident, were he ever to gain control of her again, but to allow another to—"

"You mean you won't pursue it?" Claire's eyes flashed. "That she can just do whatever she wants?"

"I didn't say that." Caedmon's expression remained mild, but his voice was a little sharper than before. "I understand that you want to protect Aiden. So do I. But these things have to be handled carefully or a war—"

"We're already at war! Or haven't you noticed?"

"I have not." It was curt. "Neither have you. Believe me, if it comes to that, you will see the difference."

Claire just stood there for a moment, vibrating. And there were no remnants of the *Vogue* cover girl now. I could see it, clearer than I ever had: the wild fey princess, all fiery hair and electric green eyes and pale, unearthly beauty, a legend straight out of an old Irish song suddenly come to life. And furious.

"Then tell her this, next time you meet," Claire spat. "If she comes for my child, she won't be dealing with a fey army, or a vampire court, or your political games. She'll be dealing with me. And I will kill her."

Chapter Thirty-two

Claire banged out of the screen door, leaving the three of us. Or the four, if you counted Stinky, and I didn't see any reason why you shouldn't, since he was kicking up the biggest fuss. Which was a problem, because I was going to have a tough time of it if I had to get between the two men again. But Caedmon surprised me.

"I need to talk to Claire," he told me quickly. "In the meantime, think on this. You've been an outsider all your life, part of two worlds, but accepted by neither—"

"She's accepted," Louis-Cesare snapped. "She's on the Senate!"

Caedmon shot him a look. "And we both know how long that will last once things calm down, don't we?"

"Her family is *here!*"

"And may be there as well." Emerald eyes found mine. "I could help you look for them."

"Caedmon—"

"Think on it," he told me, kissed my hand, and left. Leaving me with a hissing, furious baby and Louis-Cesare, who didn't look any happier.

I felt the same, although for different reasons.

Just do it, I told myself. *Right now, before you chicken out. You have the perfect excuse. Caedmon just handed it to you. . . .*

But, instead, I stood there, feeling miserable and not saying anything.

Neither did Louis-Cesare, for a long moment.

I didn't know what he was thinking, but I was trying to come up with another solution. Something, anything, that would let me hold on to him, because he was wrong. I didn't care about being on the Senate, a community that had shunned me for years. That was Mircea's idea. I'd gone along with it to help him out, not because I wanted prestige I wasn't going to get anyway.

I only wanted one thing.

But, as always, it was something I couldn't have.

And the longer I put this off, the more I tried to find a solution that didn't exist, the more I put him in danger. Dorina was a knife in the dark, a gun in the hand, a brilliant, multifaceted weapon of destruction. I'd lived with her for centuries; I knew what she was. I knew what she could do. Even worse, I knew *him*.

What happened if she decided to banish me? What happened when he realized that I wasn't coming back? That my consciousness had been scattered, and all that was left was a shell—one still walking around, because someone else was in there?

Dorina wouldn't have to provoke an attack. He would do that for her. And then he would die.

It wasn't even a question. When Louis-Cesare felt something, it was all over his face. When he did something, it was wholehearted, full speed ahead, no stopping to think about his own safety, because why would he?

He thought himself invincible.

It was why he was pulling me against him now, letting me close, not caring that I had a struggling baby fey in my arms who was considerably less than tame. It was why he was letting me there, right there, at his neck, one of a vampire's most vulnerable spots. Just as he had in the shower, taking no precautions despite knowing what I was, what I could do.

What she could do.

And what she would do, sooner or later, if I didn't woman the hell *up*.

"I think we need a break," I said hoarsely, and immediately knew he didn't get it. The body didn't tense, the hand on my back continued stroking, the lips kissed my hair.

"It's been quite a week," he agreed—to a point I hadn't been making. "The Senate has called another meeting for tomorrow, which is unavoidable. But after that, we should be able to get away for a few—"

"No." I pulled back, but forced myself to look at him, because I owed him that much. "No, I mean *we* need a break. You and me."

"What?" For some reason, he still looked confused.

Damn it! Why couldn't he understand and let this be over? I wanted to rip the Band-Aid off, not stretch it into agony.

"My life's a mess right now," I said flatly. "I need some time to figure things out. Some time to myself," I added, because he still didn't get it.

And then, suddenly, he did.

"What?" He said it again, although I knew he understood. His eyes—God. *Just make it stop!*

"You heard me. I need some space."

"Some space. What does that mean?"

"You know what it means!"

"*Non.*" It was rough. "I do not. If you wish to be with this fey, then say so—"

"This isn't about him!"

"Then what is it about? Just a few days ago, you almost—" He broke off for a moment, and his jaw clenched. But then he came out with it, because Louis-Cesare isn't like Mircea or any other vamp I've ever known. He just lays it all out there. "You almost marked me. And now you do not wish to see me anymore, *comme ça?* What am I supposed to think?"

"I didn't mark you. I wasn't—I just got carried away—"

I stopped, because that was a lie, and not even a very good one. But he'd flustered me. This whole thing was throwing me in ways I hadn't expected. I didn't know how to break up with someone; I'd never had to before. The few long-term lovers I'd had in the past—if you could call a few weeks long-term—had hightailed it for the horizon as soon as Dorina reared her head the first time. They'd left me, not vice versa, and I'd always assumed I got the short end of the stick.

I'd been wrong.

Leaving was much harder.

Especially with someone who mirrored every emotion,

every thought, on his face. Like now, when he'd just paled, enough that it was visible even in the darkness of the hall. And his eyes . . .

I didn't want to look at them anymore. I didn't want to hurt him. I didn't want any of this, but a small hurt now was better than what lay ahead.

But, God, I wanted to tell him the truth! That was the worst part of it. He'd never know how much I did want him, how much I'd always—*Fuck*, what was the point? Just *finish* this!

But he beat me to it.

"Ah. Of course. I should have realized."

"Realized . . . ?"

But I didn't get an answer. To anything. His throat was working, but he didn't say anything else.

And then the door slammed open behind us and Soini came through, grinning hugely and holding two full beer steins. "Dory! I just heard!" He bent and kissed me lightly on each cheek. Like that was a perfectly normal thing for a member of the standoffish fey to do. "It's so wonderful! And not just because there will be someone to take the pressure off me. I mean, it's not so bad; people just have all these expectations. But you already know what you're doing, so you won't have to worry about that, and now we have a new sister! It's been so long since we found anyone among your people—"

Soini kept talking, and tugging, trying to shepherd us back to the festivities. Probably because I was the guest of honor. It didn't work. I couldn't hear him anymore, just the rise and fall of his voice, with no words making sense. And I couldn't move, even though the hall seemed to be doing that on its own, telescoping in on me. Because Louis-Cesare's face . . .

It had changed from anger to something else, something familiar, because we had a similar history in at least one way. The prince and the pauper had a lifetime of being abandoned by everyone we cared about. For Louis-Cesare, it had started with his mother, who had given up the tiny boy who loved her in order to keep her reputation intact, and her betrayal had been followed by a host of others, from his treacherous half-brother's to that of my uncle Radu, the one who had made him a vampire. And who had then abandoned him to find his own way in a hostile world.

Radu had had a good reason, one that had been explained to me a couple times now, but that I still didn't completely get. But it didn't matter, because it hadn't softened the blow. And for someone who had lost her own mother early, who had spent years thinking that her father had abandoned and rejected her, who'd had to leave every lover or friend she'd ever had—yeah, I knew that look, that pain. I saw it on his face, in his eyes, and I suddenly couldn't do it to him. Not *again*.

Fine. So let him stick around until Dorina guts him, a little voice said. *See how you feel then.*

I shoved the mental voice away. It wasn't the right time. Not now. Not like this, with other people around to overhear and when there was no way to give him a proper explanation.

And you think he'll accept it if you do? You already tried that in the shower. He won't leave unless you make *him go!*

But, as it turned out, I didn't have to do anything. Louis-Cesare suddenly took my hand, bowed over it, and left. Turning around and striding so quickly down the hall and out of the house that he was gone almost before I realized what was happening.

"He isn't staying for the party?" Soini asked, blinking after him.

I just stood there, not sure I could say anything.

"But we're having roast pork."

"I have to go to the bathroom," I said roughly, shoved Stinky at him, and ran up the stairs.

I made it back to my room feeling like I'd been stabbed, straight through something vital, and now it was just a case of bleeding out.

His face.

God, his face.

I shut my door behind me and then just stood there, in the dark, empty room. Only it wasn't. There was the wall Claire had once thrown him through, misunderstanding some sounds, thinking he was hurting me when he never

would. There was the bathroom where he'd first told me
he loved me, shocking me to all but speechlessness. There
was the bed. . . .

I felt sick. Like, actually, physically ill. There were no
chairs, Olga having taken hers down again, so I settled for
leaning against the wall. And realized that I was still
holding his rose. Somehow, I hadn't dropped it with all
the others.

It was a little worse for wear: a couple of the outer pet-
als were missing, and one of the leaves was hanging by a
thin bit of stem, the rest having been ripped from the
stalk. I stared at it, feeling as empty as the room. Fuck.

I bent over, hands on my knees, and just breathed for
a minute.

It's okay, the stupid voice said. *You'll feel better in
time. You always knew this wasn't going to work—*

I beat my fists into my temples until the voice stopped.
Until I was dizzy and probably completely demented
looking, but I didn't care. There was no one to see. There
never would be. . . .

My head felt dizzy, my gut was roiling, and my legs were
weak. I slowly slid down the wall, until I ended up clutching my knees and the rose, and then just sat there in darkness. I didn't cry. I wasn't going to fucking cry. This was
my fault, all of it. So I didn't get that release. I didn't get
anything, because I *knew* better, knew these things never
worked out, and that was with normal guys. What the hell
had I been thinking? Me and Louis-Cesare—what a
laugh.

But, for a little while, it hadn't been funny. For a little
while, it had been . . . like nothing I'd ever known. I'd lived
five hundred years, more or less. The less being the swaths
of time I didn't remember, when Dorina had been in
charge. But even if you crossed those out, I'd been around
a long time. I'd seen amazing things, some frightening,
some wonderful, some terrible.

I'd never seen anything like him.

For a moment, I let myself remember: sunlight turning
brown hair to red; electric blue eyes, the most vivid I'd
ever seen; a rare laugh breaking through the facade of
sangfroid he determinedly kept up even though he was

really bad at it; him accepting an eighteenth-century-looking satin ensemble from Radu even though it was *lavender*, and probably intending to wear it sometime because it would make his father happy and he didn't care what people thought of him. Most people . . .

I thought about him looking so pleased with himself as he smugly said "three," after exceeding the number of bears I'd wanted despite the odds, and I felt my legs tense, because I wanted to run after him so badly I was vibrating. I'd never had anyone like him, and for a moment, I let myself grieve. I didn't deserve him, but I'd had him anyway, something that had frequently made me thrilled and terrified and grateful and suspicious and amazed—just jaw-droppingly amazed—all at the same time. And I'd thrown him away, without even a decent explanation because there was no explanation he'd understand.

I didn't even know if I understood.

So I sat there, dry-eyed and staring at nothing, until somebody rapped on the wood behind me.

"Dory?"

I stood up and cracked the door.

Claire's worried face looked in. "Is something—" She broke off. And before I could say anything, if there'd been anything to say, she was pulling me into her arms.

"I sent him away." I sounded blank.

Claire hugged me harder, and didn't say anything.

"I loved him, and I sent him away." It was my voice, but there was a note I'd never heard in it. Not grief, not anger. More like wonder.

Like even my brain thought I was crazy.

"This is about Dorina," Claire said, after a moment.

It wasn't a question, but I pulled back and nodded.

She didn't say anything. But I knew her expressions. I knew she wanted to.

I laughed suddenly; it sounded harsh. "I thought you'd be pleased."

She didn't look pleased. She looked stricken. "No. Oh, no. Dory, I'm so sorry!"

"For what?"

She wrapped her arms around herself, like she still needed someone to hold on to. "He was . . . he was nice, when you were ill. I expected him to be angry." She laughed a little, not happily. "I have terrible timing. I realized I must have interrupted something the other day, when you were in the bath—"

"How?"

She shook her head. "He came to the door in a towel, with soap in his hair. He was blushing."

"He does that a lot." Redhead complexion. And his kind doesn't exactly tan.

"I didn't think they could do that," she said. "Vampires, I mean."

"Louis-Cesare isn't a normal vampire."

I wanted her to go. It felt like somebody had yanked my heart out of my chest and crumpled it into a little ball. I wanted nothing more than to curl around the pain and—

But Claire almost looked like she was in pain, too.

"You told me not to lump them all together," she said. "I didn't listen."

"It's all right—"

"It's not all right."

"It doesn't matter." Especially now.

"It matters!" She stared at me. "He was so worried, Dory, when they brought you back from those fights. I told him I thought you were okay, but that someone really should check you out, just to be sure, but he said he didn't know anyone else here—"

"That's great, Claire—"

"No, *listen*. I asked him why he didn't contact one of his people, you know, mentally."

I nodded.

"And have them find a healer. But he said that takes concentration, and he couldn't manage it right then. So I dug out the emergency number, for the all-night service, and gave it to him. But he couldn't dial it. His hands were shaking too much—"

I'd started digging through the dresser, looking for something to wear to Horatiu's, but now I rounded on her. "Why are you doing this?"

She bit her lip. "I don't know. I just—I realized then that I'd made a mistake. He did—he does—love you, and you love him—"

"None of which matters!"

She caught my arm. "Love always matters! And I—When I saw him that way, this big, strong master vampire, suddenly so terrified, so helpless . . . I knew I'd been wrong. Wrong about him, maybe wrong about all of them. I don't know."

"They're like every group. Some good, some bad." I looked from her to the hand she had on my arm. "Why are you doing this?" I repeated.

"Because he's a big, strong master vampire. He can handle this. He can handle *her*."

"But I can't!" I grabbed my duffle and threw some stuff inside, barely even looking at it. "If I hurt him—"

"Dory." Claire's voice was suddenly small. "If what I saw that night was any indication, you couldn't hurt him more than . . . than this." She gestured around—at what, I didn't know. Probably my empty fucking room.

"Then I'll hurt him. At least he'll be alive to feel it!"

I left.

Chapter Thirty-three

I drove around aimlessly for a while, with the top down because it was stifling and my air conditioner had been busted for a week. It didn't help. The night was muggy, I was sweating and miserable, and nobody even bothered to try to hijack me so I could take out some aggression.

Not that I seemed to have much right now.

Or anything else.

It was why I hadn't headed to Horatiu's, like I'd planned. I was in no condition to talk to him. I'd just wanted to get away, somewhere without people, even well-meaning ones, somewhere I could think. But now that I had, my brain didn't seem interested. I felt strange, detached, numb. And seriously in need of a drink.

I also needed information, and there was only one place to get both.

I jerked the wheel around, and headed for the bar I knew best.

———

"SHUT THE DOOR!"

The collective shout made me jump, as it always did, despite the fact that I knew to expect it. I slipped inside and shut the door. Some of Fin's clientele tended to be light phobic, and the shout had become a habit, even at night. Others just liked the ambience of a basement bar lit only by a dozen TVs, a few dim lanterns, and scrolls of golden graffiti streaming down the walls, giving the odds on anything and everything. The proprietor wasn't picky; if you could bet on it, you could get odds at Fin's.

Assuming you didn't break your neck on the way down the stairs, that is. It was actually worse than descending into the twins' den, where all you had to deal with was black. In here, it was either glaring, rapidly shifting colors, or darkness, take your pick. Which left you tripping over your own feet the whole night because your eyes never totally adjusted.

Or your ears, I thought, as another roar went up from the crowd—the really big crowd. I hadn't seen Fin's this packed in a while. I couldn't even see any floor below, just a sea of heads, lit by flickering darkness.

And it was the same up here. I pushed my way down the stairs ruthlessly, because people weren't using them for the purpose intended, but as a way to get a better look at the big screen off to one side. Not that it was helping. It covered maybe a fourth of one wall, and was where the most important events were shown. But I couldn't tell what was on tonight thanks to the mass of people standing in front of it.

The bar was swamped, too, when I finally fought my way over, although I kept shoving until I found a piece to prop my elbow on.

Fin was nowhere in sight. The long slab of maple was being manned by a bunch of his family, at a guess, since they were forest trolls, too. The nearest was so tiny that, even though he was standing on a box, his nose kept hitting the bar top and then bouncing up and down. It was kind of fascinating to watch, and didn't seem to bother him, although it did make his voice a little hard to understand.

Although that would have been the case anyway, I thought, wincing as another huge roar shook the place.

What the hell was going on?

After a moment, the bartender finished with his current job and popped up at my end, bobbing his nose expectantly.

"Fin?" I yelled, because anything less wasn't going to be heard over the noise.

He cupped a hand around his ear and leaned closer, in the universal "speak up" pose.

"Fin? Is he in tonight?"

"What?"

"Is Fin here?" I all but bellowed.

"You want a beer?"

"No! I want *Fin*!"

"Okay, what kind of gin?"

"No, *Fin*! *Fin!* I just want to find out—"

"Stout?"

I gave up. "Never mind."

He nodded and hopped off his box, disappearing under the counter, and I scanned the room. If Fin wasn't behind the bar, he was usually taking bets over by the big screen, where everything was happening. But I couldn't see him. I couldn't see anything with the old green couches completely covered in people, and more standing behind. And with the screen itself giving off only an occasional flicker through the yelling, jumping, and high-fiving patrons in front of it.

Somebody was having fun tonight.

"Here you go!" The bartender was back.

He handed me something reddish gold, with a good head.

"What is this?"

"What you ordered. Barley wine!"

I sighed and paid up, because arguing wasn't worth the hassle, and took my barley wine on a tour of the facilities. It wasn't easy. I got more alcohol on me than in me, thanks to buffeting elbows, and was all but deaf due to the constant thunder of the crowd.

But I made it to one side of the big screen, where I was pushed against a side table by the crowd's ebb and flow. That wasn't such a bad thing, since the table was currently empty, except for a bunch of used glasses. So I climbed on top to look for Fin.

And found somebody else instead.

Make that two somebodies, I thought, as another earthshaking roar went up from the crowd. The screen was so big, almost filling my vision from here, and the crowd was so close and so loud, that it was genuinely disorienting. It felt like I'd stepped into some weird virtual reality game, where we were all along for the ride.

And what a ride it was.

I had to steady myself on the shoulders of a couple guys, to keep from falling off the table as we went tearing along behind a huge troll. Who in turn was tearing through a building, a bunch of screaming men running ahead of him, most of them too panicked to use the guns they were carrying. And the few who did finding it hard to aim while pissing themselves.

The troll smashed into something that shattered in a haze of flying wood, and whatever was providing the feed took a beating. We all lolled drunkenly, maybe half the bar together, as it flipped end over end, and hit the floor. And then we were leaning the other way, as it bounced up again and zoomed around in a circle to right itself. And showed us a dizzying view of an industrial building in the process.

It was old and grimy, with a row of high rectangular windows letting in streams of hazy moonlight, or maybe streetlight. It filtered down to illuminate the scene, looking strangely peaceful and serene. While below, the troll was literally ripping apart the building that the men were running through, and then using the pieces to rip *them* apart.

I saw one guy bisected by a flying piece of metal, maybe a large table or door; we were back behind the troll now and moving so fast that it was hard to tell. Another was crushed under a brick wall that decided to collapse when a massive arm was dragged through it. And a third was sent hurtling into another wall, courtesy of the girder that had been thrown at him like the world's biggest javelin.

Others, however, were obviously mages, because I saw shrapnel bouncing off what had to be shields. Shields that were taking a beating, and not just from the troll. Because, on his back, hunched over like a tiny, wild-eyed wart, was . . . something crazy.

Or make that some*one* crazy, a screaming banshee with a machine gun and an afro, just letting it rip.

I had a sudden, dizzying flashback to the same woman in the cab of a truck, swaying back and forth and cackling maniacally. Kind of like she was doing now, only the machine-gun bursts drowned it out, along with the screams of the remaining men. One of whom finally got his shit together long enough to lob a spell. The big troll ducked, and it mostly flew overhead—his, anyway. The maniacal wart, however, got her hair singed, which started smoking.

But not because it was on fire.

But because the spell had lit the dozen cigarettes she had stored up there, like a tobacco crown.

She took a couple out of the smoking circlet, stuck them between her teeth, and let loose like the last five minutes of *The A-Team*.

I just stared.

So did the mages—for a moment. Until their shields went down and so did they. Well, most of them.

I saw a few make it through some industrial sliding doors up ahead, using magic to increase their speed, while ours started to flag. I wasn't sure whether the troll was getting tired, because he ought to be tired after acting like a wrecking crew all on his own. Or if maybe there was another reason.

And then I saw the reason.

Cage after old iron cage lined the walls and spilled out into one end of the huge space. Some housed lumps huddled in darkness, too dirty and ragged to make an easy identification. But others had humans clinging to the bars, staring out in dawning hope, hands reaching, reaching, reaching—

For the keys that the troll shook off one of the few men who were still moving, before throwing him through a window. And then standing in the middle of the room and roaring, the sound almost drowned out by the cries of the slaves and the yells, cheers, and boos of the crowd around me. Who were surging to their feet, those who hadn't already been there, and acting like they'd just won the Super Bowl.

Maybe because some of them had, I realized, finally spotting Fin on the other side of the screen, doing some swift calculations on an old yellow pad.

A list of odds and their payouts showed up on the wall a moment later, while the winners surged at Fin and the losers headed for the bar. I just stood there, staring at the images. Because the important part of the night's events, which no one seemed to care about, was still ongoing.

The slaves were being freed.

The small woman with the smoking hair jumped down from the troll's back, assisted by a hand the size of an easy chair, and grabbed the keys. And went hopping from cage to cage, letting out what I could now see were mostly weres. Some were in human form, thin, dirty people with matted hair and darting eyes. But others were too exhausted and sick to transform, leaving them stuck as a menagerie of animals: a lion with half its fur gone; a dozen wolves, so scrawny I could see all their ribs; a huge gorilla that was cradling a tiny baby with the greatest of tenderness; and a mass of selkies, fey skin changers who in their animal form resemble seals.

Somebody went to switch the channel and I growled at him. The man slowly pulled his hand away, and I hopped down and pushed through the remaining crowd to get closer to the screen. The slaves were running now, some stopping to help those who couldn't help themselves, but most darting into the night, not even waiting to plunder their former jailers, whose bodies were littered everywhere.

Except on the long dock visible outside the sliding metal door, where a couple guys in a speedboat were about to take off. At least, they were before a young man with massive, eagle-like wings swooped down, the partial transformation allowing him to kick the duo back onto the dock. Where they were swarmed by their former captives.

But many more slaves ran off, not enticed by revenge any more than they had been by plunder.

They looked terrified.

But not of the troll. Who was slumped down now, on the dirty wood floor, head lolling, obviously exhausted. And letting his assistant do the mopping up.

"Dory!"

My head jerked up to see Fin waving at me above the crowd. He jumped off his stool and came bustling over, looking pleased. "You out and about already?"

I blinked at him, wondering how he knew I'd been at

the theatre, and then I realized: he thought I was still recovering from the burnt-out-building fight.

"Yeah." I went back to staring at the screen, where the eagle man had now transformed his feet into great claws, to rake at the slavers, one of whom had grabbed a kid as a shield.

And who, a second later, was hitting the dock on his knees, when the were-child changed into a python and wrapped around his neck.

"I should have expected it," Fin said. "You always heal fast—"

"Fin." I gestured at the screen, half-incoherent. "What is *that*?"

He looked over his shoulder, and then back at me, beaming. "The latest thing. I'm making a killing!"

"On *what*?"

"On the crazy crusade those two got going." He jerked a thumb at the screen. "You haven't heard?"

I shook my head.

He pushed his way through the crowd, and pulled a folded newspaper from in between two sofa cushions. "Here. It's yesterday's, but you get the idea."

It would be hard to miss. At the top of the paper was a screaming headline: UNDERWORLD GANG WAR! And beneath that: WHAT IS THE CIRCLE HIDING?

Not a lot, judging by the pictures. Which showed members of the Silver Circle in their trademark leather overcoats, a few with glittering insignia, standing around the middle of what appeared to be another warehouse. It was a newer one this time, all dirty concrete floors and few windows to let in light. On what, at a guess, was another troll attack.

It looked like the one I'd just witnessed, except with more bodies.

A lot more.

I couldn't tell exactly how many because a mage had his hand up, palm facing the camera and fingers spread, in a vain attempt to keep any images from reaching the masses. But if that was the goal, the Circle's guys should have thought to check the security feed. Below the candid shot was a whole row of grainy stills from a video of the attack. And while they were hard to make out, thanks to poor lighting and cheap equipment, they were recognizably the dynamic duo. Only this time, Revenge Granny had gone full Scarface, with a machine gun in one hand and a sawed-off shotgun in the other.

"They're really something, huh?" Fin said, looking over my shoulder.

Yeah. I just wasn't sure what that something was. But I knew what it'd be if the Circle caught up with them.

Vigilante justice wasn't a concept they understood.

"How did you get this?" I gestured at the screen.

"Easy." He looked proud of himself. "I saw the paper and recognized Big Blue from the fights. You remember him. He threw you at a wall."

I didn't say anything.

"Anyway, I saw the story and thought, huh. He's looking for some payback. And I didn't think he was gonna stop at one slaver. I mean, look at the scars on that guy. Some people are *owed*."

"So you did what exactly?"

"Called in some favors. Heard some rumors about which smugglers still got game, what with the Senate trying to shut them down and all. And the Circle's just as bad. These guys been operating for years and nobody cares, but all of a sudden—"

"Fin."

"Yeah, so anyway, I set up a camera or two. You know, the kind they use at sporting events, 'cause they can fly around after the action? Cost me something, 'cause I had to bribe some of their boys to do it since my guys . . . well, they're good, but 'good' don't mean 'suicidal'—"

"Wait. You bribed some of the slavers to give you a feed of their activities?" I stared at him.

"Not of their *activities*. Just of a room. One near where the merchandise was bein' kept, 'cause that's what these two are after. The cameras only activate if there's some major event for them to follow, like Big Blue there tear-assing through the place—"

"Why on earth would they do that? Why would *anyone*?"

Fin frowned at my obvious disbelief. "The head honchos wouldn't, but the low men on the totem pole? They don't make the big bucks, and figure what the boss don't know won't hurt him. Come on, Dory. You know how it goes. How many guys you bribed through the years?"

"Not that many." I usually didn't have the scratch. "And not slavers!"

"Well, it works the same way. And these guys, they never think they're gonna get hit. It's obviously gonna be the other guy." He rolled his eyes. "So why not set up a camera in a closet or something and pocket some paper? Anyway, these two Rambos, they're folk heroes. Two days and they're folk heroes—"

"And you're taking bets on . . . what?"

"Everything. Who're they gonna hit next? How long does it take for them to clean house? How many head shots does Granny get—"

"I get the idea."

"It's a windfall! I haven't made this much since the ley line races, and the odds kill you on those—"

"Do you know where I can find him?" I nodded at the screen.

Maybe I didn't need Curly, after all.

"Sure I do. Right—" Fin stopped abruptly, looking behind him. Because he'd just noticed the same thing I had. The fight wasn't over.

I heard several nearby patrons shout a warning, but of course, no one who needed it could hear. And Blue was either too tired, or too distracted by the handful of slaves coming up to thank him, to notice the men headed his way. One of the survivors must have called for backup, and it was coming in spades. I saw a group of men running down the now-deserted dock, saw them flood through the open doors, saw them lob a collective spell that sent shock waves through the air—

And then I didn't see anything.

The feed had gone dead.

Chapter Thirty-four

Fifteen minutes later, Fin and I swerved onto a street and then screeched to a halt. Because the warehouse wasn't dark anymore. Somebody had beaten us to the punch, and their guys were crawling all over the place, including one who magically appeared beside my car before I could slam us into reverse.

"Hello, Dory."

I put the car in park and sat back against the seat. "Hi, James."

I still had the top down on my old jalopy, so of course he'd recognized me. James was one of the guys whose retirement account I contributed to from time to time, because he made really good protection wards. Not having the ability to make any magic for myself, I had to buy it, and if you're gonna buy, it may as well be from the best.

Of course, dealing with a member of the Silver Circle has its downsides, too.

James leaned on the driver-side door, and flashed some too-white teeth at me. Or maybe they just looked extra white next to his nice, chocolate mocha skin. And his suspicious brown eyes.

"Out for a ride?"

I smiled back. "Okay."

He shook his head. He had a man bun of braids that nobody ever said anything about, like they didn't question the full beard he wore, which I got the impression wasn't regulation. Because when you're as powerful as he is, people bend the rules for you.

But not for me, it seemed.

"Not tonight," he confirmed.

"Why not tonight?"

"I think you know." He gestured back at the old building. "We got a problem."

"That's too bad."

He just looked at me.

I sighed. "Word is, some slavers got dead. I'd think that was the opposite of a problem."

"It's a problem when we don't know who's behind it, or where they're going to strike next. This time, it was slavers. Next time—"

"It'll be more slavers, if it's anyone at all." I thought of the strength of the spell that had hit Big Blue. "And it may not be anyone."

The friendly guy I knew suddenly wasn't. "All right, I'm gonna need you to come in."

"Why? I don't know any more than you do."

"Well, it sounds like you do!"

"I only know what I saw." I looked at Fin.

Who looked back, the tiny troll eyes disappearing into flaps of skin, his version of narrowing his eyes. Nobody likes talking to cops. But, after a minute, he coughed up an explanation.

It didn't seem to help.

James glared at him. "You set up a feed of a highly illegal enterprise—"

"I didn't know it was illegal. There were just these rumors."

"—so you could take bets on the *outcome*?"

Fin bristled. "There's nothing wrong with that. I run a quality establishment. I pay my taxes. City, state, *and* federal, and then you guys on top! But the world's gonna end if I ever try to make a buck—"

Two more of the Circle's guys were suddenly there. Or, more likely, had already been there, but had decided to drop the kind of charms they use for camouflage. And promptly demonstrated why they're not called police, or peace-keepers, or even law enforcement.

Oh, no.

They're called "war mages," and these two looked like that should have been "war tanks," because the stupid trench coats they wear to cover up all the weapons they cart around were so distended that they made them look positively fat.

Like Father Christmas in leather.

Leather and scowls.

Wonder what they'd leave in a stocking, I thought, as one of them grabbed me.

And then lost me when I broke his hold and flipped over his head, landing on the street behind them.

"Ah, crap," Fin said, and disappeared into the well of darkness in the floorboards.

Meanwhile I was suddenly facing two levitating guns, which was bullshit. Mages only do that when they need backup and have run out of hands, and there was nothing in their hands now. They just wanted to be dicks.

Okay.

I can be a dick, too.

A moment later, the guns were still levitating, but in pieces, and the barrels were mangled out of all use. Because mages never learn: levitating weapons are cool and all, but they still move at human speeds. I don't.

"Cut it!" James barked at his men, before they could retaliate. And then shot me a warning look, too. "Don't escalate."

"I'm not the one who drew weapons."

"You put your hands on an officer. You know better than that!"

"And you know better than to manhandle a senator, but I didn't see that stopping you."

It felt weird on my tongue, that word, like the fake title it wasn't. Like something unearned, when it hadn't been that, either. The coveted seats were always won through a combination of strength and politics, meaning that I had just as much right to one as anyone else.

And might as well get some good out of it, for as long as it lasted.

But it still felt strange, confusing. And I guess James agreed. Because he frowned and looked around, like he expected a senator to suddenly pop out of the bushes.

His buddies, who had finally realized they were down two guns, didn't bother trying to figure it out. Magical talent is a requirement for joining the War Mage Corps, but intelligence isn't. As they demonstrated by going for me again.

And getting their heads slammed down to the side of my car, which did not seem to improve their moods.

"Unhand us," one seethed at me, while thrashing around. "Or we'll unhand you!"

"Meaning?"

"Snap our shields shut on your wrists, and take your hands off in the process!"

"You could do that," I agreed. "And then I'd get the answer to something I've always wondered about."

"Like what?" the other mage demanded, as a distraction for his foot trying to do a sweep on mine.

I stepped on it.

Hard.

"Whether a dhampir's limbs are like a vamp's," I told him, while he cursed. "And keep moving after being cut off. If they don't, you win. If they do . . ."

"You'll still be handless!"

"And your skulls will still be popped like melons, so I doubt you'd care. Although it does raise the question: can disembodied hands be put on trial? I don't think it's ever come up."

Mage Number One glared at me. "You expect us to believe you don't know what happens when you lose a limb?"

I grinned, showing off baby fangs. "Never been slow enough to find out."

And then a heavy hand fell on the back of my neck, leaving us all standing there in the same pose, like a bunch of idiots.

"Now, here we are," James said cheerfully. "One big, happy family."

Mage Number Two cursed. "Not with that thing!"

"Shut it, Tomkins. You're in enough trouble." James smiled at me gently. "And so are you."

"Check it," I said.

"Check what?"

"My *position*. With the Senate. Or do you want to have to explain why you have a senator locked up?"

"A senator."

"Yes."

"You."

"Yes!"

"Since when?"

"Since a couple weeks ago," Fin said, popping back up. "I know. I didn't believe it, either."

James just looked at me. "You're a *dhampir*."

I looked back. I wasn't in the mood for this tonight, I really wasn't. "Just check it!"

He checked it. And then he checked it again, having whoever was on the other end of the phone make some more calls. And then he just stood there, phone in hand, while his boys made angry sounds because I guess their backs had started to hurt.

"I'll be damned."

"Are we done here?" I snapped. If I was going to find Big Blue alive, I needed to move.

"Technically."

"And that means?"

"You have immunity," he agreed, reluctantly. "But we don't have to let you into the scene."

"I'm on the Senate's task force for smuggling. I'm trying to help shut them down!"

"Sure, but we still don't have to let you in."

I released Huey and Louie, who showed their appreciation by cursing at me. I was gratified to notice a big red mark across their faces, where skin had met door. It didn't look like I'd broken anything, though.

Pity.

"What do you want?" I asked James.

"I already told you: information. What you know for what we know."

"I don't know much."

"But you might."

I thought about it. "I might."

"Pooling our information could be useful, couldn't it?"

"We don't need any help from the damned—" Huey's outburst cut off abruptly, although James hadn't even moved.

I blinked.

It was impressive, in a Darth Vader-y kind of way.

"We're both on the same side," James told me smoothly.

I looked at his boys, who might not be talking, but were breathing like a couple of bulls in winter. Sure. Same side.

But I still needed to get in there.

"Okay." I stuck out a hand. James took it.

He smiled brilliantly. "See? Was that so hard?"

Fin and I exchanged a glance.

Freaking war mages.

———

There were more mages inside, but nobody else smiled at me. Or at Fin, who was ambling along at my side, like a three-foot Watson to my diminutive Holmes. One with wild tufts of hair sticking up from the ride over, which made him look like a crazy-haired troll doll. To the point that I saw a war mage do a double take while I looked around for Big Blue.

Or parts thereof.

I didn't find any. And it wasn't like I could have missed him, and not only because of his size. But because the mages had done more than turn on the lights.

The warehouse was a relic from an earlier age, slowly moldering to pieces on the waterfront. It had probably been empty before the slavers found it, because pieces of the roof were missing and weeds were growing up between some of the floorboards. But the smugglers had done enough to make it usable, which mainly involved installing some cheap hanging fluorescents. It was still gloomy, the size swallowing the dim glow from overhead, but in places—

In places it was downright dazzling.

Footprints and handprints gleamed on walls and floors like angels had left them, sparkling with a bright white-gold fire. The marks the slavers had made when they hit down had left smears and splatters that blazed a brilliant scarlet against the dark. And a pile of crates by the wall, large and perilous looking, had a rainbow of different colors spilling out from gaps in the wood, as if screaming, "Look here!"

A reveal spell, then, and a good one. It had even bright-
ened moldy graffiti back to readability, and left ghostly
imprints of long-rotted advertising posters glowing against
the bricks. And there was a sizeable crew in place to take
advantage of it: war mages were guarding entrances, medical staff were examining bodies, and what I guessed were
forensic types were crawling all over everything, muttering spells at suspicious items.

One of the latter had just made a glowing footprint float
up into the air and rotate like it was 3-D. And then actually become 3-D when it suddenly flew off and attached
itself to the shoe of a guy being loaded onto a stretcher.
Immediately, a whole line of bright footprints, including
some near us, suddenly went dark.

Having now been identified, I realized.

"Okay, take him," the mage said, and the body was
carted out, one shoe still glowing.

Another mage was busy summoning a trail of blood
off a support beam, causing the drops to separate from
the peeling paint and fly into the air. And then to shimmer and change, from crimson to gold, and from tiny to
huge, before turning into a mass of gleaming strands that
whipped about wildly in space, like the tentacles off a
crazed octopus. Until, with a final flash, they coalesced—

Into the shape of a man.

It looked like a life-sized hologram of a mummy, its
missing body outlined by threads of floating magic. They
glimmered golden bright against the darkened room,
which was visible through gaps between the filaments. The
whole was strangely beautiful, like an artist had carved a
statue out of light. . . .

But the features were liquid and shifting, impossible to
read, and the body itself was generic, with no identifying
flaws that I could see. It was an impressive display, but
other than approximating the guy's height, I wasn't sure
what the point was. I'd seen more useful police sketches.

"Got a weird one," the mage called to James, who
stopped abruptly.

"How weird?"

He didn't get an answer. But the next second, the light
man became a light wolf, huge and silently snarling out of

a fang-filled mouth. I reached reflexively for a knife—it was that real—and heard Fin yelp something profane from behind me. The mage, however, didn't so much as flinch.

"Must have gotten away," he said, standing calmly next to his hologram horror, and checking a computerized notepad. "None of the bodies are weres."

"Run him through the system. Find out if we've met him before."

The mage nodded.

"Through the system?" I asked, still staring at the wolf. Which was snapping and lunging—in place, because he never moved from the mage's side. But still. A furious, oversized, golden wolf, giving every impression that he wants to eat you, draws the eye.

"Yeah." James looked at me. "Why?"

"You think a shifter was slaving shifters?"

He shrugged. "Why not? The fey traffic fey."

"But not the same kind."

He shook his head. "The first thing I learned in this job: some people will do anything if the money's right."

"Yeah, but—" I broke off, ducking low as something soared overhead, barely missing us.

Fin cursed, James just stood there, and I stared upward at the creature hovering near the ruined rafters. It was a phantom version of the eagle boy, I realized. And just as he'd been when, at a guess, he was injured in the fight and spilled a little blood. Which meant partially transformed, with a human body but huge, feathered wings.

They were currently shedding sparks that flew off through the air, or pattered down onto the floor, lighting up the old boards and turning the warehouse's collection of "ghetto diamonds"—broken bottles and scattered glass—into what looked like the real thing. In the golden glow of the spell, he looked like a medieval depiction of an angel, a spectral otherworldly figure floating midair, and making the lofty warehouse appear momentarily cathedral-like.

"Like a Botticelli come to life, isn't it?" James commented, looking upward. "Or a Fra Filippo Lippi."

He wasn't wrong.

But a nearby mage didn't seem to agree. He was standing there with a frown on his face, watching the great golden wings beat the air. Maybe because the Corps now knew that the boy had been here, but didn't know which side he was on.

I guess even magic has its limitations.

"He was one of the prisoners," I said. "I saw him on the feed."

That didn't get an acknowledgment, but the mage noted something on his pad.

"I want that tape," James told Fin, who nodded, his eyes still on the spectacle above us.

Guess he hadn't seen that trick before, either.

Neither had I, because I'd never gotten this far into a Circle crime scene. I guess rank did have a few privileges, I thought, as another mage called out to James. He went striding off, his coat billowing up dramatically behind him.

"Think they put a spell on it, to make it do that?" Fin muttered.

I just shook my head, too busy gazing around at all the other activity to come up with a rejoinder. The warehouse was like a working anthill. Just in the area around us, a woman—clairvoyant, at a guess—was holding a guy's wallet and looking pained; a white-coated medic was directing a line of levitating stretchers toward a heap of bodies; and a war mage was building a tiny, perfect replica of the warehouse out of light.

It was an exact copy, including even a clueless-looking little Fin and me, standing in the midst of all the activity, getting in everybody's way. At least, that's what I felt like: someone out of her element who wasn't helping, and who couldn't have, even if she'd wanted to. Because none of this was remotely in my skill set.

But then I noticed something that was.

Over by the door, dim and quiet and unnoticed, were the selkies I'd seen on the feed at Fin's. They were still in seal form, and still piled up together; I didn't know why. They had plenty of room to spread out now.

I also didn't know why they hadn't just left with the others. The open door, hanging half off its track, was only a little way behind them. And beyond that, across a few yards of dock, was the ocean, littered with light on the surface, but deep and dark and mysterious below. It would certainly give them an advantage over any pursuing mages.

But they hadn't moved.

Maybe too weak? It made me wonder why the smugglers didn't take better care of their cargo. Why go to all the trouble to bring in fey, and then not feed them? And for that matter, why bring in selkies at all? What the hell were they supposed to do? Kill with cuteness?

"I bet they ain't even talked to them," Fin muttered. "That's why we have all these problems. Nobody *talks* to each other. They don't know nothing about the other guy. They just assume he's bad 'cause he's different. And if they meet one who ain't, well, he's gotta be the exception, right? When we're just *people*—"

He broke off, scowling.

"Can *you* talk to them?" I asked.

He frowned some more. "Maybe. Depends where they're from. Faerie's like Earth; we got a lot of languages."

"But you could try. It looks like they've been here a while. They might know—"

"*Gah!*" Fin cut me off, suddenly running in front of me and waving his arms. "What the hell? Did you see it? It almost took my head off!"

I looked around, but didn't see anything. Except for glowing holograms and startled-looking war mages. Until something that was definitely not a hologram came zooming right at my face.

Chapter Thirty-five

I ducked, spun, and pulled a knife. And slashed at something that looked like a cannonball, what little I could see of it, because it was zooming around like a crazed drone. Until one of my strikes connected, sending it careening off into space—

Where it was promptly turned into a fireball by a nearby mage.

"What the *hell*?" Fin squeaked.

"Not again," James said in disgust, as a few bits of charred metal and a clouded lens clattered to the floor.

Several war mages went striding out the door, looking pissed.

"Check the roof!" James called after them. "That's where they were last time!"

I walked over to where he was glaring at the remains. The best I could tell, considering the state of the thing, it had looked like a smallish black soccer ball, with lenses fitted around the sides. One of which appeared to still be operational. Because it focused on James like a curious cyclops, whirring to get him in focus.

And blinked a few times, recording successively larger pics of the boot he brought down on top of it.

"The damned press," James said, before I could ask, while further stomping the thing into the dust. "They've got their panties in a twist, thinking we're concealing some great underworld war. When, from what you tell me, it's just an escaped slave on a spree." He looked at me again. "Unless there's anything else I should know?"

"Not about him."

I hesitated, suddenly wondering if this was a good idea. The Circle's attitude toward illegals was well-known, but so was their network and resources, and they'd been battling the smugglers far longer than the Senate. They could be a real help—if they wanted to.

"But about something else?" James asked pointedly.

"A kid—a troll kid—was at the fights three nights ago," I told him. "You know, the same ones where your current problem cropped up?"

He nodded. "Ugly scene. Slavers were killing the slaves, to shut them up. We rescued some, but others . . ." He shook his head.

"Well, the kid was one you missed."

"Dory—"

"Relax. He died of his wounds. He's not one you'll have to find a portal for."

James scowled, but he didn't deny it. We all knew what happened. "What about him?"

"He said something, right before he died. Three words: 'fish,' 'tracks,' 'door,'" I enunciated carefully. "Tell you anything?"

"No. You?"

I shook my head. "But there's a chance that, on his deathbed, the kid wanted to give a clue about where he was brought in, or where other slaves were being held. But he was fresh out of Faerie, and didn't know any Earth languages."

"So he went with things he saw."

I nodded. "That's the idea. But he was dying, and probably fuzzy brained, and he was a kid. They pick up on different things than an adult. But if we can figure it out, it may tell us who is still bringing people in—and where."

James scowled some more; it seemed to be the war mage resting face, but it looked weird on his usually pleasant features.

"May tell *you*," he corrected. "If the Senate wants to go ballistic on some slavers, that's their business. But it's not a priority for us."

I stared at him. "Not a priority—"

"The guys upstairs consider it to be a problem that's solving itself. So why waste manpower on it?"

"It doesn't look like it's solving itself to me!"

He raised an eyebrow. "Doesn't it? Fights mean casualties. Sure, you try to make things look bloodier than they are, and save your best people, but accidents happen. And even when nobody dies, they get injured and have to sit out for weeks or months. So you need a constant supply of new blood to stay operational, but with both us and the Senate on it lately, portals are getting shut down everywhere, and fights are getting harder to staff. Can't get people to come out for that." He nodded at the selkies.

"Rumor is, the slavers have started stealing from each other," I said, thinking of Olga's nephew.

"But that just determines who ends up with the dwindling supply of new blood," he pointed out. "It doesn't make more portals appear out of nothing. The big-time slavers, like the guy we raided three nights ago, are still in the game, being powerful enough or well connected enough to end up with the lion's share. But the little guy ends up with damned selkies, or nothing at all. It was putting them out of business."

"Was?"

"More and more, the slavers are switching over to a new line of work."

I frowned. "Like what?"

James didn't answer. He just gave a whistle that caused several of his boys to look up. "Toss me a crate."

"Which one?"

James' lips twisted. "Does it matter?"

One of the guys laughed. And then remembered that they had company, and quickly scowled some more. But he put what I guess was a levitation charm on one of the crates by the wall, and pushed it our way.

It glided swiftly across the room and James caught it, pushing it down to the floor, where it bobbed around gently.

It was an old-fashioned wooden thing, with a few tufts of straw sticking out here and there, like it was having a bad hair day. It was also familiar, looking like the crates Dorina had seen stacked along the walls in that underwater room at Curly's. It was an odd coincidence, and for a moment, I got excited.

And then I opened it.

"What a load of crap."

That was Fin, peering over my shoulder, but it looked like James agreed. The sad contents weren't likely to impress a guy whose dad owned a magic shop—one of the real ones. Instead of fake magic wands and marked decks of playing cards, it had an outer room stuffed with dried herbs, a counter stained by a thousand potions, and a back room where people exchanged power for cash.

It was one of the spots around town where people whose bodies made too much magic, like war mages, for example, could go to get a little relief. Because magic had to be used. A mage's body made a certain amount all the time, like a fleshy talisman, and if you didn't use it, bad things started to happen. And not just to you.

Rufus, James' dad, had once told me about a mage who lit his own house on fire, in his sleep. He let too much magic build up, didn't release enough of it, and it came out as a fire spell that torched his place and almost killed him and his entire family. And he wasn't the only one.

Stories like that cropped up in newspapers from time to time, and were one reason magically talented kids were pushed toward the Corps—even if they didn't have the mental aptitude, like Huey and Louie over there. They were standing guard at the side door where we'd come in, in case any nosy norms showed up and needed to be pushed along their way. And they'd be doing that for the rest of their careers, never rising higher than the magical equivalent of beat patrol, because the brains didn't match the talent.

But at least they wouldn't be setting themselves on fire.

And they might make a little something on the side, selling their excess magic to Rufus or somebody like him. Or maybe more than a little. Some of the biggest juicers, as they were known, could survive just off selling magic. The amount needed for major spells was high, so there was always a market.

I looked down at the crate.

And then there was this.

Nobody got paid for this.

"Feel free to take what you like," James told me wryly. And then leaned over conspiratorially. "I'll cover for you."

"Very funny."

I reached into the crate, and pulled out one of the pathetic-looking orbs inside. The real things were perfect balls of shining silver that broke open to release a cloud of white smoke so thick and so dense, it counted as its own patch of fog. The best ones could cover a block or more, allowing you to lose anything in it—including yourself.

They were great for when a fight got too intense or backup arrived unexpectedly, and you needed to peace out. I usually paid five hundred a pop for one of these babies, which is why I never had any damned money. But I wouldn't be taking James up on his offer.

I did squeeze it, sad misshapen thing that it was, and watched the pale steam it contained filter weakly out the sides.

I waited.

James looked amused.

Fin didn't look like anything, because he'd wandered off somewhere. I spotted him over by the selkies, frowning some more. Probably at their thinness, because to trolls that's practically the worst thing in the world. Knowing Fin, he'd be wanting to borrow my car to go get them Long John Silver's or something.

Which, no; he couldn't see over the steering wheel.

But I had no trouble seeing *him*. And the mages and the selkies, and everything else. Because the orb had finally given its all, and its all sucked.

"Are they all like that?" I asked James, who was sneering at the little thing the way a wine connoisseur looks at Two Buck Chuck. Which wasn't a bad analogy, because that's what these things were: the magical equivalent of Ripple.

"Pretty much." He batted some weak-ass fog away. "You've got your potion bombs barely stronger than human acid; your shield charms that might deflect a single spell, if you're lucky; your ward-detection bracelets, which don't; your vamp-detection bracelets, which also don't, although they did go nuts over my dog—"

"Secret were?"

He snorted. "I wish. Then I could get the bastard a job. He's eating me out of house and home."

"You took these home? I thought you just found them."

"This batch, yeah. But we ran across another yesterday, in the last place your boy hit, and one a week ago in a warehouse raid. Looks like the guys with no portal access are branching out."

"Into *this*?"

He nodded.

"And it's *selling*?" I couldn't imagine anybody spending good money on this crap.

"It's pretty general knowledge that we might have to fight the fey," James said. "And people are freaking out. Plus, there's a crackdown on the legit stuff. The Circle's trying to keep the other side from cleaning out our dealers, and using our own weapons against us. Any big orders are flagged and held up until we verify the purchaser. It doesn't affect the guy on the street, just buying a few things to protect his family, but you know how people are. The directive caused a panic and sent prices skyrocketing." He cocked an eyebrow at me. "Hope you're stocked up."

Shit.

So much for restocking on a budget.

"And with demand outstripping supply, even this stuff is selling like hotcakes," James continued. "And getting ripped off."

"Ripped off? People are stealing *that*?"

He chuckled. "You sound like the old man. He was outraged, too. But, yeah, the batch from last night was traced to a truck robbery in Jersey City. We don't normally watch this sort of thing—it's not powerful enough to worry about—and the criminal element knows it. So they've started stealing what are basically gag gifts, repackaging them as legit weapons, and selling them at a premium."

"And nobody's noticed?"

He shrugged. "It's a new problem. Plus, most people aren't likely to use anything they buy. They just want some insurance."

"So how good it is, is irrelevant."

"Until they actually need it, and realize they've been had. False confidence can get somebody—"

He broke off, because another flying camera had just zoomed in. This one was faster than the others, ducking and diving to elude the two war mages following it. And was doing a pretty good job.

"Damn it!" James barked. "I told you to find them!"

"I think there's more than one group, sir," one of the mages panted, swiping at the flying menace—and missing.

James said a word that sounded like an expletive, but I guess not. Because the next second, the camera zoomed right into his hand, as if magnetized. And a second after that, it was making these sad little whirring noises as it was slowly crushed in an iron grip.

The parallels with Vader were just piling up tonight.

"Then find both of them!" he snapped, and strode off, coat flaring.

"James—"

"Look around, but stay out of people's way," he said, spinning and walking backward. "And remember—we got a deal. What you know, I know."

He whirled and went outside, I guess to yell at his boys some more, and I stared back down at the box.

Well, this was helpful.

I poked around a little, hoping to find something useful, but it was difficult. Because Fin was back, squatting down and getting his nose into everything. Literally.

He was also looking a little weird, all of a sudden. His eyes were blown wide—for a troll's—but his mouth was almost nonexistent. He looked like he'd been sucking on an alum lollipop. He also kept casting little glances over his shoulder at a nearby mage, who was busy magicking up a model of a guy's face from an imprint in the dirt.

One of the slavers might have gotten away, but he'd left something behind. He'd face-planted, whether from running too fast or from the troll's fist, into the couple inches of dirt that had collected by a support column. And now the mage was pulling out the imprint of his features and inverting it, leaving a perfect mask floating in the air.

It reminded me of death masks I'd seen, the plaster casts of dead people's faces that were once considered a nifty idea. It even had a map of the guy's acne scars spread out over the thin cheeks and revealed that he had buckteeth. Although the latter might look a little different now, considering how hard he must have hit down.

I watched the mage solidify it, muttering something that made the dirt harden into a claylike model. And then wished I hadn't. Some of the features were mushed and flattened, on the side where he'd hit down first, I supposed. The solidification turned them into a sludge of misshapen earth that looked a lot like the "faces" on the *manlikans*.

And sent a shiver up my spine.

I looked back down at the junk in the box and wondered if this meant anything. I didn't like coincidences, but I couldn't see Geminus giving a damn about crap weapons. And for that matter, neither did I.

I was looking for something big enough to warrant the response we'd had last night. Something gamechanging. Something profitable enough to tempt a group of guys who'd just seen their family eviscerated to give it another go.

This was not it.

And then Fin grabbed my arm.

The war mage glanced over, his attention drawn by the sudden movement, and Fin started talking quickly. "I used to carry this kinda stuff at my place," he told me. "They send guys around, from the manufacturers, you know, with these display boxes. Pay you a percentage if you put 'em by the cash register or behind the bar. I made some nice extra cash for a while."

"You didn't feel a little guilty?" I asked, looking down at his hand. Which was eating into my skin.

"Naw, naw, why would I? No different than that knockoff pepper spray they sell in convenience stores. Half of it don't work, but it makes people feel better to carry it around. More secure."

"Without being, in fact, any more secure." If I was going to carry a weapon, I damned well wanted it to work. I also wanted him to let go, because I was about to have a permanent imprint of his fingers in my flesh.

I tried shaking him off, but his grip tightened. "And

practical jokes," he said, a little shrilly. "Most of the guys bought 'em for that or pranks. I made a killing!"

"Then why'd you get rid of them?" I asked, as the war mage started transferring his delicate sculpture into a case.

It looked like they were finishing up, magic turning what should have been a day's work into a couple hours'. The last bodies were being carted out, and cases were being snapped shut here and there. And, somehow, I couldn't see James letting us stay behind on our own.

Just as well; I had another errand to run.

But Fin didn't seem to feel the same.

"Same reason most shops don't carry fireworks," he squeaked. "Some moron's gonna misuse 'em. Had a couple guys playing chicken with one of the acid bombs, and it ate a chunk out of the polyurethane on the bar. Had to get the whole thing redone—"

"Listen, Fin—"

"—and then these two losers got in a fight," he said, his voice reaching levels usually reserved for twelve-year-old girls and dog whistles. "And knocked the box over, sending all these things bouncing around the bar, some of them ricocheting off walls and breaking stuff, others setting fires. Weak don't mean dead, not when fifty of 'em get set off all at once. I had to shut down for the whole night—"

The war mage clicked his case closed and walked off, and Fin jerked on my arm, bringing me as close to his face as the nose would allow.

"We got trouble!" he whispered.

"What kind?"

"The big blue kind!"

I looked at him and frowned. And then I looked where he deliberately wasn't: at the pile of selkies. All heaped up in one spot, even though there was no reason for them to be, and squirming, squirming, squirming . . .

And hiding, hiding, hiding, I realized, an additional couple people in the crowd.

Well, shit.

Chapter Thirty-six

I joined Fin in staring blankly at the crate, and tried to think.

Blue was massive—like, "I've lived in smaller apartments" massive—so he must be under the floor. No way were the selkies' emaciated bodies concealing him and Granny any other way. But they could cover any light the reveal spell might have tried to shine up through the floorboards.

Like around a trapdoor?

Seemed like the kind of thing smugglers might build, if it hadn't been there already. Concealment charms worked better on enclosed areas, like a closet or a small room. Leaving them to float around nebulously tended to disperse them and use up power faster, and then your talisman putzed out or the spell became too thin to actually conceal anything, and why was I thinking about this right now?

Maybe because I didn't want to think about how we were going to get them out.

"We gotta get gone," Fin said softly. "They're gonna move those selkies in a minute, and then—"

"People die."

Because no way was Blue going down easy.

And no way were a bunch of armed-to-the-teeth war mages, with macho meters set on overdrive, going to play nice with an illegal, homicidal, massive battle troll, and his gun-toting sidekick.

This . . . could be bad.

Apparently, Fin thought so, too, because he started pulling on me. "Yeah, like us if we don't get out of here!"

I looked at him. "So that's your solution? We just leave him to be slaughtered, or to slaughter somebody else?"

He nodded vigorously. "Now you're getting it."

He got up.

I pulled him back down.

"You could live with yourself?"

Tiny, furious eyes met mine. "Better than I could as a greasy spot on the floor! I'm not a dhampir. You wanna play hero, fine. Just don't expect me—"

"Pity about those profits, though."

"—to be Rambo Jr. because I ain't—" He stopped. "What profits?"

"The profits you were rolling in tonight. The profits you're probably going to make every time those two take on some slavers. You've invented a whole new way to broadcast the fights, and only you have it. None of those other guys had your foresight—"

"Damn it, Dory!"

"—and word is spreading. I could barely get in the door tonight; by tomorrow . . . well, if there was going to be a tomorrow. But I guess not."

The eye flaps of squintiness made a reappearance. "Don't think I don't know what you're doing. I know *exactly* what you're doing."

"I just need you to drive a speedboat. Can you do that?"

"Sure, but—"

"There's one outside." I nodded at the lolling door, beyond which, tied up at the pier where the slavers had left it, was the boat they'd been planning to use for a getaway. Only Eagle Boy had kicked them off before they could, leaving it conveniently situated for us. Well, conveniently assuming we could reach it.

"So I'm supposed to do what?" Fin whispered. "Load 'em onto the boat while surrounded by war mages? Seriously?"

"Yeah."

He just looked at me.

"I'll provide a distraction."

"Oh great. Oh yeah. That's what I need. A dhampir-led distraction!"

"Would you stop bitching?" I said softly. "Just get them on the boat; I'll take care of the rest."

"Sure. Fine. Whatever. This is why I never go anywhere with you," Fin informed me. But he slunk off in the direction of the selkies, while I looked around for a distraction.

Huh.

This could be a bit of a challenge.

On the one hand, I was without my usual bag of tricks, which I'd been forced to leave in the car due to the sad lack of trust between us magical allies, and I was currently surrounded by war mages.

On the other hand, distractions were kind of my thing. When you're typically the smallest badass in the room, you have to use whatever you can to keep the bigger ones from all piling on you at once. Because they do that. All the time.

The movie bad guys who suddenly can't shoot straight when the hero is on-screen, or who politely wait their turn to have a go at you, just don't exist in reality. I've never been in a well-mannered fight, or fought a gentleman warrior nobly giving me a chance to beat him. Well, not unless you counted Louis-Cesare—

I stopped that train of thought abruptly, because it hurt. A stupid amount. It was also useless, because there weren't any Louis-Cesares here.

There weren't any guys like him anywhere.

Stop it.

So.

Options.

Under the circumstances, there were really only two: the tower of treats in the form of all those crates, and Huey and Louie by the door.

The crates would be more fun, and thanks to the troll's rampage, there were plenty of things to send crashing into them. But there were a lot of them, and I didn't think the guys could possibly have gone through them all. They were probably going to cart them off and sort through them later, meaning they didn't know everything that was in there.

And neither did I.

And sending up a two-story mountain of magical weapons, however weak-ass they might be, wasn't a plan.

So, the boys it was. And since they were already looking at me malevolently, or as malevolently as they could manage past the now-red-and-swollen stripes across their faces, this should be easy. And it probably would have been—except that another distraction flew through the door before I had the time to start.

Actually, make that several. Okay, more than several, I thought, watching a whole stream of flying cameras charge in all at once. It looked like the reporters had decided that the only way to get a good look around was to come in force, so they had.

And it might have worked, if they'd been dealing with anyone else. But war mages are a breed apart. And while their shoot-'em-up training is understandable for some of the challenges they face, where a split second of hesitation can get you dead, it can cause problems at other times.

Like now, for instance.

A fireball engulfed one of the little flying cameras, frying it midair, and a spell clipped another, sending it spiraling toward the ceiling, where it detonated in a burst of expensive parts. But there were a lot of little black balls left, maybe half a dozen, and—predictably—somebody focused too much on the targets whizzing around and too little on what was behind them.

"No!" James ran back in, trying to corral his group of weapon-happy war mages. "Don't contaminate the scene! *Don't contaminate—*"

Too late, I thought, watching a fireball miss a camera, and hit the mountain of crates head-on.

What looked like the Fourth of July went off inside the warehouse's old walls. The mages promptly shielded, the selkies fled through the open door, and I grabbed part of a pallet as a shield and ran for the side entrance. Because my work was done here. Or it would have been, if I hadn't immediately gotten disoriented thanks to the thick, white clouds suddenly boiling everywhere.

There must have been a whole lot of fog bombs in those crates.

And a bunch of stupefaction bombs as well, judging by the way I was suddenly staggering around.

Not to mention incendiaries, because something set my shield on fire!

I dropped it and stumbled backward, awkwardly grabbing for another. But my head was spinning, my eyes were trying to cross, and I couldn't see anything but fog and the multicolored sparks lighting it in patches here and there. Or hear over the firework explosions of more crates going up and some spell-enhanced war mage shouts. And so my hands grabbed something else instead.

Something that had been zooming by and still was, only now it was zooming me along with it.

Because whatever charm the reporters had put on their little camera balls, it was a strong one.

At least enough to tow me through a couple war mages while I tried to get my confused head to tell my fingers to let go. And then into a support column—*ow*—and then into thin air, as the determined flying camera I'd latched onto decided to kamikaze the ceiling. And the wall. And the floor again.

After which it shot back into the air for no apparent reason—except to try to shake me off, I realized.

Which was why I determinedly held on, even after all the knocking about had cleared my head. Because there was a reporter outside somewhere controlling this thing, and he was pissed that something was interfering with his attempt to get a scoop. If he couldn't shake me, the next step would be to recall his little device to sort out the problem, which would get me out the door.

Assuming I lasted that long.

Which might be a problem, because the fog covered a lot of sins. And Huey—or maybe Louie; I couldn't really tell them apart—was seizing the opportunity for some revenge. Only not with magic, because that leaves a trace, doesn't it?

Unlike fists.

At least, I guessed that was why one of them had just swung for my head instead of throwing a spell. And then grabbed onto my legs when I tried to kick him. Probably assuming that I was too disoriented to fight back, since I was determinedly clinging to the little camera ball.

Which I smashed into his head a couple times, and then used my legs—which had bigger muscles anyway—to hurl him at a column. One he bounced off of and lunged for me again, because yeah. Dumb as a rock.

A rock that went barreling underneath me, because I picked my feet all the way up this time, to the point that I was hugging the camera.

My ribs didn't enjoy it, but my eyes had fun watching him take out his partner, who'd been creeping up on the other side.

They staggered off into the fog, and I deliberately wrapped my arms around the remaining intact lenses, wanting to *end this*. It almost ended me when the camera went crazy, bouncing along the ceiling before slamming back into the floor and dragging me across the rough old boards. And out into the night, because the mage had finally figured out that the only way to clear the obstruction was to pry me off.

A guy came running up as the camera flew out the door. I let go, and watched it shoot skyward when a hundred and ten pounds of dhampir suddenly went missing. And detonate against the bottom of a helicopter, because the regular cops had just arrived.

"What the hell do you think you're *doing*?" the guy—the reporter, I guessed—yelled over the *whup, whup, whup* of the copter's blades. He was a tall, thin dude with a shock of black hair and bright Asian eyes.

Then he looked behind me and his mouth dropped open, and I didn't wait to find out why.

I grabbed him and took a flying leap behind a cop car, where a couple of New York's finest were already hunkered down, staring as the warehouse all but exploded behind us, with sound and fury and lots of sharp flying bits.

The next seconds were a little confused. The guy I'd rescued started yelling at what I guess were more reporters, demanding to know if anybody had a camera that still worked. I got myself turned around to see that the building was still standing, sort of, but had crazy, multicolored sparks shooting out everywhere: through areas of missing tile on the roof, spewing toward the heavens; through the open door, cascading over the broken sidewalk; and—most spectacularly, at least from this angle—through the row of rectangular windows, which had shattered and were vomiting great tongues of fire at us, like the front of a dragon boat on Chinese New Year.

The whole building looked like a huge roman candle.

I realized that maybe it would be a good idea to move back, because the sparks weren't just for show. They were spells, too, if very weak ones. But there were a lot of them, and they were raining down everywhere.

Including onto a passing garbage scow out on the water, which hadn't steered away fast enough. And was now a burning garbage scow. Which would have been bad enough, but some levitation charms had been mixed in with the rest of the sparks, so the burning garbage was drifting up into the air and out over the water.

Despite everything, I just watched it for a moment. The blue-black water and the flickering orange-red garbage and the shooting sparks illuminating all the graffiti-covered rocks by the waterside . . . it was strangely beautiful. In a Brooklyn sort of way.

Unlike the huge piece of burning roofing headed straight for us.

I grabbed the reporter and took a leap into a ditch across the road.

"Who are you?" he demanded, staring at me. And I have to give the guy credit. Although for what, I'm not exactly sure, because he yelled the question while the big, jagged piece of metal bisected the cop car.

"Keep your head down!" I told him, while a frantic car alarm informed the fleeing patrolmen that there might be a problem.

"Answer the question," he told me right back. "And you owe me for my camera!"

I stared at him. "Dick! I just saved your life!"

He frowned. "How did you know my name was Dick?"

"Just a guess," I snarled, and started to crawl out.

"Wait!" He grabbed my arm. "Where are you going?"

I shook him off. "Out there! You stay here. Unless your shields are way better than most civilians'."

"So you're not a civilian?" He looked me over. "You don't look like a war mage, and even less like a tech. They tend to be easygoing on the dress code, but not to that degree."

"Dick," I muttered, and he nodded, and held out a hand.

"Kim."

"No, Dory."

"What?"

"Never mind." But apparently he did mind, and he'd used the ignored hand to grab my arm again.

"Richard Kim," he clarified. "And you're Dory—what, exactly?"

"None of your business!"

"Ah, but it is my business. People need to know the truth!"

"The truth is that you're going to die if you don't keep your fool head down!" I said, as another piece of detonating warehouse screamed above us.

It was really starting to go up now, which had me worried for Fin. Everybody else around here—including the cops in the copter, who had wisely gotten some air—was shielded or out of range. Even the techs the Corps used went through the same selection process as the tank squad, meaning that they could probably stand inside the building while it burned down and never feel a thing.

I didn't have their shields, but I'd raced through battlefields tougher than this. I wasn't worried about me. I was worried about—

"Yes! Yes!" I grabbed the reporter and shook him, while he stared confusedly around. I didn't care. I'd finally spotted the speedboat out on the water, well beyond the risk of the burning barge, and it even looked like they'd rescued Blue—

I stopped, blinking.

What were they doing?

"What are they doing?" Dick asked, squinting alongside me.

I had no idea. It looked like they were popping wheelies, or whatever the nautical equivalent was. Blue's weight in back pulled the front of the boat up so much, I wasn't sure Fin could see past it. Which might explain why they were just going in circles.

Big circles, over and over, while staring at the land but not the warehouse, which should have freaking drawn the eye.

Unless they were looking for me.

Shit!

I felt around my pockets, but sure enough, no phone. I hadn't thought to take it out of the duffle before locking it in my trunk—in a car parked on the other side of the building. *Shit, shit, shit!*

"Do you have a phone?" I asked Dick.

"Why do you want it?"

"To call for pizza!"

"There's no reason to get sarcastic. It was a reasonable—"

"Aghhh! Just give it to me!"

He gave it to me.

"You have fangs," he pointed out. "Are you a vampire?"

"Wanna find out?"

He shut up.

I called Fin's number. "What are you doing?"

"Waiting for you! What the hell?"

"No! Don't wait!"

"What?"

"I have the car! I'll take the car!"

"What?"

The wind was almost blowing his voice away, and must have been doing equal damage to mine. Or maybe it was the half dozen car alarms going off now, or the still-loud helicopter, or the continued explosions. Because he couldn't hear me.

"I said, I'll take the *car*!"

"No, we're not far! Are you in position?"

"Fin! Just go! *Now, now, now!"*

"Now? All right, I'm coming!"

"No! Not here! I didn't mean—"

But, sure enough, here they came, swinging about in a big parabola and then speeding this way. And fuck it, they were going to get caught! Or worse.

"Stay here, and keep down," I told the reporter.

"Like hell! I'm coming with you!"

I tried snarling in his face again, but I guess the first time had been more surprise than anything else. Because he didn't scare easy. Which had been more people's epitaphs than I could count, and how did I end up in these things?

And then James grabbed the reporter and me simultaneously, dragging us out of the ditch and up to a face as thunderous as I'd ever seen it.

Oh, thank god.

Someone to babysit.

I broke his hold and danced backward, and the expression somehow got worse.

"Immunity," I reminded him, as the warehouse burned merrily behind us, as somebody with a bullhorn told us to drop our weapons, and as red and blue flashing lights announced the arrival of more cops.

And as a speedboat laden with a troll doll, a Hulk, and a tiny madwoman sped by on the water, with everybody onboard yelling at me.

"Watch that one! He's trying to be a hero!" I told James. And then I took off, dodging through the chaos and getting up a good head of steam before hitting the side of the dock and jumping—

Straight onto the middle of the boat.

Damn, that was . . . that was pretty good, I thought, grinning, and grabbing for purchase. Granny grinned back. Fin floored it, sending a huge spray of water at the mages on the dock, who hadn't been quite fast enough to catch me.

"Okay." Fin told me breathlessly. "I admit it. You do a pretty good distraction."

And then we were gone.

Chapter Thirty-seven

Mircea, Venice, 1458

The ship creaked and groaned, the old boards protesting the rough seas. It was raining again, with the skies as angry as the water. But this was a merchant ship, built to travel long journeys to distant ports. Mircea wasn't worried about sinking.

It was almost the only thing he wasn't currently worried about.

He couldn't see too well. His head had landed sideways, cheek to unshaven cheek with the not-so-animated corpse below him. It nonetheless allowed him to stare outward at pile after pile of baby vampires, stacked like cordwood all along the sides and middle of the ship's great hold. There were hundreds of them, their eyes closed, or open and staring blankly upward—either way, insensate. Unaware and therefore unconcerned about the fate that awaited them.

Unlike Mircea. Whose mental gifts allowed him the dubious advantage of knowing exactly what was happening, but not having any way to stop it. He struggled against whatever power was holding him, but didn't manage to so much as wriggle a finger.

Merda!

The worst thing about this whole fiasco was that it was his own damned fault. He should have been more cautious. He should have expected a trap. And part of him had. He thought he'd been so careful. . . .

Not careful enough!

He'd picked up the strange angler with his human bait in the Rialto, the great marketplace of Venice, earlier that evening. It was one of the creature's favorite fishing spots, especially right after dusk. Mircea hated that time of day. Even though the darkness allowed him to be out and about, he really wasn't comfortable until the terrible sun had left to stalk another land entirely.

But the angler was stronger than he, and always made an early start of it. So Mircea had to as well. And then had to find him in the crowded zoo the Rialto turned into after dark.

Only the space-deprived Venetians would have put their abattoir, banking center, and marketplace all in one small area, leading to the sight of well-dressed men having to dodge flocks of goats, bawdy prostitutes trying to seduce wide-eyed farm boys, and clueless tourists having their pockets picked while they stared at Egyptian spices, Byzantine silks, Murano glass, exotic foodstuffs, and a crowd thick with Turks, Greeks, Spaniards, Slavs, Jews, and Moors.

And that was just on land.

The canal was busy, too, with everyone trying to pack up and leave at once, before members of the city watch showed up to levy fines—or a swift kick—to merchants staying open past the evening bell. It was chaos, as usual, and as usual Mircea found himself trying to avoid getting run over by a hefty woman chasing a live goose, or getting slapped in the face by the long sticks a boy had slung over his shoulder, strung with straw hats. All while trying to spot someone who was working very hard at not being seen.

But then, there were other senses.

Mircea slipped into the protection of a colonnade and closed his eyes. Immediately he felt calmer, his mind filtering out the noise and bustle around him, piece by piece. First the animals, with their squawks, bleats, and coos. Then the people, talking, laughing, fighting, and bartering. And finally the incidentals: waves slapping the side of the canal, wind whistling across the rooftops, a stray dog pissing against a column, music from a nearby tavern, and the smell of newly lit torches, sweaty bodies, and the sea.

Until there was only one thing left.

They were slippery gleams on his mental horizon, cool against the human heat, still against the bustle. Vampires, coming out of their sanctuaries, peppering the square. Most of them were bright to his mental eye, like jagged bits of lightning glimpsed through churning dark clouds. He mentally excluded them as well. He wasn't looking for young and bright, but old and dim, someone who was hiding his true power, someone who didn't want to be found, someone—

Like that.

Mircea's eyes opened. The angler had cloaked himself in shadow, the vampire way of going dim and unnoticed, even while standing in the middle of a crowd. Or, in this case, in the shadow of a portico, while his lure bobbed around the nearby market stalls, drifting idly among the vampires looking for their nightly supper.

Not realizing that, tonight, they were the prey.

Mircea's focus was drawn to two babies who seemed to be hunting together. That wasn't unusual in most places, where baby vampires were part of a family and learned the tricks of the trade from their older "siblings." But here in Venice, most of the young vampires had no family, and were far too skittish to trust anyone.

Here, they hunted alone.

But perhaps these two had been brothers before the Change, and were turned together. Or perhaps they had met on the perilous way to Venice's vaunted "safety," and learned to trust. Or perhaps, like Mircea, they had some talent with the mind, which allowed them slightly more control than most their age—

His speculation ended abruptly, when the trap snapped shut. The girl had walked between two market stalls, the vampires trailing close behind her. And when she walked out . . .

She was alone.

Mircea, who had been slouching against the side of the building, trying to look like he was waiting for someone, suddenly stood up straight.

For weeks he'd hunted the hunter, but had yet to answer one simple question: what was happening to all

those vampires? They seemed to disappear into thin air,
wafting away like the early-morning fog that plagued
Venice this time of year. He had never been able to find
them, and without them, he had nothing.

Until tonight.

Mircea wandered over, careful to wait until the girl
was on the other side of the market, attracting the attention of another hungry soul. Then idly passed by the
space between the stalls, glancing in swiftly before moving on. And frowning.

Because the space was just a space, boring and empty,
unless you counted a few pieces of rotten fruit disdained
by seller and buyers alike. But not by a small mouse,
which was daring to feast in the open. It paused when
Mircea walked by, its bright black eyes alert, its tiny
hands stilling on its prize.

And then scampered away, taking a half-eaten plum
along with it, as Mircea sighed his disappointment—and
his frustration. He'd been looking right at her. He couldn't
have been mistaken.

But there was nothing there. As demonstrated when a
passing vendor, a bald man with a basket of melons on his
head, bustled through, trampling the remaining plum into
the pavement. And almost barreling into Mircea on the
other side, before muttering a quick "*scuxa*" as he squeezed
past.

Leaving Mircea with a bigger frown and a determination to figure this out. A quick duck behind a bunch of
departing vegetable sellers took him between the stalls
and out of sight of the angler. And a careful balancing act
stopped him just inside the makeshift corridor, allowing
him a chance to bend over and carefully examine the
stones in front of him, to see if he could find any sign of a
trap.

There was none.

Just the pavement, grimy from a hundred boot prints,
awaiting the next squall to wash it clean; the sickly sweet
smell of the crushed fruit, its juices running like blood in
the spaces between the stones; the feel of cracked grit and
the rough-smooth-rough surface of the rock under Mircea's questing hand.

And the shock of someone's boot making a brutal connection with his backside.

Mircea fell forward into a black emptiness that reached out and grabbed him, pulling him down, down, down—and spitting him out—

Into the boat of the damned.

"Got another one!" somebody called, as Mircea hit the boards like a sack of grain.

"Already? She's earning her keep tonight!"

"For once," came the cynical first voice, as muscular legs in dirty hosen walked over Mircea.

He'd landed facedown, suddenly unable to move, even to put his hands out to break his fall. Or to fight when he was roughly grabbed under the armpits a moment later, at the same time that someone else seized his feet. And sent him flying.

"Sleep well," the first voice said cynically, as Mircea landed on a pile of bodies, and found himself staring down into the open, unseeing eye of a corpse.

He didn't cry out. Whatever spell had immobilized his body worked on his vocal cords, too. He lay there silently, bleeding from what was likely a broken nose, as several humans thumped back up a ladder.

Leaving him in a makeshift graveyard.

Well, at least he knew what had happened to the vampires, he thought, trying to tamp down panic.

Normally, it would have bubbled up into wild laughter, his usual, completely inappropriate response to impossible situations. It was why he'd been able to lead a retreat of the tattered remnants of his father's army, after a fool's invasion of the Turkish lands, before they were butchered like all the rest. The laughing knight, his men had called him, amazed that he seemed so insouciant in the face of danger.

They'd never known: he'd just been hysterical.

The same had been the case when, a year or so later, a party of senior vampires had come across him and Horatiu fleeing their homeland, in search of he knew not what. They'd knocked him off his horse, circled him round, and then just stayed there, staring at the days-old baby vampire laughing at them from his puddle of mud. And hadn't killed him.

Well, some of them had started to, but the vampire in charge had stopped them with a raised hand. And had continued to regard Mircea with a slightly perplexed look on his face. Mircea had looked right back, and laughed and laughed and laughed.

In the week prior, he'd been cursed, tortured, and buried alive; he'd watched his parents be butchered and their lands overrun by the faithless cowards who had once pledged them fealty; he had been overwhelmed by the bloodlust of his new state, which had caused him to almost kill a young woman after it drove him mad; he had been chased—rightly—by an angry mob trying to avenge her, and been forced to abandon his wife, in case he end their union by killing her, too.

In a single week, he'd gone from prince to pauper, from hero to monster, from someone surrounded by family to someone utterly alone, except for a mangy horse and a half-blind servant.

What did this idiot think he was going to do to him?

What did *anyone*?

The vampire had finally raised an eyebrow, and looked back up at his men. "This one's not worth it. Too young to provide any sport."

"But, my lord. He invaded our lands!"

"*My* lands," the older vamp had corrected dryly. "Back to the hunt with you."

The others dispersed, leaving Mircea lying in the mud and giggling helplessly at his savior. Who had looked down at him again, and slowly shaken his head. "Get to Venice, son," he said, gathering up his reins. "If you can."

"W-what?"

"There's safety for you there, if you can reach it. A place for those with no masters to guide them. Go there if this life still has any meaning for you."

Then he'd disappeared, in a flurry of flying hooves and flowing mane. The beautiful horse he rode was so swift that it had vanished beyond a hill before Mircea could pull himself back to his feet. And reassure a frightened Horatiu, who had been clinging to the neck of their far less impressive nag, and staring at him with huge eyes.

"Why the devil are you laughing?"

Mircea hadn't responded. Just buried his face in his horse's neck, and laughed some more. And, finally, when he was able to get himself under control, he'd looked up. "Feel like a sea voyage?"

Now he was on another one, because Venice hadn't been quite the haven he'd expected. Nothing was when you had no power in a world that valued nothing else. But he hadn't died, no, not any of the times—and he'd lost count of how many there had been—when he damned well should have. And he wasn't dying tonight, he thought, putting everything he had, every ounce of power, into moving, just an inch—

And failed.

Damn it!

He felt panic welling up again, and gave himself a mental slap. Not now! There had to be a way out of here! There had to!

He sent his eye rolling around, trying to see more of the room.

It looked like a battlefield, only tidier. Including the gore, because some of the bodies were bleeding, or had limbs lying at strange angles, perhaps broken or dislocated by the fall. He watched one sort itself out, the broken fragments slowly working back into shape, the blood that a moment ago had been dripping down the arm suddenly reabsorbed. But the vampire himself never moved, never so much as fluttered the eyelashes lying closed and motionless against his too-pale cheek.

So the body was working, but the mind . . .

Where was the mind?

Probably still inside whatever darkness was pulling at him, Mircea thought, feeling it slowing his brain and paralyzing his body. As it had done since he fell through . . . whatever he fell through. He glanced up, but the ceiling was unbroken. Just old, cobweb-covered boards, dusty and full of mouse droppings.

Until what looked like a dark puddle opened up out of nowhere, an inky blackness darker than the pits of hell, which spewed forth—

The redhead.

She hit the floor hard, but was able to catch herself,

landing heavily on hands and knees. Whatever this paralysis was, it didn't seem to affect her. Which was evidenced even more when she flipped over and started screaming.

It wasn't in Venetian or Italian or any other language Mircea knew, so he couldn't follow. Plus, he was distracted, staring at the pool of darkness still swirling about the ceiling above her. He'd only recently learned about portals—mage-made devices for traveling from one place to another almost instantaneously—and he wasn't sure this was one. The only other he'd seen had been brilliant— a spill of yellow-white fire—and had sounded like every ocean crashing onto every beach, all over the world, all at once.

It had been deafening and terrifying, and completely unlike the quiet darkness on display here. But then, they couldn't very well have captured any vampires with a golden maw screaming at them, could they? So they'd camouflaged it. Or else it was some other manner of mage trickery he'd yet to learn about, which was most of it, since he avoided the creatures like the plague.

Beastly people.

Like the ones thundering down the ladder now.

Mircea hadn't gotten a good look at them before, but judging by their tread, it was the same two, one carrying a cudgel and the other having a meaty hand laced with lightning. Which dimmed and went out when he saw the woman. "Damn it!" He glared at her. "Not again!"

The other mage seemed even more incensed. He was a scarred-up specimen half his friend's weight, with greasy dark hair and a nose that looked like it had been broken twice as much as Mircea's, to the point that it had given up retaining any shape whatsoever. But it flushed like the rest of his skin when he suddenly rushed over, grabbed the screaming redhead, and slapped her hard across the face.

That stopped the screaming, but did nothing else. "I won't!" she yelled. "I won't do it anymore! You can't make me!"

"Want to bet?"

"Ye're a whore," his companion said, coming forward. "In the stews when we found you, giving it up to any old codger with the cash. Now you wear nice clothes and eat good food. What's so wrong with that?"

"I might have been a whore," she shouted, "but I wasn't a murderer—of children!"

The thin man raised his hand again, but the other mage caught his arm. He looked like a typical bruiser, one of the burly types who unloaded ships down at the docks, in between boasting about their sexual prowess and pissing into canals. But there was more than a glimmer of intelligence behind those black eyes.

"What happened?" he demanded.

"A child," the redhead said, her voice catching. "He wanted me to—he was going to take a *child—*"

The bruiser sighed. "It's a damned vampire, not a child. That thing is probably older than you—than all of us! And would kill you, given half a chance—"

"You don't know that!" She glared at him. "You don't know what he is—what any of them are! And I won't—"

Mircea couldn't see her anymore, as she'd moved out of his limited range of vision. But the sound of another slap was unmistakable. As were her renewed screams afterward. Like before, they sounded as much of fury as of pain.

"Cut it out!" the bruiser said.

"Why?" It was the scrawny man's voice. "If she won't work, she's no good t'us."

"Oh, she'll work. And we need her pretty."

"I won't, I tell you!" It was the woman again. "I *can't—*"

"You can and you will. If we have t'train another, it's going to hold things up, and we haven't time for that."

"I don't care!" A sudden gasp. "Let go of me!"

"Why? If you don't get back to it, you'll be servicing worse than us soon. Or have you forgotten what that's like?"

"Stop it! Let me go!"

"I'll stop it when you come t'yer senses." He laughed. "Or maybe when I'm finished."

"You'll stop it now."

The voice came from neither of the three humans. But from someone else who had slipped through the portal while everyone was distracted. And dropped to the ground, silent and unnoticed, which wasn't surprising. Even now, looking right at him, Mircea couldn't really see him. Just a vague, human-shaped shadow, slightly darker than the rest, but which could have been a trick of the light flickering in a nearby lantern.

"We were just—" the bruiser began, before a brief gesture cut him off.

"On deck." The voice was a hoarse rasp. "Prepare for docking."

The bruiser looked like he was about to argue, but for once, the gaunt sailor was smarter. "Come on." He tugged at his companion's arm.

They went back upstairs.

The vampire looked at the redhead. She'd moved back into view, holding her cheek. The shadow pushed her hand away, and ignored the shudder that went through her. "My apologies," he murmured, healing the reddened flesh with a touch.

"I won't do it," she told him, her voice shaking. "I can't—"

"*Shh.*" He dragged a finger down the side of her face. From a human, it would have been an affectionate or possibly sensual gesture. In this case . . . it reminded Mircea of nothing so much as a horseman soothing a startled filly. It reeked of possession.

But it seemed to work.

The redhead's eyelids fluttered, and she sank down beside the wall, her head already lolling.

"Sleep." He told her. "Forget."

And then she was out.

Chapter Thirty-eight

"Hey. Hey, wake up."

I grumbled and turned over. Or I tried. But my knee hit something, and a loud horn blasted my eardrum, and I sat up abruptly.

And hit my head.

"Take it easy!"

My eyes focused on Fin, who was peering in the car door down by my feet.

"So, you want the cherry slushie or—" He stopped, and squinted at something neon blue in an oversized cup. "Whatever the hell this is?"

I blinked at him, slowly realizing that I'd been sleeping in my car.

He pushed the cups at me again.

"They didn't have cola?" I croaked.

"Like I know. I don't got a charm with me, so whaddya think's gonna happen if I go in the store like this?"

I took a cup from him. It was cold. "Then who did?"

He looked at something over my shoulder, and I twisted around. To see a massive silhouette against a glittering skyline, a bunch of dark water, and a half-sunk boat. And a little wild-haired woman standing on a rock dabbing at a hulk's shoulder.

"Wha' happened?" I asked blearily.

"We started to take on water. Don't you remember?"

Vaguely.

"Ah, you were high as a kite, on all those disorienting charms. Whaddya do? Take one full in the face?"

"A crate full." And now I had the hangover from hell.

"Yeah, and who knows what else was in there. Why didn't you just run out the door, like the rest of us?"

I glared at him around the side of the ICEE I was holding to my throbbing head. "Gee. Why didn't I think of that?"

"Ah, sarcasm. Good. Means you're okay."

"Wait." I'd slumped down and now I sat up. And hit my head again. *Son of a bitch!* "How'd I get the car?" I called after Fin, who had started walking back toward the gas station we were parked beside.

And was almost hit by a truck barreling into bay number two.

"Hey, I'm walkin' here!"

He made a rude gesture at the driver.

"Fin!"

He turned around. "You ran back for it. Then drove back here to meet us and collapsed."

He walked off before I could ask anything else, slurping on the cherry ICEE, while the truck driver and I stared at him. I got tired of it first and climbed out of the car. It took a lot longer than normal.

And a lot more effort.

I leaned against the hood, panting and drinking neon blue stuff for a while, because at least it was cold. The night wasn't, and after the jog I didn't remember, my sweats were living up to their name.

The gas station was up a hill from the waterfront, with some apartments on one side and a storage facility on the other. A scraggly tree grew down near the rocks, which were covered in graffiti, like the ones by the warehouse. New graffiti, because it was super bright and seemed to move in my peripheral vision whenever I looked away from it.

Squiggle.

Look.

Squiggle.

Look.

Trippy.

Especially with Dorina's memories, or whatever the hell they were, still sloshing about my cranium.

Sometimes it felt like she was trying to tell me something, like when she gave me that mental slap for thinking I'd had it worse than her. But sometimes it felt like I'd just plugged into random bits of her memories—or Mircea's, because she seemed to have riffled through his brain a lot, taking whatever she wanted. I wondered if the great mentalist had known that he was being spied on, and by his baby daughter, at that.

Or one of them.

A spike of pain tore through my temples, and I went down to my haunches, holding my head. I wanted to go home and crawl into bed. I wanted the stiff drink I hadn't gotten at Fin's. I wanted the landscape to stop slinging around every time I freaking moved!

After a while, it did, staying mostly steady when I looked up. But I decided there was a slight chance I wasn't in any shape to drive right now. I drank some more of big blue, and then I decided that I might as well go and meet the other one—formally, this time.

I got up and walked across the road.

The big guy was down the incline, slumped under the tree, trying to get as low as possible, so his diminutive assistant could treat his wounds. He had a lot of them. Cuts and gouges, some deep, which I guess had been the result of flying shrapnel. What looked like a potion burn on the side of his face, which had barely missed an eye. And something I'd seen before: a chest that was almost black, eclipsing the copper highlights that gleamed on his shoulders in the distant gas station lights, and which I now knew meant bleeding under the skin.

He'd gotten himself a gargantuan bruise, I guess from where the mages' combined spell had hit. It looked painful, but the fact that it hadn't torn through his chest was nothing short of miraculous. A combined spell was a bitch.

I offered him the rest of my ICEE, and to my surprise, he took it. And seemed to like the flavor.

Or maybe he was just thirsty. He drank it in about five seconds, before I could warn him about brain freeze, but I guess that wasn't a thing for trolls. Because he immediately looked around for more.

"I'll get you another," I offered, because I had a cer-

tain amount of fellow feeling. And because I'd just remembered that convenience stores carry beer. "You want
something?" I asked Granny, who shook her head.

"Got it covered," she told me, and pulled a hip flask
out of a pocket. "But some more Bactine would be good.
And some of that tape they use for bandages."

"Okay."

I wandered back to the store, loaded up, and came outside again, to find Fin dragging a U-Haul trailer past the
front door. Or part of one. It was the little half kind.

"Where are you going with that?" I asked him.

"I'm gonna—*puff, puff*—attach it—*puff, puff*—to
your car."

"Okay, no."

He paused. "Whaddya mean, no? And what's with the
food?"

"Thought they might be hungry."

"So you're giving them that? Where's the fish?"

"What fish? It's a convenience store. They have Slim
Jims and ICEEs."

"Well—*puff, puff*—we're gonna need—*puff, puff*—
some fish."

"Why do we need fish? And stop walking!"

"I gotta get this hooked to the car."

"You're not going to hook it to the car."

"And why not?"

"I don't have a hitch."

Thereafter followed a long string of out-of-breath
cussing. Followed by: "WHAT DO YOU MEAN, YOU
DON'T HAVE A HITCH?"

"Why would I have a hitch?"

"Everybody has a hitch! What do you do when you
need to haul stuff?"

"I rent a truck." And *shit*. I'd forgotten Stan's truck
again. He was going to skin me. And that was assuming I
could find the thing, since it hadn't been at the house.

Where the hell had I left it?

"What kind of truck?" Fin said, looking around.

"What?"

"You said we need a truck. What kind?"

"I didn't say that. And you realize we're having this

convo in front of the store, right? Where everybody can see you?"

"There's nobody around."

"There's that guy." I pointed with the ICEE at the guy who'd stared at Fin earlier. He'd gotten his gas and what looked like a couple hot dogs and one of the nachos-of-death things these places always try to pawn off on you, like that cheese hasn't been in the crock for two weeks.

But he wasn't eating any of it, and not because it was nasty.

But because he was staring at Fin.

"Hey. That guy's got a truck," Fin said speculatively.

And then, before I could stop him, he dropped the mini-haul and went charging across the gas station, toward the guy. Whose eyes blew wide and whose food went everywhere when he threw the truck into gear and screeched out of the lot, like all the demons of hell were after him.

Or one big-nosed forest troll.

Who stood there, shouting something for a minute, before stomping back over. "Well, what the hell do we do now?"

"You can't just steal a truck!"

"I wasn't gonna steal it. I was gonna borrow it."

"And you can't go around talking to norms without a charm. You're going to get picked up."

Fin rolled his eyes so hard he almost fell over. "Yeah, sure. That's what's gonna get me picked up."

"Look, just take that back where you got it from! If Blue and his lady friend want a ride, we'll fit 'em in the car somehow."

Thank God it was a convertible.

"And what about the others?"

I felt my stomach drop. "What others?"

Small hands found small hips. "Well, who do you think, Dory?"

Five minutes later, we were down by the water again, having towed the mini-haul over by the car simply to get it out of the way. And I was staring at—damn, I didn't even know. Eight, nine, maybe ten selkies, all crowded up against the colorful rocks, in the shallows.

And not looking good.

I guess because they'd had to swim after the boat, although I didn't see why they'd bothered. They were in the ocean! That was their thing, right? Why not swim away?

Only they weren't looking like they felt like swimming right now. Some were gasping for breath; others were using their flippers to weakly stroke their companions, some of whom had their eyes closed and, honestly, looked like they might never open them again. *Well, damn.*

"We need to get them to a healer."

"That's what I said," Fin told me, pawing through the bags of assorted stuff I'd bought. "But they're afraid whoever it is will rat them out. They say they'll be okay with some rest and food." He looked up. "Are you sure there's no salmon or anything?"

"It's a convenience store!"

"Well, it seems like a poorly stocked one." He opened some jerky and waved it around, but nobody seemed interested.

"They'd probably eat it in their human form," he said. "But transformed, it's like the animal mind gets a veto, you know?"

No, not really. But that didn't matter right now. "I could go get something," I offered, handing over the medical supplies. And some cigs, because the witch, or whatever she was, had looked like she was running low.

"Hey, thanks!" She hiked up her skirts and tucked the packet in the top of her stocking.

"No way," Fin told me. "You're gonna stay here till you don't zigzag when you walk."

"I don't do that."

"You just did that all the way down the hill!"

"You're imagining things."

"Yeah. Not imagining shit." He held out a hand.

"What?"

"The keys."

It took me a moment. "You're not driving my car!"

"I'm not. I can't reach the pedals. She is." He pointed at Granny.

"I'm pretty sober," she assured me. "It probably won't end up like last time."

I blinked. "Last time?"

"The truck. Man, that was something, wasn't it?"

"What truck?"

"Dory! I need the damned keys." That was Fin.

"What truck?" I persisted, getting a really bad feeling about this.

"That big one," she told me cheerfully. "Hoo boy, that was fun to drive."

"Wait. You drove the big truck?" She nodded. "Like, the six-wheeled truck?" More nodding. "And *something happened to it*?"

"Would you stop that?" Fin was looking pissed. "We got sick people here, and I gotta get something to hold that thing onto the back of your car, 'cause we're never gonna fit 'em all inside otherwise, and you're doing what? Oh, yeah. Bitching!"

"I don't bitch!"

"Gimme the damned keys!"

"Here!" I was impressed I didn't throw them at him, but placed them in his tiny little asshole palm.

"Finally." He looked at Granny. "You done?"

"As much as I could. You oughta take a few days off," she told Blue, who grunted at her. And then she and Fin left in a squeal of tires.

I stared after them.

She didn't even slow down for the stop sign.

After a minute, I decided I might as well get comfortable, and pulled a six-pack of longnecks out of one of the bags. I handed Blue one, took one for myself, and discovered the heretofore unknown fact that seals like beer. Well, selkies, anyway.

I poured some down the throats of the interested parties, and then Blue and I sat and drank for a while.

The city lights on the water were nice. The place smelled like gasoline, brackish water, and a fish rotting somewhere nearby, but I'd smelled worse. And, slowly, the graffiti was calming down, so I didn't get dizzy from staring at it anymore.

Blue drank his beer and ate everything in sight. Including two loaves of bread, a package of baloney, two boxes of PowerBars, a quart of orange juice, a bag of Cheetos, eight candy bars, four apples—the only fruit the store had—a dozen doughnuts, six hot dogs, another blue ICEE, and sixteen Slim Jims. Which was fine but made me feel like maybe I should have gotten more.

"You want anything else?"

"No."

The voice was deep and rumbling, as if a mountain could talk. It fit him. And it kind of surprised me, although I didn't know why. He'd been looking like he was following well enough; if he could understand English, of course he could probably speak it, too.

"You want something for the pain?"

He shook his head. And then looked skyward; I wasn't sure why. It was too cloudy to see the moon right now.

I wanted to question him, but this didn't seem the time. I wanted to help him, but wasn't sure how, or even what would be acceptable. I knew Olga, Fin, and the twins, but I didn't think they were necessarily representative of troll culture in general. Olga and Fin had been here for years, and the twins were young and impressionable. They'd become a weird amalgam of human teenage weirdness and Dark Fey habits and anyway, I was used to them.

I wasn't used to him.

But I wanted to do something. "You want anything at all?" I asked, and waited.

This was a troll, after all.

But the answer came more quickly than I'd expected.

"Four and five."

I waited some more. "What?"

"Six and seven."

Okay.

Confused now.

But then the giant head bent down, and the tiny eyes were serious. And angry, but not at me. I stared into their depths, and saw a banked fury, a quiet outrage that was somehow more compelling than any physical thing I'd seen him do.

"They destroy. They dishonor. They *pay*."

"The slavers?"

A nod.

"So, one, two, and three . . . are dead?"

It seemed a fair guess.

Another nod.

"So that leaves four . . ." But he hadn't spoken of them that way, had he? "Two groups of two?"

Another nod.

Okay, getting the hang of this now.

"So you're after two more groups of slavers. You know where they are?"

"Not know. Not yet."

"It's just . . . there's a lot of slavers in New York. We're trying to shut them down, but they're good at hiding—"

"They *blaspheme*. They *disgrace*!"

"Yeah. They, uh, they're bad people."

"They *destroy*. They kill and kill again!"

"Okay. Okay." I held out my hands, in the universal "see, I have no weapons, please don't kill me" gesture, because he was suddenly furious.

And bending over me in a way that would have been intimidating, even if my weapons hadn't still been in the car, except for the pain in his eyes. "They take fey, make fight, make *die*. And after die, they dishonor. They steal—"

He broke off with what I could only assume was a fey curse.

"They steal . . . what?"

But I didn't get an answer this time. "So many lost. So many forgotten. Cannot go back. Cannot go *home*."

"We'll help them get home. We'll help you."

He'd turned his head to look out over the water, but now he turned it back. His eyes were suddenly tired and sad, which was somehow worse than the anger. "No. They never go back. Bones lost now."

And I suddenly remembered something Caedmon had said. Something about the bones of a dead fey needing to be sent back to Faerie. But that wasn't anything a slaver would care about, was it? If someone died in the fights, or any other way, what would they do?

Probably just bury them, and leave them to rot. Why risk opening a portal when, every time you did, it had a chance of being detected? Why bring the Circle down on your head just to honor an old tradition?

An old tradition that was sacred to a certain portion

of Faerie, who believed that if the bones weren't returned a fey soul was lost forever.

They kill and kill again.

No wonder he wanted them dead.

I suddenly noticed that my eyes were wet. I wasn't the weeping type, but the depth of his pain was palpable. And not just the emotional kind, I realized, catching sight of the blood leaking out from under the pad the woman had put on his chest. She might have done her best, but it wasn't good enough. He needed stitches, or whatever the troll equivalent was.

Because, no matter how strong you are, you can still bleed out.

Screw it.

I took out my phone and called Claire.

She showed up faster than I'd expected, an old trench coat over her nightgown and her hair in the kind of big foam curlers that make for nice, loose curls the next day. She'd brought her kit, but been smart enough to leave the Light Fey at home.

"Thanks," I told her, as she paid the cabbie, because I'd managed to drown the lambo. "By the way, did I ever say sorry about your car?"

"Fuck the car." She pushed a strand of red hair out of her eyes. "Where are they?"

I led her down to the water's edge, not knowing what kind of reception we were going to get. But to my surprise, the selkies took one look at her and crowded up on land, as much as they could with the rocks in the way. Blue didn't react, except to watch her as she examined his fellow fey and dispensed one of her patented horrible-smelling concoctions.

"They're so thin," she murmured.

"Yeah, I don't think they've eaten much lately. And they didn't like jerky and Cheetos."

Her lip curled. "Who does?"

I bit back a reply about Claire's ten thousand recipes for chickpeas, because this wasn't the time.

"We need to get them home," I said instead.

"And put them where?"

"They could stay . . . in the dining room?"

"I thought the vampires were in the dining room. Or did you move them upstairs?"

Shit.

"You, uh, you know about that?"

She shot me a look. "Dory. I have a houseful of fey guards. They don't miss much."

Yeah.

Probably should have thought of that.

"And you're not upset?"

She sat back on her heels, and looked sort of sad. "I'm upset that you feel like you have to sneak people around. It's your house, too."

I sat there blinking, but she was already moving on to Blue. I tensed a little; I don't know why. I knew what she was, what she could do. But she looked so tiny next to his massive bulk that I worried anyway.

Until I saw the most amazing thing I'd seen all night. The huge, battle-scarred, fearsome troll; the guy who had dangerous slavers quaking in their boots; the guy who had torn apart a warehouse full of who knew what kind of traps, snares, and hexes, not one, not two, but three nights in a row, and that after kicking ass at a no-holds-barred epic fight—*that guy*—relaxed back against the tree and closed his eyes.

And fell asleep.

Chapter Thirty-nine

Half an hour later, I was pouring a two-liter of water over Claire's green-to-the-elbow arms, and Big Blue had a bunch of concrete in his chest. At least, that's what it looked like. I assumed it was something more medicinal, since Claire had troweled it straight into the big wounds, where it finally stopped the seepage.

It had also left Blue looking like an about-to-be-vacated apartment, with spackle everywhere, but apparently it would be absorbed by the body as it healed and wouldn't do any harm. And it didn't look like it had hurt him, since he'd snored through most of it. In other news, my car was back without noticeable damage, and so was a truck, which Fin had had a couple of his boys bring over, since he hadn't been able to find anyone to install a hitch in the middle of the night.

They were big, strapping guys that he used for security and other things, like loading up a bunch of selkies.

They'd also brought Fin a charm, which had transformed him into a short guy with a wild shock of brown hair and a big nose. It was weird; he still looked identifiably himself, with small eyes and roughly the same shaped face, just humanized. At least enough that we weren't likely to scare anybody else.

So things were looking up.

"Things are looking up," I told Claire.

She bit her lip.

"Aren't they?"

She tilted the bottle's mouth to stop the flow, and lathered up with some soap she'd brought with her. She made her own, when she had time, and this one smelled of lavender. It was nice.

Her expression wasn't.

"I did something," she told me abruptly. "I was waiting up to tell you about it, because I couldn't get you on the phone, but then—" She glanced around at a burly guy walking past with a human-sized seal over his shoulder, and sighed.

"Then things got crazy." I grinned at her.

She didn't grin back.

"You're going to be angry," she told me.

"I doubt that." Claire and I had our differences, from time to time, but we rarely fought.

"I don't."

She was rinsing off, and I could almost see her steeling herself. She finished, and the thin shoulders went back, the curler-bound head came up, and the green eyes met mine head-on. Because, whatever else Claire may be, she isn't a coward.

"I called Louis-Cesare."

For a moment, I just blinked at her. It was the last thing I'd expected—they didn't even talk in person if they could avoid it, much less over the phone. I hadn't even known she had his number.

"I didn't even know you had his number," I said, and it was her turn to blink.

"It . . . was in the house phone. He called once when you had your cell off."

"Oh, yeah. Right."

She blinked some more. "Aren't you angry?"

I handed her some napkins to dry off with, because we didn't have a towel. "Should I be? What did you talk about?"

She just looked at me some more. This was getting odd. "I told him I liked his suit."

"It was a nice suit."

"Dory!" Claire's eyes were getting brighter, rivaling the gas station lights behind her. She tried drying off using the napkins, but they shredded and stuck to her skin. "Damn it!" She shoved the wet wad in a pocket. "This is when you yell at me for sticking my nose in your business! This is when you tell me I went too far, as usual, and trampled all over your boundaries while trying to help. This is when you tell me I'm a crap friend for hating your boyfriend like a bigoted know-it-all, because sure, I know vampires better than you, when you've lived with them for centuries!"

There was a pause. She seemed to be waiting for something. Which I guess she didn't get, because the thin eyebrows drew together.

"Well?"

"Well, what?"

"Aren't you going to say it?"

"Why? You already did."

And, okay, in retrospect, that probably wasn't the right response, because she burst into tears. I awkwardly put an arm around her shoulders, because that seemed to help last time. And had it angrily shrugged off.

"Don't be kind!" she told me. "I'm a shit friend; I know it! I've been telling myself that for the last two hours—"

"I didn't say you were a shit friend."

"Well, I did! And I am!"

She angrily wiped off napkin residue like she was shedding a second skin.

"You never yell at me, even when you should. And I know why," she said, when I started to open my mouth. "You never had a roommate before. You don't have anyone to compare me to, but trust me, I'm shit."

"Claire, you're not shit—"

"Yes, I am!" She looked up, eyes blazing. And then suddenly slumped against the car, the fire gone as fast as it had come. "See? I can't even let you yell at me properly; I have to boss how you do it. I'm overbearing and interfering and everything always has to be my way. I try not to be—I *do*—but then something comes along and it—it just isn't *right*. And I have to fix it—I have to *try*, even if I end up screwing everything up and making it worse than before. Because I'm shit."

She slid down beside a tire and hugged her knees.

I'd been in that position earlier, and it sucked. Nothing ever went well in that position. That was the world's-out-to-get-me-and-probably-will position, and it made me sad to see Claire in it.

I went over and sat beside her.

"You're not shit," I told her.

She looked at me, her eyes filled with tears. "You haven't heard what I told him yet."

_____

A couple minutes later, I was on the road to Horatiu's, with the pedal pressed all the way down. Not to see him this time, but to prevent a possible murder. Because when Claire fucked up, she did it right.

Not that she'd meant to. She'd hoped to get Louis-Cesare and me back together by spilling the beans. Namely, that I loved him and was just doing this to protect him, and how he should have been able to see that when it was clear as day to everyone else, and that he should have stayed and fought for me. But instead he'd just turned and walked away—I guess she'd talked to Soini—and if he was that much of an idiot, he didn't deserve me.

When she finally let him get a word in, he'd reminded her that she didn't know anything about our relationship, and that it was her father-in-law trying to steal me away in the first place. And apparently succeeding, because I clearly preferred him! And that this was none of her business, so perhaps she should—and he meant this in the most respectful and courteous way possible—die in a fire.

Then, of course, Claire got pissed—because let's face it, it never takes much to set her off—and said that she must have misjudged him, that he really was a giant idiot and that I'd probably be better off with someone else, anyway.

Like that Marlowe fellow.

I didn't know why the hell she'd picked him. Kit Marlowe was the consul's pit bull and chief of security. He was also a giant dick. He and I cordially loathed each other, and while we had developed a somewhat decent working relationship recently out of necessity, our lips still had a tendency to curl when the other walked into a room. He hated—and I mean *hated*—the idea that a dhampir was on his beloved Senate, polluting it with my very presence. And I . . .

Well, I just hated him.

He made it really easy.

So, no, Marlowe was not an issue.

But, apparently, Louis-Cesare now thought he was, because Claire's mouth and brain don't talk to each other when she gets upset, and Marlowe was one of the only nonfamily vamps she knew. And she'd somehow managed to convey the idea that he'd been nosing around, and was now ready to pounce since his competition had just fled the scene.

Like the cowardly bastard that he was.

She'd fit that phrase in a few more times before she realized that my ex was no longer on the phone. But not like he'd hung up. More like he'd simply dropped it while doing something else, something that I really hoped wasn't driving hell-bent for leather toward a certain annoying bastard of a Senate member.

Who was, uh, probably about to have a bad night.

To give her credit, Claire had tried calling Louis-Cesare back when she calmed down, but his phone was busy. It was for me, too, which was a problem. But not as much as hearing one of his masters, who had answered the landline at his place, inform me that he'd left rather abruptly earlier this evening, and could he take a message?

No, but he could convey one. Only, apparently, he hadn't, because I hadn't gotten a call. That was a problem since, according to the Senate's New York HQ, Marlowe was currently at Mircea's Central Park apartment for some reason. And Mircea's place was roughly three hours from Louis-Cesare's. Which would be great if Claire's little creative foray hadn't taken place over two hours ago, and if I wasn't in Brooklyn.

I tried mushing the pedal through the floor, but it would only go so far.

So I gave up and called Marlowe, or rather Mircea's place, because I didn't know his personal number.

Burbles of House Happiness answered, and was overjoyed to talk to me.

"Lady Dorina! How wonderful!"

"Dory. Is Louis-Cesare there?"

"No. I haven't seen his lordship for, why, it must be almost a week now. Is he supposed to be here?"

"No. No, he is not. Is Marlowe?"

"Oh, yes. Lord Marlowe is entertaining tonight. Shall I tell him you'll be joining us?"

I didn't know why Marlowe was entertaining at Mircea's apartment, or why he was entertaining at all. He was a spy, not a diplomat, and an abrupt bastard at the best of times. But I didn't ask because I didn't care.

"Can I talk to him?"

"Of a certainty. Give me a moment."

He wandered off, and I got another call.

I answered it before looking at the screen, and damn it, I knew better. "Louis-Cesare?"

"James."

Shit.

Guess he'd had time to clean up the mess.

"Uh, look, James, I can't really talk right—"

"The hell you can't. You destroy my crime scene and then you have the gall—"

"I didn't destroy anything. Your own guys did that."

"That's not what they say—"

"Well, of course it's not what they say. I bet they didn't mention trying to beat me up as soon as the lights went out, either."

"Their report says the opposite. That you almost killed them trying to get out the door!"

"I couldn't even find the door, and you were there!"

"And didn't see shit thanks to a couple thousand spells going off in my face!"

My phone beeped again.

"Hang on," I told him.

"Hang on? Hang on? Don't you dare—"

"Yes?" I asked the second line.

"Dory?"

Shit.

Stan.

"Oh, hey, look, man, I'm kind of busy right now—"

I hit the dashboard.

"What was that?"

"Just, uh, just putting away some bad guys. You know how it is."

I hit it a few more times, which sounded like . . . I was

hitting the dashboard. Stan seemed to think so, too. "So hit 'em in this direction and bring back my truck. You know it's three days overdue, right?"

"Sure. Absolutely. Was just going to do that. Uh, look, is there some kind of weekly special?"

"Yeah. Bring my truck back before the week's out and Roberto's boys don't break your legs."

Pissant little son of a—

"You know I'm a *senator*!" I said, to no one, because he'd already hung up.

I switched back to James.

Or so I thought.

"You are *not* invited!"

"Marlowe?"

"Do you understand me?" The voice was livid.

What else was new?

"Invited to what?"

"None of your business! Go away!"

"Listen—"

"No, *you* listen. This is an important night for me—for all of us. I am not going to have you ruin it!"

"I'm not trying to—"

"You never try, but it always happens! You went to the theatre and now there's no theatre!"

I started to say that wasn't my fault, but . . . it was a little my fault. "I'm not trying to crash your damned party! I just need to tell you—"

"If I see one glimpse or get so much as a single whiff—"

"Like you know what I smell like!" I was trying to keep my temper—I really was—but Marlowe was like nails on a chalkboard. "And it's Mircea's apartment. I'll come any time I damned well—"

"You'll be escorted off the property! In pieces!"

I actually laughed at that one. "By you and whose army?"

"I don't need an army." He somehow managed to hiss it, despite it not having any *s*'s. "I'm warning you—*stay away!*"

He hung up.

Goddamn it.

I started to call him back, but then realized I already had a call waiting.

"Hello?"

"Don't you dare hang up on me again!"

I sighed.

James.

"I didn't hang up before; I had another call. And why are we talking about this? I have immunity, and that aside, you were almost finished—"

"You don't get to decide when we're finished with a crime scene! You don't get to decide anything! Particularly when you use your shiny new immunity to aid and abet the escape of a dozen felons!"

"A dozen?" I frowned. "Ten of them were slaves. They didn't do any—"

"They hid the troll who caused all this! They deliberately used their bodies to hide his signal and that of the woman he's working with—"

"They didn't hide anything. Sitting on a floor is hardly—"

"—and as a result, I have a warrant in my hand for their arrest—"

"Don't be a dick, James! This is on me. They had nothing to do with it!"

"—and another for your friend Fin, who does not, in fact, have immunity."

"James—"

"I'm not bluffing, Dory. I want the big guy. Now."

"I don't have him!"

"Don't lie. You do it badly."

"I do it perfectly, but I'm not doing it now." It was the truth. The freaked-out trucker had returned with a skeptical-looking cop just as I was leaving, and I'd nervously looked back at the waterline—to see exactly nothing.

Big as he was, Blue moved like smoke.

"If you think that's going to work," James said ominously.

"I don't have him!"

"Then your friend is going to enjoy our hospitality until you do."

"James!"

"I want the selkies, too," he went on ruthlessly. "No one even had a chance to question them. You bring me the dozen you cost me, and your friend goes free. Otherwise, I'm sure there's plenty of—"

"You're not going to lock him up!"

"—counts I can dig up on one of the biggest bookies in this city. He could go away for years. Or even be deported, if we rack up enough charges."

I didn't answer that time.

I just sat there for a moment, holding my phone.

Every war mage I knew was a giant asshole. Every single one, except for James. The last time I'd seen him, other than tonight, had been a month or so ago, on one of his days off. He'd been painting his dad's shop, while his wife cooked burgers in the small courtyard out back, and his youngest daughter wove a wreath out of centaury and feverfew, which he proudly wore while we ate.

I'd dropped in to pick up an order, and they'd invited me to share their meal because that's the kind of people they were: James; his wife, Jean; and their two little girls, Janis—because James loved classic rock, and had wanted to keep the *J* thing going—and Lakshmi, because that had been the name of their grandmother, and some things are more important than alliteration.

Rufus' wife had been gone six years now, and I strongly suspected that was why James and family visited so often. It was less about chores that needed doing and more about giving the old man voices around the place other than his own. And because that's who James was, at least on his days off.

He *couldn't* be that different at work.

So he was bluffing.

I *knew* he was.

But Fin . . . I didn't think James understood about Fin. The forest trolls didn't have a forest anymore. It had been burned out from under them, and the land used for new farms by the goddamned Svarestri, who didn't have enough evil points racked up yet, so they'd had to steal the little guys' home, too. And then kill anybody who didn't get the hint.

Fin didn't have anywhere to go back *to*.

But the law didn't care about that, like it didn't care about him.

But I did, and I couldn't risk it.

Goddamn it.

"I don't have him, but I'll get him," I told James roughly. "If I have Fin out to help me."

"Dory—"

"He has more contacts in that world than I'll ever have. He's how I found him this time, remember? And he won't help you, no matter what you threaten him with. He won't rat out a fellow troll."

James was silent for a long moment. "Forty-eight hours. Then I'm bringing him in. And I'm not bluffing."

Fuck.

Chapter Forty

A short time later, I was facing the door to a sleek Manhattan apartment, feeling more than a little out of place. I had no makeup, my coiffure was a style I like to call drove-with-the-top-down, and I still had on the rumpled old sweats. Now paired with muddy gardening sandals because I'd swapped with Claire so she wouldn't slip on the rocks.

None of which should have mattered, since Horatiu is blind as a bat.

But it wasn't Horatiu who answered the door.

And promptly slammed it in my face.

Or, to be more precise, tried to. But while Kit Marlowe is fast, so am I. And I got a muddy Croc in the door before he could shut it entirely.

Angry brown eyes glared at me through the minuscule opening. "Go. Away."

"Fuck. You." I gave a little push.

And was gratified to note that Marlowe had to exert effort to keep me out. I also noticed that he was in a tux, which was unusual because he had almost as much fashion sense as me. But somebody, probably his long-suffering family, had wrangled him into a sleek black number anyway, trimmed the Elizabethan-era goatee he'd had since it was originally fashionable, and tried to do something with the dark brown ratty-looking curls.

The latter had been slicked down with some sort of pomade, but they didn't behave any better than their master, and had sprung back up again. The result was wet ratty-looking curls, which wasn't an improvement, but I couldn't talk at the moment. Or do much of anything else, because he was *really* determined that I not get through that door.

Which was ridiculous, since I had more reason to be here than he did!

"This is my father's apartment," I reminded him. It was Mircea's condo in the city, originally purchased, I suspected, for times when he couldn't deal with the consul anymore. Being a diplomat includes knowing when to get away so you don't strangle somebody to death, like Marlowe looked like he wanted to do to me.

"He isn't here!"

"I'm not looking for him. I'm looking for Louis-Cesare—"

"He isn't here, either."

"You haven't heard from him?"

I didn't get an answer that time, probably because Marlowe was busy.

"Stop slamming the damned door on my damned foot!"

"Then *leave*." He glared at me furiously. "We're having a soiree, and you aren't attending like that!"

"A soiree?"

"A gathering! A party! A do!"

"I know what the word means! And I'm *not* attending. I just need—"

Marlowe kicked my Croc like it was a football and he was trying for a field goal from the fifty-yard line. It sent my leg shooting out backward, and would have resulted in me face-planting painfully if I hadn't twisted at the last second. I landed on my shoulder instead, and it wasn't happy about it.

Son of a bitch!

I got up and glared at the now-closed door. I could have kicked it down, but my toe hurt. So I jabbed the bell a few more times, and then leaned on it when the door stayed stubbornly shut.

Until it was flung open in my face. "Damn it, go away!"

"Damn it, answer the question!"

I guess Marlowe decided it was the quickest way to get rid of me, because for once, he actually did. "Louis-

Cesare isn't here, I haven't heard from him and I'm not going to! He's in a meeting—"

"What?" That stopped me. "What kind of meeting?"

"A Senate meeting. What else?" The eyes now looked impatient as well as angry. "An emergency one was called for tonight. Now will you—"

"Why wasn't I informed? I'm on the Senate."

As usual, that reminder had Marlowe looking apoplectic.

"But not that committee! The whole Senate doesn't meet for every issue, or we'd never do anything else. But that's where he is, so go plague the consul and *leave me alone*!"

The door slammed again, probably because I wasn't opposing it anymore.

I was just standing there in my smelly sweats, wondering why I'd just driven over here like a bat out of hell. Had I really thought Louis-Cesare was going to beat up another senator over me? Risk his new position by taking on the consul's favorite shortly after being appointed? Throw away an opportunity that most would kill for, and over what? A damned dhampir?

Yeah.

Judging by the pang in my gut, I guess I had.

And that was *stupid*. We were broken up, and Claire was right. He hadn't even bothered to argue about it, had he? Just turned around and walked away. He hadn't made any declarations while on the phone with her, either. He just told her to mind her own business and essentially hung up.

And he'd never even called me back.

I rang the doorbell again.

But not because of Louis-Cesare. I needed to get my head back on straight, and that meant some kind of communication with my other half. And *that* meant talking to Horatiu. With Big Blue to find, God knew when I'd get another chance.

And fuck Marlowe if he didn't like it!

And I guess he didn't. Because he didn't answer. And the doorknob shocked the shit out of me when I dared to grab it.

I jerked my hand back, and looked at the faint red mark the newly engaged ward had left.

Okay, *now* I was pissed.

Fortunately, Mircea's condo isn't in a sleek new building with slick glass fronts, but in a turn-of-the-century limestone beauty that he owns half of. A half filled with windows. Windows with curly-haired assholes in them.

"What the hell are you doing?" Marlowe demanded, sticking his neck out, as I edged along an ornate ledge.

I punched him in his stupid face. "What does it look like?"

"Get out!"

I let him eat fist again, and he turned the ward on over the window, which blew me off the side of the building and into some bushes. It also blew my Croc onto a nearby BMW, which was apparently a touchy little bitch. Because the car alarm started screaming its head off.

I looked at it for a moment, while I got my breath back. Mircea hadn't skimped on the wards. Even on the lowest setting, they packed a wallop.

And then I gazed up at Marlowe, who was still glaring down at me from the window, and I slowly took off my other shoe.

"Don't you dare!"

I skipped the Croc down the row of cars, like a stone on a pond, setting off multiple alarms and disturbing the genteel neighbors. Until I was snatched off the BMW and smacked against the side of the building, still grinning. I'd badly needed to let off some steam, and that had been fun.

Not as much as making Marlowe eat concrete, though.

I twisted in his grip, danced away, spun, and belted him. I put everything I had into it, all the pent-up emotion of a very bad day, and was gratified to see him actually go down. And then spring back up, almost before he hit the sidewalk, because the guy was flexible. As he proved when dodging half a dozen more blows in quick succession, before grabbing my fist.

It was the same maneuver Dorina had used on the fey, and it hurt like a bitch. Until I used my other hand for a gut shot that had him letting go with an annoyed "*tchaa!*" And then I ended up slammed against the building again.

Face-first, this time.

I turned to the side to get my lips free. "I can do this all night."

"Or you could just leave!"

"Or you could just let me in."

"I'm not letting you in!"

"Then we have a problem," I said, broke his hold, spun around, and kneed him in the groin.

I took off again, hoping the happy, burbling vamp from the phone would answer the door, but I got stopped with a flying tackle. Which was less of a problem for me than for Marlowe, because I was in ancient sweats. Ancient, muddy sweats, because it had been raining at some point earlier in the day, and the section of tastefully planted greenery I ploughed up was basically a mud pit.

"You're gonna ruin that nice suit," I said, through a dirt facial.

And, for some reason, that did what nothing else had, and stopped him. I flipped over to see Marlowe suddenly back on his feet, looking with concern at the patches of mud adhering to his formerly sleek, James Bond getup. Which was followed by him whipping out a pocket square and worriedly daubing at the mess.

"Will water take it out, do you think?" he asked me, bizarrely.

I slowly got back up, but he just kept trying to wipe himself clean. It wasn't working; if anything, it was just smearing the mess around. Something that seemed to be causing him real distress, which made him rub it harder, which only made a bad matter worse.

"Give me that," I finally said, and he actually did, passing over the by-now-sadly-soiled pocket square, and looking . . . weird. Marlowe basically had two emotions where I was concerned: pissed off and seriously pissed off. Which was why it was so strange to see him standing there in his muddy tux, biting his lip, and staring at me hopefully.

Because I was a woman, and we magically made these kind of things okay, right?

I sighed.

"Come on."

"Where?"

"You're not getting that out. But Mircea has plenty more suits in his bedroom. One will probably fit you."

"There's a party in the main room! An important one! I can't just—"

I sighed again, impatiently this time. "You can climb, right?"

We climbed.

Thankfully, he hadn't bothered to ward every window in the place, and one of the ones in Mircea's bedroom slid open easily. I ducked inside, Marlowe on my heels, and padded barefoot over to the big wardrobe I'd been told to stay out of. I decided that, since I wasn't here for me, it didn't count, and threw open the double doors.

"Oh," Marlowe said, 'cause I guess he'd never gotten the tour.

I'd been known to borrow Mircea's shirts as emergency dresses on occasion, so I knew what was in there. Basically, the pick of the great fashion houses of Europe, with a choice few American designers thrown in for good measure. And enough of it to stock a small men's store.

Self-denial has never really been Daddy's thing.

"Okay, strip," I told Marlowe, flicking through the couture. "And tell me what your problem is."

"You!"

I glanced over my shoulder, to see him looking around, as if wondering where to put his muddy coat. "Just leave it in the bathroom." I nodded at the adjoining room. "And that's not an answer."

Marlowe went grumbling off, and I went back to trying to decide what might work as a substitute. It wasn't as easy as it looked. Because, sure, there was plenty to draw from, but Marlowe had the same issue I did, only not to the same degree. I could wear Mircea's shirts as dresses because he was six feet tall in his socks.

Marlowe wasn't.

"How bad are your trousers?" I asked, as Marlowe came out of the bathroom wearing nothing else. Because I guess his shirt had gotten muddy, too. I sized him up.

The coats and shirts would probably fit okay—he was built well enough under the scowl—but the pants weren't just gonna draw up on their own. He was definitely too short. "You're too short," I told him, while he continued trying to clean them, this time with a washcloth.

"Well, what the hell am I supposed to do about that?"

"I don't know, but that's not gonna work." It really wasn't. The mud had splattered everywhere when we hit down, and some of the flakes had already dried into little cement nodules. A good dry cleaner might be able to salvage the outfit, but not in time for Marlowe to return to his guests.

I went to the phone.

Burbles picked up, and he was happy to help. No, he was *thrilled*. He'd never had a request in his entire, long life that pleased him so much, oh my God.

"Great." I put a hand over the phone, and looked at Marlowe. "What size are you?"

"What?"

"Stop trying to clean those things. They aren't cleanable. Just tell me your size."

"I don't know my size."

"What do you mean, you don't know your size? You don't buy pants?"

"Of course not. I have staff for that."

"You have staff for buying pants?"

"Trousers." He looked pained. "Pants are underwear."

"Thought that was knickers."

"Those are for women! And yes, my staff buys my clothes!"

I sighed again. I do that a lot around Marlowe. "Then take the damn pants—okay, *trousers*—off and tell me the size."

"I can't."

"Why?"

"I'm not wearing anything underneath!"

I was about to respond to that the way it deserved, when Burbles offered a compromise. "Okay," I told him, and looked back at Grumpy. "How tall are you?"

"Five eleven."

I rolled my eyes.

"Fine. Five ten."

"Is pride worth tripping over your feet all night?"

"All right! I'm five eight—and a half."

"He's five eight," I told Burbles.

"And a half!"

"You're not fifteen going on sixteen. Halves don't count."

"They'll be too short!"

"Then give me the damned size!"

"Fine!"

Marlowe stomped back to the bathroom, and I stood there in muddy sweats, getting cold from the air-conditioning. "Hang on," I told Burbles, and put the phone down on his effusions of joy.

Mircea's wardrobe of the gods yielded a long dress shirt, which I thought might do. I stripped off the sweats and was looking around for something to wipe off with, because I'd somehow gotten mud down my back. But even I draw the line at using Armani for a towel.

"Hey, Marlowe, can you throw me—"

I stopped, because I'd just come back into the bedroom, and noticed that we had a visitor. Which would have been okay, because I was still in a bra and panties, and I wear less to the beach. And because most vamps don't care about such things anyway.

You notice I said "most."

"Throw you what?" Grumpy came out of the bathroom with a towel around his waist and his trousers in his hand. Which he didn't toss to me because he was currently getting tossed himself, back through the bathroom door hard enough to crack tile.

For some reason, I felt a stupid grin break out over my face.

"I didn't think you'd come," I said, a little bashfully.

To no one, because the party had already moved to the next room.

I walked over to the phone. "Just take your best guess," I told Burbles, and hung up.

I was still barefoot, and now there was shattered tile all over the rug, not to mention glass from a newly destroyed bathroom mirror. So I didn't get too close. Just climbed onto the bed to peer through the doorway, at what was amounting to the butt kicking of the century.

Marlowe was trying to talk his way out of it, I guess in

preference to getting into a dustup with another senator, only that wasn't working so well.

And we kind of needed him alive for the war.

So I threw the comforter over the shattered tile, jumped down, and grabbed Louis-Cesare the next time he had his back to the door.

"Let me go!"

"Are you going to kill Kit?"

"Yes!"

"Well, see, that's a problem."

"You crazy son of a bitch!" That was a bloody, naked Marlowe, who was currently sprawled in the tub, but still talking. Which was great and all, but holding an enraged Louis-Cesare was not easy. Any second now—

Yep, that's what I'd thought.

He tore away from the door, with me jumping onto his back to preserve my feet, and proceeded to pummel Marlowe some more. Who got his feet up in time to send Louis-Cesare staggering back into the sink, which was less than fun for me since I hit the broken mirror. The remaining glass cascaded everywhere, along with several good-sized pieces that I normally would have used as knives against my opponent, except my opponent was my boyfriend—

Ex-boyfriend.

No matter how hot he looked while beating up Marlowe. *Cut it out,* I told myself, *and find some way to stop this!*

But taking somebody down the nonlethal way wasn't really my thing, and I guess it wasn't Marlowe's, either, who opted for the better part of valor. He snatched down the shower curtain and flung it over us, buying himself a second to tear out of the bathroom. He went for the window and he wasn't slow, but Louis-Cesare caught him and threw him at the bedroom door. And then lunged after him and down a hall.

Which is how we ended up crashing a very genteel party, filled with refined guests, trays of delicate hors d'oeuvres, discreet servants, and light musical accompaniment. And a bloody, naked master vampire, running for his life. And being chased by another, this one fully clothed, but being ridden by a bra-and-panties-wearing wild woman trying to slow him down.

It wasn't working.

But Marlowe was fast, and didn't seem to have any compunction about trampling his appalled-looking guests. So the pale half-moons ahead of us made it to the hall before we did, partly because a couple servants took one for the team and jumped Louis-Cesare. Who flung them off with a curse and dove after the boss.

"Would you l-listen?" I yelled, as Marlowe, the idiot, took a right at the foyer, instead of heading for the front door and the parking lot. He might have outrun us in a car, with the emphasis on "might," but there was no chance now. So it was up to me.

"This isn't w-what it l-looks like!" I yelled, as Louis-Cesare tore up a set of stairs I hadn't noticed before, and burst through a door. "We were just t-trying to—"

I cut off, in favor of holding on and not taking any wooden shrapnel to the eye as he plowed through several more doors without bothering to open them first.

And then we were out, into something vaguely familiar—

Oh, right.

Elyas' ballroom.

The guy who owned the apartment above Mircea's had been a senator, too, from the European court. I say "had" because he'd recently shuffled off this mortal coil in favor of—well, from what I'd heard of him, something considerably warmer. I didn't know, since I'd never met the guy, the coil shuffling having happened before I arrived.

And it looked like history was repeating itself, only not for Marlowe.

Because my uncle Radu was seated on a chair, in the middle of the huge, now-mostly-empty ballroom, with a gun to his head and a stake at his heart.

Chapter Forty-one

Everything stopped, including Louis-Cesare. Who burst through the door and then just stood there, still as a statue, staring at the tableau. The only good thing was that it was Dumb and Dumber, aka Purple Hair and Blondie, who had apparently decided on another target but had been misinformed. Because Radu wasn't on the Senate.

He was, however, protected by a couple of people who were, one of whom had started to breathe heavily.

"Oh, hello, Dory," Radu said, because Radu is special.

I climbed down and glanced at Louis-Cesare's face. And started talking fast. "How about we take a moment?"

"How about he dies?" Blondie said carelessly. Because he obviously had a death wish.

He was also the only one with a lethal weapon. Purple Hair looked like a proper badass, in a shiny black jumpsuit straight out of the Catwoman catalogue, but she'd opted for a gun. While not ideal, it wouldn't do lasting damage to a second-level master like Radu.

Blondie, in khakis and a frat boy polo, hadn't been so nice.

It was about to get him killed.

"I have a roomful of important guests downstairs," Kit said quickly. "We need their cooperation for the war and this is not going to help!"

Everyone ignored him.

It's kind of hard to look commanding while holding your junk.

"Put the stake down, and move away," I told Blondie.

"That's Mircea's brother, Radu. He doesn't have a seat on the Senate—"

"I know that!" he sneered. "We're here for you!"

"You've tried that twice, and it hasn't worked out so well," I reminded him.

"Twice?" Louis-Cesare hissed, and yeah. The gorgeous Frenchman wasn't looking so refined right now. The blue eyes were tinged with silver, the color they turned whenever he pulled up power. And the fangs were out, a drop of his own blood glistening on that luscious lower lip. He looked . . . feral.

"They're just being stupid," I told him, staring at the blood. And fighting a strange urge to lick it. "Making a try for my Senate seat—"

"I'm on the Senate," Louis-Cesare said, his eyes solid silver now. "Why don't you try me?"

And, okay, I might have been wrong about one of them. Because Purple Hair flipped the gun around, walked over, and handed it to me. "Let him go," she told Dumber.

Who lived up to his name. "What the hell? What is wrong with you?"

"He's going to kill you if you don't," she said, matter-of-factly.

"He can't do that! I haven't challenged him!"

"But he can challenge *you*. Now step away!"

But Blondie was either really stupid or really entitled or both. Because his chin got a stubborn tilt to it. "We have no quarrel with you," he told Louis-Cesare. "We just want a fair fight with that bitch of a—"

Annnnnd, that's why you're careful what you wish for, I thought, as Louis-Cesare disappeared. Not like he did with his master power, because he didn't need the Veil with this joker, but moving so fast that it almost looked like it. The next time I blinked, he was by Blondie, who he grabbed and threw into Marlowe. Because I guess he wasn't finished with him yet.

And then a bunch of guys, Marlowe's men at a guess, ran in and started chasing the fight around the ballroom. I considered interfering, but seriously, it was like twenty to one. I thought they could handle it.

Probably.

I bent to help Radu instead, but found that he'd already freed himself.

"You were loose all the time?" Purple Hair asked.

"Your friend isn't very good at bondage," Radu said, tossing the cuffs on the floor and a shining curtain of dark hair over his shoulder.

Radu was Mircea's younger brother, but only by a few years. Something that ceases to matter when you're both on the wrong side of five hundred. But while Mircea looked thirty, maybe thirty-five on a bad day, Radu could have passed for a teenager—if an elegant one.

And tonight was no exception. Louis-Cesare's Sire was sporting a sapphire and gold patterned robe and some plain—if buttery satin can be called that—lounge pants. It was an attractive set, leaving a deep V at the neck that showed off naturally bronzed skin and brought out the startling turquoise of his eyes.

"It . . . wasn't bondage," Purple Hair said slowly. "And why didn't you do something?"

"I didn't want to make you feel bad." Radu patted her gently on the arm. "You were trying so hard."

"How did you know I'd be here?" I asked her, as she stood there, blinking at Radu. Who tended to have that effect on people. For his part, he wasn't trying to rescue his son, who clearly didn't need it, but had instead started puttering around in some plastic storage containers stacked behind the chair.

"Hello?" I tried again, snapping some fingers near her head. "Find me? How?"

"Phone," she said, still looking at Radu. Before shaking herself and refocusing on me. "We tapped your phone, and overheard you talking to Vincent—"

"Vincent?"

She looked pained. "The happy one."

Oh, Burbles.

"So we knew you'd be here sometime tonight. We persuaded a few party guests to include us in their group and, well . . ." She shrugged.

I frowned. With the mental gifts I'd seen her use, I could well believe that she could persuade some humans—even magical ones—that she was their best friend, at least long enough to get in the door. But there was something I didn't get. "How did you bug my phone? You never had it."

"There are ways to do it remotely. It's not my thing, but Trevor said—"

"Trevor?" Despite everything, I felt myself start to grin.

She bit her lip.

"You're partnered with a guy named—"

"There aren't a lot of people willing to take you on!"

"For reasons," Radu murmured, still puttering.

"What?"

"Nothing." He beamed at her. "Such a pretty girl. You wouldn't like being on the Senate, you know. So many boring meetings."

"It's the pinnacle of our existence! It's what we live for, fight for! The chance to lead—"

"Yes, yes, that's what they tell you," he said, examining something he'd pulled from one of the cases. "Until you get on it. Then it's all fiscal reports and bad coffee."

She blinked at him some more.

"Hey!" I called to Louis-Cesare. "Don't kill Trevor. I need him to fix my phone."

"Trevor?" He looked confused for a moment, and then down at his bloody lump of a club. He tossed it away, and it tried to crawl off, before being trampled by the cavalry chasing their boss.

I turned back around, to see Purple Hair glowering at me.

"Don't blame me," I told her. "How did you think coming to Mircea's apartment was going to go?"

"We didn't have a choice!"

"You couldn't just catch me out somewhere?"

"Like the theatre?" she asked sourly.

I grinned. "Dry out yet?"

She scowled. "Sure. This is all funny to you."

"It actually wasn't that funny," I said, but she wasn't listening.

"Like running around in old sweats or—" She gestured at my sensible underwear. "Here the rest of us are, trying to be as intimidating as possible, and you go around like that. Like we're all just ridiculous and you don't have to care."

"I don't actually dress with you in mind."

"I know. That's what's so infuriating. Everyone else is so concerned with their image, and you just . . ." Her lips tightened. "You walked out of that house the other day, no weapons, no makeup, *barefoot*. And I wondered why my skin suddenly tightened. I realized later: the most intimidating look is not to have one at all."

"And yet you came back."

"What else is there? You don't know what it's like, starting with nothing and clawing your way up, year after year, century after century. Until, finally, you get within sight of everything you ever wanted, only to have the rug ripped out from under you."

"Sounds familiar."

"Bullshit! Daughter of a senator, dating another one, you're practically royalty!"

"And a dirty dhampir."

"Yeah, but even that. No one knows how to fight that. You're something out of legend, while the rest of us—"

She suddenly turned around and walked away.

I turned back to see Radu looking at me disapprovingly.

"What?"

"You could have been nicer."

"*Nicer?* She's been trying to kill me all week!"

Radu tutted. "She isn't powerful enough to kill you—"

"She brought a friend!"

Radu glanced at Trevor, and rolled his eyes. "She simply thinks she has to try, that's all. They brainwash them into believing that there's nothing else to do with eternity than rule over everybody else. Then they finally make it, and wonder why they hate it."

"Are you trying to tell me I won't like being on the Senate?"

"You're already on it. How are you finding it?"

"A pain in the ass."

"Ah. The usual, then."

"Is that how Geminus found it?"

Most people would have asked why I wanted to know,

but not Radu. "Geminus thought he was Caesar reborn, and we were merely his court."

"Well, he was the oldest on the Senate, except for the consul."

"A two-thousand-year-old fool is still a fool."

"And his family?"

"He trained them to believe that they were meant to rule over us lesser creatures. And yet, he never bothered with any sort of contingency plan for when he died. One had the impression that his plan was to live forever. When that failed"—he shrugged—"it left them scattered, leaderless, and at the mercy of us lesser creatures."

I remembered Ray saying that at the bottom, you allied with whoever would help you survive, no matter who it was. Who had they allied with? And where the hell did they fit in?

Usually, I had to try to roust suspects out of the woodwork, but this puzzle was the opposite: too many pieces, and none of them seemed to connect. There were smugglers and slavers and smugglers who were also slavers. There were trolls battling the bad guys and trolls who might be the bad guys. There was a *vargr* who might or might not be a queen of the Light Fey, or possibly an operative sent by her husband to make it look like she was guilty. Or possibly someone else altogether, because who the hell knew?

After four days, I didn't know much more than I had when I started.

I didn't even know what the hell they were smuggling!

My thoughts were interrupted by the sound of Marlowe being thrown into the middle of a very nice baby grand.

"Oh, really," Radu said in annoyance. "I was going to keep that."

"Seriously, he didn't do anything," I called to Louis-Cesare, who was now pounding out a sonata courtesy of Marlowe's head. "And we're broken up anyway. This is childish."

Louis-Cesare belted Marlowe, and watched him go down. "This isn't about us!"

"Then what is it about?"

Marlowe staggered back to his feet, and Louis-Cesare hit him again. "I don't like his face."

"Oh, that's mature."

Purple Hair wandered back over with a drink in her hand, while a dozen of Marlowe's guys jumped Louis-Cesare, I guess to give the boss a moment. "You broke up?"

"Yeah."

We watched Louis-Cesare throw off the guards, grab Marlowe, and launch him at a marble column hard enough to crack it. He'd lost his nice blue suit coat, and his shirt was torn, showing off the kind of physique a vampire doesn't need, but which is still . . . decorative. And his auburn hair had escaped its usual clip, falling around those broad shoulders like he was about to pose for a romance novel cover.

Fabio wished he'd looked that good.

Purple Hair must have thought so, too, because her "Why?" was tinged with disbelief.

"It's a long story."

"Then you wouldn't care if I—"

"I'll rip your throat out."

Louis-Cesare, who had been pounding Marlowe into the parquet, looked up. "What did you say?"

"Nothing."

And then Marlowe's guys re-formed and charged, all at once.

I looked back at Radu. "Why are you dressed like that? Are you staying here now?"

He nodded. "It has everything I need. Several floors, a nice amount of space for entertaining, and a good number of servants' rooms. Of course, it needs work."

He frowned around at the gold and white extravagance, the gleaming parquet floor, and the glittering chandeliers, all three of them.

"You bought it?"

"Yes. I'm staying with Mircea while I get it sorted, but Kit was having a party—"

"So you came up here."

He nodded.

"And Horatiu?"

"We followed him," Purple Hair said. "He was serving hors d'oeuvres, but he got lost."

That sounded about right.

"But then he started screaming his head off for no reason," she said. Because it would never occur to her that someone like Horatiu could pick up on her intentions. But he had an echo of Mircea's gifts, like everyone in the clan, and while he might be weak as a kitten, he was brave as a lion. My fist clenched. If they'd hurt him—

"He was going to raise the whole house!" Purple Hair said.

"So you had to shut him up."

"Trevor said if he was going to scream bloody murder, we should oblige him—"

I felt my fangs drop.

She saw and her lip curled. "I don't make war on . . . whatever he is. He's fine. He's tied up with that big blond in the bedroom."

I assumed she was talking about Gunther the Gorgeous, Radu's "bodyguard," a giant with the suntan and six-pack of a professional athlete—maybe a surfer, because the shag was a little long. But he was nobody's fool. And despite the fact that Radu hadn't hired him for that reason, he was actually good at his job.

Bet he was pissed right about now.

"I hope you did a better job on Gunther than on Radu," I told her.

"Didn't have to. He was already tied up when we got here."

I looked at 'Du.

He shrugged. "It was his turn."

I sighed.

"Why didn't you just call for help?" Radu had Mircea's gifts to a far greater extent than Horatiu. He could have had half the clan here in a few minutes.

"I tried. She blocked me."

I looked at Purple Hair with new respect. "Impressive." Her lips twisted. "Well. Not so much now."

And then we had to duck because a shirtless guy flew overhead, spinning like a Frisbee.

I looked after him for a moment, confused, because he was one of Marlowe's boys, and they'd all been fully clothed when they came in. Then I spied Marlowe himself, throwing a settee at Louis-Cesare, while wearing a new white dress shirt. Louis-Cesare and the sofa went sailing backward, and Marlowe snapped his fingers at another of his guys, who was trying to get out of a pair of trousers.

He was getting dressed on the fly, I realized.

"He's too tall," I yelled, and saw Marlowe's head jerk up.

"The trousers." I pointed. "They're gonna be too—"

The sofa came whipping back across the room, taking out Marlowe and his guy.

"Never mind."

"It will be good to get back to normal," Radu was saying, when I turned back around. "I've spent so much time going to and fro, from the consul's to Louis-Cesare's—you have no idea. It's been so inconvenient."

"The consul's?" I felt my nose wrinkle. "Why would you want to go there?"

"It's where my laboratory is—was, before her men dismantled it." And, for the first time, I saw what looked like genuine anger. "I went in the other day to find my equipment in boxes, all jumbled up!"

"They just moved you out?"

"They carried in a bed while I stood there! Said it was for some ambassador or other." He sniffed.

"Is that what all this is?" I asked, nodding at the boxes. "Lab stuff?"

"Oh, no. That arrived yesterday." Perfectly arched brows drew together. "I wasn't going to let the Senate's brutes move a damned thing. Heaven only knows what shape I would have received it in!" He held out a familiar-looking orb. "This is what I'm meant to be experimenting *on*."

I took it gingerly, because Radu was the Senate's mad scientist, and had been known to work with some scary stuff.

But not this time.

I held the little orb in my hand, and decided that the universe was fucking with me.

"What do you think?" he asked, watching me with bright eyes.

"I think you overpaid."

"They were free."

"I still think you overpaid."

"What is it?" Purple Hair asked, peering over my shoulder. Because most vamps don't need to buy the kind of insurance that I do.

"Junk," I told her, and tossed her the orb. It looked exactly like the ones James had found at the warehouse.

"Where did you get it?" I asked Radu.

"From a smugglers' warehouse out in Queens. We'd planned a raid for earlier tonight, but somebody beat us to it. They managed to evade us, but one truck hit a light pole and was left behind. It was full of these." He gestured at the containers.

Huh. Well, that couldn't have been Blue; he'd been busy tonight. So maybe the reporters had been right, after all. There really was an underworld war going on. But over these? Why not just knock over another semi, or hit up the manufacturers, if you wanted them so badly? According to James, that's what everyone else had been doing.

"That's what the Senate wants to know," Radu said, when I asked. "I was hoping you'd have an idea. You know about magic, Dory."

"Not this kind."

But still. There was something going on with these "weapons." Somebody was risking their lives for the magical equivalent of whoopee cushions, and I didn't know why.

Radu sighed. "No more do I, I'm afraid. But you know how the Senate is. Everything they don't understand is automatically my purview. Of course, it would be easier if, at the same time they're increasing my workload, they weren't also kicking me out of house and—"

His lips kept moving, but I couldn't hear anymore. Because an alarm had gone off, loud and insistent, drowning them out. And then the lights flickered off, and an electric frisson flooded over my skin, a wash of power so strong that it lifted my hair like a lightning bolt had just struck nearby.

"The wards?" Purple Hair yelled, looking around. Because the big boys had just come online, and they don't play well with modern power sources.

"How odd." Radu frowned. "Must be a malfunc—"

The whole house shuddered, hard enough to almost knock me off my feet, and to send Purple Hair to one knee. Hard enough to set the chandeliers swinging violently, throwing small scintillations of light everywhere, moonlight refracted through crystal. Hard enough to stop the fight in its tracks, and to have Marlowe yelling, "What the hell?" from under Louis-Cesare's arm.

Too hard.

Mircea was a senator; senators have enemies. They also like to sleep in safety. And while he always had some human servants hanging around during the day, just in case, good wards were simply what you did.

The kind that didn't shudder from a single blow.

Or blow inward in a carnage of expensive glass and fine painted wood a second later, followed by a bunch of guys in masks.

Looked like somebody wanted their stuff back, I thought, right before the world whited out.

Chapter Forty-two

Mircea, Venice, 1458

For a moment, everything was quiet. The ship creaked, the girl snored, the footsteps of the two men echoed vaguely from somewhere overhead, their master having disappeared back through the portal. But that was all. The hold full of unconscious vampires didn't breathe, didn't blink, didn't move.

Except for the one with the broken arm, which finally finished twitching itself back together and then fell off to the side, pulling the rest of the vampire along with it.

He hit the boards hard, and the sound reverberated in Mircea's brain. For a moment he didn't know why, the panicked *hurry, hurry, hurry* in his veins clouding his thoughts. But then he realized: if he fell off his own stack, he'd end up sprawling either on the girl below or right beside her. He would almost certainly come into contact with her, might even touch her skin. And then—

Maybe nothing. Touch helped his mental abilities, but even at his best, he couldn't control people with his mind. He couldn't make them do something they didn't want to do. But he could influence them, especially if what he was pushing for was something they wanted anyway.

Of course, he didn't know that the girl wanted to help. She might just want to get away. In her position, he definitely would, since her life expectancy with what she knew was probably about the same as his.

But he wouldn't know if he didn't ask.

And he couldn't ask if he never got off this pile!

He put his mind onto moving again, anything, anything at all, just so long as it helped his precarious position become a little more so. And when that didn't work, he shifted his attention to a finger on the hand that lay in front of his face. Trying for a twitch that might send it sliding off the pile and possibly take him along.

He didn't get it.

Cazzo!

And before he could try again, the two bullyboys were back, along with a number of sailors. They started carting the vampires up the ladder, quickly but carelessly. Nobody seemed to worry if a head hit a beam or struck the ceiling as they were towed through the small opening. No one seemed to mind if half-healed bones were rebroken, or if a protruding, rusty nail snagged an arm, tearing a great gash out of the flesh. No one seemed to care what kind of damage was done, and Mircea knew why.

Abramalin had told him.

Mircea had always wondered why there were so many mages in Venice. He'd understood why the vampires were there: it was a perfect feeding ground, with festival crowds regularly coming and going, most of them too drunk to notice if they lost a little blood. And, before the new consul changed the rules, it had been the only place in Europe where masterless vampires could find refuge.

But why so many mages?

He'd originally put it down to Venice's size and wealth. A large, well-off populace meant plenty of targets for whatever scam the unscrupulous were running this time, and plenty of customers for the more legitimate practitioners. It was also a busy port, meaning that potion supplies were easy to come by.

One potion supply in particular.

Because, while he'd been right about some of the reasons for the large mage presence, he'd overlooked the biggest draw of all. That wasn't surprising; it was almost unthinkable to him, even now. But unthinkable or not, the fact remained: the mages were in Venice because the vampires were.

Specifically, the mages were there for vampire *bones*. No one knew exactly why, but vampire bones were one of the most potent potion supplies to be found anywhere. Not that they changed a potion; they didn't seem to have any effect on the intended outcome at all. Except for one.

According to Abramalin, the addition of even a small amount of vampire bone to any potion instantly upped its power by several magnitudes. It could take a minor-level ward and make it virtually impregnable. It could take a simple love spell and bind someone with utter devotion. It could take a spell meant to light a candle and cause a raging inferno.

Put simply, it was a multiplier for magic, many times over. And as such, was worth considerably more than its weight in gold. The supply, however, was somewhat . . . challenging . . . to come by. Masters protected their families with deadly vigor, with even unimportant family members avenged lest anyone think the clan weak. Vampire bones, as magical as they might be, were a rare commodity.

Or they had been, before Venice was established as an open port. The masterless had started flocking to its sandy shores, their few belongings on their backs, desperate hope in their hearts. Hope that was soon shattered by the reality of the place. For most of the creatures who found these shores, it had proven to be merely more of the same: wealth, power, and position were the keys to success in Venice, and they had none of them.

Stubborn types like Mircea pushed through anyway, struggling to scrape a living on the bottom of Venetian society. Or to learn a skill that might endear them to one of its masters, and possibly find them a home. But others, who had pinned their last hopes on the supposed refuge, only to be disappointed again . . .

Well, suffice it to say that there was no shortage of vampire bones in Venice.

They were as plentiful as seashells on the shore, literally washing up on the sand after the daily immolation. Every morning, the wretched and the damned went down to the sea, to await the fearsome embrace of the sun. And every night, the mages and their assistants feasted, courtesy of the haul they'd made after scouring the beaches.

Until the current consul came to power, that is.

And the once-plentiful bones were suddenly less so.

There were still some poor souls, unable to cope with eternity in what they viewed as hell, who were willing to end it all. But for many, the change in regime had made a marked improvement in their situation. There were new safe zones in several areas, including the glittering capitol at Paris. There were rights-of-way being marked out between them, allowing safe-ish travel through jealously guarded territories. And, most of all, there were laws against littering vampires around the landscape that you weren't planning to be responsible for.

Masters were now expected to account for every child they made, and those who became too careless risked their own lives and positions. So the masterless had less competition finding themselves a family, more places to search for one, and an elevated position even if they chose to remain on their own. For there were jobs where the unaffiliated were preferred, and they were becoming a rare breed.

For the first time, the unwanted hordes of Venice had a real reason to hope.

Of course, for the mages, the shoe was on the other foot. Not only was the supply of masterless vampires drying up, but the ones who did arrive weren't even killing themselves anymore! The once-plentiful commodity, which had made the great mage families of Venice filthy rich, was suddenly rare once again.

And then things became worse.

Because somebody had started hunting vampires, taking by force what was no longer being given. And worse still, the bastards weren't sharing. Abramalin had been very clear on that point.

"There's nothing," he'd told Mircea, his various beards quivering in indignation. "Not a scrap! The only shipments going out these days are remnants of old stock from some of the bigger traders—at triple the price! But nothing new. Nothing at all!"

"That's . . . unfortunate," Mircea had said, trying for diplomacy while wondering if Abramalin was planning to augment his stock with him.

But if the idea had occurred to the old mage, he gave

no sign. "Unfortunate? Unfortunate? It's like having your magic cut down to a tenth of what it was!" he raged. "Everything has to come from us now, doesn't it? And we don't make nearly as much as we use!"

"I can see how that would be troubling."

"Can ye now?" Black eyes had glittered at him behind falls of grizzled hair. "Then imagine this. Some of us aren't interested in workaday spells. We're innovators, visionaries, inventors! We are the future of the magical community, keeping it on a par with—well, you lot, for one. And any other rivals we find out there."

"Yes, I under—"

But the old man hadn't been listening.

"Come up with a spell, and somebody finds a way around it. So you have to come up with another. But it's trial and error, isn't it? Twenty, fifty, a hundred times I might have to attempt the same spell before it works, and then I have to refine it! And where does that power come from, hmm? I don't generate enough—no single mage does! So, without our shipments, innovation has slowed to a crawl, and will soon get worse when the old stock is used up. We must have that trade reestablished!"

"I'm not going to help you kill anyone," Mircea had snapped, fear giving way to anger. "I'm not going to help you collect anyone's bones!"

"Have I asked ye to?" Abramalin sneered. "We aren't the ones butchering your kind, boy! But if it's found that some damned fool mages are trying to manipulate the price or whatever the hell they think they're doing, and murdering your people in pursuit of it, what do you think is going to happen then? To all of us?"

"Then do something about it! Find these murderers—"

"Don't ye think we've tried?" The old mage threw his hands up. "We've had people in Venice for months—good people—but found nothing."

"How is that possible? I thought you had ways—"

"It's possible, young vampire, because whatever mages are involved, they've got themselves some help. Your kind of help. They must have; it's the only magic we can't trace. Your kind don't do magic; ye *are* magic, and damned near invisible to our eyes!"

"You're saying you can't detect them?"

"Not in a city full of you, no! And whatever magic, if any, is being used to support them, it's subtle. Too much for us to identify when half the mages in Christendom are also packed into that damned city, and working spells all the time. It's impossible!"

"Then go to the Senate. They have resources—"

"Oh, yes, why don't we do that?" Abramalin said sweetly. He'd been pacing back and forth, waving his arms and basically looking like a madman. But when he whirled around, the old eyes were shrewd. "Perhaps I'll do it me-self, walk in and inform her scalyness that, oh, by the way, there's some rogue mages and a vampire or two commit-ting mass murder in Venice, and interferin' in the trade of your people's bones. Can you help us get this sorted out so we can get things back to normal?"

"You're afraid she'll shut you down."

"I'm afraid she'll declare war! Mine and your kind are always teetering on the brink of it anyway, and this is the sort of spark that could set it off. And even if it doesn't, she'll doubtless view this as an intolerable slight, and yes, shut us down! Which rather puts us right back where we started, doesn't it?"

"But if you explain," Mircea continued stubbornly, "as you have to me, and if it's just a few of your people—"

"But we don't know that, do we?" Abramalin pointed out. "We have no idea who's behind it, nor how many are involved. If it's someone with the right sort of connec-tions, this could spiral out of control very fast. We need one of your kind, someone who can keep his damned mouth shut, to go in and find out how they're doing this, and who's behind it! We'll take it from there."

"Oh. Is that all?"

It came out dryer than Mircea had intended, but the feeling in his gut wasn't sarcasm. It was dread. This was even worse than he'd expected, and he hadn't ex-pected anything good. But the praetor was already on the search, and with pressure coming from the consul, that wasn't going to change. She had only him on it now, not understanding the seriousness of the problem, but if he didn't find out something soon . . .

Mircea didn't want a war, either. He just wanted to save his daughter. And helping Abramalin could do that, and possibly stop a serious conflict, too.

It was repugnant, working for people who traded his people's body parts like so many trinkets. But the trade predated him, and would continue whether there was a war to stop it or not. The last thing people give up is power.

Especially power like this.

"All we want from you is information, boy," Abramalin had said, his voice taking on a wheedling tone. "There's no need for you to be in any danger yourself."

Yes, Mircea thought now, staring around at the cargo of vampires.

That was working out well.

And then it got worse, when a couple burly sailors stopped beside his stack of bodies, shoved the sleeping girl to the side, and picked him up. A moment later, Mircea was experiencing the pain of being dragged carelessly up the ladder and tossed onto a rain-slick deck, along with piles of other corpses. Corpses that were too insensate to see what hell lay ahead of them.

Unlike him.

He'd landed facing the port, giving him a perfect view of the activity on shore. Not that he needed it. The stench would have been enough, all on its own.

It was a smell he was intimately familiar with, from both halves of his life. The metallic thickness of spilled blood from the battlefield, cloying and strangely sticky in the nostrils. And the unmistakable smell of burning human flesh, half roast pork and half something that made your skin ruffle and crawl and shudder, because it was wrong, it was wrong, it was *wrong*.

He'd smelled that often enough since coming to Venice, when plague visited the town or was suspected, and the authorities ordered burnings instead of proper burials. The people had complained so much that the government had started restricting the burnings to the small island of Lazzaretto, where plague victims were quarantined if found still alive. And yet, when the wind was right, you could still smell them, roasting in their own fat.

   People tried to pretend the stench was from the local
taverns' cook fires, but they knew. They always knew. Like
Mircea did, even before the clouds of smoke parted, and
showed him a glimpse of the carnage on shore.

   For a moment, he froze, not only his body but his mind,
too, refusing to understand what he was seeing: piles of
living corpses, strewn about here and there; other piles of
dismembered yet still-living body parts, because vampires
didn't die just because you hacked them up; stacks of
bones, gleaming pale in the moonlight; and the massive
kettles they were piled beside, where the steam was rising,
rising, rising . . .

   Along with the silent screams of the damned as they
were boiled alive.

   And then it did register, oh, yes, it did, and the overwhelming flood of panic that came with it was wild enough
to wash him off the pile, to send him scuttling like a
wounded crab across the deck, to leave him with his head
pushed through a railing, so desperate to get away that he
forgot his shoulders wouldn't fit, too.

   That was partly the fault of the spell, still dragging at
him, and partly his own. Every time he tried to focus on
a limb, it stopped working, as if remembering that it
wasn't supposed to be doing that. He wouldn't get away
like this; he could barely even think! And, at any moment,
the ship was going to dock, and the sailors would be back,
and after that—

   Mircea was a soldier. He'd faced death many times.
But not like this. Not butchered like an animal, and sold
like a piece of flesh in the market. He wanted to tear at
his throat, to let in air he couldn't use but suddenly, desperately, needed. But he couldn't move, couldn't breathe,
couldn't think—

   And then a voice was in his ear, familiar, but bizarre
in this damnable place.

   "Hush. Be still."

Chapter Forty-three

I resurfaced from the latest memory-related time-out, but this time it didn't go so well. Instead of popping back into my right mind, whatever that meant anymore, it felt like I'd fallen into a kaleidoscope of fractured images. As if my brain was a giant jigsaw puzzle, where most of the pieces were missing.

And the ones that were left weren't anything good.

Radu was on the floor to my right, covered in blood. The female vampire with the strange-colored hair was lying on my other side, her limbs splayed out like a broken doll's. Neither was moving; they looked almost like unconscious humans. But they weren't human, and a vampire doesn't go down without catastrophic damage.

Strange; they didn't appear to be hurt that badly, unlike one of the dark-haired master's servants, who was lying a few yards in front of me. Or part of him was. The whole top half of his body was missing.

My own body was in pain, everywhere at once, a throbbing mass of injury. But that was easily ignored. The problem with my mind was less so. My head felt heavy, confused, almost . . . spelled.

And I suddenly understood why the vampires weren't moving.

Stun spells didn't usually work on their kind, since they lacked most of the bodily functions such spells targeted, but this one seemed to be different. It had also had an effect on me: I was awake, but my vampire abilities were not. A psychic scream, my own stun weapon, was impos-

sible right now, as was trying to get inside anyone's head. But that wasn't why I lay where I'd fallen, while a battle raged around me.

No, that was due to shock.

Because we were losing.

I watched the impossible through my lashes: dozens of high-level vampires, any one of whom constituted an army all on his own, being batted aside by half as many mages. The way the spells were being flung was casual, almost as an afterthought. Yet I saw a vampire ripped in half, and another immolated while he leapt through the air, in a fireball that filled half the room.

What was left of him rained down as ashes.

"We have to stop meeting like this."

I blinked my eyes open to see a woman bending over me. Well, sort of. She was actually bending over the massive chandelier I seemed to be lying under, which was all I could see except for dust clouds and rubble. But I could hear—

"Don't even think about it," she said, suddenly sounding like a drill sergeant on a bad day.

She didn't look like one. She looked like a soccer mom out on the town, in a sparkly top that went well with her short gray-brown hair and big blue eyes. She even had a drink in her hand: Crown Royal with ginger ale, judging by the smell, garnished with two maraschino cherries.

I'd been about to turn around and see where all the talking, grunting, and subdued moaning was coming from, but stopped on command. Mainly because my body didn't seem to be talking to me anyway. And if it had been, it would have been cursing.

She belted back her drink, made a face, and tossed the glass over her shoulder. "Okay," she told me, looking determined. "I'm going to get this thing off you, and then we'll see."

I had no idea what she was talking about. She looked to be around fifty—the fluffy, comfortable sort of fifty, not the runs-marathons-in-her-spare-time fifty, and even if she'd been the latter she couldn't possibly lift—

I hadn't even finished the thought when the huge,

heavy, multifaceted chandelier was chiming its way into the air, and I was noticing the wand in her other hand.

"There," she said, sounding satisfied and proud and faintly relieved as the massive crystal monster floated away ... through a mostly missing wall. And across a sidewalk. And into the street.

The sound of a car swerving and hitting brakes at the same time drifted to us through the gap, along with some inventive cussing, and—

What the fuck?

"Uh, can somebody get that?" she asked hopefully.

Somebody went to get that.

She turned back to me. "Okay. Now, isn't that better?"

And then she noticed the blood spurting from a couple dozen holes in my body, which I guess the dug-in crystals had been keeping inside.

"Well, shit."

The remains of the incinerated vampire blew on the wind coming through a destroyed window. I saw the powerful one notice, the one my twin liked. He jerked his head around in disbelief, while snapping the neck of the mage in his hands.

And then he disappeared.

For a moment, I didn't believe my eyes. One second he was there, and the next he was not, and not because he moved. But as though he'd simply—

Veiled.

I took the word from my twin's mind.

Not going invisible, then, so much as phasing to another plane of existence. It was ... interesting ... one of the more useful vampire gifts I'd seen. But the fact remained: he'd had to use a master's power against a handful of mages, in order to save his life.

And it had. A trio of spells exploded where he'd just been standing, destroying a wall and setting several rooms beyond on fire. But they didn't hit him, because he was no longer there.

But the mage he'd attacked was.

He was lying where he'd fallen, still twitching, but his eyes were already glazing over. So they could be killed,

*then. You just had to make sure they never touched you,
never came close. For even a glancing blow from one of
those overpowered spells could be deadly.*

Understood, *I thought, and surged to my feet.*

Crown Royal was yelling at me.

"Get back here!"

I wasn't getting back there.

I wasn't sure where I was going, but there was something very, very important I had to—

Oh, yeah.

I spied Louis-Cesare under a couple tons of fallen
concrete—and tasteful sandstone and parquet flooring
and another goddamned chandelier—and scrambled toward him over mounds of rubble. It wasn't easy; my legs
didn't work right, and the debris was studded with fallen
draperies, half a piano, a dust-covered settee, and Radu,
standing by a bar. And making himself a drink despite the
fact that most of his hair was burnt off and a chunk of his
torso seemed to be missing.

I did a double take while he belted back a stiff one, and
I almost ran into Marlowe, who still hadn't found any
pants. But who had swathed himself in a curtain and was
doing his best Caesar impression. Which seemed to mostly
involve yelling at me.

I ignored him and finally reached Louis-Cesare, who
was bleeding, bleeding everywhere, and my hands were
shaking and someone was crying, but it wasn't me, it
wasn't me, because I was yelling now, too.

"Help him! *Help him!*"

Someone was pulling on me, which wasn't going to
work, only it did because I was weak as water.

"Will someone put her the hell out?" Marlowe demanded.

Nobody did.

"I said, does anybody have the power left to put her—"

Someone touched my arm, someone other than Crown
Royal, who was still tugging from behind. I looked up to
see Horatiu's kindly old face. Unlike everybody else, he
looked pretty much like always, in a dapper, if dust-

covered, tuxedo, and peering at me myopically from under a fall of thick white hair.

"I've been looking for you," I told him.

"Sleep, child," he said, and put a heavily veined hand on my forehead.

"No, I can't sleep. I have to—"

I felt the unmistakable scrape of steel on bone, the frisson up the spine it always caused echoing through me. But the bone wasn't mine. A mage in front of me hadn't been shielded, and the arrogance proved fatal when I slipped a knife between his ribs.

A second and third went down, their hamstrings cut, and then their throats as they fell. Another died when an upstroke, coming off the last two, gutted him like unzipping a coat, and a fifth—the last easy one—died trying to warn the others that they had another problem. And kept on trying, his mouth still moving even as his head bounced across the floor.

It had taken perhaps a few seconds, one stroke flowing into another, a familiar, deadly dance, the blood painting streamers in the air around me. But it was enough for the other mages to stop attacking and shield. My knife slid off one; stuttered against another; failed to puncture a third, even so much as dent it, despite the fact that all my strength was behind it.

That wasn't normal.

But then, neither were these shields.

"Like I give a damn what you want!"

Crown Royal was yelling at somebody, I didn't know why. And then I noticed that she was facing off with Marlowe and I understood. He just kind of brought that out in people.

I looked around. We were in Mircea's apartment, sort of. I mean, there were still some walls left; and a window, somehow pristine despite standing almost on its own; and the ceiling—

Okay, forget the ceiling, I thought, staring up into what had been a very nice ballroom and was now a skylight.

"I was planning to renovate anyway," Radu said.

It concerned me that I could see through his stomach. "How do you keep the alcohol in?" I asked, and he patted me on the head.

I think I lost some time, because there were suddenly red and blue lights flashing in my face, lighting up the rubble. Even for me, getting the cops called twice in one night was . . . okay, not a record. But not exactly every day, either.

I wondered what I'd been up to.

Then I saw Louis-Cesare, lying on a stretcher between two of Marlowe's men. And the next thing I knew, I was stumbling over there, and nobody tried to stop me this time, probably because Marlowe was getting into a dustup with the cops. There was some yelling and the usual "gas leak" explanation, which it didn't sound like anybody was buying, and then somebody spied Radu and started to freak out—

"Oh, for goodness' sake!"

That was Crown Royal.

Who I guessed spelled the cops, because nobody got shot.

I didn't know. I was too busy pawing at Louis-Cesare to turn around and find out. And then hitting him, because he wasn't responding, he wasn't doing *anything*.

Until strong hands grasped my wrists, and a blue eye cracked open. The other one was closed, caked with blood and swollen about three times its usual size. It matched the jaw, which was heading for Popeye territory; and the neck, which looked like somebody had tried to burn his head off; and the chest, which had great gashes in it.

I started to cry, great blubbery snot-filled sobs, and Louis-Cesare began to laugh. "You do love me, you do love me—"

"Shut up!" I told him hysterically, and would have hit him again, but couldn't find anywhere that wasn't already hurt, which made me cry harder and oh, my God, this was embarrassing.

I was almost relieved when Horatiu tottered over and put me out again.

All the strength and finesse in the world does you no good if you can't reach your target. And I couldn't. Neither

*could the powerful one, who had reappeared, eyes wild
and chest panting, despite the fact that he didn't need to
breathe.*

I understood: it was that kind of fight.

*There were only three of us left: the dark-haired mas-
ter, the powerful one, and me. The rest were dead or fled
or were trying to, the injured grabbing the bodies of the
unconscious and jumping through missing windows.
The three of us were attempting to distract the mages while
the rest got away, by sending massive pieces of debris
crashing into those perfect shields. But there were too
many of them and too few of us.*

This wasn't going to work.

But I knew something that would.

*Get out! I sent mentally to the other two, and saw their
heads jerk around in shock.*

*My twin couldn't do that, or give them a mental push
forceful enough to stagger the dark-haired one when they
just stood there. And I doubted I could do it again, under
the circumstances. Fortunately, the dark-haired master
recovered quickly, grabbed a fallen vampire, and jumped
for the nearest window.*

*I picked up the silver ball the strange-haired girl had
dropped when she fell. It was warm and thrumming with
power it shouldn't have had. Like the mages themselves,
full of stolen magic.*

Not for long.

*The powerful one was a bloody mess, and fighting
alone now. But the room was clear, the last of our people
slipping away while he ducked and dodged and drew
heavy fire, and I yelled: "Go! Now!"*

*I couldn't tell if he obeyed or even heard. Spell fire ob-
scured my vision, the mages turned on me, and I was out
of time. But so were they.*

*We'd been fighting on the fringes, trying to protect the
weaker ones while they scrambled to get away. And thus
the mages had ended up largely in the middle of the room,
around the plastic containers they were trying to retrieve.
Most of those had been taken already, but one was still in
place.*

And if it contained what I suspected, one was enough.

I threw the silver ball on the fly, while running for the nearest window. I didn't hear the explosion; didn't hear anything; couldn't see. Light was suddenly everywhere, like being in the heart of the sun. All I knew was the feel of a mage's body slamming into mine, and the floor falling out from under me, and falling—

"Aughhhh!"

I sat bolt upright, screaming. That felt familiar. And other things that weren't so good, I thought, as the room slurred violently around me.

Only it wasn't a room. It was a van, or maybe an ambulance. It wasn't the usual, boxy shape, but it was kitted out with a lot of medical gear, much of which seemed to be attached to me.

I stared at it, but didn't take it loose. Not because I was being a good patient, but because my brain had finally caught up and was making connections to things. Things that had seemed random, but were suddenly coming together into a picture.

One I really didn't like.

And then somebody grabbed me, and I lost my train of thought.

It was Marlowe, who was still there and still yelling, maybe because the van had swerved when I screamed and clipped a line of cars. It righted itself, briefly going up on two wheels in the process, and then we were off again. And Marlowe was in my face, furious brown eyes glaring into mine.

"How did you know that would happen?" he demanded, shaking me. "How did you *know*?"

"Let her go!" Somebody was tugging ineffectually on his arm. "Damn it, if you pull out the IV—"

"I'll let her go when she answers the question!"

"You'll let her go now." That was Louis-Cesare. He was propped in a corner, among half a dozen other vamps, none of whom appeared to be conscious.

Kit sneered at him. "You're in no position to give orders—or condition, either, after all that!"

"But by tomorrow, I'll be back to normal."

Louis-Cesare didn't reference the butt kicking.

I guess he thought it was memorable.

And, apparently, Kit agreed, releasing me with one of those cat noises he likes to make.

I fell back against a very inadequate pillow, which I wasn't complaining about right now. And noticed that I did have a needle in my arm; I guess I'd lost a little too much blood. Might account for why it took energy to *breathe*.

It didn't explain what had happened to the rest of them, though.

"What happened to them?" I panted, looking at the piled-up vamps.

"Spell," Radu said, from somewhere behind me. "They're all right. They're just stunned."

"It wasn't a spell!" That was Kit again. "There's no spell that can do that, not to us!"

"That's all very well for you to say. It didn't hit you."

They continued arguing while I concentrated on breathing. It wasn't going well. "Oh God."

"No, it's Kathy."

I stared up into the pleasant face bending over me, and thought it looked slightly—

Oh.

"Crown Royal."

"No, *Kathy*."

"Well, I could use . . . a drink, Kathy."

She patted my arm. "Couldn't we all?"

"—well, obviously, they were adjusted." Radu was still talking, and now he sounded pissed.

"*Adjusted?*" That was Kit. "You're talking about goddamned toys. They're supposed to be harmless!"

"Mostly harmless."

"What?"

"As Douglas Adams would say."

"What?"

"Read a book sometime, you philistine."

"Radu," Louis-Cesare said. His head was leaned back against the van's side now, and his eyes were closed. He looked wiped.

"Very well. My point is, these toys, as you call them, aren't toys at all. They're low-grade weapons made for personal defense—"

"PPDs," Kathy said.

"What?"

"That's what they're called in the trade. Personal protection devices."

"Thank you." Radu looked like he was making a note of it. "In any case, the only difference between these . . . PPDs . . . and whatever we encountered tonight is the amount of magic they hold. The spells are the same—"

"Bollocks!" Marlowe snapped. "Those damned things killed some of us!"

Radu paused. I could almost hear him reminding himself that some of the dead had belonged to Kit.

"He's right." That was Kathy. "My uncle has said for years that there ought to be more regulations on PPDs. There are plenty of guys flagged by the Circle so they can't buy real weapons, who get some of the low-grade stuff, add a bunch of extra magic, and go to town."

"And who the hell are you?" Kit demanded.

"I already told you. I'm one of the night docs for the Brooklyn on-call service—"

"I know that! It doesn't mean you know anything about weapons!"

"*I* don't," she agreed placidly. "My uncle does. Why do you think I was at your party?"

Marlowe didn't look like he cared. "You should have left with the rest!"

"I have a patient to look after, and you're not the boss of me." Kit blinked at her, his expression somewhere between angry and surprised. Like a lion being lectured by a mouse. "Anyway, my uncle is Aaron Samuelson," she continued.

Nothing.

"Of Samuelson & Todd?"

I'd never seen Marlowe go from asshole to angel that fast. "Ms. Samuelson!" An attempt was made at a smile. "My apologies. It's been a difficult night for all of us—"

"Oh, I don't know. I think it's been kind of stimulating." She smiled back. "You have a nice butt."

And, for the second time in one night, I saw Marlowe at a loss for words.

"This is what I think happened," Radu said. "Our opponents needed a large number of weapons, but were having difficulty acquiring enough from their own sources. The Black Circle is formidable, but weapons manufacturing is a specialized field. Just because you're a mage doesn't mean you'll be any good at it."

"People train for years," Kathy agreed. "There's an apprenticeship and everything."

"Exactly. It isn't merely casting a spell; the ones designed for weapons have to last, have to be bound to something portable, and have to be stable enough not to blow up in your face. The Black Circle likely has spellbinders working for them, but not enough for a major war. They needed outside sources."

Kathy nodded. "Somebody must have figured out that the PPDs use the same spells as the more powerful stuff, so you don't need a spellbinder. You just need the magic to . . . plump them up."

"It all makes sense," Radu agreed.

"It makes no kind of sense!" That, of course, was Marlowe. "Those weapons weren't merely 'plumped up'! They were like nothing I've ever seen. Each spell felt like it had the combined force of a hundred mages behind it—and there were cases of them! No one has that much magic—not the Black Circle, and certainly not a bunch of slavers. So how the devil are they doing it?"

Nobody said anything.

But I suddenly remembered what I'd realized earlier, in that brief moment of clarity. Dorina had shown me that vampire remains could be hugely powerful, but it was almost impossible to get them anymore. But there was another magical creature that was dying in quantity, and that nobody seemed to care about.

"They're using fey bones," I told them, and passed out.

Chapter Forty-four

Something was wrong.

I awoke in a strange bed, with a strange vampire. I had a hand on his throat before I recognized him: the powerful master from the fight. The one my twin liked.

He was in a healing trance, his many wounds bandaged but still radiating heat. Yet he was not insensate. His kind retain a low level of awareness in that state, so he knew I was there.

Yet he never so much as stirred, even with my nails digging into his flesh.

I slowly removed them; he wasn't the source of the danger.

But something was.

I glanced around.

There was no one else here, but there had been. The room was full of scent puddles, some distant in time, days old. Servants, likely, in to clean and then out again, quickly enough that their presence barely registered. Others were brighter. Like my Sire's, his scent unmistakable: dark, rich, and deep. Part of it clung to my hairline, where he'd pushed some damp strands away. It was an hour old, perhaps two.

I sat up.

The brightest scent in the room was around a chair beside the bed. A woman—a healer, judging by the faint traces of herbs and tinctures—had sat there for some time, and possibly fallen asleep watching over her charges. She'd definitely been the one to bandage the vampire; none of his kind would have bothered. He couldn't get infections, and he'd heal himself soon enough, something I supposed she hadn't known.

She'd bandaged me, as well.

Too well.

Mummy, *I thought, glimpsing myself in a mirror. The comment came from my still-asleep twin. She thought we looked amusing, like a bikini-wearing mummy, the undergarments almost obscured by bandages and tape.*

I didn't care what we looked like.

I cared about the niggle at the back of my mind. Something familiar, but that I couldn't quite place. Something wrong.

There was a door across from the bed. I walked over and opened it. No one was outside, not a single guard, which seemed unwise. Did no one here know what I was, what I could do?

But all I saw was an empty hall, and all I smelled was woodsmoke and alcohol. I followed the scents down the corridor, to where it let out into a sitting area. It was ma-hogany paneled and dimly lit, mostly by the flickering light of a low-burning fire. A small group had gathered around it, including two humans. I automatically synced my heartbeat with that of one of them, but may as well not have bothered. They were too caught up in their conversation to pay me any attention.

And too secure.

Because this place . . . what was this place?

The terrible fog in my head caused by the stun spell had cleared, allowing me to access my abilities again. But what they were telling me seemed impossible. I tried to contact my twin's mind, but she was too deeply asleep, and batted away the request. It didn't matter; I was already reaching out, in something like awe, my mind encounter-ing what felt like every vampire on Earth. I brushed mind after mind, all crowded into one place, like a working ant-hill. And at the center of it all—

The queen.

I could see her in my mind's eye, not here but some-where close, seated on a dais in the midst of a crowd of her creatures. Silks fluttered, satins gleamed, vampires talked and laughed and moved around her, but I barely saw. Didn't care.

How can you see the stars when the sun is out?

"—*no bloody idea!*" That was one of the people around the fire. There were five in all: Radu, a woman in a glittery blouse, the dark-haired master from the fight, another master vampire I didn't know, and the human man who'd spoken. They seemed to be arguing.

"*Then take a guess!*" The dark-haired master appeared agitated. He was the only one standing, with an arm on the mantel when he wasn't striding around the room. He was strong enough to sense my presence, even with precautions, but too distracted to care.

"*I can't!*" the man spat. "*It's absurd!*"

He was a mage; I could smell the magic on him. His voice boomed around the room as he sat forward, arguing animatedly with a creature who could silence him between one heartbeat and the next. But he wouldn't.

The vampire wanted something.

"*Don't lie to me!*" He was bending over the man now. "*I know what you do, in those labs of yours. You experiment on everything! You're telling me you've never—*"

"*That is what I'm telling you. And get out of my face, vampire!*"

"*Uncle* . . ." That was the glittery woman. She was the healer I'd detected in the bedroom. I could just discern her scent over the smell of the fire, and the cologne her relative wore. He was still in dirty clothes, fine evening wear smeared with dust. He had been at the fight, too, then.

"*Don't 'uncle' me,*" he told her. "*I came here for you, even after everything, and now I'm being bullied!*"

"*No one can bully you.*"

"*Well he's damned well trying!*"

I was following their conversation, but it was almost background noise. I was more interested in the queen, or more accurately, in her power. It was astonishing—and strange. The strangest I'd ever encountered.

Most masters have a constant level of power. They can call up more in an emergency, from their own reserves or those of their Children. But normally, they display an average that allows you to guess at their abilities.

Not this one.

I watched the aura around her shrink and expand, shrink and expand, but not like breathing. It was wild, uneven, capricious. Instead of being smooth, it spiked and dipped, ebbed and flowed, in a pulsing, jittering rhythm. At its height, I could not have touched her. I doubted anyone could. But at its depth . . .

At its depth, I could have her.

Our eyes met, and a small smile flirted with her lips. "It would be . . . unwise . . ." she informed me, lighting a cigarette.

And, suddenly, I was back in my head, panting and confused, from what felt like a mental slap.

"—wanted to, how would we obtain any?" The mage was asking. "We've experimented with fey flora, now and again—even use some of it on the regular. They have a root that's a damned good stabilizing agent, better than anything we had before. But their bones? Are you mad?"

"You're saying you can't get them?" The dark-haired master sounded skeptical.

"I'm saying I haven't tried! I'm not a murderer—or an idiot. The Light Fey—"

"I didn't say anything about the Light Fey. I don't expect you to go hunting the highborn, but some of the Dark? The type nobody would miss? You're telling me—"

"I'm through telling you anything!" The man was on his feet now, and furious. I felt his heart rate spike, saw the flex of his fingers at his waistline. They must have taken his weapons before letting him in here.

Probably just as well.

"Uncle, please—" That was the glittery woman, who had put down her drink to jump up and grab his arm.

"Perhaps I should summon Lord Mircea?" the other vampire asked.

"I don't need Mircea!" the dark-haired master snapped. "I need answers—and I will have them!"

"What you'll have is nothing if you don't shut up!" That was the woman, putting herself between her family member and the dark-haired master. She looked at her uncle. "Forget about him. Will you answer a few questions for me?"

He scowled, but after a moment he relented. "Make it fast. Your aunt was still in hysterics when I left, after that damned farce tonight. You're lucky we got shields up in time, vampire!"

"I would hope you could manage that much," the dark-haired master sneered. "When we were saving your lives upstairs from some of your own kind!"

"That's it." The man's fury had coalesced into grim resolve. "I won't stay here and be compared to a bunch of damned black magic users—"

"You think that's what they were?" the woman asked.

"What the hell else would they be? Normal mages don't go around experimenting with ground-up bits of fey!"

"Just ground-up bits of vampire," the dark-haired master said, showing some fang.

"Damn it, man! That was hundreds of years ago!"

"Officially, maybe." That was the other master, commenting in a smooth, unruffled tone. He sounded like a bureaucrat, and had some sort of device he kept checking. "The traffic continues, in small amounts—"

"Maybe among the Black Circle—"

"That's always the excuse!" The dark-haired master flushed. "Every time we catch you lot in anything. 'Oh, it wasn't us—it was the bad type of mages!'"

"Because it usually is!"

"Not tonight! The Black Circle attacked us several times recently—here and at a stronghold in Las Vegas. They suffered enormous casualties, yet didn't use these powerful new weapons—not even once. Which makes me suspicious—"

"Are you accusing me, vampire?"

"I'm asking for an explanation! Your own life was imperiled tonight, and your family's. I'd think—"

"Something that would not have been the case if you'd taken precautions!"

"We did! Those spells tore through them like they were tissue paper! Who the hell is making them? And how and why and where? I want to know and I will!"

I stopped listening. The master was wasting his time; the man didn't know anything more than he'd said. I could *see the bewilderment in his mind, along with fear and anger. The vampire would get no answers tonight.*

But perhaps I would.

I followed the annoying niggle back down the corridor, to where a dining room lay behind a door. There was a fireplace in here, too, but not for heat. I pushed my head through the illusion and found what I'd expected: a secret passageway, a spy tunnel, and a way for she-who-saw-everything here to move her servants about quickly.

No one surprised her in her own home. Not even me. I would be spotted in moments by one of the masters I could feel roaming the pathways that snaked through this great house. I would never make it to her, not through all this.

Well.

Not without some help.

I woke up in a strange bed, with a familiar vampire. And in alarm, but not because Louis-Cesare was looking like a corpse. But because—

What the hell?

Dorina, I thought blankly, and fell out of bed.

And then proceeded to go snuffling about, like my counterpart was currently doing. Because she wasn't in my body anymore. She was—

"Ew!"

"Dory?" Louis-Cesare peered at me blearily, from over the side of the bed.

It was the consul's, or at least one owned by her, because we were in her house in upstate New York. The ants-on-skin feel of the place, the result of my dhampir senses being assaulted by the presence of hundreds if not thousands of vampires, all at once, was unmistakable. It literally made me want to scratch my skin off, and Dorina . . .

What the hell would she make of a place like this?

Shit.

Why did I think I knew?

"Dory?" Louis-Cesare said again, looking at me strangely.

I sat up, trying to ignore the taste of whatever my counterpart's avatar had just found in a dark corner. It wasn't going so well. And now it was on the trail of something else, scurrying about in the dust, because housecleaning was not a priority in secret passageways.

"*Dory?*"

"I'm fine." I looked around. "Have you seen some clothes?"

"What clothes?"

"Any clothes!"

Louis-Cesare caught my arm. "What is wrong?"

For a moment, I didn't answer, because I wasn't sure. I wasn't supposed to be able to do this, to feel Dorina when she was away, to know what she was doing. Except for that moment at the end of the car chase with Caedmon, when I'd had that terrible split-screen view of the world.

I didn't have it now, but I had something.

"Dory, talk to me!"

"This might sound a little weird," I warned him.

"Trust me, it already does."

Louis-Cesare was looking at my nose. I grabbed it. It was snuffling again.

Goddamn it!

"I think there's a chance Dorina plans to kill the consul," I told him quickly.

"What?"

"I told you it was going to sound weird!" I broke away.

Louis-Cesare's pants were on the back of a chair. I pulled them on. And then pulled them off again, because I'd do a Marlowe in the damned things and break a leg! Damn it, I didn't have time for this!

I settled for a sheet, wrapped it sarong-style, and headed for the door.

"Wait." Louis-Cesare was suddenly beside me, which wasn't a problem. And leaning on the door, which was. "Explain this to me."

"I already did!"

"Explain it to me again."

"I don't have time!"

"Then I'm coming with you."

I looked at him. He should have been in bed. He had healing scars all over his body, and even a few seeping wounds. I could smell the blood, thick and strong, under all the bandages.

It should have been reabsorbed by now, like the wounds should have closed. Hell, they should have closed instantly! But there'd been a minute or so when he'd been fighting a whole coterie of mages all on his own, ones armed with weapons that killed most vamps on contact. How many times had he gotten hit?

"How many times were you hit?" I demanded.

"It doesn't matter."

"It matters!"

"Why?" Blue eyes suddenly burned into mine. "I thought you no longer cared for me?"

I glared back at him. "This? This is the moment you take for that conversation?"

"Why not? According to Claire, there are things I do not understand."

"The only thing you need to understand right now is, there's the bed." I pointed. "Get in it!"

"No."

I glared at him some more.

It didn't seem to help.

"I'm coming with you," said the most stubborn creature on earth.

Make that the second-most stubborn. "No way in hell."

"And why not?"

"Because I'm not sure you can take her!"

I opened the door; he shut it again. And splayed a hand over it to keep it that way. "That's what this is about? You think she is stronger?"

"She's a first-level master!"

He arched an eyebrow at me.

"And she has freaky abilities—"

"The same could be said of any of us."

"Not like this!" I tried to open the door again, but it may as well have been cemented in place.

"Like what?"

"Let go of the damned door!"

"Answer the question. Like what?"

I turned on him. "Like inhabiting a rat scurrying through secret passageways, looking to kill the consul!"

Louis-Cesare blinked at me a few times. "I'm . . . going to call somebody."

"Call Marlowe. He's just down the hall. Or he was. He can get her away before Dorina finds her—"

"Get who away?"

I stared at him. "Are you listening to me at all? The *consul*!"

Louis-Cesare licked his lips. Then he pulled me into an embrace I didn't want, but when a first-level vamp decides he wants to hug you, you just go with it. We stayed there for a moment.

I don't know what he was doing, but I was debating eating some rat bait. The rat was in favor, but Dorina was trying to talk him out of it. They were still arguing when Louis-Cesare pulled me over to the bed and sat us down.

"One more time, with a bit more explanation?"

I sighed. "Dorina has some kind of weird master power. You know, the one Caedmon mistook for a fey ability?"

He frowned at Caedmon's name, but didn't comment on it. "But it is not."

"No! It's . . . Look, I just found out about it, so I don't have a huge amount of info here. But she can separate from my consciousness and . . . tag along . . . with other people. And things."

"Things?" He frowned. "You mean like a—"

"Rat, yes. She didn't think she could make it to the consul in my body, so she borrowed another one."

"But you're a senator. You can go wherever you wish. She didn't need—"

"But I don't think she knows that. We're having communication problems, and I don't think she understands everything." I sure as hell didn't, I thought, feeling queasy.

Probably because my avatar had just eaten a bellyful of poison!

"Crap."

"What?"

"Never mind. We just have to tell Marlowe—"

I started to get up, but Louis-Cesare pulled me back down. "Tell him what?"

"That the consul's in danger!"

"Yes, I do not think we will be doing that," Louis-Cesare said, grabbing his trousers off the chair.

I watched as the world's best butt, bruised and bloody though it was, disappeared into the rumpled leftovers of a once-nice suit. "What are you doing?"

"I told you. Going with you to find Dorina."

"Why? We'll just tell Marlowe—"

Louis-Cesare turned on me. "What? That your alter ego is about to kill his Lady?"

I frowned. "Well, we won't put it like that—"

"It doesn't matter how you put it. He will very likely attempt to kill you to ensure her survival."

"I'm not trying to kill her!"

"But you and Dorina share a body, do you not? He may well decide that killing one would dispose of both."

I opened my mouth to say something, but yeah. That sounded exactly like something Marlowe would do. And, bonus, I wouldn't be besmirching his beloved Senate anymore, either.

"All right," I told him. "We won't say anything to Marlowe."

"You don't have to," somebody said. And shot me.

Chapter Forty-five

I abandoned the dying avatar and flitted out into the air, before snaring a human servant who was moving quickly down the hall. He took a wrong turn, but I managed to jump to a low-level vampire who was going the right way. And who was too young to notice one more voice in his head.

Among the usual background noise of his family's gossip, of higher-level vampires giving him errands to run, and of others jeering about his clothes—someone had told him that everyone was going to be wearing livery at the consul's home, and he'd believed it—I managed to plant a suggestion.

Suddenly, we were moving much faster than before, through a maze of passageways, and then out a hidden door into a hallway. Or, no, I thought, because it deserved a better word than that. It was long and wide, with a great many people in it. It reminded me of some of the old European courts, where a monarch sat at one end of a gallery and cliques of courtiers laughed, talked, and schemed all along it.

It was easy to tell the cliques here by their clothing. I rode the small vampire down an expanse filled with priceless statuary, beautiful inlaid floors, and marble walls with the height and breadth of old Rome, and barely noticed. I was too busy gazing at costumes from all over the world and a hundred different eras.

Older vampires, especially in formal or stressful situations, liked to dress as they had in their youth. It was comfortable, familiar, and an easy way to remind everyone of

*exactly how old and powerful they were. So we passed by
groups looking as if they had just stepped out of ancient
China, or the Roman Empire, or Montezuma's court, or
some Japanese shogunate, along with dozens of others.*

*And those who weren't in period dress wore the latest
magical fashions, everyone trying to outdo everyone else,
to the point that my ride's elaborate blue and gold livery
seemed tame by comparison.*

*I marveled at a jeweled octopus, its golden arms hold-
ing a woman's upswept chignon in place, when it wasn't
moving them around to adjust its grip. Nearby, embroidered bees decorated the thick black velvet of a Tudor-era
doublet, their fat bodies making constantly changing designs as they buzzed about the sumptuous fabric. And just
past them, a flock of magical butterflies fluttered in the air
and then straight through me, their insubstantial forms
hovering around the pastoral train of a woman's gown,
which showed a garden in full bloom.*

*One of the small creatures had become confused, and
was trying to feed off the jade and coral adornment in
another woman's coiffure. She was in a kimono printed
with gamboling dragons, which spewed tiny plumes of
flame at us as we passed, causing my ride to veer to the
side. And to shoot her a dirty look before he got his face
under control.*

*There were other such clashes going on everywhere,
partly because of the crush, which forced the crowd too
close together. And partly because, while vampires might
not make magic in the traditional sense, they certainly
seemed to enjoy it. And to enjoy employing it against
others.*

*As demonstrated when my ride abruptly halted, and
then just froze, staring upward in horror.*

*Several nearby humans glanced around, looking con-
fused, for they saw nothing. But they could feel the sudden
escalation of tension in the huge space, the quieting of
murmured conversations, and the power washing over
their bodies, like a hot wind. They quickly moved out of
the way, and my ride followed, going from paralysis to a
run worthy of an Olympic sprinter, to the amusement of
the guests around us.*

I don't think the young vampire cared. He hugged the nearest wall, swallowing convulsively. And staring upward, like everyone else in the gallery, at the spectacle playing out in the air above us.

It was something I'd rarely seen, and never this close. What looked like two huge storm clouds, laced with lightning and shuddering with power, circled each other, writhing and boiling and looking for an advantage.

And then transforming into something else.

What looked like a giant, ghostly tiger emerged from the golden haze, its eyes bright as flame. While a huge flock of crows, black as the night, darted out of the dark gray cloud and tore around the room. It looked like magic, but it wasn't—at least not the human kind. But rather two first-level masters, their power taking on forms that had meaning for them, preparing to savage each other.

It wasn't a duel—not quite. But it was often the precursor to one, the show of power they sometimes put on before the killing started. Because if it went on long enough, it could drain a master into vulnerability.

It didn't drain anyone this time.

Because a new cloud formed up out of nothing, all at once. It was green and black and terrifying, and carried so much power that it caused my ride to sink down onto his haunches, whimpering softly. And that was before it took the form of an enormous snake, hissing and rearing back, like a cobra ready to strike. The other two clouds abruptly parted, the tiger snarling and turning away with what I swear looked like its tail between its legs. But the other remained in place a little too long—

And was whipped viciously by the snake's great tail, sending the "birds" crashing against the opposite wall, where they puffed away into bursts of black smoke.

Conversation, which had gone silent for the duration, resumed. The light music playing in the background likewise picked up where it had left off. A casual observer, walking in a minute late, might have been forgiven for thinking that nothing had happened.

But something had. And was likely to again. Because friction was everywhere, now that I looked for it.

The gallery was packed with masters who, until very recently, had thought they knew where they stood in the overall hierarchy. Who had believed they had a grip on the motives, desires, and histories of everyone around them. Who had spent centuries working their way into their present positions at their own courts, and building up a rock-solid foundation.

Only to find the bedrock under their feet suddenly turned to quicksand, when they were confronted by hundreds of new power players as the court of courts coalesced.

Normally, physical contests would have sorted things out, with masters competing against one another for positions of power. But my twin's mind informed me that duels were forbidden for the course of the war, lest they cost the court too many of its most useful members. So tensions were high and getting higher, with no outlet in sight.

And that was especially true around the mini courts of the other consuls.

They were seated here and there along the gallery, in areas that looked like they might once have held large statues. But the raised platforms had been cleared off, draped in swags of rich fabric, and decked in various types of seating arrangements. Turning them into smaller versions of the queen's dais up ahead.

There the other consuls, the queen's counterparts at senates around the world, sat surrounded by their combative creatures. They could have easily reined them in, but weren't doing so. This queen might have proven the strongest momentarily, and won their grudging allegiance. But winning wasn't keeping, and there were jealous eyes everywhere—on her position as much as the rest.

The whole court was a powder keg, the air thick with expectation, which might explain why nobody had yet realized what moved among them.

And because they were careless.

They didn't expect to find me, in this place of many masters. They thought themselves safe, at least against my kind of peril. And they were right—for now.

I looked toward the main dais, where the queen sat, smiling at something one of her courtier's had said.

I was after bigger prey.

Jolt, jolt, jolt.

Duck, bend, *augghh*!

Jolt, jolt, jolt.

I woke up to the sensation of being carried . . . painfully . . . somewhere I couldn't see. Because I couldn't see anything. The only light came from little squares of haze that broke the blackness here and there, but they flashed by so quickly that they didn't help much. In fact, it was mostly the opposite: they acted like strobes in a nightclub, brightening things just enough to fool my eyes and make me dizzy.

And I was already dizzy enough.

Damn it, what was *happening*?

I struggled the rest of the way back to consciousness, cursing the darkness. But then a bullet whizzed by and sparked off the floor in front of us, and I decided I didn't mind so much. And then it didn't matter, because whoever was carrying me made a movement so fast that, even as part of it, I couldn't follow.

And, suddenly, we were running through light.

Not bright light. Most of it was provided by huge candelabras dripping wax everywhere and looking creepy. But they showed me enough to realize that Louis-Cesare was carrying me, that we'd just darted out of one of the hidden passages around here, and that we were currently tearing through a library.

And that somebody was shooting at us.

Make that a lot of somebodies.

Annnnd I was caught up.

"Put me down," I told him, struggling.

"In a moment."

"Why? What are you waiting for?"

"That," he said, as we burst into a narrow hallway and leapt over a line of masters who'd just knelt in front of us.

I thought I recognized one of them.

"Mircea's?"

"Mircea's."

I craned my neck around, because we were now running down the hall, so fast that it was almost a blur. But I was in time to see another squad of vamps—the ones who I guess had been following us—get held up the hard way. The two groups crashed together as we rushed in the other direction, into another room, through a fireplace, down a passageway, and out—

Into Mircea's suite of rooms.

I knew them because I'd been here before. What I didn't know was that they'd gotten an upgrade. Or maybe the portal swirling on the far wall had always been here, because trust Mircea to have a plan B—and C and D and E—for every occasion.

Except this one, because I wasn't going in there.

"Let me down—"

Louis-Cesare wasn't letting me down.

I twisted and managed to get loose, hit the edge of a table, and bounce off onto the floor.

Oh yeah.

That was fun.

"Dory!" Louis-Cesare grabbed me again, blue eyes wild. "We need to get you out of here!"

"We need to get me to the consul," I snarled, ripping off the sheet. Which was covered in blood from a wound in my side, thanks to a certain curly-haired bastard. Who was going to rue the fucking *day*.

"You can kill Kit later," Louis-Cesare told me.

"I plan to!"

"And Mircea can deal with Dorina," he continued, as I felt around for an exit wound.

Found one, lucky me. And not through anything vital. So it was just blood loss I really couldn't afford right now that was making me feel like shit.

I ripped up the sheet and started a basic field dressing.

"Listen to me!" Louis-Cesare caught my upper arms, and shook me.

"Cut it out!"

"Then explain to me why I shouldn't pick you up and throw you through that portal, whether you like it or not!"

I looked up. "You do and I swear—"

"*Quoi?*" He spread his arms, blue eyes flashing. "What

are you going to do? What do you think would be worse for me than seeing you riddled with bullets?"

I stared at him, because he looked genuinely angry, which he almost never was with me. And genuinely afraid, which he wasn't with anybody. And genuinely gorgeous, and fuck it—I'd had a hard day.

I surged up and kissed him, and for a brief second, he was into it. Before breaking away and glaring at me. And cussing inventively in French, which was never a good sign.

"Lord Mircea can deal with this!" he repeated furiously.

"Can he?" I panted, pulling the dressing tight. "You sure?"

"His specialty is the mind!"

"So is Dorina's. And he couldn't detect her before, when she was just a kid and used to follow him around Venice for shits and giggles. He didn't know she was there until she said something."

Louis-Cesare frowned. "That was a long time ago. He is more powerful now—" He caught my expression. "And do not say that she is, too!"

"Okay, I won't say it." I tied off the bandage and looked around for weapons. And didn't find any. Damn it!

Fine, we'd do it the hard way.

An iron fist gripped my arm. "You are *not* going out there!"

"The consul is a poisonous bitch, possibly literally," I told him. "But if she dies, the war effort descends into chaos while those other bastards fight over a successor. And they will. You know they will."

My brilliant appeal to logic did not appear to have much effect. "What I know is that you're in no condition to do anything about it! Neither of us is."

I looked him over. He had a point. "So what's your plan?"

He gestured at the portal. "That! Get out, get you to a healer, and let your father handle this. I've already sent him the information. He knows Dorina is a danger."

"He's known that for five hundred years." I walked over to the portal, swirling in the wall. It was a powerful one; I could feel the pull from here. I looked back at him. "Where does this go, again?"

He joined me, looking relieved. "Lord Mircea's home in Washington State."

"And we can get back afterward? Once this is over?"

"Yes, it works both ways. As long as the shield isn't up."

He glanced at a little button on the wall. Guess that was the shield. "Good to know," I said, and shoved him through the swirling light before slamming my fist down on the button.

All right, then.

Or it was.

Until an arm snaked through the portal and grabbed me, jerking me in.

After a furious trip through a vortex of color and light, I landed in a posh office I was too pissed to take in right now, where a lying bastard of a vampire was trying to—

"Oh, no, you don't!"

I pushed him away from what I was pretty sure was the portal's control panel, and he went staggering back into a bookshelf. It fell over, making a hell of a racket, and a bunch of vamps ran through the door, guns drawn. And immediately looked confused.

"Thanks," I told the nearest, and grabbed his gun.

"Urm," he said.

"Extra clips?"

"I—not on me—"

"Hit the kill switch, damn you!" Louis-Cesare snarled at them, even as he went for it himself.

Before he could reach it, I dove back through the portal, landing hard on the other side—with someone's hand around my ankle.

And was promptly jerked back, my body feeling like candy at a continent-spanning taffy pull, until it popped out the other side again.

"Son of a bitch motherfucker!"

"Language," Louis-Cesare said grimly, from down near my foot.

I kicked him in the mouth.

I felt bad doing it—it was a nice mouth—but I didn't have time for this.

"I don't have time for this—let me go!" I yelled, while a line of perturbed-looking vamps just stood around, uselessly. "Grab him!" I told them, because he wasn't letting go. "And get me some extra clips!"

The guy who'd lent me the gun looked conflicted. "Are . . . are you going to use them to shoot Louis-Cesare?"

"Probably not," I said, broke his hold, dove for the portal, and got tackled again halfway through.

The forward momentum kept us going anyway, landing us back in Mircea's bedroom—only to find another bunch of vamps in there, and they didn't look conflicted at all.

Shit!

Of course Marlowe would know there was a portal. And of course he'd send a group to secure it. The sneaky son of a bitch!

I did some bullet riddling, which pissed them off but bought us time, and then Mircea's boys ran in the door and a trashing of the room commenced. *That's two in one night,* I thought dizzily. *I'm on a roll.*

And then Louis-Cesare dragged me back through the portal again.

"This . . . is getting . . . goddamned . . . old!" I told him, as we rolled around on the floor of an office three thousand miles away.

The Washington State vamps were still just standing there, watching us and looking like they wanted to intervene. But when it was a case of the boss' daughter and the boss' nephew, it was a conundrum. I decided to help them out.

"Get in there!" I pointed a toe, which was all I currently had loose, at the portal. "We're getting our asses kicked!"

And then Louis-Cesare grabbed me the wrong way, I screamed, and he let go—for half a second. But that was enough. I slipped out of his grip, flung myself through the portal, and arrived in time to see—

Fuck!

We were getting our asses kicked!

But then the cavalry arrived, bursting through the portal

behind me with a yell, followed by a furious ex-boyfriend who was stunning when he was angry.

And right then, he was *livid*.

He snatched up one of Marlowe's guys and threw him at a window, only we didn't have a window. "We. Are going. To bed!" he roared at me, loudly enough for everyone to stop fighting for a second and stare at him.

"Not in front of the children," I said, snatched a nice Persian carpet from under his feet, and watched the portal grab him when he fell backward.

And then I grabbed one of Mircea's guys. "Controls?"

He pointed at a desk.

I slammed my hand down on the actual button, shot one of Marlowe's guys in the face, and ran out the door.

Knowing Louis-Cesare, I'd just bought myself maybe thirty seconds.

I intended to use them.

Chapter Forty-six

My Sire was here. I felt him before I saw him, the brush of his power spreading out over the great hall like ripples in a pond. Small ones, subtle ones. Ones no one else seemed to notice.

Feelers; he was looking for me. And he was good—he was very good—and he knew my power signature like he knew his own. I stayed very, very still.

The young vampire I was riding looked around, from his less-than-dignified place on the floor. He appeared somewhat bewildered, the panic having cleared his head. He hadn't planned to come here, into the audience hall, which, frankly, terrified him. He'd been on an errand when I'd suggested a shortcut, one he was now deciding he could live without. He scrambled to his feet and fled, forcing me to make a hasty decision.

Hoping the minor hop would go unnoticed, I jumped to a passing human who was carrying a tray of glasses. Magic swirled all around us, from the little sparks off gowns and coats, to the background hum of the wards, to the multicolored clouds that sparkled everywhere. Surely, no one could see through all that—

Dorina.

A flash of dark eyes in a thunderous face flicked across my inner eye.

I batted it away and jumped, right before a couple of guards grabbed my very bewildered ride, spilling his champagne. They took him away, while I rode a low-level master in another direction. It was more of a risk, but his magic somewhat cloaked my own. I hid in the haze of his *power, staying quiet, wishing I dared try to influence him, even though it probably wouldn't have worked.*

But I couldn't risk finding out, not with Mircea so close.

I could see him now, dark, lean, and dressed in a sleek tuxedo instead of the velvet robes he was entitled to. He looked strangely human among the glittering throng, like a raven among peacocks—ah. He hadn't planned to be here tonight.

He was supposed to be at the apartment in New York, charming the mages who made weapons into making them for the Senate. And into finding ones powerful enough to be of use in Faerie. He was to lead the assault on the fey that was soon to come, and wanted to be sure of a steady supply of arms. But then something happened. . . .

Caedmon, the one who wanted our gift. He had been pressing his suit, while Mircea had been finding arguments to stave him off, to keep us here. And was now wondering why he'd bothered.

I felt a sharp pang at that, the longing of a child for the father who'd never wanted her, who had locked her away—

His head turned abruptly in my direction.

I cursed myself. Stupid! Stupid! I knew better. Emotion was the easiest thing to read, especially if that emotion involved you. He'd laid a trap and I'd fallen into it, and now he was coming this way.

The master I was riding smiled, and bowed. He felt honored; I did not. I had been careless, and now we were being surrounded.

Mircea's vampires, so easy to pick out in a crowd, their power ghostly white against all the richer colors, started converging on all sides. They looked like spectral angels, perhaps vengeful ones. I looked desperately around for an advantage.

And found it above my head, in a swirl of angry magic from several arguing vamps. Not nearly as big as before; the room was still somewhat cowed from the lashing the consul had dealt the other master. But displeased, quarrelsome. Offense had been given and apology was demanded.

So I jumped, not out this time but up, into the angry

clouds, and looked down through the glittering swirls of their power at the master I'd just left, who was bowing lower now and wondering what the great man wanted from him.

The great man wanted me, but didn't find me. He was angry, but hid it well, making small talk with the vamp while mentally searching the surrounding area. He was worried; he knew what I could do, and better than the rest. I wanted to talk to him, to explain, but that . . . did not always go well. Sometimes he listened; many more times he did not.

And this time, I could not take the risk.

I also couldn't hold free flight for long, and started looking around for an avatar.

And found something else.

One of the main advantages of being a dhampir is the natural camouflage. We register as human, even to high-level masters who ought to know better, unless they have something approaching Mircea's facility with the mind. Fortunately, few do.

Unfortunately, all of them are able to smell blood, especially freshly spilled, and I was covered in it. And I didn't exactly have time for a shower and change. So there was no hope of switching places with a human servant, grabbing a tray of drinks, and just waltzing my way into where I needed to be.

Of course not, I thought grimly.

That would be too easy.

And then there was the small matter of being out of time. Dorina didn't fuck around. When she decided on something, she went for it, and that little party in Mircea's rooms had held me up. I needed to get to the consul and I needed to do it now.

So I ran, but not through the dark-as-pitch passageways. I didn't know them and didn't have time to figure them out. And, anyway, Marlowe had probably flooded them with his people by now.

Of course, he had people on the main thoroughfare, too, the one cutting a swath from the entrance hall along the front of the building, forming an extended audience chamber. They were so thick there that this had to be it, had to be where the consul was holding court. I couldn't see her yet, because of the length of the damned thing, and because there were a crap ton of people everywhere. But I could see Marlowe's masters.

And vice versa.

They were already headed this way, and they were fast, but so was someone else.

And I didn't mean me.

"Stop them!" I told a nearby guard, one of the ones dressed in Roman-looking armor that were standing at attention everywhere, guarding the Senate. They were there for show more than anything else, standing around all night trying to look shiny and not too bored. But they *were* bored, and the nearest was now looking hopefully at me.

"Protect me, goddamn it!" I told him. "Do your job!"

They did their job.

I started for the great hall at a dead run, and from every side, Marlowe's masters jumped out at me. And looked everything from comically surprised to seriously pissed when the Senate's ceremonial guards jumped for *them*. And quickly demonstrated that they'd been picked for more than how good they looked in a leather skirt.

Meanwhile, I ducked between masters, dodging the knives Marlowe's boys had switched to, because I guess they didn't want to spray bullets into the crowd. There was no time for subtleties, or apologies for the drinks that went flying or for the important types who got elbowed or for the outfits worth the price of a house that were splattered with hors d'oeuvres. There was only time—

For nothing, because somebody grabbed me.

But it wasn't Marlowe.

Dorina had been hovering in the air overhead, and had dropped down on top of me like a bird of prey taking a mouse. Suddenly, I was seeing everything through the garbled vision of two sets of eyes. And even more worryingly, I was running again, correcting the stumble I'd taken when she took me and fumbling at my belt for the gun and—

Oh, no you don't*!*

I'd finally spotted the creature, riding a nearby woman. It had been startling, disturbing. A black miasma that crouched over her like a malevolent shadow.

But I could do little about it as I was. My freed consciousness was extremely limited in ability, and was only slightly better with an avatar. To attack the creature enough to drive it out, to force it back inside its own body, I needed mine.

And, to my surprise, it came running into the gallery a moment later, chased by what looked like an army of vampires.

One of which was quickly attacked by another.

I stared for a moment, at the sight of senatorial guards flowing out to protect a dhampir.

Then I dropped down to join her, and to finish this—

Only to discover that she was fighting me.

I felt our hand spasm, dropping the gun we'd been holding, and our feet falter, sending us stumbling into a column. She was trying to take us to the floor, to ground us until one of the dark-haired master's servants could subdue us. Or, worse, until Mircea could.

I felt him move this way, having seen her come in and realizing that something was wrong. But he didn't know what yet, didn't see the threat. And even if I'd wanted to try the explanation I'd rejected earlier, there was no time.

Not for him.

I hesitated, because Mircea had warned me against this. Do not contact her directly, he had said. Do not force a reintegration lest it all start again, and you damage her as you once did. Let it happen naturally. . . .

But there was nothing natural about what we were. And he underestimated her; he always had. She wasn't a child anymore, but a woman hardened by combat and toughened by experience. And she would hate me for this, for leaving her out of the decision, for letting this murderer succeed.

As I would hate myself.
Dory, *I said, and felt the shock reverberate through her.*

My head snapped up, and my eyes stared blankly at a slur of faces, some surprised, some intrigued, some horrified as they realized that a dhampir savage had been allowed to roam freely among them.

I didn't care.

Because the voice came again.

Dory . . .

I swallowed, and then jerked to the side, so that a vamp who'd been jumping for me slammed into the pillar instead. He sprang off, embarrassed and furious, and I elbowed him in the face, grabbed him by the hair, and smashed his head a few times into the heavy silver tray a frightened human servant was holding like a shield. And when that still wasn't enough, I kicked him at a senatorial guard, who sent me a nod of thanks before introducing the guy repeatedly to the wall.

I barely noticed, being too busy staring into the air, because I persisted in the idea that I was going to see Dorina.

But I couldn't see her.

She was me.

And she was talking—oh, yes, *now* she was talking, in a flood of words and images and feelings, so much, too much.

"Stop it!" I yelled, and staggered into someone—

Mircea.

I stared up at him, and knew my pupils were blown wide by the change in his expression. "What is it?" he growled, although he already knew.

"She's talking," I said in wonder. "She's finally talking—"

"Dorina!" Mircea shook me. "Stop it—I warned you! This is dangerous!"

"No." I gripped him back, trying to sort through everything she'd sent. Trying to understand—

"I'm getting you out of here—"

"No!" I gripped him harder, my fingers biting into his arms. "There's a problem—"

"I know that!"

"*Listen to me.* Someone's trying to kill the consul but *it isn't her.* It isn't Dorina. I think—I think she's trying to stop it, but—"

"—*augghhh!*"

Light exploded everywhere, searing, painful, overwhelming. And blinding. Suddenly, I couldn't see a thing.

I also couldn't hear. Or, rather, I could, but far too much. Something was confusing my mental control, letting in the surrounding voices, all of them, all at once. And unlike in a human gathering, these conversations weren't just audible. There were mental voices, too, many more than could possibly fit into a single room, no matter how large. For there was almost nothing but masters here, pulling me in, smothering me under the weight of their vast families, turning a thousand guests into a million, a sea of voices, threatening to drown me.

I jerked back in self-defense, panting and disoriented, but that left me almost totally without senses, and the threat was growing. I could feel it, crawling along my spine, etching my mind like acid. But I couldn't find it, even though it was getting closer, even though it was about to spring.

Damn it! I had to see.

But something saw me first. For it had been looking for me, too, feeling me as a subtle presence, as I had felt it. But not being able to locate me, either.

So it had uncloaked itself, showing its true form for the first time. And my body's reaction to its power had told it exactly where to look. I'd just started to regain control, to begin filtering out the voices, and to dampen down that terrible light, when it hit: vicious pain and blinding static, the defense mechanisms of my prey. They were strong enough to stagger me, to cause me to clench my teeth on a scream as I fell back against the wall, to leave me gasping in agony.

But not strong enough to stop me.

Not this time.

Mircea had stumbled against the column, caught in the attack because of his proximity to me, and was as debilitated as I had been the first time. But this wasn't my first time, and there's a truth about pain that most people never learn, unless they're really unlucky. Or really long-lived, long enough to have felt almost every kind there is. Pain has a signature to it, a type, a song. The first time you experience a new one, it's a bright, white-hot, cutting edge; or a searing, brain-twisting burn; or a shattering, soul-crushing thud; or any of the thousand other forms it takes to torment you.

But the second time? Or the third? Or the fiftieth? No. It's still terrible, still rage inducing, still debilitating, but it's not the same shock as at first. You know this song, all its terrible highs and dismal lows; you can hum it with your eyes closed, because it's just that familiar. Not like a friend—never that—but like an old enemy you've grown to know as well as to hate, his weapons and his limits.

You know what he can do to you.

But you also know what he can't.

Which is why I came off the wall with a roar that scattered people in front of me, like a school of fish parting when a shark swims by. It would have been interesting another time, to catalogue the different reactions: young vampires spilling drinks on themselves in shock, or sinking to the floor in horror. Older, mid-level vamps, all but disappearing through doors and stairways, melting into the darkness, going dim. And then there were the oldest ones, bright, bright, so incredibly bright, their power eclipsing that of the others around them, wherever they were standing.

They did not run. They did not hide. But they also did not attack, holding back, seeing what I would do.

And looking vaguely surprised when I passed them by, uninterested.

For I was after something else, something deadlier than any of them, something I'd encountered before. Something that was still attacking: cutting, harsh and cruel. But not enough.

This time, I would have it. This time, I would kill it. But I had to find it first.

And it was no longer riding the woman I'd seen earlier. I found her, looking wide-eyed and shell-shocked, being *supported by two others. So my prey wasn't just riding, then, but controlling.*

Who was it controlling now?

I didn't know, and it was getting harder to concentrate. The creature knew I was hunting it, but wasn't concerned, was laughing at me, and sending static from all sides now. I couldn't see anything but leering vampire faces; couldn't hear anything above the static's awful roar; couldn't use my inner eye, not with the massive crowd everywhere, hiding the one I needed to see. There were so many voices—

Until I screamed, the psychic shock waves spreading across the room like a scythe through wheat. Vampires, mages, human servants—they all went down. All except two. The vampire queen, standing still and terrible at the top of her dais, and the man suddenly running at her from across the room.

I had no weapons, and there was no time to get inside his head. I saw the queen glance at me as I started to run, not for her but for the creature clothed in the flesh of a man. I failed to reach him, but not because I was too slow. But because I was thrown backward, not slapped this time but belted, so hard and so fast that I hit the wall again, a dozen yards away, before I could blink. And the jolt of the blow—

Put me back in charge.

But the tag team handoff was a little abrupt, like me face-planting onto the nice marble floor when I bounced off the wall. It left me feeling like a punching bag that somebody had beaten all the stuffing out of at the gym. I somehow managed to get my shaky arms underneath me, to raise my head—

And then just stayed there, blinking in confusion, as what looked like a desert storm blew up in the middle of the room. It engulfed the man leaping at the queen, which would have been strange enough, because that's not something you see every day. But then the whirling winds hardened into what looked like a shell of earth, a large globe behind which another storm broke with blinding fury.

I saw what looked like a hundred spells hit the sides of the shell, all at once, in bursts of color and light. Saw the consul blink, a tiny thing, a half expression. Saw her power spike as she fought to keep the fury contained. And heard Dorina tell me that she couldn't sustain that level for long.

No shit, I thought back groggily.

I'd no sooner had the thought than the great shield cracked and buckled and shattered, exploding in a thousand pieces that lashed my face, even this far away. I saw something fall out of the other side, in swirls of dissipating magic. Saw it crash against the bottom steps of the dais and shatter like glass. Realized that it was the man, who was nothing but a collection of charred bones now.

The sand-laced winds had scoured him clean.

The consul was untouched, but not unscathed. I saw her stagger back against her throne, and the fact that she'd actually show weakness told me what the man had been carrying. Those explosions must have been caused by more of the superweapons we'd encountered, hundreds of them, enough to leave even a consul vulnerable.

And somebody was prepared to take advantage of it.

Through half a dozen doors, vampires surged into the room, all but flying at the dais. But they weren't wearing the clothing of just one family. They weren't from a single clan, and several were from competing ones. Which told me that this wasn't—

—*a normal assassination. They were being*—

—controlled, by that creature who had attacked us at Claire's—

—*and who was here, riding someone new*—

—but who? There was no way to know—

—*except it wouldn't be one of the controlled, lest we attack them and the creature lose its focus*—

—but there was no one else! No one still conscious—

—*no one except*—

My eyes widened.

And then I grabbed the knife my last assailant had dropped, jumped up and threw—

Straight at the consul.

Chapter Forty-seven

This time, I woke up alone.

The bed was the same as before, so I was still at the consul's. Oh goody. Even better, someone was bitching.

"—don't care! I need to talk to her!"

Oh, damn it all to hell. I threw an arm over my face, because that was Marlowe and seriously? I hadn't lived an exactly perfect life, but what had I done to deserve this?

I lay there for a while, contemplating various vile things I could do to the consul's stooge. But I honestly wasn't up to any of them, and repressed aggression would only give me a headache. I got up.

And discovered that I still had no clothes, other than for my bandages. I looked everywhere, but couldn't find any, not even Louis-Cesare's trousers. So I wrapped myself in a blanket and peeked out the door.

A couple vamps were there, lounging against the wall, apparently enjoying watching Marlowe have a fit down the hall. Until they saw me. And suddenly stood to attention, like soldiers when an officer walks by.

I blinked groggily at them.

"Uh."

They didn't say anything. I got the impression that they were waiting for me to continue my thought, which would have worked better if I'd had one. As it was, we all just stood there, them at what looked like parade rest and me swaying slightly until I grabbed hold of the door.

And acquired a thought.

"Clothes," I croaked, and to my surprise, one of the guys all but disappeared.

I watched him flee down the hall and frowned. I was pretty sure I'd just said "clothes," not "I'm going to kill you horribly," but I wasn't sure. My head had the fuzzy feeling of a ten-day bender, and right then, I wasn't sure of anything.

I considered talking to Guy Number Two, but was afraid I'd scare him as well.

"Um," I said tentatively.

Guy Number Two stayed in place.

So far, so good.

"So. Could you tell me what—"

I stopped, but not because he'd run away. But because somebody else had heard me and shoved his way past Guy Number Three down the hall. "Damn it! I told you to tell me the moment she was awake!"

That was Marlowe, striding this way.

At least, he was until something amazing happened.

Like, seriously amazing.

Like, I actually rubbed my eyes amazing, since I was obviously hallucinating.

What I thought I saw was Guy Number Two—a tall dude who could have been a James clone except for pointier teeth and less hair—put out his arm and place a hand on Marlowe's chest, stopping him.

Now, half the time Marlowe goes around in Elizabethan slops like a nutcase, and the rest he's wearing whatever wreck he's made of his family's latest effort to dress him like a person so he doesn't embarrass the hell out of them. Again. However, it's a case of looks being deceiving, because he is a first-level master and a Senate member.

And Guy Number Two was not.

My brain was finally coming back online, at least enough for me to make a decent guess: Guy Number Two was a strong third- or maybe a weak second-level master. In other words, strong enough to do some impressive shit, but not this impressive. I started to wonder if maybe he had some kind of mental issue, because he was about to be a rather large stain on the carpet.

Only he wasn't.

"Damn it! Get out of my way!" Marlowe snapped.

"I'm sorry, sir." And for another strange thing, Guy

Number Two did not sound sorry. He sounded . . . annoyed? Put-upon? Slightly bored?

It was bizarre.

Until he cleared it up for me.

"Lord Mircea gave strict orders."

"*Fuck* Lord Mircea," Marlowe snarled. "I've waited long enough!"

"And you'll wait some more. Sir."

I grinned.

I decided I liked Guy Number Two.

And then his paler friend was back, along with someone else.

"Lady Dorina! How wonderful to see you up and about! How are you feeling this fine morning?"

Burbles, living up to the name.

And looking it, too. I don't know what I'd expected, but what I got was a jolly round dude with a jolly round face, a double chin, warm brown eyes, and cute little pink lips hiding the fangs that wouldn't have gone well with that face at all. That, frankly, would have looked absurd. Burbles was a cross between a black Santa Claus and the Michelin Man, and I didn't know what to do with him at all.

I went with: "Hello."

"Hel*lo*!" He was almost overcome with joy. "You are looking very well, if I may say so."

It was a lie, but said with such utter conviction that I almost believed it.

It also cleared up an old mystery for me. Mircea's masters—which is what I guessed all these guys were, or else Marlowe would have been doing more than standing there vibrating at me—were renowned diplomats. Everybody knew it; everybody said it. Their master was the consul's chief ambassador and resident miracle worker, so it made sense that the family would be, too.

Only I'd never believed a word of it.

Not that I'd met every one of Mircea's vamps, or even his masters. Until recently, I'd spent most of my time *avoiding* Mircea, and that included the family. However, I'd met enough through the years to have a serious WTF reaction every time someone told me how charming they were.

They were not charming.

Unless you counted not beating me up and/or hissing at me, like half the vamps I met, so I guess that was something.

But still.

Yet, now I was getting the full treatment, and it was eye-opening. Burbles was sweet. Burbles was joyful. Burbles was thrilled to finally meet me, which was *absurd*. No vampire—except Louis-Cesare, who was mostly crazy anyway—was ever happy to see a dhampir.

So why was I smiling back at him?

I stopped myself.

It was actually hard.

"Would you like some breakfast? We have some glorious blueberry muffins or heavenly eggs Benedict or—my favorite—a simply divine bananas Foster that our chef makes with bourbon whipped cream. Oh!" He raised his eyes to the ceiling with a hand on his heart. "So good!"

"I'll have that," I found myself saying.

I had no idea why.

I don't even like bananas.

"Excellent choice. I know you'll be pleased! And perhaps you'd like to pick out an outfit for today?"

"Uh . . . I don't have any clothes here."

"But of course you do!" And then Burbles' hand found his mouth, and his eyes widened in horror. "Oh! You haven't seen your closet!"

I laughed. I don't know why. Maybe because he'd intended me to, or because Burbles had just elbowed Marlowe out of the way without apparently noticing.

Or giving a damn.

"Please allow me," he said, and I somehow found myself back inside what I was only now realizing was a very nice room. *Very* nice. I stood there in my blanket, taking in the elaborate crown moldings and the massive amount of space and the huge bed and the large, well-appointed sitting room and the closet I hadn't opened yet because I'd assumed it would be empty. But which instead was big enough inside to count as another bedroom and was stocked full of stuff.

All of which appeared to be in my size.

"What's this?" I asked, sticking my head in and looking around.

"Your wardrobe," Burbles told me, making a slight moue of dissatisfaction. "Very preliminary, of course, but we haven't had a chance to inquire about your preferences yet."

I looked over my shoulder. "We?"

"Your father, Lord Mircea, lent you thirty or so of his masters. Just to help you get started," he quickly assured me. "Until you assemble your own."

"My own what?" I was still trying to figure out how all these clothes got in here.

He looked surprised. "Staff."

"For . . . ?"

Burbles regarded me for a moment. For the first time, he appeared a little nonplussed. "For . . . whatever you need us for. As a senator—"

I burst out laughing.

Burbles continued to look slightly off-balance.

I appeared to be harshing his buzz.

"Is . . . is something wrong?" he asked, while I started sorting through the clothes, trying to find an outfit that wouldn't make me look like I was heading for the Oscars.

"Nope. Just that you're a little behind the times. I'm not a senator anymore."

In fact, I was kind of surprised I was still alive, all things considered. But Mircea had been there, and I was pretty sure I'd seen Louis-Cesare running into the gallery, looking crazed, just before I passed out. So that probably explained it.

"I—when did this happen?" Burbles asked, appearing confused now. And the fact that I had a really strong urge to walk over, pat him on the back, and tell him everything was going to be okay seriously worried me.

The guy was good.

"About the time I stabbed the consul in the neck?"

He just blinked at me for a moment, and then this . . . fluttering . . . went across the room. Marlowe, who had been bitching in the hall, suddenly shut up, and the three other vamps—two in the doorway, and Burbles a respectful few paces outside the closet—did this thing where they went up on their toes and just . . . fluttered. Shivering all over like birds rippling their plumage.

It was weird.

I'd been looking around for something comfortable to wear, because I didn't want a waistband to rub against my wound, but hadn't found anything. So I was eyeing the bathrobe on the back of the door, which would do to get me home, where I had a whole closetful of old sweats waiting to embrace my kicked-around bod. So I reached for it—

And heard a sudden intake of breath from the vamps, and not the good kind. More the Grandma-seeing-your-full-Goth-ensemble-for-the-first-time kind. And hating it.

I felt a small, tentative touch on my shoulder—Burbles, looking even more adorable with huge eyes and a pleading face. "Please?"

It was a whisper.

"Please what? What is wrong with you?" I asked him, because cute or not, he was starting to freak me out.

"Your presence is requested in the salon, my lady, and . . . more formal attire would be . . . preferable."

Which looks like a totally fine sentence, right? Except that it completely fails to replicate the inflection—and seriously, what Burbles could do with his voice was kind of amazing—which made "preferable" sound like "avoid the terrible heat death of the universe."

I had no freaking idea what was going on, and was too beat-up to care. I didn't want bananas Foster. I didn't want to get dressed up. I sure as hell didn't want to hang out with anyone in the salon, except possibly Louis-Cesare, and why did I get the impression that this was not about him? I just wanted to go home.

It had been a long night.

"Don't call me lady," I said, and finally located some sweats. They were purple and plush, and looked suspiciously like something Radu would pick out, but clothes were clothes. And they felt positively decadent against my abused skin.

I sighed in relief, turned around—

And saw a doorway full of faces staring at me. There was a line of vamps all the way up either side, peering around the jamb, and more in the opening. I didn't know how they did it. They must have been climbing on top of one another, like some kind of circus act.

With fangs.

"What?" I asked.

And the next thing I knew, I was being engulfed, and me and my sweats were being stuffed inside a "robe," which was actually more of a caftan stiff with embroidery and little seed pearls and what looked like actual jewel chips making up flowers and leaves and tiny birds and shit. And then I was being hustled out the door, until Burbles yelled: "*Waaaaaaaaaaait!*" And everybody stopped to look at him.

"Shoes," he pronounced, in a tone that suggested that Armageddon could be avoided only by locating the right footwear.

For a moment, I was treated to the sight of half a dozen master vamps, some of them probably hundreds of years old with courts of their own, diving for the floor and scrabbling around as if finding the right shoes was a matter of life and death.

And I guess they did, only I couldn't see them because of all the butts in the way, but something was stuck on my feet. Then the lot of us were shuffling down the hall, which was all I could do in whatever the hell I was wearing, and while batting at some lunatic behind me who was trying to comb out my bed head. And while being pressed in between a phalanx of vamps like the filling in a very weird sandwich.

I'd have fought back, but I didn't have the energy. And I kind of thought that, if they were going to drag me to an interrogation room and chain me to a wall, they'd have done it already. And wouldn't be so concerned about my wardrobe.

So I had no idea.

Until the fluttery vamps and the clueless dhampir spilled out into a room at the end of the hall, only to see—

Oh.

That was why.

What I guessed was the salon Burbles had mentioned earlier turned out to be a small room with the dark wood paneling and low burning fire of a gentleman's study, only sans the books. And plus a glittering vampire queen, all in red, because she'd changed from the mostly green ensemble she'd worn before. I suppose because of all the blood.

She was surrounded by her own entourage, a bunch of absolutely massive vampires that I barely noticed because it was kind of hard to look anywhere else.

You had to give it to her; she knew how to command a freaking room.

The outfit helped. It had what I initially thought were red and burgundy flames licking up it, raised from the underlying crimson satin by exquisite embroidery. Only flames don't move like that. I was still having trouble focusing, but my eyes suddenly got their act together and caused me to almost jump back in alarm, but Burbles was practically on my heels and wouldn't let me.

Because the "flames" were snakes. The embroidery—and the charm animating it—was so good that they were positively lifelike, with emerald eyes, and tiny garnet or ruby flakes for scales. And little onyx tongues that flicked out here and there, while the bodies squirmed around the tight sheath and plunging neckline.

Her hair was down, a dark river rippling to her knees, and it was spotted with rubies, too, little ones that glittered in the firelight like drops of blood. She wasn't wearing a necklace, although the J.Lo-worthy décolletage gave plenty of room for it. I guess she thought she'd already made her point.

Or maybe she was making another one by showing off the unscarred expanse of golden skin on her throat.

Well, I thought.

And then I didn't think anything else.

Except, damn, I wanted that outfit.

The queen's arrival had apparently thrown everybody into a kerfuffle—everybody except me. Because I wasn't all that interested in genuflecting if she'd only showed up to murder me in person. But I guess not. Because a long silk-draped arm extended, and a ring-bedecked hand rose into the air, and then just stopped, halfway up.

I looked at it.

The rings contained rubies, too, huge old-world things in heavy gold settings. They glimmered and gleamed and showed off how slender her fingers were. The nails were bloodred and slightly pointy, with a little golden glister at the tips. Impressive, the whole damn ensemble.

I was suddenly kind of grateful for the caftan.

I also had no idea what I was supposed to be doing, but I guess it was something, because everybody was staring at me expectantly. I spied Radu, making some kind of gesture I couldn't see because I could glimpse him only in between the bodies of the queen's servants, who were some kind of mutants. Seriously, there wasn't one under seven feet tall.

"You may kiss her hand," Burbles informed me, a whisper in my ear.

Yeah, I thought. And she could kiss my—

"Dory!"

That was Radu, speaking aloud, because I guess whatever mental message he'd been trying to send wasn't getting through.

Not surprising. My head felt heavy, closed off, almost leaden. I wanted to sit down.

No—better yet, I wanted to go home.

But here was some more nonsense I had to get through first.

"Kiss the hand," Radu said, fairly shrilly, bouncing around behind the tall guys. "Kiss the hand!"

Why? Is she the pope? I didn't say, because Radu finally fought his way through the crowd and grabbed my head, bobbing it downward before I could tell him where to go.

I did not kiss the damned hand. But I guess it must have looked like I did. Or maybe Her High-and-Mightiness figured that was as good as she was going to get, because it finally withdrew.

"We thank you for your service," the vision informed me. She glanced around the room. "Twice in a month a dhampir has come to our aid when others failed. It will be remembered."

Okay. Well, that was bright and shiny, I thought, in some relief. She'd actually wanted to do something nice for a change, and thank me.

I was almost impressed.

She looked back at me. "Is Lady Dorina available? I should like to speak with her."

"It, uh, doesn't work quite like that."

"How does it work?"

The question was mild enough, but it was kind of like Burbles' comment. It wasn't the words so much as the inflection. And the fact that she was standing there, glimmering at me, surrounded by a dozen of the biggest vamps I'd ever seen, while her snakes squirmed and her jewels glinted and I started to feel inadequate, which pissed me off. Because, *Hey lady, don't recall inviting you to stop by.*

"She comes out when she wants to," I said flatly. "Or when she sees a threat. I don't control her."

"Ah. Then come with me."

She swept out, along with her entourage, and I found myself being hustled after her, in the middle of mine.

Chapter Forty-eight

"What's going on?" I asked Burbles, because he'd stuck himself to my side like a charming burr.

"The consul has formally noticed you," he told me, brown eyes gleaming. "Even better, *she* came to *you*. It is a great honor. For you and the entire house!" He was literally quivering with joy.

I started to explain that I could give a shit, and just wanted to know where we were going. But another look at his face, and I gave up. Let the damned vampire be happy for five minutes. It wouldn't last.

Not around here.

Instead, I hurried, as much as I could in what I now saw were embroidered slippers. They matched the robe, the background a deep blue velvet that was almost invisible because it was so heavily encrusted with embroidered fruits and flowers and ribbons and bows. And gold insects, their minuscule wings raised above the rest and fluttering, fluttering, fluttering.

Like my horde of vamps, who appeared almost as awestruck as Burbles—why, I didn't know.

The bitch wanted something.

I mean, come on.

But nobody was telling me what, so down the hall we went, and one nice thing about my suddenly acquired entourage was that they took no prisoners. Get in the way of the Dory train? *Screw you, here's a wall.* Stop in the middle of the hall to stare at the consul and the crazy dhampir coming atcha? *Wow, bet that hurt.*

Not that I saw my guys actually shove anyone, unlike

Her Highness' up there, who seemed to view it as a sport. But elbows and feet can be so careless, can't they? And this train was on a roll.

We covered a lot of ground, winding like a centipede through a warren of hallways and crossways, this-ways and that-ways. Until my head was spinning and I didn't have any idea where we were. But I guess the boys did, because the fluttering suddenly intensified, and then we were spilling out of a tight passageway into a huge, sunny room.

It actually wasn't sunny, of course, but it gave that impression. It was big, with high ceilings and chandeliers that rivaled Radu's, and a nice, soft yellow paint job. There were coordinating draperies over faux windows that didn't exist because vamps hate windows, and mirrors to reflect the light around, and a lot of healthy-looking plants spilling over their containers onto gleaming white-and-yellow-veined marble floors.

The flora wasn't so much a surprise after I spotted Caedmon, over by a wall, arguing with Louis-Cesare.

I couldn't see them very well because the consul's huge guards had stopped in front of me, making a very serviceable wall. One that towered almost two feet above my head, which one of my entourage was still trying to comb out. I pushed him away, and peered through a gap in the wall at the action, the sound of which floated clearly across the room, because the acoustics in here were pretty great.

And because neither man was bothering to lower his voice.

"—could have been anyone!" Caedmon was saying. "There are other *vargar*—"

"Who would have reason to hurt the consul?"

"Yes, in fact!" Caedmon's voice snapped like a whip. "Or have you forgotten that my dear brother-in-law just tried to kill her two weeks ago—along with the rest of her court?"

"And now his wife is here to finish the job."

Caedmon made an explosive sound of mingled anger and disgust. "My sister came to warn you of her husband's intent, else he likely would have succeeded! Yet now she turns around and tries to kill the queen herself? Are you mad?"

Louis-Cesare glared at him. "*Non, m'sieur,* nor am I stupid. Everyone knows your sister wants her son on the throne instead of her husband—"

"What does that have to do with anything?"

"—and coups begin with discrediting the former leader, do they not? Had Aeslinn's attack on this senate succeeded, his stock would be high—too high for her to successfully supplant him. But with him discredited and a stockpile of these superweapons at her command—"

"You *are* mad."

"—she could dislodge him and put her son in his place—"

"And promptly lose the war, having just crippled the Senate! She is not insane, vampire!"

"I agree, *m'sieur.*" Louis-Cesare was doing his haughty Frenchman routine, and he did it well. He was six foot four, but Caedmon still had something like eight inches on him. Yet he somehow managed to look down his nose at him anyway. "She is not insane. She is *diabolique.* Murdering the consul would throw the Senate into disarray, leaving her time to carry out her coup without having to worry about our invasion—"

"And afterward? She doesn't want the gods back any more than we do!"

"Even more of a reason to overthrow her husband, then. He is the one trying to bring them back, is he not?"

"Among others! He is hardly the only true believer, and if you continue to attack highborn fey, you're only going to add to their numbers! You understand *nothing* of the situation in Faerie—"

"And why is that? We ask you for information, and you refuse it—"

"Perhaps I don't trust you—imagine that!" Caedmon's eyes widened in pretend surprise.

Louis-Cesare's narrowed. "We are supposed to be allies, yet you tell us nothing and now your sister has tried to kill our consul—"

Caedmon was looking genuinely angry now. "For the last time, she had nothing to do with it!"

"Yet Lord Mircea saw evil intent, quite clearly, in her mind—"

"Where he had no reason to be! She isn't one of your creatures, vampire!"

"He had every reason, and do not change the subject—"

"I'll pursue any subject I damned well please. Or I would, but we are leaving your hospitality."

The last word had another of those inflections, one that made it sound like he'd said something else altogether. Something that started with *f* and ended with *u*, which made it really weird that Louis-Cesare was smiling at him.

It wasn't a nice smile, but still.

"*You* may go," Louis-Cesare said. "*She* cannot. She has been formally accused."

"You have no right to judge her!"

"On the contrary, the treaty clearly states—"

"That you need two witnesses, and at senatorial level, for one of her rank! You have *one*, and his motive can easily be called into question."

For the first time, Louis-Cesare looked confused. "What motive?"

Caedmon's own sneer was actually pretty good, if a bit worrisome. Usually he was Mr. Calm-and-Collected while the rest of us went to pieces, but not now. "Lord Mircea brings suit against my sister, and then graciously offers to drop the charges in return for me dropping my claim to his daughter. I know how such games are played, vampire, and better than you."

"You are accusing Lord Mircea of lying?"

And, uh-oh. Louis-Cesare's voice had just gone very quiet, which was usually the prelude to letting his rapier do the talking. But he was injured, and Caedmon was . . . Caedmon . . . and there'd been enough bloodshed tonight. I started trying to forge a path between the guards, who weren't budging.

"All packed, then?" That was the consul, suddenly moving forward on her own, without her guards, but with a creepy smile on her face. I couldn't see it, being behind her, but Caedmon's reaction was eloquent.

"I beg your pardon?"

"Your sister. You did say she was leaving us?"

"I—yes. We both are. I'll be taking her with me."

"Very well. I should like to wish her a safe journey. If she is available?"

"I . . . will go and check."

Someone touched my shoulder, and I looked around to find Mircea standing behind me. He pulled me over beside some yellow-and-white-striped chairs, but we didn't sit down. He put a hand on my cheek and looked into my eyes like he was trying to see something behind them.

Or someone.

"Are you all right?"

"She's not here," I said irritably.

"That's not what I asked."

"I'm fine. What's going on?"

"It's . . . complicated."

It usually was around here. I decided to cut to the chase. "Am I free to go? Or are they planning to pull out some fingernails first?"

A small frown appeared on the otherwise unlined forehead. "You helped the consul, possibly saved her life. If you hadn't realized that thing was riding her, and disrupted its concentration—"

"I also got a blade in her. How long has it been since that happened?"

Mircea's lips quirked. "Some time, I believe. But it was preferable to the alternative."

"So I'm free to go?"

"In a moment."

Why did I know he was going to say that?

"First I wish to hear about Dorina. You said she was talking to you. Has she done that before?"

"Not directly."

"Meaning?" It was sharp.

"Meaning, usually she just sends me these weird dreams—"

"What kind of dreams?"

I rubbed my eyes, and suppressed a yawn. I kept getting sleep, but not enough. Possibly because I was constantly being woken up in the middle of it. "More like memories. Your memories, mostly. She was hitching a ride on you a lot while growing up—did you know?"

He grimaced. "Eventually. I would have preferred to realize it before I spent quite so many nights in dissolute company."

"And in dissolute beds?"

He raised an eyebrow. "More like playing cards in rough taverns. Sometimes I wonder what you think of me."

So did I. But he'd been doing the good-father routine in the stuff Dorina had showed me, fighting to keep her—us—safe, and putting himself in danger to do it. I was about to ask how he'd got off that damned death boat, and if it was Dorina whose voice he'd heard, but I didn't get the chance.

"What has she shown you?" It was idle—too much so. Mircea and I don't make a lot of small talk.

"Why? What are you afraid of?"

"Nothing. But if you want to know about those days, you have only to ask. I could tell you—"

"But it would be from your perspective, wouldn't it?"

He didn't say anything, and his face—of course—gave nothing away. But, somehow, I knew I was right. "That's it, isn't it? You're afraid of me seeing things through her eyes. Is that why you told her not to talk to me?"

"No."

"Then why? Because it's caused some damned problems, Mircea!"

"And could cause more, if you allow it to continue."

His expression hadn't changed, but his voice was clipped, the way it got when he was angry—or afraid. He didn't process fear any better than I did; he just hid it better. We both had a tendency to lash out, to savage whatever was threatening us, even if that was each other. It had led to some truly spectacular fights in the past.

"I warned her to be careful," he told me. "Now I am warning you. Give yourself time."

"Assuming I have any."

I'd spoken without thinking, because I was still half-asleep. But of course he picked up on it. And pulled me even farther away from the others—I didn't know why. With the acoustics in here, and with most people's hearing, we could be eavesdropped on from anywhere in the room.

Or maybe not.

"Explain," he told me, but I was preoccupied, watching Burbles and the other guys suddenly start drifting this way.

"What are they doing?"

"Putting up a screen."

"What?"

"Creating mental white noise." Mircea's voice was impatient. "No one will hear us."

"No one but them."

"They're family."

Maybe yours, I thought, watching Burbles flutter his fingers over a tray of hors d'oeuvres that was being passed around. "Are these *fey*?" he asked delightedly.

"Yes." The blond fey holding the tray bent down a little, to provide better access, since he was tall enough to give Olfun a run for his money. And I suddenly understood why the consul had NBA-sized guards.

She was damned if anyone was going to tower over her people in her own house.

"Dory." That was Mircea.

"I don't know if I can explain," I told him. "I don't know what Dorina wants, since I haven't been able to talk to her. But I've been getting mixed messages."

"Such as?"

"On the one hand, she's sending me dreams about that mission you were on back in Venice, to find the people murdering vampires for their bones. You remember?"

"Vividly."

Yeah, I guessed so. "Anyway, I haven't got the whole story, but I saw enough to realize that the same thing is happening now. Only with fey bones instead of vampire—"

"Yes, Kit told me what you said. So that's how you knew what was in those weapons."

"Partly. There were other clues, but I wouldn't have made that connection without Dorina, and I think she sent it to me on purpose. Like she picked up something when we were at the fights a few days ago, and wanted me to know."

"And the other?"

"What?"

"The other hand. I assume there's also been a downside?"

"Yeah, well." I thought about the last few days. "That's one way of putting it."

"So delicious," Burbles was saying. "So, so good. What was that again?"

The fey waiter said a word I couldn't pronounce.

"And what is that?"

"I do not know the equivalent in English. Stuffed . . . field mouse?"

Burbles turned slightly green.

"How exactly would you put it?" Mircea demanded.

I hesitated. I don't claim any diplomatic abilities myself, but even I have limits. And telling somebody "There's a chance your daughter might hate you and also me and has every reason to do so" is a bit much.

But as it turns out, I didn't have to.

"I know what Dorina thinks of me," Mircea said grimly. "I locked her away. It was meant to be temporary, until you stopped growing and caught up."

"But it wasn't," I pointed out. "Why?"

The dark eyes glanced around the room, distracted— or disingenuous. "I've told you. I was afraid I couldn't raise the wall again once it fell. If you weren't compatible, and couldn't live as one, I would lose you both."

"As it was, you just lost her."

"I didn't lose her!" The dark eyes snapped back to me. "The situation wasn't ideal, but as you've seen, she wasn't trapped. Physically, yes, unless you were asleep or let your emotions get the better of you. But mentally she could go anywhere. Anywhere she could find an avatar, that is."

"And you decided that was enough for her."

It wasn't harsh, or even inflected. I didn't have the control over my voice that the vamps did, and right then I was too tired to try. But Mircea flinched anyway.

That must have really struck a nerve.

"I didn't think it was enough! But it was better than nothing—which is what I would have had otherwise!"

"What *you* would have had?" I felt my forehead wrinkle. "What about what she had? She could go flitting about, riding different people, but she wasn't in control of any of them. She can't just take over like that. Maybe in an emergency, but not reliably, and not for long."

It hit me suddenly that Dorina had been left just . . . watching things. She could get out, see the world, watch other people's families, lovers, children, but could never have any of her own. And wasn't that almost worse than the reverse? To be left watching others live while you have no way to influence anything, decide anything, plan anything . . .

Even with me. I chose where we went. Dorina just went along for the ride.

And now, after five hundred years, what did she want? Had anyone ever asked her? Had she ever even asked herself?

Maybe part of the reason she hadn't talked to me was that she didn't know what she wanted yet. I could relate. Until I met Claire, and finally found some sort of stability, I hadn't done a lot of planning, either. What was the point when you don't see a future anyway?

But now, after all this time, Dorina could have one.

Damn, it was a miracle she hadn't banished me already.

"Banished?"

Shit.

"Stay out of my head."

"You're projecting."

"Don't give me that. I couldn't project shit right now. My head feels like a lead balloon."

"Perhaps if you would cease beating it into hard things, it would not."

Mircea turned me around, and ran practiced fingers over my scalp. The bump was in the back this time, where I'd almost cracked my skull against the hard marble of the consul's wall, thanks to her sending me and everybody else in the area flying out of the way of her little storm. I couldn't complain too much, since I'd be a skeleton right now otherwise, but damn, it hurt!

Until Mircea's soothing fingers stole the pain away, better than a shot of morphine.

I drowsily watched Burbles, who was back at it again, I guess in the hopes of bettering interspecies relations. "What a lovely little molded salad, with all the tiny flowers in! Why, it's almost too pretty to eat—"

The server plucked it out of his hand, halfway to his mouth. "Sir. Please do not consume the tray ornaments."

"There's another way," Mircea murmured.

"Another way for what?"

"Out of this dilemma we find ourselves in."

I turned around to look at him, because there was something in his voice. "What dilemma?"

He frowned. No, it was more like a full-blown scowl, which I guess he could risk, being currently hidden from the room. Doubly so, since the consul's guards had also drifted over here, leaving us behind two walls of vamps and cut off from everything.

But it was still strange.

Like the small shiver that suddenly went up my spine.

"You and Dorina."

It was my turn to frown. "What about us?"

Mircea suddenly gripped my arm. "Do you think to hide it from me? I know exactly how powerful she is, what she can do. I know what she can do to *you*."

I shifted uncomfortably in my stiff, backless slippers. I wasn't ready to talk about this right now. I wasn't ready to talk here at all, where the walls had ears and Marlowe, damn him, was probably listening in no matter what Mircea said. Not that I thought I'd be any more prepared back home.

"We *will* discuss it now," Mircea said grimly. "If she already has this much access to your mind, there's no choice. We have to act, and act soon."

"Act how? What are you—"

"These new weapons. They aren't normal magic, the type the mages produce. Our kind can't manipulate that, can't use it. We can buy it, at a high cost, from others, but that's all. But this . . . The energy in those weapons was taken from the life force of the creatures providing it."

"What? Then the soul thing . . . is true?"

"Soul thing?"

"Something some of the fey believe. That their souls are, well—that somehow they end up in their bones. Ask Caedmon."

"I will." Mircea looked at the fey king, still arguing with Louis-Cesare. The expression did not bode well for him. "All we know for certain is that the weapons are utilizing life magic, the same kind we tap into when we feed. And that kind of magic we *can* utilize; we do so every day!"

"So?"

"So that cache that the mages stole back tonight, if we could find it again . . ." He licked his lips. It was such an uncharacteristic gesture that I stared. He didn't notice. "There should be enough."

"Enough for *what*? Mircea, what are you talking about?"

His eyes found mine again. "The problem with separating the two of you was always the amount of power it required. Especially now, with the age gap between Dorina and me insignificant. On my own, I cannot hope to contain her. But with the power in those weapons . . ."

I gripped his arm, the shiver a full-on shudder now. "Mircea! What are you saying?"

Dark brown eyes bored into mine, fierce and compelling. "I'm saying . . . that I might be able to rebuild the wall."

Chapter Forty-nine

I stared up at him. This close, he and Radu could almost have been twins instead of brothers. The arched brows, the patrician nose—just a little too straight for aquiline—the high cheekbones and the sculpted lips were all the same.

But no one would ever have any trouble telling them apart.

Radu had a slightly more delicate cast to the features, which had earned him the sobriquet "the Handsome," once upon a time. Mircea was plenty handsome himself, but it wasn't the same type. There was a sweetness to Radu, a gentleness that had somehow survived everything that had happened to him. His thick lashes and bright eyes had always reminded me of a stag: beautiful, regal, occasionally silly, one of nature's great works of art.

But lovely as it was, and as powerful as it could be at times, a stag was still prey.

And Mircea could never be that.

He was the wolf in the darkness, the eagle flying overhead, the predator you never saw coming. The eyes could melt with genuine feeling, or brighten with laughter, or charm or seduce or any of the other thousand tricks in his repertoire. But if you looked close enough, you could see them, even then: the watchful eyes of the predator, staring back at you.

I recognized them because I had them, too. I sometimes wondered if that's why we clashed so often. We were too alike: too stubborn, too suspicious, too . . . something. We'd never had an easy relationship; I doubted we ever would. But I wanted that relationship, no matter how much I'd denied it—wanted it fiercely.

And so did Dorina.

She might resent him, even hate him, but she loved him, too. I remembered that pang of longing she'd felt in the hall, while he searched for her. Remembered and experienced it all over again, because it echoed the same emotion in me. She loved him, however much she didn't want to; loved him despite knowing it wasn't returned; loved him even after he locked her away.

And now he was planning to do it all over again?

How could he do that?

How could he even *think* that?

"Because I want you to *live*." Hard hands gripped me. I struggled, but was too weak to break his hold, to do anything but stare up at him in disbelief and pain—hers, mine, ours, I wasn't sure anymore.

How could he *do this*?

"Listen to me!"

"I've listened to you for five hundred years, and what has it got me?"

"Life!"

I laughed, and it was cruel. I heard it in my voice, but couldn't stop it, didn't care. "Yeah, and I've enjoyed it so."

"More than you would have if I'd done nothing!"

I'd finally managed to pull away, and had started to walk off to clear my head, but at that I rounded on him. "How do you know that? How do you know *anything*? You don't know much about me, and less about her! Maybe she could have compensated in time; maybe we'd have reached some kind of balance. Or maybe not. Maybe we'd have been torn apart like all those other dhampirs, and died screaming, but you *don't know*. Because you had to interfere, to handle everything, just like you always do—how has that worked out, Mircea?"

"Better than the alternative!"

I spread my hands. "How? I've spent centuries scrabbling, half-mad, on the edges of a society that hates me, looking for a foothold I only found because of *her*. Meanwhile, she's been caged like some kind of animal, only able to emerge when there's something to kill, abandoned, alone—and now you're planning to do it all over again!"

A hand like steel found my arm. "I am planning to save your *life*! Something you will not have if she banishes you. And you've thought about it—don't deny it. That word came from your head, not mine. You've thought—"

"Maybe I have." I struggled with his hold and went nowhere. "It doesn't mean she'll do it!"

"And it doesn't mean she won't. Vampires have a constant war between our two natures, pulled by the beast on one hand and our humanity on the other. Forced to reconcile the two because we don't have a choice. You do. And now so does she—"

"I'm not listening to this."

"Yes, you are. For once you are going to listen—"

"For once? For *once*?" I stared at him.

"You never listen—"

"You never talk!"

"Well, I'm talking now." It was grim. "We vampires have no choice but to blend our two natures, to come to equilibrium or to go mad—and some do. Unable to reconcile the monstrous part of themselves that every human has, but that every human does not have to *feed*. We cannot hide from what we are; we have to prey on others to survive. But we cannot give in to it utterly, or we risk becoming the monsters we are so often thought to be. It is a constant balancing act and there are times—oh, yes, there are times—when we would love to banish one part or the other.

"What if we *could*?"

"You wouldn't. Go back to being human?" I laughed, because that comment deserved it. "No vampire would do that."

"You might be surprised. But that isn't the offer on the table, is it? Not you becoming human but Dorina becoming vampire. Fully, completely, with no human side to hold her back, to rein her in. You've thought about it—*don't you think she has, too?*"

"Damn it, Mircea! You can't just—" I stopped the explosive comment I'd been about to make, tried to compose myself. Arguing with him made me see red faster than anything else on earth, and then nothing productive happened. "She could do it," I admitted, after a moment. "I know she could." I met his eyes. "But she *hasn't*. And she's had plenty of time."

Mircea didn't even blink. "She's had a few weeks. To our kind, that is nothing. To her, it is nothing. Her viewpoint today—if she even knows it yet—may not be the same tomorrow. Or next week or next month or next year. The fact is, she can banish you at any time, force you out and take over, and you have no defense against it. Save one."

"You mean by doing the same thing to her."

"Not the same thing. She will still be alive."

I looked at him, and wished I had his way with words. Wished I had a way to make him see. "That's not living."

It never had been.

But I didn't have the words, and maybe there weren't any, because Mircea was as stubborn as I was. He'd found a solution once, at great cost to himself, when everybody had told him there wasn't one. It hadn't been perfect, but from his perspective, it had kept both versions of his daughter alive.

Why change it now?

But for me . . . it wasn't that easy. I hadn't known what was happening before, hadn't even known Dorina existed. Much less the price she'd paid for my continued survival. And now that I did, how could I send her back to that? What right did I have to send her anywhere?

"You have the right of any creature to survive."

"Get out of my *head*!" I turned away, furious and frustrated, and afraid—more than I wanted to admit. And angry at myself for feeling that way.

Because she'd never given me cause, had she? Not once. And she'd helped me, all those times she'd fought for me. Maybe I hadn't needed it, but maybe I had. Maybe there'd been things she'd picked up on that I hadn't seen, dangers I hadn't noticed.

Like tonight. I'd been sleeping, dead to the world. The faint static of that creature's mind hadn't even registered. I would have slept right through everything, and awakened to the death of a queen and a world in chaos.

But Dorina had heard.

And while I might have been the one to throw that knife, she'd gotten me there.

Or maybe she'd just done it out of self-preservation, since our losing the war would hurt her, too. Like maybe all those times she'd helped me in the past were because she thought me weak and incapable, and hadn't been willing to risk it. I just didn't know.

And neither did Mircea.

I turned back around. "I want to talk to her."

"Dory!"

For a moment, Mircea looked like he was about to lose his cool. The eyes flashed amber bright; the nostrils flared; the hawklike aspect of his features became a little more pronounced. Because I have the same effect on him that he does on me.

But he reined it in.

"That would be unwise," he told me tightly. "If she knows what we're planning, she could, and likely would, evade it—"

"*We* aren't planning anything—"

"But you should be! Now, while she's asleep. When she wakes up, we won't be able to talk. When she wakes up—"

I didn't hear the rest of the sentence. It was drowned out by a burst of noise, shockingly loud, only it wasn't. Just the usual soft music, idle conversation, and *click, clink* of glasses, which I hadn't realized had been blocked out until it suddenly broke over us again.

I stared around, like Mircea himself was doing. Something had cut through the sound barrier his masters had created, but I didn't know what. And I couldn't see what was happening in the room, because there were still two rows of vamps in the way.

Until, suddenly, there weren't. They parted, straight down the middle, leaving a long, cleared path lined with vamps on either side. And at the end—

Was a woman.

No, make that a fey, beautiful and golden haired, her shining locks cascading to the floor and explaining the consul's current hairstyle. But there was no Goth vibe here, no reds and golds and vague creepiness. There were only big blue eyes and a simple blue gown and a peach and pink complexion, like something out of a Victorian painting of the perfect woman. Or girl, because she looked about sixteen.

She wasn't.

Efridis was almost as old as her brother Caedmon, and he was ancient by human standards. But looking at her, it was almost impossible to believe. The air of innocence was palpable.

Which was why it was so strange to feel the tide of rage suddenly pouring through me.

I had time to say, "Uh-oh," not that I could hear it over the roaring in my ears. I had time to look at Mircea, who was staring back with alarm on his face. I had time to feel the strangest sensation, like I was about to vomit up the world.

And then Dorina tore out of me, as I'd seen her do in Mircea's presence once, barely a ripple on the air, almost invisible unless you knew what to look for. But I did. And even if I hadn't, it wouldn't have mattered.

I'd have caught on when Efridis started screaming.

Everything after that happened really fast. I saw something emerge from the fey queen, another ripple in space. But not one rising calmly or charging out determinedly, but *ripped* out of her by Dorina, right before they went writhing into the air, and what felt like a couple extra atmospheres descended on the room. Mirrors shattered; vases toppled; fey and vampire alike hit the floor. Except for Mircea, who grabbed me right before something smashed into us like a freight train.

It sent me flying back against the wall for the second time that night, something I wasn't sure my body could take. But Mircea had gotten behind me and absorbed the blow. And then held me as I screamed and fought, feeling like my insides were being ripped out, because Dorina was back—and she'd brought company.

Whatever she'd planned, it had gone horribly wrong, because the creature was far more powerful than her, than both of us. I felt Mircea invade my mind, trying to help, but it easily flung him out as well. But it obviously didn't know my father, because the next moment he was back, and he'd brought company, too.

A lot of it.

I didn't know all of Mircea's masters, but suddenly I could see them, and not just the ones gathered around us. A brunet sat on a sofa a few floors down, a book falling from his suddenly motionless fingers; half a dozen beat-up guards, drinking around a table in Washington State, looked up all at once, as much in sync as if they'd been practicing for weeks; a few dozen more dropped what they were doing in Las Vegas, heads turning unerringly toward New York—

But it wasn't enough.

This thing, this fey queen's power, was like nothing I'd ever encountered. Shocking, cutting, cruel. And pervasive.

It felt like every cell was being attacked at once. I tasted blood in my mouth, saw it spurt from my lips. Felt my heartbeat start to slow—

And then my field of vision abruptly widened—or "pulled back" might be more accurate. Because, suddenly, I could see beyond the confines of the country, Earth like a blue ball spread out beneath me. One with golden sparks lighting up everywhere.

Mircea's family, spread around the globe, a lightning storm of power all coming online at once at their master's call.

And while the thing inside Efridis was strong, so were we. Everywhere she looked now were faces, staring at her. Every move she made was countered, not by the power of one or two, but by dozens, hundreds, thousands. I'd had no idea Mircea's family was so large, no idea at all—

And then the globe caught fire, as a few million more sparks flared in the darkness.

"The Senate," someone said, but I didn't know who. I was watching a globe full of light come screaming at us. A ball of fire roaring with the combined fury of all the Senate's masters and their families, all at once.

I didn't feel it when the blow landed, because it didn't land on me. But I felt the creature get torn out of me, felt it go flying back to its home, saw the fey queen get lifted off her feet by the force of it and slammed back against the wall, hard enough to go crashing through it.

And then they were gone, all those minds, all that power, leaving me panting in Mircea's arms as Caedmon dove for his sister, as the consul stepped daintily forward, as Louis-Cesare ran for me. And as Marlowe's voice boomed out from somewhere across the room.

"I believe we have our second senatorial witness, majesty!"

"You know, I do believe you're right," the consul said, peering through the hole in the wall at her currently unconscious guest. She looked at her guards, streaming at her from all over the room, and bared some fang. "Take her."

Chapter Fifty

Mircea, Venice, 1458

Mircea crawled desperately through a punishing storm. It would have been hard enough with the streets of the Rialto running like rivers, splashing mud and muck in his face to match the torrent bucketing down from the skies. And with two broken legs dragging behind him, torturing him with every move. And with a hysterical woman pulling on him, when he was already going as fast as he could!

But then a voice sounded an alarm.

He jerked his head up, panic spreading through him. But it hadn't come from a party of foot soldiers, running at him with bare blades, as he'd been expecting. This voice was as pure and clear as a bell, and echoing as loudly inside his head—along with that of every other vampire in Venice.

Because that's the kind of power the praetor possessed.

He stared around in shock as he listened to her low, husky tones order the entire city to find and kill him.

"Come on, come on!" The red-haired woman was tugging at him, half out of her mind with fear even without hearing the latest disaster. "We have to go!"

"We have to hide!" Mircea snarled back, because the pain was excruciating, and his head was spinning, and something very like horror was spilling through his veins. "The praetor just called for my death!"

"Well, of course she did." The woman looked at him like he was mad. "What did you expect?"

"Something else!"

He crawled into the shadow of the great bridge, not having strength enough to pull shade around him just now, and hoped it was enough. The angry skies had lowered a black veil over Venice, blocking out the moon, the stars, everything except the lightning storm, like a bunch of devilish sprites dancing through the clouds above them. Mircea watched it through a haze of shock and pain.

Or, he tried to.

"What's happening? Why are you stopping? What—" Mircea grabbed the red-haired woman's skirts and jerked her down.

A moment later, they huddled together in silence, watching a group of five vampires come running out of the square. But instead of looking around, searching for them, they were looking at the Grand Canal, which currently had as many white peaks as the ocean. One of the biggest slammed into the quay a moment later, drenching the vampires and sending them staggering back. And then a voice called out—a normal one this time—from a side street.

"Over here! I think I saw them!"

The vampires didn't pause to argue. They ran in the direction of the voice, not least because there were porticoes and colonnades that way to provide shelter from the storm. And a moment later, Mircea felt Dorina flit back to him.

"That was you?"

"Yes. I planted an idea in one of the guards, but it won't fool them for long."

"I'll heal in a moment," Mircea said, hoping it was true. But the vampires who mended hurts so quickly were far older than he, and had large families from which to draw strength. He had a hysterical woman, the disembodied consciousness of his daughter, and half a body. He was going to die, wasn't he?

And then he felt like an ass, because if it hadn't been for his little group, he'd be dead already.

Dorina had been with him on that awful ship, something he would have given a great deal to spare her. But he had reason to be grateful for her presence: she'd been the one to flit down to the hold, to wake the red-haired woman, and to persuade her to reactivate the portal. And then to help Mircea break through that strange paralysis long enough to crawl a few yards, near to where a group of unconscious vampires lay slumped by the mainmast.

He hadn't been much better off himself, dizzy and prone to body parts suddenly going unresponsive. And he'd been confused as to what, exactly, he was doing here, instead of finding a way to slip into the water without anybody noticing. But that wasn't likely, and he assumed Dorina had a reason—

And then he'd felt it, the dim thrum, thrum, thrum of the portal's energy, radiating upward from the ceiling of the room below.

For a moment, his eyes had widened and his heart had leapt, because portals didn't have sides, did they? They weren't like doorways: they could be entered from any angle, and still dump you out . . . wherever they went. It wasn't guesswork. He'd used one before; he knew how they worked!

So, if he could just break through these boards . . .

But he couldn't.

They were nothing special, just normal boards, sturdy yet weathered by sun and sea. Normally, smashing them to bits would have been the work of a moment. But today, nothing was normal. And if Mircea's limbs were clumsy, it was nothing compared to his hands.

They flopped against the deck like two beached fish, all but useless. He couldn't get any strength behind them, and even if he did manage to break through the damned planks, how was he supposed to remove them in his current state? How was he supposed to pry up the deck of the ship without bringing every sailor on board down on his head?

It was impossible!

He lay there, furious and terrified, feeling the portal's power quite literally just below him, but having no way to access it.

Dorina, he thought, his gut twisting. He had to find a way to persuade her to leave, before she saw . . . what she was going to see. He didn't want her to remember him like that. He didn't want—

And then something hit his face.

A single drop of water ran down his cheek, distracting his thoughts. And then another, and another, the soft patter steadily growing harder. It cut through the greasy feel of that terrible smoke, still billowing this way even as the winds picked up and the rain came down and the ship began to rock slightly, side to side. And as Mircea looked skyward . . .

At a miracle.

He'd felt like laughing, even in that awful place. Because God—and yes, there was a God; he knew that because the Divine delighted in tormenting him—had decided he'd suffered enough. And sent him salvation in the form of one of Venice's famous November storms.

A big one.

The skies hadn't cracked open so much as torn asunder, suddenly deluging the small ship with a solid sheet of rain. Along with wind and lightning and cresting waves that sent the vessel sliding around on its anchor. And mages yelling and rushing to get their cargo secured, so that it didn't tip into the sea.

Mircea barely noticed. He had started scrabbling at the deck, desperate to break through, and failing because his hands still didn't work. But his elbows did. Enough, at least, for him to punch through the boards with brute force, and then to tear at them with teeth and elbows and wrists, heedless of the sound now, most of which was covered by thunder in any case.

Speed was all that mattered.

Yet he still hadn't been fast enough.

Somebody saw him; he didn't know who, but it didn't matter. Not with hands suddenly grabbing him, dragging him back. But the portal had seized him, too, catching the fist he'd accidentally dangled too low and pulling, pulling, pulling.

Hence the broken legs—or shattered, more like—that had resulted from the tug-of-war between a powerful magical object and half a dozen men. The portal won, in the end. But it was safe to say that Mircea still lost.

Maybe God wasn't finished toying with him, after all.

But then, as he was dumped onto the flooded streets of the Rialto, still desperately fighting to get away, he received his second miracle: the portal shut down. Not correctly or properly—at least, he assumed not. Since it cut several mages and a vampire in half in the process, when the shortcut through space they'd been using suddenly disappeared.

The two mages were human; they had not continued to move for long.

But the vampire was different, and he wasn't one of the poor sods destined for the rendering pots, but one of those putting them there. Worse, he was a master. And even half a master, Mircea had discovered, was far more powerful than he.

The vamp might be trailing half his intestines behind him, but he still had two good arms. And an excess of shattered boards that had followed them through the portal. Quicker than Mircea could parry, almost quicker than he could see, the master grabbed one of them, snapped off the end to give it an edge, and—

Looked down in alarm, at the similar piece of wood sticking out of his own chest, the bloody tip glistening in the latest lightning blast.

Mircea had a second to see the red-haired woman standing over the body, her eyes huge, her hands still gripping the other end of the piece of wood. And then the master was hacking at him again and again and again, trying to finish the job. And Mircea was grabbing up a shard of his own, his fingers suddenly quicker, steadier, with the feel of an invisible hand covering his own.

Dorina, he thought, and she was savage, slashing across the creature's throat, releasing a torrent of black blood, sticky as tar. It flooded over him—them—as he panted in shock and pain. And struggled to get away with the creature's body pinning his legs.

But he was too clumsy and it was too heavy. Leaving him nowhere to go as the master slowly raised his head, the dark slash in his throat mirroring the grinning rictus on his face. And grabbed for his makeshift stake again, because the horror hadn't bled out yet!

"Die! Die! Die!" Mircea was yelling and stabbing and scrabbling back, agony shooting up his spine as the true state of his legs became apparent. And as the master got the makeshift stake in him, more than once. And as Mircea kept twisting and turning and scuffling and slashing, to make sure it didn't hit his heart—

And then watching as the master's head went bouncing across the cobbles and fell into the canal, when a lucky strike finally finished the job.

He lay there, watching it bob among the waves for a moment, his mind blank with shock.

Until somebody slapped him.

The red-haired woman, Mircea realized, staring up at her.

"Move!" she screamed.

He moved. Not running or even walking, both of which were out of the question now, but crawling, if dragging himself by the arms counted. Because passing out, or cursing, or any of the other things one usually did in these cases, wouldn't get him anything but dead. And he didn't want to be dead.

But several hard minutes later, he could still see the space where the portal had been, sandwiched between the two stalls that had fallen over in the gale.

And right after that, the praetor's voice had shaken whatever tiny hope he'd had left, leading him to his current state, sprawled against the side of the bridge, wondering if the booming sounds from above were God's hysterical laughter.

Then the woman slapped him again.

"I said, where are the *rest*?" she screeched.

Mircea blinked up at her, mud and water and gore dripping off his face. "The rest of what?"

"Your companions! When are they coming for us?"

Mircea started wondering if fear had driven her mad. "Would I be in this condition if I had companions?"

She stared at him. And then she shook him. "What are you talking about? Where is the Circle? Where is *Abramalin*?"

"You know Abramalin?"

She stared at him some more, although he wasn't sure

how well human eyes could see in this light. But she must have seen something, because she managed to slap him again. "You weren't sent to get me *out*?"

"Cease attacking me, woman!" Mircea snapped, and pushed her.

From his perspective, he'd barely touched her, but he sometimes forgot vampire strength. Or perhaps she slipped on the torrent raging across the cobblestones—he didn't know. He knew only that she hit the side of the bridge, bounced off, and fell down the embankment.

Cazzo!

He scrambled after her, afraid she would drown. And she might have; the canal was roiling like the ocean, as if the whole city had somehow floated far out to sea. But she wasn't in it.

"Abramalin! È un figlio di puttana! Un porco demonio, un miserabili pezzi di merda!"

Mircea blinked. He didn't know if Abramalin was the son of a whore, but he was absolutely spawn of the devil and a miserable piece of shit. "He sent you in and then abandoned you," he guessed, as she floundered around in a boat full of fish.

"He said he just wanted information! He said I wouldn't get hurt!"

"Sounds familiar."

She wiped her face, which didn't help because the rain was still pelting down. "You, too?"

Mircea nodded, before remembering that she couldn't see it. "Yes. And now we're both in desperate danger, but if you're with Abramalin, you must be a witch. You can get us out of this!"

Sprawled among the fish, she looked up at him for a startled moment, her face blank. And then began laughing hysterically. Mircea went back to worrying for her sanity.

"I'm what's known as a scrim," she finally managed to gasp, as if that made things any clearer.

"What?"

"You know, like the curtains?"

Mircea scowled. "I'm not a mage! I don't know what that means!"

"It refers to my kind being like curtains that block out the sun, leaving a room dark inside. Magicless."

"Then you're not a witch."

"I'm a witch as much as any of them!" she snarled, probably because she'd just tried to get out of the boat, slipped on fish, and landed on her backside. "But I don't make enough magic for anyone to detect it. My kind make good spies."

"So you're a spy?" Mircea said, because frankly she didn't look like one.

"I'm an idiot," she spat. "I came to Venice because I have one talent, one I hoped to turn into a fortune and spite them all, everyone who always told me how useless I was! But, instead, I listened to Abramalin, and his stupid stories about the future of the magical community—the same one that always despised me! And now look—"

Mircea cut her off. "What talent?"

"Glamourie." She was thrashing about in fish guts, in what to her was probably total darkness, but that didn't seem to have dampened her spirits any. "'Go to Venice,' they said. 'The courtesans there live like queens,' they said." She slipped again, and ended up draped across the side of the craft, cursing. "If this is a queen, I'd rather be a commoner!"

"Glamourie," Mircea repeated, hope dawning. "Then you can disguise us!"

"I could disguise *myself*," she corrected. "I don't have enough magic for two. And it doesn't matter, anyway, when I can't disguise my scent. Or don't you think I'd have walked away before this?"

Mircea felt like battering his head against the boat, but he was hurt enough.

"Abramalin, the bastard, was supposed to send someone to get me," the woman continued, ripping her skirts to get them free of a nail. "But the damned praetor changed locations, and I couldn't get to the rendezvous for a week or so. She didn't want anyone getting wise to her little scheme—"

"To kill the consul and take over," Mircea said, as things finally made sense.

The woman nodded. "The weapons she was making

from all those bones would give her the edge she needed when they dueled, and she wasn't taking chances. I found out everything, but no one ever came to get me out! Just left me for dead. Who cares about a damned scrim? I should have known—"

She cut off when Mircea shook her. "Wait! You're saying you can do magic, you just need more power?"

"I—yes. Something like that. Why?"

He looked behind him, up the little stretch of beach.

"I have an idea."

———————

"Oh God! Oh God, oh God, oh God, oh God—"

"Be silent!" Mircea hissed.

"I've never done anything—oh God!" And then the witch grabbed him, her eyes reflecting the lightning above them. "I'm going to be sick," she told him calmly.

And then she was.

All over him.

Mircea didn't care. He was already waist-deep in water, with waves crashing into him on the regular, washing away worse things than that. Much worse.

He held on to the little boat full of fish. And tried to keep the waves from slamming the damned thing into his half-healed legs. Something he couldn't very well prevent and hold on to the *briccole*, the wooden pillars used for docking, at the same time!

He and the witch were down a little way from the bridge, near where the vampires had been doused earlier. The side of the canal was built up here, to make a decent pier. Enough to hide them from eyes on the quayside, if they didn't look down. And they wouldn't, not with what they were about to see.

That was the hope, anyway, Mircea thought, fighting with the boat. It was an old hulk of a thing, a repurposed gondola with its once-shiny paint now mostly gone and the wood beneath cracked and splitting. Which was less of a problem than whether it would stay afloat!

"They're coming." He felt Dorina rejoin him, after briefly flitting about the nearby streets.

Mircea was surprised it had taken them this long. The

first five vampires had been nobodies, just hunting in local taverns and rousted out by the urgency of the praetor's command. But her real troops were out now, and augmented by whomever they could press into service. There must be literally thousands of vampires on the streets, looking for them.

And thanks to Dorina's whispers in the leaders' ears, most of them were now coming this way.

How long? He asked her mentally.

Now.

Damn! He grabbed the witch, who had been hugging a *briccola* to stay upright. "Do it!"

She swallowed and looked at the boat, which had a mage and a vampire in it. Or, to be more precise, half of each, two of the bodies from the fight at the now-vanished portal, wedged in and weighted down by piles of fish and nets to look like they were sitting up. One wore Mircea's face, the other her own. And either she was low on power, or she had overestimated her gift, because Mircea's doppelganger had one eye higher than the other, and a terrifying grin on his face, while hers . . .

Well, that would cure a man from going to brothels, he thought wildly.

But perhaps it would be good enough from a distance.

"I'm going to let the boat go, and then you do it, all right?" He repeated the plan, because she wasn't looking all right.

"I hope this works," she told him rapidly. "I haven't done this much. Or any. I mean, when I was younger, before they realized . . . I had the usual training, but I don't actually use . . . I mean, I never—"

Mircea fought an urge to shake her. "It's all right. Just try to concentrate."

"Yes." She swallowed again. "When—when did you want me to—"

"Now."

"Now?"

Mircea's head jerked up, because all of a sudden he could feel them. And by God, it was an ocean of vampire power surging their way. Irresistible, unstoppable, overwhelming. They were both going to die!

"Yes, now! Now, now, now!"

"All right—"

"Now!"

"Stop yelling at me!"

"NOW!"

"Then launch the damned boat!"

He didn't have to launch it so much as let the sea take it. He shoved it, nonetheless, as hard as he could, out into the swollen canal. Which grabbed it like a child with a new toy.

Mircea grabbed her, jerking the woman back among the *briccole*, and slamming them both up against the canal, where the raging sea had carved a shallow channel into the side.

He couldn't see the vampires, assembling somewhere above them. Could barely even see the boat, through the water that kept hitting him in the face, and the mountain-like waves. Couldn't see anything—

But someone else could.

"There! In the boat! They're getting away!"

He had a brief moment to hear the shout taken up by what sounded like an army. And then swords being dropped and boots being shed, as the praetor's guards prepared to jump in after them. And yet still the witch did nothing.

And neither could Mircea, for fear of being overheard.

Wait, she mouthed, as he glared.

Wait! as he shook her.

Wait, a pox take you!

And then a lightning bolt flashed, blindingly bright, and thunder boomed, so close and so loud that Mircea almost jumped out of his skin. And finally—finally—the witch threw out a hand, while everyone cowered in fear and the elements roared and the little boat, storm tossed and tempest rocked—

Went up like a powder keg had gone off.

Make that a hundred powder kegs, Mircea thought, pushing the woman the rest of the way into the water. And shielding her as best he could as explosion after explosion tore through the night. They displaced the waves in a huge trough around what had been the boat; they sent what looked like burning orange fireworks into the formerly darkened night; they lit up the entire expanse of waterfront, including the witch's amazed face, resurfacing with a gasp, because she hadn't expected that, either.

So that's what half a skeleton's worth of vampire bone gets you, Mircea thought, as the praetor's men shouted, and the winds blew, and what was left of the little craft sank beneath the waves, to be carried away by the tide.

Chapter Fifty-one

I slept for over a day. And, for a wonder, nobody bothered me this time. Well, almost nobody.

I blinked my crusty eyes open to find another pair staring back at me. They were blue, a lovely almost-violet shade that human eyes never achieve without help. And huge, like those of an anime character come to life. And startled, because I guess they hadn't expected to be suddenly looking into mine, either.

A small creature let out a bleat and stumbled away, into the middle of my bedroom floor, because somebody had brought me to Claire's. He hunched down with arms over his head, like he thought I was about to strike him. And then just stayed there, shaking in fear.

I didn't move.

The shaking increased for a moment, and the arms tightened. But when nothing happened, they loosened enough for one large, purple eye to peer out from underneath. It flicked toward the door, which was halfway open, but the owner didn't budge.

I didn't, either, because I'd recognized my guest, and wasn't particularly worried about being attacked by a half-dead troll kid. Not that he was looking half-dead now. I hadn't expected Olga's rescue to be on his feet anytime soon, even in an obviously shaky sort of way, much less to be exploring the upper floors of the house.

But trolls are damned hardy, more so than me. I felt stiff and starved and badly in need of a drink, but I didn't want to freak out the kid. So I just stayed there, unmoving, until he slowly, slowly, slowly stretched into a more or less standing position.

He had dark brown hair, thick and shaggy and completely unlike the twins' baby-fine variety. He also wasn't the usual gray-green, but more of a gray-teal, with bluish undertones to the skin. He had the small mouth and round face of a child, and even a somewhat smallish nose, which for trolls is more telling. To the point that I wondered how young he actually was. And then there were those eyes, framed by long, thick, dark lashes.

He was freaking adorable.

But he was also still hunched over somewhat, despite the impression I had that he was standing straight, or as straight as he could. Claire had put him in one of her old hippie shirts, loose and flowy and painter's-smock-y, which was enormous on him, so all I could see was a head and some teal-colored toes. I supposed it was a miracle that he was getting around at all, but the posture looked uncomfortable. I wondered why—

Oh.

That was why.

The big eyes moved to my bedside table, and mine followed. And showed me that I'd had an earlier visitor in the form of my roommate, who knew a little about dhampir metabolism and liked to feed people. She'd loaded me up, probably because food had a tendency to disappear if left in the kitchen.

As a result, I had three whole sandwiches waiting for me. I slowly reached out a hand and took one, a nice fat BLT, because Claire understands that the B is the most important part. Thick-cut, peppery B, complemented by her own homemade bread and vine-ripened tomatoes and bacon jam and—

I heard my stomach grumble. And be echoed a second later by a similar sound from under Claire's smock of a shirt. My visitor was hungry, too.

I held out the sandwich. "It's okay," I said. "You can have it."

The little troll didn't move.

But he didn't run away, either, although his eyes kept

flicking from the sandwich to me to the door. Over and over. He was obviously frightened, but also hungry, but also frightened. . . . It was an impasse.

I decided to help him out and put the sandwich platter on the foot of the bed, pushing it as close to him as I could without getting up, which I somehow knew would spook him.

Then I sat back against the headboard and ate my own sandwich, because it smelled like heaven.

He watched me for a moment, eyes huge.

And then, faster than I would have expected—almost faster than I could see—he grabbed the remaining two sandwiches and fled, practically knocking Claire over in the process.

She'd been coming in the door with some laundry, and had to do an acrobatic maneuver to avoid getting mowed down. "What the—Hey! What are you—"

But the kid and his loot were already gone.

Claire stared after him for a moment, and then turned to me, astonishment on her features. "He's walking!"

"He's running around, stealing sandwiches," I corrected. "Good ones, too." I licked bacon grease off my fingers.

"He's supposed to be in bed!"

"Put a platter of sandwiches beside it. He'll never leave."

Claire blinked, considering that. Then she put down the laundry basket and went out again. I heard her talking to Gessa, and I guess they sorted it out, because she was back a moment later. She started putting towels away while I hauled my stiff-as-fuck body out of bed.

"I'm surprised Bulsi risked coming in here," she told me, from the bathroom. "He's really skittish."

"Bulsi? Is that his name?"

Claire nodded. "He woke up briefly yesterday. I managed to get some soup down him, and a little medicine, before he passed out again. He and Olga talked while I fed him."

"Did he remember anything about those mystery words?"

Claire looked confused for a moment, and then shook

her head. "He was barely conscious. They did a number on him, Dory!"

Yeah, I remembered. And felt my face flush in anger, which was stupid. The slavers didn't care about wiping out whole villages of fey; how much less would they care about a single child?

"I don't think he trusts anyone right now," Claire said. "She was lucky to get his name. Although she isn't too happy about it."

"Olga isn't?"

She nodded.

"Why not? What's wrong with . . . What was it again?"

"Bulsi. It means wart."

"What?"

Claire came out of the bathroom, having loaded me up with fresh-smelling towels. "Or lump or bump or protrusion. It's what his owner called him. Anyway, it doesn't matter; we're not keeping it."

"The name or the kid?"

"Don't look at me like that," she told me severely.

I'd hobbled over to the dresser for something to wear, so hadn't been looking like anything. I glanced over my shoulder. "Like what?"

"I'm *not* adopting him! We can't have any more house-guests, or this place is going to pop."

Couldn't argue with that.

"Anyway, Olga is trying to find his people, but it's not easy. She said his dialect is really strange. He might be from one of the mountain tribes. With all the fighting, a lot of groups went to the hills over the centuries and some never came down again."

"So how do we find them?"

Claire didn't immediately answer, being busy staring at my rumpled mess of a bed. And a few bloodstains here and there, from where I guess I'd bled through my dressing. I felt around under it now, and found a ridge of puckered skin, but no bullet hole.

Sometimes I love dhampir metabolism.

"I can do that," I said, as Claire started stripping sheets, but she just shook her head. Housework is how Claire works off excess energy. She sometimes complains about it, but if you try to take over, as I have plenty of times, she gets upset.

Unless she gets to boss you doing it, of course.

"Pillowcases," she instructed.

I blinked at her.

"They're in the bathroom closet, third shelf."

Really? Who knew? I put down some old jeans and moved to oblige.

"I'm not sure," she told me, answering my previous question. "Olga has been talking to the other slaves, trying to find out about her nephew. And she's also been asking about the boy—" She stopped abruptly. "What do you think about Kjeld?"

"Kjeld?"

"As a name."

I handed over pillowcases. "It's . . . all right. Why?"

"Well, Bulsi needs a new one, and there's not a lot to choose from. Most of the fey names, boys' ones anyway, are all about war. It's all 'Fighter with Helmet' or 'Warrior in Armor' or 'Spear of God.' And Olga says he'll probably never be a fighter, so a name like that would just make people laugh at him."

"There's other things in life than fighting," I pointed out.

And got an incredulous look from Claire.

"I do other things!"

"Name one."

"I paint. I play a mean hand of poker." I thought about it. "I know how to tango."

"Well, maybe you should teach the fey," Claire said, dumping my rumpled sheets into her now-empty basket and putting on new ones. "They're obsessed. Even the stuff that isn't war related is usually designed to strike fear into their enemies by reminding them of scary stuff. I like Calder, for example, but it means harsh and cold waters. Who would want to be called that?"

I agreed that Calder was a no go.

"And then there's nicknames, although they aren't any better."

"Nicknames?"

"You know how the fey are; everybody has a dozen

different names. But, apparently, other people are supposed to give them to you. You aren't allowed to just name yourself."

I shrugged. "So name him."

"I would, but there's all these rules. Even nicknames are supposed to say something about you. I asked the guards for recommendations, and you know what they came up with?"

"No idea."

"*Inn magri*: the thin one. Or *ópveginn*: the unwashed." Claire looked indignant. "He's not unwashed! I bathed him just yesterday! Or—even worse—*rotinn*, the broken. I mean, can you imagine?"

"Some of the guards are pricks," I agreed.

Claire gave me a sideways look. "They have one for you, too, you know."

"A nickname?"

She nodded. "They're calling you *ambhǫfði*. It means two-headed. I guess because of you and . . . you know."

I blinked. I wasn't sure how to feel about that.

"They say it's an honor. That all warriors have a string of nicknames, telling their story." She sighed. "They're probably going to give you more."

"Good," I decided.

"Good?"

"Then I can bore them with all my names, just like they do me."

Claire laughed. "They'll probably enjoy it! If you stay still long enough, they'll tell you all about how they got each of their names, and ask about yours. You can be trapped for *hours*."

Okay, that was slightly alarming.

"So, anyway, back to Kjeld. Do you like it?"

"What does it mean?"

She spread out some wrinkles in the sheets. "Large pot."

I grinned.

"Well, trolls like to eat! And a large pot of . . . whatever . . . means you aren't likely to starve. And you can even feast others!"

"Sounds good to me. Or you could just ask him what he wants to be called."

She shook her head. "I can't. He speaks almost no English, and even Olga can barely understand his dialect. But he'll be around a little while recovering, and I refuse to call him Wart the whole time!"

I laughed. I couldn't help it. I had a kid named Stinky.

"Anyway, word is that the mountain tribes have been hit hard by the slavers, because they're usually small groups, and too weak to fight back. But there's a lot of them, and they're spread over a large area, and sometimes they war with each other and"—she sighed—"it's a mess. And with the little one's condition, even if Olga does find his people, they may not claim him."

"So what happens then?"

"I don't know."

She fluffed pillows.

"He's very sweet, though."

More fluffing.

"He liked my soup."

I didn't say anything; I wasn't stupid.

I was seriously stiff, though. It felt like the years were finally catching up to me. A lot of years, I thought uncomfortably. All the freaking years.

Until I stretched, and oh. My. God. Oh yeah. Oh fuck yeah.

Claire was looking at me in sudden alarm. "Did you just crack every bone in your spine?"

"Yeah." It felt so good that I did it again. And then rolled my neck around, hearing what sounded like miniature fireworks going off.

"How do you *do* that?" She looked disturbed.

I extended my arms, laced my fingers together, and cracked my knuckles. "Like that."

"Stop it!"

I laughed, and contemplated chasing her around the room, cracking things at her. But that might impact the chance of breakfast, and I was out of sandwiches. "Food?" I asked hopefully.

"Get a shower. I'll have something for you by the time you're done."

That, I decided, was a plan.

Twenty minutes later, I was clean, moisturized, and

dressed. But not downstairs, because Claire had a tray waiting for me when I emerged from the bathroom. She'd also brought a chair for herself.

Uh-oh.

Not that I wasn't happy to have company, but Claire wasn't a big fan of bedroom eating. If this was a normal conversation, we'd be having it at the kitchen table. So it wasn't going to be normal, and judging by the closed door, she didn't want it overheard.

Well, crap.

"Relax," she told me. "I just want to fill you in."

"You want to fill *me* in?" I ambled over to the spread on the spread. "I thought that was my job."

"Louis-Cesare brought you home. He told me what—" A phone rang. She sighed, pulled it out of a pocket, rolled her eyes, and put it back.

"What was that?"

"Nothing. Sit down and have breakfast. Or lunch, I suppose."

"Lunch? Shouldn't it be dinner?"

Which is how I found out that I'd slept the clock around.

"Shit!" I was halfway to my feet, when Claire pulled me back down. "Sit. Eat. Listen."

Which is how I also found out some other things.

"So that's why we're talking behind closed doors," I said.

I was looking at a newspaper pic of Blue's latest activities. It showed an illegal market in some abandoned subway station. It didn't specialize in the fey per se, but in forbidden ingredients, the kind of stuff you couldn't walk into a normal potion shop and buy. But some of those did originate in Faerie.

Need a basilisk's egg for an unbreakable ward? Got you, fam. Want kelpie blood for detection-proof glamouries? Step right up. How about naga venom, for a poison no antidote can treat? Sure, for a price.

It was exactly the sort of place where you'd expect to find fey bones and the fey supplying them. Because butchering a bunch of helpless slaves is safer than constantly going into Faerie, isn't it? Or it was.

Until things suddenly got a lot Bluer.

All that was left now were broken cages and blood. Enough of the latter that I was assuming slavers number four and five had just bitten the dust. Along with probably a bunch of their crew.

What a pity.

Claire nodded. "If all this gets out—when it gets out— nobody knows what will happen. But that"—she fluttered a hand at the paper—"will probably get a lot more common!"

"I understand why Olga felt she had to tell the Elders," I said. "This affects the whole Dark Fey community. I just wish she could have held off for a few days, until we know a little more. We don't need riots—"

"Oh, there will be riots. You can count on it!"

I looked up. "You think it will be that bad?"

"The troll council does! That's why they're meeting now, to try to figure out how to spin it. But that's just it— there is no way! The Dark Fey believe that these weapons are powered by the souls of their people, souls that will never again be able to reincarnate. You can't spin that!"

She got up and started pacing.

"And the worst thing is, it's not just some crazy superstition. Louis-Cesare said it had some truth to it." She turned and put her hands flat on the bed. "He can't be right, can he? Tell me he isn't right!"

"I don't know," I admitted. "But Mircea confirmed that it was life energy. Vamps can tell the difference between that and regular magic. And there was plenty of it floating around, after the consul almost got incinerated."

"I don't believe it." She abruptly sat back down on her chair. "I don't believe it!"

She did, though. The green eyes had just gone incandescent.

"They're killing us! And Faerie—"

She cut off, and then just sat there for a moment, trying to absorb the implications. Because, yeah. There were a lot of them.

If Caedmon was right about the symbiosis between Faerie and its people, then whoever was making these weapons wasn't just using up the souls of individuals, but draining that of their entire world. Might explain why there were fewer *vargar* being born these days, I thought. And then I wondered how many more traits had been lost, how many more vital ways Faerie had been diminished.

I also wondered what had happened to all those souls that had been left behind through the years, but not used up. If the bones deteriorated enough, were they lost, too? Just dissipating into the ground of an alien world, and fading away?

I shivered, despite the warmth of the day and the residual heat of a very hot shower. How long had Faerie been bleeding out? Centuries? Millennia?

Because it had to be that long, right? Ever since our two worlds encountered each other, and people started going back and forth. And while the Light Fey seemed to have a policy of taking their dead back with them, what about the Dark?

They might have done it if left to their own devices, but they hadn't been. Not those who had been used as slaves and killed for sport. And if what Caedmon said was true, the soul of a Dark Fey this incarnation might be that of a Light Fey the next, so every group was hurt, every group weakened.

It was kind of stunning. And appalling. Which probably explained why Claire looked sick as well as furious.

"They should string her up publicly," said my pacifist roommate. "That *bitch*!"

"You mean Efridis?"

"Of course I mean Efridis! Who else?"

And there it was. The thing I'd been contemplating in the shower while my groggy brain woke up. The thing I'd been hoping to avoid, because I *knew* how this was going to go.

I didn't say anything for a moment, because I am a coward. And then I sighed, and womaned the hell up. "Ermh."

Chapter Fifty-two

Claire spun around, because she knows me, too.

"What?"

I licked my lips, and not just because there was jam on them. She had that weird elfin thing going on suddenly, with the too-translucent skin and the hair color not found in nature—not outside of a bonfire, anyway—and the too-bright eyes. I tried telling myself it was just the light streaming through my sheers, but I knew I was lying.

I had a theory about it, too. I didn't know if I looked any different when Dorina was around, except for a weird, glowy-eye thing I'd glimpsed once and tried not to think about. But I suspected that Claire's looks changed when her twin was awake.

Which meant that she was awake right now.

Making this not the time for this particular conversation.

But, as usual with my luck, it was already too late.

"You are *not* going to tell me that you still don't think it was her!" Claire demanded.

"Yeah, well. That would certainly be easier."

"Dory!"

"Look. I would love for Efridis to be guilty, okay? She's a threat, if not now then later, and it would make things nice and tidy since she's already in custody—"

"As she ought to be!"

"—but what I want is less important than the facts, and I'm sorry, but they just don't fit."

"*What* facts?"

I held up a buttery finger. "One. Efridis is a well-known

vargr, and she wants Aiden dead. Neither of these things is a secret. Yet she uses her best-known skill to attack us, *and* does it when her brother is here, who will almost certainly recognize it? And possibly recognize *her*?"

Claire frowned. "She might not have known Caedmon was here. It wasn't a planned visit and he only arrived that afternoon."

"And stayed outside most of the day," I reminded her. "Where any little passing birdie could have seen him. Unless she's a complete idiot, she'd do some recon before the attack, and Caedmon is hard to miss."

"But she used the *manlikans* first. She only came in herself after that didn't work!"

I nodded. "And the *manlikan* part I can understand. It could have been blamed on Aeslinn—it's his element, after all—and he hates Caedmon. Killing his rival's heir would give him revenge on an old enemy, and might make Caedmon less likely to support the Senate in the war. The fey lead their armies, and Caedmon would be less willing to risk himself without an heir."

She frowned. "So you think it was *Aeslinn*?"

"I don't know. I'm just saying that the *manlikan* attack didn't point the finger directly at Efridis. She could plausibly claim to have had nothing to do with it, and try her luck again later if it didn't work. Only . . . that's not what happened, is it? Instead, she charges in using her *vargr* abilities, despite knowing they would put a glowing neon sign over her head."

Claire shook her head. "It sounds crazy when you put it like that. But when it's your child . . . it's not that simple, Dory! You try to think clearly, but emotions get in the way. And she was so close—"

"Okay," I agreed. "Let's say she saw her best chance to make Æsubrand heir to two kingdoms slipping away, and decided to go for it. I had a similar thought that night: that the first attack had failed so a second method was being tried. Or that the first was just a feint to get the stairs cleared for the second—"

"And what's wrong with that?"

"What's wrong with it is that Efridis didn't need them

cleared. She already had a potential avatar in the room with Aiden, *and she knew that*."

"Dory, what are you talking about?"

"I'm talking about the night a couple weeks ago, when she and Æsubrand came here to warn us about Aeslinn's attack on the Senate. They kidnapped the kids so I'd listen to what they had to say, and Efridis was actually holding Stinky when I got here. So she knows he lives here, and since she had plenty of time to look around before I showed up, she probably knows he shares a room with Aiden."

Claire was looking seriously skeeved out. Probably at the reminder of her safe place being violated by the two people she hated most in the world. And of Æsubrand actually having his hands on Aiden, which, yeah.

But she got it together quickly.

"So they were here. What difference does—" She suddenly stopped, because Claire is not slow.

"It makes a difference," I told her, "because Efridis could have used Stinky instead. He was in the room with Aiden already, and while he's small, he's strong—all the Dark Fey are. Yet instead of taking over the kid lying a few feet away, she went all the way to the basement for an avatar, one who fought her viciously the whole trip, and came close to giving everything away. Why?"

Claire didn't say anything, although her jaw had a mulish set to it that I knew only too well. But she also hadn't walked away. She was listening.

I held up another finger.

"Two. The rune. If the attacker was Efridis, and she thought she was stabbing Aiden, she'd have had Ymsi remove the rune first. You told me yourself: it's her family heirloom. She knows how it works. She couldn't take it off when she and Æsubrand were here, because he'd already decided that his honor wouldn't allow him to kill a child—"

Claire scowled. "Or he's afraid it would damage his reputation as the great, purebred hope!"

"Maybe. But whatever the cause, he didn't allow it. He was holding Aiden when I showed up; Efridis was holding Stinky. He didn't trust her enough to let her touch him, even then, when they badly wanted our help, because he knew she could remove the rune. Yet, after going through so much trouble to get back in here, without her son this time, she *still* doesn't remove it? When she knows Aiden would survive any attack as long as it stayed on his person?"

Claire shook her head. "She was nervous. She thought Soini was the only *vargr* here. She didn't expect you— Dorina, I mean."

"No, she didn't. But I'd think somebody thousands of years old could handle a few surprises. And Dorina and I didn't start chasing her until *after* the child was stabbed. Yet, Efridis still didn't remove the rune, despite having time. And despite the fact that not doing so rendered the whole trip useless."

Claire frowned some more.

I held up a third finger. "Three. She didn't stab Aiden." The frown deepened. "You know damned well—"

"That trolls have lousy eyesight. And that the room was dark. And that Efridis wasn't supposed to know the troll kid was in there, because he only arrived that afternoon. And Stinky was snoring up a storm, as usual, so the nonsnoring kid had to be Aiden, right?"

"Yes!"

I ate some more omelet. It was cold, but still good. I swallowed.

"What about smell?"

Claire blinked. "What?"

"Trolls are used to living in darkness. Those caves that some of them call home are pitch-black, much worse than a bedroom with streetlight sifting in. Yet they navigate them just fine."

Claire crossed her arms at me. "I had doctored him. Bulsi, I mean, or whatever we're calling him. I wanted to make sure he didn't get an infection, since he still had open wounds. So the room reeked of medicine. Maybe Ymsi got confused."

I stuffed down some toast. "Wouldn't have mattered. Dorina woke up at the consul's in an unfamiliar room, and she knew exactly who had been in there—going back hours—what they were and how long they'd stayed, as sure as if she'd watched a film of it. And one of them smelled of medicine, too."

"Dorina is a first-level master. Ymsi is not!"

I shrugged. "So put a bunch of people in the basement and turn off the lights. Then send Ymsi in, and ask him who was there when he comes out. I'll bet money he can tell you."

Claire didn't say anything, so I worked on finishing up the omelet and toast and fresh fruit and coffee she'd brought me. And was still hungry when I had, because my stomach thinks it's fey. But at least I managed to clean the plate before Claire spoke again.

"Okay, now I've got a point."

I leaned back with the rest of my coffee. "Okay, shoot."

"Dorina." Her eyes were bright, not with anger, but with excitement. She thought she had me. "Louis-Cesare said that Dorina attacked Efridis as soon as she saw her. Why would she do that if she didn't recognize her?"

I shrugged. "Maybe because she'd just seen a powerful *vargr* attack the consul, and there was a powerful *vargr*, standing right beside the consul? Or maybe . . ."

"Or maybe what?"

"Or maybe she *did* recognize her, just not from the attack last night. Maybe she recognized her from the attack here."

Claire stared at me. "You just finished telling me that wasn't her!"

"No, I said the attack using *Ymsi* wasn't her. But that night, there were two of everything: two boys, two battles, and two very different attack styles. Why not two attackers?"

———

Claire did not like my theory.

No, that's not right. Claire *hated* my theory, and I knew why. I just didn't know what to do about it.

"Is there a problem?" Olfun asked, backing up abruptly when Claire slammed out of the room.

He had a phone in his hand, and it was ringing. But instead of answering it, he hit TALK and then OFF without so much as a pause in between. And then smiled sadly at me.

"My apologies. Reflex."

I decided not to ask what that meant.

He proffered it to me. It was the house phone. I needed to go get mine from my car, assuming it wasn't buried under half a ton of rubble, that was.

A blond eyebrow raised. "Want to tell me about it?"

It took me a second to realize that he didn't mean the phone.

"I have this theory," I told him, while gathering up my mess, "that maybe we had more than one attacker here the other night."

"But of course."

I looked up.

"No one can hold more than one or perhaps two *man-likans* at once," he informed me. "For each one, then, there was probably a fey warrior behind it. First creating and then directing it."

"Okay, but I was talking about the person running things. The mastermind. Which, if we're talking Earth magic, makes it look like Efridis or Aeslinn was behind the first attack."

"Why just the first? The king's sister is a well-known *vargr.*"

"Which is why I doubt she'd attack that way."

Both eyebrows went up. "That is something to think about."

"Yes, but Claire doesn't want to think about it." I sat on the edge of the bed. "Can't say I blame her."

Olfun took the tray, which won him a raised brow in return.

"I am not allowed to help?" he asked.

"I was under the impression that that sort of thing was beneath your dignity."

"Some might think so," he agreed gravely. "I think you saved our lord's grandson and heir, almost on your own, a few nights ago. While we took more than three minutes to wake up and assist." His lips twisted. "Perhaps you should carry the sword and I wear the apron."

"I don't wear an apron. Ruins the tough-chick look."

He smiled, but it didn't reach his eyes.

"You're serious," I realized.

"Of course. It is a serious matter."

"You're upset about three minutes? You guys saved the day!"

But Olfun shook his head. "Our performance was no less than shameful. I think it is why Reiðarr challenged you. He wished to regain some of his honor." He smiled slightly. "You were kind not to make him rue it."

It had looked like he was ruing it plenty to me, but I decided to emulate dear old Dad for once, and not say so. "He didn't lose any honor," I said instead. "Neither did you. Most people would be proud of that response time—"

"Would you be?"

"That's different. I was already here."

"As we should have been. We should have been sleeping in the halls with our weapons beside us. Instead, we were treating this as a holiday, a chance to enjoy some of the human world without a mission to distract us. And all the while, we knew the risks."

"You mean Efridis."

"Not just Queen Efridis. There are many at court who would be happy enough had the attack succeeded. Particularly now, with the Ice Prince separating himself from some of his father's . . . eccentricities. Fear of the gods' return was the main obstacle to many people supporting his claim to the combined throne. Now that they have reason to believe he would not follow in his father's footsteps, fewer have cause to prefer a child with mixed blood to one of pure, highborn heritage. Particularly when times are so troubled, and the child is young and untested, while Prince Æsubrand is a renowned warrior."

I scowled. "Yeah. That's why Claire left court. Someone killed Aiden's nurse and tried to kill him, so she took him and ran."

He shook his head. "A shameful thing, and in the palace!"

"And still unresolved. That's why Claire wants so badly for Efridis to be behind it all. If she was responsible for the attack here, and if the one at court was caused by someone in her pay, then everything works out nicely.

She's under guard, with Caedmon sitting on her to make sure she doesn't flit off somewhere, and Aiden is safe. Or as safe as he's ever likely to get. If not . . ."

"If not?"

"Then anyone could be behind this. Aeslinn, some of his court, some of your court, somebody else she doesn't even know about yet. It's terrifying."

Only Olfun didn't seem to think so.

Because he suddenly grinned. Not another of those solemn smiles that never reached the eyes, but a full-on delighted expression that looked strangely goofy on his serious features. I liked it. I just didn't understand it.

"What?"

"Did you not wonder *why* it took us so long to respond the other night?" he asked me.

I shrugged. "I told you. I didn't think it took long at all."

"Well, I can assure you that it did. But that was not entirely our fault. We should have already been in the house; it is true. But even from the garden, we should have been here within seconds. Except that we couldn't hear you."

"Couldn't hear us?"

He shook his head, and tapped an elongated ear. "We do not usually have that problem. Certainly not with a house being demolished a short distance away, and with the princess screaming out of her bedroom window!"

"Claire was screaming?" I hadn't noticed. But then, I'd been getting the ever-loving crap kicked out of me at the time.

He nodded. "She was apparently quite loud, yet we did not hear. Our best guess is that a silence spell, and a strong one, was put on the house prior to the attack."

"Can the fey do that?"

"Oh, yes. So can human mages."

I frowned. "That doesn't narrow the field any, Olfun!"

"No, it does not. But that was not my intention with my story."

"Sorry," I said. "Go on."

"I thought you might wonder how our princess managed to get our attention."

He was back to deadpan, so I knew this was going to be good. "Yes, I would be quite interested in knowing that."

"She set our tents on fire."

I burst out laughing. "*What?*"

He nodded. "From the house. I awoke to a burning hellscape, and dragon fire is not easily doused. I shan't soon forget it."

I guessed not. "So where are you sleeping now?"

"She informed us that we could sleep inside from now on, or out in the elements—she cared not. But that we were forbidden to acquire new tents since they appear to affect our hearing." He hoisted the tray. "I rather pity anyone foolish enough to come after the little prince."

From your lips to God's ears, I thought.

And then, as he started to turn away, the phone rang. He sighed deeply. "I almost forgot."

"Forgot what?"

"My reason for disturbing you. The guards would collectively like to know if you can please stop him from calling. We sleep inside now, in shifts, and, well . . ." He grimaced. "It must be fifty times today."

"Get who to stop calling?" I asked, and looked at the phone.

And saw the name on the little view screen.

"You have got to be kidding me!"

Chapter Fifty-three

I stabbed TALK. "Go to hell," I told the phone.

"Dory?" Kit Marlowe's voice came booming out of the speaker, like it was in surround sound. "Is that you?"

"Yes. Do you have something to say to me?"

"Naturally! Why else would I be calling? I need—"

I hung up.

He rang back immediately, because of course he did. Vamps didn't need speed dial. They had speed fingers.

"Damn it! Don't hang up on me!"

"Then say the magic words."

"What magic words? What are you talking about? I want—"

I hung up.

I put the phone on silent mode, pulled on jeans and a black tee, and headed downstairs.

My butt vibrated. I sighed, took the phone out, and held it a good distance from my ear. "What?"

"Don't hang up on me again!"

I hung up because I don't take orders from him.

The kitchen was full of fey again. Including Reiðarr, who was rolling out dough—like a *machine*. He'd been the one with the sad, lumpy effort last time, but things had clearly turned around.

"Damn," I said, and meant it.

He looked up, and froze. His face twitched around for a moment, like it wasn't sure what expression it was going for. And then, slowly, it resolved into . . . not a scowl. It wasn't a smile, but it wasn't a frown, either.

"I was ordered to assist," he informed me stiffly, in case I got any ideas.

"It's impressive."

"You cannot do this?"

"Never had the knack."

He did smile that time, rather superiorly. "It's in the wrists."

"It looks good," I said, because it did. And so did the hand pies on trays stacked literally everywhere. "Apple?" I asked hopefully.

"And cherry."

"God*damn*."

Ring, ring, ring.

"Sod it all!" Marlowe yelled. "What the hell do you want?"

"I already told you. I know it's unfamiliar territory, but you'll get it. I have faith in you."

"This is ridiculous! I don't have time for—"

Click.

I went over to the small stretch of counter by the stove, to help Gessa make sandwiches, and ended up getting handed a bucket of boiled eggs. It looked like we were all having sandwiches for dinner, and Gessa was putting some of each kind on the boy's tray as she finished with them. I pointed out that it probably didn't matter—he hadn't seemed picky to me—and she nodded. But then kept doing it anyway.

"Slavers feed gruel," she told me, after a minute.

"Okay."

"Back in Faerie, also eat gruel." Her eyes darkened. "And anything else."

Ah.

"And now you're having fun feeding him all kinds of different tastes he's never had before."

She didn't answer, but looking at the determined slant of her chin, I didn't think I had to worry about the kid going hungry.

"We'll add some hand pies, too," I told her, and she smiled.

My butt cheek did the mambo again, and I considered throwing the phone out the door. But it didn't belong to me, and besides, that wouldn't make the asshole go away. That would make him come down here, and then I might have to murder him.

"What?"

"All right, all right! I'm . . . sorry."

It sounded like the last word got caught on something in Marlowe's throat, probably his overweening pride.

"What was that? I couldn't quite hear you."

"You heard me! I'm tired of playing these stupid games! I need—"

Click.

I mushed up maybe three dozen eggs in one of Claire's huge mixing bowls, added half a jar of mayo, some salt and pepper, some diced onions, and some Dijon mustard. And made a face after tasting it, because it was missing something.

Sven, who was stalking the kitchen like he was afraid we'd eat it all, passed me some brown sugar, because he used it on everything. Literally. How he still had teeth I didn't know.

"Thanks, but I don't think that'll help."

Sven looked like he was going to argue, but Reiðarr intervened. He put a spoon in my mix and sniffed it cautiously before taking a tiny taste on the very tip of his tongue. And wrinkled his nose.

"It's mostly just eggs," I said defensively.

"Tasteless eggs."

"I could add some pickle relish. Or some bacon?"

Sven perked up at the mention of bacon. He liked to add brown sugar to it while it was cooking to make what was essentially meat candy, so it was always a hit. But Reiðarr disagreed.

"Vinegar."

"Vinegar?"

And damned if a splash of the white wine variety didn't help.

But not enough.

"I could go ask Claire," I said, but Reiðarr bristled.

"We don't need Claire. We can do this."

We all stood around and contemplated the bowl for a minute.

Then Gessa finished wrestling a tray of hand pies out of the oven and took a taste. And rolled her eyes at us. She tapped a cabinet with the handle of a wooden spoon, and I opened it to find—

"Okay, yeah."

"What is that?" Reiðarr demanded, because he was apparently now a chef.

"Ambrosia," I told him, sprinkling a liberal dose over the eggy mix on his spoon.

He tried another tiny taste, looking dubious, and then his eyes widened and he ate the whole spoonful. He grabbed the jar before I could dose my own eggs. "What *is* this?"

"I told you: ambrosia. Or smoked paprika, if you're looking for it in the grocery store."

He looked like he was making a mental note.

Ring, ring, ring.

"All right, I'm sorry, I'm sorry, I'm sorry!" Marlowe snapped. "Is that clear enough for you?"

"I don't know." I ate some eggs. Those were damned fine eggs. I shared a look of triumph with my co-chefs.

"What do you mean, you don't know? What more do you want?"

I licked my fingers. "Normally, an apology comes with a little more than that. Like an acknowledgment of guilt. What, exactly, are you sorry for?"

There was a sudden silence on the other end of the line.

"Bang, bang?" I prompted.

And got an outraged noise in return. "You can't still be upset about that!"

"Still?" I felt my blood pressure rise. "You *shot* me! All of a day ago!"

"I clipped you all of a day ago," he corrected nastily. "To slow you down. And you should be grateful—"

"Grateful?"

"I had a perfect shot, and that gorilla you were with never even heard me. I could have killed you—"

"So I should be *thanking* you?"

"Apologizing for wasting my time, perhaps—"
Click.

I was going to tell Louis-Cesare about that gorilla comment.

I swore to God.

"Turn off," Gessa advised, looking at the phone.

"If I do, he'll be here in person—"

Ring, ring, ri—

"Let me spell it out for you," I snapped at Marlowe. "I am done. Finished. Out of patience, time, and interest in *anything* to do with you—"

"This isn't about me! This is about the weapons—"

"What weapons?"

"What weapons?"

It was approaching screech territory. I pulled the phone away to save my hearing, and saw Sven wince. I took the party into the hall, because it wasn't fair for everyone to have eardrum damage.

"You know damned well what weapons!" Marlowe was yelling. "They couldn't have used all of the ones they took from Radu on the consul, not with a single man carrying them! Which means the rest are still floating around out there, along with who knows how many others!"

"And?"

"And?"

"And what do you expect me to do about it? I have fifty other things—"

"Not now. This is priority one!"

"Not for me." I made it final. "You're the one with the resources for a job like that. One more person isn't going to help you play hide-and-seek across the city, and I have—"

Marlowe cut me off. "I want to know what you know— everything. Every tiny detail. We're dealing with a ticking time bomb—"

"Why a time bomb?" I asked, and immediately regretted it.

Because I'd forgotten and put the phone back to my ear.

"Because that bitch isn't talking!" Marlowe yelled, at front-row-at-a-death-metal-concert decibels. "Even Mircea can't get anything out of her, and whoever was working with her is still at large, leaving us with two very ugly scenarios!"

"Such as?"

"Such as I can't talk about this over a phone! There's no telling who's listening—"

"Everyone, if you keep screaming."

"—and there's certain terms I don't need showing up in a file somewhere!"

But then he told me anyway.

"Such as number one: she was working with loyal confederates, who are even now tracking down the rest of those damned weapons, and smuggling them . . . somewhere we don't need them to be. Giving her partisans a war-changing advantage should we ever invade!"

"Should? I thought that was the plan."

"Until last night! But until we find those weapons, it's suicide to even attempt it. No one is willing to send their people in there as things stand!"

"Okay," I agreed. "That's bad."

"And number two isn't any better. If her associates aren't loyal, then they are sitting on a trove of . . . power . . . like nothing we've ever seen. Those fights have been going on for decades! They involved thousands of . . . people . . . especially after Geminus began enlarging and promoting them. There's no telling how much . . . power . . . they currently have—"

"You think they're going to sell it."

"Of course I think they're going to bloody sell it! And while I have people watching the black market, what if they don't go there? What if they decide that, instead of selling it off in dribs and drabs, and taking a chance on getting caught every time, they just make one big sell? To our enemies who will fucking use it to fucking *end us*?"

I hated to admit it, but the asshole had a point.

"All right," I said. "But I still don't know what you want me to do. I've been on this for less than a week and I haven't even been looking for weapons. I've been trying to help Olga—"

"Save it. I can't talk like this. I'm coming down there."

Damn it, I knew it!

"I have things to do," I said. "I can't just wait around the house all day—"

"Like hell you can't. I'm leaving now. If you're not there when I arrive, so help me God—"

"What? You'll shoot me again?"

"No." It was vicious. "I'll make you wish I had!"

Click.

God*damn*, I hated that vampire.

————

I found the little troll in the boys' room. The door was open since it was early afternoon, and the guys were off on adventures. But the bed skirt on Aiden's bed was hiked up, to give a view of the door, and ruffling slightly.

Like somebody was breathing under there.

I sat the tray on the table the boys used for coloring and puzzle doing, got down on my hands and knees, and lifted up the skirt a little more. And found what I'd expected: two violet eyes, glowing faintly in the dark, a small hunched body, and a smock covered with bacon jam. For a moment, we just looked at each other.

I debated trying to fish him out, decided that probably wasn't likely to go well, and brought the platter down instead. I put it on the braided rag rug beside the bed and started looking through the sandwiches on offer. There were two more BLTs, fat and happy looking; a couple of egg salad, thick and spicy, with a generous sifting of paprika; a couple chicken salad topped with lettuce, tomatoes and red onion slices; and no fewer than four PBJs. Because you can never have too many PBJs.

And just in case that wasn't sufficient, Gessa had stuck a handful of turnovers around the sides like parsley only not, because trolls don't get the point of garnishes you can't eat. Their idea of how to improve a plate of food is to add more food, which is a hard point to argue with. Particularly when they're still warm from the oven and dripping with glaze.

"Smells good," I said idly, my own mouth watering a little, because the cinnamon-apple and sweet cherry scents were busy battling it out for dominance.

I pushed the mounded tray a little closer to the bed, started munching on a turnover, and attempted to look harmless.

I guess I succeeded, because, after less than a minute, a small, thin arm snaked out and grabbed a cherry pie.

It jerked it back under the bed, too far for me to see anything, but I could hear smacking going on.

I listened to him inhale a few more turnovers and a couple sandwiches, and then pulled over the paper and crayons that the boys use to design knights and fighter jets and knights piloting fighter jets.

Violet eyes peered out at me curiously.

I flipped back the rug to get a work space, and fed the kid another sandwich. He took it from my hand this time. He appeared to like the meat ones best, but he ate them all. Yes, ten full-sized sandwiches—or twelve, if you counted the two he'd had as an appetizer—along with half a dozen small fruit pies.

Trolls had to have a stomach that extended into another dimension; it was the only explanation.

"Fish, tracks, door," I said clearly, and picked up a blue crayon.

I drew a fish.

He ate egg salad at it.

I drew train tracks, and even got the perspective right. Nothing.

I drew a door, complete with a damned good version of a doorknob, if I do say so myself.

Nada.

I finally sat back and ate a pie.

This was starting to look like a waste of time—well, other than for feeding up the kid. Healing took food, and trolls weren't like humans; soup wasn't going to put flesh back on those bones. Cherry pie, however, appeared to be a hit. I watched as the rest of the pies and the platter they sat on were slowly pulled under the bedclothes.

I finished off my own snack, and contemplated my artwork. This was starting to look like a dead end. But like the stuff with Efridis, I just couldn't let it go.

The kid didn't know much English, and those weren't survival terms that you'd prioritize: "food," "water," "bathroom," "bed," "medicine," "help." They looked more like words he'd deliberately tried to pick up, maybe even asked people about, despite the fact that doing so might earn him a beating. But he'd learned them anyway, possibly at different times, so as not to arouse suspicion, and then spoken them on what he thought was his deathbed.

Damn it, they meant something!

I just didn't know what.

Like I didn't know why Dorina had felt it necessary to send me another memory. I'd thought the point was the bones, and the fact that people were literally being killed for a potion ingredient. True, one time was vamp bones and the other fey, but the method was similar. Find a vulnerable community, people no one would miss, and exploit the hell out of them.

So what was I overlooking?

I reclined back against the trundle and rubbed my eyes. *Come on, Dory. You're better than this.*

And, normally, I was. Normally, it didn't take somebody hitting me over the head with a clue-by-four for me to figure out what I was dealing with. Normally, the problem was how to *stop it*, not how to *find it*, but this . . . I wasn't getting this.

I'm tired, I thought at Dorina. *Why don't you just tell me?*

Nothing.

Damn it, I know you can hear me!

Like she could probably hear Mircea last night. Because he didn't get it: Dorina didn't go to sleep anymore. At least, not like she once had. Every mind had to have rest, so there were times she wasn't aware of what was happening, just like me. But there was no way to tell when those were anymore.

And she'd been aware enough to attack Efridis when she saw her, hadn't she?

So she knew what Mircea was planning.

There was a mirror across from the bed—just a little thing, hung at kid height. One of Claire's vain attempts to teach good hygiene to a couple boys who were happier splashing about in the mud. I doubted it was used much, but it was there and in my line of sight when I was sitting down. I caught my reflection in the glass, and swallowed.

Staring too long into a mirror is always a freaky experi-

ence, and that's when you *know* no one is staring back. I
didn't know it now, and for the first time, I tried to get a
glimpse of my other side. But the black eyes were the
same, with no additional life experience that I could see.
And so was the too-pale skin, the cap of dark hair, still
slightly damp from the shower, and the teeth biting a lower
lip in indecision. *Damn it!*

"I'm not going to do it," I told her. "I'm not, okay? That
was his idea, not mine!"

Nothing.

"He doesn't speak for me—he never has!"

More nothing.

So we were back to not talking, huh?

What a shock.

"I'm still not," I told her, feeling angry and frustrated
and destructive—and mad at myself for it. Trashing the
kids' room wasn't going to help. And neither was anything else.

Mircea could scheme all he wanted; she was going to
do what she was going to do.

"Do what you want with your life," I told her. "You
have to live with it. I'm going to live mine—while I still
have one!"

I got up and slammed out of the room.

And into another world.

Chapter Fifty-four

Mircea, Venice, 1458

Merda! Mircea grabbed the witch, clapped a hand over her mouth, and spun the two of them back against a wall. And into the shadow of the second story of a house, the kind Venetians liked to push out over the street to gain themselves a little more room.

He thickened the shade around them as much as he could, but his heart was still in his throat as what had to be a hundred vampires rushed past the opening of the alley, just a few feet away. He stayed stock-still, the woman flat against him, her frantic heartbeat sounding like thunder in his ears. And probably in their pursuers', too, only it was drowned out by real thunder from above.

The last soldier finally passed, but Mircea stayed in place a little longer. Not because of worry that they'd double back, but more because he couldn't get his body to move. It seemed to like the freezing-cold wall just fine.

But the witch didn't and started beating on him, so he let her go. Only to find his arm clutched in a surprisingly strong grip. "How the hell are we supposed to get through this?" she hissed. "They're every—"

Mircea's hand clapped back over her mouth, winning him a glare worthy of a praetor. He ignored it. Thunder was crashing like ocean waves above them, and echoing off the high, close-packed walls all around. Rain was bucketing down, causing water to cascade off rooflines and shoot out of gutters, crisscrossing the narrow streets with liquid arcs like suspended canals. Meanwhile, the real canals rushed like rivers, adding their roar to the cacophony. But vampire hearing could not be underestimated.

Not aloud, Mircea thought at her, as hard as he could.

She jerked, and stared at him, eyes wide and startled. And Mircea felt welcome relief flood through him. It was easier to communicate mind to mind with his own kind; humans were more problematic, especially magical ones. And God knew nothing else had gone right tonight! But now, at least, they could talk.

Only the witch didn't seem to agree.

Because he'd no sooner released her again than she started screaming. *"Augghhh!"*

Stop it! he thought at her frantically.

"Augghhh!"

Shut up! You're going to get us—ooof. The last was because she'd just elbowed him in the ribs, which hadn't mattered, and then kicked him in the shin, which had. Mircea's still-healing bone sent a spear of pain lancing through him, and the witch took the opportunity to scramble away, bouncing off the narrow walls and looking crazed.

Mircea tackled her halfway down the alley, but slipped on some muck, sending them sliding into a wall, and giving her the chance to kick him viciously in the face and run. He felt the little space slur around him, and his eyes go fuzzy for a moment. Damn it, they couldn't afford this!

Then his vision snapped back, allowing him to spot her, silhouetted by a burst of lightning in the middle of a small bridge, and glowing like a beacon.

Merda!

A moment later, the light flicked out, plunging the scene into darkness. But the heavens cracked open again almost immediately, along with a cannon boom of thunder. Showing Mircea a party of the praetor's guards instead, their shiny breastplates running with lightning and all but glowing against the now-empty bridge.

Because the witch had disappeared.

The light faded and Mircea hugged cobblestones, hoping against hope that his dark hair and clothes would hide him. And he guessed they did. Because the guards' steps pounded in another direction, and he clambered back to his feet, his mind whirling with fear and confusion.

He limped down the alley to the little bridge, but still saw nothing. Which was impossible; no human moved that fast! And she'd said she was out of power, so what . . . ?

Oh.

That was what.

A rogue pain had caused Mircea to look down at his calf, just as a dimmer scrawl of lightning flared overhead. It was less blinding than illuminating—in more than one way. He retraced his path, stepped off the bridge, and knelt beside the small, rickety structure to peer underneath.

And saw the witch, huddled in the freezing water up to her neck, probably hoping it would muffle her heartbeat, which it hadn't. And that it would hide her from the guards, which it had. But only because they'd been distracted by the storm—one that couldn't last much longer.

Mircea slid down the muddy bank, and got on her level.

The witch's flame-red hair had been part of a glamourie she could no longer maintain, leaving mousy brown locks to straggle dispiritedly around a face that was less alluring at the moment than pinched and pale and freckled. She had brown eyes, too, not unattractive in their own way, but a far cry from the luminous blue she'd been wearing. Not to mention that everything she had on was soaked.

She looked like a drowned rat.

A very frightened one.

For a long moment, Mircea simply knelt there, listening to the skies, which sounded like they'd had some of Horatiu's infamous garlic torta. He didn't want to spook the witch more than she already was, but they couldn't stay here. They couldn't stay anywhere.

They were being hunted, and the noose was tightening.

Because their little ruse hadn't worked.

Well, that wasn't entirely true. They'd managed to float away from the pier under a bit of flotsam, while everyone else stared at the burning gondola or ran for cover. The latter had been the popular choice, since vampires are even more flammable than humans, and they'd just seen two people incinerated.

But while the distraction had helped him and the witch get away, it hadn't done much else. By the time they'd swum a safe distance, they'd barely had the strength to drag themselves onto dry land again. But they'd nonetheless been forced into a mad scramble through streets still teeming with vampires—too many of them.

Their pursuers should have been heading for home or for the taverns and betting parlors where hunting was still to be had. And some of them were. But those were mainly the locals who had been pressed into service while the praetor mobilized her coterie of guards, who were suddenly everywhere.

Because she wasn't as stupid as her creatures.

She hadn't bought the lightning bolt story.

Mircea and the witch had stayed alive this long only because of the storm, with the rolling thunder covering their footsteps, the pounding rain masking their scent, and the lightning causing so many helpful shadows to flicker and jump that even vampire eyes had trouble knowing where to focus. But it couldn't last much longer. They were going to die unless they got out of this city, and did it soon.

"I have an idea," he said, in between thunderclaps.

The witch had been staring at the water with a blank look. The same one she now turned on him. Her moods had ranged wildly during the chase, from defiance to desperation to strange euphoria to . . . whatever this was. But at least the panic was gone.

"That was you," she rasped. "In my head."

"Yes."

"The praetor . . . she used to talk to me like that. I thought"—she licked her lips—"I thought she'd found me."

"No."

The "not yet" remained unsaid, but floated almost tangibly in the air between them.

She slowly got out of the canal, dragging heavy, waterlogged skirts behind her. And then squatted, dripping, on the muddy bank beside him. She was shivering, and he wished he had his cloak to offer her. But it was long gone, and would have been drenched in any case.

"I have an idea," Mircea repeated.

She didn't say anything for a long moment, just stared at the rushing water of the canal, which was wholly black in the absence of any lightning. It was almost mesmerizing, a river of ink, with only its movement making it visible at all. It felt strangely cozy, sopping wet though they were, under this tiny bit of shelter, while the wind howled down the alleys and the little river rushed inside its banks, masking any sign of them.

It was so easy to imagine that they could just stay here forever, shut away from the world.

But they couldn't, something the witch seemed to realize, because she slowly turned her head to look at him.

"You're not going to like it," Mircea admitted.

"I know."

———

Light flashed, impossibly bright, and a waterspout exploded on a nearby building. That and a crack of thunder, loud as cannon fire, almost caused Mircea to lose his grip on the windowsill. And it did cause the witch to lose hers.

He scrabbled for purchase on water-slick stone, and she screamed and started to fall, her eyes wide with terror, her hand reaching for him desperately—

And snagged the hem of his shirt.

Gah!

Mircea experienced the unique sensation of almost being decapitated as he dangled off a third-story window ledge by a couple of fingers, while the remains of the too-close lightning crawled around his body like manic worms. He did not scream, something he would have been proud of if his throat hadn't been too indented to allow it. But he did curse inventively for a moment, in his head.

Good thing he didn't need to breathe, he thought savagely, and hauled the witch back up.

Below them, the little alley by the praetor's palazzo roared like a living thing, sweeping anything unlucky enough to land in it straight into the Grand Canal. Mircea knew that because they'd just waded across, the witch clinging to his back, while debris battered them and winds shook them and lightning threatened to roast them. And, damn it all, he wasn't doing that again!

He pushed the window the rest of the way open with his chin, dragged the witch up, and shoved her through, and then scrambled after her.

And promptly slipped on a dish of slimy little fish that had been left to rot on the floor.

"You're right—I don't like it!" the witch hissed at him— why, Mircea didn't know. He was the one whose private parts had just become intimately acquainted with the hard edge of a table.

Very hard.

God, so hard!

He bit back an unmanly sob and stared into the darkness for a moment, before glancing around the small study belonging to the praetor's secretary, hoping for a light. But of course not. The only one at the moment was the moon, flirting with the storm clouds outside, and she was a coy bitch. They'd never find anything like this!

"Here." The witch thrust a candle in his face that she'd seemingly pulled out of nowhere.

"How . . . did you find . . . that?"

"Stepped on it." She paused, and then cocked her head at him. "Are you out of breath?"

"No."

"I thought vampires didn't have to breathe—"

"We don't!"

"Then what's wrong with—"

"Nothing! Just light the damned thing!" Mircea snapped, and straightened up.

And, yes, that hurt about as much as he'd thought it would.

She waved the bent candle at him impatiently. "I'm out of magic, remember?"

"You can't even light a damned candle?"

"I could hold it out the window and hope the lightning hits it, if you think that would help!" Her eyes narrowed on him. "Or you could."

Their brief rapport under the bridge appeared to have faded. Probably due to almost getting caught a dozen times since then. He'd foolishly thought the streets would be clearer near the praetor's mansion, because what kind of idiots would dare to come here?

Our kind, Mircea thought, and limped next door with the candle. He discovered that the secretary's bedroom was even more of a disaster than the cubbyhole, with stinking piles everywhere. But it did have a low-banked fire burning across from the bed, which managed to light the wick.

All right, then.

He reentered the small study and placed the thing on top of a cabinet, where it did little more than gild the darkness. But it would have to do. The witch started searching through the heaps on the floor, including one that contained a pair of unwashed hosen that she had some low-voiced curses for. While Mircea broke open an elaborate ivory box, rifled through the papers on the table, pawed through a little slanted writing desk, checked out a bookcase, and even shook out some fine green draperies, in case something had fallen into the creases.

But found only dust.

The praetor's shield was missing.

"You're sure it's kept here?" the witch whispered, looking as frustrated as he felt.

"Of course I'm sure! I've used it before!"

"Well, didn't you ever see where it was kept?"

"Here!" Mircea picked up the ivory case, and thrust it at her. "It's supposed to be right here!"

"Well, it's not."

"I know that!"

"And without it, we're not going anywhere."

"I know that, too!"

"I hope so," she said grimly, shoving sodden hair out of her face. "If you expect me to somehow shield us in the ley lines, you're going to be very disappointed. I couldn't manage that at my strongest; I definitely can't do it now!"

Mircea bit back a sharp comment, because it wasn't fair. Weak the witch might be, but he was no better. Damn it, they had to have that shield!

Without it, they would be dead by morning, if not sooner. But with it . . . his fist clenched. He'd visited Abramalin in far-off Egypt and come back the same night. The ley lines were terrifying but also unbelievably fast, and seemed to crisscross the entire world. Meaning they could go anywhere, anywhere at all!

Including Paris to tip off the consul about the damned praetor!

He started searching the desk again.

"You've done that already!" the witch whispered.

"Perhaps I missed something."

"I was watching; you didn't!"

Mircea whirled on her. "If you have a better idea, I'd love to—"

Damn it! He'd knocked a half-full glass of wine off the overcrowded table, which shattered against the hard tile of the floor. Both of them froze, waiting for startled cries and running feet.

But none came.

After a moment, the witch let out a breath, and Mircea felt his spine unclench. The praetor was having another of her endless parties, and the servants were overworked as it was. They weren't going to go looking for . . . messes to . . . clean up. . . .

His thoughts stuttered to a halt as he watched the puddle of wine, gleaming like blood in the low light, drain away under the wall. Until there was nothing left. Just a vague pink stain on the floor.

"What is it?" the witch asked, as he knelt beside it.

"I'm not sure."

He ran his fingers over the fine scrollwork on the paneling. It had an acanthus-leaf design interspersed with rosettes, none of which appeared to be movable. But when he tapped faintly on the wall above the stain, it sounded hollow.

He looked up at her. "Perhaps . . . another room?"

"What are you talking about?" The witch leaned over his shoulder. "What other room?"

A section of wall suddenly slid back behind another, leaving an opening just big enough for a person to fit through.

Mircea looked up at her. "That one."

The hidden room was dark, even by vampire standards. It looked like it had a window, the twin to the one they'd crawled through, but it had been boarded up, letting in only a few thin flashes whenever a lightning bolt burst outside. But it wasn't the darkness that bothered Mircea; he was used to that.

It was the *smell*.

The anchovy-and-dirty-clothes odor of the study was worse, mixed with months of accumulated grime, because Mircea didn't think the maids were ever allowed in here. This wasn't like that; it wasn't a bad smell, although there was a good bit of dust involved. It was just . . . whatever the underlying scent was, he didn't know it.

And he'd thought he knew them all.

After more than a decade as a vampire, Mircea had built up an impressive scent catalogue in his head, despite not being a Hound, what those of his kind were called who had particularly sensitive noses. He'd seen a blind one navigate a crowd once with perfect dexterity, even stopping to pick up an old woman's dropped purse and offer it back to her. He'd talked to him later in a bar, and discovered that he *could* almost see, the scent clouds in his head resolving themselves into hazy images of people, canals, even buildings, that in some ways were more distinct than anything Mircea's eyes could perceive.

That vampire would probably have known everything in the room in a moment, where it was and what it was, even in pitch-darkness. But Mircea wasn't that vampire, and the skin of his neck was ruffling. He motioned to the witch to hand him the candle, then pushed it through the gap and held it up, the small flame illuminating . . .

Nothing, because a couple lanterns had just flickered to life, all by themselves.

He and the witch looked at each other.

"You first," she said.

Mircea went in.

Chapter Fifty-five

Mircea, Venice, 1458

Mircea looked around, still not sure what he was seeing.

The room looked like a storehouse for weapons, only he didn't know why anyone would bother keeping these. Baskets held sword and ax blades that were almost eaten away by rust, their pommels long since lost to time. Ragged quivers were full of arrows that looked like they'd disintegrate with a breath. An old piece of cloth—possibly a banner, judging by the shape—lay on a table, so tattered and burnt that it would have been impossible to display any other way.

Yet it had once been magnificent: a heavy weight of silk with glimmers of gold here and there, their brightness undimmed by time. And it had some sort of pastoral scene painted on it, although it was so faint now that he couldn't quite make it out. He bent closer, putting out a hand—

And had it grasped by the witch, hard enough to hurt.

"Careful." Her voice was rough. "It looks like the praetor collects more than just human art."

Mircea frowned, not understanding. And still didn't when he raised the candle, because the lanterns left deep shadows draping the walls in places. And sent light dancing over maps he didn't recognize, books he couldn't read, and strange-looking shields with designs he'd never seen. And clothing . . .

That was trying to crawl up his arm.

He dropped the candle, and the witch's hand abruptly

tightened, jerking him back. "Fey," she told him, before he could ask. "And old—very old. I don't even know how the spells are still active."

Mircea stared at the mail shirt now gleaming on the floor. Unlike the weapons, it showed no ravages of time, shining as brightly as if just made. And it hadn't felt like metal, but more like silk against his skin. He'd never seen anything so fine.

He looked at the witch, because something had just registered. "Fey?"

"Yes, fey. You know."

Mircea didn't know.

She put fingers beside her ears and wiggled them at him.

He just stared.

And then snapped out of it, because they didn't have time for this! "The fey are a myth! A tale told to frighten children!"

"Like vampires?"

Mircea stared at her some more.

And then caught a pair of greaves trying to inch their way out of a basket. Which was less of a concern than the fact that they stopped as soon as he spotted them! He looked at them, slumped innocently over the weave, and felt a hard shiver crawl up his spine.

"Be careful what you touch," the witch said, completely unnecessarily, and moved off to begin a search. Mircea retrieved his guttering candle and took it as far from the damned armor as he could get. Only to be distracted by something on the banner.

Or to be more precise, something *in* the banner, which moved between the rents, shivered over the threadbare patches, and thundered across once-verdant fields, now gray with age. Something that sent little puffs of dust up, here and there, as it traveled across the surface. Something . . . impossible.

Half in disbelief, half in wonder, Mircea edged closer, tracking the movements of tiny riders on tiny horses, silently braying hounds, beaters with their little sticks, driving prey before them, and deer that flickered in and out of sight as they fled across ghostly fields—

And then off the cloth entirely, golden light that hadn't come from Mircea's candle following them as they jumped to something covered by a sheet.

Mircea sidled over and gave a cautious tug. The fabric slithered away to reveal a huge, leather bound book on a wooden stand. It was open to a page where a hunt was depicted, one he could see clearly now, because there was no corruption here. Like the mail shirt, it looked like it had been finished yesterday, the colors so glossy and bright that he was almost afraid to touch it, lest he smear the paint.

But he did, after a brief glance over his shoulder at the witch, who was muttering to herself and whacking at something in a basket with a piece of broken spear.

Mircea turned back to the book, and gingerly turned over a gossamer page, being careful to touch only the unpainted edge. And then another and another, because they were like nothing he'd ever seen: illustrations, in vibrant hues picked out in gold, that would have been wondrous enough on their own. But, like the ethereal hunt, they also *moved*.

He saw nobles riding in procession, their gilded leather trappings gleaming under a painted sun; peasants tilling the land, the soil under their tiny plows so warm and rich that he swore he could smell its scent; people dancing around a painted bonfire, the little sparks glowing like jewels as they rose off the page and into the gloom; and two navies clashing in the midst of a majestic, rolling sea, which sent what felt like miniature sprays of water up at him.

He turned page after page, eagerly, almost hungrily. They were painted poetry, all of them, more perfect than any masterwork he'd ever seen. Far more, he thought, after sighing a little too hard on a page, and sending a noble's hat flying, which the tiny man scrambled around and only just managed to catch.

Mircea stared at him, sure he'd been mistaken, and accidentally brushed the edge of a painting. And had a very small, very angry squirrel glare at him from under the edge of his fingertip. And then push out from beneath the pad to bark at him in outrage.

He grinned, utterly enchanted, and turned over another page.

And felt his smile grow puzzled.

That was . . . strange.

The illustration took up both pages this time, bright and colorful, like all the others. But instead of a distant view of an expansive scene, it showed only a close-up of a crowd—very close. So much so that Mircea could see virtually nothing, except the backs of jostling, milling people.

Something appeared to be happening up ahead— something important, judging by the animation of the crowd—but he could see little of it. Just occasional glimpses of a bright blue sky, and something that might be a castle on a hill. But the view was so intermittent that even that was debatable. He found himself pushing at the crowd of bodies, even poking at a fat man who refused to budge, trying to see—

Everything.

The dark little room flashed out, the fire-splashed walls giving way to a crowd of people, screaming and shoving and threatening to trample him. Mircea tried to move away, while he figured out what was happening, but he couldn't seem to control his body. And it wouldn't have mattered even if he could.

Behind him, a double ring of guards circled the crowd, their swords out, blocking the way back. And ahead— damn it, he still couldn't *see*! Until the screams became shrieks, and a huge fight broke out, sending dozens to the ground, and parting the crowd enough to show—

Oh God.

Not again!

Mircea stumbled back, but there was nowhere to go. And nowhere to look except for the caldron straight ahead, big as a ship and gleaming copper bright in the incongruously sunny day. Inside, a crowd of men floated motionless on the bubbling surface of the water, their long hair drifting around them, their skin sloughing off in pieces. Or else they writhed, screaming and fighting, lobster red but still trying to climb up the blistering sides, while a thick line of soldiers with spears shoved them back in.

Mircea tried to avert his eyes—he'd seen enough horrors this day! But they stayed glued to the scene nonetheless. Forcing him to watch as more men, waiting their turn alongside the caldron, used their chains to strangle their fellow prisoners out of pity, before they were boiled alive. While the vast crowd tore at their hair and cried and fought and—

Mircea finally looked away, but only because a woman, beautiful, desperate, and tear streaked, grabbed him. "Help us!" she breathed. "You're on the Domi! Make her stop!"

Mircea followed her outflung arm, and saw another woman, raven haired and dark eyed, standing on top of a terrace, framed by the castle. She was watching the spectacle and laughing: at the sufferers, their families, him. Knowing he couldn't do anything, that if he so much as muttered a word against her, he'd join them.

"I can't help," he babbled. "I'm sorry, I'm so sorry—"

"Murderer!" the woman shrieked. "You may as well be killing us yourself! Do something! Those are your *people*!"

"I'm sorry, I'm sorry—"

"Stop saying that!" She was shaking him, and now more people were pausing, were turning this way, were looking at him.

Didn't any of them understand? He'd done all he could! Why were they looking at him with such hate? What did they expect? For him to die along with them, and his family, too?

"I'm sorry!" he screamed in the woman's face, shame and horror and panic all coming together into what felt like madness. And why not? The whole world was mad. "I'm sorry! I'm sorry! I'm sorry!"

She was backing away now, but still he pursued her, screaming, crying, helpless and hating himself for it, until hard hands grasped him, and strong arms pulled him back. And still he yelled: "I'm sorry, I'm sorry, I'm—"

"Sorry! All of you! And your descendants for generations!"

The voice that finished the sentence wasn't Mircea's; it changed as the scene did, dizzyingly fast, but not back to the quiet shadows of the hidden room. But to a night with a waxing moon shining through the bare branches of a winter forest, shedding little light onto a crowded hillside. But it wasn't needed; a great ring of torches surrounded a scaffold at the top of the hill, where the largest tree of all stood in solitary splendor.

Like the woman from the castle, who was standing in the middle of the platform, her long dark hair streaming like a banner in the wind, the same one that sent ribbons of fire flowing out of the torches, and almost carried Mircea's voice away.

"Even now," he heard himself intone, "you cannot accept your guilt. Even now, you spit in the faces of those who would redeem you—"

"Redeem?" The woman's scornful voice rang across the crowd. "Oh, pray forgive me, masters all. I thought you were here to kill me!"

"The body, lady, not the soul—"

"I'm a queen, not a lady! And I don't give a damn about my soul!"

"Some truth from her at last," someone muttered nearby.

"But we do," Mircea said gravely. "And we choose to give you one last chance."

He saw his arm rise—although it didn't look like his, with darker skin and strange attire—and beckon a huge man forward. Only no, not a man. For he was shirtless, and his torso was strangely muscled, and his face . . .

Mircea suddenly stared around at the faces of the crowd, noticing what he'd been too panicked to see before. Because they were beautiful—beautiful but not right. Here was hair the color of bright green grass, there eyes like summer violets, and all of them too tall, too lithe, too . . .

Alien, he thought, and wanted to run, but his feet stayed planted on the scaffold.

"For your crimes, you are cast out," he informed the woman, as the huge executioner tried to affix a blindfold over her eyes. "Separated forever from your home, your people, and your realm. May you find peace in your new world, and enrich it with your undoubted gifts—"

"I will make it tremble!" The woman twisted out of the guard's hold, who had foolishly dropped his ax to tie the blindfold, and grabbed a knife from his belt. Before anyone could react, she'd sliced open his stomach, sending him stumbling back with his guts in his hands. "And then I'll come after you!" She whirled on the crowd. "You puling cowards, you little fools, do you think you've heard the end of me?"

"Yes," a deep voice boomed, and the next second, the beautiful, livid face was bouncing across the boards, along with the head it was attached to, coming to rest at Mircea's feet.

He looked up, stunned, at a giant blond man with a sword in his hand and a spattering of blood across his face.

"Bury it!" the man snapped. "And may the gods have pity on this world!"

The vision, or whatever it was, snapped, ending as suddenly as it had begun. Mircea awoke to find the witch beating on him and screaming "Shut up! Shut up! Shut up!" which wasn't good; then he heard the sound of those running feet he'd been dreading, which was worse.

Merda!

He threw her off, but it didn't help. She just grabbed him again, yelling for him to keep quiet and apparently not recognizing the irony. While he looked around for a weapon that might still work, because they were about to need one!

And found nothing that didn't disintegrate under his hands.

So he grabbed the witch instead, and shook her. "What happened?"

"—screaming, and now they've probably heard us—"

"They *have* heard us! They're on the way!"

The witch looked startled for a moment, like she hadn't expected him to agree with her, then her face crumpled. "I knew it! I knew it, I knew it, I knew—"

Mircea shook her some more. "Answer me!"

"What difference does it make *now*?"

"Tell me!"

It was basically a roar, and finally snapped her out of her frenzy. "They—the fey—can weave memories into things, like paint or cloth. Letting you relive what one of them saw—"

The entire wall blew in, sending paneling flying, dust billowing, and a vampire in Medusa-head armor lunging for Mircea.

And then writhing on the floor, seemingly possessed, as he fought with a crowd of people long dead.

Mircea grabbed the witch out of the shelving she'd staggered into and towed her through the wall.

"W-what happened?" she demanded, looking back. "What did you *do*?"

"Threw the book at him," Mircea said, and started out the door.

Only to crash into the secretary running in from the hall.

"That's it! Look in his hand!" The witch pointed at something the secretary was clutching, as his startled eyes took in the two of them. Something glowing like a beacon, with a stronger, purer light than it had ever had before. The praetor's shield!

Mircea lunged for it, and the next thing he knew, he was hitting the wall on the other side of the study. The secretary might look weak, and he wasn't a master, or Mircea would be dead already. But he wasn't a baby, either.

And more guards were doubtless on the way.

The window was open, letting in a scattering of rain and offering a quick escape, but there was nothing but death out there. And if he was going to die, he was going down fighting, not cowering under a damned bridge! The secretary had just knocked the witch aside and now he looked up, in time to see the resolution settle onto Mircea's face.

"You want this?" the man sneered, holding up the orb, which had just flushed a deep, dark crimson. "Take it!"

He threw the shield right at Mircea, just as the woman sprang off the floor, a heavy tray in her hands, which she swung at the secretary's head.

And hit the stone instead.

The little thing slammed back into the vampire, hitting him smack in the middle of his chest. Mircea was halfway through a lunge, trying to grab the stone and the witch at the same time, only to have her grab him instead, sending both of them to the floor. "Don't touch him! Don't touch him!" she screamed, and this time, Mircea listened.

Because something very strange was happening to the secretary.

The long, dark hair he wore in a clip had come loose, and was flooding white, as quickly as if someone had poured a bucket of paint over his head. Like his skin, already vampire pale, was fading to alabaster. And the eyes, formerly beady and black, were now beady and blue, almost colorless.

He was albino pale as he batted at the orb, which appeared to have become stuck, and he started screaming: "Get it off! Get it off! Get it off!"

What looked like a whole squadron of guards appeared in the hallway behind him, but they didn't get it off. They also didn't come in. Perhaps because the secretary was screaming; the guard in the hidden room was yelling that he was sorry, sorry, so very sorry; and the witch was standing in the middle of the room, breathing hard and looking . . . fairly witchy.

She'd partly dried, leaving wild tufts of muddy hair sticking up everywhere. They matched her expression, which was a cross between anger and panic that mostly read as furious. And she'd just grabbed the broken spear shaft again, which was too thick for a wand, but it didn't look like the guards knew that.

Do something, Mircea told her mentally. *Pretend to cast a spell!*

She did not cast a spell. She did, however, panic at the sound of his voice in her head, habit and fear overriding good sense. Which also seemed to be the case with the guards, when she suddenly ran at them, screaming and waving the "wand."

They fell back against the outer wall of the hall, alarm on their features, while the secretary flailed wildly and the shield finally dislodged. It fell to the ground, almost clear again, spinning around on the hard tiles of the floor. The secretary gasped and went staggering backward, the witch screamed and beat him with her stick, and Mircea swallowed and stared at the orb.

And then took a calculated risk and grabbed it.

Nothing happened.

Nothing happened! Except that it felt warm and strangely full in his palm. As if it contained far more power than before, and it had already contained enough.

"Come on!" he yelled at the witch, and held it up.

And was immediately tackled by one of the guards, who hadn't bought into the pantomime. Until Dorina flew at the man, doing something that made him scream and flail around, and Mircea yelled: "That's it! Curse them! Curse them all!"

Suddenly, he and the witch were alone, the vampires thundering down the hallway, the secretary yelling profanity outside the door, and the guard in the hidden room sobbing apologies that echoed off the walls.

"I told you this would work," Mircea breathed at the witch.

Who whacked him with her stick, very hard, several times.

And then they were gone.

———

"Dory! Dory!"

I opened my eyes to hardwood floors, a puddle of drool, and Claire kneeling beside me. So were Stinky, Olga, and the troll boy, whose smock was now truly a sight to behold. A handful of fey guards stood on the steps, all looking spooked.

But not half as much as I was.

"Are you all right?" Claire demanded.

"No," I said, my head spinning as everything finally came together. "None of us are."

Holy shit.

Chapter Fifty-six

An hour later, Coffee Lover was standing in the kitchen doorway, trying to get my attention, but I couldn't hear him over all the screaming. *"What?"*

His mouth moved some more, but it didn't help.

"Can you shut up for a minute?" I asked Marlowe, only to have him round on me.

"As soon as you start making some goddamned sense!"

"I have been. I told you—"

"That an ancient fey queen turned praetor turned . . . whatever the hell . . . is rampaging around New York wearing a war mage's skin! Do you have *any* idea how that sounds?"

"Yes, but it doesn't mean I'm wrong."

"No, it means you're crazy!" Marlowe snapped his fingers at his vamps. "We're leaving."

And found his arm caught by a pissed-off senator with flour in his hair.

Louis-Cesare had shown up just before the chief spy, and he hadn't been baking. But Marlowe had been doing a lot of fist pounding on the kitchen table and, as a result, we were all a little starchy. Louis-Cesare just made it look good.

"You're going to listen to her."

"I *have* listened! And been fed the biggest pile of horse—"

"Then you can listen again. Perhaps with your mouth closed this time."

Well, shit, I thought, as Marlowe turned puce. In fairness, he'd already been pretty close, since he didn't seem to like my Alfhild-as-the-villain theory. And while I normally wouldn't have cared what Marlowe liked, in this instance, we needed his help.

Which is why I didn't respond in kind when he grabbed me. Even though it left me, him, and Louis-Cesare facing off on three sides of the kitchen table, and me bent halfway across it because I was too short for this. Like the room was too small for a conference.

"Release me!" Marlowe barked, ignoring the fact that he had me in the same grip.

Louis-Cesare did not release him. The tension ratcheted up a few more notches, and it had already been pretty high. Because some of the guys Marlowe had dragged along looked vaguely familiar.

Like I-might-have-recently-shot-a-few familiar.

I sighed, and wondered if I could make it to the door without anybody returning the favor. But before I could try, Louis-Cesare squeezed my other arm, completing the awkward triangle. "Tell him."

"I already did. He doesn't want to hear—"

"Tell him anyway. Then we'll have Mircea tell him. Perhaps something will get through that thick skull!"

"While the only thing going through your skull," Marlowe snapped, "will be my fist if you don't let go!"

Louis-Cesare let go, but only so he could grab the spy's lapels and drag him over the table.

"Damn it, man, think! If she's right, the creature who attacked the consul is still at large, and you're responsible for her safety! If there's *any* chance—"

Marlowe broke his hold with a savage upward gesture, and I thought we were about to have round number two, electric boogaloo, only with no holds barred this time. And since that would involve masters' powers, which in Marlowe's case included the aforementioned ability to crack skulls, I wasn't on board.

But then he made an annoyed-cat sound and flung out a hand in my direction. "Fine. Tell me!"

I looked at Louis-Cesare, who raised an eyebrow. And then around the room, at the sea of glowering faces. And sighed again.

Always nice to have an appreciative audience.

"Caedmon told me about Alfhild, the ancient fey princess with a rep for boiling people alive, but I didn't think much about it," I said. "But that's where our current problem started, all those years ago in Faerie, when she was betrayed and murdered—as she saw it. She was furious and vowed revenge, and that kind of anger carries over. Some of the guards told me that fey who claim to remember substantial bits of their past lives are usually either very powerful or very troubled, and Alfhild was both."

"That's one way of putting it," Louis-Cesare murmured. Thanks to Marlowe's theatrics, he'd heard only bits and pieces of this himself.

"Anyway, she was exiled from Faerie and executed on Earth, which should have been the end of it. Except she was fey, and they reincarnate. But since she was on Earth now, she came back as a human, because that seems to be the way it works. The fey soul latches on to the energy of the planet to help it form its next body, and this is a human world. But she was still fey underneath, and kept being tormented with weird flashes of memory she didn't understand."

And with that, at least, I could sympathize.

"That's why she sought out a vampire," one of Marlowe's guys piped up. "To give her time to figure things . . . uh . . . out."

He trailed off when his master glared at him.

"Maybe," I agreed. "Or maybe she just got bit randomly. Either way, a longer life allowed her to put the pieces together. Enough to find her grave and that damned book, which told her the rest."

"Why would the fey leave such a thing?" Louis-Cesare asked. "If they knew there was even a chance she'd remember—"

"The guards said that's probably why it was left: as a warning, in case she recalled anything substantial, and as a reason for her exile. It was supposed to promote repentance, by reminding her of her crimes—"

"Yes, that works so well with homicidal maniacs!" Marlowe snarled. "They may as well have given her a primer! Like leaving young Hitler *Mein Kampf*!"

I didn't point out that he had no reason to be angry,

since he wasn't supposed to be buying any of this, because I was just glad that he actually seemed to be listening this time. And because I agreed with him. "They should have destroyed her when they had the chance."

"Did anyone say why they didn't?" Louis-Cesare asked.

"No. None of Claire's guards were alive then. But they said it probably had something to do with the old religion. That her judges would have felt like they were killing off part of the soul of Faerie if they completely obliterated her. And that maybe they thought she'd get it right, the next time."

"That's what I'm afraid of," he murmured.

Marlowe didn't seem any happier. His brows had lowered and his eyes had darkened. Several of the vamps around me fidgeted, feeling their master's growing displeasure in their own bodies. This close, they functioned almost like a single organism, to the point that, when Marlowe made another of those angry little noises, several of his boys did, too.

Sounded like a bunch of asthmatic cats in here, I thought.

But he wasn't ready to officially board the crazy train yet.

"None of this proves that she's still around today," he pointed out. "Even if she did become a vampire, and eventually the praetor, as you claim, the consul killed her five hundred years ago!"

"The consul killed her *physically*," I corrected. "In fury after Mircea explained who had been murdering all those vampires. What she didn't know was that she was dealing with the reincarnated soul of an ancient fey princess in a vampire body—"

"Understandable," Louis-Cesare murmured dryly.

"—and so didn't realize that her nemesis remained, just in an altered form. Because Alfhild was a *vargr*—"

"Based on?" Marlowe cut in.

I looked at him incredulously. "Did you hear anything I said about what happened here the other night? The *manlikans* might have been Efridis, trying to get Aiden out of the house, but the *vargr* attack definitely wasn't. The person doing that didn't know she already had a potential avatar in the room, and couldn't have cared less about Aiden. She went straight for the troll kid, the only living witness to what Alfhild has been doing—"

"That doesn't prove anything. There are other *vargrs*—"

"The plural is *vargar*, and I wasn't finished yet! In Faerie, she was known as Alfhild Ambhǫfði: Alfhild the Two-Headed. It's a common nickname for *vargar*. It's probably how she escaped from that tower the fey imprisoned her in, and it's definitely how she got away from the consul. Her body died, but she threw her consciousness into her secretary—"

"Who just let her ride him around for the last five hundred years?" Marlowe scoffed.

"He didn't have a choice! Something happened to him that night, when Mircea and the witch stole the shield. I called Mircea while we were waiting for you, and he filled me in on some of the things they figured out afterward.

"He thinks Alfhild intended to put all the power she was stealing from those vampires into a single receptacle, knowing that the consul would call up a sandstorm during their duel. As soon as the view of the fight was obscured, the praetor would hit her with all that power, all at once, crippling her. Then finish her off on her own, making it look like she'd won the duel fair and square.

"It was a good plan—if she'd been faster. But she knew how powerful the consul was, and wanted to make sure she overpowered her, so she was still collecting bones when Mircea and the witch discovered her plans and made their escape. She hadn't even had the receptacle made yet, but suddenly she was hours, perhaps only minutes away from an enraged consul if she couldn't find them—"

"She put the power in the shield, didn't she?" Louis-Cesare asked. He hadn't heard this part before—I hadn't gotten this far last time—but no one's ever accused him of being slow.

I nodded. "It was the only thing she had on hand strong enough to hold that much energy, because it was designed for traveling through the ley lines. So she had one of her mages spell it to absorb the power in the bones. I don't know if she planned to stay and fight, or run and try her luck later, but either way, she wanted her stolen power with her."

"But Mircea stole it first." Marlowe suddenly grinned, showing fang. I couldn't remember if I'd ever seen him smile before, but it was . . . disturbing.

I decided I liked him angry better.

"Uh, yeah. But not before the shield almost killed her avatar. Mircea said he thought she must have been using her secretary to oversee the operation in Venice, based on the height of the 'fisherman' he'd been chasing. The praetor was paranoid, and didn't trust anyone besides herself to manage things. So she rode her secretary around to have her cake and eat it, too, and to have plausible deniability if anyone found out what was going on."

"That is why he received favored status among her servants," Louis-Cesare said. "I did wonder what a non-master was doing in such an important place in her household."

"But he paid for it that night. He tried to use the altered shield to suck the life out of Mircea, but instead the witch turned it back on him. He didn't die, but Alfhild was left with a crippled avatar, or else we'd have heard from her before this."

"That's absurd," Marlowe said, no longer smiling. "Who the hell would choose to live like that? With two consciousnesses in a single body!"

I stared at him, wondering if it had been deliberate. But I guess not. Because he flushed suddenly, as realization hit. And, for once, Marlowe actually looked flustered.

"I . . . didn't mean—"

"Someone who wanted revenge badly enough," I cut him off, because we didn't have time for this. "Reincarnation ran the risk of her not remembering who she was next time. We don't know how many human lifetimes she lived before one was long enough to jog her memory. What if it never happened again? As for the secretary, he was weak, but any other body she chose would have fought her, whereas he probably didn't have the strength. Or maybe he didn't want to. Alfhild knew how the vampire world worked, and could protect him. In his weakened state, who else would have bothered?"

"So he was the albino we saw at the fights," Louis-Cesare said. "With Alfhild in control."

I nodded. "And back to her old tricks. The parallels between the praetor and our current problem were everywhere: preying on the same type of vulnerable communities, using the same method with the bones, even having the same target. But they were separated by five hundred years, so whenever I noticed anything, I put it down to coincidence—"

"Which it probably is!" Marlowe said, resuming asshole mode and pissing me off.

"Damn it, Marlowe!" I slapped my hands down, sending flour billowing. "Do you think I *like* this? I'd prefer for you to be right—then the villain is in custody and all's right with the world. Instead, I have to deal with the fact that I left a friend to be used by that . . . thing, and ignored every hint he gave me!"

"Friend?" Marlowe's guy said, his forehead wrinkling. "I thought we were talking about some albino?"

I put a hand to my head, and contemplated having an aneurysm. "Okay," I said. "One more time. Alfhild is a disembodied consciousness. She needs a body in order to get around and execute her revenge. At first, she took over her secretary, because he was loyal and didn't fight her. But after he died at the burnt-out-building fight, she needed a replacement, and she needed one fast."

"Because *vargar* can't hold free flight," Louis-Cesare said.

At least somebody had been paying attention, I thought gratefully.

"Yes. After her former avatar ended up under a burning truck, she had to find another, and she only had minutes before her consciousness scattered. And for an on-the-fly choice, James was a damned good one."

Louis-Cesare agreed. "A Circle member tasked with combating the smuggling trade was the perfect way to find out how close we were getting to . . . whatever she is doing."

Yeah, like ruining a good man's life.

He must have seen something change on my face.

"Your friend is a war mage," he told me quietly. "He knew the risks."

"He has two little girls," I told him back. "And a father who relies on him more every year. He's been talking about transferring to training duty, because he wants to watch his kids grow up. He—"

I cut off, because if I didn't my voice was going to change, and I didn't need my voice to change. I needed to kill something. Not someone, some*thing*. A thing that should have died millennia ago, but which instead was riding James around town like a sports car and doing God knew what kind of damage in the process!

Even if I got him back, I wasn't sure I'd get him back.

"You were unconscious," Louis-Cesare reminded me. "You didn't even see your friend that night."

"But I did a couple nights later at the warehouse, and I knew he was acting strange. James doesn't know who Fra Filippo Lippi was, or swan around like Darth Vader, or threaten to send innocent people back to a war zone to die! And he was there that night, when that bitch lost her previous avatar. He told me so himself. Probably deliberately, like all those theatrics, because she didn't know his mannerisms, but I *did*. He was trying to get my attention, hoping I'd start asking questions, but instead—"

Instead, I just left him there.

With her.

There was a brief silence, which of course was broken by Marlowe. "So, according to you, Alfhild is back and looking for revenge?"

"Not just according to me. Dorina recognized the albino as the praetor's old secretary. Not at first—they were in the middle of a chase, and it had been five hundred years—but soon—"

"And started sending you memories because she thinks history is about to repeat itself?"

I nodded.

"How the hell does that work?" he demanded. "If Alfhild had won that fight in Venice, she'd have ruled the vampire world, or a sizeable portion of it. But now? If she exists at all, she's a shadow, a phantom, an echo of what she once was. What can a shadow do?"

"Almost kill the consul?" Louis-Cesare said dryly.

"That was a one-off! Those damned weapons use life energy, not conventional magic. It led our wards to recognize them as people instead of arms—"

"People?" I asked.

Marlowe grimaced. "That's the problem with wards. They only know to look for what they've been told is a threat, and nobody uses life energy for weapons—it's too hard to come by! But while we figure out how to recalibrate, the consul is being well guarded."

Louis-Cesare didn't look reassured. "You may have tightened security, but you've highlighted another problem. We're in New York City, one of the most densely populated areas in the country. If the weapons register as life energy, how are we supposed to find them?"

"Because we've been doing so great so far," one of Marlowe's guys muttered. It was the same one as before, with an impressive 'fro and a problem keeping his mouth shut.

But he wasn't wrong.

He was talking about the great weapons hunt, which had started when the albino died and his fellow slavers lost no time raiding his warehouse. Literally no time— they were at it before the flames died down on the truck. They'd robbed him blind knowing that the Circle was busy at the burnt-out building, and that his people were trying to hunt down escaped slaves.

As a result, the overpowered weapons ended up in the hands of smugglers all over the city, which was where the "underworld war" came in. It was actually Alfhild raiding the raiders, trying to get her stuff back. And to do it before anybody figured out what they had.

That was why she'd been so pissed at Blue. Here she was, trying to keep things nice and quiet, when along comes a homicidal battle troll, drawing everybody's attention. She'd managed to keep a lid on that through James, who had pulled rank to take control of the crime scenes and any weapons they contained, but she couldn't watch everyone. So she'd tried to recruit me to pimp on the Senate's investigation for her.

It was also why she'd showed me those weapons. So

that, if I ran across any more, I wouldn't think anything of them, just assume they were the same crap she'd already given me an explanation for. And meanwhile, maybe I'd hunt down Blue for her in exchange for Fin, because she had too many balls in the air and needed some help.

But she was already too late.

Because the Senate clashed with some of her guys that same night, when they both decided to raid the same smuggler. And found the mother lode of weapons he'd taken from the albino's stock, without any idea what they actually were. He didn't have time to find out before the Senate took them to Radu's, where Alfhild's people took them from us.

And now where were they?

"Call the mage," Marlowe snapped. "Get a location."

"She already did," Louis-Cesare said. "His phone is off."

"Ping him, then! We have contacts—"

"Which we've used. It's not that simple."

And no, it wasn't. Cell phone tower records weren't that reliable, despite what TV cop shows liked everyone to believe. In a rural setting, a single tower might service several hundred square miles, and even in New York City, where they clustered close together, you were still talking two or more. Not exactly a small area in a place as crowded as this one.

And that was assuming your call was routed to the closest tower. Which it often wasn't. So all we really knew for sure was that James was still in the city.

Well, and one other thing.

"James was frothing at the mouth to get his hands on Blue," I told Marlowe. "Probably because he kept drawing attention to the people who had those weapons—"

"So?"

"—so he gave me a two-day window to track him down, and it's up tonight. Why two days? And, if he was expecting to hear from me, why not take the call?"

Marlowe frowned.

"Perhaps he retrieved all the weapons," Mouthy said, "and no longer cares what the troll attacks."

"Maybe. Or maybe whatever is happening, is happening tonight."

"What do you mean, happening tonight?" Marlowe demanded. "The consul was already attacked!"

"Using only a small portion of the weapons," Louis-Cesare pointed out. "What is Alfhild doing with the rest?"

"And nobody knows where James is," I added. "I called war mage HQ, but they said it was his day off—"

"Check it," Marlowe snapped, and one of his boys moved out into the hall, a phone to his ear.

"—so I called his wife, who said he hasn't been home in five days. He told her he was working a case, but she's worried. Being gone this long isn't like him—"

"Map!" Another of the guys pulled one out of a pocket and laid it on the flour.

"—so I called his father, but Rufus hasn't seen him, either—"

I cut off, because Marlowe wasn't listening. He'd bent over the map, so Louis-Cesare could show him where the cell phone tower had pinged. I tried to concentrate on it, too, and on where James might be in all those crisscrossing streets, but I wasn't seeing it. I was seeing him, with that crown of flowers his little girl had made for him, laughing at something his wife had said.

That's why Alfhild needed to die, I thought. Because of James. And all those other Jameses she'd crushed under her heel through the centuries: the poor bastards back in Faerie, the hundreds or maybe thousands of baby vamps in Venice, the Dark Fey . . .

She'd destroyed countless lives, thoughtlessly, carelessly, on her climb to the top, because they didn't matter to her.

They just didn't matter.

Marlowe and Louis-Cesare continued the debate, but I'd had enough. There was a minuscule opening in the crowd and I went for it, elbowing my way through to Coffee Lover, who was still patiently waiting. The fey were better at that sort of thing than I was.

"Tell me some good news," I said, before he even opened his mouth.

He arched an eyebrow at me. "You have a visitor."

I scowled. "Who is it this time?"

He didn't answer. Just stepped out of the way to show me another doorway filled with vampires. And, in the middle of them, Curly Abbot, looking like Porky Pig with his shirt rucked up over his fat little belly, and his blue eyes huge. And Ray, standing beside him, appearing unbelievably smug.

"Curly has something he'd like to tell you."

Chapter Fifty-seven

"C-c-c—"

The security guard waited patiently.

"C-c-c—"

Less patiently.

"C-c-c—"

"Oh, for God's sake!" That was Ray, who hit Curly on the back of the head.

"Curly Abbot!" Curly spat, as if the strike had knocked something loose. "And friends!"

The guard ran Curly's little black membership card through a reader. Curly made a sound that defied description, and then bounced a little in the driver's seat. "Hurry up! I have to go to the bathroom."

"There's one in the—"

"I know where it is!" Curly said, grabbed his card back, and hit the gas, skidding the tires and shooting us away from the gatehouse.

So much for a low-key entrance, I thought. And then forgot to worry about it when the crappy industrial park ahead of us rippled and changed. Big-time.

"So this is how the other half lives," Ray said, sounding impressed.

I didn't blame him. A second ago, we'd been looking at a rusted-out hulk of a factory, about to fall into the sea. It was the kind that Red Hook, Brooklyn's lesser-known seaside hood, had a lot of, along with parking lots like the one next door, where razor wire and rusted shopping carts passed for landscaping.

But, suddenly, all that was gone. Instead, manicured

lawns spread out in all directions. Flower beds materialized, planted in undulating rows of different shades of blue and edged by taller, white blooming bushes, like the ocean followed by breaking surf. Silky smooth blacktop replaced the pitted wonder outside, and a space opened up in the middle of the big circular drive, boasting a reflecting pond with sprays of water and a huge sculpture of silver metal and aqua glass.

The sculpture was abstract, with mostly curved pieces shooting upward from a central base, but it nonetheless managed to give the impression of a group of sea deities rising from the water, presumably the ones that gave this place its name: Oceanid.

In case your mythology wasn't that good—and mine wasn't—it was also written in crystal letters on the five-story white stone building that framed everything else. I could see right through to the other side, courtesy of an all-glass section that went the full height of the building, showing the water and city skyline beyond. Where a tiny Statue of Liberty was looking dull and kind of chintzy in comparison.

We slung into a parking spot off to one side, and Curly jumped out, rabbiting for the employee entrance. I guess he really did have to go. The rest of us piled out and followed him, while a line of beautiful people inched closer to the casino's front entrance and valet parking.

I watched a gorgeous brunet in a few wisps of red satin get out of a Maserati, with the ease of someone used to driving about a foot off the ground. She nodded to a bleach blonde in yellow silk and her earrings caught the light. The huge things sparkled like lasers, despite the fact that we had to be a third of a football field away.

"Remind me why we didn't take Radu's Bugatti," Ray muttered, adjusting his suit.

It was a little wrinkled, having been dug out of a suitcase less than an hour ago, but he looked fine. I'd thought I did, too, but suddenly, an LBD and black pumps just didn't cut it. But at least one of our group was styling, I thought, watching the car in question sling around the drive, bypass the peasants, and careen to a stop directly in front of the building.

"That's why," I said, as Louis-Cesare got out and tossed a valet the keys.

He had a fleet of cars back home, but that was three hours away, so he'd borrowed Claire's. Like he'd grabbed a tux off the rack, since he didn't have time to go back for any of the bespoke numbers in his closet. But, goddamn, you'd never know it.

"I don't know why he gets to be Mr. Look-at-Me," Ray grumbled. "I coulda done that job."

I stayed quiet, because no, Ray could not have done that job. Nobody could have done that job like Louis-Cesare, who had effortlessly captured everyone's attention without saying a word. The blonde and the brunet stopped and stared. An older woman, swaddled in mink despite the weather, almost fell off the steps before her husband caught her. Even the valet did a double take.

Because Louis-Cesare shone, from the dark auburn mane, which had been slicked back into a discreet clip at the base of his neck, to the platinum and diamonds that glittered on his cuff links and studded the front of his shirt, to the glossy Berlutis on his feet. He hadn't bothered with a tie, because when you look that good you don't need a tie, or with the open-container laws despite the fact that the car was in convertible mode. He grabbed a bottle of Dom out of the passenger side, took a swig straight out of the bottle, and stared up the steps like he owned the place.

He looked gorgeous. He looked rich. He looked ready to drop a huge amount of dough.

Most importantly, he drew the freaking eye, which was his job. Specifically, to make enough of a spectacle to give security something to watch besides us. Which was why he was all blinged out, and the rest of us were sneaking in a side door looking as bland and boring as possible.

Or we were supposed to be.

But some weird movement caught my eye, and I glanced over at the shadowy side of the building to see Curly dancing around, cussing, and repeatedly jamming his card into a reader by the door.

"Shit," Ray said.

"I thought he had access," I said.

"He's supposed to have access!"

"It doesn't look like he has access."

"I don't have access!" Curly said, jogging back over.

"Why not?" Ray demanded. "You said they have you over here all the time—"

"They do!" Beads of sweat were forming on the bald head. "Every time something goes wrong, I'm their go-to. It's not enough they steal my idea; they expect me to make it work, too! And for fifteen years' experience, what do I get? A pissant consulting fee!"

"And a card somebody canceled."

"It still worked at the gate! That probably means I've just been bumped down a level in clearance."

"They're not worried about you; they're just battening down," Rufus translated.

James' dad was the fourth member of our little squad, and I was unhappy about it. He looked like an older, darker, more wizened version of Curly, except instead of curls he had a little ring of snow-white fuzz around his head, and unlike Curly's deer-caught-in-the-headlights expression, his was shrewd and focused.

I'd nipped by his shop to get resupplied, because I was out of almost everything, and had let slip what was going on. I'd hoped it would get me access to the not-entirely-legal stash in his back room. Instead, it got me a partner.

And there was no getting around it. If I hadn't agreed to take him along, he was going to scream bloody murder to the Corps, which was all this needed: a bunch of jarheads with too much magic and a serious lack of subtlety. We needed to get in, get out, and do it quietly. We did *not* need the Corps. So Rufus it was.

I just hoped I wasn't going to have to tell James that I'd gotten his dad killed.

"We'll go in the front," Curly was saying. "It's okay; they know me—"

"They know her, too!" Ray said, gesturing at me. "That's the whole point!"

"So leave her out—"

"She's the *vargr*! We can't leave her out!"

We also couldn't stand around discussing this. After Curly spilled the beans, Marlowe had given us exactly one hour to locate the weapons and rescue James before he sent in his boys. They were already getting into position, a literal army of vampires ready to swoop down on the cache as soon as we found it—assuming we did. Because the damned things read like people and this place was packed.

It was the only reason Marlowe gave a shit about James: he assumed he'd be with the weapons. And considering how vindictive Alfhild was, and that these things could level half the city, rushing in without knowing exactly where they were wasn't smart. Of course, neither was letting her do whatever she was planning, hence the compromise.

And my latest ulcer.

Because guess who was supposed to deal with Alfhild if she spotted us?

Rufus had been watching me. He patted the big black suitcase he was carrying. Among other things, it contained a duplicate syringe to the one I had taped to my thigh.

"We get this in him, and he won't be a problem."

"But Alfhild might," I pointed out. "She can jump to somebody else if she loses James."

"Maybe not. They share a consciousness at the moment, from what I understand. If he goes out fast enough, she may, too."

"May," Ray said darkly. "That's great. We *may* not end up in the stewpot. I feel much better now."

"You can stay behind," Rufus said curtly.

The man was laser focused, looking like he was ready and able to take on the whole place by himself. But he wasn't. Which was why I stepped on Ray's foot, to shut his mouth, even before Curly grabbed him.

"No, he can't! He can't stay here! You promised!"

Curly was a little squirrelly without his friend/teddy bear.

"He can stay. We can all stay," I said. "We just have to find a way through that door without anybody noticing!"

And then someone did it for us.

I jerked my neck around when what sounded like a bomb went off. And was just in time to see the sturdy security gate come flying through the ward and skidding down the middle of the street. Where it was promptly run down by Frankentruck, burning rubber, billowing smoke, and looking like a ride straight out of hell.

"What the *fuck*?" Ray said, stumbling back, although we were nowhere near the drive.

But then, neither was the truck. It smashed through a flower bed, careened back the other way to crack the fountain, and finally straightened up to gouge the blacktop, all while leaking enough fiery oil to set the pretty bushes on fire. It didn't hit the brakes until it was halfway up the great swath of steps, just missing Claire's Batmobile, and sending a bunch of beautiful people scattering and screaming.

The engine died a second later, judging by the clouds of smoke cascading out from under the hood. It was almost enough to hide Louis-Cesare's expression as he jumped out of the way, and to obscure the front entrance in billows of white. Great big billows.

I looked at the guys; the guys looked at me.

"I think I just wet my pants," Curly breathed.

And then we were darting across the road, up the steps, and through the entrance, unnoticed by the security guys, who suddenly had their hands full.

We ran through the atrium, which had a ceiling covered in strips of hanging, rippling glass that resembled seaweed, and which were chiming in the wind and smoke blowing through the doors. And then we veered off to the side and around a corner, because Curly was heading for the john, damn him! Ray shrugged at me and followed; Curly was the only one who knew anything about this place and we needed him.

"What are the trolls doing here?" Rufus asked, as I pretended to check a stocking to get my hair to fall in my face.

"Don't know. Olga's been searching for her nephew, who we think was taken by slavers—"

"Well, she won't find him here! And she's likely to screw up this whole thing!"

I glanced at him through my bangs. "You wanna tell her that?"

Rufus looked like he was considering it. But the dustup behind us was already getting heated, with a few fists being flung around—along with something else. Something that zipped here and there through the fog like dark bugs. Dark bugs with eyes. Dark bugs the size of soccer balls that—

"Damn," I said, with feeling.

"What now?"

"Reporters."

And, sure enough, a couple dozen camera balls were whizzing about, getting in people's faces. Along with what appeared to be every reporter in town, jumping out of a bunch of cars that must have followed the truck, and screaming questions at the security guards. We needed to get gone.

Luckily, Ray pulled an annoyed-looking Curly out of the bathroom a moment later. "Can't a guy take a piss?"

And then we were through, into the huge main room.

I caught it in glimpses, because there was so much to take in all at once: a white marble floor with a mosaic of the sculpture outside, and "Oceanid" carved around it in gold. A huge wall of glass on the opposite end, outside of which a passing ship was lit up like a Christmas tree. Slot machines, table games, a large bar with an abstract wave pattern in the big open space directly ahead. And on the walls—

I had no freaking idea.

The nonglass sides of the building had four balconies going up, all overlooking the main room. They were connected to the ground floor by open staircases fore and aft, the ultramodern kind that seemed to hang in space all by themselves, although that wasn't the weird part. The weird part was what was on them.

Large, round doorways studded the walls in lines, like portholes on a ship. There were no actual doors, leaving the openings dark and kind of ominous. Except for one, on the lowest balcony to the left, which had just lit up with a circle of little lights curving around it, inset into the stone.

The lights were shaped like a bunch of orange squid, colorful and oddly cartoonish, glowing against all that white. But they seemed to make a bunch of people really happy. Because a sizeable chunk of the crowd peeled off and headed that way, some with glasses still in hand, chatting and laughing and booking it, as much as high heels would allow.

"What's going on?" I asked—nobody, because I was the only dummy still standing out in the open like this.

"Come on!" Ray beckoned from halfway up the nearest staircase, and I hurried to join him.

The balcony, when we reached it, gave a better view of what was happening across the room at the squid door. The big, round opening let out into a circular waiting room, still kind of dim, with a few benches hugging the sides, covered in the same dark blue as the walls and floor. It made them almost melt into the darkness and disappear.

Like the people.

Because I'd just watched maybe a couple hundred tuxes and evening gowns be swallowed up by the entrance, and now—where were they now? Because there was almost nobody in there. Just a few stragglers headed for the door, and a woman adjusting a shoe strap while hanging on to her date, who had stopped to consult a small notebook.

"Where did they go?" I asked, before I noticed: the dark wall behind them had another big round door in it, like the one leading in. It was dark enough that I hadn't immediately noticed it next to the midnight blue wall, but now that I did, I couldn't unsee it. Because it was filled with a rippling, inky blackness that was swallowing people up like a giant maw.

"What is this place?" I asked, and Curly snorted.

"Geminus' darling. I designed it; he built it. It was my payment for protection."

"But what *is* it?"

"A modern-day Colosseum. He used to be a gladiator, you know? In old Rome?"

I nodded.

"He was there when they flooded the real Colosseum, for a great naval battle. It's what gave him the idea."

"The idea for what?"

"A new type of fights. Through each of those doors is a

portal to a different water environment, here and in Faerie. Only, instead of ships and crews fighting each other, like the Romans did, Geminus used—"

"Fey."

Curly nodded. "All different kinds. That's what people are really gambling on here. The table games are just to keep 'em occupied in between bouts."

"Like in Vegas," Ray said. "They got fights in some of the casinos out there."

Curly's lip curled. "No, not like in Vegas. Geminus thought a fight wasn't worth a damn if somebody didn't die."

"He set up portals to different areas, for the different types of competitors," I said, finally getting it. And looking around with a sinking feeling, because there were a *lot* of doors. Instead of a single building, we were now faced with searching . . . what, exactly? Half the seafloor?

"No one building could have held all the environments he wanted," Curly confirmed, "so the bouts are held out there." He gestured at the dark sea beyond the windows. "Everywhere from the Arctic Ocean to the Caribbean. The audience passes through portals here, into warded viewing areas, and the fighters enter the open sea through separate portals in their holding tanks. And then they go at it."

"But, if they're out in the open sea, why don't they just swim away?" Ray asked.

"Geminus kept family members back here, in holding tanks down below, as hostages. Escape from the scene of a fight or refuse to fight—"

"And they kill your family," I said, remembering the little girl at the theatre.

Ray gave Curly a shove. "And you helped him?"

The blue eyes grew big with alarm. "I didn't know all this at first! My idea was for an interactive theatre, a spectacle! Like at my place, only bigger. Geminus turned it into something else. And by the time I realized what he was doing, I was in too deep."

"So you just kept doing it, you little—"

"I didn't have a choice!"

"You said some of the portals go to Faerie," I interrupted, before we got off track. "Then why did Geminus need the one at your theatre?"

"*He* didn't. The family did. After his death, the Senate was watching them like a hawk, but nobody was watching me."

"But now his guys are back in business."

"Yeah." He looked around resentfully. "They trashed my place, so they just came back here. I don't know how they think they're going to get away with it. The Circle does checks on places like this—"

"They recently acquired an in with the Circle."

Rufus and I exchanged glances.

"Well, that's just great," Ray said. "All these people mean we can't use magic to pinpoint the weapons, and now you tell me we gotta search"—he broke off to count—"twenty portals!"

"Forty. Twenty on this side, too," Curly pointed out.

Ray cursed. "How the hell are we supposed to search forty portals?"

"I don't know. You said, get you in. I got you in. Now I got to go to the john."

"You just went to the john!"

"I have a tiny bladder! It's a condition!"

He said something else, too, but I didn't hear. Because the front doors went crashing into the main room, followed by fifty thousand pounds of pissed-off war machine. And I didn't just mean the truck.

Looked like the party had come to us.

Chapter Fifty-eight

I guess the truck hadn't died, after all, just got hung up on the steps. Because it came barreling into the room, shattering the pretty glass lobby and slinging around. And started off-loading trolls—tons of them.

It looked like a clown car at the circus; they just kept coming. But instead of big red noses and floppy shoes, they were wearing full-on armor: huge helmets, massive breastplates, even shin guards. And it *wasn't* just Olga's usual crew; I didn't know most of these guys, although I was pretty sure I'd seen a few at the burnt-out-building fight.

And it looked like they were ready for a new one.

"What are they *doing*?" Ray yelled to be heard over the trolls, who were also yelling. And banging on massive shields and slamming equally massive spears into the floor, hard enough to crack the tile.

Olga got out and clambered on top of the cab, and if I'd thought she looked like Boudicca before, it was nothing compared to this. She was armored, too, including a shining bronze helmet, a breastplate that truly deserved the term, and a sword in her fist that had to be six feet long. She roared, a word that in no way does that sound justice, and which was completely unlike the triumphal noise I'd heard her make at the theatre. This one was full of anguish and fury, a primal, heart-stopping, gut-wrenching cry that had all my hairs standing on end and my knees weak.

The beating and stamping and assorted other sounds abruptly stopped.

And so did everything else.

A couple slot games chimed quietly to themselves and somebody dropped a glass. But nobody moved; nobody spoke. For a space that a minute ago had been loud and boisterous, it was pretty impressive.

And then Olga started talking, and it was more so.

"Trym! Geirröd!" The shout was loud enough to shake the rafters. "Come out and face me. Come out and die!"

Nobody came out.

I didn't really blame them.

"You go into our hills," Olga spat. "You lead slavers to hidden villages. You rip children from mothers' arms, sell like animals. Those you not sell, you kill! You kill my sister's son, my *BLOOD*. Now I take yours! Come out and face me! Come out and die!"

Shit. It looked like I hadn't been the only one doing some investigating, and Olga's had not ended in good news. For her or the bastards responsible.

"Worse, you sell bones," Olga said, her voice low and savage, but it went through the room like a shout. "You sell *souls*. You make weapons from our people to use on our people! You blaspheme and defile! No more!"

There was a sound from the crowd then, a murmur that swept, not through the staring humans, motionless in their gowns and jewels, but through the trolls. Only that isn't the right word. A murmur implies something soft, and there was none of that here. A low, furious vibration was more like it, one that shook the floor under my feet despite the fact that I was standing on a balcony. If rage had a sound, that would be it.

"What's going on?" Ray whispered.

I thought about what Blue had told me. "I think . . . six and seven are about to have a very bad day."

"What?"

I shook my head.

"Come out and face me!" Olga thundered. "Come out and *die*!"

And, this time, somebody did come out, but it wasn't White Hair or Gravel Face. It wasn't trolls at all. But vampires, what looked like a whole army of them, unleashed from doorways on both sides of the ground floor like an unending flood.

And while I was sure Olga's crew was good, I didn't think they were that good.

Until somebody else tore out of the truck—literally—grabbed Olga off the cab and then picked it up and threw it across the room. The approaching horde scattered, like pins when a bowling ball smashes through them. And another indescribable sound went up from every troll in the place, including from my throat because it was contagious. Blue roared and we roared with him, a deafening, earsplitting cry that shook the walls.

Then the two armies clashed, and everything was chaos.

"Part of Geminus' family, my ass!" Ray yelled. "This is the whole thing—it's gotta be!"

Yeah, it did. Which . . . was not going to work, for a variety of reasons, but I didn't have time to list them right now. Because we'd been recognized.

A wave of vamps leapt for the balcony, and Ray and I grabbed stakes from Rufus' suitcase and prepared for a back-to-back, no-holds-barred fight. I was trying to protect Rufus, and get him in between us, until I realized: he didn't need it. He pushed me off, grabbed his case, and let loose.

For a moment, I just stood there, getting schooled. Because, sure, I bought some stuff to even the field from time to time, but I wasn't a mage. And the difference between what I did and what a century-and-a-half-old magical arms dealer could do was . . . eye-opening.

Rufus had unfolded a stand from one side of his suitcase, making it into a little table. It looked like something a traveling magician would use, as a platform for card tricks or maybe pulling a bunny out of a hat. Only I didn't see any bunnies.

What I did see were a flock of bolas made out of light that went sizzling through the air to wrap around vamp legs and then drag them backward, while sinking into their flesh as if trying to eat through it. I saw something scatter from a vial that was almost too bright to look at, a dazzle that strobed the room and caused the vamps heading for us to scream and shield their eyes, while their flesh burned and bubbled off their bones. I saw nets, made out of what looked like the same stuff as the webs at the theatre, that snared half of the oncoming assault. And then, Rufus sent a pulse through them, slammed back against the floor a story below, leaving the snared vamps sizzling and smoking and trolls enthusiastically stomping on their heads.

Yet the vamps just kept coming.

I saw a bunch of magical throwing stars, like mine but incredibly fast, zip through the crowd, flaying a path. I saw a dislocator hit a bunch of vamps, turning them into something that looked like a rat king, a single creature with numerous heads and limbs sticking out at odd angles. I saw a mass of black circles, filmy and indistinct, that fluttered out into the air like they were made out of tissue paper, and didn't seem to do anything at all.

Until a handful landed on a vamp leaping for me and he suddenly looked like Swiss cheese. Because they weren't circles; they were *holes*. And everywhere they touched, something suddenly went missing.

Yet the vamps just kept coming.

I got a stake in my latest problem, ducked under a knife swipe, and took out two more. Then jerked back the head of a guy trying to strangle Ray. Who pulled free, dodged under another assault, spun, and slit the vamp's throat. And drenched us both in bright red blood, because he hadn't even been a master.

But there were plenty that were. Enough that, barely a minute into the fight, Rufus switched to the big guns, although they didn't look like it. They didn't look like much of anything, just a handful of small silver disks, which put out tiny pincers and glommed on to the mass of shirts and trousers around us.

And then projected what looked like a bunch of quarter-sized swirls of color and light that opened up in front of the vamps, I didn't know why.

And then I realized: they weren't *in front of* the vamps.

"Oh shit! Oh fuck! Oh shit!" Ray said, as one of the nearest masters looked down—in time to see his whole midsection get sucked inside the growing portal.

It was the size of a saucer when it finished consuming his chest in a swirl of angry red flesh and yellowish fat, and a dinner plate by the time it pulled in his legs. And then I guess it ran out of steam. Because it winked out with the guy's head still here and somehow still alive, with malevolent eyes staring, staring, staring—

Until I kicked it down the hall and looked up, panting. And saw another wave headed our way.

It's what people often forget about vamps, and what makes fighting them so damned hard: hurting them is easy—if you're good and fast, or slow but tricky. But killing them is something else altogether. And if you don't kill them, they just. Keep. Coming.

And then suddenly I was eating carpet.

Ray screamed, "Troll!" about the time that he smacked me and Rufus to the floor, and I looked up to see a couple thousand pounds of muscle slam overhead and into the wall behind us. The troll appeared to be dead, judging by the fact that half his torso was missing. But the body took out a bunch of vamps anyway, sending them crashing against the stone, and then smearing along the wall under his momentum. They left a bloody swath that stretched halfway down the corridor, but that wasn't what had me staring.

I'd seen Blue survive a combined spell that would have taken down a platoon. Yet this troll had a burning crater in his chest, and had also been flung from halfway across the building. What the *fuck*?

And then Rufus suddenly stopped with the magical mayhem and threw up a shield. One that bloomed with angry colors a second later, along with scrabbling, burning vamps. Because somebody hadn't waited for their allies to get out of the way before lobbing an attack.

"Mages!" someone yelled; it might have even been me. I wasn't sure because, while the shield had saved our asses, it also acted like a kettledrum, trapping the sound of all those spells inside. To the point that I thought my head might burst.

Rufus did something to tone the sound down, enough that I could hear Ray yelling at me. "Call Marlowe!"

"I can't call Marlowe!"

"You have to—we're getting slaughtered here!"

"And half the city will go with us if they set those weapons off! Some pissed-off trolls probably won't do it, because they'll think they can take them—"

"Probably because they *can*!"

"—but Marlowe's men show up, and it's over!"

"It's over anyway if we're stuck behind this shield!"

He had a point.

I fished out my phone and called somebody, but it wasn't Marlowe.

"Roberto?" I yelled, barely able to hear myself.

"Dory." The thick, rounded Italian syllables always made it sound like he was eating. Of course, he usually was. "You got Stan's truck? He keeps bugging me. Pretty soon, I gotta bug you. Know what I'm sayin'?"

"I'll get around to it! I'm partying with my boys over at Oceanid right now—"

"That place closed down."

"They said that's what they told you! I said they'd better pay you your percentage, 'cause this is your turf—everybody knows that! But they're laughing over here—"

"Laughing?"

"—about this being your territory! Said they're taking over—"

"I got a deal with Geminus!" The wolf growl was starting to eclipse the mellow Italian vowels.

"But Geminus is dead, and they say you've run things long enough! They got a little troll problem at the moment, but as soon as it's over, they're coming for you—"

"They're coming for me? I'm coming for them!"

"Better get here fast, then! And remember, the trolls are on *your* side!"

I hung up.

Ray just looked at me. "You think inviting a crazy were gang boss is gonna *help*?"

"Can it hurt?"

"Yeah! Like when he figures out that you set him up to—" Ray broke off and stared at something behind me. "*Shit.*"

"Shit? What's shit?" And then I followed his gaze. "Shit!"

Because Curly hadn't gone to the john, after all. I could just make him out, through the psychedelic shield, standing on the third-floor balcony across from us with something in his hands. It looked like some sort of controller, small and black and—yeah. It was controlling things, all right.

Or maybe it was a total coincidence that one of the big, round doorways suddenly opened up like the floodgates had lifted—or like a portal had reversed—to gush water down onto the frenzied crowd. Satins were drenched, silks were ruined, and people went slip-sliding for the doors, those who hadn't already been headed that way because of the massive brawl going on.

"I knew he was too willing to come along!" Ray raged. "He planned this!"

Yeah, he had. I couldn't hear him, even with dhampir senses, but I could lip-read. "Payback time, bitches!"

Great.

And then it was. It really, really was. Because it wasn't just water squeezing through the big, round opening. It was—

"What the fuck is *that*?" Ray screamed, sounding almost outraged.

I laughed the laugh of the faintly hysterical, because Cthulhu had just made his entrance, or something that looked like him. Well, it would if he were scarlet and three stories tall. As it was, I guessed it was a combatant from Faerie.

And it was *pissed*.

The creature started laying waste with arms the size of tree trunks—if the trees in question were redwoods—and a maw full of holy hell that could spear a vamp clean through and then fling him the length of the room to splat against the pretty windows.

Okay, I thought.

All right!

Then I realized: we were still losing.

"How are we still losing?" Ray demanded, as half the mages and a good number of the vamps peeled off from us to attack Big Red. Yet Rufus was still sweating bullets trying to maintain the shield. And out in the fray, I saw a mage materialize a glowing spear and run it through three trolls at once.

"What . . . the hell . . . are they doing?" Rufus panted, his dark eyes pained. "How are they . . . this strong?"

"They're using the merchandise," I said, staring around.

"What?"

"They have to be." But I couldn't see—

And then I did.

"There!" I pointed to a couple vamps with a very familiar-looking crate on the far side of the room by the windows. Another crate was already open and the contents were being passed around, which was probably why a charge of maybe twenty trolls was repulsed like it was nothing, sending them slamming backward what had to be thirty yards. And why a bunch more were already floating facedown in what was now hip-deep water.

"Olga was right," Ray said, gripping my arm. "They're gonna kill 'em using weapons made out of their own people!"

"No, they're not." I scanned the room again. "Stay here."

"What?"

"Just guard Rufus for a minute, okay?"

"What are you—no!" And then, when he realized what was about to happen: "No, don't you dare!"

But I did, because I didn't have a choice. Another minute of those things, and there wouldn't be anybody on our side left standing. And it wasn't going to go down like that.

"I'll be right back," I told him, and jumped.

The shield Rufus had thrown up was the kind that let people out, but not in. Although, judging by the expression of the vamp I grabbed, nobody had really expected me to leave. Or to use him as a buffer to keep the mages' spells off me while I leapt over the balcony and into thin air—

And grabbed one of the little black camera balls as it whizzed past.

The sizzling body of the vamp fell into the drink, and

I took off—under an enormous, slashing tentacle; through another huge waterfall that had just opened up; and out the other side, drenched and gasping, only to slam into a line of vamps leaning over the railing, one of which grabbed me. And found himself flung into the windows a second later, when I popped a leg, and looked around for—

Yes!

"Richard! *Richard Kim!*"

The shout was unnecessary, because the reporter had already spotted me. He was standing on the balcony below Curly and staring at me with his mouth hanging open, I have no idea why. I waved the ball around at him, and then pointed with my toes, since my hands were busy.

"Over there! Send me *there!*"

But he didn't send me there. He didn't send me anywhere. He just stood there, the controller limp and useless in his hands, while the camera and I went around and around in a little circle.

"Dick!" I said fervently, as a vamp jumped up at me from the floor.

And missed, because Richard suddenly got with the program and swerved me abruptly to the side.

And then sent me careening through a minefield of leaping vampires, slashing water, and a merman that tried to stab me with a trident, because I guess to him all humans look alike. But I did a handstand on the ball and he ended up stabbing the vamp jumping up behind me instead. And then I jerked his weapon out of the vamp and sent it flying into the group around the crate.

What looked like blue-white electricity spidered across the knot of vamps, causing some to fall out and everyone else to look around in shock. Right before I added to the chaos by plowing into the middle of them. I grabbed the crate, hit a vamp in the head with it, got hit back, saw stars, and ended up hanging off the camera ball by my knees with the crate in my hands, while three—make that four—vamps tried to pull it away from me.

But the camera was stronger than it looked, and kept on tugging, and I hung on to the crate with one hand while I used the other to get a stake in the lead guy. He let go, and since the others had been holding on to him, they all fell back, too, and suddenly I was flying.

Straight at someone who had just appeared on the balcony, grabbed the remote from Richard, and used it to jerk me over to him. Somebody with a topknot of dark braids and burning, alien eyes. Somebody who looked like he'd like to rip my throat out like the vampire he wasn't, but which the damned bitch riding him had once been.

James. I felt my lips form the word, but no sound came out. It was okay; there was nothing of the man I knew in those eyes anyway.

But there was surprise when I tossed the crate to Olga, grabbed the ball with one hand and him with the other, and jerked him over the balcony.

"I have the controller," the thing that wasn't James snarled. "What do you think this is going to do?"

"This."

I used my feet to push off from the railing, as hard as I could, sending us speeding back into the thick of the fight—and straight into the path of one of Cthulhu's thrashing limbs.

The next thing I knew, I was eating stone on the other side of the room.

Chapter Fifty-nine

I don't know how fast we were going when we hit the wall, but it was officially too damned fast. I felt myself peel away and fall heavily to the floor, the slo-mo vamp senses that were supposed to protect me kicking in a split second too late. They didn't help with the blow, but did make it feel like I took a long time to crash down, giving me a chance to notice an imprint of my made-up face that had been left behind on the plaster.

Huh.

And then James was on me.

He must have somehow gotten a shield up in the maybe two seconds he'd had, because he wasn't looking all that affected. Or maybe you didn't with a *vargr* riding you. After all, they didn't care how much damage they caused their avatar, but I did. Which would have left me at a disadvantage if I'd been planning to fight him, but I wasn't.

I wasn't planning to break his nose, either, but my senses were screwy, and my aim was off.

"Sorry!" I said insanely, and heard it echo in the distortion of the slo-mo, while his head kicked back, allowing me to get a leg around him and bring him down. I was also fumbling for the wrist of the hand he was raising to curse me with, but I didn't get it. Not because he was too fast—human reflexes in slo-mo are ridiculously sluggish—but because I was seeing double or maybe triple, and couldn't figure out which one it was.

But the next second he went limp anyway, which had my heart hammering until I noticed Rufus standing over him, syringe in hand. I lay back against the carpet, panting and thanking Cthulhu. And wondering where all the vamps had gone, because nobody else seemed to be attacking me.

"Louis-Cesare," Ray said, when I asked.

His voice was distorted and echoey, because I couldn't seem to snap out of slo-mo. Like I couldn't seem to stand up properly, even when Ray levered James off me. I smacked the side of my head a couple times, but it hurt so I stopped. And looked around for Louis-Cesare, but didn't see him.

"Where is he?" I asked Ray. He was covered in blood, but I got the impression that it was mostly other people's.

"Don't know." He tried to put an arm around me for some reason, but I batted him away. "He showed up, cleared the balcony, then ran off chasing some vamps. Now let's get out of here!"

"We can't get out. We only did half the job."

I'd been on the way to my feet, but they got confused and I abruptly sat down again.

Ow.

Ray crouched down in front of me, while Rufus rigged up one of those floating stretchers for James. The guy really had thought of everything. I watched him sloooowly roll his son's body onto it, until Ray turned my cheek back to face him.

"Listen to me. We got what we got, okay? We're not gonna find the rest of those weapons, not in this. And you're not at your best—"

"I'm fine—"

"You just took a hit that woulda leveled a troll. You are not fine!"

I scowled at him. And then tried to push his finger out of my face, although I couldn't seem to catch it. "Stop moving."

"I'm *not* moving. And you're done."

"You don't get to tell me that!"

"Well, somebody needs to!"

I scowled at him. "You're supposed to be what? My Second?"

He looked surprised for what seemed like a long moment, but was probably just a flash across his face. Maybe because a Second was a master's leading servant, and kind of a big deal. But since the only vamps I had were Ray's, it seemed appropriate.

But I guess he hadn't stopped to think about it before.

"Yeah," he told me. "I guess so."

"Well, a vampire's Second does what he's told!"

Ray snorted. "You must not have known many Seconds."

"What does that mean?"

"It means that they do a lot of different jobs, depending on what the family needs. But their main one is to tell the master what he don't want to hear."

"To be a pain in the ass, in other words."

"A useful pain in the ass."

"Then you're perfect for the job."

"Thank you," Ray said, and pulled me back up again.

I grabbed the railing, not that I needed it, and looked around. Olga must have realized what I'd flung at her, because it looked like the battle was evening out. But that could change, really fast, and I hated the idea of just abandoning her. Plus, I couldn't shake the feeling that I was missing something.

I had the weirdest impression that, not only were the rest of the weapons here, but I was staring right at them. It was maddening. And if Marlowe came into this mess with no clue where they were . . .

Ding!

I started at the sound and looked around. But it hadn't come from another weird magical device, or from the drowning slots, which had been spazzing out this whole time. But from something behind me.

And, for once, it was something benign.

It looked like nobody had turned off whatever system controlled the fights, because the doorway behind us had just lit up, announcing a new one. A ring of little green crabs decorated the stone all around the opening, like the orange squid had on the other door. I guess they meant something to the regulars, maybe some clue to the venue or the type of combatants? I wondered if Cthulhu's door had red octopuses. . . .

"Dory? We're ready."

It was Ray, but I barely heard him over the *ding, ding, ding,* only this time, it wasn't the door chiming.

It was my head.

"Dory? You up to taking point, or you wanna bring up the rear?"

I didn't answer. Instead, I turned around and stared at all the porthole-looking doorways, each of which had a different symbol around it. Only there was so much smoke and potion residue drifting around that I couldn't make most of them out. But if I could have . . .

"Dory." A touch on my shoulder. "You okay?"

Yeah, I thought. *Yeah!* I whirled around, got dizzy, straightened up, and grabbed Rufus. "Can you do a reveal spell?"

"What?"

"*Can you?*"

"Y-yes, of course." He blinked at me. "On what?"

"On them." I gestured outward. "Can you make the little symbols on the doorways light up?"

Rufus looked like he was about to ask why, then seemed to decide it would be quicker just to oblige. And, all of a sudden, every door in the place was ringed in a circle of brilliant symbols, glowing brightly against all that white: blue swordfish, pink hammerheads, teal mermen, some weird black snakelike things—

"What are you doing?" Ray demanded.

—gray whales, yellow sea lions, and some purple three-tailed creature that ought to be on a coffee cup—

"Dory!"

"I'm looking for fish!"

"What? Why?"

"Because fish, tracks, door!"

Ray looked at me worriedly. "You do know you're not making sense, right?"

"There!" And there they were, aqua-colored fish tracking around a door on the fourth balcony up, all the way in the corner. "That's it! Ray, I think that's it!"

"That's *what*? What are you—"

He broke off abruptly. I was still staring at the door, so it took me a second to wonder why. And then I turned around.

And didn't have to wonder.

Ray was still standing there, but I wasn't sure how. Because somebody had just punched all the way through his middle, leaving me looking at a gory fist and Ray's shocked eyes. And then the fist was jerked back out again—

Along with his spine.

But that wasn't what had me frozen in shock.

No, that was because of who had done it.

"Louis-Cesare," I said blankly.

And then Dorina threw us over the railing.

———

The vampire was fast—I'd give him that. As I sailed into space I felt his fingertips brush me, warm against the skin of my arm. And then I was gone, grabbing one of the camera balls that had been speeding past and reaching for my phone to alert the one they call Marlowe.

And having it knocked from my fingers.

Because Louis-Cesare was already there, a split second behind me, dangling by one hand from the camera James had been using, leaving him plenty of options for attack. But there was something different this time, between Dory and me. Because she was still awake, leaving us with more options, too.

I took the offense, slipping my foot under the handgrip for the camera, because these things were designed to be used more than one way. And grabbed the controller a reporter tossed me as I passed, using it to somersault under the vampire, grab a club from a troll, come up behind him, and bash him in the back of the head. It felt like hitting a brick wall and did no observable damage.

Of course, I wasn't done yet.

But we went spinning away before I could try again, because Dory had the controller and was screaming at me: "Don't kill him!"

Same head, *I reminded her shortly, because he was already coming back this way.* Don't yell.

Then answer me!

I didn't answer, because she didn't need it. The best way to lose a fight was to use half measures against an opponent using full ones. Especially this one, I thought, watching as he duplicated my movement, only he didn't grab a troll's club.

He grabbed the troll.

It was a smaller one, which I dodged easily. But he sent two more my way just afterward, and was moving fast enough to be annoying. I decided to drop into the mental state vampires used in battle, the one that made everyone else seem to slow down, just to be on the safe side.

Only to realize: I was already there.

That would explain why people in the flood were looking around with startled expressions. To them, it must have seemed as if their allies or opponents had simply disappeared, plucked up and tossed like living boulders across the room. It must have seemed like that to the creatures as well: I saw one's ferocious expression change to bewilderment as he sailed past, especially after I pulled his sword from his hands.

And just managed to get it up in time to meet the one slashing down at me.

The vampire was also strong, I discovered, surprisingly so. He'd fought my twin before, but he'd apparently been pulling his punches. He wasn't pulling them now, or to be more precise, the creature controlling him wasn't. If we'd been on the ground, he might have done some serious damage.

But we weren't on the ground.

We were flying above the battle, balancing on a couple of speeding camera balls, while dodging the spells being flung at us from the ground and a few balconies.

And it looked like he didn't know how to fight this way.

I smiled, showing fang, as our swords rang together and as Dory took us down at the same moment, ruining his momentum as we dipped underneath and then zipped away. But he learned fast. Because the next time, he didn't come for us.

He came for the ball.

And it seemed that I had been wrong: he wasn't fast; he was quicksilver. He was lightning, flashing across the sky. He was faster than the spells we were dodging, which boiled by almost leisurely in comparison.

He was faster than me.

*Not by much, just a fraction of a second, but some-
times, that's all you need. There followed a blur of motion, a strange aerial ballet across the room, each of us
standing on a speeding camera, swirling and ducking and
somersaulting, and silent except for the staccato ring of
swords clashing together almost too fast to see, even for
me. It was heady, exhilarating; I'd never known anything
like it, as each of us tried to find an advantage, and each
of us failed.*

Until that split second came into play.

*I saw the blur of the blade coming for my mechanical
platform, but wasn't fast enough to dodge it. So I jumped,
straight up, just as the blade turned the camera I'd been
using into so many flying parts. And I flipped, landing on
the vamp in a judo hold, one leg around his neck, a stake
in my hand—*

*Only to have Dory throw off my aim. And before I
could recover, a wave of static hit me like a fist. Like a
thousand fists, boiling behind my eyes. I heard myself
scream, felt Dory convulse but somehow manage to grab
the vampire's controller, felt us spring away. But if she'd
planned to send Louis-Cesare careening off while we recovered, it didn't work.*

*Because he kicked the camera out from under him,
sending it shattering into a thousand pieces against the
wall, and fell as we did. And I learned that static could be
used in more than one way. It cut out abruptly, either deliberately or because he'd just splashed down, disrupting
the creature's thoughts. And either way, the shock caused
me to do the unthinkable.*

It caused me to trip.

*I landed on a troll's back, wet with water and blood.
But instead of using him as a platform to jump to the
nearby balcony and get away, I slipped off his shoulder,
heading for the water ten feet below. And hit something
else on my way down.*

*The vampire already had his blade back up, and it
pierced our leg, a sharp, biting pain that became agony
when it hit bone. And kept on going. The blade was so
razor-sharp and was wielded with such force that it took
me a moment to realize we'd just lost a leg. The part below*

the knee spun off into the fight, lost to view, and we fell backward into water over our head, that was immediately fogged with red.

The pain was stunning; the blood loss even more so. I prepared to dive, in the vain hope that I could beat the vampire to the bottom, and lose him in the thrashing, battling pairs all around. Or at least get enough water between us that it would blunt the next blow and save our lives. Instead he lunged for us, in a move almost too fast to see, even in slo-mo.

And jerked us back up.

"Louis-Cesare! Please!" That was Dory.

I could hear her pain, her anguish. Not only for us, but for him, what this would do to him when that thing let him go. And something of that must have gotten through, because for a split second, I saw him falter.

But the creature was too strong, and reasserted control almost at once. The blue eyes, confused and horrified one second, were suddenly resolute once more. And the sword was being raised and we were out of options.

But somebody else wasn't.

Louis-Cesare was swarmed by a bunch of flying cameras, perhaps twenty or more, all hitting him at the same time. One smashed into the back of his head; another punched the side of his jaw. And then more and more at various angles, until the little things had kamikazied their guts out, like big, black, wildly swinging fists.

They didn't hurt him, but the surprise bought us a second to tear away, and I didn't hesitate. I landed back in the frothing water, disoriented and desperate. And somehow grabbed a shield.

It was a long wooden thing, heavy and unwieldy. A fact not helped by the depth of the water, which was now over my head. My foot couldn't reach the bottom of this newly formed lake, and I was off-balance and rapidly losing blood from the leg. I nonetheless managed to get the shield up, and block the next strike of the blade. Only to have the wicked, curved steel sink deeply enough that it caught in the wood, allowing the vampire to use the sword as a handle.

And rip our only protection away.

Dory! *I yelled mentally.* Help me!

One second!

She was doing something with the hand under her control. Then she dunked us underwater, swimming for the bottom, and how was that supposed to help? I didn't get an answer, and the next second we were jerked back out of the tide. I'd been expecting it, and closed my hand on the wrist holding the sword as it slashed down. But even though I was putting everything I had into the fight, the blade kept coming closer and closer, a relentless, deadly weight, until the shiny surface reflected my strained face and startled, disbelieving eyes—

And something else.

I had half a second to see a giant mass of muscle, fur, and fury leaping for us, before it was gone—and Louis-Cesare along with it. For a split second, I watched him being dragged through the fight by a were the size of a car, and then the view was obscured as the rest of Roberto's creatures appeared, a river of fur parting the water and immediately taking the fight to a new level.

But not for long.

Not where the vampire was concerned.

I saw him across the fray, battling the were, and knew we had seconds at best. Not enough time to get away, not enough time to do anything. He was relentless.

But so was Dory. She'd found the controller the vampire had dropped, and apparently it went with the fritzing, sparking wreck of a camera ball speeding toward us. The thing could barely fly, and was listing hard to one side, but when the up button was pressed on the controller, that's where it took us, straining and fighting, but unerringly UP.

Toward the weapons, I realized.

And then we shot through the doorway and into a vortex of light and sound that grabbed us like a fist, jerked us through, and spit us out . . .

Somewhere else.

Chapter Sixty

The pain made it difficult to concentrate, but some things you just don't miss. Like Caedmon trapped behind some kind of ward, throwing his body against it uselessly. Like the fact that we were in a huge cave, like football-field huge, with a long slit of an entrance providing a vista of snow-covered peaks that went on for miles. And like the fact that a mass of what looked like the rock monsters the fey made were headed this way, only they'd gotten an upgrade.

In spite of everything, I just stared. They were shaped like *manlikans*, but the size . . . I had no idea how large they were, but if they'd been standing still, I would have mistaken them for mist-covered mountains. Mist-covered mountains with a tiny man—or fey, I guess—riding on the shoulder of each of them.

It was completely bizarre and strangely intimidating.

And then things became more so.

A woman turned to look at me from across the expanse of the cave, her diminutive blond beauty on display in a gossamer white gown. It blew in the breeze coming through the crevasse, like her long, unbound hair, perfectly complementing the snowy mountains and brilliant blue sky behind her. My thoughts screeched to a halt and then fell all over one another, like a multicar pileup.

Because that . . . wasn't Alfhild.

I stared at Efridis, Caedmon's beautiful sister, and wondered how we got it so wrong.

And then Louis-Cesare appeared, jumping through the portal, and I realized: we hadn't.

There *were* two of them.

My brain went blank.

"I thought you said you could handle things back there," Efridis said.

"I can." It was strange to see such an expression of contempt on Louis-Cesare's features.

And even more to feel his boot slam down on my neck.

"Then what is she doing here?" Efridis regarded me mildly. There was no contempt on her features. There was no anything. Somehow, that was more chilling than Alfhild's open hate.

Efridis did not hate.

Efridis was indifferent.

Like her voice when she said, "Kill her," and then turned away again.

"No!" Caedmon yelled, but nobody listened.

And then Louis-Cesare's sword was coming down, hard enough to bisect stone—and flesh and bone and everything else. . . .

Only, it didn't. It bit into the rock close enough to my back to slice through my little black dress, but didn't touch actual flesh. For a moment, I just lay there, in a crumpled heap, barely conscious because of blood loss, and not even daring to breathe.

But there was no second stroke. Louis-Cesare walked off, his eyes on the vista outside and the giants headed our way. I stared after him, through half-closed eyes, and tried to think past the agony in my leg and my steadily slowing heart rate.

Louis-Cesare might have distracted Alfhild long enough to spare me, but I was going to bleed out in a minute anyway.

Maybe less than a minute, because the pain was already diminishing, and a pleasing feeling of warmth was spreading through me. I'd heard that people felt that way when freezing to death, mistakenly believing they were getting warmer, when the opposite was true. And although I knew the stone was bitterly cold against my wet clothes, it didn't feel that way. Not that I was complaining.

Death was nicer than I'd thought.

And then somebody had to ruin it.

"Dory!"

It was barely a whisper, more a susurration of breath than anything else, but it annoyed me. Like a buzzing insect that wouldn't go away. I wanted to swat at it, but for some reason I felt like I shouldn't move. *Why shouldn't I move?*

I couldn't remember.

And then that warm feeling was back, only with a vengeance. It wasn't warm this time; it was hot—to the point that I almost yelped in pain as what felt like a miniature lightning bolt went through me. And jolted me out of the fugue I'd slipped into.

I blinked around in confusion.

And saw Caedmon staring at me.

Okay, that explained why I hadn't bled out, I thought. And then I realized that he was whispering something. I tried to pay attention—I tried hard—and it gradually got easier.

"—by the wall. Preferably more than one."

I squinted at him. And finally realized that he was waiting for an answer. "What?"

He looked frustrated. "I know you're in pain, and I am sorry for it—truly, I am—but I need you to concentrate. Please."

"Okay."

"There are crates of weapons—do you see? Along the far wall?"

I gazed around. I saw the crates—our missing weapons, I guessed. But they were dwarfed by piles and piles of bones. There were thousands of them, maybe tens of thousands. I stared at them blankly, wondering how I'd missed that. And why I felt so sick.

"Dory," Caedmon said, very clearly and deliberately, "I need you to get to one of the crates and find something to destroy this ward. Can you do that for me?"

I looked at him. I looked at the crates. I looked back at him.

"No."

"Dory, you must!"

"I . . . don't have a leg."

"But they *do*," Caedmon whispered furiously.

I followed the direction of his gaze, to where a handful of trolls were staring at the approaching giants—including the two who had killed Olga's nephew. They had their backs to us; I couldn't see their faces. But those physiques were memorable.

And then a random troll wandered away from the rest, to relieve himself in a corner, and Dorina grabbed him. Near-death experiences were freaky, I thought, because I could almost see her, a dark shadow crouched on his shoulders, riding him across the room.

Had anyone been paying attention, the jig would have been up pretty much immediately, because the guy looked like he had palsy. He was jerking and shivering and staggering about as he tried to fight her off. But the giants in the mist were holding everyone's attention.

I looked at Caedmon. "What are you doing here?"

"My sister." It was vicious. "She met Alfhild at the consul's home and they joined forces. She tricked me into coming here by telling me that she'd heard her husband talk about strange weapons being developed in the mountains—which I believed because we'd heard the same."

"That's what you wanted Claire to help you find."

He nodded. "We'd heard rumors of Aeslinn establishing laboratories outside his capital, away from the prying eyes of any spies I may have been able to suborn. But it's becoming harder to scout out his territories; his sentries are . . . formidable."

Caedmon's eyes found the walking mountains again. Yeah, I guessed so.

Dorina's troll lurched into some stacks of crates, spun, and lurched the other way.

Caedmon sighed.

"So, Efridis brought you here because?" I asked.

"She told me what I wanted to hear, that she was finally willing to give over her husband, and help us in the war. She told Aeslinn the same thing in reverse: that she'd only betrayed him in order to gain my confidence, so that she could deliver me to him. She knew it was the only thing that would get him out from behind his palace walls: the chance to kill me personally. In reality, she intends to blow us both up, leaving the throne of each kingdom vacant."

"So her son can take over."

He nodded. "We are not easy to kill, Aeslinn and I. But this"—he glanced around—"will probably do it."

"And Alfhild gets revenge for what your ancestor did to her."

"Yes. It seems they found common ground in my death."

Great. Good to know. I wondered if it was a bad sign that the hard stone beneath me was starting to feel good, comfortable even. I closed my eyes, just for a moment. . . .

"Dory! Don't go to sleep!"

"Yes, don't nap now. You'll miss it," Efridis said, turning around. She had to be thirty yards away, but I suppose those ears are good for something. And then Dorina was flying back to me, as the troll took a knife in the gut courtesy of Louis-Cesare.

Like I was about to.

"Stop!" I said desperately. "Stop! You—you're killing your own *brother*, because you want your son to rule? Why not just wait?"

"Wait?" She paused politely.

"Æsubrand said he'd challenge for the throne when Aiden grew up! Your son is far more experienced, far more skilled—he ought to have a clear advantage. Or are you so sure that you birthed a weakling?"

And, suddenly, there it was, the flash of anger I'd seen on the stairs back at Claire's, when I'd spit in the eye of the *manlikan* that I guessed Efridis had been controlling.

"My son is quite capable of defeating the half-breed," she snapped, "were he on his own. But he won't be on his own, will he?" Her eyes slid to her brother. "If you want someone to blame for your death, for the child's, for all of this, look to—what do they call you here? Caedmon?" Her lip curled. "Great King. Even in your human name, you reveal your ambition!"

"Ambition?" I looked from her to Caedmon. "What is she talking about?"

Caedmon didn't answer; he was too busy glaring at his sister.

"Poor, deluded fool," she told me. "You don't even know why you're dying, do you?"

"Why . . . don't you . . . enlighten me?"

It was becoming harder to think, harder to breathe, not that it mattered.

"She's stalling," Louis-Cesare snarled, and started forward.

But Efridis caught his arm. "A moment. I'm going to enjoy this." She looked back at me. "My brother and I both grew up with the same ambition: to see Faerie united under a single crown. One king, or . . . one queen . . ." She smiled.

I suddenly wondered how much power her son was actually supposed to have in this new order.

"Our plan was to end the constant bloodshed!" Caedmon erupted. "We were supposed to end the perpetual warfare that has torn our world apart!"

"Oh, I will, brother," Efridis assured him. "As soon as you are dead."

"I . . . don't understand," I said. Because I really didn't.

"My brother and I chose different paths to power," Efridis informed me. "I joined ancient bloodlines through my marriage, ones that had long been kept apart by old quarrels, and produced a son who controls all four elements. I brought together the complete spectrum of our greatest powers in one prince, who every member of the Light Fey has reason to support."

Her eyes slid to Caedmon. "Every member except one.

"My brother tried something similar, but his marriage to the queen of what you call the Green Fey was a signal disaster." She laughed. "It produced no sons, or children of any kind, nor did any of the concubines he took thereafter. How it must have galled you, brother, to see me succeed where you had failed—"

"I have a son!" Caedmon snarled.

"Yes, a half-breed! A mongrel half-human disgrace that you would set before—" She caught herself. "My brother," she continued, more calmly, "knew the Light Fey forces were almost certain to rally to my son—enough of them, at least, to make his rule inevitable. So he tried a new tactic. My child combined all strains of royal Light

Fey blood in one person, but my brother would go a step farther. He would go where no one had ever dared, would do the unthinkable, would create an abomination—"

"The only prince who can rule all Faerie is one who embodies all of it!" Caedmon exploded. "Not just the parts you feel are worthy!"

"There, you see?" Efridis asked me. "I did not start this conflict, dhampir. The birth of the polluted prince did that. The one who combines both Light and Dark Fey blood in a single person, and not just any Dark Fey blood. My brother somehow found a scion of one of their ruling families living here on Earth, away from their oversight. For they, too, would never have allowed such a union. But they didn't even know she existed, the product of some tryst by one of their princes, and by the time they did—"

"Aiden." I felt my heart sink.

She inclined her head.

"A prince who combines the blood of all faerie could one day raise a Dark Fey army, combine it with my brother's forces, and defeat my son. But that will never be. This ends tonight."

"And with it, any real chance for peace," Caedmon said, his voice ringing out across the cave. Because he was talking to the trolls, I realized. Our only hope for allies.

"She will betray you," he told them. "No matter what she has promised. Has she told you that you will rule over your own lands? That she only cares about the Light Fey? Her ambition will never allow her to stop short of taking all Faerie! As the humans say, she'll create a wasteland and call it peace! Whereas I—"

Efridis cut him off with a gesture and a line of liquid syllables I didn't understand.

I guess the trolls didn't, either, because they just stood there.

"Oh, allow me to translate for your friends," Caedmon told her viciously, but looking at them. "She said: 'And you would give Faerie over into the hands of savages, under a king as unclean as they are!'"

"You lie!" Efridis said. "You always—"

"I'm not the one planning to consolidate power and use

it to destroy them! You will never obtain peace this way—none of us will!" he told the trolls. "Don't be foolish!"

But it was too late. The troll leaders had made their decision. They were gambling on the power and wealth Efridis and her ally had promised. And without them, we had no friends in the room.

"I thought you said you'd never follow another fey king?" I reminded them desperately.

"She no king," Gravel Face rumbled, and I contemplated banging my head into the ground.

Efridis glanced at Louis-Cesare. "Finish this."

I looked at Caedmon, who looked back at me. And for the first time, I saw something other than perfect self-assurance in those green eyes. For the first time, I saw something that looked a lot like panic.

And then shock, as another voice rang out across the room.

It was as loud as someone using a megaphone, and so startling that I jumped, and sliced open my back on the sword. While Louis-Cesare stopped his run, halfway across the huge space, staring around in confusion. But not for long.

"Alfhild!"

Louis-Cesare's face abruptly turned gleeful. "Mircea! Come to watch your daughter die?"

And then, out of the side of my eye, I saw a hazy version of Mircea shimmer into existence. I could see right through him, out to the snowy mountains beyond. He looked like a ghost, so much so that I wasn't sure what I was seeing.

Until I realized: he was in our heads.

"Your head," he told me. "I am transmitting this through my link with you."

So I was Wi-Fi now? I took a look at the twelve-inch-long dagger in Louis-Cesare's hand, and decided I didn't mind so much.

"I came to bargain," Mircea said, and Alfhild laughed.

"There is nothing you have that I want!"

"Isn't there?" He held something up.

Something familiar.

"Keep it," she snapped, looking at the little ivory casket that had once held a potent magical shield. "Consider it a souvenir of your failure!"

"Oh, it's already a souvenir," Mircea said mildly. "One the consul took the night she visited your palazzo, all those years ago. I thought it in poor taste at the time, but I've since learned that she has excellent . . . instincts. As soon as I heard who we were dealing with, I took a ley line to Paris, in order to retrieve it."

Louis-Cesare's eyes narrowed. "What are you talking about? If you think—"

"What I think is that you've never asked yourself an obvious question: what happened to *your* bones, Alfhild?"

There was a sudden silence. For a moment, all I could hear was my heartbeat and the wind whistling through the cave mouth. And then—

"You're bluffing!"

Mircea's ghostly form opened the little casket and snapped something. And Louis-Cesare jerked, as if he'd been stabbed. A dark eyebrow rose.

"Believe me now?"

Alfhild snarled. "If you had what you say, why not destroy me?"

"I told you; I'm here to bargain." He looked down at the contents of the box. "And to make a solemn vow, to return your bones to Faerie where you can be reborn among your own kind. A peaceful sleep, and then a new life. Your exile undone, your past forgotten. Or . . ."

"Or *what*?"

Mircea's voice changed. "Or you might want to recall that we have portals, too. And a new alliance with the demon lords. I'm thinking of a very nasty hell region, where little creatures play among the acid pools. Creatures that other demon kind come to that world to feed upon. Think of it, Alfhild: an eternity of living in a hellscape, only to reincarnate, over and over, because you can't die. An eternity of being born to live a short, terrified existence, until you become prey for some stronger being. An eternity of never knowing who you are, who you were, anything but pain and fear and death, and all of it on endless repeat—"

"You don't have the guts! I'd find a way back—"

"I don't think so."

Mircea's head came up suddenly. And I blinked, because I'd seen a lot of expressions on his face, but never that one. It was . . . frightening.

"And if you did, I'd be waiting. I had the 'guts' to defy you when I was newly turned, with barely any power at all. I am not a powerless boy now, Alfhild, groveling at your feet for scraps. And even when I was I *beat* you. And will again, unless . . ."

"Unless what?"

"Unless you kill her." He looked at Efridis. "Right now."

"Bravo," I heard Caedmon whisper. And then, before I could quite process what was happening, the room was filled with two clouds of power, like the ones I'd seen at the consul's, only not. Because these were stronger, thicker, sparkling bright and white on the one hand, and a furious reddish black on the other. They clashed in the air overhead, like a thunderstorm had blown up inside the cave, something that would have held my attention more if Louis-Cesare hadn't started toward me again.

But while there was still a knife in his hand, I didn't get the same feeling of menace as before. He was starting and stopping, jerking and shaking, looking even worse than the troll Dorina had ridden. And then dropping onto the ground in convulsions, because he was fighting her, I realized. He was fighting!

But Alfhild was desperate, and despite having another problem right now, she was shoring up her control. Louis-Cesare was an extremely powerful vampire, but I doubted he'd ever faced an enemy like this. I didn't know if he'd win or not.

And I guess he didn't, either. Because the next thing I saw was him lurching to the side, near one of the crates, and snapping off a piece of wood. And stopping for a moment, to stare at me.

One last time.

"*No!*" I screamed. "No!" and tried to run. Forgetting that I couldn't, and falling, slipping on my own blood.

And watching helplessly as he drove the stake straight through the heart, while the knife in his other hand came up—

And went clattering across the floor.

Dorina, I thought, seeing her shadow behind him for an instant, before she did something that caused him to slump over, in a spreading pool of dark crimson.

I stared, not understanding anything. And the world didn't give me a chance to get a grip. Because the trolls all started this way, like they were marionettes on the same string.

"Dory!" Caedmon said, like I hadn't already seen them. But there wasn't a lot I could do, or Mircea, either. Because they burst through his image, making it roll away like steam on every side, and came hurtling this way.

I saw Dorina rush to meet them, but I already knew it wasn't going to work. They were too many, and we were too weak, and whatever ward Efridis had thrown up around her brother, she'd used enough fey bones to make it impenetrable to his power.

We had no champions left.

Or so I thought. Before a bunch of massive jagged-edged bones, femurs from creatures ten and twelve and fourteen feet tall, suddenly leapt up from a pile, as if carried by an unseen hand. And the next thing I knew, the trolls were bisected and trisected and whatever it is when you have a forest of your victim's body parts suddenly spearing through your own.

I saw White Hair's eyes glaze over, as he hit the cave floor, along with most of his kin. But Gravel Face was made of sterner stuff. He'd been hit by at least three bone segments, but I guess they hadn't taken out anything vital, because he kept coming, hate for me burning in his small eyes—

Until Purple Hair, immaculate in yet another catsuit, jumped out from behind a bunch of crates and slammed a knife through his skull.

Because, yeah. She was telekinetic, wasn't she? And didn't get the Senate seat if she didn't kill me herself. So I wasn't seeing a real upside here.

Until she stretched out a hand that, weirdly enough, didn't have a weapon in it. I looked up at her, hurting and confused. And she put an arm under mine and pulled me up, while the storm crackled and hissed overhead, boiling brilliant white as Alfhild's power was consumed.

Dizzy and agonized, I yet remembered one of Dorina's thoughts from the *vargr* attack at Claire's, one about Caedmon. That he looked fey but wasn't, at least not entirely. And it looked like his sister wasn't, either, because Efridis was absorbing her power easily—too easily.

We didn't have much time.

Purple Hair stared upward, looking like she was thinking the same, as the light of more power than either of us had ever seen played over her face. And then she looked down at me. "I've decided Radu was right," she said. "I don't wanna be a senator."

"Yeah. Me, either."

"Let's get out of here!"

"Wait!" Caedmon called. She scowled in annoyance. And then a whole case of weapons jumped up from the floor and hurtled for the shield around him, making his eyes blow big.

I didn't see them land, because Purple Hair was protecting me with her body. But I felt the hot wind blow past, strong enough to slam us back into the ground again. And then Caedmon was up and Efridis was facing him alone, because Alfhild was nowhere to be seen.

And then, a second later, neither was Efridis.

"Fuck me," Purple Hair whispered. "I thought they made that shit up for the movies."

"Guess not," I said, as we watched Efridis decide on the better part of valor, take a running jump for the opening of the cave, and be caught halfway through her fall by a giant freaking eagle.

Well, she always did like birds.

They soared off, leaving us with only a large army of approaching stone giants and a murderous fey king to deal with.

"We can't let Aeslinn have the bones!" Caedmon said, rounding on me.

"Well, what the hell else are we supposed to do?" Purple Hair said, gesturing savagely with her free arm. "Those things are gonna be here any minute!"

"Burn them," I said, and for some reason, I felt Dorina jerk.

But Caedmon was nodding. "Some of our people used to burn the dead, saying it sped up the process, and allowed them to reincarnate more quickly." He glanced around. "I think these have waited long enough."

"So have we! Let's go!" Purple Hair yelled, and grabbed a grenade.

Caedmon shoved the crates of weapons over by the biggest piles of bones, and then gently picked up Louis-Cesare. We ran for the door, while behind us an army crashed through the entrance to the cave, obliterating it.

Only to be obliterated themselves, a moment later—at least, I assumed so. Because Purple Hair threw that grenade like a World Series pitcher in the ninth inning. And the last thing I saw before the portal grabbed us was an explosion of light brighter than anything Efridis had ever put out.

And then we were gone.

Chapter Sixty-one

I woke up in a familiar bed with a familiar guy. Louis-Cesare was sprawled next to me, wearing a lot of bandages and no clothes. I smiled at him, even though it made my cheeks ache. "We have to stop meeting like this," I whispered, and put a hand on his chest.

And felt him flinch.

I was still half-asleep, and groggy. The residuals of some of Claire's hideous concoctions hung in the air, which probably explained why. Or the pain that was slivering through them anyway, from my nonexistent leg, like someone was poking at it with shards of glass.

I'd heard of phantom limb pain, but had never had a chance to experience it before. It was possibly the only pain I hadn't previously experienced. *Do I shout bingo?* I wondered blearily, and sat up.

And found myself staring at a perfectly good, if seriously bruised and battered, left leg.

"What the shit fuck!"

I almost fell out of bed.

Louis-Cesare grabbed me, just in time, and hauled me back to the bed's center. Which left me half underneath him, not that I minded. But I still didn't know—

"What the hell is going on?"

He licked his lips nervously. For someone as naturally—let's be kind and say confident—as him, it was a strange sight. "They found your leg."

"I see that."

"Mircea reattached it."

"That was good of him." Considering that I lost it on

senatorial business, and the Senate didn't have a medical plan. I glanced downward again, although I couldn't see anything, having a rather large amount of naked vampire in the way. "Is it . . . likely to stay that way?"

"He thinks so. He is hoping there is no lasting nerve damage. He is having a specialist brought in from Paris to make certain."

"That's good."

Louis-Cesare didn't say anything else, and what he had said was stilted, unemotional. His body was likewise rigid, instead of the lean, muscular strength I was used to. He looked like a guy who would rather be anywhere else.

It hurt more than the damned leg.

"And that's it?" I said flatly. "You don't have anything else to say to me?"

The blue eyes had been focused somewhere on my left shoulder, but now they slid to mine. And then abruptly wandered off again. "I am sorry," he told me.

"You damned well ought to be!"

He flinched noticeably. "I don't blame you for being furious," he said quietly. "They put me in here, while I recover, but I told Claire that it might be best if I were not here when you awoke—"

"What?"

"But she seemed to think otherwise. And she was right." He manned up, and met my eyes. "I understand how you feel. I would not blame you if you never wish to see me again."

"What?"

"I took your leg." His fingers touched it lightly, almost reverently. "If they had not been able to find it—"

"Well, yeah. But they did find it. And if they hadn't, think of all the neat attachments I could have gotten."

It was his turn to say: "What?"

"Think of it: a peg leg, especially a sharp wooden peg leg, for a dhampir? It would almost be worth—"

I broke off, because Louis-Cesare was having a small fit. I wasn't sure of what kind, and I didn't think he was, either, because his face tried out a couple dozen expressions before settling on one. It was incredulity.

"I *maimed* you!"

"You tried to maim me." I flexed my leg at him. "And you only managed it because I was already hurt when you showed up. If I'd been at my best, I'd have kicked your—"

He shook me.

"What?" I said again.

"You are angry with me! You hate me! You possibly even fear me!"

I burst out laughing. I couldn't help it. It had been a very long week. And the sudden ability just to let everything out caught me by surprise, and then sort of swept me away, until I was lying there, crying with laughter.

Louis-Caesar looked at me in growing concern. "I—I will go find Claire—"

"I don't need Claire!" I rolled on top of him. The leg, I was glad to notice, responded to commands, although it bitched at me about them. That was okay; I got that a lot.

Including from my lover, I thought, judging by his expression.

"You think that's what I want an apology for?" I asked him. "For the leg?"

"Yes!"

"And you've been lying here, blaming yourself and getting more and more worked up about it?"

"As I should do! I hurt you! I could have—" He broke off, but it was obvious what he meant.

"But you didn't kill me. Alfhild ordered you to, but you didn't. And when you thought you might, that there was even a chance, you tried to kill yourself instead. And that," I added, before he could interrupt me, "is why I'm angry."

He looked at me, and he'd found a new expression. It was bewilderment. But he didn't say "What?" again. He said "Why?" instead.

And looked like he genuinely didn't get it.

"Because, when you're part of someone else, you don't get to make that call," I told him quietly.

And then felt like cursing, because the damned man still didn't get it.

I could see it in those shimmering blue eyes: confusion, awkwardness, more than a little fear. He, who wasn't afraid of anything, was afraid of this. Of me. Of being sent away.

And there was one really good way to solve that problem, wasn't there?

I felt my fangs pop. "I'm proprietorial about my things," I snarled, and bit him.

And, God, yes, it was good! So good, so warm, so rich. I heard Louis-Cesare cry out, felt him grab my arms and try to push me off, but I knew his true strength now, and he wasn't pushing very hard.

Not that it would have mattered. I wrapped my legs around him as my fangs sank deeper, and I felt it: the swirl of magic around us. It should have been a surprise, but it wasn't. Maybe because it was so right, so good, so—

"*Perfect,*" I heard him murmur, and then he was drawing me close, and it was. It really, really was.

───────

I awoke an indeterminate time later in a warm embrace, one that had ended up with me wedged into an armpit, with Louis-Cesare draped over top of me. Like he wanted to make sure I would still be there when he woke up. *No worries,* I thought, letting my fingertips ghost over the tops of the new little fang marks on his neck.

He shuddered slightly, and drew me closer, tightening the embrace even in sleep. But not so much that I couldn't slide out from under, when I felt it again. A mental tug from above.

It was still dark, although on which day, I didn't know. It felt like I'd been in bed awhile. I was stiff, to the point that it took me an embarrassingly long time to get the sash up on a window and look out. And then to clamber onto the roof.

Dorina was there, looking something like Mircea's ghostly form, only paler, less distinct. But it was more than I'd ever seen of her before. "So you can materialize."

"Not to anyone else. At least . . . I don't think so."

She sounded a bit unsure.

I knew the feeling.

"You let them go," she said, as I settled beside her.

"What?"

Visuals came, instead of words. Mircea's gloved hand picking up the glowing ward where Alfhild had kept her power, all those years ago in Venice; him arguing with Abramalin, who couldn't do as he'd promised, after all, since he'd just made up the procedure to get Mircea to work for him; Mircea bending over me as I lay in my small child's bed, his eyes glowing with stolen power . . .

And then there were two.

"So, that's how it happened," I said, my voice hoarse.

She nodded.

I didn't know how to feel about that. It hadn't sounded like it was possible to return the energy stolen from the bones, once it was extracted and made into something else. But even so. People had been destroyed for it, real people, with hopes and dreams and lives. . . .

It had been done at a megalomaniac's command, to quench her thirst for revenge, not so Dorina and I could live. But it *had* given us life, all the same, and so it still felt weighty. Not like a burden, but like . . . a gift. And a responsibility, not to waste it.

I'll try, I thought, staring up at the stars.

"I should have told you before," Dorina said. "But I was afraid."

"Afraid?"

"So much power, in those bones. Fey, even more than vampire. I knew what Mircea had done with it; I didn't know what you would."

"Didn't you?" My voice sounded choked, even to me.

"With that much power, you could have locked me away forever. Made it so that I could never get out, not even when you slept. You could have been free of me, completely free, for the first time."

"And you could have banished me," I pointed out. "Sent me off to wither and die alone, to dissolve on the winds. Taken this body and lived your own life. Been free yourself."

She shook her head. "That wouldn't have been free. I would have been haunted by what I'd done, how I'd hurt you." She turned to look at me. "I never wanted to hurt you."

She raised a hand, and I swear I felt a brush of phantom fingertips against my cheek.

"You do that enough to yourself."

I blinked. "What?"

That wasn't exactly what I'd expected to hear.

"For five hundred years, you existed on the fringes, as you told our Sire. What you didn't tell him is that you're still there. In here."

Her touch dropped to my chest.

"Okay," I said. "That's not—I don't know what you think—"

"Five hundred years of watching," she told me. "I saw. You weren't any freer than me. You think you decided what we did? They decided. Where you could go, what you could do. You didn't become a hunter merely because you're good at it. You did it because it was all they would allow you to be. You were dhampir, hated, despised, outcast. It was a hard, meager, cold life. But it was all you knew. And, eventually, it was all you wanted to know."

"You know—you can't talk to me like—"

But she could, and she did.

"It became familiar, comfortable. Most people are frightened on the fringes, in the woods in the middle of the night, in the old, abandoned places. They set horror movies there, don't they? But you weren't frightened. You were the eyes in the darkness, the shadow on the wall, the thing that goes bump in the night. Others were afraid of *you*. They didn't know those places. You did. You made them your world—"

"You don't understand anything!"

"It wasn't the dark or the cold that frightened you. It was the light and the warmth, the places where it wasn't possible to hide, the places where you had to be *seen*. You think I wanted all those things: family, home, children, because they were what you wanted. But you couldn't have them, either, and every time you tried, every time you came close to anyone, you were hurt. So you learned to love the shadows. . . .

"But the shadows are gone now. You stand in the light. Surrounded by all the things you always thought you wanted, and it terrifies you. Even after what you just did, claiming that vampire, there's a part of you that wants to run. That is so afraid of losing all you have, that you are thinking of throwing it away, to leave before you're left, to go back to the desolate wastes because there, at least, you know the rules.

"You don't know them here."

"And you do?" I asked harshly. "You seem so sure what I want—what about you? This doesn't scare you? All of this?"

I flung out a hand, because I didn't have words for all the ways my life had changed recently. And was probably going to change further. Into what, I didn't know and couldn't even guess.

"Yes. It scares me." She looked up at the moon, floating overhead. "I don't know how to live this way, either."

I waited, but she didn't say anything else.

"That's it? You don't know?"

"Yes."

"That's not very helpful!"

"You're asking for an ending, the answers all spelled out. We aren't at the end, but the beginning."

"That's . . . profound." It was also pretty damned useless.

"You want answers," she told me. "I don't have them. I don't even know all the questions yet."

"Yet you sound excited."

She turned to look at me. "Aren't you? Five hundred years, with everything the same. Suddenly, nothing is. It's frightening, yes, but isn't it a little exciting, too?"

I didn't answer, but not because she was wrong. But because—

"What's going on?" I asked, because something was. Something that looked a lot like Olfun, booking it out of the house and down the street, with something in his arms. Only no. Not some*thing*, some*one*. Aiden.

And I suddenly remembered what he'd told me. About how a lot of people who'd opposed Efridis' plans for her son were suddenly coming on board, now that they knew Æsubrand no longer wanted the gods back. I just hadn't realized that Olfun was one of them!

"You won't be fast enough," Dorina told me, standing up. "Not with our leg as it is."

"And you'll never defeat that bitch!" I was standing, too, feeling pain course through my body and cursing my weakness.

"Perhaps she isn't here—"

"She is!" I pointed to the top of the little hill, just down the road, where a couple streets crossed. Efridis was still in white, the pure color gleaming under the moonlight, lighting her up like a beacon.

"I have to try," Dorina said, pulling away from me and spiraling up into the sky.

And then just stayed there, because no, she didn't.

There were fey streaming out of the house, and chasing after Olfun. But his legs were longer and he had a head start. They'd never catch him in time.

But someone else would.

There was a sudden, terrifying screech from overhead, like a thousand nails on a thousand chalkboards. And a strange, crystalline sound, and a rush of wind so sudden and so severe, that it knocked me to my knees. But I was still up high and there was a gap in the trees, and through it I saw—

Something that would forever be etched in my memory, no matter how long I lived. A huge dragon, black winged and purple tinged, with frightening sunburst eyes, sailing overhead, its body blocking out the moon. As well as the light reflecting off the tiny-looking woman on the ground, who barely had a chance to realize what was happening before the dragon dove—silent, awe-inspiring, death incarnate.

And then Claire ate Efridis.

Epilogue

Burbles was looking grim.

I almost didn't recognize him, with his normally jolly face dour and his arms crossed over his chest in what should have looked like a protective gesture, but mostly looked like he was trying to keep from strangling someone. I smiled and waved.

He did not smile back.

Mircea sidled up behind me. "What have you done to poor Vincent?"

"Saddled him with sixteen in-need-of-a-home vampires."

"Saddled him?"

"I told them they could stay in my consular suite, until they figured out their housing situation." I looked over my shoulder at his amusement. "Well, it's not like I'm going to be living here."

We were at the consul's, waiting for the ceremony to finally confirm us newbies, which was following a bunch of other ceremonies. Because that's apparently all vamps ever do: get dressed up and parade around, trying to impress people. Which might explain Burbles' current attitude: Ray's guys weren't looking so impressive.

"And where will you be living?" Mircea murmured, leaning on the balcony beside me.

I turned my head to look at him.

"Why?"

"I saw Louis-Cesare a few moments ago. He was looking . . . absurdly pleased with himself."

"Are you about to get all paternal and complain that I didn't invite you to the ceremony?"

"Do you know," Mircea told me thoughtfully, "we have ceremonies for almost everything, except that? The bite is considered an intimate act. It is customary to take care of it in private."

Yeah, I could see that. We hadn't been up to much that night, both of us being exhausted and very much under the weather, but Louis-Cesare had enthusiastically made it up to me several times since. Most recently in an alcove downstairs before he had to go away to get his own family ready. Although, it was really all the same thing now, wasn't it?

I realized I was grinning stupidly and stopped it.

"So what's the problem?" I asked.

"No problem. I merely wished to ask if—"

But I didn't find out what Mircea merely wished to ask, because an elegantly dressed Olga was headed our way.

I had on a bias-cut, sapphire blue silk thing that Louis-Cesare's tailor had whipped up, and I thought I looked pretty good. But Olga was jaw-dropping in some fey ensemble that consisted of a lot of bling, a lot of gilt leather, and a lot of feathers, which she nonetheless managed to make appear regal. It helped that she had an entourage of her own, a mixed group of trolls of all sizes and descriptions, including one familiar towering blue mountain.

"Hang on," I told Mircea, and walked over.

Blue was one of the few who had not gone all out. He was wearing what looked like the same leather loincloth he'd been in every time I saw him, and the hoary feet were unshod. But he managed the same gravitas Olga projected anyway, and frankly, he didn't need any bling. The guy was impressive enough all on his own.

The tiny, velvet-clad woman at his side, on the other hand, was styling. I almost didn't recognize her, because the gun-toting granny had had a makeover. Even the cigarettes were gone.

She flashed me some thigh, when I asked about them.

"Still got 'em, although I'm trying to quit. Faerie, you know."

"What about Faerie?"

"They don't got 'em there, and even if they did, Magdar and I are off to the hill tribes, so we'll be camping out a lot. I wouldn't be able to get any anyway."

"Hill tribes?"

She nodded. "That's where he's from. We're gonna try to find his people. And maybe some of mine."

"Some of yours?"

"Oh, I know," she told me, "I look ancient to you. But I was young once, and met this guy and—well. You know. He left after a while, which woulda been fine, 'cause I don't need no man to take care of me! But then he came back for the babe."

"You lost your child?"

She nodded, and the old eyes went soft. "He had dark hair, like his daddy. One of the river folk, Magdar said. He came back for my boy, and that's the last I ever saw of him. So Magdar and me, we both got people to find, you know?"

I nodded.

Blue hadn't said anything, and I hadn't really expected him to. Trolls don't waste a lot of words. But then he surprised me.

"Always thought I die in fights," he said suddenly. "Or in battle with slavers. Now . . ."

"Now you need a different plan."

I knew how that felt.

"Good luck," I told them. "To both of you."

They nodded gravely, and passed on, and I rejoined Mircea.

"You have interesting friends," he told me. He glanced over the railing. "And family."

"At least somebody got them into tuxes," I noticed. "More or less."

Ray's guys were all lined up below, ready to follow me into the ceremony, because apparently you were supposed to bring your family to these things. And I guess one's family wasn't supposed to pick their noses or scratch their asses. Because Burbles, looking frighteningly like a drill sergeant suddenly, smacked the offenders' heads together.

Weirdly enough, they almost looked pleased about it,

straightening up and throwing their shoulders back proudly.

Vamps, I thought, and shook my head.

"How is Raymond?" Mircea asked, watching the farce.

"Recovering. He's upset he's going to miss this. I promised to take lots of pictures." I gestured at the one little camera ball we'd managed to save, which was snapping away happily. And the next moment, it had something worth the effort.

"What is *that*?" I asked, leaning over the railing for a better look.

The great concourse of the consul's ballroom fell silent as four different delegations came in from four different directions. One was headed by Caedmon, with a great glowing cohort of velvet-clad, blue-robed fey. I saw Soini in the lineup, who saw me, too, and looked like he wanted to wave, but that wouldn't be dignified. He flashed me a grin instead.

The second group was headed by Olga and her trolls, which she'd picked up even more of along the way. "The local Dark Fey community has elected her as spokesperson," Mircea murmured. "After the recent demise of two of their more prominent leaders."

"She's good at that," I murmured back.

The third group was led by the consul, with a glittering stream of vampires—dressed to the nines, of course. As usual, she'd arranged to outshine everyone else. Caedmon's attractive but understated robes paled in comparison, and even the trolls' more exotic attire faded into the background. But she'd forgotten one little thing.

There was a fourth group at this party, and they didn't use the doors.

"What the hell?" I said, as some of what I assumed were Claire's relatives flew in and circled around the room, before coming to rest in front of a table. And changing, as they stepped down to earth, with perfect fluidity from one form to another.

The fluttering cloths they'd worn around their scaly necks transforming into robes that swirled around their human bodies before settling into place, as effortlessly as everything else they did. It kind of left everyone else's attempts in the dust.

"They are here to sign a treaty," Mircea told me. "For a long time, the animosity between Dark and Light Fey has made it difficult to negotiate any kind of an alliance for the war. The Dark Fey are tired of being cannon fodder in Light Fey conflicts, and they didn't trust Caedmon—"

"I noticed."

"—who has become so secretive over the years, that I doubt he trusts anyone," Mircea added, without a shred of irony.

For once, I didn't call him on it.

"So what changed?"

"You did."

I looked up. "What?"

"Your status as *vargr* is revered among the Dark Fey; you've proven yourself to Olga, someone they respect, many times; your roommate, Claire, has vouched for you to her father; and now you have fought and bled for them—and for the souls of their people. They've decided that your side is the right side. And the bones showed them that they couldn't sit on the sidelines in this conflict. This is a struggle for the soul of Faerie; they have to be in it, too."

"But . . . I don't want to be the reason someone goes to war."

"You're not. You're just the reason they're doing it now, as part of a unified force, while we have our best chance to win. It's also why you're our new liaison to the fey."

Caedmon looked up at me suddenly, almost as if he'd heard. I narrowed my eyes at him. Why did I have the feeling he'd had a hand in that? Probably because he'd threatened to do it before.

He was up to something; I knew it. But right then, I didn't care. And I cared even less a moment later, when Louis-Cesare appeared below, in his glittering best, and our families lined up together as one.

I started to go down to join them for the big procession, but Mircea caught my arm. And, very strangely for him, he looked almost uncertain. Off-balance. Like everything that had happened lately had thrown him a little, too.

"I wanted to ask . . . if you are all right?"

I started to make one of my usual flippant remarks, but the intensity on his face stopped me. "Yes. Shouldn't I be?"

"After everything?" He shook his head. "I don't know. So much has changed, in such a short time. Louis-Cesare, the Senate, Dorina . . ."

He stopped, like he wanted me to tell him that I could handle it, that I was okay. Maybe that both parts of me were. And, for once, I thought I could oblige.

"It's frightening, yes, but isn't it a little exciting, too?" I said, repeating Dorina's words. And felt like the two of us answered him, for once speaking together.

Mircea just stared at me.

I kissed his cheek, laughed at his expression, and went downstairs.

NEW YORK TIMES BESTSELLING AUTHOR

KAREN CHANCE

"Chance takes her place along[side]...
Laurell K. Hamilton, Charlaine Harris,
MaryJanice Davidson, and J. D. Robb."

—SFRevu

For a complete list of titles,
please visit prh.com/karenchance